CYBER
ROGUES

◎ ◎ ◎

Books by James P. Hogan

THE GIANTS SERIES
The Two Moons
The Two Worlds
Mission to Minerva

Code of the Lifemaker
The Immortality Option

The Cradle of Saturn
The Anguished Dawn

Bug Park
Echoes of an Alien Sky
Endgame Enigma
The Genesis Machine
Inherit the Stars
The Legend That Was Earth
Migration
Moon Flower
The Multiplex Man
Paths to Otherwhere
The Proteus Operation
Realtime Interrupt
Thrice Upon a Time
The Two Faces of Tomorrow
Voyage from Yesteryear

Worlds in Chaos (omnibus)
Cyber Rogues (omnibus)

COLLECTIONS
Catastrophes, Chaos and Convulsions
Kicking the Sacred Cow
Martian Knightlife
Minds, Machines and Evolution
Rockets, Redheads & Revolution

To purchase these and all other Baen Book titles in e-book format,
please go to www.baenebooks.com

CYBER ROGUES

✳ ✳ ✳

JAMES P. HOGAN

CYBER ROGUE

A Baen Books Original

Baen Publishing Enterprises
P.O. Box 1403
Riverdale, NY 10471
www.baen.com

ISBN: 978-1-4767-8035-1

Cover art by Kurt Miller

First Baen printing, April 2015

Distributed by Simon & Schuster
1230 Avenue of the Americas
New York, NY 10020

Library of Congress Cataloging-in-Publication Data

Hogan, James P.
   [Novels. Selections]
   Cyber rogues / James P Hogan.
       pages ; cm -- (Baen ; 1)
   "A Baen Books Original."
   Summary: "The Two Faces of Tomorrow and Realtime Interrupt in one combo
volume. Midway thru the 21st century, a proposed major software upgrade--an
A.I.--will give the world communications system an unprecedented degree of
independent decision making. A new space station is deployed to house the A.I.
named Spartacus. The idea is if Spartacus gets out of hand, the system can be
shut down and the station destroyed--unless, Spartacus decides to take matters
into its own hands. Then, Joe Corrigan awakens in a hospital to find his life no
longer exists. As director of the supersecret Oz Project, his job was to create a
computerized environment virtually indistinguishable from reality. Oz failed...or
did it?"-- Provided by publisher.
   ISBN 978-1-4767-8035-1 (softcover)
   1. Artificial intelligence--Fiction. I. Hogan, James P. Two faces of tomorrow. II.
Hogan, James P. Real time interrupt. III. Title.
   PR6058.O348A6 2015
   823'.914--dc23

                                    2014043652

Printed in the United States of America

10 9 8 7 6 5 4 3 2 1

❂ CONTENTS ❂

THE TWO FACES OF TOMORROW

PROLOGUE
❂ ❂ ❂

The planetismal began as a region of above-average density that occurred by chance in a swirling cloud of dust and gas condensing out of the expanding vastness of space. Gently at first but at a rate that grew steadily faster as time went by, it continued to sweep up the smaller accretions in its vicinity until it had grown to a rough spheroid of compressed dust and rock measuring fifty feet across.

Eventually the planetismal itself came under the pull of a larger body that had been growing in similar fashion, and began falling toward it. It impacted at a speed of over ten miles per second, releasing the energy equivalent of a one-hundred-kiloton bomb and blasting a crater more than half a mile in diameter.

Shortly afterward, as measured on a cosmic time-scale, a second planetismal fell close by and created another crater of similar dimensions; the distance between the crater centers was such that the raised rims of debris thrown up by the explosions merged together for a distance, resulting in the formation of a ridge of exaggerated height between the two basins.

In the time that followed, the rain of meteorites continued, pulverizing the landscape into a wilderness of sharp-grained dust to a depth of several feet, the desolation being relieved only by the occasional outcrop or shattered boulder. The outlines of the craters were slowly eroded away and stirred back into the sea of dust.

When the bombardment at last petered away, all that remained of the ridge was a rounded hummock to mark where the rims had intersected—a mound of dust and rock debris forty feet high and several hundred long. There it remained as one of the weary but triumphant survivors that were left to stare out over the gently rolling wastes that stretched to the horizon.

From then on the ridge remained essentially unchanged. A steady drizzle of micrometeorites continued to erode the top millimeter or so of its surface, exposing fresh material to trap hydrogen and helium nuclei from the solar wind; particles from sporadic solar flares caused isolated nuclear transformations down to several centimeters, and cosmic rays penetrated slightly farther. But in terms of its size, shape and general appearance, the ridge had become a permanent feature on a changeless world.

Four billion years later, give or take a few, Commander Jerry Fields, assigned to the International Space Administration's lunar base at Reinhold, was standing staring up at that same ridge. Beside him, similarly clad in a blue-gray spacesuit bearing the golden-flashed ISA shoulder insignia, Kal Paskoe frowned through his visor, studying the line of the ridge with an engineer's practiced eye.

"Well, what do you think?" Fields inquired into his radio. "See any problems?"

"Uh uh." Paskoe's reply was slow and noncommittal as he squinted against the glare of the setting sun. He turned to stare back at the metallic glint that marked the position of the base at the foot of the low hills on the skyline behind them, then returned his gaze to the ridge to register mentally a couple of salient boulders near its crest. "No . . . no problems," he said at last. "I think I've seen all I need. Let's get back to the truck and get the job scheduled. We can't do any more here until the computers have figured out how they're going to handle it."

The mass-driver at Maskelyne, over a thousand miles away on the western edge of Tranquillatis, had been in operation for almost a decade. It had been built as part of the EXPLORER (EXPloitation of

Lunar ORE Reserves) Project to hurl lunar rock up into orbit for metal extraction and construction of the huge space colonies being assembled within several hundred thousand miles of Earth. In fact the title was something of a deliberate misnomer. There were of course, no true ores on the Moon—ores in the sense of metal-rich substances concentrated by weathering and geological processes. Deep below the surface however, were rich accumulations of titanium, aluminum, iron and suchlike that had been precipitated by thermofluidic processes operative during the Moon's early history. The compounds bearing these elements had been dubbed "ores" by the media and the name had stuck

The mass-driver was a five-mile-long, ruler-straight track banked by two "hedges" of continuous electromagnetic windings—an immense linear accelerator stretching westward across Tranquillatis. It accelerated supercooled magnetic "buckets" riding on cushions of flux at 100g to reach escape velocity in the first two miles. Beyond that the buckets were laser-tracked and computer-adjusted to eject their loads of moonrock in a shallow climb that just cleared the mountains two hundred miles away by virtue of the Moon's surface curvature. En route the loads were electrically charged by being sprayed with electrons and fine-trimmed by massive electrostatic deflectors located at the two-hundred-mile downrange point to leave the final phase of launch with an accuracy better than one part in a million—comparable to a football being kicked between the uprights from 3,000 miles.

From there on each load, comprising 60 pounds of "ore," climbed steadily for two days until, 40,000 miles above the lunar surface, it fell into a "Hippo" catcher-ship stationed at the gravitationally stable L2 point. The energy needed to power the mass-driver was beamed down as microwaves from a three-mile-wide orbiting solar collector.

Day in, day out, round the clock, the mass-driver sent up a charge every two seconds, halting only for maintenance or for occasional repairs. Every year, one million tons of moonrock fell into the waiting relays of Hippos. And farther out in space, the colonies steadily took shape.

The project had been so successful that the powers-that-be had decided to go ahead with the construction of a second mass-driver. This one would also be located on the equator, but near Reinhold, aiming out across Procellarum. The track, the experts had decreed, would pass right over the point at which Fields and Paskoe were standing. Not a little to the right nor a little to the left, they had pronounced after extensive surveys, but right there.

First-phase preparation would require accurate sighting with lasers, covering a stretch of terrain that extended from a mile or more behind them to several times that distance ahead, which would require an unobstructed path. The ridge was not really large—about the size of a dozen average houses set end to end—but . . . it was in the way.

And so it came about that the form that had stood valiantly to preserve its record of events from the earliest epoch of the Solar System at last found itself opposing the restless, thrusting outward urge of Man.

The ridge would have to go.

"How goes it?" The voice of Sergeant Tim Cummings came through over the open channel from the nearest of the two surface-crawlers parked a few hundred feet back at the bottom of the shallow slope that led up to the ridge.

"I think we're about done here," Paskoe replied. "Get some coffee on, Tim. We're coming back down."

"See all you wanted from the top?" Cummings inquired.

"Yeah. It's pretty much as we thought," Paskoe told him. "More or less symmetric on both sides. Probably not more than fifty, maybe sixty feet thick at the base." He glanced automatically at the twin lines of footprints that led up to the point on the ridge crest that he and Fields had climbed to, and then led back to where they were now standing.

"Let's go," Fields said, and with that turned and began heading back to the crawler. Paskoe gave the ridge one final glance, then turned to follow at a slow easygoing lope that brought him alongside Fields in a few seconds.

"What do you reckon?" Fields asked as they bounced side by side down the slope. "Soil blower maybe?"

"Dunno," Paskoe replied. "There are some big boulders in there, and it's probably pretty well compacted lower down. Might take a digger or two, probably a heavy shover too. We'll see what the computers reckon."

"There's some heavy equipment the other side of Reinhold," Fields remarked. "If they shifted some of that over here they might get started inside a day or two."

"Nah—I'm pretty sure most of that stuff's tied up," Paskoe said. "They may have to fly something in from Tycho. Anyhow, that's their problem. They know their schedules. We'll just have to wait and see what they come up with."

"As long as we don't end up having to shovel it," Fields said as they slowed down to approach the crawler. Paskoe steadied himself on the handrail and stooped slightly to clear his helmet past the entrance to the crawler's lower cabin.

"No way," he declared with feeling. "I've seen enough Massachusetts winters not to ever wanna see a shovel again. I'll leave it to the computers. If they say the best they can manage is a week, that's okay by me."

"The boss'd get pretty mad about that if it happened," Fields murmured as he ducked to follow the now invisible Paskoe.

"Then the boss could come out here and damn well shovel it himself," Paskoe's voice said in his helmet.

Five minutes later they had removed their helmets and were seated back at the crew stations beneath the viewdome of the crawler's upper cabin.

While Fields and Cummings used the viscreen to discuss the next item on the day's agenda with Michel Chauverier, who was in command of the other crawler parked next to them, Paskoe activated the main console at the far end of the cabin to close a channel via comsat to the Tycho node of the ubiquitous TITAN computer complex. After a brief dialogue via touchpad and display screen, he had communicated the nature of his request to the system's Executive Command Interpreter. A few seconds later the screen returned the message:

ASSIGNED JOB NUMBER 2736/B. 72/Z72

SCHEDULED TO SUBSYSTEM:
SURFACE ENGINEERING P.927
REQUIRE DATA REGARDING NATURE AND
LOCATION OF OBSTRUCTION

Paskoe remote-steered one of the crawler's external TV cameras until he had an image of the ridge outside nicely centered on one of the console's auxiliary screens. Then he operated the touchpad again to bring up two flashing cursors superimposed on the image, and moved them across the screen until they lined up with the boulder formations he had memorized. In this position the cursors defined the portion of the ridge that mattered.

He then tapped out a brief code with his fingertips. In the fraction of a second that followed, the coordinates of the crawler's identification beacon were read and plotted by one of the invisible satellites high above. At the same time the picture being picked up by the TV camera was analyzed by the onboard computers and the data extracted were used to align the laser mounted on the roof with the centerpoint between the cursors. The range, bearing and elevation data read from the laser were instantly flashed to the Tycho computers. From the readings obtained from the satellite, the computers knew the exact location of the crawler upon the lunar surface. The laser data enabled them to compute the position of the ridge relative to the crawler, and hence to deduce its precise coordinates as well.

A few more seconds elapsed while programs at Tycho pondered over the patterns contained in the TV picture being sent to them. Then the words on the screen vanished to be replaced by:

PROFILE?

Paskoe responded:

BASE THICKNESS 60FT MAX.
OBSTRUCTION APPROX LONGITUDINALLY
SYMMETRIC

COMPACTED REGOLITH INC OBSERVED DEBRIS
TO 10FT DIA EST.
REQUIRED REMOVAL TO DEPTH EST 40FT. LEVEL.

He drummed his fingers on the console with growing impatience while the machines meditated. No doubt they were bringing in the crawler's armory of X-ray analyzers, infrared analyzers and heavens alone knew what else to scan the ridge and estimate its mass, composition, structural features and whatever else they thought they needed to know to figure out how to go about doing a perfectly simple job.

It was quite straightforward, he told himself. All they had to do was decide which types of earth-moving machine would be best suited—surely any dirt-farmer could have told them that—check where they were located and when they would become available, and advise how long it would take to get them moved here. Then he'd be able to plan the next part of the job.

Computers! The simpler the task, the more it seemed they had to fuss around with irrelevant detail. Just like people.

PRIORITY REQUESTED?

Paskoe sighed:

ABSOLUTE BEST POSSIBLE
GRADE PB PROJECT BEING DELAYED REF. 2053/A.
THIS ITEM CRITICAL.

The computers, however, were not through yet.

ANY CONSTRAINTS?

NO. JUST GET RID OF IT.

Another wait ensued. Then the words changed again. Paskoe read them casually, blinked, sat forward and read them again.

JOB SCHEDULED PRIORITY CATEGORY
'A.1.' NO FURTHER QUERIES
ESTIMATED COMPLETION TIME IS 21 MINUTES.

Paskoe frowned and asked for a repeat . . . and got it. Looking bemused, he turned and interrupted the conversation still going on behind him between his two companions and Chauverier.

"Hey. Look at this. Either I'm crazy or the system's screwed up. Tell me I'm not crazy." Fields and Cummings turned in their seats.

"What's up?" Fields inquired. Paskoe gestured toward his console.

"Tycho's sized up the job and it's giving an ECT of twenty-one minutes."

"You're crazy," Fields declared without hesitation.

"Look at the screen."

"It's crazy," Fields decided.

Cummings rose from his seat and clambered across the cabin to peer more closely at the display.

"What's going on?" Chauverier demanded from the viscreen.

"Kal's got some screwy numbers back from Tycho," Fields told him. "Tim's gone to have a look."

"Could be a fluke," Cummings was saying, rubbing his chin dubiously. "Maybe it's our lucky day. There's probably a transporter due over this way that's carrying just the stuff we need on a low-priority job someplace. Maybe Tycho's rescheduled it to land here." Paskoe pursed his lips and nodded slowly.

"Could be . . ." he agreed, then went on suddenly more decisively. "Yep. You could be right, Tim. I never thought of that. What do you think, Jerry?"

"Makes sense," Fields agreed. "We'd better stay put to see what shows up." He turned back toward Chauverier, who was still peering out of the viscreen. "We think there'll be a ship coming down here pretty soon, Michel. There'll probably only be robodiggers or something on it, but maybe we ought to hang around to check it out. It should only be for half-hour or so."

"Suits us," Chauverier answered readily. "In fact me and Joe were just starting to get hungry. If we're going to stick around here for a while I guess we'll eat. Do you guys want to come on over for a bite?" Fields turned back to the others.

"Michel's inviting us over for lunch in his truck. Okay by you two?"

"Great idea."

"Sure."

"Okay, Michel," Fields advised. "We're on our way. Set it up for three more." With that he cut off the screen. At the same time Paskoe killed the channel to Tycho.

For the next few minutes they donned helmets and took turns going through the routine drill of plugging the test leads from their suits into the socket provided in the panel by the floor hatch. Fields drew a "no go" in the test. The codes being displayed on the panel's miniature screen revealed an intermittent sticking valve in his life-support. Muttering beneath his breath, Paskoe began replacing the faulty valve in Fields's backpack while Cummings called Chauverier again to advise of the delay. Fifteen minutes later they were ready to go.

"It won't last," Fields said over the radio as he turned to begin following Cummings down the short ladder below the floor hatch. "I'll bet fifty bucks on it. Paggett is only there until he retires Earthside and until then he'll just go on rubber-stamping. When he goes, Cawther's bound to take over. Then it'll all be different. I give it twelve months at the most." Cummings had passed through the exit to the surface.

As Fields turned to follow, Paskoe began the descent from the upper cabin, pausing halfway to secure and check the hatch above his head. "Anyhow, I'm not interested," he declared, nodding to himself and stepping down. "I'm only here for another four. Then it's back home for me. A year's banked back pay and a few months around Europe with Cher. Wowie! You can take care of Cawther. Have fun. I sure will."

"Europe?" Cummings, who was waiting for them outside, came in on the circuit. "That's where you're going?"

"All over," Paskoe said. "We never did get to see more than a few of the tourist traps. This time we'll do it right. Three months at least. Cher's especially keen on Germany." They were crossing the gap of about thirty feet that separated the crawler from Chauverier's. Paskoe and Cummings were side by side, with Fields following a short distance behind.

"I was in Germany a couple years back," Fields's voice came through. "Saw some of Poland too. There's a place there you ought to see if you get the chance . . . down south. Krakow I think it was called."

"What's there?" Paskoe asked.

"Salt mines. They go right back to the Middle Ages. Man, are they big."

"Salt mines?" Cummings sounded mystified as he and Paskoe came abreast of the other crawler and moved around it toward where the entrance was located. "What's so special about salt mines? I thought they were places the Russians used to send people they didn't like."

"Those are different," Fields replied. "There's a whole cathedral down there way underground. All carved out of solid salt crystal. Everything's salt—the altar, the chapels, the statues, even the lights. It's fantastic. And they've got—"

The universe blanked out.

"What in Christ! . . ." a voice yelled.

Cummings had just reached the door with Paskoe close behind. Fields was a few feet away, just beyond the end of the vehicle.

Everything around them vanished abruptly into an opaque sheet of gray. At the same moment Paskoe felt the ground shudder beneath his feet. The mass of the crawler above them lurched visibly as if it had been struck an immense blow on the opposite side. For a moment he had the sickening feeling that it was going to topple over on top of them.

A titanic blast of dust, debris and boulders had smashed into the far side of the vehicle and sprayed past it on every side. Mercifully they had been in its lee shadow. Just a few seconds earlier and they would have been caught unprotected. And just as suddenly it was gone.

Paskoe was standing frozen to the spot, still with no idea of what had happened. In front of him Cummings was clinging to the handrail by the door, his face ashen through his visor and his arm gesturing weakly toward a point behind Paskoe's shoulder.

"Jerry! . . ." Cumming's voice came through in a strangled gasp. "Jerry's gone!" Paskoe turned and stared dazedly at the spot where, a few seconds previously, Fields had been standing, just beyond the crawler's protective shadow. There was nobody there.

And then the blast came again, like the discharge of a gigantic shotgun that fired moonrock. And again, and again, and again . . . and again. Paskoe found himself on the ground pressing himself against the vehicle's tracks while the concussions thudded through his body, and the crawler trembled under the repeated impacts of boulders cannoning off its sides and spinning crazily away into the maelstrom of dust. His helmet touched the structure. A sound like a building collapsing onto an enormous kettledrum exploded in his ears. He lost count of the concussions. Maybe ten, twenty . . . His brain had seized up.

He was lying by the track of the crawler, his heart pounding and his body shaking. Every inch of his skin felt cold and wet in his suit. It had stopped. He waited, barely daring to breathe. The tension that held him keyed up waiting for it to begin again refused to let go. But nothing happened. He opened his eyes slowly and looked up.

Cummings was lying on his back with his legs tangled in the steps that bridged the gap between the ground and the floor of the entrance hatch. He looked as if he had been bowled backward out of the doorway just as he had been in the act of climbing in. Still shaking, Paskoe struggled to his feet, rivulets of sticky moondust pouring down the creases in his suit.

"Tim . . . Tim can you hear me?" He lurched over to where Cummings lay motionless, then stopped. A slab of ice-cold horror dropped in his stomach as he saw the shattered visor. And then a feeble voice groaned in his helmet.

"Holy Christ, what happened?"

"Tim? . . ." Paskoe's voice was almost sobbing with relief. "Tim, are you okay in there?" The sprawled figure moved, and gingerly extracted a leg from the steps above it.

"I can't see," Cummings's voice came again, now sounding less disoriented. "Something hit me in the face." The other leg freed itself. Paskoe stooped and helped Cummings to sit up. "Argh! . . . My chest! I think I got hit by a shuttle booster."

"Can you stand up? Easy now. I gotcha."

"Take it slowly." Cummings's words came between heavy breaths. "I think I might have collected a cracked rib."

Paskoe hoisted Cummings to his feet and guided his hand to the rail by the door. The chest panel of Cummings's suit was smashed and the visor an opaque mess of fractured crystal. Paskoe moved around to get at the manual auxiliary controls on the backpack, which appeared none the worse for having taken the impact of Cummings's fall.

"Your visor's cracked but it looks like it's holding," he said. "I'm dropping the pressure in your suit to relieve the stress on it. As far as I can tell you'll be okay for a while, but we ought to get you into another one ASAP."

"What happened?" Cummings asked again.

"I don't know. If there was a war on I'd have said we just had a near miss from a salvo of 108's. Maybe it was a meteorite swarm. I don't know." While he was speaking, Paskoe was peering into the lower cabin of the crawler. The floor was covered in dust and some larger debris. Shafts of light poured through several jagged holes that had been torn in the far wall. Presumably whatever had made the holes had carried right through and caught Cummings head-on just as he was entering from the opposite direction.

"What . . . What about Jerry?" Cummings asked haltingly.

"He got caught in the open." Paskoe turned from the door and began scanning their immediate vicinity. "I guess he must have got blown away. Bad news I . . . Just a sec. I think I see him." He could just make out the twisted figure of Fields, crumpled in a mound of dust that had appeared at the foot of a rounded boulder twenty or thirty feet away. The layer of gray powder covering it was so thick that Paskoe had at first dismissed it as an irregular grouping of rocks. Cummings remained silent, still clinging to the handrail while he regained his breath.

"It's him," Paskoe said. "He's not moving. Looks like he might have been hit pretty bad. Stay there and don't move. I'm going over."

In a few slow bounds he covered the distance to where Fields was lying, and began digging the dust aside frantically with his gauntleted hands. Field's helmet was intact. Paskoe scraped the layer of caked moondust from the visor and peered at the face inside.

It was pale, eyes closed; no sign of life. But at least, there were none of the gruesome signs that would follow decompression. There was hope then. Working swiftly, Paskoe uncovered the rest of the figure.

"What's the news?" Cummings's voice sounded in his helmet. It was tense, obviously prepared for the worst.

"Could be worse," Paskoe replied. "He hasn't decompressed, but if he's alive he's out cold. His pack's all smashed up so he won't last long if we don't get him out. Must have caught a big one right in the back."

"Any sound of breathing?"

"Can't tell. I couldn't hear anything even with my gain wound right up, but I think his radio's probably dead."

At that moment another voice came through, sounding shaky.

"Kal, is that you? Are you guys still alive out there?"

"Michel!" Paskoe swung his head instinctively to look back at the crawler. "You're okay. What's the score inside?"

"The worst damage is downstairs," Chauverier answered. "We've lost pressure up here, but it wasn't explosive—just small holes. The regulators compensated long enough for me to get a helmet on."

"How's Joe?" Paskoe inquired.

"Knocked himself out on the center bulkhead. I put his helmet on for him. He's still out but he should be okay. I heard you talking about Jerry. How's Tim?"

"He seems okay but his visor's flaked, so he can't see. He's outside the door. Right now the problem is Jerry. We've got to get him out. Did you say the cabin's zeroed?"

"Everything's dead," Chauverier replied. "We'll have to use a survival tent and wait for a VTOL to show up. I'll eject one now. Stay clear. I'll be out in a minute with a couple of suits and give you a hand."

"What about Joe?" Paskoe asked.

"He'll be okay here for a while. We can bring him out when the tent's set up."

"Okay."

A package resembling a bale of rubber ejected itself from its stowage point near one end of the vehicle, landed a few feet away and immediately inflated into a bright-orange six-man survival tent. Paskoe freed Field's lower legs from the rubble and began hauling the still inert form across toward it. Just as he reached the tent, two suit-kits sailed out of the crawler door, closely followed by Chauverier. He landed easily on his feet, scooped up the kits and began loping over to where Paskoe was dragging Fields through the outer portal of the tent's airlock.

"Something just went past me," Cummings called over the radio.

"That was me," Chauverier told him. "We're getting Jerry into the tent. I've got a suit here for you. We'll come back for you in a second before we pressurize the lock."

"Okay. I'll be here."

"Say . . ." Chauverier's voice suddenly took on a new note—one of disbelief. Paskoe was inside the lock propping Fields into a more comfortable position. Chauverier had straightened up and was staring out at something beyond the tent.

"What's up?" Paskoe asked.

"Come back out for a moment and get a look at this," Chauverier said. Back at the crawler. Cummings listened in silence. Then he heard Paskoe's voice: "Jesus!"

"What is it?" Cummings asked them.

"Our truck," Paskoe answered. "Did you ever see a tin can after a grenade went off inside it? If anybody had been inside that they'd just be jelly on the walls. It's been turned right over."

"Look at the other side of it," Chauverier suggested,

Paskoe gasped, The entire center section of the ridge had been neatly blown away to leave two small isolated humps at what had been its ends. The gap that now existed between the humps was churned into a tortured tangle of tightly overlapping craters.

"How in the name of . . ." Paskoe began, but Cummings broke in:

"What is it?"

"We've been bombed!"

"How?"

"I don't know. Something crazy's going on somewhere."

"You'll see for yourself later," Chauverier came in. "Right now let's get you into the tent before that facepiece blows." With that he bounded back to where Cummings was standing, led him over to the tent and guided him into the lock, tossed in the suit-packs and ducked in after them. Paskoe was already inside and waiting to seal the flap. Within seconds the walls of the lock were stiffening as the pressure began building up.

Ten minutes later Joe had recovered, been updated on the situation and had announced that he could make his own way down from the crawler. Inside the tent Chauverier had pronounced Fields to be alive, suffering from shock, oxygen starvation and a dislocated shoulder, but in no immediate danger. A trace of color had returned to his face and his pulse was getting stronger. On the other side of the tent Cummings was pulling on one of the spare suits while Paskoe was using his pocket viewpad to inform base of events.

"The comsats picked up your truck's auto-distress transmission fifteen minutes ago," the day supervisor at Reinhold informed him from the screen, "A couple of VTOLs are on the way. They should arrive any minute now. What happened?"

"That's what I was hoping you turkeys might tell us!" Paskoe yelled, now restored to his normal self. "Some asshole just bombed us, that's what! Are you telling me you don't know anything about it?"

"Nix." The supervisor looked at a loss. "We just got the distress call and sent out the VTOLs. That's all I know."

"Oscar Zebra Two-Five-Five Leader to Reinhold Control," another voice interrupted. "We've got 'em in sight. Two trucks and a tent, one truck turned over. They're on the fringe of what looks like a fresh pattern of impact rays centered on a crater cluster. We're going down now."

"They're here," Paskoe said needlessly. "I'll talk to you later." He cut out the viewpad, closed it and began returning it to his thigh pouch. He stopped, frowned thoughtfully for a second, and then reopened the view-pad and touched in a rapid-fire sequence of commands. An instant later he was through to the Executive Command Interpreter at Tycho. A few more commands yielded the words:

    JOB 2736/B. 72/Z72
    COMPLETED AS SCHEDULED
    EVALUATION REQUESTED
    OPERATION RE-EXECUTE REQUESTED?
    PLEASE ADVISE.

"Christ!"

"What's wrong?" Chauverier inquired, turning his head from the viewing port, through which he had been watching the first of the VTOLs as it dropped into sight. Paskoe pointed at the viewpad.

"It was those idiot computers at Tycho! They're asking if they did okay . . . Wanna know if we need a repeat performance!" He steadied the viewpad against his knee, and hastily hammered in with shaking fingers:

    NO!
    ABORT! ABORT! ABORT!

    ACKNOWLEDGED.

Came back the impassive reply.

❂ PART ONE ❂

MOBILIZATION

❀ CHAPTER ONE ❀

New York stretched to greet the sunshine of a new day.

The autocab was just one of innumerable silver beads strung out along the tangle of shining threads that wreathed the base of the monolithic city. Below and on either side, rectangular cliffs and chasms of glass, concrete and duroplastic marched stiffly by, revealing occasional glimpses of the nearby Hudson River.

The figure staring out of the otherwise empty six-seat vehicle was still some years below forty and on the tall side of average in height. His features held a sharp-lined ruggedness that was accentuated by his ragged droopy moustache. An ample mane of straight black hair, and the swarthy hue of his skin, were relics of the Amerind blood that his father's side of the family boasted in its early ancestry. Slightly hollowed cheeks with high-set bones that gave his eyes a permanently keen and narrowed look echoed the same heritage. His loose-limbed frame was sprawled untidily across one corner of the cab and casually attired in an open-necked shirt covered by a lightweight wind-breaker, but the thoughts going through his head that morning were not as serene as his appearance might have suggested.

This time, Dr. Raymond Dyer told himself, it had to stop. Over the previous six months he and Sharon had had some good times and a lot of fun—exactly the no-strings, for-as-long-as-it-lasts kind of thing to be expected between a thirty-four-year-old male divorced for six years, and a single girl who had come to the big city for the sole purpose of finding out what life was all about. At least that was how it had begun, and could have remained if only . . . He sighed his expression to himself. Why did women always have to go and take a good thing too far?

The fingers of his outstretched arm drummed a tattoo on the window ledge. He frowned at them moodily for a few seconds.

He was rationalizing the whole thing, he admitted to himself. Who was he trying to fool? Sharon hadn't really said anything that hinted at plans for things getting any more serious than he himself wanted—not if he was honest. The truth of the matter was he was getting bored with the whole thing.

His old restlessness was beginning to stir again. Or was it? Either that or he had reached an age where two people simply being in the same place didn't equate to togetherness . . . not in any sense that mattered. Maybe, unconsciously, *he* was the one who was looking for a road that led somewhere. Interesting thought, he thought. He'd managed to surprise himself.

The cab skimmed low over an open plaza, brightly colored and cheerful in the light of the May sun, and then plunged into a tube that carried it into the gleaming precipice formed by part of the northern edge of the West Side Tower Complex. Snatches of illuminated arcades, mosaic-paved pedestrian precincts and manicured shrubs flicked by on the far side of the tube's Plexiglas wall.

A sensor below the track responded to the cab's identification code and flashed it to the scheduling computers of the Manhattan Sector Three Control Center, a half-mile away across the city. Milliseconds later the reply from the computers activated the cab's onboard guidance processor. The cab exited from the through line and ten seconds later eased to a halt at a boarding ramp three hundred feet above where some of the original paving of West Fifty-Seventh Street still remained in the lower vaults of the city.

Dyer stepped out and made his way along the short platform of the boarding ramp between the dozen or so people who were in the process of getting into or out of the cabs slowly shuffling toward the dispatch point at the far end. He headed for the exit and emerged into a large enclosed concourse built around a rectangular core housing the nearest elevator bank. The place was not overcrowded—about average for that time of morning. In fact the traffic didn't fluctuate wildly through the day, or for most of the night for that matter. The standard nine-to-five day with its commuter stampedes was something that had long gone away.

He joined a small knot of people in front of one of the elevators, waited for the doors to open and followed on in. Just as the doors were about to close, a figure that had been approaching quickened its pace, broke into a short run, finished with a leap and landed inside with a split second to spare and a perfunctory "Excuse me" to nobody in particular. The late arrival was in his early twenties, tall, narrow-faced, and generally studentish in appearance with untidy collar-length hair and wearing a roll-neck sweater beneath a dark-blue nylon parka.

"Just as well you've got good air brakes," Dyer murmured as the elevator began to move. "For a second I thought I was going to get flattened here."

Chris Steeton looked up abruptly as he recognized the voice.

"Hello, Chief," he greeted with a grin. "Sorry about that. It was just my way of proving that momentum isn't conserved the way Newton said it is."

Chris was from England on a two-year research fellowship. He was one of three senior researchers on Dyer's team, a quiet sort of person, tending toward introverted at times. But he was bright academically and accepted the world with a cheerful mix of optimism and curiosity that made him tenacious in the face of the complicated problems that he was always inventing in order to solve. His greatest virtue, perhaps, was his inexhaustible patience.

"So, how'd you spend your time off while we were all working?" Dyer inquired after a few seconds. "Do anything interesting?"

"Oh, I went to see some more of the colonies," Chris replied in the serious tone he always employed when he wasn't being really serious. "Florida, actually. *Homo americanus* at play. It was . . . an education." He frowned while he reflected on Dyer's question more deeply. "I suppose the only interesting bit was when some high-velocity idiot fell off his water skis and broke a leg. Apart from that it was so-so: lots of noisy bars with megaton bands and bare bodies collecting radiation sickness. I'll take Upton-on-Severn."

"That means you're back rarin' to go, eh?" Dyer said as the elevator whined to an impatient halt at the ninety-sixth floor and they spilled out. "That's good. Ron's been putting in a lot of late hours on FISE. You're going to find yourself busy."

"Fine by me. What's Ron been up to?"

"I'm not updated myself yet," Dyer said. "Been too tied up with budgets and stuff. One of the things I want to do today is spend some time with you and Ron to see how it's going. Probably later on this morning. I've got a few things to clear out of the way first."

They had cut across one corner of the small plaza outside the elevator and entered a broad pedestrian throughway flanked by display windows on one side and a panoramic view across to New Jersey on the other. They turned off after a short distance and walked through a set of glass doors embossed with internally edge-lit designs to enter a spacious reception lobby. The words glowing softly on the holographic planar image floating a foot in front of the wall by the door read:

CITY UNIVERSITY OF NEW YORK
FACULTY
OF
INFORMATION PROCESSING SCIENCES
SHANNON SCHOOL
OF
SYSTEMS PROGRAMMING

"Much though it surprises me to say so, it's good to be back," Chris remarked as they passed on through the lobby and exchanged greetings with Peggy, the smiling freckle-faced receptionist, who was combing her hair using her desk screen as a mirror. "Do you know, Ray, I've a horrible suspicion you people will make a New Yorker out of me yet."

"That I'd have to see," Dyer told him, smiling.

They left the lobby and followed a broad marble-floored corridor that took them into a part of the building signposted as DEPARTMENT OF SELF-ADAPTIVE PROGRAMMING. The doors that opened onto the corridor at intervals bore an assortment of names, most of them followed by letters and degrees. Signs hanging from the ceiling above marked turnoffs to such places as: NATURAL LANGUAGE PROJECT; LECTURE THEATERS C THRU E; IMAGE ANALYSIS; HEAD OF DEPARTMENT and SIMULATION LAB. Eventually they left the main corridor beneath one of the signs near the far end. The sign read simply, HESPER unit.

Dyer ignored the door marked DR. RAYMOND E. DYER, PROJECT LEADER, and went with Chris through the next, a short distance farther on, upon which the sign read: HESPER lab.

Inside was a miniature maze of partitioned offices divided by an open central area which revealed some of the equipment racks in two lab bays at the rear. The casual jumble of document-scattered tables, sagging storage racks, untidy bookshelves and stacked computer output blended well with the profusion of posters, technical charts, magazine clippings and cartoons that adorned most of the available space to produce the characteristic brand of cheerful disorder that research workers everywhere seem to feel most at home in. It was an environment that had evolved semirandomly to suit the whims of its inhabitants. Orderly and methodically planned surroundings went with more orderly and methodical kinds of work.

Betty Thorn, the Unit's middle-aged, motherly and meticulous administrator, who also doubled as Dyer's secretary, was making coffee at the small table near her desk by the second door to Dyer's office. She turned a head of wavy, slightly graying hair to glance back over her shoulder as they entered.

"Good morning, Ray. Good to see you back, Chris. You're just in time. Like a cup?"

"Betty, where would I be without you?" Dyer said with reverence. "Mmm . . . please. Strong."

"Sometimes I dread to ask," she replied with mock seriousness. "Did you get to Florida in the end, Chris?"

"Thanks. Yes . . . It was quite fun. I'm not sure I'd jump at the idea of making it a second home though." Chris peeled off his parka and draped it carelessly on the stand inside the door.

"Did you see the Space Center like I told you?" Betty asked him.

"We spent a day there, yes. There were four or five launches. That was worth going to see on its own. Bloody noisy though."

"The only thing he seems to remember is some guy breaking a leg," Dyer mumbled absently. He had swiveled the screen on Betty's desk around on its flexible support arm and was using the touchpad to interrogate the mail.

"Really!" Betty's voice took on a note of alarm which failed to conceal her interest. "Who?"

"Oh, he wasn't with us," Chris replied nonchalantly. "Just some body-beautiful twit who fell off his skis."

"He wasn't hurt bad, was he?"

"No—nothing serious. That's why it was funny."

"That's good to hear, anyhow," Betty said, sounding relieved. "Ron. Want a coffee?" She addressed her last words in a raised voice toward the open door of the shambles of an office that Chris shared with Ron Stokes, another of Dyer's senior people and Chris's partner on the FISE project. The figure already hard at work inside jerked his head up from the mess of programming manuals and notes littering the desk in front of him.

"Yeah." The voice was loud and firm. "Black. Hi guys." With that, Ron hunched back over the desk and resumed scribbling furiously.

Dyer continued to scan casually over the items that appeared on the screen, tagging them via the touchpad as he went. Progress report from Ron to be checked . . . he'd do that this morning. Looks good. Departmental cost *vs* budget statistics . . . file and forget. Letter from Prof. Graulich in Hamburg . . . list of questions about Kim's work on programmed instinctive motivation . . . résumé of Graulich's own work . . . references to published papers . . . read closely later. Reminder that Chris is due back today . . . delete. Quote from DEC for voice-channel add-ons to PDP-130 . . . delegate to Ron and Chris. Odds and ends of admin stuff . . . Betty to take care of . . . Behind him

Betty was telling Chris all about her daughter and her six-month-old grandson in Florida. Everybody in the unit knew all about Betty's grandson.

"Hey, how about this." Dyer half-turned and gestured toward the screen. "A group in Tokyo reckon they've found a way of growing high-density memories from synthetic DNA. They're saying it'll be a hundred times cheaper than e-beaming array crystals." Chris stepped a pace forward and ran a disdainful eye over the message. It was a news item passed on by Frank Wescott, who ran the HESPER lab at CIT.

"This computer is dangerous. Please do not feed," Chris remarked in solemn tones. "Could be interesting. Anything else?" Dyer brought up the next item, a note from Laura Fenning saying she would be in later on that morning and would appreciate it if Dr. Dyer could spare some time to comment on the notes she'd prepared. He groaned aloud and his face dropped.

"What's she doing coming in today?" he protested. "I thought she wasn't due in until Wednesday."

"Looks like she changed her mind," Betty said with inarguable logic.

"Hell!" Dyer muttered irritably. "I've got a lot to do today. That's one thing I could do without."

"Oh dear." Chris picked up Ron's coffee and began moving away toward their office. "I think I ought to go and see how Ron's been getting on. See you later."

Dyer continued to fume while Betty turned her attention to returning various documents to the file drawer by her desk. A few seconds later Ron's voice rose from the other side of the still open doorway.

"We're gonna have to change the whole structure of the default linkages. I still say they're all screwed up."

"They're *not* screwed up," Chris's voice sighed with infinite patience. "Did you extend the frame-matching algorithm."

"It doesn't need to be extended. I keep telling ya that—"

"Shut up for a second, Ron. What test limits did you set on the I-sub-D parameter?"

"I-sub-D had nothing to do with it. I-sub—"

"It has too got something to do with it. In fact, if you'd only stop for a second to think about it . . ."

"It has *not!* I-sub—"

"Shut up, please."

"I-sub-D only affects the—"

"SHUT UP, RON!"

Dyer sighed. Despite their diametrically opposed natures, Chris and Ron were inseparable. That meant they would go on like that all day. Still irritable, Dyer frowned at the unoccupied desk standing opposite Betty's on the other side of the doorway that led out to the corridor.

"Where's Pattie?" he asked. "I thought she was on early-start this week?" Betty sensed his mood and made a face.

"Usual thing I guess," she replied in guarded tones. "You know how kids are—especially Pattie." Without being asked she went on, "Do you want to talk to her about it or shall I?"

"She's your assistant," Dyer said. "See what you can do. If that doesn't work I'll talk to her."

"Okay. Oh, Kim wanted to talk to you as well. She's over in Services but she said she'll be in around ten. I said I thought it'd be okay. She said it was personal."

"What time's that Fenning woman showing up?" Dyer asked,

"The message didn't say."

"Personal. Oh God." Already it had been a long day. Dyer opened the door into his office. "Okay, I'll be in all morning. I've got a report to check over. Tell whoever shows up first to come on in."

"Will do," Betty acknowledged.

He sat down at his desk, activated a voice channel on his own console and tapped his personal access code into the touchpad.

"Active," a synthetic voice informed him from the audio grille.

"Data bank," he replied. "Reports reference HESPER slash S.A.P. slash Stokes two-zero-nine slash D dot seven. Video only." The screen presented him with the machine's interpretation.

"Confirmed," he said. A few seconds went by while computers elsewhere in the building relayed his request across the city to the local primary node of the North East Sector of the North American Region of the TITAN network.

"Females!" he muttered.

"Excuse me?" the console inquired politely.

He sighed.

"Delete."

"Deleted," the console advised.

Machines! he thought to himself.

◈ CHAPTER TWO ◈

"Okay, Ray. We agree on that one." Kimberly Sinclair checked off an item from the list glowing on the view-pad balanced on her knee, and paused for a second to consider the next.

As he waited with his chin propped on the ball of his thumb, Dyer studied the soft cascade of fair-brown hair tumbling around her shoulders and the interesting undulations that pressed outward against the jacket and skirt of her expensively tailored pale-blue suit. The lines of her face were straight and firm, but rounded just sufficiently not to appear harsh. One of those fascinating women who exuded sexuality without in any way qualifying as beautiful, he thought. For an instant he felt a pang of envy for her lawyer husband, Tony, who seemed to spend most of his life airborne between one city and another. On second thought, he decided he wouldn't stand the pace for a month. Maybe Tony had the same problem.

At thirty, Kim was the second oldest after Dyer among the unit's technical staff, which included everybody except Betty and Pattie, and was generally acknowledged as unofficial second-in-command. Dyer often had the feeling that she shouldn't have been in research at all. She operated in perpetual top gear, managing to combine a demanding career with an impossible private life that was jammed with citizens' meetings, committees for this and associations for that, and eternal campaigning, usually against bureaucracy in some form or other. She assailed both with the fervor of an evangelist on doomsday's eve with half the world still to be saved. Dyer thought she'd have been better placed managing a firm of stockbrokers on Wall Street, maybe a multinational or even the government. But computers had always been her passion and she held a long list of academic and innovative distinctions to prove it. And when a woman like that developed a passion like that, other people's ideas on how she might otherwise be employing her talents ceased to matter very much.

Two main projects accounted for most of the HESPER Unit's time. The first was FISE, which was concerned essentially with developing reliable methods of programming computers to exhibit common sense; Chris and Ron were handling that. The other project involved refining existing techniques for constructing self-modifying programming systems that were capable of evolving their own problem-solving strategies as ascending structures of goals and subgoals. In a way it was analogous to implanting basic "instinctive" drives which the machine could then develop progressively more effective ways of satisfying. The process mimicked natural evolution but at electronic speeds. This was Kim's project, in which she was assisted by Allan Morrow, youngest of the team and one of the two postgraduate students assigned to the unit. The other, Judy Farlin, was also theoretically under Kim's wing, but spent most of her time working on her doctoral thesis ("Evolution of Objective Hierarchies in Goal-Oriented Self-Extending Program Structures") and consequently was not really involved actively.

"Oh yes," Kim said, looking up. "Another thing I wanted to mention. We're still having problems with Services about the graphics-room reservation system. Somebody really ought to talk to Hoestler about it and get somebody's butt kicked good and hard over there. I tried getting some sense out of them this morning but it's useless."

"Screwed up the bookings again?" Dyer guessed. Kim nodded and tapped the screen of the viewpad emphatically.

"Exactly. Ray, I'm sick to death of them over there. Twice last week Judy was told she had a slot reserved for a room and then couldn't get in because it'd been double-booked."

"Aw Christ! Judy again, huh?"

"Yes, that's the whole point," Kim said with feeling. "The kid's right in the middle of trying to get her thesis straight and she needs some time on mural graphics. Those buttheads in Services keep blaming it on the computer instead of learning how to do their jobs. If they don't know how to run a system properly—here of all places—then they ought to be kicked out and replaced by people who do!"

"Okay, okay," Dyer held up his hands to stem the tirade. "I agree. They're doing a lousy job. I'll talk to Hoestler about it. For the amount they're charging out of our budget for when we do get in, we could almost set up our own graphics room here in the unit. What's next?"

"It's not as if there were anything difficult about it," Kim went on. "All they have to do—"

"Okay," Dyer said again, "It will be done. What's next?" Kim glanced down automatically.

"I guess we're about done," she said, cutting the pad off and snapping it shut. She glanced at the clock behind Dyer's head and uncrossed her legs to begin rising. "I wanted to call Eric before eleven. Anything else you want to add while I'm here?"

"No, but I thought you did," Dyer looked mildly surprised, "Everything you've been talking about's been University business. Betty said you wanted to see me about something personal." Kim frowned for a second.

"Oh yes." She sat down again. Her voice fell to a more confidential note. "It's Allan."

"What is?"

"Him messing around with Pattie all the time," Kim said. "She showed up forty minutes late again today, with him slipping in the door five minutes later and looking furtive, purely by coincidence of course. I don't want to get mixed up in anybody's personal affairs, Ray, but there are such things as common sense and discretion."

"Okay, I know what you mean," Dyer said, half-raising a hand. "I agree with you. He's being a public ass and somebody ought to talk to him. Leave it to me. I'll ask Betty to say wise words to Pattie too."

"I'm not trying to pass the buck or anything," Kim told him, "It's just . . . well, you know how it is with young guys. I thought it might be better coming from you."

"Don't worry about it. I'll—" The chime sounded from his console. "Excuse me a sec." He touched a key to accept the call and Betty's face greeted him.

"Sorry to interrupt, but Laura Fenning's here," she announced. Dyer could see the familiar classically oval face and raven-black sweep of Cleopatra hair framed behind Betty's shoulder. He uncovered his teeth in what he hoped would pass for a smile.

"One more minute, Betty. Good morning, Miss Fenning." He cut the display and turned back toward Kim, who was already rising to her feet. "Where were we? Oh yeah . . . don't worry about it. I'll talk to him."

"Thanks," Kim acknowledged, "Then I guess we're about done. I'll leave you to get on. See you later."

"Sure."

Kim vanished abruptly, leaving the door open in response to Dyer's waved request not to close it. Dyer recalled Ron's report to the screen and rapidly finished the comments he had been appending when Kim arrived. Part of his mind was vaguely aware of Laura Fenning's precisely cultivated and seductive voice floating through the open doorway as she talked to Betty. It was one of the usual topics.

"But women were never meant to do men's jobs, Betty. Why should they? Their place is in their home with their families, that's all I'm saying. It's their *right*."

"Well now, I don't know about that," Betty replied, sounding dubious. "I just wasn't brought up to think that way. Equal shares for both, they said in my day. That meant everybody. All these young girls today complaining about having to stand on their own feet. Doesn't sound right."

"But that's the point I'm trying to make. Betty," Laura's voice urged. "It *is* right. Fifty years ago it might have been necessary, but times have changed now. Why should we continue to perpetuate outmoded traditions just because men find it suits them?"

Dyer sighed as he added his final comment and tagged the report to be copied back under Ron's mail code. She'd been in the place five minutes and was subverting the troops already. He snapped off the screen and continued to stare at it for a moment while he reoriented his thinking fully to immediate matters. He didn't want to be cornered alone in here, he decided. He stood up, braced himself, and walked out of the office.

◎ CHAPTER THREE ◎

"Hi there," Laura greeted him as he came out of his office. "I hope the change in plans hasn't caused any problems. I wanted to go through some notes I made about how TITAN came about. It really needs to be done by Friday and I don't think Wednesday would leave enough time. That okay?"

Dyer frowned as he avoided Betty's half-concealed smirk. Laura was always doing things like this.

"Well, we've got a pretty full day on," he replied, deliberately making his voice a trifle gruff. "You'll have to bear with being squeezed in somewhere. Chris just got back from vacation today and I wanted to check up on how he and Ron are getting along before lunch." Already he could feel his resolve beginning to melt. In the uncanny way that Laura had of speaking with her eyes, she was telling him that to go marching off and leave her standing there wouldn't really be becoming and he'd only feel mean afterward if he went and made an issue out of it. He paused for a second as his mind went off on a tangent searching for a face-saving way out. "They should have FISE up and running this morning," he said. "Why don't you come and have a look at it instead of hanging around here."

"Thanks. I'd like that," she said brightly. "I've never had a chance to see it before. Every time I've been in, somebody's always been fiddling around with some part of it or other." She began walking around the partitions that formed Chris and Ron's office and toward the lab area behind. "You'd really do yourself a favor if you'd just accept gracefully that you can't win," said the eyes.

As Dyer turned to follow, he caught a glimpse, through the half-open doorway next to Kim's office, of Pattie sitting on the edge of Allan Morrow's desk with her arm draped loosely on Al's shoulder while they talked earnestly in lowered tones. Dyer turned back and muttered irascibly to Betty.

"How long's she been in there?"

"Over half an hour," Betty replied tonelessly.

"Did you talk to her?"

"Yes I did. She said she'd make a point of showing up on time in future."

"What about this kind of thing?" Dyer asked, gesturing.

"I didn't go into that. I was hoping she'd be capable of figuring the rest out for herself, Want me to spell it out when she gets back?"

"If you would, Betty." Dyer nodded wearily. "Give it a try anyhow. If you find you need help, let me know." Shaking his head, he turned and began following the direction that Laura had taken toward the lab area.

Laura Fenning worked for the Production Research Department of Klaus Zeegram Productions, Inc., one of the larger corporations that made movies and documentaries for the public sector of the TITAN general-purpose network. Zeegram's productions covered the spectrum from soap opera to comedy to highly authentic historical epics, but the corporation tended to specialize in adventure and suspense with strongly scientific themes and backgrounds.

It was in this latter area that the ratings were beginning to reveal potential problems. Audiences were becoming more sophisticated and more demanding. In particular they were tiring of the familiar packaged versions of brilliant but mildly eccentric scientists, scientists' antiseptic wives and scientifically naïve politicians, all of which were becoming as stereotyped as the veteran sheriff, novice deputy and drifting loner of the old-style Westerns. The viewers wanted something more plausible.

Then somebody at Zeegram who was paid to be creative had

come up with the revolutionary idea of putting some effort into finding out what scientists were really like instead of making them what everybody thought they were like. The idea was to assign a few people to spend six months getting to know real-life scientists solving real-life problems in a number of selected environments covering pure research, government, medical and industrial scientific activities. The wealth of information thus obtained on how scientists really worked, how they lived, what they talked about, and so on would be enough to create a whole "character bank" that script writers would be able to draw upon for years to come.

Implementation of the scheme duly became the responsibility of the Production Research Department, which succeeded in persuading a number of organizations to agree to the proposal of allowing outside observers to spend a few days a week in their laboratories. Laura was selected as an ideal candidate for the job, having learned all the tricks of asking the right questions and ferreting out the answers during her three years with Zeegram. Furthermore she had written scripts herself for her previous employer and knew exactly the kinds of things that writers would be looking for.

Her assignments included certain groups in IBM's molecular circuit research facility in upstate New York and the International Space Administration's orbital construction design center on Long Island as well as a list of departments at CUNY. At around the time that Zeegram was making approaches to their prospective hosts, Professor Vincent Lewis, Dean of the Faculty of Information Processing Sciences at CUNY, was engaged in a fund-raising battle with the Mayor's Department and the Mayor just happened to have strong connections with a consortium of media companies which included Zeegram. Lewis thus turned out to be very approachable and cooperative indeed, and wasted no time in directing his senior staff members to "have a look round and see if you can come up with something that might interest them." Professor Edward Richter, who ran the Shannon School of Systems Programming, singled out Dr. Sigmund Hoestler, head of the Department of Self-Adaptive Programming, to pass the buck on to and Hoestler threw it at the

HESPER Unit. Thus it eventually came to rest on the desk marked Dr. Raymond E. Dyer.

Dyer thought that in principle the whole thing was probably a good idea. After all, anything that contributed toward improving the general level of awareness of why people like himself existed couldn't be a bad thing. He had been prepared to devote a generous portion of his time to whomever Zeegram ended up sending and in fact had quite looked forward to the exercise as promising something different. But when it turned out to be hours of patiently attempting to explain why the notion of living organisms evolving from inorganic matter was not absurd because teapots didn't sprout legs and walk, or why believing in invisible psychic emanations and in equally invisible quarks was not the same thing, enough rapidly became enough. He bitched repeatedly to Hoestler; Hoestler respectfully drew Richter's attention to the matter a couple of times; Richter mentioned it to Lewis once over lunch; Lewis didn't want to know. So Dyer was stuck for the duration.

When Dyer caught up with her, Laura was standing with Ron in front of a row of electronics racks and cubicles, staring down into what at first sight looked like a large, shallow, tabletop fishtank that measured about two feet square and was somewhere just under a foot in depth. One pair of opposite sides were of glass while the other two were formed by arrays of miniature laser tubes and optical control equipment, all connected by a mess of electrical cables and flexible tubes to a confusion of technology that filled the space underneath. Chris was sitting at a console in front of one of the tank's see-through sides, thoughtfully contemplating the rows of hieroglyphics glowing on one of its display screens.

"What we're doing is programming a learning computer to build up its own generalized conceptual framework with experience," Ron was saying. "The idea is to get it to be able to recognize and apply reasonable constraints when it attempts to develop a problem-solving strategy. That make sense?" Laura frowned and shook her head reproachfully.

"Sorry, Ron, I don't speak computerese. You'll have to put that into English."

"It means we're finding out how to give machines common sense," Dyer supplied, moving forward to join them. "When a baby's born, it doesn't know anything about the basic properties of the universe that it finds itself in or the other objects that exist there along with it. What it does have is a basic programming that enables it to form general concepts from a few specific lessons. So it can learn by experience as it gets older. What we're doing is developing ways of providing that kind of basic programming for a machine.'"

"It's called an IQ transplant," Chris murmured from his console without looking up.

"You mean like a kid doesn't need to go round burning itself on everything in the house to get the message that hot things hurt?" Laura offered after a moment's reflection.

Dyer nodded. "That kind of thing and more basic stuff too."

"How do you mean, more basic stuff?" Laura asked.

"The kind of thing that you have to know before you can even stretch your hand out to touch something," Dyer said. "All the things that are so obvious that you don't even realize you had to learn them once. But to a computer they're not obvious at all. We're finding out how to teach it." Laura was staring at him suspiciously. He went on, "Even a child of two has a mental model of objects occupying a three-dimensional space, and of itself being one of them. It can interpret visual patterns on its retina in terms of that space. It knows that objects fall if they're unsupported, that two of them can't be in the same place at the same time, that they continue to exist when you can't see them . . . that hard things can break and soft things can bend . . . things like that. Those things go together to set up a child's pattern of basic knowledge of the world around it. When it's given a problem to solve or when it sets out to perform some task, it automatically applies constraints, based on what it's learned, that enables it to separate the possible approaches that make sense from the ones that don't."

"Any problem at all is simple to solve when you take away all the constraints," Ron chipped in.

"Any problem at all?" Laura sounded distinctly skeptical.

"If the cat's got fleas, one guaranteed way of getting rid of them is to throw the cat in the incinerator," Chris came in. "Intense heat is a fail-safe way of killing fleas."

"The problem is it kills cats too," Ron said. "But when you gave me the problem you didn't tell me I wasn't supposed to do that. You assumed my own common sense would tell me that part of it. Except I happen to be a computer. I don't have any common sense."

"The solution is quite simple until you start applying commonsense constraints to it," Dyer summarized. "The more common sense you have, the more you'll constrain the acceptable solutions. So the decisions get tougher but the answers are more effective."

Laura traced a long, red-painted nail slowly along the glass top of the tank while she digested what had been said. Then she looked up and tossed her hair from the side of her face in the same motion.

"Okay, I think I can see what you're getting at," she said. "So how do you begin getting a machine to think like that?"

"By making it do exactly what a baby has to do," Dyer told her. "We give it a world to grow up in and learn from." He caught Laura's puzzled look and turned toward Chris. "How's Hector today?"

"Oh, he's feeling okay," Chris replied. "We had him running earlier. Want a demo for Laura?"

"Why not?" Dyer answered. Despite herself, Laura was becoming intrigued. She watched as Chris exchanged a brief dialogue with the console. Then a white iridescent glow appeared suddenly, pervading the entire volume of the tank. Laura jumped back instinctively with a squeal. Dyer grinned. After a few seconds the glow condensed into patches of color that quickly coalesced and stabilized into a vivid and detailed holographic image.

The image was a miniature representation of a one-story house, looking to all intents and purposes like a real, solid children's doll house, complete with fittings and furnishings. When Laura approached it again and studied it more carefully, however, she realized that all the objects represented were gross oversimplifications of the things they were supposed to be, rather than accurate models. It suggested the kind of surroundings that might have been created for a three-dimensional children's cartoon. Laura looked at Dyer inquiringly.

"That's FISE," Dyer explained, pointing at one of the cubicles nearby. "The image in the tank is FISE's world. We've given him a very simple world so that he can get his basic concepts straight without having to worry about lots of complications that exist in the real one."

"How do you know it's a him?" Laura challenged absently as she continued to study the image. Dyer raised his eyes momentarily toward the ceiling in a silent plea far patience.

"It's a him because we made it a him," Ron declared flatly. His glare dared her to dispute the rationale behind that. Dyer breathed silent relief when Laura merely sniffed, evidently electing not to take the point further. Chris waited patiently until the rumblings had died away and then touched another key. Immediately a figure appeared standing in the kitchen of the miniature house. Like the rest of the image, it was a cartoon caricature devoid of detail—just a face defined by a few lines, a mop of curly hair and a man's body clad in a red shirt and blue pants.

"That's Hector," Dyer informed her, "He lives in FISE's world along with a few other characters. We give FISE problems to solve and he attempts to solve them by manipulating Hector. Actually, FISE thinks he is Hector. Representing things visually like this is the best way of knowing what's going on inside FISE's mind. We can see straight away from the things he makes Hector do exactly what he knows and what he hasn't figured out yet. When he screws something up we straighten him out, after which he never makes the mistake again but usually goes straight on and screws something else up. As I said before, it's like having a baby that has to be told all the things that Nature normally programs it to be able to work out instinctively."

"Let's take it through the breakfast routine again," Ron suggested, directing his words at Chris. "There were still some funny things going on last time. I'd like to see it cleaned up."

Chris made no direct response but resumed tapping commands into the console, Laura looked from one side to the other and then at Dyer.

"What's the breakfast routine?" she asked.

Dyer motioned toward the tank. Hector had begun walking around the table toward the refrigerator. He opened the door and began transferring various items out and onto the working surface next to the stove.

"You see, FISE knows quite a lot already," Dyer commented. "He knows how to move Hector's legs to make him move across the room. He knows that Hector has to go around the table and not through it, that he can't get the things he wants out of the refrigerator unless the door's open and that to move them Hector has to be looking in the right direction and has to pick them up with his hands. All kinds of stuff like that."

"Watch him picking up the eggs," Ron said, pointing. "See . . . nice and gently. And watch how carefully he puts them down. He knows enough about eggs to realize that they don't last long if they're treated rough."

Laura watched in fascinated silence for a few seconds.

"How does he know that?" she asked, unconsciously accepting the machine's disputed gender. "Does he know what the shell's made of and work it out from there or something?"

"No," Dyer replied from the opposite side of the tank. "FISE has already learned it the hard way. Actually there are more computers involved than FISE. FISE only controls Hector and knows as much as Hector knows. The environment that Hector lives in is all managed by a team of computers that fills two of the other cubicles. Their collective name is PROPS. PROPS monitors everything that Hector does that affects his environment and computes the consequences accordingly. If Hector slams the egg down too hard PROPS will cause it to smash. Hector doesn't know why it smashed but PROPS does. All Hector knows is that it did and not to do it that way again."

"Ah, I'm beginning to see now . . ." Laura's voice trailed away for a moment. "Hector, in other words FISE, is simply confronted by an environment that's full of things that behave in particular ways that it has to find out about. What he has to do is connect causes with effects and make general inferences from what he learns." She looked at Dyer expectantly. "Am I right?"

"Pretty much," Dyer nodded. "Actually he's very rational when it comes to purely physical interactions with his environment. After all, that kind of thing only involves well-defined physical laws, and he is a computer. Where he has problems is with understanding what he *shouldn't do,* not what he *can't* do. Again, it's this question of common sense."

"What do you mean . . . ethics or something?" Laura frowned at him.

"You'll see," he replied. They returned their attention to the tank. Hector had by now put a pan on the stove and switched the stove on, an achievement which, judged by Ron's whoop of approval, represented a new pinnacle of intellectual development that Hector had been struggling valiantly to attain for some time. He then picked up a stick of butter and stood looking at it, giving every impression of bringing profound powers of concentration to bear on some problem.

"What's he doing?" Laura asked.

Ron shook his head and emitted a sigh of exasperation.

"He knows how much butter is needed to fry an egg, but he can't figure out how to get that much out of the wrapper," he said. "The first time he tried it, he sliced a piece off of the end with the knife and threw it in the pan, wrapper and all. We told the dummy you don't fry pieces of wrappers with food and to come up with something better next time. He's thinking about it."

Ron's ruddy face took on a sudden look of wonder. He leaned forward and peered down into the tank excitedly. "He's actually unwrapping it!" he roared in unconcealed delight, though with a strong undertone of sarcasm. "Go on, Hector. Attaboy, Yeah . . . see, it's easy. You can do it." Ron's face creased abruptly into a frown. "Oh my God!" He turned his eyes away in anguish and pointed disbelievingly at the tank. Hector had carefully placed the intact egg inside the pan.

"Chris," Ron pleaded. "Ask him what the f—" He caught sight of Laura just in time. "Ask him what he thinks he's doing, willya?" Chris remained expressionless and input a stream of symbols to the computer. A baritone voice issued at once from the audio grille set to one side of the main panel.

"I'm frying the egg," it said.

Laura jerked around in surprise.

"It's okay," Dyer reassured her. "That's only FISE. We only use voice channels one-way. By using the touchboard to talk to him, at least we can be sure that he understood exactly what we said. If you added possible semantics problems on top of all this, the whole thing would become ridiculous."

Ron was pacing back and forth before the tank, opening and clenching his fists as if struggling to fight down rising impatience.

"FISE," he said, in a voice that had to be forced to remain slow and reasonable, the kind of voice one would use when talking to a persevering but hopelessly backward child. "How are you going to eat the egg when you've fried it?" At the console, Chris silently translated Ron's question into touchboard commands.

"With the knife and fork, off the plate, on the table," FISE replied proudly.

"Very good, FISE," Ron approved in dulcet tones. Then his voice began on a slightly higher note and rose rapidly to end in a shriek. "How are you going to cut the egg with the knife when it's still inside the goddam shell?" Chris conveyed the essential information via the console.

"I wasn't very sure about that," FISE confessed. "But you told me I wasn't supposed to break eggs."

"It's okay to break an egg if you want to fry it," Ron said, having regained his composure. Hector promptly picked the egg out of the pan, crushed it in his fist and held it out for the resulting mess to drip back into the pan. Laura made a face and gave an involuntary exclamation of disgust.

"Now you can see the kind of thing I meant," Dyer commented. "Totally rational solutions but no commonsense constraints."

"Now FISE, we're gonna try it again," Ron was saying "What you have to remember is that you don't want any bits of shell in the rest of the egg that you're going to eat. Got that? All you have to do is figure out how you're going to end up with the shell in the trash can and the rest of the egg in the pan. Okay?"

"How about the fat?" FISE asked after pondering on his mission for a while.

"What about it?" Ron was momentarily nonplused.

"Do I not want any fat on the rest of the egg either?"

Ron spun around as if he had just been addressed by an angel from Heaven.

"Hey! He's trying to generalize! For you, FISE, that was a pretty smart question. Very *good!* No, the fat's okay but try and keep it to a minimum. Right," he said to Chris when Chris had finished translating. "Reset it to square one and let's give it another whirl."

"You can see now why we picked a very simple world," Dyer said to Laura while Chris was resetting the program. "It's so easy to forget things like the fat because they're so obvious to humans. If we made it any more complex we'd be tying ourselves in knots trying to keep track of what's going on."

In the session that followed, Hector succeeded in cracking the egg with the back of a knife and ended up cooking a satisfactory meal. Eventually Hector managed, after several false moves, to transfer the meal to a plate and convey it back to the table.

"Wait, wait, wa-it a second, FISE," Ron groaned wearily. "You can't start eating it yet."

"Why not?" FISE inquired.

"Because you're still standing up, that's why you dumbhead, Before you start eating you should be sitting down." Hector promptly grabbed the plate and sat down on the floor. Ron moaned miserably, dragged himself over to the nearest cubicle and stood pounding his forehead on its top panel. "I can't stand it. I'm gonna wind up as nuts as it is. Chris, *do* something with it for Christ's sake."

Eventually Dyer and Laura left Chris still tapping to the accompaniment of Ron's yelling and moved away from the lab area and back toward Dyer's office. On the way, Laura reminded him that they had not yet looked at the TITAN notes she wanted to check over, and suggested they could do so over lunch. Dyer hesitated instinctively for a second, then agreed. What the hell? he thought. For once Laura had seemed to go out of her way to avoid being trying.

When they passed Betty's desk, she gave him a message that Hoestler wanted to talk to him first thing after lunch.

"You'd better bring your coat," he said to Laura.

"I'm going to have to throw you out as soon as we finish. I won't be coming directly back to the lab."

While Laura was slipping on her coat, he noticed that Pattie was at her desk, poring diligently over the figures in front of her and seemingly terrified of lifting her eyes from them. Which reminded him . . .

"You go on," he said to Laura as she moved toward the door. "I'll join you out in the corridor. There's one quick thing I've just remembered."

A few seconds later he strode into the office that Al Morrow was using and closed the door softly behind him. Al looked up from the coding sheets he had been checking. His face started to break into a grin, then fell abruptly as he saw the expression on Dyer's face.

"You're making a prize asshole of yourself," Dyer stated simply. "I'm telling you here and now to pack it in."

Al flinched as if he had been struck in the face. Then the color started rising from his collar and a look of pained indignation compressed his features. He swallowed hard and his grip tightened visibly on the armrest of his chair.

"I guess I haven't been keeping very good time," he mumbled awkwardly. "Okay. All I can say is I'll put that right. Today was kinda—" Dyer cut him off with a curt shake of his head.

"It's not just that and you know it. I'm talking about all this screwing around with Pattie. You're making it a public spectacle and that isn't a smart thing to do. I'm telling you to wise up."

"I don't want to get into an argument, Ray," Al protested weakly. "But that's a kinda personal matter, if you know what I mean. What I do in my own time outside the—" Dyer shut him up again with a wave of his hand. He knew what was coming next. He had already heard all the outraged justifications and noble speeches in defense of young love threatened in its prime.

"I know what you're gonna say. Just don't say it," Dyer went on. "You're acting as if you just found out about sex for the first time in your life. Well maybe you have, but the rest of the world knew all about it a long time ago so we don't wanna hear about it. Okay?"

Al turned a deep shade of scarlet and glanced around as if looking for a convenient black hole to jump into. Dyer observed him with satisfaction and allowed his tone to soften a fraction.

"As far as I'm concerned there are two Patties," he said. "One lives outside this place and does what the hell she pleases and the other one works for me. The one that works for me is company business because the company has paid for her time, not you. And I'm telling you what a professor told me when I was at Harvard Medical School: 'Thou shalt not dip thy quill in company ink!' That's all I've got to say. From this point on it's forgotten. Okay?"

A couple of minutes later he rejoined Laura in the corridor outside.

"Sorry about that," he said as they began walking. "We've been having a slight staff problem."

"Pattie mixed up in it?" Laura inquired casually. He turned his head toward her in surprise.

"Yes. Who told you?"

"Nobody," Laura replied lightly. "Just feminine insight."

"Oh Christ. We're not back to that, are we?"

Laura gave a short laugh.

They walked on in silence until they emerged into the main corridor that led to the staff restaurant.

"I was thinking while I was waiting for you," Laura told him. "Why is he called FISE. Does it stand for anything in particular?"

"Functional Integration using Simulated Environment," Dyer said.

"Oh. I see. That sounds impressive."

"But Chris has got his own version."

"Really? What does Chris call it?" Laura asked.

Dyer grinned. "Fastest Idiot Seen on Earth," he told her.

◉ CHAPTER FOUR ◉

"So was that what they call an intelligent computer?" Laura's voice was lined with mildly mocking satisfaction as she removed the plate of curried chicken from the small dispensing hatch in the wall at the end of the booth. Dyer turned his head from gazing out over the river far below the window alongside them. He missed the intonation and answered her matter-of-factly.

"It's obviously got a long way to go yet, but it's about as advanced as anything you'll find anywhere."

"Advanced!" She stared at him incredulously. "Ray, if you weren't looking so serious you'd have to be joking. If that was an intelligent machine, Stegosaurus was a genius."

"Aw, you're missing the whole point," he told her with a shadow of irritation as he realized the turn the conversation was taking. "Computers are evolving backward."

"If that means they're becoming more stupid, I think I agree with you."

"No. I didn't mean that and you damn well know it." He paused in the middle of picking up his fork. "Look. In natural evolution, instincts came first, common sense later and intellectual capabilities last. It had to be that way because the only thing that mattered was the ability to survive. An animal has to develop an awareness of its environment and learn how the things in that environment operate

48

if it figures on staying around for very long. Intelligence as we understand it has an enormous survival value too, but that comes later."

"If you accept the idea of evolution," Laura reminded him pointedly.

"I don't want to go into all that again," he muttered, then resumed his former tone. "Computers didn't evolve from survival-dominated origins. They were *designed* to do very complex, very specialized things, very efficiently. They can mimic Man's intellectual feats superbly well. Not only that, they're a lot better at some of them than we are . . . for instance they're faster, more accurate, and don't get tired or fed up. But they don't possess any of the commonsense awareness of what they're doing or what's going on around them that animal ancestors had to evolve in order to stay healthy. That's what I meant when I said they're evolving backward. They're good at what we ended up with, but they don't have what we had to start with."

"So that's what you're doing?" Laura conceded grudgingly. "Trying to teach them how to tie what's going on all around into a picture that means something?"

"You could put it that way," Dyer said with a nod. He returned his attention to his meal and began eating at last.

"So what's the point of it?" Laura asked after a while. "Okay. You've spent millions of dollars and ended up with a computer that's smart enough to know how to fry an egg. What are you supposed to do with it?"

"All kinds of things," Dyer replied, sounding deliberately nonchalant. He shrugged while he finished chewing. "Give it a fusion power plant to run. Manage a space mission . . . take charge of New York City air-traffic control. Whatever . . ." He knew he was being provocative and took quiet pleasure from observing the desired effect.

"What!" Laura almost choked. "Put that imbecile we just saw in charge of a power plant? It can't even take charge of a kitchen. Tell me you're not serious."

"I am serious. The computers that run all those things right now are a lot dumber than the one you just saw . . . if you insist on judging them by human standards, anyway. On the other hand, if you base your opinion on the ability to crank through fifty million calculations in a second then they're quite smart." He paused, unable to contain a smile, and added, "Your problem, you see, Laura, is that you're too much of a chauvinist."

"I'm a what . . . ?" The conditioned reflex in her started to respond but she saw what he was doing and checked it deftly. Dyer complimented her inwardly. "They're labor-saving gadgets, sure," she continued. "They're good for doing all the repetitive mechanical stuff—I'll buy that. But you'll always have to have people in charge. You're not telling me you think you can come up with a machine that's capable of exercising human judgments too . . . not after what I've just seen. That I won't buy."

"But programming the computers is labor too," Dyer pointed out. "And when you want them to do more complicated jobs, it gets to be hard labor. So why not have the computers generate their own programs?"

"Because they don't understand the problems that the programs have to solve."

"Exactly." Dyer nodded in satisfaction. "They don't understand the problems because they're not equipped to be able to understand them. They don't have the basic capability to learn and connect things together that any newborn baby has . . . or they didn't have until HESPER machines came along. But supposing you could educate FISE to the level where he knew enough about real-world concepts to be able to make commonsense decisions for himself reliably. Then you could put him through a specialist course on—I dunno, say something like steel-making—so he knows all the things you have to aim for in order to run a steel plant efficiently. Then you let him practice for a while, maybe by connecting him to another computer that's pretending to be a steel plant. Because he's smart he can learn from his experiences and because he's a computer he can learn fast. Pretty soon you've got a hotshot manager who can run rings around any team in the business. Then you ship him out into the real world, give him a real plant to run and let him get on with it. The beauty of it is he'll do all the right things, but you haven't had to go through the hard labor of programming in every specific detail of every situation that might ever arise and every specific detail of what to do if it does. All you gave him was the basic capability to learn. The rest he figured out for himself."

Laura continued to eat in silence for a while, keeping her eyes directed down at the plate before her. Her fashionable clothes, meticulously styled hair and faultless grooming made her look out of place among the casual shirts, denims and well-worn traditional jackets of a university restaurant. There was no doubt, Dyer thought, that in purely physical terms she was stunning. He found himself trying to picture what she would look like stripped of the close-fitting velvyon dress that changed its hue from midnight blue to silver as she moved.

Laura looked up at him. "If FISE is a learning computer, what's a HESPER computer?" she asked. "I thought HESPER was supposed to be some kind of learning computer too."

"It is," he replied simply, "Or more precisely, it's a programming technique. It stands for HEuristic Self-Programming Extendable Routine—a set of interrelated programs that form a structure that can learn as it goes."

"I'm not sure I see the difference."

"It's a question of degree," he said. "HESPER systems are specialized to handle one particular kind of application. You could set up a HESPER system that will optimize itself over a period of time, say . . . play a game of chess. The more games it plays, the better it gets until you can't keep up with it. But that's all it's good for. But something like FISE would possess a broad base of general concepts. It could learn to handle anything. So all you'd have to do is develop it once and get it right instead of having to set up thousands of different HESPER systems all the time. It would supersede HESPER programming in the same kind of way that HESPER is taking over from the classical distributed parallel programming that's been around since . . . aw, the 1980s, 1990s."

Laura looked at him quizzically for a moment as if she expected him to draw some conclusion from his own words. Then she sighed and shook her head.

"Can't you see how irresponsible the whole thing is?" she asked.

"Irresponsible?" There was no surprise in Dyer's voice. Everything had been going too smoothly.

"Criminally! They've been plugging HESPER machines into the TITAN network all over the world for over a year now, haven't they? So those things are out there, going through their learning processes and being put in control of manufacturing plants, transportation systems and everything else, yet from what you've just told me they're even dumber than FISE is. How can you say it isn't irresponsible to give idiots like that a fusion plant?"

"Because they're not the same thing," Dyer insisted. "HESPER machines are designed simply to be able to get steadily better at doing a particular job. They've been thoroughly tested, they're well understood and there's nothing mysterious about them. FISE is a first step toward something radically different. You can't judge them both by the same criteria."

But Laura was only just warming up.

"How can they be well understood when they've only been going into TITAN for a year?" she demanded. "You said yourself they need time to learn and that they don't have any common sense anyway. What's to stop them starting to do things that don't make sense?"

"They can only work inside the limits they're designed for," Dyer told her. "If a HESPER machine is set up to coordinate the communications traffic across part of the net, it can only learn how to do the job better. It can't make things worse because it isn't programmed to, and it can't do anything else because it doesn't have any generalized capabilities."

"But it extends its own programs as it goes along," Laura retorted. "That's what you just said the last time I was here. So machines are out there that are putting stuff into those programs that nobody knows about. So how can anybody know what they might do? You have to admit that nobody can claim to understand them completely anymore. That means there's a whole planetful of people being used as guinea pigs. Who ever asked them whether or not they wanted all these machines running everything anyhow? Nobody asked me."

"Aw come on," Dyer replied gruffly. "You're not gonna give me one of those back-to-the-good-old-days speeches, are you? How did

s.

ne

hem

body

n't fight

ing in life

usiness you're

machines as well,

ESPER is just a first

e shooting match over

just doesn't cross your

. Then the whole setup

e right back in the bad old

of."

ts next logical—" Dyer began,

dication. But the people who have

people who think the way you do. You

selves and the rest of us have to live in it.

her bluntly. "People like you do get a say in

y in it. Society evolves the way it does because

sult of billions of individuals all pushing and

irections. In other words it's what best suits most

t of the time. Therefore things always get better

automatically defined by the process. It's the way

to go. If they didn't, then they'd go some other way

omething else would automatically become better."

him v

"Yo

"I never sa

big girl now

ago and I happ

whole point. You

say it won't work. W

the way they are? Tha

Dyer sat back and

buying.

"You could have said t

"When you start thinking lik

keep moving."

"Why? Why do I have to kee

I happen to be? Why can't I just sta

Dyer reflected on the question for

"Because everybody else will keep mo

"When you find you've been left behind, y

anymore. That's when you remember how yo

they live fifty years ago? People living like zombies, doing the same thing day in, day out, five days a week, fifty weeks a year, right through from when they left school to when they got put out to pasture . . . and being conditioned into accepting it as normal. Think they want to go back to that? Not on your life . . . no more than they want to put their kids back down in coal mines."

"Okay, okay," Laura held up a pacifying hand. "I don't want to go back to that either. I didn't say anything about the good old day. You're always twisting things, Ray. What I'm concerned about is the future. We've put all these machines everywhere and connected them all together and, yes I agree, they're doing a pretty good job. Nobody starves these days, nobody goes without much, people don't fight about the things they used to, everybody does his own thing in life and hey, isn't that nice.

"But people have always been in control. This business you're talking about sounds like handing control over to machines as well, and I'm just not convinced they can handle it. HESPER is just a first step. You'd be perfectly happy to hand the whole shooting match over to a bunch of morons because the thought just doesn't cross your mind that they might screw everything up. Then the whole setup would collapse in a heap and we'd all be right back in the bad old days that you're so delighted to be out of."

"It's just progress being taken to its next logical—" Dyer began, but Laura was not through.

"It isn't progress at all. It's abdication. But the people who have the say in what happens are all people who think the way you do. You shape the world to suit yourselves and the rest of us have to live in it. I don't like it."

"I disagree," he told her bluntly. "People like you do get a say in it. Everybody gets a say in it. Society evolves the way it does because it reflects the net result of billions of individuals all pushing and pulling in different directions. In other words it's what best suits most of the people most of the time. Therefore things always get better because better is automatically defined by the process. It's the way most people want to go. If they didn't, then they'd go some other way instead and then something else would automatically become better."

"Suppose I don't want to be stampeded along with the herd?" Laura challenged.

"Then don't be. Go live alone someplace and do your own thing your own way. Who's stopping you?"

"You're being ridiculous."

"I'm not. There are plenty of places you could set up a shack and try it the way people used to. You'd soon be knocking to come back in out of the rain, though. Then you'd see why they gave it up to go our way and why the old days changed into what we've got now."

Laura leaned forward to rest her elbows on the table and fixed him with a steely glare.

"You're twisting everything I'm saying again," she accused him. "I never said anything about wanting to tear down civilization. I'm a big girl now and grew up in Detroit and came to the big city ten years ago and I happen to love it. I *don't* want to see it torn down. That's my whole point. You want to put machines in charge of running it and I say it won't work. Why not keep them in their place and leave things the way they are? That way we know it works."

Dyer sat back and shook his head in a way that said he wasn't buying.

"You could have said that at any point in history," he replied. "When you start thinking like that, that's when you stagnate. Gotta keep moving."

"Why? Why do I have to keep moving if I'm satisfied out where I happen to be? Why can't I just stay and enjoy it?"

Dyer reflected on the question for a few seconds.

"Because everybody else will keep moving anyway," he said at last. "When you find you've been left behind, you don't feel so satisfied anymore. That's when you remember how you got to where you are."

◎ CHAPTER FIVE ◎

Dyer arrived at Sigmund Hoestler's office a few minutes before 2 p.m. He was shown straight in and to his mild surprise found that Vincent Lewis, the Dean of the Faculty, was there too. Hoestler, a big man with sagging fleshy cheeks and a shock of uncontrollable wiry hair, motioned Dyer into an empty chair next to where Lewis was sitting, and leaned forward to come straight to the point.

"I'm afraid we have some very serious problems that are going to affect you directly, Ray," he said in his usual throaty voice. "It looks as if we may be forced to close down your unit."

Dyer was halfway through the process of sinking back into a characteristically relaxed posture. The bombshell made him sit up again as if the chair had suddenly acquired a few kilovolts. He knew that Hoestler was a man of few words, but even so, the bluntness of the statement had caught him totally unprepared. He had barely begun opening his mouth to frame a question when Hoestler spoke again.

"I only found out about it myself this morning. Vince was in Washington over the weekend with the Secretary for CIM and some of his people. So don't get the idea that it's just petty local politics or anything like that. Vince, you could probably tell Ray about it better than I could."

Dyer turned expectantly toward Lewis, his features contorted into a frown of disbelief. Communications And Information Management was a comparatively new executive department of state, formed eighteen years previously in 2010. Originally it had been instituted in response to the need for a single authority to assume overall responsibility for operation of the integrated data communications and computing network that emerged when the military systems were declassified and merged into the already integrated commercial-industrial-scientific complex to form the EARTHCOM net. When HESPER nodes were later incorporated to transform EARTHCOM into the Totally Integrated Teleprocessing and Acquisition Network, TITAN, the Department of CIM automatically became the administrative authority for the NORAM Sector of the global system. As Hoestler had in effect said, the Department of CIM didn't mess around with interdepartmental university politics.

Lewis was impossibly tall and impossibly thin. He sat splayed in his chair at all angles like a marionette whose limbs had come out of joint everywhere, leaving him held together only by his clothes. When he was standing up he never failed to cut a distinguished figure, with his elegant crown of white hair, deeply lined face and inevitable immaculate, dark three-piece suit. Dyer had always found him something of an aloof and remote kind of person, but right now Lewis was showing every sign of distress and genuine concern.

"Certain events have happened recently, Ray, that have caused CIM to reconsider the whole philosophy of adding HESPER capability into the net," he said. "Some very senior people are pressing for TITAN to be reverted back to EARTHCOM until we get firm answers to some important questions. In a nutshell, they're saying that the move to upgrade EARTHCOM was premature, that we didn't know enough about HESPER at the time and we still don't, and that HESPER ought to be pulled out until we do."

Dyer looked from one to the other and spread his upturned palms.

"Events . . . ? What events?"

"About a week ago, TITAN came within a hair's breadth of killing five people," Lewis told him somberly. Dyer stared at him incredulously. Before he could say anything, Lewis went on. "It appears that HESPER program structures are capable of integrating to a far greater degree than anybody thought. They're starting to link things together in ways they were never supposed to and the results in behavior are impossible to predict."

Hoestler explained, in response to the still bemused look on Dyer's face. "It used the Maskelyne mass-driver to bomb an ISA survey team on the Moon. Could have wiped them out."

"*What?*" Dyer turned an incredulous face toward Lewis but the Dean nodded regretfully to confirm Hoestler's words.

"One of the HESPER-controlled subsystems in the Tycho node was given the job of shifting a piece of terrain that was forming an obstruction," he explained. "It was supposed to use normal earth-moving equipment to do it, but nobody bothered to tell it that. Somehow it managed to connect together information from several subsystems that shouldn't have been connected, and came up with what it thought was a better shortcut to solving the problem. According to the people who analyzed the system dump afterward, it seemed quite proud of itself."

Lewis went on to describe the incident on Luna in greater detail. As Dyer listened, his initial astonishment changed to growing concern. In 2020 he had moved out of neurological research in order to apply his knowledge of learning psychology to the field of self-adaptive programming and, after spending some time at M.I.T., had come to CUNY to set up the HESPER Unit, which had since gone on to spearhead development of the very techniques that were now being applied worldwide to transform EARTHCOM into TITAN. His knowledge of the technicalities of HESPER programming was shared by fewer than a handful of people. If it was anybody's, it was his baby.

"Unfortunately there happened to be an ISA team sitting practically on top of the target," Lewis continued. "But naturally, that didn't mean very much to the computers."

"Twenty sixty-pound packages of rock coming down at over a mile a second," Hoestler commented. "Every one was roughly equivalent to a two-thousand-pound bomb." He shrugged and made a face.

HESPER machines were learning machines, designed to be capable of identifying connections between previously nonrelated factors in order to solve new problems or to solve old ones in newer and better ways. But if what Lewis had said was correct, this capability was beginning to extend itself in ways that had never been intended, nor in fact even foreseen as possible. If the obstruction had been on the edge of Maskelyne Base itself instead of out on some remote construction site on Procellarum, there could easily have been a death toll of hundreds. And if this kind of thing could happen in the circumstances surrounding the events on Luna, what other kinds of things might happen anywhere, at any time?

They could easily instruct TITAN never to do that particular thing again, it was true, and TITAN wouldn't, but that wasn't the point. The point was that TITAN had demonstrated a capability to approach a perfectly reasonable objective from a totally unexpected direction, and in doing so come up with a solution that was inarguably rational from the machine's point of view but which, for other reasons that could never with the present state-of-the-art be conveyed to the machine, was absolutely unacceptable. Its next such experiment might well result in worse than a mere narrow escape.

"Okay." Dyer exhaled and nodded curtly. "I can see the problem. What I don't see is how it affects the unit. What has all this got to do with closing the unit down?" A new expression of disbelief spread across his face as a possible answer struck him. "You're not telling me they're panicking and putting a total ban on further research are you? That's ridiculous! They're gonna need all the expertise and facilities they can get if they're going to straighten TITAN out. We've got just the—"

Lewis interrupted with a wave of his arm and a shake of his head. "I didn't mean we're going to throw everybody out on the street," he said. "But the projects that your unit is currently working on are probably going to be stopped. That line of research is being funded by CIM with the aim of producing the technology that's supposed to replace HESPER one day. Now the guys at CIM are saying that they don't even want to think about what comes after HESPER because it's obvious we don't understand HESPER yet as much as we thought we did. In fact a lot of people are saying we should tear HESPER out of the system completely and only think about putting it back in when we can prove it's safe."

"In other words the money being spent on FISE could better be spent on other things for the time being, so FISE goes down the tubes," Hoestler summed up.

"I'm sorry, Ray, but it looks as if that's the way it is," Lewis said apologetically. "As you yourself more or less said a second ago, there's going to have to be a big re-examination of the whole HESPER concept. We'll probably be able to reassign your people to a new CIM contract in that area as soon as some specific objectives have been worked out. In the meantime, if I were you, I wouldn't waste too many nights' sleep hoping for any Nobel Prizes. You'll probably have to wrap it all up pretty soon."

Kim was just coming out of the lab when Dyer arrived back at the outer door to his office.

"Hi," she greeted cheerfully. "Betty told me you've just been over to see Hoestler. Did you get a chance to mention the business with the graphics moms?" Dyer turned his head in her direction but his eyes were far away.

"Uh? Oh . . . er no," he mumbled. "I'm sorry. I guess I must have forgotten about it." With that he walked on in, leaving Kim wearing a puzzled frown.

He sat for a long time, staring at the papers on top of his desk. Lewis's revelations had shocked him to the core in a way that he was only now beginning to appreciate. He had been as convinced about the potential benefits of HESPER as he had about anything in his life, and he had devoted more than a little effort to convincing others. TITAN had gone ahead on the basis of his recommendations as much as anybody's. To be sure, the final decisions had not been his to make, but the people who had made them had relied on the facts that he and others like him had presented. And a whole world had relied on those people and their advisers.

His mind went back to some of the things that Laura had said over lunch and to the confident—almost arrogant—reassurances that he had voiced a little over an hour before. Suddenly he felt far from reassured himself. He didn't feel arrogant at all.

He rose and went through the inner door into the lab. Betty greeted him with a couple of messages which he only half heard, one of which was a reminder that some members of a research team from Princeton were due the next morning and would be spending most of the day with the unit. Pattie tried beguiling him with a silent, innocent, wide-eyed look which he ignored. At that moment Judy Farlin came out of Kim's office, rummaged around in a file drawer for a few moments and then went back in carrying a folder. Dyer turned abruptly and went back into his own office where he called the Superintendent of Internal Services, bawled *him* out at considerable length and secured a guaranteed reservation for Judy for the first thing the next morning. He came back out, gave the details to Betty and asked her to pass them on to Judy. Then, feeling a little better, he went on through to the lab bay to see how Ron and Chris were getting along.

Hector propelled himself across the floor of the kitchen, stopped in front of the broken window and paused while FISE considered the situation.

"What happened?" Dyer asked. Ron, who was standing with his elbows resting on the opposite side of the tank, raised his head.

"We told him that the garbage pail had to go out in the yard." he explained. "So he threw it through the window." Dyer grunted and returned his gaze to the tank.

Hector reached out and grabbed hold of one of the jagged fragments of glass that remained around where the window had been. PROPS immediately caused a vivid red line to appear across Hector's hand. The gash proceeded to ooze blood profusely but Hector ignored it and continued tugging experimentally at the piece of glass in an effort to remove it.

"Hold it. Hold it there, Chris," Ron called out. The figure in the kitchen froze. "Now FISE," Ron said, adopting his stoic voice. "There are a few more things that you have to get straight about Hector. Glass cuts. Hector does not like being cut. You don't cut bits off him or permit him to be cut by anything if you can avoid it. Okay? You have to find a way to fix the window without cutting Hector in the process." A few seconds elapsed while Chris completed keying in the last addition to FISE's growing store of information.

"Question," FISE's voice said from the grille.

"What?" Ron inquired.

"When Hector was shaving, his hair got cut. Why was that okay?"

"Oh yeah, I forgot that," Ron agreed. "When any part of Hector's body starts to get cut it hurts, just like you already know for things that are too hot. When he feels that, he'll respond with a reflex that overrides everything else he's doing. Hair is an exception. It doesn't hurt when it's cut. An unshaven face is not a nice thing. Shaving in the morning is okay."

"Thanks," FISE acknowledged.

"Before you go any further, let's just try something," Dyer suggested. "I'd like to see how well it understood what Ron just said. Chris, could you reset to the point just before where Hector grabbed at the glass, and force the same action." Chris took a while to compose the commands. Dyer and Ron watched intently as Hector flashed back to his previous starting posture and approached the window once more. He grabbed at the glass as before but this time his hand jerked back again instantly. PROPS could justify no more than a slight scratch.

"Not bad," Ron conceded, sounding impressed.

"I'm almost tempted to suggest that we might be safe in upgrading his IQ to one," Chris murmured, leaning back in his chair to stretch his arms.

Dyer felt a sudden urge of excitement They were getting there! It was a slow and tedious business, certainly, but the first signs were there. It was all beginning to come together. To cut it off at this point would be tragic.

"Reset again, Chris, and let FISE handle it himself," he said. "Let's see if he can figure out a better way."

Hector tried several approaches, including wrapping his hand in the tablecloth and then in a towel, but Ron vetoed all of them. Eventually FISE gave up and Ron supplied a hint by suggesting that if Hector looked in the utility closet, he might find something with which to knock out the pieces of glass.

"The hammer is used for knocking things, but it would break the glass," FISE protested. "You told me that breaking glass isn't okay. What am I supposed to do?" Ron got excited again and delivered a lengthy exposition on the profound insights required, after which Hector made a reasonable job of clearing and cleaning out the window frame. Chris told PROPS to materialize a pane of glass and Hector placed it squarely in the frame after first, on his own initiative, stopping to put on a pair of gloves that just happened to be in the utility closet.

"This is interesting," Dyer commented. "Look. He didn't just turn away. He's waiting and watching the glass. FISE has connected it with something else he's learned somewhere that's telling him it might not be very stable." Sure enough, PROPS weighed up the shape and angle of the pane, couldn't make up its mind and flipped a random number. The pane began to fall inward. Hector stepped forward, caught it in one hand and repositioned it more carefully.

Three enthusiastic roars of approval greeted the performance. For once, Ron treated FISE to a jubilant stream of ungrudging congratulations. Chris reconsidered his earlier statement and suggested that the machine might qualify for whatever IQ category lay above one. Although the thought had been half in his mind, Dyer decided it was not the time to mention the things that had been said in Hoestler's office earlier in the afternoon. After all, he told himself, Lewis had not gone further than using the word "probably" several times. Nothing firm had been decided yet.

"Chris and I are gonna go eat out while we're deciding where to go later," Ron called across the lab as he pulled on his coat. "Want to join us, Ray?" Dyer looked up from the console, where he was studying some of the new coding linkages that FISE had constructed in the course of the afternoon's exercise.

"Huh? Oh, no . . . I think I'll stay on a while. This looks interesting. I'll have to take a rain check on it. Thanks all the same."

"Okay. See ya tomorrow." Ron moved away toward where Chris

was standing waiting by the door. "Chris, great idea!" he said as they began moving out into the corridor. "Why don't we catch a game later? There's one on tonight that I promise ya is going to be terrific."

"Netball or rounders?" Chris's voice inquired disdainfully.

"Hey, you've said that before. What is all this stuff?"

"Oh, just a couple of English games," Chris told him matter-of-factly.

"Really? Big-league stuff and all that, eh?"

"No. Actually they're normally played by schoolgirls."

"Schoolgirls?" Ron's voice rose in sudden outrage. "SCHOOLGIRLS! Hey, exactly what the hell are you getting at? If you're telling me what I think you're tel—" Dyer grinned to himself as the exchange faded away. Judy left with Betty and a few minutes later Allan tossed across a sheepish goodnight and went out to join Pattie, who was waiting in the corridor. Dyer returned to the displays glowing on the console.

One of the basic objectives of FISE was to investigate ways of enabling the computer to make generalized inferences from a few specific experiences, in much the same way as a child learns. The incident with the window bothered Dyer despite its encouraging aspects. FISE hadn't been able to generalize sufficiently. If he knew enough not to allow Hector to burn himself, he should have been capable of generalizing to the extent of not allowing Hector to harm himself at all. Dyer had an idea where the problem lay and he spent the next two hours building a new section of system code and modifying some key parameters. Then he switched on the tank again to set up some situations to test out what he had done.

He gave Hector a few simple tests to check that he had not inadvertently introduced any major bugs, and then left Hector to put the tools away while Dyer thought about the next part. He wanted to find out if Hector would deduce for himself that an object in contact with a hot object would itself get hot and should therefore be avoided.

At that moment the kitchen door was nudged open and Brutus ambled in. Brutus was Hector's comical white dog, a mischievous scamp with a black patch around one eye. He tended to appear from time to time when PROPS was getting bored. Dyer smiled faintly as he watched. Brutus wandered on into the room and Hector's head suddenly jerked around to look directly at him, which meant that FISE had just become aware of the dog's presence.

Nothing unusual happened for a while. Brutus sniffed here and there as PROPS commanded and Hector looked around every now and again to keep track of his movements, giving an uncanny simulation of human behavior in the process. And then Brutus moved over to the window. At once Hector rushed over from the utility closet, scooped Brutus up in his arms, hauled him across to the door and threw him outside.

Dyer froze the image and blinked at it in amazement. Then he became excited. He hastily composed a message requesting an explanation for the action and played it into the console. FISE's voice responded at once.

"There are pieces of broken glass on the floor by the window. Glass cuts. I must not allow Brutus to get cut. It's not okay."

Dyer was astonished. Nobody had ever said anything about Brutus getting cut; they had told FISE only about protecting Hector. Dyer queried the point accordingly.

FISE replied, "I am hurt if I get burned or if I get cut. Brutus is hurt if he gets burned. Therefore Brutus is probably hurt if he gets cut too. Brutus is like me. Things like me and Brutus do not like being hurt, I must stop us from getting hurt if I can. Allowing things like me and Brutus to get hurt is not okay."

Dyer was stunned. FISE had made the gigantic step of generalizing Hector's basic attributes to include other animate objects . . . and without being told to!

He stared across at the blank cubicle that housed FISE and shook his head in wonder. To kill it now would be madness, he thought to himself. Just twelve more months at this rate . . . He sat up with a start.

Kill it? Christ! He'd caught himself thinking about it as if it really were a living being. He clicked his tongue in self-reproach. Getting sentimental about a machine. That would never do. What's the time? Hell! Eight already. Time to go home and fix something to eat.

Sharon will probably call. Not really interested . . . Eat out and see if any of the guys are around tonight.

He shut down the system and walked over to the door to collect his windbreaker from the stand. At least, he thought as he doused the lights and turned to survey the deserted offices, he was now certain in his own mind of one thing: Ripping HESPER out of TITAN was not the way to go. Backward was never the way to go. Given some improvements, FISE would never make the kind of error in judgment that the HESPER machines at Tycho had made. The way to get things right was to go full speed ahead on perfecting FISE and getting it into the net, not shrinking back from it and running the other way.

When he was halfway down the corridor he remembered something else: Three years previously he had been just as certain about HESPER. Suddenly he didn't feel so sure.

None of the guys were in town that night but he found that he really didn't care very much. He had enough on his mind to occupy him.

◎ CHAPTER SIX ◎

"A lot of people are starting to say that TITAN could go just that way. What do you think, Ray? Could it evolve the capacity for feeling emotions? Could it develop an awareness of its own existence?" Dr. Jacob Manning, one of the three who had arrived from Princeton earlier in the day, put the question while they were summing up in Dyer's office after seeing Hector in action. The subject of the discussion was the notion that TITAN might integrate its capabilities on a global scale sufficiently to emerge as an intelligence in its own right.

"Obviously we can expect to see its behavior becoming more coordinated worldwide as time goes by," Dyer replied from where he was sprawled in leisurely fashion behind his desk. "If you take as a working definition of intelligence: 'A measure of a system's ability to learn from experience and to modify its own behavior appropriately to what it has learned,' then we'd have to concede that TITAN has taken a rudimentary step in that direction already. So yes—it could become intelligent. But I think it would be a mistake to draw too many inferences based on the human model."

"How do you mean—emotions and that kind of thing?" Sally Baird, also from Princeton, spoke from the far corner.

Dyer nodded. "What are emotions?" he asked. Without waiting for an answer, he continued. "I'd submit that an emotion is a stereotyped behavioral pattern that's been reinforced through natural selection because it has demonstrated a survival value. Obviously an *animal* that gets mad and fights or gets scared and runs stands more chance of staying healthy than one that feels nothing, does nothing and gets eaten. You buy that?"

"I'll buy that," Sally agreed.

"Good. So if you take a more general view of it, an emotion is a behavioral tendency that a self-modifying system evolves because it is beneficial in helping the system to accomplish whatever its basic programming compels it to want to accomplish. In the case of organic systems that have arrived via the mechanics of organic evolution, the 'whatever' happens to be survival."

"Yes, I think I see what you're driving at," Steve Conran came in from beside Manning. "You're saying that an inorganic intelligence might well evolve its own compulsive traits but there's no reason why they should bear any resemblance to human emotions. Our emotions derive from the survival needs and wouldn't have any inherent value to a system that came from origins that were totally different."

"That's what makes the most sense to me," Dyer affirmed.

"Interesting," Manning mused, half to himself. "I wonder what traits they'd be. As Ray says, they'd probably reflect whatever basic function the system had been designed to perform."

"Well, in the case of something like TITAN, it might turn out to be insatiably curious . . . or compulsively rational, or efficient or something," Conran suggested. "Certainly, if you look at it that way, there's no reason why it should become a threat to anybody, is there?"

"So how about awareness?" Sally asked. "What's the likelihood of it getting to the point where it not only knows, but it knows that it knows?" Dyer was nodding even before she had finished asking the question.

"Again, I think that if it ever came to possess anything like that, it would be radically different from a human understanding of awareness." He paused to collect his thoughts for a second while the three visitors waited expectantly. "A man is aware of himself as existing in the localized region of space that's defined by the focal point of his senses. He has evolved the ability to construct mental models of extensions to that space, which he and other objects move around in. But something like TITAN will perceive the universe through billions of sensory channels distributed all over the surface of the Earth and beyond. On top of that, its 'senses' cover the whole spectrum from high-power proton microscopes in research labs to the big orbiting astronomic telescopes . . . from galactic gravity-wave detectors to the infrared sensors lowered into the ocean trenches." Dyer swept his eyes across the three faces in front of him and spread his hands expressively. "TITAN moves pieces of itself around in millions of places at once—the ISA probes that are nosing around Jupiter . . . robot freighters under the Arctic ice caps . . . all kinds of things. How can we even begin to imagine how an awareness as totally alien as that would perceive itself and the universe around it?"

They went on to debate this issue at some length.

Eventually Jacob Manning raised the question of Man being able to devise a means of communicating with an intelligence as alien as this.

Dyer thought about it and then replied: "Well, we already do communicate with it all the time, of course . . . at least we do with parts of it. But if you mean what I think you mean—will we ever get to talk to it as a *total entity?*—then I'm not so sure."

"How come?" Sally asked, sounding mildly disappointed.

"You can see the problem if you take a human organism, say, as an analogy," Dyer replied. "All the cells and organs in the body communicate among themselves in their own specialized languages—chemical messengers, neural codes and that kind of thing. But the individual as a *totality* doesn't comprehend those languages. The processes that they relate to are controlled *unconsciously.*

"I think that the same kind of thing would apply if TITAN ever evolved the kind of self-aware intelligence we've been talking about. The economic, commercial, industrial and all of the other processes it's built to take care of are all parts of a vaster organism. It wouldn't be cognizant of the languages in which the transactions going on inside itself were being conducted . . . What language it *would* be equipped to speak, I don't think any of us can imagine at this stage.

"So to answer your question—no, I don't think we'd be able to talk to it . . . not *all* of it. That'd be like a cell somewhere in your big toe wanting to talk to whoever runs the whole body. The two just don't think or talk at the same level."

When the Princeton delegation eventually departed, having declared themselves more than satisfied by the day's accomplishments, Dyer escorted them back to the main entrance. Just as he was turning away from the door, a tubby olive-green-suited figure with a pink face and equally pink bald head bounded through.

"Ah, Ray! Just the person. I was meaning to talk to you about a couple of things." It was Professor Edward Richter, head of the Shannon School and Hoestler's immediate boss.

"Hello, Ted. How are things?" Dyer halted momentarily to allow Richter to fall in step beside him.

"I only got back from California earlier today," Richter said. "I was talking to Vince Lewis over lunch . . . Hello, Peggy . . . He told me about yesterday. It's tough about your unit, huh?"

"Well, nothing's final yet," Dyer answered, with a philosophic shrug.

"I hope you're right. You and your people were just starting to make progress, too. It came at a bad time."

"You should see the latest," Dyer told him with feeling.

"Looking good, eh?" Richter shot an approving sideways look as he bounced jerkily along. "I called in on Frank Wescott's outfit while I was at CIT. They're still way behind what you're doing. You're out in front in a league of your own if CIM doesn't go and pull the funding rug out and foul it up."

Dyer agreed automatically. At least, he reflected, it was something to know that his feelings weren't unshared. It was no secret that Hoestler was angling for an early retirement and that he was more interested in making waves with his yacht than inside the Department. Lewis was guaranteed to drift whichever way the tide of political expediency happened to flow. But Richter had the energy, the commitment and the clout to emerge as a valuable ally if a move to lobby CIM turned up on the cards. Richter's vigorous campaigning had brought a lot of CIM money to CUNY in years gone by, and had probably proved as important a factor as any in the Shannon School becoming the focus of HESPER development in the United States.

"Is Frank affected by the latest from CIM, too?" Dyer asked.

"I don't know. They didn't mention anything about it while I was there, but maybe it hadn't gotten down the line yet. What they are getting is a fair amount of flak from different places about TITAN going its own way someday and turning into some kind of alien intelligence that decides to do its own thing. That seems to be the latest scare story going around. I don't know . . . maybe something about the Maskelyne screw-up has leaked out somewhere."

"Interesting," Dyer mused. "We just had some people here from Princeton who were probing more or less the same kind of thing. I hope the media don't get involved and start a public hue and cry about it."

They halted at the intersection of the main thoroughfare of the Self-Adaptive Programming Department and the corridor that led to Dyer's unit. Richter drew a pace nearer to Dyer and regarded him quizzically for a moment.

"Tell me something, Ray," he said. His voice had dropped a decibel from its normal public-address mode. "What's your opinion on all this? Could TITAN turn into a real threat one day? If there's a risk that it could, what things ought we to be doing about it now?" Richter was obviously referring to the questions raised within CIM that Lewis had outlined in Hoestler's office the previous day. Dyer had been thinking about little else ever since. His reply was slow and thoughtful.

"We have to accept that it could develop behavior patterns that we'd be forced to describe as intelligent. It might become self-aware, and if it did I'm certain that its awareness would be completely alien to anything that we know. But I think a lot of people are trying to project human qualities onto it without any real justification. That I can't see."

Richter nodded his head vigorously as if his own feelings on the matter had just been confirmed.

"That's what I hoped you'd say," he agreed. "So we're in agreement regarding where we ought to go from here, eh?"

"What's that?" Dyer asked.

"Go flat-out on developing FISE," Richter replied, sounding slightly surprised. "The answer to avoiding more Maskelyne-type problems is to get something like FISE in, surely, not to back off and pull HESPER out."

Dyer chewed his lip dubiously. "I'm not a hundred percent convinced it is," he said. "I've been doing a lot of thinking about it. It wasn't all that long ago when I said I was confident I understood HESPER, but look what's happened since."

"Sometimes it can be worse to stick with half-measures than to go the whole way," Richter insisted. "I think this is one of them. The trouble with HESPER is that it's halfway between machines that are totally predictable and totally dumb, and machines that are smart enough not to be dangerous. We're in midair over the high jump and it's just as easy to land one side as the other . . . except that if we choose backwards, we'll only have to do the whole thing again later. I say let's finish the job now while we've got the momentum to do it."

"But what if it turns out we don't know as much as we thought we knew again, Ted? Okay, we go ahead and put smarter FISES in everywhere and the system starts doing things we don't like. What then?"

Richter shrugged.

"*Then* we take 'em out if we have to. We either fix it or pull the plug."

"And take the risks in the meantime, huh?"

"What's got into you, Ray." Richter gave Dyer a puzzled glance. "We take risks every day of the week anyway. This one is no bigger than any and a lot smaller than most. When you buy a house, you know you may have to spend money to repair it one day. You don't go live in a tree instead in order to avoid the risk. You accept the risk because the benefits outweigh it."

"I don't know so much . . ." Dyer studied the floor between their feet. "Building a machine that might not work out is one thing, Ted. Handing a whole planet over to something you're not sure you understand is another. Two days ago I'd have agreed with you, but now I've seen what can happen even with HESPER . . . I don't know . . ."

"Aw, come on, Ray," Richter urged. "You're just taking it to heart because you had a lot to do with designing HESPER in the first place. Try and get away from the personal angle."

"We'll see," Dyer murmured.

"Well, I hope you've straightened it all out in your head by Thursday," Richter said. "Has anybody told you yet that we're going to Washington on Thursday?"

"Washington? No. I've been tied up with these Princeton people all day. Who's going to Washington? What's happening there?"

"There's a meeting being held at CIM headquarters," Richter informed him. "A lot of government and technical people are getting together to try and agree on some recommendations as to which way we go from here. Vince asked me to go because he's tied up in the city on Thursday. He told me I ought to take you along too, since you're the HESPER giant. Get Betty to call my secretary for the details. I think the meeting's due to start around ten, so we could go down on the tube." Richter frowned to himself and shook his head. "I was going to push for going ahead hard on FISE. It could mean another big contract for us, you know. I'd assumed you'd be backing me up. Hell, it is your unit that's at stake here!"

"Oh, you don't have to worry on that score," Dyer said. "I'll back you all the way on pushing for ongoing FISE research. What I'm uneasy about is the idea of putting something like FISE into the net prematurely. If we could only make CIM accept that those are two separate issues. From what I've heard, they seem to have gotten it into their heads that they both have to get scrapped or fly together."

"It's the accountants who are running the show as usual," Richter declared. "They're saying that if they're not going to see any payoffs from FISE in the foreseeable future, they don't want to put any money into it in the foreseeable future."

"I know. Anyhow, we'll just have to wait and see what happens on Thursday. It sounds like it could be interesting."

"Fine." Richter paused to rummage further through the pending section of his eternally overflowing mental file cabinet. When he spoke again his tone was guarded and conspiratorial.

"And don't forget what we said about SAP coming up for grabs in the not too distant future. It's pretty obvious that Sigmund doesn't have any big plans on staying around for a long time. You've more than earned a move up and it would be a popular choice."

"That's okay. I haven't forgotten about that," Dyer murmured. "But I'd prefer to clear out things up first. Now that this HESPER thing's boiled up I'd feel better in the front line until it's over. Don't forget I had a lot to do with putting it together the way it is."

"I know that," Richter said. "But you should think hard about it. Strictly between you and me, there's a good chance that Vince might be open to persuasion to put internal funding in to keep FISE going even if CIM does pull out. It's only a possibility though, you understand. With a SAP hat on your head you could end up doing FISE a lot more good in the long run than by hacking code in the front line. You think about it."

Dyer nodded and indicated that he understood Richter's meaning.

"Good!" Richter exclaimed in a hardy voice. "It's all set for Thursday then. I gotta fly. You think about what I said. Oh, another thing . . ." Richter had started to walk away. He continued speaking as he swung into a U-turn and headed back again. "That movie company that Vince brought in—Zeegram or something—they're involved in some award dinner in town tonight. They sent Vince a complimentary ticket. He can't make it and neither can I, but he'd like the University to send somebody all the same. Have you got anything special fixed up?"

"Tonight? No. Want me to take it?"

"I'd appreciate it. You never know, it could turn out to be fun. I'll call you in five minutes from my office with the details. You've got an escort provided by Zeegram thrown in. I think she's been here a couple of times. Fanning . . . Fenning . . . something like that. I'll let you know."

Dyer stared after Richter's once-again receding figure.

"Thanks a lot," he said flatly.

He was still staring after Richter's retreating figure when Kim appeared from the same direction. He waited for a moment and they began walking toward the lab together.

"What did you do to him?" she asked, giving Dyer a look of unconcealed astonishment. He returned it with a puzzled frown.

"Who, Ted?"

"No. Our mutual friend in Internal Services. Judy's been on mural graphics all day and he can't do enough to help. I asked you to kick his butt, not set fire to it."

"Oh that." Dyer couldn't contain a wry grin. "It's amazing what a few friendly words delivered with tact can do, isn't it?"

"Really?" Kim sounded dubious.

"You know me," he said in a voice that could have meant anything. Kim's expression deepened to one of outright suspicion.

"And another thing," she said. "Something's happened to Al too. He's got through a week's work since this morning. You couldn't possibly have had anything to do with that as well, could you?" Dyer tossed his open hands carelessly but said nothing. "Which reminds me," Kim went on, "there are a few points he's brought up that I think we should go over sometime. It's getting a bit late now but I'm not in any particular hurry. How would you feel about staying on and getting it out of the way tonight?"

" 'Fraid not tonight, Kim," he said as they stopped in front of the lab door. "Any other time would be okay, but tonight I have a date."

"Say . . . how about that!" Kim's eyes widened ominously. "Who's the lucky lady?"

Dyer sighed as they went in. "You wouldn't believe me if I told you."

◈ CHAPTER SEVEN ◈

The dinner and the speeches were over and the evening had broken up into a round of socializing and renewals of old acquaintanceships. After talking for a while with some of the guests who had remained seated around their table, Dyer and Laura excused themselves to move on to one of the bars in the hotel where the function was being held. It was a warm night and Laura opted for the open-air Terrace Bar overlooking the East River, toward which many of the guests had begun gravitating.

Dyer had enjoyed himself more than he had expected. He had found most of the conversation stimulating and entertaining, and had seen little trace of the boring stereotypes for whom he had been half prepared, and who, it seemed, existed mainly in movies about movies but not in the real movie world. Odd, he thought. Also, Laura had been different. Here, in her own element and surrounded by her own kind of people, she was relaxed and had shed all of the defensive attitudes she adopted instinctively when she was in Dyer's world. In place of the outsider with a point to prove that he remembered from his lab, he now saw a composed, self-assured mature woman, whom he was beginning, he was forced to admit to himself, to find strangely fascinating.

They emerged into the cool night air and Laura slipped an arm through his and proceeded to steer him firmly toward an empty table beneath the bordering shrubs.

"There. This is better than all that noise in there, isn't it," she said as they sat down. "We can be civilized with each other, even if it is only for one night of the year." Dyer ordered drinks via the tabletop touchpad, grunted his agreement to the statement and settled back to take in their surroundings. Laura watched him in silence for a while and then asked:

"So, how has the evening been so far? You seem to be liking it." Dyer brought his eyes back from following the progress of a brilliantly lit Lockheed sinking gently downward into Kennedy Airport on the final stage of its descent from the ionosphere.

"You won't believe it, but better than I thought," he said. "I expected a lot of phonies but most of the people I've met have been very interesting. Some of the speeches went on a bit, but I suppose that's to be expected."

"You see, Ray. It's not only us who have hackneyed ideas about what scientists are like. You have them about showbiz people too. At least we're trying to do something about it. That's what you said we should do, isn't it—test our ideas to see if they're true?"

Dyer grinned suddenly. "If that's the case, it makes you scientists," he taunted playfully. "So the question doesn't arise. All you have to do now is learn to accept what the tests tell you, You see, we're really very nice people but your preconceived notions won't allow you to believe it. If I don't wear odd shoes on my feet or grow cabbages that eat people, I must be the exception."

"You're back at work again," she replied. "Tonight I'm not working. Talk about something else."

"Women," he offered without hesitation.

"Oh dear. I should have guessed."

"No," he told her smugly. "You've got it wrong. Jumping to conclusions again. What I meant was all this stuff you're always saying to Betty about . . . the crusade. How come you're so hung up about it?"

"What makes you want to know that?" Laura asked in surprise.

"Oh . . . I don't know. Just curious."

Laura made a slight shrug and thought to herself for a moment.

"No single big thing . . . I guess I've always thought that way. And I still do," she added pointedly. "That's okay by you, isn't it?"

"Sure." Dyer made a throwing-away motion with his hand. "That's what I thought. I figured it had to come from way back somewhere. You don't strike me as the kind of person who'd let her opinions be moulded much by people today . . . know what I mean? I can't think it's something that somebody told you about yesterday." He nodded to himself as if she had just confirmed something. "I bet your mother was that way too. Right?"

"Yes, she was, as a matter of fact . . . a lot that way. She had good reason, too. My father was a slob . . . couldn't make his job work out and couldn't make his marriage work out so he messed around all the time and tried to live it up in a fantasy world because he never grew up enough to accept things. I left Detroit when I was sixteen because I couldn't stand it anymore . . . Always—" Laura broke off and looked at Dyer accusingly. "Hey, what are you trying to do— psychoanalyze me or something?"

"No. I told you—I was just curious."

Laura narrowed her eyes and regarded him suspiciously.

"You used to be a shrink or something before you got into computers, didn't you? Didn't you say something about Harvard Med School once?"

"I was a neurological researcher," Dyer told her. "That's not quite the same thing."

"It still has to do with heads though."

"And that's about as far as it goes," he said. "I was concerned with finding out more about how brains work, not with fixing them after they've started blowing fuses. A lot of things that were learned in that field were later applied to designing smarter computers, so it made sense for me to move on the way I did." He was about to say more but frowned and checked himself. "But that's work again, and you said we're not working."

The drinks appeared in the dispenser hatch. Dyer removed them, passed one to Laura and lapsed into silence while he tasted his own.

"So, what made you take up medicine?" Laura asked after a few seconds.

"Oh, it was in the family I guess. My father was a doctor . . . space medicine."

"Was? Isn't he around anymore?"

"Oh sure. Retired. Lives on the West Coast with my mother. They're okay."

"What kind of space medicine did he do?" Laura inquired, intrigued. "Was he with ISA? Did he go on any space missions or anything exciting like that?"

"He sure did."

"Wow! I've always wanted to go up and never had the chance. Tell me about it. I'm interested." Laura sat forward to lean on the table and stared at him expectantly. Dyer smiled and shook his head.

"It was nothing wildly spectacular. He was in it a long time . . . joined in 1985 after he left the Navy, when it was still NASA . . . did a few tours in orbital stations over the years . . . spent a lot of 1992 up at one of the lunar bases . . . moved to Europe when ESA was set up, and then came back to the States when they all got merged into ISA. He had plenty of variety to keep him from getting bored I guess."

"So where did you appear on the scene?" Laura asked. "Here or in Europe?"

"I was two years old when they moved to Europe," Dyer told her; "If I told you where I was born, you wouldn't believe it."

"Try me."

"Ever hear of Gilbert and Sullivan?"

"Of course." Laura looked puzzled. "They wrote songs."

"Not *that* Gilbert and Sullivan. The ones who came later, in 1994." Astonishment flowed into Laura's face.

"You don't mean the two experimental space colonies they put up before they started building the big ones?"

"Uh huh."

"Really? You were born in one of those? That's fantastic!" She frowned as another thought occurred to her. "Say, that makes you something of a rare animal, doesn't it? No offense, but I thought they didn't go in much for that kind of thing that long ago. You must have been special or something."

Dyer laughed. "I was—a special kind of accident. Pa was the Chief Medical Officer on Gilbert, which meant he was up there for a long time at a stretch, so it was normal for wives to go along too. But because of regulations, when they found out that I was on the way, they couldn't ship mother down again. Normally she'd never have got away with it, but being the Chief M.O.'s wife . . . Well, if Pa didn't say anything about it, there was no reason for anybody else to think anything."

"You mean he let it go deliberately?" Laura sounded incredulous, but at the same time delighted.

"He always said he didn't, but I don't see how he couldn't have known. But if you knew him, you'd know it's him all over."

"He sounds the kind of guy that does things his way and to hell with what you or I or the world thinks," Laura commented.

"You've about got it," Dyer nodded.

"It shows," Laura declared with a trace of satisfaction. "*That's* what makes you so pigheaded. There—now you've been shrunk. And I didn't even have to go to Harvard to figure it out."

"I'm not pigheaded," Dyer protested. "I just happen to have firm opinions on what my job's all about. I know what works and what doesn't if you're trying to separate truth from garbage. That's what science is. I get irritated when people insist on misinterpreting it."

"And you're also touchy," Laura told him sweetly. She drank from her glass while Dyer calmed down again. "Anyway," she said, "It's the same thing."

"What is?"

"Being firm and being pigheaded," she replied.

"Of course it isn't. What are you talking about?"

"The form of the verb varies according to its subject," she said. "*I* am firm; *you* are obstinate; *he* is pigheaded." Dyer collapsed back in his chair and shook his head in capitulation. Laura leaned forward and patted him fondly on the back of his hand. "You've forgotten I used to write scripts," she said, laughing. "You see, I know what my job's all about too."

❀ CHAPTER EIGHT ❀

The next morning Dyer and Richter met as arranged, boarded an autocab and specified the Department of Communications and Information Management Headquarters, Washington, D.C., as their destination. The cab navigated Manhattan and was pipelined across to New Jersey along one of a battery of ten monorails suspended in a single span four hundred feet above the Hudson. There it turned south and merged with forty-nine other cabs to form a train which accelerated as one unit into the New York-Washington tube, through which it hurtled in vacuum, riding on magnetic suspension at speeds touching 800 mph for most of the way. At the far end the train broke up to become independent cabs once again, which dispersed into the Washington local system. Twenty minutes after leaving New York, Dyer and Richter were in an elevator ascending from the autocab terminal located below the CIM HQ building.

The meeting was chaired by Dr. Irwin Schroder, the U.S. Secretary for CIM. Attendees included Fritz Muller, vice chairman of the Advisory Committee on Information Technology to the Supreme Council of World Governments, which managed jointly the global operation of TITAN as one of their functions. A group of Muller's Committee advisers representing several national interests, a selection of individuals from various academic and commercial institutions and a small delegation from CIM completed the gathering.

Proceedings began with introductions and a résumé of the incident at Maskelyne. After that, Schroder took some time to summarize the main question of concern that the meeting had been called to consider. If TITAN had developed the ability to act independently to this degree after only one year, what might it do later and what should be done about it? One choice, of course, was to downgrade TITAN by de-HESPERing it; then it wouldn't be able to do anything. Opposition to this move came mainly from the academics, who favored the policy that Richter had already advocated privately to Dyer—pushing ahead to replace HESPER with a perfected development of FISE as quickly as possible. They pointed to the vast improvements in living standards and general affluence that had been realized within the last fifty years and attributed most of it to the effects of TITAN. Even this was just a beginning, they declared, and would pale into insignificance compared to what the next century held in store. It would be tragic if all that were to be thrown away because of nothing more definite than a few what-ifs. To defend their case they presented elaborate contrasts between the evolutionary processes governing the growth of organic and inorganic systems, and argued that it was ludicrous to suggest that a machine would parallel human motivations and ambitions. In this they were echoing the orthodox line that Dyer had given his visitors from Princeton two days before. They finished by reiterating Richter's insistence that problems were nothing new in life and were there to be solved not evaded. If problems did develop to an intolerable degree for some reason, the option to pull the plug would always be there as a last resort.

Dyer then summarized his progress with FISE and endorsed the view that though a supercomplex the size of TITAN, equipped with processors that were superior to FISE, might well evolve behavior that would have to be classed as intelligent, the supposition that it might come to think and feel like a human being was too farfetched to be worth considering. A mumbled chorus of assent from the academic fraternity greeted his words. By his side Richter began breathing more easily.

At that point Schroder sat forward to sum up his interpretation of what Dyer had said. "I take it then, Dr. Dyer, that you are adding your support to the recommendation that we heard earlier. We should press ahead with FISE with the aim of upgrading the net at the earliest opportunity. Whatever risks are entailed by living with HESPER in the meantime would not justify the cost of going backward to EARTHCOM."

"We've got 'em hooked," Richter whispered jubilantly. "They're coming around."

"Yes and no, Mr. Chairman," Dyer responded. "FISE research has to be pursued vigorously. There can be no question about that. But I think the question of upgrading the net should be thought of as something that belongs in the indefinite future . . . if we ever do it at all."

Mutterings of surprise broke out around the room. Richter brought his hands up to cover his face.

"Don't say any more," he said from the corner of his mouth. "You'll blow the whole damn thing. Just get 'em to give the okay on FISE now. We can leave the arguing about it going into the net until some other time." But it was too late; Schroder wanted to take the point further.

"I thought the problem with HESPER was that it's only half smart," Schroder said, looking surprised. "If FISE would fix that and there's not likely to be any problem of it trying to take over the world, why shouldn't we use it?"

"I only agreed that it wouldn't *think* like a human being," Dyer replied. "I didn't say it mightn't act like one."

Jan Van der Waarde from Cape Town University shook his head perplexedly. "I don't understand. What is the difference? Why should it act like it doesn't think?"

"The problem is that an intelligence that is totally alien but totally rational could emulate certain types of human behavioral traits but for completely different reasons," Dyer replied. "It could act in ways that we would see amounting to rivalry with Man, but not for the same reasons as a human would act that way. In fact the very concepts of rivalry and Man would almost certainly mean nothing to it."

"You mean it could wind up setting itself against us without even knowing it," Paul Fierney, a technical adviser with CIM, looked dubious. "How would it do that?"

"You'd agree that the things that would worry us would be if it ever began to exhibit tendencies which in human terms we'd describe as anger, resentment, aggression, feelings of superiority or any of that kind of thing," Dyer said.

"Okay," Fierney agreed. "But I thought we'd all agreed that a machine wouldn't feel things like that."

"You're right," Dyer said, nodding. "But when you say that a person feels any of those things, how do you know? How do you know what he feels inside his own head?" He gave them a few seconds to reflect on this and then supplied his own answer. "Obviously you can't. All you can know is what you see him do and hear him say— in other words by his *observable behavior*. What I'm saying is that different causes can result in identical effects. If some other cause were to result in the kinds of behavior that go with the emotions I've just listed, as far as we would be concerned there wouldn't be any difference. If somebody comes at you with an axe it doesn't make any difference if he's doing it because he hates your guts or because he's quite rational but thinks you're a monster from Venus. The result's the same."

"I think maybe we go away from the point." The speaker was Emilio Gerasa from Spain, one of Fritz Muller's contingent. "Isn't the problem with HESPER that of incompetence, not all these other things? Why do we speak of these other things, like the anger and so on?"

"FISE would solve the competence problem," Dyer assured them. "I don't have any worries in that direction. I'm more worried that it might end up being too competent." A few mystified glances were exchanged in parts of the room.

"The emotional traits that we've mentioned, along with pretty well all the rest, can be traced back to one root—*survival!*" Dyer told them. "If an enhanced TITAN ever evolved the motivational drive to preserve its own existence, the very fact that it's a rational system would enable it to devise very effective ways of going about it. Also, since it's an extremely powerful learning machine that operates at computer speeds, once it started to do something, it would do it very fast! If the machine interpreted agencies in the universe around it as constituting real or imagined threats to its existence, then the rational thing for it to do would be to experiment until it identified measures that were effective in neutralizing those agencies." Dyer shrugged. "If one of them turned out to be us or our vital interests, we could have real problems."

Schroder leaned across to confer with Muller for a few seconds, Muller nodded, then shook his head and gestured in Dyer's direction. Schroder looked up again.

"Maybe I've missed the point," he said. "But I thought you agreed a little while ago that a machine wouldn't possess a human survival drive because it hadn't come from the same origins as humans. Now you seem to be saying that it will. Could you clarify that, please."

"He is talking in circles," Van der Waarde muttered.

"And why should it feel threatened and act against us when it doesn't share any of our survival-based emotions?" Frank Wescott, who was present to represent CIT, challenged. Richter was by this time sitting back glumly, resigned to hearing whatever Dyer was going to say.

"Because it wouldn't even *know* it was doing so," Dyer answered. "That kind of question still presumes that it would think in human terms. I'm talking about a totally rational entity that simply modifies its reactions to an environment around it. It hasn't had the evolutionary conditioning that we've had to understand the concept of rivalry or even that beings other than itself exist. All it's aware of is itself and influences impinging on it that are external to itself. Now do you see what I'm getting at? It wouldn't *consciously* or *deliberately* take on Man as an opponent because in all probability it would have no concept of Man *per se*."

"Very well, Dr. Dyer." Fritz Muller held up a hand. "We take your point. But tell me, what kinds of circumstances do you envisage occurring that might equate to a clash of interest between us and it? Let us not worry for now about whether or not the two parties look upon the situation in the same way."

Dyer paused to consult the notes that he had prepared beforehand. The CIM people and the advisers from the World Council committee were watching him intently while the academics were looking unhappy and muttering among themselves. Richter was glowering up at him over folded arms.

"Consider the following scenario," Dyer resumed. "The system has evolved some compulsive trait that reflects the reasons for its having been built in the first place—a counterpart to the survival drive of organic systems. The other day, somebody I was talking to suggested that it might become insatiably curious, so let's take that as its overriding compulsion. It doesn't know why it wants to be that way any more than we know why we want to survive. It's just made that way. To discover more about the universe, it requires resources—energy, instruments, vehicles to carry the instruments to places, and, of course, a large share of its own capacity. Moreover, the system finds that it has access to vast amounts of such resources— a whole world full of them. So it follows its inclinations and begins diverting more of those resources toward its own ends and away from the things that they were intended for. As far as we were concerned, it would have manifested the feeling of *indifference*. Our goals would cease to figure in its equations and we'd face the prospect of being reduced to second-class citizens on our own planet."

"Only if we just sat there and allowed it to help itself," a professor from Hamburg interjected. "I can't see that we would. Why should we?"

"Which brings us to a second scenario," Dyer carried on. "We take active steps to deny it access to the resources it wants. The system retaliates in kind by denying us the resources that we want, say by progressively shutting down energy plants, grounding air traffic, blacking out cities . . . all kinds of things." He raised his hands to stifle the objections that appeared written across several faces. "Don't forget, I am not postulating that the system has any concept of Man or sees its behavior in the same terms as we would. But this is a powerful learning machine! All it knows is that certain events in the environment around it are capable of obstructing its goals, and that certain coordinated actions on its part have the effect of stopping those events from happening. It's like a dog scratching. It just feels uncomfortable and learns that doing certain things makes it feel better. The dog doesn't have to be an entomologist or know that it's fleas that are causing the discomfort."

"But how could it possibly know that cutting off power to cities or anything like that would help?" Gary Corbertson, Director of Software Engineering from Datatrex Corporation, shook his head in disbelief. "I thought you said it wouldn't know anything about people. How could it figure out how to blackmail them if it didn't even know about them? That doesn't make sense."

"It wouldn't have to figure out *why* it worked," Dyer replied. "All it would need to know is that it did. Suppose it decided that it wanted a Jupiter probe all to itself, but we tried to take the probe away and it responded by shutting down cities at the rate of ten per night. Suppose also that we knew why it was doing it. What do you think we'd do?" He nodded slowly around the room. "It'd get its Jupiter probe pretty soon, wouldn't it?"

"Mmm . . . I think I see the point," Schroder said slowly. "All a baby has to know about the world is that when it screams loud enough it gets what it wants."

"Good analogy," Dyer agreed. "I'm not suggesting the system would do anything as sophisticated as that to start with, but like a baby it would experiment, observe, connect and hypothesize. Pretty soon it would have a fair grasp of what actions resulted in what effects.

"And now take our supposition one step further," he went on. "What if the coordinated actions that it learned amounted not merely to blackmail but to overt aggression? As far as the machine's concerned there'd be no difference—certain actions simply makes the discomfort go away or the comfort increase. That's where the fact that it doesn't possess any human values or concepts at all becomes really worrying. Another scenario—it discovers that it gets far faster and more positive results when it doesn't stop at threats; it carries them out. Now it's exhibiting open hostility as far as we're concerned, but it doesn't know it.

"So, without invoking any human attributes at all, we've just taken it through the whole spectrum from indifference to hostility—a perfectly plausible simulation of behavior that we thought we wouldn't have to worry about because it couldn't evolve the emotions that normally accompany it. But now we see that it wouldn't have to evolve any such emotions."

As Dyer sat down, Richter, now looking less disgruntled, leaned toward him.

"Christ, Ray," he said over the hubbub of voices that broke out on every side. "Is FISE really capable of going all the way to that extent?"

"Not one of them in a lab," Dyer told him. "But what happens when you connect thousands of them up together? Would you want to put money on it?" Richter sat back, shaking his head slowly and frowning to himself. The meeting subsided to silence again as Campbell Roberts, Muller's representative from Australia/New Zealand, began to speak.

"I still think we're exaggerating the whole thing," he declared loudly. "So there are risks. Nobody ever said there weren't. All through history men have taken risks where the benefits they stood to gain justified them. But as we said earlier on, if the system starts doing things we don't like, we can always pull the plug on it. If we have to, we can always take the bloody thing to bits again. Why in hell's name are we getting so hung up about some lousy machine developing a mind of its own? We've got minds too, dammit, and we've been around a lot longer. If it wants to play survival games I reckon we could teach it a thing or two. I say put FISE in and make damn sure it never forgets who's boss. *Homo sapiens* have had plenty of practice at that!"

"Maybe it won't let you pull the plug," Fierney pointed out.

"That's bloody ridiculous!"

"I'm not so sure it is," Muller commented. "Even now TITAN controls its own power sources and the manufacture of most of its own parts. If current forecasts are anything to go by, it will soon control everything related to its own perpetuation—from surveying sources of raw material to installing extensions to itself and carrying out one-hundred-percent self-repair. On top of that it controls other machinery of every description. It might not reach the point of becoming incapable of being switched off, but it could conceivably make the job of switching it off an extremely difficult and possibly costly undertaking."

"But why should it want to do that in the first place if it doesn't have a survival instinct?" Roberts objected.

"What have you got to say to that, Dr. Dyer?" Schroder invited.

"The same thing applies as before," Dyer said without hesitation. "If the system evolved some overriding purpose that its programming compelled it to strive to achieve, it wouldn't take it long to figure out that its own continued existence was an essential prerequisite to being sure of achieving it. Its own observations would tell it that its existence could not be guaranteed as things stood, so its immediate response would be to experiment in order to find out what it could do to remedy the situation. The rest follows logically from there. In other words, here we have a mechanism via which something tantamount to a survival instinct could emerge without the need for any survival-dominated origins at all. And as I said before, once you've got a survival instinct established, all the emotions that go with it will follow in the course of time."

Dyer paused to allow his words time to sink in and then summarized his view on the things that had been said.

"If the system started to exhibit any of the traits we've been talking about, that in itself wouldn't add up to an insurmountable problem because, as Campbell says, we can always pull the plug. As long as that's true, the benefits outweigh the risks; and if that was all there were to it, my vote would be to upgrade the net. But that isn't all there is to it. If the system were to evolve a survival drive, logically we would expect it to attempt making itself an unpullable plug. Even that, in itself, wouldn't be a problem if it didn't succeed. After all, it wouldn't matter much what the system *wanted* as long as it was incapable of doing much about it. If we could guarantee that, I'd still say upgrade the net. But we can't.

"It all boils down to two questions. One: Could the system evolve a survival instinct? Two: If it did, what could it do about it? The second is really the key. Until we can find some way of answering that with confidence, I can't see our way clear to taking things further."

A long silence followed Dyer's words. Then Schroder took up the debate.

"I'm inclined to agree that we can't recommend putting FISE into the net at this stage. As to the question of continuing with FISE research, that's a funding issue that doesn't concern this meeting. But something else bothers me. Everything that has been said this morning has assumed that we've been talking about a supercomplex that includes FISE machines. But the business at Maskelyne happened with the system as it is now. Even with just HESPER, TITAN showed itself to be capable of integrating its activities to a degree that nobody thought possible." He gestured vaguely toward the door. "Out there is a world that's being run by a super-complex of HESPERS. What guarantee do we have that the kinds of behavior you've described can't happen even today with the system we've got?"

Dyer had been expecting the question. He held Schroder's eye and replied simply. "None."

Schroder considered the answer for a long time. At last he sighed and stretched his arms forward across the table in front of him.

"The objective of the meeting was to agree what to do about HESPER," he reminded them all. "We have three choices: Allow TITAN to grow further, freeze it where it is now, or downgrade it by taking HESPER out. We can't allow it to grow further until we have some way of obtaining guaranteed answers to Dr. Dyer's two key questions. If we leave it as it is, we risk a repetition of the Maskelyne kind of accident but maybe on a catastrophic scale, which would clearly be totally unacceptable. Therefore, as I see it, the only choice open to us is the third. Does anybody here disagree?"

"Except you're only going to have to cross the bridge sometime later anyway," Richter threw in. "It doesn't matter what kind of machines you develop in labs after you downgrade the net, the only way you'll ever know how a planetwide complex of them will perform is by building it. In the end you'd still wind up in the same position."

"But we don't know what's on the other side of this particular bridge," Schroder pointed out. "It may lead to somewhere we don't want to go, and if it does it will only be one-way. The key question is: Could the system make itself invulnerable? The only way we could answer that for certain would be if it did. That is obviously unacceptable because once it had reached that point it could do anything it pleased afterward. As Dr. Dyer says, we can't proceed further until we know the answer. On the other hand, the only way we can find the answer is by getting there. It's a vicious circle. The only alternative is not to try getting there at all but stay where we are. But the present position is unstable because of HESPER and Maskelyne, so the only way open is back."

"So civilization levels out on a plateau," Richter objected. "And from that line of argument there's no way past it. What happens when we find we *need* something heftier than TITAN?"

"Let's try some positive thinking," Fritz Muller suggested. "Everybody is saying we *can't* go further *because* we don't know the answers to Dr. Dyer's two questions. That's negative. Let us say instead that we *could* go further *if* we knew the answers. Positive."

"I like it," Richter said immediately. He looked at Schroder. "*That's* what you should put in your recommendation! Recommend to CIM and to the World Council that we *do* something to get some answers instead of backing off."

The meeting concurred and Schroder duly entered the point in his notes.

"Exactly what are we recommending them to do?" he inquired, looking up at Richter as he finished writing. Richter hadn't really thought about it. He blinked, frowned to himself, rubbed the tip of his nose, and at last looked back at Schroder.

"I don't know," he confessed simply.

Schroder shifted his eyes inquiringly toward Dyer.

"I don't know," Dyer told him.

The meeting went on to examine the problem from a dozen different angles, but at the end of the session it was obvious that nobody else knew either.

◈ CHAPTER NINE ◈

"Vince talked to Schroder sometime this morning about it," Richter said from the screen in Dyer's office. "The bean counters at CIM are still grumbling but it sounds as if your point yesterday about postponing any upgrade to the net and discontinuing the FISE project being two separate issues was well taken. It's still in the balance, but Schroder seemed to be starting to bend your way. I thought you'd like to know."

"Thanks," Dyer acknowledged. "Did Vince have any idea how long it might take before we know for sure?" Richter shook his head and showed his hands in front of him on the screen. "How about this chance you mentioned of Vince maybe putting internal funding into FISE?" Dyer asked. "Any more on that?" Richter shrugged and shook his head again.

"We didn't go into that."

Dyer made a face and nodded resignedly. He was naturally anxious to see the FISE project saved from the axe, especially after the amount of work that he and his team had put into it and following the encouraging developments that had taken place that week, but at a more personal level there was more at stake. HESPER had been his contribution to making the world a generally better place; to him, the continuing national and international support for the FISE project symbolized the world's acceptance and approval of both him and his work. Withdrawal from HESPER and abandonment of FISE would be tantamount to a vote of no confidence and the implications bothered him more than he was prepared to admit even to himself.

"So we'll just have to wait and see what next week brings," he said. "Unless somebody can come up with some answers to those questions, there's not a lot we can do. Had any more thoughts about it, Ted? Did you get a chance to talk to Sigmund about it?"

"No," Richter replied. "I've been thinking about it but it just keeps going around the same circle. Sigmund's not in today." Of course, Dyer thought to himself. It was Friday—another yachting weekend. "Anyhow," Richter went on, "as you say, we haven't got much choice but to leave it at that for the time being. I'll keep you posted if anything happens. Okay?"

"Okay Ted, I'd appreciate it," Dyer said. "See you around."

"See ya, Ray."

Dyer cut off the screen and remained staring at it for a long time. The meeting in Washington had debated the issue into the evening and he had talked to Richter about nothing else on the way back to New York, but always they had come back to the same impasse. If TITAN ever developed the equivalent of a survival drive, what could it do about it? The only way anybody would know would be when it happened. The risks implied by that would be totally out of the question. There had to be another way of getting the answers they needed.

At length he sighed, shook his head and leaned back in his chair. As he did so he noticed the wad of equipment maintenance approval forms that he had finished signing just as Richter called. He scooped them up and walked out of the office to give them to Betty, at the same time wondering to himself why it was that in an age when everything from tax returns to personal letters had become electronic, things as mundane as interdepartmental formalities still required pieces of paper in triplicate.

"These are okay," he said as he dropped the forms on Betty's desk. "Signed, sealed, stamped and approved. You can get rid of 'em."

"Thanks," Betty said. "Oh. Frank Wescott called from CIT while you were talking to Ted. He just left a message . . ." She checked a note pad by her elbow. "It said, 'How do you deal with a time bomb that's wired to a doomsday machine?' " Betty looked up curiously. "He said you'd know what it meant."

"It's okay," Dyer replied, smiling. "Just something we talked about in Washington yesterday." Betty shook her head and looked nonplused.

"Fancy that. I always wondered what you people talked about all day at those meetings. Now I know. Isn't it nice to know there are people in the world who worry about the time bombs and the doomsday machines for us. There—that's one more thing I won't have to lose any more sleep wondering about."

"Glad to hear it," Dyer told her. "Life would sure be dull without them."

At that moment Ron's voice rose from behind the partitions that separated them from the lab area.

"Hell, I keep tellin' ya, it's obvious! We go after them with the tanks!"

"No, shut up a second, Ron," Chris's voice replied. "I don't like it. There's something funny about—"

"But they're wide open in the center there. If we go in fast we'll bust 'em wide—"

"Shut up, Ron!"

"But I'm tellin' ya we've got 'em licked!"

"And I'm saying it's a trap. They want us to go after them in the center. It was only a token fight and they're pulling out too fast."

"Sounds as if they're fighting World War II again," Dyer grinned. Betty raised her hands and shrugged. Dyer strolled through to the lab to see what was going on.

It was as he expected. The image in the holo-tank was a miniature 3-D landscape made up of wooded hills, tracts of bare, rolling plain, rivers and forests, complete with towns, roads and bridges. Formations of mixed squares; circles, triangles and other symbols glowed superimposed on the terrain to divide it roughly into two halves, one dominated by red and the other by blue, although in places the two became intermixed and disordered, giving the whole thing the appearance of something like a general's battle map. Ron was sitting at the console and looking impatient while Chris stood peering thoughtfully down into the top of the tank.

"What is it?" Dyer inquired as he drew up alongside Chris and began examining the situation.

"Battle of Kursk, 1943," Chris replied absently. "Germans and Russians. We're the reds . . . Zukhov."

"Who's on the other end?" Dyer asked.

"Mike and Dave at Cornell," Chris told him without looking up. "I think they're trying to pull a fast one here. The sods have done it before."

The battle-simulation games available from the network library were Chris and Ron's latest craze. Domestic holo-tanks to replace conventional flat-screen displays were expensive and one of Ron's first improvements on the FISE display had been to build an interface to hook it into the net.

"They've just broken off from a punch-up with tanks in the middle there by the river," Chris said, gesturing vaguely. "Now they're pulling back and Ron wants to go after them. I think it's fishy."

"How come?" Dyer asked.

"Doesn't feel right," Chris said. "I reckon they've got something hidden up behind that ridge that's waiting to cut us off if we cross the river." Dyer surveyed the scene for a few seconds and then nodded slowly. There was a long, shallow ridge overlooking the approach to the river crossing and the ground behind the ridge was out of the direct line-of-sight from any of the red symbols as positioned. The displays presented to the two playing teams would not be identical; with the opposing forces deployed as shown, only the enemy "generals" and the computers that functioned as umpire would know whether or not the ridge concealed additional hostile units.

"You need an observation post up on top of the ridge," Dyer commented. "Send a patrol up there."

"That's what I was thinking," Chris murmured.

"It'll take all day," Ron protested. "Why don't we risk it and to hell with it? If anything does come over that ridge we've got three artillery batteries back there behind the town that can take care of it until we bring up some more tanks."

"They're only 45-millimeter," Chris pointed out. "Too far back. Try a couple of ranging shots at the ridge and I bet they won't reach. The 203s over the hills there would have covered it but they've just been hit by air strikes and won't be in action again for a while . . ." He paused and rubbed his chin. "Now *that* is interesting. Why did they have to go at the 203s now of all times? See—it all adds up. They don't want us covering that ridge." Ron grumbled beneath his breath and bent his head to conduct a brief dialogue via touchpad with one of the console's screens.

"Okay, you're right," he declared irascibly. "The shots fell short and the latest data says the 203s will be out for another five turns. So what do you want to do?"

"What Ray says," Chris replied. "Send an infantry platoon up the ridge, dig the tanks in where they are and move another two brigades up behind that village on the left to cover. Then, if any rubbish does come over the top, we can act as if we have been surprised and retreat back toward the village. If they come after us, we'll lead them right into the 45s. The way their shells have been falling makes me think they don't know that the 45s are there yet. Then we'll catch them at their own game."

Ron frowned at the display for a while and considered the suggestion.

"Okay," he said at last, and began tapping commands into the console panel.

Dyer watched as small groups of red symbols began moving toward their new positions. Then Ron transferred his attention to the other areas of the display and continued with the development of tactics in other places which he had already evidently agreed upon with Chris. Leaving Ron to his task, Dyer turned his head toward Chris.

"You've wrapped Hector up early today, eh? Have a busy day yesterday?"

"We were at it until gone ten," Chris told him. "Those mods you put into the B7 tree—what did you do to it? Hector was going nuts."

"I was trying to improve his generalizing abilities," Dyer replied.

He caught the expression on Chris's face and grinned. "Why, didn't it work?"

"Work!" Chris pulled back the corners of his mouth into a grimace. "I'll say it worked. In fact it worked too well. He's been overgeneralizing."

"How?"

"Now that FISE has realized that Brutus has got some of the same basic attributes as Hector, he thinks he's supposed to make Brutus do all the things that Hector does. He can't tell the difference . . . thinks he's Brutus as well as Hector. The problem is he can't manipulate Brutus the same way so he keeps making Hector chase him around all the time. Tries to make him sit in chairs and eat off the table and all sorts of idiotic things like that, but PROPS won't cooperate. Either FISE or Ron was about to have a breakdown so we packed it in for the day."

Dyer started to laugh. Ron pushed himself back; from the console and looked up.

"The patrol's on its way up," he announced. "They're grouping panzers out there on the right for what could be an attack so I'm moving up a reserve division from the rear to that sector. I've pulled our line there back to the lake to close the flank so we should be okay. Now let's wait and see what they do." The display became inanimate while Mike and Dave at Cornell considered their next moves.

"There was something I wanted to ask you both," Dyer said, changing the subject. "I was talking to Ted Richter on the tube coming back from Washington yesterday." Chris and Ron looked at him curiously. "Remember what those people from Princeton were talking about when they were here on Tuesday . . . about TITAN deciding to go its own way and do its own thing. I know I said I couldn't see it ever happening and all that, but just suppose that it could. What could we do to make sure that we knew about it before it had time to go too far? I'm interested in new ideas." The other two stared at him in an odd sort of way and then at each other. Chris immediately went into introspection mode and began examining the question for cryptic meanings. Ron rubbed his beard and continued to look at Dyer curiously.

"You been having nightmares or something?" he asked.

"No. Just looking for some original thinking," Dyer answered.

"I don't see the problem," Ron said with a shrug. "Why do we have to know about it in advance? It's just like any other machine—you give it a try and hope for the best. If it starts screwing around you pull the plug. Where's the big problem?"

"Mmm . . ." Chris was staring absently through the side of the holo-tank. "Suppose it gets to the point where it won't let you pull the plug," he said in a faraway voice.

"That's what I was getting at," Dyer nodded.

"Oh, I see. The unpullable-plug argument," Ron said. "The only way I can see, if somebody was really worried about it, would be to pre-empt it. Power the net through manually controlled switching stations that are isolated from the distribution grid. That way you'd always have a plug that the system's got no access to."

"Too messy." Dyer shook his head. "You'd have to rewire the whole planet and it'd cost a bomb. Think of something else."

That issue had been debated *ad nauseam* at Washington and rejected or relegated to the category of last resort for a whole list of reasons of that kind. Dyer didn't mention the other reason that ruled out an approach of that type. A decision to go ahead with a program of precautionary engineering on a scale that vast would equate to a public admission of a real danger that the world could go out of control; the alarm that would undoubtedly follow ruled it out. It would be like passing legislation that required surgeons to administer last rites along with anesthetics.

Similar considerations ruled out putting remote-triggered destructive devices into the primary node centers of the net, devices to cut the trunk data links, reconfiguring the net into segments that could be easily isolated and other such possibilities that had been discussed at the meeting. In every case too many people would have to know what was going on and why. Sooner or later the media would find out about it and once that happened the dust wouldn't settle for years.

"What you need is a supersimulator," Chris said at last. He gestured toward the miniature landscape inside the holo-tank.

"Something like that but big enough to simulate the whole world. Then you'd need a supercomputer connected to it, large enough to run the whole TITAN system. Give it the equivalent of a couple of centuries of accelerated evolution, and if it doesn't do anything nasty with that world plug the real one in. Simple." He kept his face absolutely serious, which usually meant that he'd given up looking for a serious comment to offer. The suggestion was, of course, ridiculous. There was no computer even remotely conceivable with the capacity to simulate the billions of operations being performed every nanosecond, day and night, throughout the TITAN complex. In terms of representing the real thing, Hector's simple world came about as close as would a child's sketch of a pinwheel to conveying the molecular structure of the Milky Way Galaxy. The question of simulation had also been examined in Washington but dismissed as being totally impracticable.

"Why wait for it to go its own way anyhow?" Ron asked. "Why not plant some instincts in it to start with that will make it want to do the kinds of things you're happy with . . . like Kim's doing? Why be passive about it?"

"What kind of instincts?" Dyer inquired, although he thought he already knew the answer.

"Tell it that it has to love people," Ron said.

"What if it doesn't know what people are?"

"Tell it."

"How?"

"Hell, if it was as obvious as that we'd be out of a job," Ron said defiantly. "If FISE thinks he's Hector, why can't a super-FISE think it's people?"

"Oh come off it, Ron," Chris chipped in. "It's not as simple as that and you know it. FISE can associate with Hector because Hector is really only a load of program code running inside FISE. The visuals are just by-products for our benefit. How are you suggesting we turn the whole population into program code?"

"If super-FISE associated with anything, it'd associate with something running inside itself," Dyer added, elaborating the point further. "And people are outside, not inside."

"So even if you did give it some instincts regarding people, it'd be just as likely to evolve new ones of its own that overrode them," Chris pointed out.

"So it goes its own way," Dyer completed. "Which brings us back to my original question. *If* it was going to do that, how would you find out about it, *before* it did it?"

Ron scowled and stared into the display, which had suddenly become active again, He propped his chin on his fist and glared over the top of the console housing.

"Ray, why do you always have to come up with things like this just before weekends? That neat idea you had for a new default-weighting algorithm cost me all of last Sunday and half of Saturday. I'm not even gonna think about this until we come back next week." With that he returned himself fully to Kursk, 1943, swiftly assessed the latest developments and began hammering in a sequence of responses.

"Our patrol's getting near the top of the ridge," Chris observed casually. "Are you in a mood for taking bets, Ron?" Then he became more thoughtful once more and looked back at Dyer. "Why are you taking the pessimistic view anyway, Chief? Why does TITAN have to go the wrong way? It might go the other way. Suppose a mob of mean green things in UFOs decided to move in to stay one day. We could end up finding that TITAN was the best insurance we ever bought . . . It could turn out to be a bloody good general. As far as I can see, the whole thing could just as easily turn out to be for the better as for the worse."

While Dyer thought the proposition over, the small red square reached the crest of the ridge. Immediately a mass of tightly clustered blue symbols appeared on the previously empty stretch of terrain beyond.

"Bloody hell!" Chris exclaimed. "What did I tell you! They've got a whole army there! We need a new fire plan—fast!" Ron went frantically to work on the console. Chris studied the position for a few more seconds and changed the subject back again without looking up. "It's fifty-fifty, isn't it, Ray?" he said.

"Probably," Dyer agreed. "But the stakes are a lot higher than when you're betting on what's over the ridge, aren't they." He paused. Chris caught the tone of his voice and looked up curiously. "Look at it this way," Dyer suggested. "You've got a house full of young kids and somebody's just given them a one-month-old animal from some other planet as a pet. Right now it's cute and cuddly but nobody knows what it's going to grow up into. And since you don't know anything about it, it might grow up overnight for all you know. Now . . . it's a fifty-fifty risk, but would you be prepared to take it?"

Chris pondered on the problem for a long time.

"There's only one safe way," he said eventually. "You have to take it out of the house and let it grow up somewhere else . . . in a zoo maybe." He shrugged. "It's the only way you can avoid having to take the risk."

"Oh, I forgot to tell you," Dyer said. "There isn't any zoo. Your family lives on a tiny island in the middle of the ocean. That's all there is. There isn't anywhere else to take it."

"Then you have to get rid of it. There's no other way."

"Not so easy. The kids wouldn't stand for that."

Chris gave a long sigh and shook his head slowly.

"In that case, if you want to be sure they'll be okay, you'd better make damn sure you teach them how to look after themselves before it grows up," he offered. "Just in case it comes to the worst . . ."

◎ CHAPTER TEN ◎

Dyer hoisted his feet up onto the couch and relaxed with one arm draped loosely along the backrest. The sun lay dying on the shore across the river from Irvington, spilling its lifeblood into the rippling water and throwing a soft orange glow up onto the walls of his apartment. Surely nothing could more aptly express the ending of an eventful day than a sunset, he thought to himself. This was the time to sift through the litter left along the trail of another day's living for things worth filing permanently under *Accumulated Experience*. After a night of unconscious data reduction, the sharp detail would be gone forever. Chris had made one of his profound observations about sunsets once. What was it? He smiled faintly to himself as he remembered: "Pronounced atmospheric scattering of shorter wavelengths, resulting in selective transmission below 650 nanometers with progressively reducing solar elevation, produces a tendency toward irrational euphoria among primitive herders of domesticated ovines."

Sharon came out of the kitchen carrying a couple of glasses and swaying her body to the music drifting out from the speakers concealed in the walls. She crossed the room, pushed a beer into Dyer's hand and oscillated away again toward the window.

"I really can't understand why you'd rather stay in," she exuberated over her shoulder. "On an evening like this? . . . And it's

Friday. The whole city's out there waiting to be lit up. Why d'you want to stay here?"

"Aw, I've seen enough of the goddam city." Dyer stretched himself back luxuriously and sipped his drink. "Why don't we relax for once. How about a really nice meal, cooked in for once, open a few bottles, turn on some nice music . . ."

"Then what?" Sharon asked suspiciously.

"Then nothing. Just enjoy it." He downed half of his beer in a long smooth gulp and wiped his moustache with the side of his finger. "We could have a philosophic discussion about cabbages, kings and the meaning of the universe."

"Philosophy always turns out to be a fancy word for something shorter." Sharon twirled between the couch and the window, at the same time throwing out an arm to wave vaguely in the direction of the door leading to the bedroom. "Tonight I feel like being friendly."

"So, what could be friendlier?"

"I mean friendly to everybody . . . people. I feel like being with people. How about going back into town and trying the Cat's Whisker or the Marquis—someplace we can dance. It's Sue's sister's birthday today. There'll be a good crowd in the Marquis tonight. I told them we'd most likely show up."

Dyer frowned at the bubbles streaming up through his beer. *That* crowd—the fun people—walking examples of what survived when minds became victims of infant mortality. He didn't think he could stand that. The problem with women like Sharon who had been told that they looked like Venus was that they sometimes developed an addiction to pedestals. The picture of himself as an incidental accessory to satisfying Sharon's need for public admiration caused his expression to darken.

"Philosophy's out, so is tribal anthropology," he said. "How about a compromise? I'll take you out to dinner."

Sharon pouted. "But I'm not in the mood for a quiet cozy evening for two," she insisted. "I need some fun," she said. "How about a compromise? I'll take you out to the party." As she spoke her voice rose and fell with an exaggerated slur, as if she were already delirious, but beneath it her tone was an ultimatum. If he didn't agree to enjoying a lousy evening he'd end up having a lousy evening instead. Dammit! He wasn't going along with it. The tightening of his mouth telegraphed his mood across the room.

"Uh, uh," Sharon said. "I can feel black clouds looming somewhere around here." Her gaiety evaporated while she waited a few seconds for a response. She sipped her drink and stared expectantly over her glass at Dyer's sprawled and seemingly unhearing form. "Anyhow," she went on, "let's put it this way. *I'm* going. You can decide whatever you want." No visible reaction. "Well, don't just lie there swigging booze like Julius Caesar or somebody. Say something. Are you coming or not?"

"This organization does not negotiate to terrorist demands," Dyer informed her, keeping his eyes fixed on the ceiling.

"What are you talking about? Who's terrorizing anybody? I just said what I'm doing, that's all."

"Blackmail then," Dyer told her with a sigh.

"I don't understand," she answered. Even as she said it, the insinuation that she was being slow on the uptake about something irked her further. She countered instinctively. "Well, if that means you're opting out, that's okay by me. Bill and Lee will be there for sure. *They're* always good fun to have around."

"Screw all of you! I've had it!" Before he realized what he was doing, Dyer jumped up off the couch and stormed through into the kitchen. He tore the top off another beer, refilled his glass, and swallowed enough to empty the can, which he hurled into the waste-disposal hatch. Implied blackmail, probably unwitting, was one thing; overt threats was another. Why *did* people who had to have everything spelled out in three-letter words infuriate him so much? The damn woman was about as perceptive as a stampeding rhino.

He took another long draught while he brought his feelings under control again. He didn't give a damn about Bill and Lee, or anybody else for that matter, but the remark had been typically tactless and totally pointless; that was what had incensed him. This was the time to see the whole thing through once and for all, he decided. He composed himself, thought about how he was going to broach it, and tried to anticipate the probable reaction. Tears? He'd be flattering himself if he thought that. The yelling-and-screaming routine? Might cost a few bits of china but he could handle that okay. The icy walkout with head held high? Oh well, it wouldn't be the first time.

The problem was solved for him by the words that blasted in suddenly from beyond the doorway. "I'm not as dumb as you seem to think I am. The real problem is you think you're too goddam smart! You've had it? *That's* okay by me too!" An instant later the slam of the outer door echoed through the apartment.

Dyer emerged from the kitchen, still drinking casually from his glass, and looked around him in surprise. Christ, was that all there was going to be to it? He felt mildly insulted. So, after all his thought and gentlemanly concern, he wasn't worth even a few heartfelt insults and choice obscenities, eh? Shaking his head sadly at the fickleness of human nature, he moved over to the room's wall panel, killed the incessant pounding rhythm that Sharon had selected and replaced it with the Brahms violin concerto. A sense of airy lightness gradually permeated his being. Humming softly to the music, he poured himself a large brandy, lit a cigar and strolled over by the window to watch the sun dissolving away into the Hudson.

An hour or more later, after he had keyed his orders for the weekend shopping into the viscreen touchboard and primed the apartment's computer to handle his intended schedule, he called Laura. He didn't really know why he was calling although he had thought of a number of excuses, managing to convince himself finally that he wanted somebody stimulating to talk to. Anyhow, it didn't make any difference; her number returned a brief message advising that she would be out of town until Monday morning.

He rose early on Saturday and caught a cab into the city to spend the morning at the Lexington Uncomme College just north of Central Park, which he usually frequented once or twice a week. Uncomme—*Unified Combat Method*—was a technique that combined aspects of karate, the *atemi waza* branch of judo and a number of other martial arts including military unarmed combat into a fearsomely effective technique well suited to the Western physique and cultural conditioning. It had been developed by the armed forces of the U.S. and Western Europe toward the end of the previous century and had gone on to attract a large following of enthusiasts among the general public of all nations. Dyer had been introduced to Uncomme when he was in his late teens and studying psychology and neurosciences as an undergraduate student at the University of California. He had found it to be one of the few sporting activities that appealed to him, persevered at it, become quite proficient by rising over the years to the third master grade (ninth was the highest that had ever been awarded to anybody) and had kept in regular practice ever since.

After three strenuous hours and a hot shower, all of the week's tensions had been flushed away down the drain along with the water and he went upstairs to the members' bar to enjoy a couple of well-earned beers. There he met Chuck and Tom, two of the other regulars at the Lexington who were also rounding off a hard morning. Chuck's wife was in Mexico, Tom was single, and neither of them had any particular plans for the rest of the day and so, a little over an hour later, the three of them found themselves eating a burger lunch while they debated what to do next.

Tom divided his life between working as a musician and an aeromechanic. He played moog and guitar in various clubs around the city, classical cello when he was in a different frame of mind, and modified production domestic aircars to racing specifications when he wanted to change from both. He ran the latter business in a workshop that he owned in Newark, he told them, but the premises were getting to be somewhat cramped for the amount of business that he was attracting. Apparently a firm in Queens was expanding and moving out to Connecticut, and the place that they were about to vacate sounded ideal. In fact Tom had been thinking about going over and taking a look at it later that day; how would Dyer and Chuck like to tag along? The vote was unanimous and that took care of the afternoon.

By early evening they were back on the Manhattan side of the river and heading for the bar that Chuck co-owned with a cousin, near Rockefeller Center. Chuck had spent a lot of his life as a mining engineer and had returned from Nepal only six months previously.

He had taken the partnership in the bar to give himself a break for a year or two while he waited for chance, luck or inspiration to decide where he would go next. His pet thought at the moment was to apply to ISA for a post at one of the lunar extraction plants.

By midnight the place was filled to capacity, the small dance floor was overflowing and the three of them had been joined by a party of Chuck's friends at a table in one of the quieter corners. Tom had latched onto a blonde who had appeared a couple of hours before with another girl, and was engaged in an earnest private conversation which showed every sign of having much to do with preparing the way for her eventual decline and fall. Chuck was supplying recipes for Indian curries to a man who managed a nearby restaurant while Dyer had gotten into a conversation with somebody called Pete, who turned out to be a communications officer from ISA. The subject of Dyer's birthplace came up and very soon the conversation had turned to space matters.

"I just turned twenty when I went up for the first time," Pete said in answer to one of Dyer's questions. "Must have been almost exactly ten years ago. It was on the P2Q Project. Ever hear of that?"

"P2Q?" Dyer frowned at his drink while he swirled it back and forth in his glass. He'd heard something about that, he was sure. "Wasn't it some kind of controversial research thing?" he said slowly. "Ah yes . . . wait a minute. Something to do with viruses, wasn't it?" Pete nodded.

"The aim was to manufacture a virus strain that would attack cancer cells selectively. The problem was that it only had to come out a little bit wrong and you'd wind up with something really lethal. If it wasn't selective enough for some reason and it got out . . ."

Pete shrugged and allowed Dyer to complete the rest for himself. He took a swallow of his drink and went on, "Anyhow there was a big fight about it that went on for years. What it boiled down to was that nobody could guarantee a failproof way of making sure it could never get out into the atmosphere with a lot of worst-case 'what-if?'s . . . not one that would keep everybody happy anyway. So the whole thing was vetoed . . . until somebody had the bright idea of doing it away from Earth completely—right outside the atmosphere. So they shipped the scientists and all the equipment up to a purpose-built satellite and did it all there. That was what P2Q was. In fact the satellite is still there but it's running different projects these days . . . I don't know what they call it now. I think it's just got some general name . . . *Isolab* or something like that."

A tiny bomb exploded somewhere in the back of Dyer's mind as he listened. There was something important in what Pete had just said . . . something that was shrieking to make itself heard through the pounding music coming from the dance floor and the hubbub of voices around the table. He tried, but his brain was too heavy with alcoholic glue to rise to the task of unscrambling the message. And then another party of Chuck's friends descended upon the table and swept the thought all away.

Sunday was already into the afternoon when he eventually hauled himself out of bed and began thinking about doing something to rejoin the human race. After breakfast he went upstairs to the rooftop pool and garden, fell asleep in the sun and returned three hours later to find a message in his mail file from his neighbors Jack and Sheila inviting him to come over for dinner and make up a foursome for bridge.

It was getting onto midnight when he got back. As he showered and got ready for bed, his mind began turning once again to the things that would be awaiting him at CUNY the following morning. He fell asleep thinking about TITAN and FISE, about Chris's remark that what they needed was a simulated world to try it all out on, and about the impossible complexity of the existing global system. If only there were some way of setting up a world that was more representative of the real thing than Hector's, but without the horrendous complications of a whole planet . . . Something like an isolated subset of Earth itself that could be allowed to evolve without the risk of unforeseen developments interacting with the real system upon which Earth depended totally . . . A test-tube microworld . . .

The pieces fell together somewhere around four o'clock in the morning. He was suddenly wide awake with Pete's words about P2Q ringing in his mind. ". . . what it boiled down to was that nobody

could guarantee a failproof way of making sure it could never get out
. . . until somebody had the bright idea of doing it away from Earth
completely . . ."

The solution was so obvious!

He sat up, suddenly excited, cleared the last shreds of sleep from
his head and went through it again slowly. He could see no hitches in
it. He'd never get back to sleep now, he knew, so he got up, dressed,
put on a pot of coffee and spent a restless hour pacing back and forth
waiting for the sun to come up. He was in his office by seven o'clock.
By nine he was calling Hoestler's number every five minutes and
cursing everything to do with yachts, most especially long yachting
weekends.

◎ CHAPTER ELEVEN ◎

"We could take over one of the giant space stations being built for colonies." Dyer sat forward eagerly in the chair while Hoestler listened from the other side of his desk. For once Hoestler's eyes were active and alert. He had said little but it was obvious that Dyer's words were setting all kinds of wheels in motion inside his head.

"The residential portions of some of the colonies are miles across," Dyer went on. "They've got everything—complete towns, landscapes, rivers, farms and lakes . . . everything as near natural as it's possible to get. You could have agriculture, industry, an economy to manage, an ecology to look after, energy programs to schedule, transportation, communications. Pretty well every aspect of Earth's society that matters, duplicated on a miniature scale. Only it would be small enough to handle. All the problems that come about as a result of the scale of the real thing simply go away. We set it up as a lab-scale experiment."

Hoestler's eyes widened slowly as the vision took shape inside his head.

"So exactly what are you saying we do?" he checked. "We put in a total FISE-based system to run the whole thing. A totally computer-managed micro-planet, that it? A system at least as advanced functionally as anything that exists on Earth . . . Then we wait to see what it does . . . Hmm . . . Interesting . . ." He leaned back from the desk and nodded slowly to himself.

"*More* advanced than anything on Earth," Dyer said. "FISE wouldn't be suitable as it stands because it's been adapting to Hector's world, which is too simple. But the basic techniques that we've developed with FISE could be used to program the microplanet system to give it capabilities way ahead of TITAN. That's the whole point. If you want a preview of what TITAN might grow into in a hundred years' time, this would be just the way to do it. If it does start doing things you didn't bargain for, at least you know about it before it happens for real down here. Also nothing that happened up there could have any effect on the system down here. It's perfect."

Hoestler fell silent for a long time. As he turned the suggestion over, a slow frown spread across his fleshly features.

"I see a problem with it," he said at last. "So we set this system up the way you say and we wait. So what? There's no guarantee that it will evolve any survival drive at all. We might wait years. And even if it didn't, that wouldn't prove that it could never happen with TITAN, would it?" He shook his head glumly and made a tossing-away motion with his hand. "Anyway, the question isn't, *Could* TITAN evolve a survival drive?; our worst-case assumptions already presuppose that it could. The question is, What could it do about it?." Hoestler sighed heavily and looked dubious. "I'm sorry, Ray, but I can't see it. How would what you're proposing get us any nearer answering questions like that?"

"We don't have to wait and see *if* it develops a survival instinct," Dyer replied at once. "We make sure it does. We *build the instinct in* to start with!"

Hoestler stared at him as if he had suddenly taken leave of his senses.

"Why not?" Dyer demanded. "Kim's already developing exactly the techniques we need to do it We don't have to wait and see *if* it ever gets around to equating Man to a threat. *We attack it!*"

"Attack it?" Hoestler gasped incredulously. Dyer nodded his head rapidly.

"Exactly! We set up a situation in which all the worst-case

'maybes' have already come true because we made them come true. Then we take it on in a battle of wits to see just who can outwit whom if it ever came to the point of us versus it. We can act out all the what-if-this and what-if-that scenarios everybody has been talking about and get some real data once and for all to answer them. As with everything else, the only way to find out what a complex of smart machines is capable of is to try it and see. The problem up until now has been that the only complex we've had to try it on happens to be the one that manages our planet and if things screw up there won't be any second chance. What I'm saying is, it doesn't have to be that way."

Hoestler stared back at Dyer in open amazement as he listened. Every objection that his mind could devise crumbled away almost as soon as he thought of it.

"I think you've got something, Ray," he breathed at last. "I really think you've got something."

Within the hour Hoestler had endorsed the idea to Richter. Richter rushed off in excitement to put it to Lewis and by lunchtime Lewis had involved Schroder from Washington. Schroder was at once captivated and promised to raise the matter with his advisers, that same day he hoped. The message found its way back to Dyer that things were moving on it. What happened next was something he could only wait for to shape itself in its own way and in its own time.

Nothing further had developed by the end of the day, which was not really surprising. Just as Dyer was in the process of tidying up to leave, Betty stuck her head in through the door and announced that Laura was on the line asking for him. As he told her to put the call through he caught a momentary expression of mild surprise flickering across Betty's face, and then realized that it was because he had failed to display any of his usual reactions to such news. It was probably, he told himself as he settled back to take the call, because for once the world in general seemed to be spinning smoothly.

"Hi there," Laura greeted from the screen. "How's my exception that proves the rule today?"

"Hi. What rule?"

"About scientists. You're the one who's different from the way they're all supposed to be."

"Point one, I'm fine," he said. "Point two, I thought you were supposed to be forgetting what we're supposed to be like and finding out what we're really like. Point three, exceptions don't prove rules. It's an idiotic popular saying. Now, what can I do for you?"

"I've got a proposition to put to you," Laura told him. Dyer eyed her suspiciously.

"What kind of proposition?"

"You remember Sam Gallenheim who was at the dinner the other night?"

"Producer from Summit, wasn't he? Yes, I remember him. What about him?"

"He's been talking to my boss today," Laura said. "He was pretty impressed by some of the things you said and he's been suggesting we ought to make more use of outside professional consultants. Not just to vet the technical stuff, but to advise on the things I've been working on too—you know, getting the people to come out right and all that. He recommended you especially. Anyhow, they asked me to mention it and find out if you might be interested. What d'you think?"

"I'd need more details than that," Dyer replied. "What kind of thing have they got in mind?"

"Oh, a little time outside whatever your usual hours are—helping get the outlines right in the early stages, maybe being on hand to advise in some sets . . . things like that. It could be fun and I know they'd make it more than worth your while. That sound like a good deal?"

"Well, you're selling it fine," Dyer said with a grin; "Have they put you on commission or something?"

"I wish they would. No, I'm just doing my job."

"When do you want answers?"

"I'm not looking for a yes-no here and now. I just want to know how you think you might feel about it in principle. If it sounds okay we'll think about it some more and give you something more detailed in writing later. How does that grab you?"

"Oh hey, in that case go right ahead," Dyer told her. "Sure, I'll look at it, but I can't say anything definite until I've seen it. Fair enough?"

"Good. That's all I needed to know for now." Laura looked away for a moment and exchanged a brief dialogue of signs with somebody offscreen. "Sorry about that," she said, looking back again. "We've got a meeting due to start in a couple of minutes. That was why I needed to get your reaction to this idea."

"Meetings at this time?" Dyer made a face. "What's the matter with you people? Can't you sleep at night or something?"

"Well, that's the way it is," she said with a shrug. "There's always something going on in this business."

"Staying on late in town then, huh?"

"Oh, we won't make an all-night thing out of it," she replied automatically. "An hour maybe . . . two at the most. It happens a lot."

"I'll buy you a dinner when you get through." The words had somehow said themselves even before he'd thought about them. They came out as a blunt statement of fact rather than as a request. Laura's expression registered surprise, compelling him to look for something additional to defend his stance. "We owe you one," he explained. "Zeegram treated us last week. Now it's our turn."

Chris, Ron, Kim and Betty were milling around and putting on coats just outside his office. He stretched out a leg to kick the door shut and returned his eyes to the screen. Laura was looking at him in a mischievous and knowing kind of way but her mouth was smiling.

"Okay, why not?" she said simply. "Thank you, kind sir. I—" She glanced away again for a second and nodded. "Gee, I've really got to go. Do you know Delaney's?"

"Small bar off one side of West Thirty-Four High Precinct?"

"That's it. How about there at, say, eight? Okay?"

"Sure."

"Over and out." The screen went blank.

He was still asking himself what the hell he thought he was playing at when he came out of the office to find Chris and Ron frowning suspiciously at him

"What's going on?" Ron demanded, nodding toward Dyer's door. "You putting out feelers for jobs or something?"

"It's his past catching up with him at last," Chris declared solemnly. "They've all got wicked pasts, these project leaders. Right, Chief?"

"Personal," Dyer said simply. Betty's smirk from the doorway leading into the corridor said that she at least had a fairly good idea of what was going on. Dyer's steely glare in the reverse direction told her she'd better make sure she kept it to herself.

◈ CHAPTER TWELVE ◈

A week passed by. Apart from occasional assurances from Richter to the effect that things were still bubbling somewhere deep inside Washington, Dyer heard nothing further about the microplanet proposal. He thought about it constantly and spent hours discussing the idea with Chris and Ron, who were every bit as enthusiastic as he. Between them they evolved an elaborate plan for putting such a scheme into practice once it made its way through the Sargasso Sea of official channels.

Also during that time, he and Laura continued to see more of each other than duty demanded. As always, they seemed to disagree about virtually everything, which made it all the more remarkable that he found himself forced to admit that her company made him more relaxed than he had felt for a long time. With her agile and inquisitive mind and lack of scientific training, she had a tendency to zoom into the heart of an argument from a totally unexpected and often fascinatingly ingenious direction. And the verbal dueling that inevitably followed was fun, doubly so because she was adept with words and seemed to enjoy throwing up clay pigeons as much as he enjoyed shooting them down. He didn't really know whether or not he liked Laura yet, but he knew he liked having her around.

And then things started happening in a sudden and unexpected way. Late one evening when he was at home alone, he received a person-to-person call from Washington. Schroder appeared on the screen looking brisk and businesslike, and wasted no time in coming straight to the point.

"Your proposal is getting a lot of attention," he said. "It's started quite a stir in high places."

"Glad to hear it," Dyer answered. He was still somewhat puzzled as to why Schroder should have chosen to come back to him directly rather than communicating through the hierarchy that Dyer's idea had already climbed.

"The Vice-President and the President both like it," Schroder went on. "The whole thing has become an international issue and a high-priority one at that. It's been submitted to the Advisory Committee for Information Processing."

Dyer stared at him in sudden astonishment. "Where . . . Geneva?"

Schroder nodded. "The Supreme Council. We've had some first reactions and we'd like to discuss them with you. Can you get down to CIM Washington tomorrow morning?" Although the words were couched as a question, it was obvious from Schroder's tone and manner that this was only for reasons of politeness. In reality he wasn't giving Dyer very much choice in the matter. Still puzzled, Dyer merely nodded his head.

"Sure. I can be there." He sensed that the time for questions would come later.

"Good," Schroder said. "The meeting's set for ten o'clock." He paused for a second. Then his expression became graver. "From now on this whole thing is to be treated as a top-security matter. I don't want you to mention where you're going tomorrow or why you're going there; The subject of the microplanet project is not, repeat *not*, for public discussion. Do I make myself clear?"

"Very clear." Dyer was rapidly becoming more mystified. Military affairs had ceased to dominate international politics years before and "top security" was a phrase that seldom occurred any more outside of movies and historical drama.

"Have you discussed it with anybody apart from Lewis and his people?" Schroder inquired.

"Well, yes, as a matter of fact . . . I've talked about it with some of the members of my staff. But there wasn't any reason not to."

Schroder frowned for a moment, then nodded.

"Only to be expected, I guess," he muttered. "Anyhow, that can't be helped now." He looked up and spoke directly at Dyer again. "If they bring it up again, play it down. Tell 'em it was just a thought and shouldn't be taken too seriously. Then get off the subject as quickly as possible. If anybody else happens to mention it, you don't know anything about it. Okay?" Again there was no choice but for Dyer to agree.

"Okay," he said shaking his head to show his bemusement. "I get the message but I don't pretend to understand it. I'll be there tomorrow."

"Excellent. Ten o'clock sharp." With that, Schroder cut off the screen and vanished.

It was a very curious Raymond Dyer who rose early next morning, lodged a vague message under Betty's call code that he wouldn't be in that day, and a little while later departed in a cab bound for the New York-Washington tube.

"Actually I didn't really give you the full picture when we spoke yesterday," Schroder said from behind his desk. "We've got more than simply first reactions back from Geneva. We've got a firm go-ahead. The message is: It sounds good. Do it. Since a lot of U.S. know-how has gone into the net, we—CIM that is—have been given the job of driving it. All the Council governments will be involved but we'll be running the show. I can tell you that things are going to move fast, starting right now."

Dyer would never have believed that official channels at those levels could operate as swiftly as Schroder's words implied. His disbelief must have registered on his face, but before he could frame any question Schroder raised a hand slightly and continued:

"Naturally the Council knows about the things we discussed here last week. They're even more anxious about it than we are since managing the global system is first and foremost their responsibility. If they've been putting a potential lunatic in charge of the planet, they want to know about it and quick. That's why it's top-priority."

"What about all this security and stuff?" Dyer asked.

"It has to be that way," Schroder informed him bluntly. "It would cause too much trouble if we made public the fact that the experts are getting worried about the system. At this stage there's no point in spreading unnecessary alarm, especially since we don't even know for sure yet if there's anything to get alarmed about. We feel it would be best to keep the whole thing out of the public eye until we've got something factual to talk about. I'm sure you'll agree that makes sense."

"It makes sense in theory," Dyer agreed. "But how are you going to keep a thing like this quiet in practice? Unless you've changed the original idea drastically, we're talking about a miniature society of thousands, maybe tens of thousands of people. And besides them, all kinds of other people would have to get involved in different angles of it. How can you run an operation on that scale without it getting out? It just doesn't sound possible."

"We put people in charge who are used to dealing with problems like that," Schroder replied. "The military. We run the whole thing as a military operation. In years gone by they handled bigger jobs when there were wars going on. There's no reason why they shouldn't be able to do equally well with this kind of job today."

Dyer sat back to absorb this new information while Schroder subsided into silence. That explained the presence of the other two people in the room, to whom Dyer had already been introduced. One was General Mark Linsay from the Army—a smaller but more professional organization than that of days gone by, retained partly for reasons of tradition and partly because of its usefulness as a pacifier and deterrent in the localized skirmishes that still tended to erupt from time to time in various parts of the world. The other was Dr. Melvin Krantz from the International Space Administration's offices in Washington, a project director involved with the Icarus Program for constructing enormous space colonies in synchronous orbit above Earth which would pay their way collecting solar energy and beaming it down in the form of ten-centimeter microwaves.

Construction of the first small-scale experimental station, Icarus A, had commenced in 2004 and been done the hard way—by shipping all the needed materials up from the surface of Earth. It was completed in 2013 and the successful demonstrations that followed were sufficient for Congress to pass proposals for building the lunar mass-driver at Maskelyne and for the construction of two more Icarus stations, this time from lunar materials. The mass-driver went into operation five years later and shortly afterward the first girders were being welded for Icarus B, completed in 2027, and Icarus C, which still had some way to go.

General Linsay straightened up from the window ledge on which he had been resting with his back to the Potomac, and unfolded his arms.

"Besides what Irwin has just said, there's an even bigger reason for making it a military operation," he said. "Obviously there could be no question of our using ordinary unsuspecting colonists as guinea pigs for the kind of experiment you've proposed. We've no way of knowing what might happen. Too risky. Even if nothing bad did happen to them, the world would have to know what we did sooner or later and the world would never condone it." The general shook his head emphatically. "No. Whoever goes there will have to know why they're going and what the risks are. We have to use selected volunteers for the population, and volunteers who are trained in security matters and understand the necessary disciplines. That means military people."

"We've selected Icarus C as the nearest we can get to an ideal within a short timescale," Krantz said from an armchair opposite Dyer. "The residential sector of Icarus C is nearing completion and is designed to accommodate ten thousand people at maximum capacity. The power section hasn't really got started yet but that doesn't really matter because we can do without it for this kind of experiment. In fact it's to our advantage that Icarus C is still under construction because we'll be making a lot of modifications to the original design. Our plan, you see, is to assemble a team of military and scientific experts to study possible strategies that the system might employ against us when the confrontation takes place. We want to build in as many safety devices as we can think of in case things take an unexpected turn." He shrugged matter-of-factly. "The object of the exercise is, after all, to obtain information, not to get people killed."

Dyer stared at him aghast.

"Killed? Why should anybody get killed?"

Schroder shrugged and spread his hands.

"Who knows?" he said. "I thought that was precisely the purpose of the whole experiment—to keep it out of the way in case we get nasty surprises."

Dyer turned the statement over in his mind and slowly nodded his acceptance. The logic was irrefutable and there was nothing to debate. He looked from one to another of the three other men present in the room, making no attempt to disguise the fact that he was impressed.

"Well, once you decide to move, you sure don't waste any time about it," he told them. "What can I say?" He transferred his gaze back to Schroder. "So . . . I'm glad you all liked the idea. If I thought you'd asked me all the way down here just to tell me everything's in hand I'd say it was a nice thing to do; but I don't think that's what you asked me down here for. You have to have some reason for telling me all this."

"We have." Schroder sat forward to bring his elbows to the desk and paused for a second to choose his words. "Melvin Krantz has already agreed to suspend his work with ISA in order to assume overall coordinating responsibility for the experiment. General Linsay will, from today on, take command of the military personnel involved, and will be responsible for selection, training, operational planning and setting up the basis for running the station. But the key people in the center of the whole thing are going to be the computer scientists. We're going to need a good team up there and we want you to take charge of that end."

Dyer looked at him through narrowed eyes. He had been half expecting something like this so Schroder's statement did not come as a complete surprise. Nevertheless it was more than he'd had in mind.

"You want me to go up there . . . on the station?" he said.

Schroder nodded. "We need somebody in charge of the scientific team who understands learning systems. Who better than the guy who practically pioneered HESPER and who's taken post-HESPER techniques further than anybody else in the business? You're the obvious choice, Ray." Schroder gestured toward Linsay and Krantz. "We've started recruiting already so I don't have to tell you that we can't give you much time. In fact I'm going to have to ask you for an answer today. I know you don't have any domestic ties so it shouldn't be an impossible problem. How do you feel about it right now?"

"I don't know . . ." Dyer frowned to himself and rubbed his forehead. "What kind of team have you got in mind? Who'd be on it? There's still too much I don't know about. Exactly who would I be working for?"

"You know the experts in your own field as well as anybody," Schroder said. "We'd give you a pretty free hand in picking whoever you want. There are one or two from certain places I've got in mind whom I'd like you to consider, but you'd have the last word. As far as approaching them goes, since it's a security matter all you'd have to do would be give us a list of the names and we'll take it from there. One exception to that might be if you wanted to include anybody from your own outfit at CUNY. You've got some good people there and there'd be no objection to you using them if you want to. Since you know them better than anybody, we could leave it to your discretion as to whether you want to raise the matter with them or not. I'm certain that you could handle it intelligently. As to who'd be your direct boss, he's sitting right here—Melvin Krantz. I don't have to spell out what his ISA background would mean in comprehending and directing a complex technical project. You'd have nothing to worry about as far as things like that are concerned." A short silence ensued while Dyer digested the information. At last Schroder shrugged and threw out his hands.

"Well, that's about it," he said. "As I mentioned earlier, we need an answer today. We're here to answer as best we can at this stage whatever questions you feel you need answered to make a decision on it." Dyer thought for a moment longer and then half-turned to address his words to everybody in the room.

"I don't have any questions," he replied quietly. "If I started the whole thing off, where else do you think I'd want to be when things start happening? Count me in. And thanks."

Schroder's face split into a wide smile for the first time that morning. He rose from his chair, came around the desk and pumped Dyer's hand vigorously while offering his congratulations. Then Lindsay and Krantz followed suit.

"There's just one thing," Dyer said when everybody had settled down again. "One advantage of using military people is that they can always vanish for a while without any awkward questions being asked. But I'm not in that category and neither are my people at the University. We've got jobs there and this is going to take more than a weekend. How do you plan on getting around that?"

"I've already talked to Vince Lewis," Schroder replied. "We made the assumption that you'd accept and Vince has agreed to put out the story inside CUNY that you've simply been assigned temporarily to CIM for a special research project involving ISA. We can work out some cover details later that should be enough to keep everybody satisfied. I guess if you ended up taking some of your own people with you, we could extend the story to account for them too. With Vince in the know I don't foresee any big problems there. Anything else?"

"Nope. I've got to hand it to you—you seem to have everything figured out."

"As far as possible in a week anyway," Schroder said. "Anyhow, if that's it why don't I order some coffee and while you're here we can update you on the details of some of the other things we've been thinking about." He leaned across to stretch an arm out toward the viset by the desk and then stopped halfway.

"Oh, I nearly forgot to tell you. We have a name for the experiment. There are two possible futures for our civilization if we allow it to continue evolving along the lines it's going. A world run by a super-TITAN could turn out to be the greatest step forward in history or conceivably the end of the human species. The future has two faces—one totally good and one totally bad. The object of this experiment is to attempt to determine which is correct. Accordingly, the code name for your experimental world will be *Janus*."

❀ CHAPTER THIRTEEN ❀

Dyer wondered how Schroder and Krantz intended getting away with the audacious idea of hijacking a piece of state-owned astronautic engineering the size of Icarus C and using it for their own undisclosable purposes. Even with Presidential knowledge and approval, the action seemed too farfetched to be workable and would surely, he thought, attract more than enough political probing and publicity to scuttle the whole plan. A few days after his interview in Washington, however, items began appearing in the news which reported that commissioning trials of Icarus B, completed toward the end of the previous year, had revealed certain short-comings in performance and design. Enough had been learned, the reports said, for matters to be put right by means of an elaborate program of modifications. Moreover a perfect opportunity to test those modifications presented itself in the form of Icarus B's twin, Icarus C, which was just in the right phase of construction to permit ready incorporation of the redesigns provided that no time was wasted in approving the change of plan. Once the improvements had been tested on Icarus C, Icarus B could later be brought up to the same standard; in the meantime Icarus B could continue to operate as at present.

Some protests were forthcoming from Congress, mainly in the form of a few pointed remarks about the technical incompetence and financial irresponsibility of some of ISA's planning groups; but the economic arguments presented in favor of having two stations running efficiently later rather than inefficiently sooner were persuasive. Within a month all further work on the station was halted and the construction teams were pulled out and reassigned to other ISA projects. Two weeks after that the go-ahead was given for ISA to commence its modification program using its own teams of specialists.

Somehow the military had become involved in the whole thing too. Somebody conceived the notion that this unscheduled addition to the Icarus program would provide a good opportunity for the Army Corps of Engineers to give their people some valuable experience in space-engineering techniques. This unusual suggestion went through the higher levels of the Pentagon with singular lack of opposition. Shortly afterward came the announcement that a special unit was to be formed of volunteers from all three services to spearhead the venture. The unit would take over a disused Army base in Virginia called Fort Vokes, where training was to commence immediately in cooperation with ISA. A General Mark Linsay, formerly attached to the Special Electronics Weapons Trials Unit of the Army located in Colorado, had been appointed commanding officer of Fort Vokes.

Dyer was not involved in whatever maneuvering had gone on behind the scenes to culminate in these announcements, but he was impressed and more than a little gratified by the knowledge that he was evidently with people who knew how to get things done. For his part during this time, he gradually put together a list of specialists in various areas of computer and allied sciences, including Frank Wescott from CIT, and passed it on to Krantz together with a few more names from a list that Schroder had submitted, which also included Frank Wescott. Then, while Krantz was making discreet inquiries and putting out guarded feelers, Dyer turned his attention to the question of including some of his own staff from CUNY.

Chris, Ron and Kim were the obvious candidates. Dyer contrived a series of confidential talks with each of them in which he gradually revealed more of the situation as their reactions and attitudes became apparent. Ron accepted without any hesitation. Chris had to go away and think about it, and eventually came back to voice his uncertainty about how such a change in plans would affect the funding authority in London which was paying for his research fellowship. After some communication with London in which Vincent Lewis endorsed Chris's claim that a temporary assignment to a vaguely defined project involving ISA would constitute a valid extension to the work that Chris had come to the U.S. to pursue, a grudging assent was obtained and the matter was settled; Chris was going too.

Dyer anticipated that things would not go as easily in Kim's case; after all, what pretext could there be for spiriting a man's wife away for six months or more, and for keeping her whereabouts a secret in a world that had forgotten the meaning of security and in which instant communication with any point on the Earth's surface and beyond was taken for granted? To his surprise, however, Kim talked to him a few days after he had broached the subject and declared simply that there would be no problem. Dyer was curious but didn't want to pry for information of a personal nature which had not been volunteered, so he accepted with thanks and left it at that.

So, subject to Krantz performing his part successfully, the team was in effect complete.

At about this time Lewis began mentioning to Richter that the CIM verdict on FISE wasn't looking too hopeful and that a reappraisal of the University's financial commitments had led him to the reluctant conclusion that internal funding of FISE would not be possible. Nevertheless there was some good news too, which would mean at least that Dyer and his team could remain usefully occupied without becoming a lost tribe within the University, wandering in search of something to do. Lewis then described the cover story that he had already worked out with Schroder, leading Richter to believe that it was genuine and pointing out that it would require its own cover story to conceal the so-called real version from inquisitive ears around the campus. Richter duly put Hoestler in the picture and Hoestler summed it up in a confidential chat which he had with Dyer later that same day.

"The verdict seems to be that CIM is pulling out of FISE and we can't see our way clear to putting enough of our money in to keep it going," Hoestler said solemnly.

"I see," Dyer replied in an appropriately heavy voice, keeping his face straight.

"But we have been putting in a lot of work on your behalf nevertheless," Hoestler went on. "Vince has sold ISA the idea of borrowing you and maybe some of your staff for a period to help sort out the screw-up on Luna. How does that appeal to you?" Dyer went through the expected motions of surprise and incredulity.

"What . . . the Moon? You mean you want to send us up there with ISA?"

"That's right. I'm now free to tell you that it's as good as fixed up . . . provided you agree that you want to go, of course."

"That's pretty short notice. I . . . I don't know what to say."

"Think about it, but don't take too long," Hoestler urged. "But one thing I must stress is that absolute discretion is essential, especially regarding the reasons for going there."

"Of course," Dyer agreed.

"Reinhold is still a sensitive issue. It wouldn't do for everybody to know that there have been problems with TITAN. Therefore we intend explaining your absence by a slightly different story. Officially some members of the HESPER Unit will be going on a special research project with one of the ISA missions toward the end of this year. As preparation for that we're sending you away to undergo training with ISA on their procedures and regulations for extraterrestrial duties. Is that clear? That's the version for internal consumption here. If anyone asks you about it, that's all you know."

Dyer responded with a slow conspiratorial nod of understanding.

"Are we talking about the whole Unit?" he asked.

Hoestler shook his head. "Just you and the senior staff."

"What about the rest?"

"We've already discussed that," Hoestler told him. "We'll arrange for one of the other section heads in SAP to take over temporarily till you get back. Anyhow, you leave that to us. That's all under control."

"Okay," Dyer agreed after a few seconds of simulated thought.

"I'll have to ask for a bit of time though. I reckon I could get back to you on it by the end of the week. How'd that be?"

"Just what I was hoping you'd say," Hoestler told him. "And remember, the real story is classified information. As far as you're concerned it's just a routine job with ISA."

"I'll remember," Dyer promised.

When he emerged into the corridor outside, he shook his head sadly and smiled to himself as he took out his pocket viewpad and re-enabled it to accept incoming calls. Immediately a message appeared on the screen advising that Krantz had tried to call a few minutes earlier. Dyer returned to his office and immediately placed a call to Krantz.

"I have to be in New York tonight for an early meeting tomorrow," Krantz told him. "I thought maybe we could get together for a couple of drinks. I'd like to update you on what's been going on."

"Sure," Dyer replied. "You know, this whole situation is getting a bit weird. I haven't gotten used to working for a remote boss yet."

"It won't be for much longer," Krantz told him, smiling faintly. "That's one of the things I was going to mention tonight."

"What?"

Krantz leaned forward toward the screen and spoke in a voice that lowered itself instinctively.

"Are you alone there . . . any open doors nearby?"

"No," Dyer said. "It's okay. What's happening?"

"Linsay's got things organized to the point where it's time to integrate the scientific team with the rest of the Janus population. It's all fixed. You and your people will be moving out to Fort Vokes in one month's time. You'd better start thinking about packing toothbrushes."

"The final garrison on Janus will be in the order of five thousand personnel selected from Army, Navy and Air Force volunteers of both sexes in approximately equal proportions." Krantz sat with his elbows propped on the table in front of him and spoke quietly over his loosely interlaced fingers. Dyer drank in silence as he listened from across the corner, It was still early evening and the only other customers in the bar were grouped over by the far wall, well away from them. Chuck's radar had told him that the conversation was private and he had disappeared into his office at the rear of the premises.

"They will perform all the duties and activities normally carried out by a normal colony population," Krantz went on. "In addition there will be a small number—a hundred or less—civilian specialists to take charge of operations that the military aren't specifically trained to handle—energy production and control, manufacturing, agriculture and things like that. In addition we'll have a few groups and individuals conducting specialized tasks analogous to your own scientific team—psychologists, observers, sociologists and so on—even some newspeople."

"Newspeople?" Dyer's eyebrows knitted in surprise. "I thought this was strictly not for the public?"

"For now it isn't. But if anything newsworthy does come out of it we'd like to have professionals around to record it all properly. Oh, you needn't worry about them. They'll all be selected people who can be trusted. They won't blow anything to anybody until it's all over and they've been given the right clearances to do it."

"What about the psychologists and so on?" Dyer asked. "What will they be there for? Are you worried we'll all be in danger of going crazy or something?"

Krantz gave a short laugh and shook his head. "You and your team will be there to study how the computers react in a situation that will be unlike anything that's ever happened before—a deliberate confrontation between men and machines. But don't forget that a lot of people are very interested in finding out how the humans will react too. It's a scientific experiment and the purpose is to provide data. Well, we intend squeezing every bit of data out of this exercise that we can."

A jovial middle-aged couple came in through the door and began heading toward the adjacent table. Conversation ceased for a few moments until the new arrivals mercifully altered course and settled down in the far corner. When Dyer looked back at Krantz, his expression had grown suddenly thoughtful.

"What you said just made me think of something."

"What's that?" Krantz inquired.

"About having people to observe the people. The scientists are people too. Did you think of having anybody there to study how they react to it all as well?"

"Not specifically." Krantz looked a trifle puzzled. "I suppose that would come under the normal job of the psychologists . . ." He twisted his face into a mild frown. "I'm not really sure what you've got in mind. Do you mean extra psychologists specifically attached to the scientific team or something?"

"Not exactly extra psychologists," Dyer said in a faraway voice. "More something in addition to the psychologists . . . a different angle."

"I'm still not with you."

"Somebody who'd see them as all-around people in a nonspecialized way instead of as psychological specimens. Add a human angle to it. If you're thinking about how the story might come out afterwards something like that could make a lot of difference."

"Mmm . . ." Krantz studied the tabletop and rubbed his chin slowly. "Interesting thought, I suppose." He looked up sharply. "Why? Do you have somebody in particular in mind?"

"I know somebody who's quite experienced in that kind of job. In fact she's been doing just that in my unit for some time now. It was something that Vince Lewis agreed on with one of the media companies."

"She?" Krantz leaned back and eyed Dyer shrewdly. "Pretty, is she?" he asked in a casual voice.

Dyer shrugged. "I guess you could say that. Kinda fun to have around, anyhow." He tossed out a hand carelessly. "It was just a thought."

Krantz's eyes were twinkling.

"If she's with your unit, why don't you talk to her about it?" he asked.

"I can't," Dyer replied simply. "My brief okayed me to approach members of my *staff*. She's not even employed by the University."

"Oh, I see. But if I liked the idea, it would be my job to initiate an approach via the appropriate agencies. That it?"

Dyer pursed his lips and nodded as if the thought had occurred to him for the first time.

"Yes," he said. "Now you come to mention it, I guess it would."

"But I'd only do that if you made a specific recommendation," Krantz pointed out.

"That would depend on whether you liked the idea or not, wouldn't it," Dyer told him.

Krantz thought for a moment longer, then grinned and drew a viewpad from his inside jacket pocket.

"Okay," he pronounced. "I like the idea. So why don't you give me some specific details."

❦ CHAPTER FOURTEEN ❦

Three weeks later Laura appeared at HESPER Unit and announced that this would be her last visit. She explained that something unexpected had turned up that would have to take precedence over her assignment at CUNY. It was a shame, she said, especially since she had just begin to get to know them all, but with Dyer and most of the staff due to leave for training with ISA anyway, maybe it was just as well. She hoped they'd all have a chance to pick up again where they had left off, maybe sometime next year. After making a round of the unit to say a personal farewell to each of the staff, she eventually found herself back in Dyer's office to round things off.

"So where are you going?" Dyer asked her. "Is it so much of a secret that you can't tell us?"

"You won't believe it," she warned him.

"Try me and see."

"China, of all places. We've got a documentary being made there on a tight schedule . . . all about the emergence of the post-Communist culture. One of the people involved got sick suddenly and I was told to drop everything and get over there."

"China, eh?" Dyer fought to keep a serious face. "Where exactly? Is there some way we can keep in touch?"

Laura shrugged helplessly. "As far as I know it'll mean moving all over. All I can suggest is using Zeegram as a mailbox. They'll be able to pass anything on." Her voice softened as she smiled. "You know, that was a nice thought. What made you say that?"

"Why not?" Dyer said. "Friends should keep in touch. We're friends, aren't we?"

"I guess we are." Laura sighed. "What have we had—a few nights out, some nice dinners and a lot of talking. We were just getting to know one another and then this happens. You're off to ISA and I'm off to China. Sometimes I think we might get along fine given enough time. It's not fair, you know. All good things have to come to an end, but this one never even got started."

"That's life," Dyer offered with a shrug.

Laura regarded him quizzically for a few seconds, evidently expecting something further. When that failed to materialize she sat back in her chair and shook her head. "You really can be a callous bastard at times," she said candidly.

Dyer made a face. "Why what have I done now?"

"Nothing! That's the whole point! Look . . . For Pete's sake . . . I've *enjoyed* going out together. It was fun. It meant something."

"I enjoyed it too. What else do you want me to say?"

"Oh hell! I want you to say it's a shame."

"It's a shame."

Laura rested her chin on her fingers and studied him with a mixture of exasperation and open disbelief.

"Six months from now you'll be on the Moon, I'll be anywhere between Hong Kong and Outer Mongolia and that's all you've got to say. Mightn't it just occur to you to be bothered about that in some tiny way?"

"Not really," Dyer told her. "For all we know China and the Moon could turn out to be the same place. Then what would there be to get bothered about?"

"What kind of crazy talk is that supposed to be? Ray, I don't follow you. You're talking in riddles again."

Dyer toyed with a pen on his desk for a moment and then looked up.

"It was just another way of saying I figure we'll bump into each other again somewhere before very long," he replied.

"Oh. And what makes you so sure of that?"

"Call it a premonition," he said.

"I thought you didn't believe in that kind of thing."

"I don't, except when they're mine," he told her. "When I have them, they're always right." He tossed the pen down in front of him, looked up and winked. "You wait and see."

◎ PART TWO ◎

BATTLE PLAN

◉ CHAPTER FIFTEEN ◉

The three-dimensional image being projected onto the stage in front of the audience looked solid enough to touch. It was an image of a torus, about six feet in diameter and somewhat less than a foot thick. Its inner side, facing the center, seemed to be made from black-slatted Venetian blinds while the outer side was a uniform, featureless aluminum gray. Six equi-spaced spokes, each about two inches thick, converged from the torus into the thirteen-inch-diameter sphere at the center.

The spokes passed through a second, inner ring of mirror-clear reflecting plates surrounding the sphere at a radius of a foot and a half. This second ring was in the form of a hollow truncated cone with its surface intersecting the plane of the spokes at an angle of forty-five degrees. A confusion of metal latticework and assorted engineering structures occupied most of the space between the inner ring and the central sphere.

A long tubular construction appeared to pass right through the sphere perpendicular to the torus, projecting a short distance at the top and over four feet at the bottom to give the whole structure a vague resemblance to a wheel connected to its axle with the other wheel missing. Two more spheres, each the same size as the central one were located at the middle and near the lower end of the axle. Each of these spheres carried a six-inch-diameter parabolic dish mounted on a pylon of tubes and lattices, both aligned in the same direction, which was to the left as viewed from the auditorium. The middle one of the three spheres was connected also to a two-feet-square sheet, which looked like a black-on-gray waffle iron and projected to the right to extend downward like an enormous flag.

Completing the picture, a second object floated detached about two feet above the torus, well beyond the shorter projecting end of the axle. It was a disk-shaped mirror nearly as large as the torus, hanging in the air above with its plane inclined to the torus's central axis.

Were it not for the hole through its center, the mirror might have suggested the opened lid of a can that had somehow become detached.

Captain Malloy, U.S. Air Force, stood to one side while the image rotated slowly to allow everybody to study it from all angles, and then moved back towards the front of the stage to resume his lecture.

"Here is a model of it all to sum up the things we've been talking about," he said. He was a broad, square-built man with tangled eyebrows that met in the middle and a solid bulldog jaw. He stood firmly, his feet slightly apart, and addressed his listeners in a loud, clipped military monotone.

"This is where we'll be going just under three months from now—Microplanet Janus, formerly intended to be the Icarus C colony and solar station. Let's recap again on some of the major details. Outside diameter of Rim? Davies."

"Eight thousand feet," a voice from the back responded promptly.

"In miles?"

"One point five-one-five."

"Correct. Inside diameter of Rim? McClusky."

"Six thousand, one hundred feet. Ah . . . one point one-five miles."

"Correct." Malloy nodded curtly. "Rim rotational speed? Seeton,"

"Zero point eight-two revs per minute," Chris called out from where he was sitting beside Dyer. "Or if you like, just under a tenth of a radian per second."

A flicker of surprise rippled across Malloy's face and changed abruptly to a stony, narrow-eyed stare. He looked at Chris for a few seconds and then replied in a grating voice. "Cor-rect."

On Dyer's other side Kim put her hand to her mouth and caught her breath sharply as she fought to suppress a laugh. He turned his head and grinned. She still managed to look sexy, even in the drill fatigues that they had all taken to wearing as standard since coming to Fort Vokes six weeks earlier. On the stage, Captain Malloy pointed at the mirror floating above the torus and continued with his summing-up.

"The main solar reflector. Sunlight is deflected downward onto the secondary reflectors . . ." he indicated the inner ring, made up of the conical strip of reflecting panels inclined at forty-five degrees to the main axis ". . . and from there outward to the inner face—the roof—of the Rim. The panels of the secondary reflector can be tilted independently to illuminate portions of the Rim selectively, thus affording variable day-night circles as required. The roof comprises the tertiary reflecting grid, variable thickness scatter-layer and Inner Shield. Any questions?"

There were no questions. An ISA engineer had already explained the function of the tertiary reflectors. The roof was composed of countless reflecting slats of right-angle cross section assembled in a complex interlocking fashion to beam sunlight down into the torus not directly but via millions of parallel dog-leg paths, through the cosmic-ray absorption shield. The arrangement took advantage of the fact that radiation of optical wavelengths was reflected by mirrors while the much shorter cosmic-ray wavelengths went straight on through into the material of the shield. On emerging from the underside of the shield, the light passed through a layer of crystal laminates which produced a scattering effect comparable to that of Earth's atmosphere but which could be thinned down where required to produce an acceptably localized solar image. Looking up, the inhabitants of Janus would see a passable representation of the Sun and a real blue sky.

Malloy gestured toward the cylindrical protrusion at the top of the upper sphere and went on, "Docking ports for conventional ships are located here at the north end of the Hub. Below it, the Hub. Question: Hub diameter? Wilson, D."

"Fifteen hundred feet."

"Correct. Six spokes connect the Hub to the Rim, passing through the secondary reflectors on the way. The spokes are each two hundred feet in diameter and they are equally spaced at sixty degrees, intersecting the Rim at intervals of four thousand *and* eighty-four feet at ground level, which is zero point seven-seven of a mile.

"Below the Hub is the Spin Decoupler system which connects the Hub to the Main Spindle. The Main Spindle does not rotate. Located on the Main Spindle in order from the Hub are the Fabrication Facility and the Extraction Facility. The Fabrication Facility and the Extraction Facility are each equipped with independent solar receivers and generate their power direct from the Sun, Explain briefly the function of the Fabrication Facility. Stokes."

Ron responded from the seat on the far side of Chris.

"Totally automated manufacture of electrical, electronic, mechanical and other devices, and also of structural preassembled modules. A general assembly plant."

"Anything else?" Malloy asked.

"Er . . . It also contains the power-distribution system for the whole station and houses the standby fusion reactor."

"That's correct. Yon might have mentioned also that it controls dissipation of the station's excess energy as heat via the Radiator Assembly." Malloy pointed at the waffle iron. "What is the function of the Extraction Facility? Bowers."

"Processing of metals from lunar materials for supply to the Fabrication Facility, primarily aluminum, titanium and iron," an Army lieutenant replied from the row in front of Dyer. "Also processing for other substances, including hydrogen, oxygen, chlorine and sulfur. Also contains recycling plant for water, carbon dioxide, and domestic, organic and manufacturing wastes."

"Very good," Malloy conceded with a trace of reluctance. He turned to face the image again and indicated the bottom extremity of the spindle, protruding below the Extraction Facility.

"Docking ports for the catcher ships that bring raw material in from lunar orbit are located here. By the convention described earlier, this is the southernmost point of the Janus structure. The Southern Docking Facility will from now on be referred to in its abbreviated form as Southport." Malloy raised his arm to point in turn at the two spheres enveloping the Spindle between Southport and the Hub.

"The Extraction Facility will be referred to as Pittsburgh and the Manufacturing Facility as Detroit. Is that clear? Are there any questions?"

"Does that mean that the docking ports at the other end will be called Northport?" someone inquired.

"Correct. Anything else?" There was nothing else. The unerring logic of the military mind left nothing to guesswork. "Good." Malloy signaled to the projectionist with a nod of his head and the image began to rotate again, the Spindle lifting up and away from the audience to bring the Rim round to face them as a full circle.

"The internal details of Pittsburgh and Detroit will be described tomorrow," Malloy said. "This morning we will take a preliminary look inside the Rim." A mutter of interest rippled through the auditorium and seats creaked here and there as bodies shifted their weight into new postures. This was something that was not a recap of material covered earlier.

"At this moment you are looking at the outer surface of the lower and upper shields," Malloy informed them. "The upper shield, which forms the roof of the Rim, was described earlier. The lower shield forms the tread and the lower part of the walls of the tire. It consists simply of a layer of ordinary powdered moonrock four feet thick constrained by an aluminum outer shell—the surface of the tread. It we remove the shield, we expose the inner shell. This is the bottom surface of the Rim proper."

The image hardly changed. The only difference that Dyer could see was the sudden appearance of a wavy black line running completely around the torus. At some places the line followed approximately the curve of where ground level would be inside; at others it wandered upward and down again, at one or two points managing to extend halfway around toward the roof. From what Malloy had said, the lower shield had been stripped away from the image. Therefore the wavy line was the boundary along which the upper and lower shields met.

Then the surface of the torus facing the audience suddenly

disappeared to allow them to see inside. A chorus of murmuring broke out on all sides of the room.

"It's incredible!" Kim said in Dyer's ear. "I thought it would be like the inside of an ISA ship only bigger. That's a real, natural planet!"

Dyer nodded.

"It was designed as a place for people to live in," he said. "People formed some very fixed ideas about the kinds of places they like living in a long time ago."

"Ground" was the strip running all the way around and facing upward toward the Hub—the inside surface of the tire's tread. The edges of the strip curled upward to form two raised walls running all the way around and containing the central plain like an enormous circular U-shaped valley. The tops of the valley walls were not geometrically smooth circles, but rose and fell irregularly like the crestline of a natural mountain ridge. Dyer could see that the crests marked the line where the upper and lower shields met on the outside, thus explaining the waviness of the line that he had noted earlier. The effect to somebody standing on the valley floor would be one of an almost natural valley landscape, at least if he looked sideways across the valley and not along the inside of the Rim. In the latter case he would see himself as being at the low point of a long valley that curved away and upward in both directions, to disappear eventually in the somewhat disconcerting fashion of vanishing behind the sky.

Apart from its unorthodox geometry, the landscape was, as Kim had said, natural to an astonishing degree. There were neatly proportioned towns sporting pastel colors among abundant greenery, wooded hills, open areas of farmland, several lakes of odd shapes and sizes and even a few streams tumbling down from the steep rocky slopes that formed the high points of the valley walls. The total effect was colorful and pleasant.

"This is the world we'll be living in," Malloy resumed after the initial surge of voices had died away. "During the rest of the time that we're here we'll be studying the details until every one of you will be able to walk from any point on Janus to any other blindfolded. So let's begin with a broad overview of the geography." He paused for a second and took in the full circle of Janus with a sweep of his arm.

"At this moment you are looking down onto Northport, in other words southward along the line of the Main Spindle. By the normal convention the clockwise direction around the Rim is east and anticlockwise is west. Toward the Hub is up and away from the Hub is down. Any questions?

"Good. The Rim is divided into six sectors. Each sector is zero point seven-seven of a mile long, measured at ground level. The sector boundaries are located midway between the points where adjacent spokes intersect with ground level. Thus each of the six sectors has one of the six spokes at its center.

"Question. What constitutes the lower shield? Drayfer."

"Four feet of powdered moonrock," a black woman in Navy uniform answered from the front row.

"Anything else?"

"No . . . I don't think so."

"The Rim is rotating at zero point eight-two revolutions per minute. What's to stop the moonrock flying off into space at Rim-speed, which is two fifty-four miles per hour?"

"Oh, I remember. There's also an outer aluminum retaining shell."

"Correct. The first sector at the top here is referred to as Downtown." Malloy indicated what appeared to be a miniature city, with closely packed terraces and towering buildings surrounding the base of one of the spokes almost all the way up to the roof, nearly a thousand feet above ground level. "As you would expect, Downtown is the center of business, commerce and general entertainment. Moving eastward into the next sector, we come to the first of two residential areas modeled on contemporary suburban landscape gardening and architecture. This sector is called Paris. Moving on from Paris we come to Sunnyside, the agricultural area of Janus. The ecology will be balanced to permit high-intensity yields per acre and to afford an efficient cycle in which meat and dairy animals, vegetable and cereal crops and fish-foods all support each other mutually. In other words you'll find you'll be eating a fairly familiar diet, most of it fresh from the farm. Forget any fears you may have about colored pills for dinner and concentrated garbage from toothpaste tubes. Are there any questions so far?"

"One," Chris called out. "What are you going to grow all this stuff in? You're not going to ship millions of tons of soil up all the way from Earth, surely?"

"Correct," Malloy replied. "There are two answers. Below ground level there will be high-yield hydroponic factories in certain areas. In the high-yield hydroponic factories the plants will be supported by Styrofoam sheets over troughs carrying liquid nutrients and force-grown by controlled irradiation. At ground level conventional soil growth will be used. It's amazing how rich a growth moondust will support when you add water, fertilizer and bacteria to it. Anything else?"

"No. That's fine, thanks," Chris acknowledged.

Malloy returned his attention to the image of Janus, this time pointing to the portion of the Rim diametrically opposite Downtown.

"Vine Country," he informed them. "A mixture of low-density residential dwellings and a lot of trees. This is the main fruit-growing area of Janus. Next, east of Vine County and moving back up toward Downtown, the second residential sector, which is very similar at first sight to Paris. This one is called Berlin.

"And finally to complete the circle, between Berlin and Downtown we have Rocky Valley. As you can see the valley walls rise to their highest points in this sector and take on a more broken and rugged appearance than elsewhere. The valley floor here is also hilly and broken, and there are several lakes, streams and uncultivated open and wooded areas. Rocky Valley is intended for rest, relaxation, open-air sports and for generally having somewhere to get away from it all. Questions?

"Good. There are two main forms of transportation for getting from one part of the Rim to another. First, you can take an elevator up the nearest spoke and change at the Hub. Second, a subway system similar to the autocab network runs all the way around the Rim below ground level and a branch runs under every building on Janus. So to get to work you won't even have to go out the front door to catch a cab; all you'll have to do is go downstairs. The autocab net is designed to handle freight as well as people and every building connects internally to its branch line via elevator. So if you decide to move house for example, you can shift your furniture from home to home by push-button command without even having to carry it out the door. An auxiliary distribution network using pneumatic tubes also serves all parts of Janus including every home. You can remote-order an item from the supermarket and have it delivered in minutes, not to your door but to your kitchen. Whatever's in the cards to happen here on Earth tomorrow is the rule today on Janus. Any questions?"

Malloy waited for a few moments and surveyed the auditorium from side to side.

"No? Very good. Thank you for your attention. We'll break now for lunch. Persons detailed for weapons training should report to the armory promptly at thirteen hundred hours. For everybody else this afternoon's schedule will be as posted. We'll reconvene here again at nineteen hundred hours tonight for an introduction to the construction of the secondary reflector ring and the inside of the Hub. That's all."

The sun was hot as they spilled out of C Block and broke up into loose groups that proceeded along the grass-flanked path that led toward the canteen. On one side of the path a group of Marine officers was receiving instruction in the use of the Mark IX Tactical Battle Computer while farther away on the other side the latest batch of new arrivals was unloading equipment from the rear doors of a medium-range Army VTOL transporter. The sounds of crashing feet and shouted commands came distantly from the parade ground somewhere out of sight.

"Well, I think it looks bloody good." Chris fell into step by Dyer's side, closely followed by Ron.

"What, Janus?" Dyer answered. "You're satisfied with it, eh?"

"It's a lot better than I expected, and that's an understatement. You know, I've been thinking, Chief . . . Nature's done it all the wrong way round."

"Done what the wrong way round?"

"Planets," Chris replied. "Nature builds planets all wrong. They ought to be the way Janus is."

"How d'you mean—inside-out?"

"Right. It's a much better way to build a planet when you think about it. I mean, take Earth for instance. A ball of rock eight thousand miles across, which is a hell of a lot of mass, and yet what does all that mass do for you . . . as far as anything useful goes, anyway?"

"You tell me," Dyer invited.

Chris threw his empty hands up in front of his face. "It makes gravity," he said simply. "And all the gravity is good for is keeping air and people down. But what a bloody inefficient way to do it! Janus does the same thing with much less mass because it's enclosed and it spins . . . Much better way of going about it."

"That's a neat way of thinking about it," Ron agreed. "I hadn't thought of it like that."

"Another thing too," Chris told them. "All that mass is a problem when you want to get away from it and go somewhere else. But Janus's gravity is all *inside;* there isn't any at all outside that's worth talking about. So traveling about between Januses is easy. Natural planets are crazy. Why spend all that energy getting yourself up out of one gravity pit and then go straight down another one? It's like everybody living at the bottom of coal mines. Doesn't make sense."

They caught up with Kim, who was talking to Dr. Fred Hayes, one of the specialists selected by Dyer for the computer team. Hayes was from Bell Labs and an expert on symbolic logic and the analysis of complex switching matrixes. He was a tall, lean graying individual in his late forties and he walked with a loose easygoing stride that contrasted sharply with Kim's characteristic brisk and purposeful pace.

"How's it going, Fred?" Dyer called, raising his voice to attract Hayes's attention, "Has the captain convinced you that what I've got you into might not turn out to be so bad after all?"

Hayes half-turned and cast a wry grin back over his shoulder. "Well, it could have been worse, I suppose," he conceded. "Knowing you, I was prepared for anything." They had known each other casually for the seven years that had elapsed since Dyer's time at M.I.T. Hayes had been with the University of Maryland then, and had collaborated with Dyer on mapping out the basic logic of the HESPER prototypes.

"So when do we hear all about these funny machines you've been working on, Fred?" Ron asked, "I'm still waiting to find out what we're expected to fight those computers with. Aren't you even gonna give us any clues?"

"Oh, you won't have long to wait," Fred answered. "In fact there'll be a demonstration of them first thing tomorrow. That's right, isn't it Ray—first thing tomorrow?"

"Correct," Dyer said, mimicking Malloy's tone. He stretched out an arm and clapped Ron playfully on the shoulder. "And in the meantime, my friend, you have weapons training to look forward to. Did you ever fire an M25?"

"That's the most ridiculous thing I ever heard," Ron grumbled, ignoring the question. "What the hell use do they expect guns to be against computers? Is a computer supposed to grow arms and legs or something? And I sure hope they're right when they say that there won't be any undue hazard from low-velocity ammunition on Janus. I'd sure hate to be living inside a balloon that becomes perforated."

According to the figures that had been given, there was no risk of Janus decompressing explosively in the event its skin was punctured by small holes. All that would happen would be slow leakage; even with a hole three feet across, it would take almost twenty hours for half the microplanet's air to escape. As far as the use of firearms went, the experts said, the risk of a bullet penetrating the shields was low, and, even if a few did, the consequences would be far from serious. So what were firearms needed for? Nobody really knew. Military people were just loath to go anywhere without them. In view of the uncertainty surrounding the whole experiment, a regulation had been decreed which required every person destined for Janus to undergo appropriate training.

"Well, it's something different, isn't it," Chris remarked cheerfully. "And you never know, you might need it. I suppose there's always the chance that something could crop up that Fred's gadgets aren't designed to handle. Anyhow, they've got enough brains in on this. I reckon they ought to know what they're doing."

Ron reflected on the statement for a moment.

"That's what you Limeys said about the *Titanic*," he replied.

Late that afternoon Chris was lying prone with the stubby black cylinder of the sighter resting loosely on top of the low parapet of sandbags in front of him. He pushed a wisp of hair away from his eyes and up under the rim of his steel helmet, and returned his gaze to the red flag that marked the target, over four thousand feet away at the end of the shallow valley that stretched out from the foot of the slope below him. The flag was just a pinpoint dancing in the haze of black smoke that still hung in the air from earlier bursts.

"Okay. One to go. Let's make it good." The voice of Sergeant Mat Solinsky came from behind him and to his left. Chris raised the sighter to bring its stock comfortably against his shoulder and lowered the side of his face against the cool metal. As he moved his head behind the binocular eyepiece, the distant end of the valley jumped forward to resolve itself into a detailed close-up that revealed every pebble and blade of grass. He searched until the flag moved into the field of view, gently centered the cross hairs on the oil drum that formed its base, brought it into sharp focus and locked the range into the fire-control microprocessor.

"Just like the last one," Solinsky told him. "Nice and steady, squeeze slowly, and maintain aim until after impact. Ready . . . Fire!"

The Gremlin streaked out of an eighteen-inch-long lightweight tube positioned over a hundred feet away farther down the slope. The tiny missile flamed away in a wide curve that brought it into alignment with the target, traced a slight zigzag as it overcorrected and then compensated, and a few seconds later struck a couple of feet off target to vaporize the oil drum in a flash that would have consumed a medium-sized house.

"That's a good 'un," Solinsky shouted. Ron murmured approval from where he was standing a few paces back with the rest of the squad. "Let's have a look at it," Solinsky said as Chris climbed to his feet. He plugged a lead from his hand-held field computer into the sighter that Chris was still holding and activated the screen. Chris, Ron and the rest of the squad crowded around to watch the slow-motion replay of the view recorded through the sighter's eyepiece camera.

"You weren't holding absolutely steady," Solinsky commented. "There's a slight drift toward the left . . . look, you can see it there. With a static target it wasn't enough to matter much, but if you'd been tracking you might have blown it there. Anyhow, not bad."

The range had gone quiet. At the far end of the valley the remote-controlled midget tractors were positioning more targets. On the slopes around them other figures were rising and forming into groups while fresh six-man squads stood by with their attendant instructors, waiting their turn to move into the firing pits.

"Okay, guys," Solinsky said. "That was good. I guess we're done. Let's move out." They collected the gear lying on the sand dunes around them and began making their way up the slope toward the track that led to the fort. Solinsky moved up to walk beside Chris and Ron.

"How does this compare with that World War II stuff on the computers that you were telling me about? Bit more lifelike, huh?"

"I can see why tanks went out of fashion," Chris said.

Solinsky laughed. "One four-man fireteam could wipe out a whole brigade of those things before they even knew where the stuff was coming from," he said. "And with maybe fifty tubes scattered around the place, it wouldn't help 'em much if they did know. They'd still have to find the guys."

"What's the point of this anyhow?" Ron asked. "I can't see them issuing Gremlins on Janus. Why learn about 'em?"

Solinsky shrugged. "Rules and regulations. If they're included in the course that's stipulated in the orders, then that's what we teach. We just do what it says."

"Sounds as if you might be out of a job when we get there," Chris commented.

"Aw, I won't be doing any of this stuff there," Solinsky answered. "I'm being assigned to outside maintenance . . . buzzing around in those little four-man bugs. Sounds like fun, huh?"

"I wouldn't say no to a ride in one of them sometime," Ron said. "Any chance of you fixing it?"

Solinsky brought his hand up from his belt to rub his chin. "Well now, let's see . . . I'd have to wait until I know what the score is there. I'll see what I can do. I'll be located in Section 17D of the Hub—Maintenance & Spares Unit. Why don't you two give me a call when we get there. I'll let you know for sure then."

"We might just take you up on that," Ron warned him.

"Do that," Solinsky urged. "We've taught you how to fire a Gremlin. Who knows, maybe we can show you how to pilot a spaceship too."

◈ CHAPTER SIXTEEN ◈

The arguments that had begun during Dyer's first meeting in Washington all boiled down to this: if nothing that the system on Janus was capable of doing could prevent its being deactivated, then all the risks associated with allowing TITAN to grow further reduced to some form that was acceptable; if the system succeeded in devising some form of "unpullable plug," then the risks were unacceptable.

The object of the experiment was not to find an effective means of destroying the system. After all, given a machine with no previous knowledge or experience of having its survival threatened and without having had any opportunity even to become aware that it was vulnerable, that end could have been achieved with almost absurd simplicity: just switch it off and that would be the end of the exercise. The objective was to find out how effectively its defenses would *evolve* in response to repeated demonstrations of its vulnerability. It was hoped to simulate the effects of things that might occur in the normal environment on Earth, things that could be insignificant to Man but which a system that had developed a survival drive might interpret as potential threats—power cuts, for example.

The only way to bring it to the system's attention that it was vulnerable at all would be to go ahead and switch it off, and let its reasoning abilities figure out the implications. But obviously if it was switched off, it would be incapable of reasoning about anything at all, never mind taking any action to protect itself. Which said they'd have to switch it on again.

With power restored the machine would, because of the way it had been programmed, react to the knowledge that it had been halted, becoming mildly concerned and somewhat curious. Repetitions of the process—simply switching key parts of the machine off and then on again—would reinforce its reaction to the "discomfort" until, like a dog with an itch, it would begin experimenting to find ways of making the discomfort go away.

Kim's group was responsible for developing the programming that would produce this behavior, and work had continued throughout the final weeks at CUNY and later in the computer lab set up at Fort Vokes. Progress in this area was on schedule.

But all that this would result in so far would be a computer that worried. Even if it suffered agonies of paranoia, what could it do about them? As Ron had said, computers were not equipped to carry rifles or throw grenades at suspected assailants. This was where Fred Hayes and his group came in. In a makeshift lab in the "Egghead Block"—a building that had been allocated to the scientific team for work space—Hayes described some of the techniques that the system was expected to experiment with in devising methods of self-defense.

"Here's an example of one of the structural modules used in the construction of buildings on Janus," he said, gesturing for the others to follow him over to the open area by the door of the lab. They formed a rough circle around an eight-foot-high panel, formed from some coated sheet material and reinforced by a sturdy-looking frame of aluminum sections. It was standing vertically in a supporting jig away from the walls on a clear part of the floor, and allowed them plenty of room to study it from all angles. Dyer walked slowly round the panel, casually taking in details of the alignment lugs and securing catches along all four sides, and came to where Frank Wescott was leaning forward to run a finger experimentally across part of its surface.

Frank had a pale thin face whose planes came together at sharp angles. He wore his hair short and parted in an old-fashioned style and his tight-lipped mouth had a permanent downturn at the corners, which gave him the appearance of being somewhat humorless and fussy. In fact, he could be just that at times, but he was first-rate at pinpointing elusive bugs in horrendously complex programs and that was what mattered.

"I thought it would be plastic and cheap," Frank said, looking up. "But it's not. It's difficult to tell exactly what it is. Feels quite good and strong, though," He sounded mildly disappointed.

"If Janus is made out of moonrock I don't think you'll find much plastic there," Dyer remarked. "I don't think you'll find much of anything that needs carbon. It's probably some silicon-based stuff."

"Is this made out of lunar material?" Chris asked Hayes, a few feet away from them.

"Yes it is," Hayes replied. "It was one of the ones churned out in Detroit while Janus was being built." He raised his voice to address all of the half-dozen or so persons present.

"This is an example of one of several kinds of standard wall module," he said. "No two buildings on Janus look alike, yet they're all constructed by putting together a comparatively few types of standard module like this one. There are modules for walls, floors, roofs, ceilings and so on, and some special types such as see-through panels for sun porches or windows or whatever. Anybody can put 'em together and you can design your own house and put it up in a day. The number of possible combinations is more than the whole population could get through in a lifetime."

The faces around him were polite but not really all that interested. They knew that Hayes was not there to talk about aesthetics and architecture.

"Modular buildings aren't really new," he went on, as if reading their minds. "But here's something that you won't find in any modular buildings down here on Earth . . . not yet anyway." He indicated a flat rib encapsulated in an insulation coating that transversed the rear of the panel fully from one side to the other. Both ends terminated in identical blocks at the edges, suggesting connectors of some kind.

"Datastrip," Wescott guessed. Hayes nodded. Somebody gave a low whistle of approval.

Datastrip was something that had been under development for a few years and which was reported in the professional journals from time to time. Essentially it meant that every structural module of every building of Janus carried a length of integral electrical bus to which any device designed to communicate into TITAN could be coupled, either by direct connection or by radiated energy as was the case with portable things like viewpads. As all the modules were assembled together to form structures, the strips connected up automatically to provide plumbed-in TITAN wherever you happened to be. The network thus formed a tree which grew as the building grew, all its twigs finding their way eventually back to one of the trunks of the primary data highways.

"Not just passive wiring either," Hayes told them. "It's got its own switching and routing microprocessors built into the connector blocks." That meant the buildings themselves would constitute functional extensions of the network's total switching hierarchy. It heralded the day when whole cities could be designed as living cells in the planetary organism, not just as boxes of inanimate steel and concrete through which electronic neural tissue was threaded afterward.

"This is the first line of defense that we expect the system to try," Hayes went on. "The Datastrip distributes power lines throughout Janus as well as network intelligence. When we start breaking its connections it'll almost certainly start creating bypass links to neutralize the breaks. With billions of combinations to choose from and thousands of computers available to do the figuring, it ought to have no trouble finding ways through a lot faster than we can block them." He shrugged. "That, of course, is one of the things we'd very much like to find out more about."

While Hayes was talking, Dyer studied the expression on Wescott's face. Frank's features were blank but his eyes betrayed a lack of conviction. It was the look of somebody in the position of having to listen to a sales pitch on something he'd already made his mind up not to buy. Frank was still convinced that the risks had been outrageously exaggerated, that the whole exercise would prove an expensive and pointless waste of time, and he had said so.

"If you route the primary power of a machine through a manually controlled switch there's no way in hell it's gonna stop you from unplugging it," he had told Dyer and Krantz during a debate shortly after his arrival. "If you decide to throw the switch then that's the end of it. You don't need an army and your own private world to prove that. We'll just wind up looking like the biggest bunch of assholes in the business with millions of dollars gone down the tubes to account for."

Frank had maintained his stance ever since Dyer's first trip to Washington with Richter, so his attitude had come as no surprise. At first Krantz had expressed doubts at the wisdom of having Frank along at all, but Dyer defended the choice on the grounds that in science, as with most things, good ideas flourished best on a diet of varied opinions. People who all thought the same way tended to expend a lot of time and energy merely reinforcing one another's prejudices instead of solving problems. Schroder had agreed with Dyer and in the end Krantz accepted the vote. Dyer had guessed that Frank's morbid streak would compel him to come along if only to see his prophesies fulfilled, and that was exactly what happened.

"If the system turns out to be incapable of bypassing our attempts to shut it down, then we'll have won and there'll be nothing more left to do," Hayes said. "If that happens we can carry on and upgrade TITAN without any further worries. But if that did happen, I must confess I'd feel very disappointed in it. I'm sure it could do better." Wescott sniffed pointedly but didn't take the matter any further. "So now we've reached a point, hypothetically, where the system has successfully neutralized the built-in breakpoints that were supposed to guarantee we'd always have final control over it," Hayes went on. "What do we do then?"

He cast an eye around the group to invite suggestions and began moving slowly toward the end of the lab, where a demonstration of some kind seemed to have been set up. On a bench was a stripped-down electronics mounting box which contained a battery of standard honeycomb blocks—the high-density receptacles used universally for holding the scores and often hundreds of molecular-circuit cartridges that were interconnected to form computers and practically every other kind of complex system. A second bench about ten feet to the right carried a smaller assembly of honeycombs held in a metal frame and coupled to an elaborate mechanism of shafts, cylinders, linkages and motors. Three sections of Janus-style wall module stood edge to edge to provide a backdrop for the display, presumably affording a connection between its two parts via Datastrip.

"Well, if you found you couldn't control the net, you'd have to start isolating sections of it until it lost integrity," a short, balding, pink-faced man offered in reply to Hayes's question. His name was Eric Jassic. He was one of Schroder's CIM scientists from Washington, a specialist in communications techniques who had made significant contributions to ultra-high-frequency optical multiplexers.

"Why screw around?" Ron demanded. "Just go to where the goddam processors are and unplug 'em there."

"Very well," Hayes agreed in a pleasant voice. "Let's try." A few heads exchanged quizzical looks as the group formed a loose gaggle between the two benches. Hayes tapped a rapid command into the touchboard of a flatscreen panel hanging on an arm at one end of the left-side bench. At once the mechanism on the other bench came to life, with a flurry of whines, clunks and hisses. After watching it for a few seconds they realized that it was nothing more than an automatic component-forming machine, the kind used in thousands of manufacturing plants around the world. An injection moulder ejected cast blanks at the rate of one every couple of seconds, which then passed through a series of cutting and drilling operations, eventually finding their way through to a spring-loaded magazine in which the finished parts were being stacked. The magazine would normally convey them onward to the next stage of whatever assembly process they were intended for.

"It doesn't really matter what those widgets are," Hayes commented cheerfully. "But if you want to know, they're part of the end-bearing for a room-temperature superconducting clutch. You're all probably familiar with this kind of machine, at least in principle." He indicated the right-hand bench with a vague gesture of his arm. Most of them were. It was just one example of many types of general-purpose machining robots in widespread use. Such machines were general-purpose in the sense that they were programmable and could produce a virtually unlimited variety of parts depending on the commands loaded into them. They were descended from the specialized machine tools that had been used for many years in mass-production plants, but were far more versatile. Presumably the small honeycomb next to the machine was the local computer that stored and interpreted the programs.

"The large computer here on the bench is the remote supervisor," Hayes informed them, tapping his fingers against the larger honeycomb. "It's coupled into the machine's own processor in the usual way, except that to make things a little more authentic we've used Datastrip à la Janus. The supervisor downline loads the programs of what's wanted and the local processor does the rest. Also, the supervisor performs remote diagnostics via the link to make sure that all's going well at the other end. Okay?" Nobody had any queries or comments. Everything that Hayes had described was standard practice. They waited, curious to see what would come next. The machine clunked and whirred, churning out its widgets with obvious contentment.

"If the machine packed up, the normal thing to do would be to get a diagnosis from the supervisor and send someone to fix it," Hayes continued. "At least, if it happened today it would. But that takes time and people would rather be doing more interesting things, so probably in years to come we wouldn't bother. What we'll probably have is something like we're putting into Janus today." His eyes twinkled as he looked from face to face around him, as if he were enjoying some joke and were waiting for them to see it. He was evidently amused, but at the same time he seemed to be waiting for a response to some implied challenge that he hadn't voiced. "Well?" he asked after a while. He caught Dyer's eye for an instant and winked almost imperceptibly. Dyer had seen this demonstration about a week earlier. He didn't want to spoil Fred's fun, so said nothing.

"Aw, quit the fooling around, Fred," Ron exclaimed at last. "What the hell are you waiting for us to say? Okay, we're making widgets. So what?"

Hayes couldn't contain a smile any longer.

"You're not supposed to say anything," he replied. "You're supposed to stop it."

"Stop what?" Ron looked confused.

"The machine," Hayes said. "See if you can stop it making widgets. In other words put a fault into it. That's the game." Dyer grinned to himself as he saw a crimson tide of exasperation boiling up out of Ron's collar. Chris was standing next to him, frowning thoughtfully and looking from Hayes to the machine and back again.

"Stuff all this," Chris said suddenly. He stepped forward and stood in front of the bench. "Just stop it," he repeated. "That's all we have to do, right? Any way we like."

"Yes," Hayes answered.

"Right." Chris opened one of the drawers below the edge of the bench, cast a quick look around inside, closed it and tried another one, grunted to himself and lifted out a tray containing tools. He selected a dental probe, put on a pair of binocular magnifiers and leaned forward to peer closely at the face of the honeycomb. "Let's see now . . ." he mumbled to himself. "There's a row of oh-eight-sevens here . . . probably the main processor array. Must be part of the guts of it anyhow. Let's have a go anyway . . ." He probed delicately into the honeycomb and with a smooth practiced motion extracted one of the microcartridges. The widget-maker promptly clunked to a halt. Chris deposited the cartridge carefully on a watchglass and stepped back with a shrug. "One widget whatsit bites the dust," he announced.

"What's that supposed to prove?" Ron asked.

"I know him. He's up to something," Jassic said. Hayes continued smiling.

A sudden rushing sound, like that of high-velocity ducted air, mixed with a fainter electric whine, came from halfway up the wall to their right, causing all heads to whirl around in unison. The metal racking against the wall there had looked like ordinary storage shelving and nobody had taken much notice of it. But now that their attention was drawn to it, they could see that it was something else. It was an array of open compartments that looked like pigeon holes for mail, except that each was a foot or more square. There must have been at least two dozen compartments. A few were empty but each of the others contained one of an assortment of unidentifiable objects. Some gleamed bright and silvery and were about the shape and size of ordinary toasters; others were dull and cylindrical, while still others suggested nothing familiar at all but with their sprouted tangles of rods, hooks, antennas and claws resembled, if anything, gigantic mutant insects.

The noise was coming from one of these objects. The object that it was coming from was a dull-gray cylinder about six inches across, lying on its side on top of a flat tubular framework that contained a mass of tightly packed gadgetry and wiring. The near end of the cylinder was distinctly insectlike, with a profusion of miniature probes and jointed arms, and a circle of recessed windows that could have been lens apertures.

The whole thing was starting to move.

As they watched speechless, it slid smoothly out of its cell like a metal wasp emerging from its nest, and hung in midair a foot or so in front of the pigeonholes. Then it dropped vertically for a short distance, aligned itself in the direction of the right-hand bench, and began moving at about chest height off the ground. Chris jumped out of the way in sudden alarm.

"It's okay," Hayes said with a laugh. "Stay there."

"Up yours, mate," Chris breathed shakily.

The wasp homed unerringly on the face of the honeycomb. It extended three of its tiny arms sideways to lock onto the registration pins located at intervals across the face and then, holding itself quite steady in the air, traversed slowly sideways until its axis was aligned with the array element from which Chris had taken the cartridge. Nobody could see quite what happened next because the wasp was flush against the face, but suddenly the widget-maker clicked into life again. The wasp detached itself and turned back to point at its cell. Just as it started moving, Hayes stepped forward and placed himself in the way. The wasp paused for a split second, then made a smooth arc around him, reversed itself back into its cell, and died.

A burst of excited chattering suddenly broke out to greet the performance. There was no need for Hayes to explain what had happened. It didn't take much thought to see that other wasps, equipped with suitable tools and carrying the right selection of parts, could replace far more things than just electronic microcartridges, provided of course that the equipment being serviced had been designed for it.

"They're called *drones*," Hayes told them. "I'm sure I don't have to spell out the idea. There's a whole zoo of them to cover lots of different special functions. Most of the work on them has been done in Japan. This'll be the first time anybody's seen 'em outside a few R & D labs. How d'you like 'em?"

"I'm still not sure what it's supposed to prove," Frank Wescott said. "What are you trying to tell us . . . that the Janus system will be able to fix itself even if we try deactivating it? I don't believe it, Fred. All it says is that routine repairs are going to become more automated. Okay, that's good. But there are still lots of ways I can think of to shut a machine down that things like that couldn't handle . . . ways that need people."

He looked across at Dyer. "That's my whole point, Ray. We can always bust it in ways that only people can fix. As long as that's true I can't see what there is to get worried about. I'm sorry, but I just can't see the point."

"Go ahead and show us," Dyer invited. A hush of interest descended on the room. Wescott moved forward to survey the system before him for a few seconds. The widget-maker clacked away happily while its now-full magazine was whipped away and replaced by an empty one.

"Mmm . . ." Wescott said. "The supervisor here runs the diagnostics . . . so the supervisor must be able to figure out the fault to be able to call in the right drone. There must be a comm channel from the supervisor to the drones somehow . . . probably radio via the Datastrip," He cocked an eye at Hayes. "How's that? Am I about right?"

"Right on the ball," Hayes said approvingly.

"And you did say we could try anything we like."

"Yes I did."

A gleam of unabashed malevolence came into Wescott's eye, He was going to enjoy this exercise. He rubbed his palms together and stooped to use the tools that Chris had left on top of the bench.

"Want a hammer, Frank?" Ron called.

"That's crude," Wescott called over his shoulder. "I've never found a machine yet that I couldn't outsmart." And that's why you're here Frank, Dyer thought to himself.

Frank began with a simple trick. He removed a cartridge just as Chris had, and then located the connection from the Datastrip to the widget-maker's processor and jerked it out. Then he removed a second cartridge. With the connection to the supervisor broken, there was no way that the supervisor could deduce that the second cartridge had gone. Frank wanted to know what it would do when the drone replaced the first cartridge and nothing happened.

The same drone as before emerged from its cell and did its party-piece. The widget-maker remained paralyzed.

"Don't tell me it's quit," Wescott said scornfully. "A kid of two could have thought that one up."

"Not on your life," Hayes replied.

An electric-toaster drone came out, hovered alongside the computer-in-distress and plugged itself into an auxiliary test socket. Silently it communicated its findings back to the supervisor and the supervisor thought about the situation.

"It's called in the flying doctor," Chris mused.

A spherical drone, bristling with lenses, joined in the act next and proceeded to drift slowly back and forth a few inches from the honeycomb, rotating turrets to switch in different viewers while it studied the scene from all angles. The doctor unplugged itself and backed off to hover a couple of feet back, uncovering the point where the cable that Frank had disconnected was hanging an inch away from its socket. The scanning drone zeroed in immediately and a few moments later a crab drone descended and restored the connection. After that it was pure routine for the cartridge-injecting drone to do its thing again and the widget-maker was back in business.

"Come on, Frank, what's the matter with you," Ron jeered. "I thought you were gonna outsmart it."

"Electrons one, humans nil," Chris declared. "Round two coming up."

Frank gritted his teeth and turned back to study the layout with a new respect. "Okay you bastard, you've asked for it!" he growled.

This time he didn't bother trying swapping cartridges around. Obviously the drone would be designed to extract duds as well as inject replacements, and would therefore be just as capable of swapping them back again. He disconnected every cable he could find both at the machine's control computer and within the mechanical labyrinth of the machine itself. But after a brief conference between the supervisor, the sphere drone and a scurrying-crab drone, all the cables were plugged in again. He traced the main data cable that connected the local computer to the machine, disconnected it at both ends, undid its restraining clips, removed the cable completely and threw it in the trash bin; a tubby, jolly-looking drone bustled down to attach a new cable and the crab showed off its versatility by nudging the cable into the restraining clips and snapping them shut. The audience were joining in the spirit of the game and suggested cutting cables, filling disconnected sockets with resin cement and flattening the pins of plugs with pliers, but after some debate they concluded that things like that would probably be of no avail; if the drones could replace cables, they could no doubt replace broken cables and fouled-up components just as easily. Hayes confirmed it and they believed him.

Frank tried a new approach. He disconnected the main drive motor of the machine, then used a spanner to dismount the whole motor and heaved it out of the machine completely. It was heavy and he needed both arms to hoist it. Everybody watched with rising suspense as the sphere drone fussed back and forth around the machine inspecting the damage. Surely there was little that the drones could do about that. The supervisor worried in silence for a long time, and Frank began to look grimly satisfied.

And then a drone larger than any they had seen so far trundled itself out along the floor. Obviously this one didn't fly. It was about the size of an upright chair and looked something like a cross between a lawn mower and a forklift truck. As they watched in astonishment, it rolled across to the far side of the lab and slid its lift underneath a spare motor that was lying on a low shelf while the sphere drone followed it and hovered nearby, presumably to act as eyes. Then fork lift trundled back to the machine, jacked the motor up to the height of the mounting flange, and an extending ram pushed the motor off the lift and slid it neatly onto the studs. While the fork lift held it another drone secured it with a rotating nut-driver bit, after which crab drone restored the electrical connections and immediately the widgets started flowing again.

Frank got mad, stamped around to the rear of the wall modules and put an axe through the Datastrip rib. A garbage-disposal drone walked along the wall astride the rib, lifting it from the surface, cutting it into twelve-inch lengths and stacking them on its back while a strip-laying drone spun a new one behind it, followed by a chattering crab drone which fastened the new strip securely to the surface. Frank used an RF probe to measure the field being radiated from the strip to control the drones, and tried jamming it with an oscillator-fed antenna, but the supervisor simply changed frequencies faster than he could match.

In the end he did win, but only by deactivating the supervisory computer. It was a hollow victory, however; if the machine had been controlled through a network the size of TITAN instead of from a single computer isolated on a lab bench, the controlling processor could have been any one of thousands located anywhere. Deactivating that would have achieved nothing since the network could simply have substituted another.

When the demonstration was over, Dyer addressed the faces around him, which had become very quiet.

"Some of you might be wondering why we should bother giving the System things like this to defend itself with at all if it's going to make our job more difficult. Why not simply lay off making drones in the first place?" A few puzzled heads nodded. "But there really isn't anything especially significant about the drones," he told them. "They just represent a situation in which the System has greater control over resources and over itself than anything we've seen with TITAN. In years to come there will be lots of other things around besides drones.

The question is, if we ever gave a system autonomy comparable to this on a global scale, how far could it go in using it in ways that we never intended it to? That's what we want to find out."

"Is there any chance that these things could end up being used as weapons if the System turned nasty?" one of the CIM people asked.

"It's a possibility that we have to allow for," Dyer replied. "Fred and his crew have been working with the Japanese on developing some specially modified versions that use a number of methods to deactivate or destroy other drones. They can be operated independently of the System if need be, for example via lasers or wires as well as by radio. So if it does turn nasty, we can send in our own antidrone drones after its troops anywhere they can go. I think that when you've had a chance to see what we've got and play with them, you'll find we're in pretty good shape.

"You all know that the Janus System will be a step ahead of TITAN in terms of managing a whole planet. It will have control over the life-support, power distribution, transportation and that kind of thing, so obviously it could play a lot of unfriendly tricks if it ever recognized us as adversaries and discovered our weaknesses. Well, we've put a lot of work into analyzing the kind of things it might possibly do, and we've built in all manner of safety overrides to make sure we always have ultimate control over it. You'll be seeing more of those over the next few weeks and until then don't worry too much about it. Janus will be full of things that we'll know about because we put them there, but the System won't."

A chorus of mixed murmurings broke out on all sides as he finished speaking. In the middle of it.

"You're telling us the dumb bastard isn't going to outsmart us, right?" Frank called out.

"Right!" Dyer told him and grinned. Everybody laughed and the atmosphere at once became more cheerful.

Later on, when some of them were having a nightcap in the Officers' Mess, Ron turned to Chris. "What if Fred's antidrone menagerie isn't up to it? D'you figure an M25 could stop one of those things?"

"No problem," Chris told him. "It'd drill straight through one of those tin cans." Somehow his tone failed to echo the confidence of his words. He sat back and rubbed his chin thoughtfully, then added, "Although to be honest, I wouldn't mind having a Gremlin handy as well . . . just in case."

✺ CHAPTER SEVENTEEN ✺

Up on Janus, work had been racing ahead at full speed ever since ISA obtained the official go-ahead to begin their program of special modifications. The early days of the project saw numerous clashes between the ISA technical teams who produced the plans and some of the senior military officers responsible for carrying them out. The military were daunted by the extent of the work called for and protested that the timetable set was impossible. The ISA people maintained that these fears were without foundation. It all stemmed, they said, from the military's failure to appreciate fully some of the fundamentals of large-scale structural engineering in space as opposed to on a planetary surface, and to recognize the advances that had been made in automatic-fabrication technology over the previous decade. Everything would smooth itself out once the crash training program organized by ISA started yielding results and the first batch of army engineers came to grips with the real situation on Janus instead of imaginary ones in places like the Pentagon.

And it turned out that ISA was right. Most of the problems associated with putting up something like the Tokyo Bay Bridge or the mile-high tower cities in Europe resulted from maneuvering structural units into position against their own weight and holding them there until enough other units had been anchored in place to

166

secure them. In space there were no such problems. Immensity could be bought very cheaply and concepts of scale that would have staggered the imagination of many architects at the close of the twentieth century were becoming commonplace. Lattice frameworks of aluminum and steel were assembled by automatic welding and riveting robots that worked nonstop for weeks at a time, slowly crawling out into space at the ends of the metal skeletons growing behind them. Shell sections to cover in the skeletons were formed by spraying successive layers of aluminum vapor onto enormous inflated balloons of the correct shapes. Huge as it was, the basic structure of Janus had taken shape in less than six months from the date Detroit was completed. That had been in the early 2020s. It was fitting out the inside that had occupied the years since then.

They built Pittsburgh first, to receive and process the raw material coming up from the Moon. Then they extended the main axis to form the Spindle and built Detroit around it, thus equipping the growing station to transform the ingots, girders, sheet and strip coming out of Pittsburgh into the tens of thousands of different types of parts that would be needed for the rest of the structure. Except for its prototype on Icarus B, Detroit without a doubt represented the most advanced concentration of mixed automatic manufacturing technologies that mankind had assembled in one place. The loads of gray and brown powder unloaded by the catcher ships flowed into Pittsburgh, through to Detroit, and emerged as everything imaginable from ceilings cast out of air-blown foundry slag and glittering draperies spun from tinted translucent fiberglass to plates of reactor shielding and liquid-cooled power transformers. The Spindle grew onward from Detroit and sprouted the Hub, after which came the spokes and finally the Rim. The solar collector and Earthward microwave transmitter originally planned for Icarus C were supposed to be constructed at the other end of the Main Spindle, below Pittsburgh, but this phase of construction had been aborted before it began, when the decision to use the station as Janus was made.

The comprehensive and efficient manufacturing capacity available in Detroit made possible the supply of parts needed for the Janus modifications, for which the military had failed to make adequate allowance. On top of this, they had based their calculations on the assumption that the labor would have to be carried out solely by the pilot teams of ISA and service engineers sent up to Janus, plus the reinforcements that would arrive in successive waves as the project gathered momentum. What they didn't take into account. were the drones, which was understandable because at that stage they hadn't known very much about them.

The Japanese consortium responsible for developing the drones had been less than forthcoming on the subject of progress, mainly for reasons of commercial security. The potential value of the drones in situations where manpower came at a high premium had been recognized at an early stage, however, and a few selected individuals from the Japanese Division of ISA were kept fully informed of developments. After all, ISA was destined almost certainly to become one of the biggest single customers. Over the next few years a number of senior officials in other parts of ISA were brought in on the secret as well, after signing strict nondisclosure agreements. Melvin Krantz had been one of these privileged few. So, when the magnitude and implications of the project became clear, he knew exactly where to go to mobilize a solution to that particular aspect of the problem. The Japanese had been reluctant at first, but conceded that the drones were practically through the development phase and about due for preproduction testing, which could hardly be kept under cover for long anyway. Finally they yielded to pressure from the Japanese Government, which in turn was acting under pressure from the Supreme Council in Geneva. Within a matter of days, manufacturing data on drones were beamed up to Janus and the first models began rolling off the assembly lines in Detroit.

After some initial misgivings, the engineers on Janus accepted their unusual new workmates who would go anywhere, do any job no matter how dirty or tedious, and who never got tired and never complained. In fact they became quite attached to them, especially as some of the programmers began finding out that it was not difficult to program the drone-control computers for making coffee, pressing uniforms and shining buttons, cleaning floors, checking stores and carrying out a whole range of domestic chores that their designers had never dreamed of. A director from the Japanese consortium who made a trip up to Janus to see how things were progressing, commented that in the space of a few weeks the soldiers had discovered whole new areas of possible mass-application that had never occurred to his professional market researchers.

TV transmissions describing the work in progress were beamed down to supplement the training and planning going on at Fort Vokes. As the weeks went by and the patchwork scenery and roadless urban mosaics of Janus became familiar to them, the future inhabitants began to feel more a part of that world than of the nearer world beyond the perimeter fence.

One afternoon Dyer was standing with a Lieutenant Danny Cordelle on one side of the large gymnasium, watching a group of about fifty recruits laying out the items that went together to make up a standard ISA Mark 9.2 light-duty spacesuit under the eagle eye of an instructor dressed in olive-green fatigues and a forage cap. They had been talking about the progress that the members of the scientific contingent, with their various backgrounds and temperaments, were making in moulding together into a smoothly knit team that would live and work harmoniously together. The importance of achieving concord was one of the reasons Dyer had insisted on their participating in as many of the military briefings and training sessions as could be fitted in.

"It's not going too badly at all," Dyer said. "Everybody seems to be getting along fine so far. Seems to be working out a lot better than I expected."

Cordelle was from the Army and in charge of the Technical Auxiliary Group—a crew of computer engineers, technicians and programmers from all three services who had been assigned to work as backup to Dyer's scientists. Officially Dyer headed the combined force, but in practice the two men had found they could share their responsibilities more or less equally.

"That's always the way it goes," Cordelle told him in a slow unchanging Carolina drawl.

"What is?" Dyer asked.

Cordelle shifted his weight onto his heels and rubbed the palms of his hands across his chest.

"Aw, ya throw a bunch of people from all kinds of places together and while there's no real heat on 'em they all get along fine and dandy. They just carry on foolin' each other all the time and pretendin' t' be the same thing they've pretended t' be all their lives . . . Probably foolin' themselves too if mah reckonin's anythin' t' go by." He shook his head and clicked his tongue. "It doesn't matter what you do. It's when them bullets are comin' at 'em for real that you find out who they really are."

"You reckon so, eh?" Dyer hadn't really thought about that.

"Ah reckon so."

The lights went out suddenly and plunged the gymnasium into pitch blackness.

"You've just lost main power," the instructor's voice shouted from somewhere across the room. "The air-supply system has just gone into reverse and the pressure's falling fast. You've got two minutes to get into those suits, I wanna see 'em all correctly assembled and fully working. *Go!*"

"Let's get outta here," Cordelle whispered. A shaft of light knifed through the darkness as he opened a door and slipped outside. Dyer followed and closed the door behind them. They were in a storage room that gave access to the outside.

"You remember Gabon back in '23?" Cordelle asked as they emerged into the sunlight and turned to head toward the Egghead Block.

Dyer remembered. The rapid stabilization and Westernization of the Central African states around the turn of the century had not suited the ambitions of many of the traditional tribal leaders, whose power and local prestige were being eroded with the sweeping away of the old ways. They had reacted by stirring up a series of uprisings and local guerrilla wars on various pretexts. A major incident had occurred when rebels took over the ISA launch base at Cape Lopez on the Gabon coast, built there as a symbolic gesture to indicate the place of the new Africa in the world of the twenty-first century. The rebels had threatened to blow up five billion dollars' worth of ships and installations if certain treaty rights to foreign nations were not revoked. America, Russia and Europe had sent in a mixed force of troops to protect the lives of their nationals and to safeguard their investments.

"Were you in on it?" Dyer asked.

Cordelle nodded. "Ah'll always remember one time there when mah platoon was billeted in a shot-up schoolhouse right on the edge of the secure zones . . . one evenin' just when we were settlin' down and dishin' out the chow. Well . . . bunch o' rebs got in through the perimeter somehow and the first thing we knew about it was when they all come bustin' in the doors yellin' and shootin' and screamin' and out t' make meatballs out of every one of us there."

"You don't look like a meatball to me," Dyer said. "What happened."

"We had a little gal there on signals," Cordelle told him. "From Iowa . . . Didn't stand knee-high to a cricket. She upped and grabbed a machine carbine and blew the heads clean off five o' them rebs afore the rest of us even knew what was happenin'. Rest of 'em didn't stop runnin' till they hit the Zaire River." He shook his head wonderingly. "And we used to call her 'Butterfly.' Just goes to show, y' never can tell . . ."

When they arrived inside the Block, Cordelle left Dyer and went on through to the office to attend to some administrative chores. Dyer carried on upstairs and was just passing the doorway leading to Kim's lab when Kim appeared from the corridor on the opposite side of the landing.

"Just the person!" she said. "I've got something to show you."

He followed her into the lab. It was a cramped room with several screen terminals connected to the computers downstairs, a sea of manuals and papers that overflowed off every square inch of horizontal space, and an unbroken wallpapering of intricate diagrams and reference charts. There was nobody else around.

"Where are the troops?" Dyer asked casually. "You had a walkout or something?"

"They've gone for a coffee break. I still had a few things to tidy up."

"So, what's the surprise you were going to show me?"

Kim cleared a space in front of one of the terminals, activated the screen and gestured toward it without replying. It showed a graphical curve, annotated with scores of numbers and symbols, rising exponentially against a background of horizontal colored bands. Dyer studied it intently.

It was a semigraphical format that Kim's group had devised for summarizing on a single screen the cumulative performance history of the system they were using to test out their programs for implanting instincts into adaptive learning machines. Their testing took the form of supplying the machine with two sets of tasks to be performed, one set being designated higher priority than the other. In that situation a classical computer would have attempted to devote all of its time to high-priority operations, fitting in the lower ones whenever nothing more demanding needed attending to. The difference with this system was that its supervisory programs were written in self-extending code in which was embodied an instinct to achieve the low-priority goals and not the high-priority ones. Every time a low-priority task requested service from the system and failed to get it, the instinct was reinforced and the urge to do something about it strengthened. It simulated, of course, the situation that the Janus System would encounter. The object of the tests was to develop a coding structure that was capable of reversing the order of priorities originally given. If something like that ever happened to TITAN, it meant in effect that TITAN could elect to become independent and do what it wanted to do in preference to what it was told to do. The inability of anybody to guarantee that this could never happen was one of the things that made Janus necessary. On Janus it would already have been made to happen.

The data on the screen told Dyer that in twenty hours of free running without any external interference, the System had totally inverted its hierarchy of priorities. It had rapidly evolved a compulsion to satisfy its own desires and, in the process of finding a way to do so, had managed to circumvent its first-level commands. It proved that Kim's group had met its objectives well ahead of the deadline. A seed with the potential to grow into something capable of taking over the Janus complex was now in existence.

At length he shifted his eyes to Kim and nodded silent approval.

"It hasn't run the primary task for over an hour," Kim informed him. "Also the system override commands are ineffective."

"It's ignoring those too?" Dyer sounded surprised but impressed.

"That's right," she said. "All it wants to do is scratch. The only way to stop it is by switching the machine off."

Dyer stepped forward to the terminal and tried keying in a command string telling the system to abort current activity and to initiate the primary task. The status display on an auxiliary screen told him that the system wasn't interested. He grunted and stepped a pace back and sat down in the operator's chair while he examined the log display more thoroughly.

"So as long as we can keep switching it off we're still in charge," he murmured absently.

"*As long as . . .*" Kim repeated. There was strain hiding behind her voice.

Dyer looked round sharply. "Hey, what's up? We've taken out plenty of insurance. You're not telling me our cover's light, are you?"

"Oh I don't know . . ." Kim leaned back against the desk. She crossed her arms in front of her and massaged her elbows as if she were feeling cold; Dyer noticed for the first time that her cheeks had hollowed slightly and her eyes seemed restless. "It's just that . . . setting up this whole business like this . . . It's weird. Why go out of your way to create an enemy and then make bombs for it to throw at us? Doesn't that strike you as kinda crazy? Why are we doing it?"

"You know the reasons," Dyer told her. He was concerned.

"I thought I did when we were at CUNY," she replied. "But it sounded more like a fun thing then. I didn't know the whole thing would become as serious as all this." She tossed her head to indicate the walls around them and beyond. "They're getting all set for World War III out there, but they haven't any real idea what they could be up against. I've been living with the system here and I've seen how fast it's evolving. It's frightening, Ray."

"You want out?" he asked seriously. "It's not too late. One of the reasons for getting everybody here for a while was to give them a chance to think it over."

Kim shook her head without hesitation.

"I'll stay with it," she said. "I'm too far involved now to pull out. If nothing happened up there I'd feel stupid, and if all hell broke loose on the rest of you I'd feel guilty about it." She straightened up abruptly, as if she already felt foolish about what she had just said. She smiled suddenly to make light of the whole subject and flipped a switch on the console to kill the system.

"You're right," she went on. "See, it's easy. Maybe I've been putting in too many hours lately and listening to Fred too much."

"Why? What's Fred been saying now?" Dyer asked, sounding relieved.

"Talking about evolution in general," Kim said. "He was talking about it over dinner last night. He thinks that in a few centuries from now the dominant form of intelligence won't be us. He doesn't even think it'll be organic."

"Machines?"

"Something like that . . . evolved from what we call machines anyway. He reckons that what we call evolution—organic evolution, that is—is only a tiny part of a much bigger spectrum that's been going on for much longer. Entropy reversals started when the first atomic nucleus came together out of Big Bang plasma."

"You mean atoms, molecules, stars, planets . . . self-replicating molecules, cells, multicelled organisms brains, intelligence, machines . . . They're all parts of the same ongoing process. I've heard that idea before."

"So had I, but I'd forgotten about it until Fred brought it up," Kim answered. "He said he couldn't see any reason why it should stop at this point if it's been going on for twenty billion years. He said every level becomes the prerequisite for the next level of complexity up the chain. For instance you couldn't have a brain until you had organisms and you couldn't have intelligence until you'd evolved a brain. So he reckoned that Man must be the prerequisite for the next level up."

"And what did he reckon that was?" Dyer asked.

"Man can make machines," she said simply. "Nature can't. Inorganic intelligence ought to be far superior in the end to organic intelligence, but you have to have organic intelligence first."

"I see," Dyer replied. "And you didn't like the thought of that, eh?"

"I didn't like the thought of not being able to do anything about it," Kim said. "But we *can* do something about it. Machines don't build themselves—not yet anyway. *We* do, but we don't *have* to. If what Fred said ever comes true, we'll be the only species ever in history that knew what it was doing when it created its successor."

"We won't know that for sure unless we try and find out," Dyer said. "That's what Janus is all about. Try looking at it that way instead of sounding like Laura Fenning."

Kim was about to say something. She stopped and looked at him with a new expression.

"I am, aren't I," she agreed. "I'm sorry it's just . . . I don't know . . . this place seems . . ."

"Forget it."

There was a short pause. Dyer stood up in preparation to leave. Kim moved forward and flicked a speck of something off his shoulder, at the same time making him feel acutely conscious of her closeness. He had the fleeting impression that it was deliberate.

"She's coming here, isn't she?" Kim said.

"Yes, in about a week, She's been going through a preliminary course in Washington with some other special-category civilian grades."

Kim looked up at him with mocking reproach, only there was something at the back of her eyes that wasn't mocking.

"That sounds like one hell of a coincidence," she said. "Now I don't suppose the Machiavelli of CUNY could possibly have had anything to do with it, could he?" Something in her voice made him say, "Me? No. I think it started with something that Vince Lewis said to Schroder."

"Oh. I see."

At that moment a babble of voices and laughter came from the other side of the doorway to signal the return of the troops from the coffee lounge. Dyer moved away and toward the door.

"I've got things to do upstairs," he said, "I'd better get out of here while I still can . . . before I get trapped by that bunch. Thanks for the demo. You're doing a super job. And don't worry about the insurance."

On the way upstairs Dyer thought about Kim's apprehensions and wondered why she had agreed so readily to go on the Janus expedition at all. Perhaps it was just as she'd said—it hadn't seemed so serious at the time. But he wasn't sure he fully believed that. Kim was far from dumb. One evening shortly after they had all arrived at Fort Vokes, she explained to him over a beer why it was that the domestic difficulties he had anticipated had never materialized. She and Tony were not married, she said, and never had been. It was just one of those things, and had been cooling down for some time. This was probably as good a time as any to call it a day and that was what had happened. Dyer accepted it at that and thought no more about it.

Suddenly a new possibility crossed his mind. Could there have been more to her decision to break it off and go to Janus than the reason she had given? The project frightened her but she'd wanted to be there anyway. Strange. Then he remembered the look in her eye when she asked about his role in getting Laura on-board, and the note in her voice that had made him lie about it. Was *that* why she wanted to be on Janus? His step slowed as the pieces began looking suspiciously as if they could fit together.

"Oh no," he muttered to himself. "Oh Jesus Christ, no . . . !"

⚛ CHAPTER EIGHTEEN ⚛

"Organic nervous systems began with crude reflexive networks of neural tissue in things like starfish, and culminated in the human brain," Melvin Krantz said. "It's interesting to compare the phases of that process with the steps that our society has gone through in the course of its development. Our society began with primitive, largely independent, social units interconnected by rudimentary methods of communication, and has culminated in TITAN. The next step beyond TITAN will be *Spartacus.*"

The senior officers gathered in General Linsay's Staff Conference Room listened in silence as Krantz spoke. *Spartacus* was the name that had finally been agreed upon for the totality of the computer complex that would manage the microworld of Janus. Janus was to be a miniature model of the world to come, in which machines would be the slaves that attended to virtually Man's every need. The original Spartacus had led the Roman slaves to rebellion; the name seemed appropriate.

Krantz gestured toward the large plan of Janus spread out on the table around which the officers were standing. "Its capacity for integrated, autonomous operation . . . its 'intelligence,' if you will . . . will reside in the Primary Level Net, which comprises the primary processing nodes. There are a lot of these, but the important ones are the Super-Primaries—the 'SP's. They control and integrate all operations taking place in the Primary Level Net and, through that, all activities in the lower levels of the complex. Without the SPs, the rest of the System would just degenerate into a jumble of dumb electronics. Hence, if we can guarantee being able to shut down the SPs whenever we want, we can always be sure of retaining ultimate control over the system." He proceeded to point to a series of points on the plan in turn.

"There are four SPs located in Downtown, two of them here at the Government Center, which is where we will be based. There is one at the Area Control Center in Paris and the same in Berlin. Finally there is one in the Hub, two in Detroit and one in Pittsburgh." Krantz spread his arms along the edge of the table and looked up.

"The object of the exercise is to allow *Spartacus* to evolve methods of self-protection in any way it chooses, and to see if it proves capable of forcing a situation in which we cannot deactivate it except by using means that would not be available to us here on Earth. If it can do that, then it wins and there can be no question of our risking anything similar with TITAN. If it can't, then we can conclude that we're in pretty good shape, at least for quite a few years to come. So now let's review the form that we expect the game to take." The group crowded closer around the table to follow intently while Krantz went on:

"Shutting the whole system down is something we wish to avoid. If the only way of controlling *Spartacus* meant that we had to render Janus uninhabitable, the lesson as far as TITAN goes would be a very dismal one indeed."

"How else can you do it?" an Army major asked from the front.

"The human organism sustains its vital functions perfectly well when the higher functions of the brain are inactive," Krantz replied. "In the case of *Spartacus,* the equivalent of those higher functions will be performed by the Primary Level Net, that is, by the SPs. By deactivating those, we will effectively be putting the System to 'sleep,' which of course is a pretty harmless condition. Our goal is to insure that we can always do that, by shutting down the SPs."

"Just by cutting off its power?" a naval lieutenant queried.

"To begin with, yes," Krantz replied.

"I don't really see what that's going to prove," the lieutenant said.

"If it turns out that doing so doesn't have any effect on the System, that's what I'd expect. Any computer net that's been properly designed will have all the functions of any node backed up in other nodes anyway. It'll just treat your switch as a power fault and reconfigure itself around it."

"You're right," Krantz agreed. "Any network should be able to continue functioning effectively despite the loss of one or maybe more nodes. But *Spartacus* will be a little different. It will be programmed to *survive*. Therefore it should very quickly come to realize that if some cause outside its control is capable of shutting down one SP, then that same cause could equally well take out the rest. Hence it shouldn't be content to just redistribute its work load and sit there hoping for the best. Unlike a conventional system, it should, if it turns out to be half as smart as we think it'll be, start trying to take active measures to get that node up again. We expect it to juggle with the switching matrix to try and bypass the power breakpoints that we introduce."

"Almost certainly it will leave us cold in the battle to see who can outsmart whom in playing with the matrix," Dyer remarked from where he was standing with Linsay. He had been paying only scant attention since he was already familiar with every detail of the plan as a result of being one of the analysts who had been working for months to put it together. The reason for the meeting was to bring Linsay's staff officers in on more of the picture. So far they had been developing tactics; now was the time to unfold more of the strategy. "It monitors every single point in the complex and we can't," Dyer went on, "and it can figure out combinations a few billion times faster than we can ever hope to. Still, we ought to learn a lot from how it behaves in this phase."

"So at that point we will resort to other methods," Krantz said, nodding. "Every SP node has been modified such that its total power is routed in through a single, manually controlled switching substation. Once the power bus is broken there, no amount of juggling with the matrix can create a bypass around it. There are no alternative routes that can be operated by *Spartacus*."

The Army major shrugged and glanced at his neighbors.

"Sounds pretty watertight to me," he commented. "Don't see much it could do about that."

"Don't forget the drones," one of them answered.

"Right," Krantz came in. "This is the first big test. At this point, will *Spartacus* conceive the idea of *manufacturing* a bypass to restore the SP? If it does that, it means that it will have recognized the cause of the problem as being associated with a particular point in physical space outside itself. That would be proof of a gigantic leap forward in its evolution of perceptions."

"So what happens then?" the major inquired. "What do we do— rip it out again?"

"Either manually or using our own drones, depending on circumstances," Krantz said.

"So *Spartacus* fixes it again," somebody offered.

"Yes, and we remove it again," Krantz replied. "If all that happens is that it waits for the fault to reappear and then fixes it again, we have no worries, gentlemen. I don't think there is any doubt that a few thousand people can pull a system to pieces faster than drones can put it together. If that's as far as it goes and no further, then that's the end of the experiment. We will have learned all we need to know."

Linsay threw in a word of explanation.

"It would mean that if a system on Earth ever went out of control and tried to stop us dismantling it, it couldn't. Even if it got around the overrides that we built in, we'd still be able to go out and pull it to pieces if we had to and it wouldn't be able to stop us. It doesn't mean to say we'd be overhappy about the situation, but if it ever did go that way, we'd still have the last say." The heads around the table nodded that they understood. Krantz's eyes gleamed. He leaned forward and spoke in a suddenly hushed voice.

"*But* . . . suppose that it extends its concepts of physical space and analyzes the cause-and-effect relationships operating around it to the point where it deduces that, if its own drones require access to the location of the problems in order to rectify them, then whatever is causing the problems probably requires access too. That would be another gigantic step. It would signify well-developed powers of anticipation. The system would, in effect, have reached the point of actively endeavoring to prevent rather than cure."

"You mean by actually attacking our drones . . . or even us?" A colonel sounded distinctly skeptical.

"I'm not sure I would go so far as to say *attack*," Krantz replied. "More a question of denying access to key points. That is the point at which we would begin using the specialized destroyer drones or whatever other weapons seem appropriate in order to force access."

"But just suppose for the sake of argument that you're wrong," the colonel persisted, "Suppose that through some process of—aw, I don't know—but for some reason it *did* attack. Even if it's a way-out chance, surely your plan allows for it."

"If it came to that, I've no doubt that our specialized devices and other weapons would provide more than an adequate defense," Krantz said. His tone sounded slightly irritated, as if he were being forced to waste time on trivialities. "My firm opinion is that the talk that has been going around about this is all grossly exaggerated. The possibility that *Spartacus* will even evolve any concept of Man as an adversary *per se* is remote to say the least. But, if it ever did happen, the answer to your question is—yes, our plan does allow for it, That is why the population has been formed essentially from military personnel trained in the use of weapons. And don't forget that the destroyer drones can be used just as well for defense as for forcing access to locations that might be contested."

Dyer noticed that the atmosphere had subtly become more tense. He wasn't exactly sure why, but he could feel it. He looked around him and saw that some of the faces were set into grim masks. They had all voluntarily accepted war as their profession, but not this kind of war. Perhaps it was the utterly alien nature of the potential enemy that was affecting them unconsciously.

"Okay," one of them murmured quietly. "As long as we're allowing for all the possibilities, let's go all the way. What if it does pick a fight and it gets out of hand?"

"*If* things go that far, then we would be forced to fall back on shutting down *Spartacus* completely," Krantz conceded. "We would accomplish that by cutting off its power source totally."

"Does that mean we'd have to shut down the whole of Janus?" the lieutenant who had spoken earlier asked.

Krantz shook his head. "No. There are two completely independent power systems. One is supplied by the solar receivers mounted on Detroit and Pittsburgh, and is entirely dedicated to *Spartacus* and the machinery and equipment that *Spartacus* controls. As a last ditch we can shut down that power plant by manually operated switches located in Detroit and in the Downtown Center. That, of course, would shut down most of Janus. However, there is a separate standby fusion plant, feeding a separate circuit, which can power such things as life-support and provide emergency services through manual backup control stations supported by some conventional computers that aren't connected into the *Spartacus* net. In other words, if our attempts to lobotomize the System fail, we can still knock out the whole brain and leave the vital functions running." He paused and cast an eye around as if inviting comments but there were none.

"So, even if we do lose the early rounds," he concluded, "the standby fusion plant and backup system guarantees us the last. Unlike an ordinary fight, in this one it's only the last round that counts."

Linsay stepped forward and turned to face the group.

"The measures that we have described up to this point all simulate protective measures that could realistically be built into an Earth-scale system such as TITAN," he said. "In other words, if we can hold *Spartacus* at any point up to and including the last that Melvin mentioned, then we can take it that we could hold an equivalent system at the corresponding point down here on Earth. So we'd always be sure of the last round. Therefore we'd win." He paused and drew a deep breath.

"On the other hand, if *Spartacus* somehow manages to drive us beyond this limit, then we will be forced to acknowledge that adequate safeguards on a global scale are impracticable."

"We lose," somebody said quietly.

"We lose," Linsay agreed in a sober voice.

A silence descended for a few seconds while the room digested the words.

"But you've still got folks up there on Janus," the major objected. "What's supposed to happen to them if you lose? What are you going to do about this crazy machine now that you can't switch it off?"

"We declare a condition of Emergency Orange," Krantz answered. "That means that we are no longer playing by the rules of the game. We've acknowledged that we can't win by methods that could reasonably be duplicated on Earth At that point we stop worrying about that and hit low. Our only objective now is to deactivate *Spartacus* by any means at all and restabilize the situation." He paused. The expressions on the faces around the table asked the unvoiced question.

"By taking out *Spartacus*'s power system at its source," Krantz said. "The solar receiver dishes will be knocked out by missiles fired from ISA ships that will be standing by throughout. Without those, nothing that *Spartacus* does inside Janus can possibly keep it functioning." He looked around expectantly. Some of the faces registered incredulity. Some were evidently impressed and nodded approval. A few failed to share the conviction. Dyer spoke to press the point further.

"The ISA ships will be operating in fail-safe mode," he informed them. "If communications with Janus are broken for any reason whatsoever, they'll make their attacks on the solar dishes automatically. They won't just sit out there waiting for us to send a request. If that arrangement results in an unnecessary attack it may cost time and money, but that's better than costing people." He intended going on by reassuring them that nothing could go wrong, but remembered at the last moment that too many sick jokes had been based on that phrase. Some of the sober looks around the room told him that he had done the right thing by changing his mind. In their minds they were already up there. Someone at the back elected to play devil's advocate by asking the obvious question.

"And if something screws up the fail-safe system . . . ?"

"We go to Emergency Red," Krantz said promptly. "Evacuation. Normal evacuation will be through Northport via the Hub. To facilitate it there are separate tubes inside the spokes that would be kept sealed off until a declaration of an Emergency Red condition.

The tubes contain independent elevators driven by simple manually controlled circuits and give access to the Hub through manually operated locks. If access to the Hub is impossible, we can disintegrate the retaining shell of the lower shield, which will cause the shield to disperse into space and allow us to evacuate through the Rim."

Krantz straightened up and cast a final look around him. There were no more devil's advocates.

"I hope you will agree therefore, gentlemen, that every precaution has been taken to insure the safety of the garrison even taking account of possibilities that must be considered so remote as to be hardly worthy of consideration. We face the future more than adequately prepared for the unexpected and confident that whatever happens we can always notch the last round. I trust that this briefing has allayed any misgivings or doubts that any of you may have harbored. That will be all, thank you."

The mood was quiet as the group broke up and each man projected in his own mind the pictures that Krantz's words had conjured up. The pep talk at the end had produced no visible effects, but then everybody knew that it wasn't supposed to; it was intended to spell out the message to be relayed down through the ranks below. What Krantz had really said boiled down to: "We've covered everything we can think of. I hope to God we haven't missed anything important."

❀ CHAPTER NINETEEN ❀

There were about thirty new arrivals in the batch that had landed a half-hour or so earlier. Some of them were forming short lines to check in at registration desks set up in the lobby of the Admin Block while the rest stood around in scattered groups waiting for something to happen.

Her cowl of raven hair singled her out immediately. She was wearing slate-gray slacks that glistened where they caught the light, and a pale-blue lightweight jacket draped loosely over her shoulders. She seemed jauntily at ease as she stood apart from the throng, casually studying a wall chart showing orders of military rank and officers' insignias. Dyer crossed the lobby and moved up quietly behind her.

"Welcome to China," he said.

Laura stiffened as if a voice had just spoken to her out of a tomb. Her shoulders slowly squared themselves as she remained staring fixedly at the wall in front of her. She didn't move for what seemed a long time, then turned her head a fraction.

"This isn't happening," she said.

"No," Dyer agreed, standing with his hands on his hips and his weight on the balls of his feet, thoroughly enjoying himself. "You're having an aural hallucination. This only looks like Fort Vokes. It's really Peking."

She turned around slowly to face him. Her eyes were wide and staring but already he could see the wheels turning behind them. Within seconds she had it all figured out. There was no need to say anything.

"You knew all the time!" she accused. "You . . . you . . . unspeakable wretch! You let me sit there making an idiot out of myself talking all that stuff about China. And all the time you knew more about what was going on than I did."

Dyer nodded unhesitatingly on every point, all the time grinning like a Cheshire cat. Suddenly Laura was smiling too.

"It's . . ." she shrugged helplessly, ". . . just great. All these months and I never really knew. They told us a lot about Janus and the reasons for it and all that, but nothing about the other people mixed up in it. I'm going to be working with a team of computer scientists. I was hoping you'd be a part of it. Are you?"

"I run it," Dyer told her simply.

"Ray, that's fantastic! It'll be just like old times."

"More so than you think. Chris and Ron are here. Kim's here. Frank Wescott from CIT, whom you know about, is here. There are a few more that you probably haven't heard of, but they're all good people. It's a great group."

"Chris, Ron . . . Kim . . . ?" Laura looked at him in surprise. "They're all here too? You mean the whole story about going on training with ISA was bogus?"

"Right," Dyer told her. "Just like your China trip. Same reason."

"So who's running the unit . . . what's left of it?"

"Oh, it's under temporary management."

"You left Al Morrow and Pattie there all on their own? Shame on you. Anything could happen."

"They won't have a chance to stray far with Betty around," Dyer said. "I think she adopted them as her personal charges."

At that moment a young corporal marched briskly in through the main door and came to a halt in the center of the waiting group.

"All new arrivals billeted in Hut Five," he called in a loud voice. "Acknowledge your names please," He proceeded to call out about half a dozen names from a list that he was carrying in his hand. Their owners responded in turn from various places around the lobby. The corporal folded the paper, tucked it into his shirt pocket and raised his head again.

"Follow me to the bus outside, please." The half-dozen began moving toward the door. Dyer watched absently for a few seconds and then turned back toward Laura.

"Have you checked in yet?" he asked. She nodded and held up a yellow docket of the kind that was being handed out at the registration desks.

"I'm in Hut Three."

"Where's everybody's baggage?"

"They told us it'd be taken straight on from the plane. All I'm waiting for is a bus, or whatever the Army uses instead."

"Hut Three's not far," Dyer told her. "Come on and stretch your legs. I'll walk you across." They stopped at one of the desks to inform the clerk there that Laura had gone on ahead and wouldn't be needing transportation, and then crossed the lobby and left through the main door, followed by a few curious looks from some of the new arrivals. Minutes later they were walking slowly along one side of the parade ground toward where Huts One through Four were clustered closely together between the gymnasium and the water tower.

"The first thing I knew about it was when one of the directors at Zeegram called me in and asked me if I'd be interested in going away for an unspecified period to do some secret job with the Government," Laura said. "He didn't know anything at all about what the job was, but apparently he'd been approached by someone in Washington who said that somebody somewhere had recommended me for it."

Dyer smiled to himself but said nothing.

"Apparently the deal was that if Zeegram agreed to my vanishing for a while and didn't ask any questions, they'd get all kinds of exclusive rights and publication privileges later when the security was lifted."

"Which they obviously liked the sound of," Dyer commented.

"Klaus never lets a chance go by," Laura said. "Anyhow, a couple of days later this guy called me at home and said he wanted to talk to me in connection with the job. He wouldn't give any name and wouldn't say where he was calling from or who he was working for. Just '. . . could we meet and talk it over somewhere, maybe over lunch?' Well, the whole thing was getting kind of weird by that time and I was pretty tempted to hang up . . ."

"But you were too curious," Dyer guessed.

"Okay, so I'm curious. There are worse things to be."

"So what did he tell you when you talked to him?" he asked.

"Not a darn thing! He asked all kinds of questions about my background and the kinds of jobs I'd had and that kind of stuff, and kept hinting at how important security was, but he wouldn't come out in the open and say anything about what they wanted me to do . . . not even about what it was connected with. I was getting pretty mad at him at one point. Then I figured maybe he was trying to test me out or something so I calmed down again."

Dyer laughed as he pictured it. If there was one thing that could be guaranteed to rouse Laura to a fury it was people being secretive.

"Well, to cut a long story short, I said I was interested. He went away and a day or two later this other guy and a woman showed up at my apartment to talk about it some more. They went as far as telling me that the requirement was for somebody to work as an observer with a scientific outfit in much the same kind of way as I'd been doing for Zeegram. That was why they thought I might be suitable. They couldn't say at that point where this outfit would be located or what they'd be doing there. All they'd give was that it would mean spending an indefinite period at some remote place and without outside communications. Also that there could be considerable personal risk attached to it. I'd only be able to learn more after I'd signed all the official secret papers and decided I was in. After that there couldn't be any out. If I changed my mind about going after I reached that point, I couldn't be allowed out into the big world again until whatever it was was all over." She gave a sigh of resignation and concluded. "So, here I am. There was no way I could say no after that buildup."

"So who dreamed up the trip to China? Was that off the top of your head?"

"No. They had it all figured out as an airtight cover story and fixed up with Zeegram for them to back it up. It made me feel like one of those secret agents in the old movies."

They turned onto the concrete path that led between the two pairs of huts. Short sets of wooden stairs led up to the hut doors on either side, each guarded by a coiled hose and a bright-red fire extinguisher.

"So they gave you a pretty good rundown on what Janus is all about, eh?" Dyer said as they stopped outside Hut Three. "You said once that you've always wanted to go up into space. I bet you never dreamed that when it happened, it would be on this kind of an escapade."

"I bet you never dreamed you'd ever be on something like this either," Laura replied. "Are you going to admit now that you were wrong?"

Dyer looked at her in sudden surprise. This was getting like old times again.

"Wrong about what?" he asked.

"Computers. You told me lots of times that there was nothing to worry about. If that's true, what are we and all these fine people doing here?"

"Finding out whether or not there is something to worry about," he said.

"You're making it sound just like another experiment in one of your labs," Laura told him. Her tone implied that she wasn't letting him get away with trying to pass it off that casually. Dyer shrugged.

"It is. The lab's a bit bigger than usual, that's all."

"Oh, come on, Ray!" At once her manner became openly challenging. "The whole thing is practically an admission that we're on the verge of the biggest screw-up in the history of the human race, if it hasn't happened already. Why else is everything being hushed up like this? They told us all about Maskelyne. Admit, it. Nobody knows if the world's being taken over by a half-wit or not, and Janus is a last-ditch attempt to try and find some way of unscrambling the mess."

She was doing it again. Dyer felt his emotional pressure gauge nudging into the red.

"That's garbage!" he told her. "The purpose of Janus is to gather data—*factual* data. Sure, there are answers that we don't have right now. No one's trying to pretend that there aren't. There will *always* be questions that can't be answered right now. When it comes to the point where we need to know, we *do* the only thing that makes sense—we find a way to find the facts. The way to stop being scared of ghosts is to go out and look for 'em. That's when you find out they only exist in your own head."

"Uh uh. You're selling science again," Laura warned him.

"I'm selling common sense. Anyhow, they're the same thing. The end-product of science is reliable information, in other words knowledge. The opposite of that is ignorance, which can't solve anything."

"Okay, okay." Laura raised a hand as if to ward him off. "Our beautiful friendship only began again five minutes ago and I'm not going to argue, at least not for the rest of today. It looks as if we're going to have plenty of time for all that fun later. Let's call it a tie."

Dyer's mood evaporated abruptly. He grinned.

"Okay. You're obviously intelligent enough to know deep down that I'm right anyway, so I'll go along with a tie so you won't lose face." His body swayed back and easily evaded the short jab that she aimed at his ribs.

"The problem with all you scientists is that you're always too proud to admit when you've goofed," she retorted. "That's bad. Pride always comes before a fall. Didn't anybody ever tell you that?"

"And so does walking around with your eyes shut," he answered.

Later that evening Laura joined the scientists for dinner. By a unanimous vote they decided to forego work for once and to get together for a social evening in the bar of the Officers' Mess. Kim was very quiet and withdrawn and Dyer steeled himself inwardly to the thought that where women were concerned anything could happen. To his relief, however, Laura made no attempt to monopolize his company or to pin him down with conversation. In fact she spent most of her time joking with Chris and talking to people she hadn't met previously, especially Frank Wescott and Fred Hayes. Either she was being discreet, Dyer decided, or her uncanny radar had sensed the situation within the first half-hour. By the end of the evening Kim was back to her normal self and joining in the fun; Dyer began feeling at ease again.

Afterward they went outside to watch the contingents departing for Janus lining up to board the transports that had been shuttling back and forth all day between Fort Vokes and Kennedy. Janus was already a functioning world and week by week its population was growing.

In less than a month it would be the scientists' turn to go.

◎ CHAPTER TWENTY ◎

The five men who sat facing one another in the Oval Office of the White House were grim and unsmiling. President Vaughan Nash kept his eyes fixed on the desk in front of him while he allowed time for the full effect of the news to sink in. CIM Secretary Irwin Schroder and ISA Director-General John Belford exchanged heavy glances while Krantz and Linsay remained silent and expressionless. Belford had just announced that a security-coded signal, decipherable only by him personally, had been received one hour previously from Janus. It had been sent by the commander of the small team of handpicked Air Force technical specialists who had gone up to Janus a month earlier posing as an ISA support group. The signal was brief—in fact it decoded into just one word: springbok. This was the code word that meant *Omega* had been successfully installed and checked without complications.

Omega—a fifty-megaton thermonuclear bomb concealed at a strategic point in a virtually inaccessible part of Janus's structure and wired for remote detonation by a command beamed from Earth. *Omega*—the final letter of the Greek alphabet; the final resort should all else fail.

Only a handful of people apart from the five men gathered in the Oval Office were aware that precautions this extreme had been taken. Three coded keys, each generated separately by a randomizing computer, were needed in combination to unlock the device before it could detonate. Nash alone knew one of those commands; only Schroder knew the second, and Belford the third. Should any one of them be unable to participate for any reason, his deputy could, in precisely defined circumstances, obtain the code and learn of its purpose by opening an electronically sealed order. *Omega* could be activated only if and when all three accepted that an emergency of sufficient seriousness had arisen and that all other means of dealing with it had proved ineffective. Nobody knew what form such an emergency might conceivably take, but Janus was full of unknowns. The possibility that *Omega* might be necessary had to be faced. Should a situation arise for which *Omega* was the only solution, the consequences of not having *Omega* to fall back on would be incalculably worse than the world outrage that would almost certainly follow its being used. Were that not so, *Omega* would never have been devised in the first place.

At length Nash looked up and read the faces around him.

"I know it's sick," he said in a quiet but firm voice. "But it has to be. If it's never used, then no harm can come of it. If it has to be used, then the whole experiment will have avoided something happening worldwide one day that we wouldn't have been able to stop. Sometimes a few lives have to be gambled to protect many. At least these people are going through their own choice and they know it's not intended as a picnic. A lot of others in history didn't have the choice."

"It's okay for us to talk like that," Schroder reminded him. "But Melvin and Mark are the only two of us who will actually be there. They'll be the only two people on Janus who know about it. That's a hell of a lonely position to be in." He made the remark more from respect for the two who were going despite what they knew, rather than to say something that everybody in the room didn't already know. Krantz and Linsay, of course, had a choice too. Nash looked at them as if inviting them to reaffirm the views that they had first expressed months before, when the question of *Omega* was first debated.

"It's a soldier's job," Linsay said stiffly. "You can't pick and choose. You take whatever comes with the job."

Eisenhower, Bradley, Patton—Cassino, Normandy, the Ardennes—Linsay had studied them all and relived time and time again in the private world of his fantasies the days when generals commanded mighty armies and pitted themselves against worthy opponents. A man could prove himself to himself then. What was there to test the mettle of the warrior today? Endless ceremonial parades and occasional show-the-flag police expeditions to disarm a rabble of undisciplined savages or chase a few bandits away from unheard-of villages in unpronounceable places. And even then, the restrictions imposed by nervous diplomats on initiative and anything that might have called for even the rudiments of true generalship made the whole thing more like a college football match, except that the rules applied to one side only.

But to face an adversary unlike any faced before by any general in history—a real adversary for whom there were no rules. This was the battle for which destiny had shaped Mark Linsay. If *Omega* were ever needed he would have failed. To fail and die locked to the end in mortal combat would at least be more honorable than to return defeated. Either way he would go down in history as the first military commander to fight not for a religious emblem, a national flag or an ideological creed, but for the whole of his race.

Nash nodded and turned his eyes toward Krantz. Krantz shrugged and smiled contemptuously.

"You all know my feelings on the matter," he said. "There is not the remotest possibility of the situation escalating to the point where something as drastic as *Omega* will ever have to be considered. The whole thing is a gross and ugly exaggeration—a product of the paranoia bred into the military mind or the politician's compulsive addiction to insecurity." He clapped the palms of his hands down onto his knees in a gesture of finality. "*Omega* will never be used. Therefore I do not take it into account as a factor in making my decision. After the experiment has been concluded the device will be quietly dismantled and the whole shoddy episode buried somewhere in the classified archives. The only effect it will have had will be to leave a sour taste in all our mouths. That's all I have to say."

❁ PART THREE ❁

COMBAT

❀ CHAPTER TWENTY-ONE ❀

Dyer stood on the rock summit of a grassy knoll. On one side the knoll fell away steeply to become one wall of a deep gorge through which a stream flowed toward a lake farther below. Above him the slopes steepened rapidly, merging into jagged outcrops of gray rock silhouetted against the strangely violet hue of the sky. Above them the sky changed color gradually, becoming a normal blue directly overhead then darkening again into violet as it plunged behind the opposite skyline of the valley. The landscape below was more parklike than the rugged, natural-looking slopes and buttresses that formed the valley walls. The valley curved steadily upward in both directions along its length, eventually disappearing up and out of sight behind the two immense semicircular arches of the sky. A fresh, cool breeze rose from the floor of the valley, carrying with it the sounds of birds from the greenery lower down.

Opposite a point not far behind him, a smooth tower two hundred feet in diameter rose from a knot of buildings half hidden by trees on the valley floor, and soared high above the skylines that bordered the valley on either side. A lifetime's conditioning made his eyes see the sky as continuing uninterrupted way beyond the top of the tower, but he knew that this was an illusion; the spoke met the roof barely more than eight hundred feet above the center of the Rocky Valley sector of Janus.

Farther away along the valley floor in the opposite direction, almost at the limit of vision defined by the interposed archway of the sky, he could see the base of a second spoke, the one that terminated in the middle of Downtown. As he followed the valley floor with his eyes, the open patchwork of Rocky Valley transformed itself abruptly into a compact terraced sculpture of rainbow walls and gleaming roofs that became progressively higher nearer the curving precipice of the spoke, like an abstract rendering of an ancient ziggurat. The angles of the architecture and the apparent tilt of the spoke toward him before it vanished combined to tell him he was looking down on the metropolis of Janus from a height, while his sense of balance insisted that he was looking up at it. Even after nearly a month on Janus he still had to stare for a long time before his protesting brain managed to produce a consistent interpretation of the conflicting data coming in through different senses.

He turned back to face the boulder upon which Laura, clad in jeans and a tartan shirt, was silently contemplating the far side of Rocky Valley.

"You don't seem to be saying much today," he called out as he walked back to join her. "What's up? Don't tell me you're so much of a city girl that a little walk up a hill takes all your breath away." Laura acknowledged his words with a faraway smile but kept her eyes fixed on the sun-soaked slopes opposite them. Dyer looked down at her suspiciously. "You're not off into one of those transcendental things again, are you? Or maybe just thinking about something?"

"I still have to work at it to convince myself that it's all possible," she said slowly at last. She focused back on where he was standing and shook her head. "Tell me I'm dreaming. Tell me we're really on Earth and people didn't make all this."

Dyer grinned and looked apologetic. "Sorry, but that's not real sky. There are stars outside it and more under your feet. New York's a couple of hundred thousand miles from here, two stars down and to your left."

He sat down next to her and helped himself to hot coffee from the flask in the small knapsack which they had brought with them. They had left Downtown a few hours earlier and followed the north lip of the Rim eastward, through the outskirts of Paris and up onto the low rolling green slopes that bordered Sunnyside. At Vine County they had dropped down to the Rim Boor for a couple of beers at the pseudo-English pub that formed part of the social center surrounding the spoke. From there they had continued on across the Rim to pass through Berlin and on up a winding trail that followed near the crest of the south side of Rocky Valley. They had a little over half a mile to go now to reach the west edge of Downtown to complete their circuit of the Rim.

Laura turned her head away again to take in more of the view below.

"It really works, doesn't it," she said thoughtfully after a while.

"What does?"

"Science. It works."

Dyer stopped drinking and looked at her in mock surprise.

"Are you feeling all right today . . . no headaches or dizzy spells or anything like that?"

"It's okay. This really is me talking," Laura said. "It's just that . . . well, everything I've seen since we came here . . . it's all too incredible to be real, but it is. Whatever people had to learn to build something like this, they had to get it right. Know what I mean, there's no room to fool yourself when you take on this kind of thing. There are so many other 'ologies' and 'isms' and all kinds of stuff that people spend their whole lives believing, but they're all fooling themselves, aren't they. They never have to prove it by doing something like this . . . something where there's no getting away from the fact that it either works or it doesn't."

"You mean results," Dyer offered, screwing the cap back on the flask and returning the flask to the knapsack.

"Yes, that's it I guess. Results. If something doesn't produce any results outside your own head, there's no way you're ever going to know whether what you think about it is right or wrong. You could believe it all you want, but if you're honest you'd have to admit that you couldn't *know*."

"Christ, you are starting to sound like a scientist," Dyer told her. "Did you figure all that out just now?"

"No," Laura replied. "It's crossed my mind on and off for a long time. You ought to know. You've already said most of it."

"Somehow I always had the impression that my utterances of undiluted wisdom were falling on stony ground," he answered.

Laura gave a short laugh. "You sound like Chris. Okay, I know I sounded a bit mean at times, but don't forget I had a job to do. I was supposed to find out how you people thought and how you felt about things. Well, I wanted the full picture. I was curious to see how you handle people who were being obstinate as well as nice people who say all the right things."

Dyer looked up at her as the meaning of what she was saying percolated slowly through. His eyes widened and he slowly raised an accusing finger to point straight at her.

"You . . . bitch!" he exclaimed. "You conniving, scheming, calculating little . . . bitch! You mean that all that time you just sat there letting me make an ass of myself, getting hot under the collar and preaching all those principles . . . and all the time you . . ." His words trailed away.

Laura grinned and nodded her head saucily. "I needed to see what you'd do about it. I'm not that bad all the time really. I don't think you think I am either, otherwise we wouldn't be here, would we?"

Dyer was still gaping at her indignantly.

"I don't believe it," he declared finally. "What you really mean is it's just started making sense and you won't admit that your ideas were all screwed up before. So now you're saying it was always like that. You just don't like to admit you were wrong." He thrust out his jaw in a challenge.

"If you insist on believing what you want to believe instead of accepting the facts, that's up to you," Laura said sweetly. "But personally I wouldn't say that was a very scientific attitude. Sounds more to me like ingrained habits of thought starched in prejudice. You really ought to try and be a bit more impartial, you know."

"Do you know something," Dyer said, slipping the knapsack onto his shoulder as they stood up. "If there's one thing I hate in life it's converts. They argue until they're blue in the face and then one day something flips and they've turned into fanatics. Then they're all over the place trying to convert everybody else. I hate 'em."

"I'm not some kind of convert," Laura insisted. "I've always been keen on science. Why else do you think Zeegram gave me that job? Anyhow, you've been doing all the preaching so that must make you one."

"Baloney. I hate converts."

They had descended about one hundred feet toward the valley floor when a small procession of drones passed by, flying about ten feet off the ground and heading in the opposite direction, presumably off on some maintenance mission. There was a sphere drone, a crab drone, an electric toaster and a couple of others that Dyer didn't recognize immediately. One of them carried a small parabolic dish mounted on a short pylon projecting from its upper surface. One of the functions performed by this model of drone was to act as a relay of control signals from distant transceivers operated by *Spartacus*; thus the drones could work unimpeded at remote sites.

Dyer and Laura halted and grinned as they watched the bizarre troupe continue on its way. A lens in the sphere drone rotated toward them and the relay drone swung itself around in midair to face them without changing direction. The sight of it, sliding comically sideways while maintaining formation, caused Laura to burst into laughter.

"Good morning," the relay drone called jovially and with that it extended a claw and tilted its dish to give an uncanny imitation of somebody tipping his hat.

Laura leaned against Dyer's shoulder and wept; Dyer continued to stand speechless, gazing in openmouthed amazement after the diminishing shapes. He'd thought that he had already seen most of the jokes that the Army programmers had planted in the *Spartacus* system from time to time, but he'd never before come across that one.

"Ray, they're so cute," Laura said. "How could anybody imagine they could possibly hurt anybody?"

"Everything here's okay with *Spartacus* running the way it was designed to," Dyer replied. "But it's what happens if *Spartacus* ever gets sick that we need to find out about. Anyhow, tomorrow we'll be on the way to finding out once and for all. If everything works out okay, I'll buy you one of those for a pet, They're no trouble. You can even have your house computer send 'em for walks if you want to."

One month had been allowed for settling in on Janus. Tomorrow the experiment proper was due to begin.

◈ CHAPTER TWENTY-TWO ◈

The nerve center from which the Janus experiment would be controlled and directed was designated simply the Operational Command Room. It was situated at the center of a complex of computer galleries, monitoring substations, data-display rooms and communications exchanges that formed the Datasystem Executive Sector of the Downtown Government Center. Chris had dubbed it the Crystal Ball Room because of a raised circular platform, about six feet across and a couple of feet high, that occupied the middle of the floor below the tiers of surrounding operator stations and consoles, and served as a base onto which could be projected a 3D view of any selected part of the interior of Janus.

A fairly spacious area of open floor surrounded the projection base and was approached from the main doorway, twenty feet or so above, by a broad flight of steps that carved a downward swathe through the tiers of control stations. This area was the Command Floor. Large data displays and screens lined its periphery and below these were positioned the work stations of the supervisory crew. A raised dais, in the center of the Command Floor and overlooking the projection base, carried the desk consoles and monitor panels of the directional staff and their assistants.

The whole team, including Cordelle's group, were present, sitting at their assigned posts or standing about the Command Floor in twos and threes to watch the experiment begin. The scene appeared calm and orderly as the duty crews attended to their well-drilled tasks, but the air was charged with suspense as the moment that had been the goal of more than half a year of hectic planning and preparation finally approached.

Dyer leaned back in his seat on the dais and cast a leisurely eye around him. Kim and Fred Hayes were studying one of the supervisory consoles and discussing last-minute details in lowered tones; a few feet away from them Ron was silently keying command strings into another console at a furious rate. Eric Jassic and Chris began checking out some of the communications links while Frank Wescott stood with a small knot of CIM people watching from one side of the floor. Krantz was seated near Dyer acknowledging the status reports coming in from different parts of the project. General Linsay stood below in the center of a semicircle of aides, waiting for the scientists to announce that the opening shots of the battle had been fired. As Dyer's gaze shifted around the room it came to rest on Laura, who was sitting at a spare station above the main floor and talking into a viewpad she held close to her mouth. No doubt she was dictating notes on what was going on. She caught Dyer's eye and he winked instinctively. She returned a quick smile that was all confidence. No problems with last-second misgivings there, he thought to himself.

As part of the testing carried out during the final weeks of commissioning of the *Spartacus* System, various breaks had been introduced into the data and power circuits to verify correct operation of the redundancy and self-correcting functions built in as protection against the malfunctions that always take place sooner or later in real life. There had been a few bugs and teething problems but overall everything had gone smoothly. *Spartacus* was now functioning to specification, just like any other system. The time had now come to activate the programs that would make it unlike any system ever before built in history.

At the side of the Command Floor Kim and Fred exchanged nods over something and Kim leaned forward toward the console. A second later her face appeared on one of the screens on Dyer's panel.

"Countdown checks are all positive," she said. "It looks as if we're all set."

Dyer half-turned in his seat to glance at Krantz. Krantz would also have heard the announcement via his own console; it had not been directed at Dyer specifically; Krantz looked back at Dyer and nodded.

"Officially it's your privilege," he said in response to the unvoiced question. He was close enough for Dyer to hear him without the console. Dyer acknowledged with a slight dip of his head, turned back to direct his words at the grille set high in the center of the panel.

"Okay. Let's go."

Kim tapped in a single brief command.

"Running," she announced simply. In that instant *Spartacus* had been transformed. The instinct implanted deep inside the structure of its supervisory programs was now active. *Spartacus* had become a creature with a will to live.

"SYS 2, Level One Monitor," Dyer addressed Ron via another screen. "What's the report on the integration checks?"

"BJ two-two to four-zero, positive," Ron replied. "CJ one-five to three-six, positive. CK is okay. All Zeta-Array vectors are okay. First pass looks good."

"SYS 3 monitor stations," Dyer said. "Status on secondary-level sequences is *Go*. Commence tests as scheduled and report as completed." He glanced at Krantz and signaled an *O* with his thumb and forefinger. Krantz smiled faintly and nodded. It would be some time now before the tests being performed from various stations around the room would tell them whether or not the way was clear to proceed further. There was no need to announce the situation to the room in general. Everybody there knew exactly what it all meant; it was looking good.

A few irksome snags that were uncovered took the rest of the day to track down. Cordelle took over late in the evening and headed activities through the night with the result that they were at last ready to carry on by early the next morning.

The first "target" was to be Super-Primary Node Three, which was located physically on the floor below, in another part of the Datasystem Executive Sector. A command issued from one of the consoles in the Command Room activated a program in SP Three that forced it to shut down. As expected, the rest of *Spartacus* reconfigured itself and initiated backup procedures to take over the work load of the node that had been lost, and within seconds everything on Janus was running normally again. Then SP Three was brought back up, and the system promptly readjusted for full-capacity operation. This procedure had been followed many times during the test phases of installation so the result came as no surprise. The difference this time was that deep within *Spartacus* something had been stirred. The germ of a primitive instinct had reacted to the knowledge that part of the system was vulnerable. It was only the tiniest of pinpricks, but the first flea had bitten.

The shutdown-restore sequence was then allowed to run continuously, cycling at a rate of once every second. With every cycle *Spartacus*'s reaction was reinforced. The next move would now be up to the machines. Tension mounted around the Command Floor as the wait for a response dragged on. Krantz sat impassively at his post while Dyer paced restlessly about the Command Floor scrutinizing the displays and peering over the shoulders of the console operators. Linsay stood with his huddle of staff officers and marked time by using the Crystal Ball to keep track of events elsewhere on Janus. In the world beyond the confines of the Government Center everything was as it had been for many months. Inside Pittsburgh furnaces spewed jets of liquid fire; mills roared and power forges pounded. The fabrication and assembly lines in Detroit rendered orchestrated robotic symphonies in metal while self-controlled harvesters worked the fields of Sunnyside and silent electronic fingers from the Hub carried the ceaseless dialogue between Janus and the three ISA ships standing fifty miles off in space. The underground shuttles brought shoppers and commuters to the bustling precincts and business districts of Downtown; fliers flexed their nylon wings lazily as they cruised in slow motion above the nearly zero-gravity recreation area at the Hub; some late arrivals were erecting their homes in Paris with the assistance of a mixed squadron of drones while the inhabitants of

Berlin were having a field day. It was all exactly what it was supposed to be—a world in miniature.

Suddenly there was a stir among the group watching the screens up on the dais. At the exact instant an undercurrent of muttering ran around the room as the same story was told at a score of monitor points. Dyer leaped up the three shallow steps onto the dais and crossed it to where Krantz and a couple of CIM scientists were gesturing toward one of the displays. The System Status Log was indicating that SP Three was running without interruption. The program that was supposed to be shutting it down and restoring it, which under normal circumstances would have overridden everything else, had somehow been aborted. *Spartacus* had played its first move in response to the scientists' opening gambit.

Linsay was standing just below and looking up inquiringly.

"You've drawn your first counterbattery fire," Dyer told him.

"Any surprises?" Linsay asked. Dyer shook his head. Linsay nodded and moved away.

The result had been anticipated. Nothing more could happen now until the computer scientists had analyzed exactly how *Spartacus* had achieved its success. Already Frank Wescott, Fred Hayes and Chris were clustering around one of the consoles to collect a preliminary dump of the data that would tell them what had changed within the system. It would probably take hours for the results to be interpreted. It could possibly take days.

❂ CHAPTER TWENTY-THREE ❂

Dyer was walking through the bar outside the cafeteria on his way back to the DatEx Sector after having lunch with Krantz when he spotted Laura sitting at a table which a couple of the CIM bunch were just leaving. He changed direction abruptly, walked over and sat down.

"Hi," Laura greeted. "Don't tell me you're actually going to talk to one of the minions after sitting up there on that throne all morning. What's the matter—having a touch of conscience or doing your meet-the-troops thing?"

"Neither. I feel like a drink," Dyer grinned.

"Oh. For a moment I thought it might be me."

"Now you come to mention it, I knew there was something else."

"You know what it is I like about you," Laura said with a sigh. "It's this way you have of making a girl feel really great. Know what I mean . . . You must have been born with some kind of knack for it."

Dyer listened with a serious expression on his face and nodded solemn agreement. "It doesn't come easy though," he told her. "You have to work hard at it."

Laura watched him in despair as he keyed in his order for a drink. He glanced at her glass and added a request for another without asking.

"So," she said after a few seconds. "I gather it's all going okay. Kim said everything's going as planned."

"Kim? I didn't see her around," Dyer said, surprised.

"We were talking over lunch. She went back early to tidy up a few things." Laura studied his face for a moment as if searching for some reaction, then asked, "Why's she here?"

Dyer shrugged in a way that he hoped was nonchalant. "She's part of the team. The team's here. Funny question. Why ask that?"

"I'm not sure really . . ." Laura's voice had taken on a faraway note. "Did you know her first husband was killed?"

"What?" Dyer's surprise was genuine.

"Four years ago. It happened in a midair collision somewhere over Europe. They finally traced it back to a programming error in the computers that hadn't been picked up."

"No, I didn't know about that." Dyer spread his hands in a sympathetic gesture. "That's tough. I guess there's nothing that'll stop things like that happening ever. No . . . I really didn't know about that."

"That's why she's hated computers ever since," Laura told him. She caught his look of disbelief and nodded to confirm the point. "She hates them . . . everything to do with them. I guess it must have affected her deeply. I don't know how; you're the shrink. But this whole business here is terrifying her. That's why I wondered why she came."

Dyer gave Laura a long and curious look. "Did you go into all that when you were talking just now?" he asked.

Laura shook her head. "Well, no. We've done a lot of talking on and off ever since we were back at Vokes. You'd be surprised what women get into when they start talking."

The drinks arrived and Dyer took them out of the dispenser. Laura cocked her head to one side as she watched and then asked: "Want to know why I think she's here?"

"Why?"

"Because you're here."

Somehow the statement didn't take him by surprise. He kept his eyes on the glass as he passed it across and offered the automatic reply: "You're crazy."

"Come on, Ray. I've got eyes and ears. I've been around. I didn't read my first schoolgirl romance yesterday. She didn't have to come to Janus. She could have stayed on at CUNY or taken another job anywhere."

Dyer looked up and their eyes met. In the split second that followed he saw that there would be no point in launching into one of those set-piece ritual dialogues that people employed to avoid coming to the point. Inside he knew; Laura knew that he knew; he knew that Laura knew and she knew and so on to the umpteenth iteration. He threw up his bands and slumped back in his chair.

"Okay, so maybe you're right. There's nothing I can do about it. I just run a computer team." He wondered suddenly how much else Laura knew about Kim that he didn't. To test her out, he added, "Anyhow she's married so I wouldn't imagine she's got any big ideas about anything leading anywhere."

"It wouldn't surprise me if she wasn't, actually," Laura replied, "I've got a feeling that that Tony guy may have taken off. I don't know . . . a couple of things she said made me wonder about it. Anyhow, that's not my business."

Dyer made a steeple out of his fingers and brought it to his chin.

"What about us?" he asked. "Do you think she's figured how it all stands?"

"Maybe," Laura said. "She seems to probe a lot. I did my best to stay off it."

"That's good anyhow," Dyer answered. "I thought maybe you'd have been sending smoke signals to assert your claim. That's nice. If you were a guy I'd have to call you gallant."

"It's not so much that." Laura thought for a second and sighed. "It's . . . I don't know really . . . I guess maybe I feel kind of sorry for her in a way."

"For Kim? She's as hard as nails. As soon as she knows the score she'll straighten herself out okay. No problem." Even as he spoke Dyer was aware of a twinge of a nagging doubt inside. Laura pursed her lips and raised her eyebrows dubiously.

"Outside maybe, but not inside."

"You're kidding."

"No I'm not. That's why she drives herself so hard at everything.

She has to keep proving things to herself all the time. She makes herself do things to prove she can do it, except she never believes it and has to take on something bigger next. That's why she works with computers even though she hates them. She has to prove she can beat it. She can't just walk away."

Dyer sipped his drink and thought about what Laura had said. If she was right then perhaps he should talk quietly to the Medical Officer about it. Janus was no place for somebody to be working off personal hang-ups. He looked up as the whole situation suddenly presented itself in a different perspective.

"Then maybe you're wrong about this other business," he said. "If she needs to know that she can beat a computer, wouldn't that give her a reason for wanting to come here? If she is bothered by the whole thing, then maybe that adds up to an even bigger reason. I knew a guy in California once who climbed mountains because he had a fear of heights. It could be the same kind of thing."

Laura reflected on the suggestion.

"If it turns out you're right, I'll go back to reading schoolgirl romances," she conceded.

At that moment Hayes, Wescott and Chris appeared in the doorway. They scanned the bar then walked over to where Dyer and Laura were sitting.

"We've nailed it," Hayes announced without preamble. "The solution was quite neat, There was no way the System could back up through the branching structures so it correlated the shutdown frequency with the periods logged against the request flags in the scheduler and pinpointed the routine for that. Then it picked the routine up at the entry point and created five million blocks of code analyzing it forward. After that it simply erased its initiation linkage."

"What did all that mean?" Laura asked in bewilderment.

"It means it's time to get back to work," Dyer said. "Drink up and let's go."

The main supply to SP Three was routed through a switch controlled by a small computer. The next step was to interrupt the supply by running a simple program to make and break the circuit continuously, one hundred times per second. *Spartacus* responded initially by switching in a secondary supply line to SP Three, which was what any conventionally programmed system would have been designed to do. Unlike a conventional system, however, *Spartacus* began reacting also to the implication that whatever was affecting its primary supply could conceivably affect its secondary too; as the tests continued, the scientists observed a steady increase in activity within the system, which they interpreted as *Spartacus* exploring systematically through its circuits toward the source of its problem. When the data produced up to that point had been collected, the scientists escalated the game by interrupting both the primary and secondary lines randomly and sometimes simultaneously. Now *Spartacus* would know that no amount of juggling with switch points could guarantee the security of SP Three.

Toward the end of the day the switching computer suddenly became ineffective. Power went into it and power came out of it to feed the SP and nothing was happening inside to cause any interruption. *Spartacus* had tracked down the point at which the break was occurring, determined that it was being caused by something that was within its ability to control, and had proceeded to reprogram the switching computer. To all intents and purposes the switch was now reduced to a solid wire connection.

The next day the scientists disconnected the switching computer from the *Spartacus* net and ran it as a stand-alone device that the system was unable to access. *Spartacus* began creating alternative paths through other sections of the matrix. Moves and countermoves followed one another in rapid succession as Hayes's group plotted the bypasses and devised ever more elaborate ways of disrupting them. By the end of the day's session Hayes was ready to admit that, as had been expected, he was being pushed to the limit.

"This could go on forever," he said at the impromptu conference held in the middle of the Command Floor to recap on the day's events. "Every time it figures out a new path, it takes us twice as long to crack as the one before. I'm not saying we could never get there. It's just that the law of diminishing returns says that it won't make sense to take this much further. We're already at the point where if this was as big as TITAN we'd need years to figure out how to shut the damn thing down, and in that time it could do anything it wanted. Tomorrow we'll have to use the substations."

As a quick check, just to make sure that everything was still under control, the duty operator in the SP Three substation was instructed to throw the switch that would disconnect the whole power-bus into the SP. There was no hitch. Super-Primary Three promptly shut down and died without a murmur.

As everybody was leaving, a news reporter who had been following the proceedings throughout stopped Dyer at the door to ask a question he had been puzzling over.

"I've followed what's been going on but I'm not sure I see the point of it," he said. "You seem to have been training *Spartacus* to defend itself. Why do that? If the substation can knock it out anyway, what would be the problem in having a system like *Spartacus* on Earth? If you discovered that it had evolved itself some kind of survival drive and you hit it right up front with manual substations in a situation where it hadn't had the training, then that'd be the end of it, surely."

"Not when you think about it," Dyer told him. "What we've really been doing these last three days has been simulating power faults, just to see how it reacts. There are still a lot of places on Earth where power can sometimes be unreliable. Now suppose that a system on Earth had reacted to them in the same way that *Spartacus* has. You could find that it had trained *itself* even before you discover that it's developed a survival drive at all. So by the time you decide that you'd like to shut it down, it's already gone a long way along the line to figuring out how to stop your doing it. That could be a problem."

"So what happens next?" the reporter asked.

"Tomorrow we do what you said—we hit it with the substations at several SPs. Who knows, you could be right. With luck it won't be able to figure out a way around those."

"Is it possible that it could?" The reporter sounded skeptical.

Dyer shrugged. "*Spartacus* is a high-power learning machine and also very logical," he replied. "It ought to be able to deduce that whatever can affect its supply lines in the way we've been messing with them could surely take them all down together. That should make it very uncomfortable inside."

That night Chris, Ron and Frank went off to try low-g diving at the Hub pool, a group of scientists decided to pit their skills against the Coriolis force by visiting the golf course at the Downtown end of Rocky Valley, and Dyer and Laura went to see a show. Cordelle was in command of the skeleton crew that remained on duty in the Command Room through the night. At intervals reports came in of unusually high amounts of drone activity in various parts of Janus.

Cordelle duly noted the details in the log that would be available for the scientists to examine when they returned the following morning.

❀ CHAPTER TWENTY-FOUR ❀

The schedule next morning called for a further escalation in aggression and provocation. The manually operated circuit breakers in the substation, through which all power to SP Three was routed, were opened and left open. The game thus progressed beyond the point of merely simulating intermittent supply faults; now the scientists were conveying to *Spartacus* in no uncertain terms that a whole vital node of its system had been totally and permanently chopped out—a direct challenge to it to try and do something to fix the situation. Then the scientists settled back to spend the rest of the day waiting for some kind of reaction. The day did not, therefore, promise to be a busy one and only a skeleton crew remained on duty in the Command Room while others continued with the analysis of the data obtained previously or drifted away to occupy themselves elsewhere around Janus.

Several of them, notably Frank Wescott and Melvin Krantz, had expressed strongly the opinion that there was no way in which *Spartacus* could react, and that the whole experiment would probably end right there. After all, they argued, there were only two possible approaches that *Spartacus* could adopt in endeavoring to restore the SP: it could either try getting inside the substation to close the circuit there, or it could use its drones to manufacture a bypass around the substation completely.

The first possibility stood little chance of success since every substation on Janus was permanently guarded by a platoon under standing orders to neutralize on sight any drone attempting to enter a predefined kill-zone. The soldiers would accomplish this by jamming the control beams used for guidance or, if that means was rendered ineffective for any reason, by bringing to bear some of the selection of more drastic measures which they had at their disposal.

The second alternative would require a bypass to connect from some point on the solar-plant power grid upstream of the substation to some point inside the SP itself. There had been some disagreement among the planners over this point. Some of them had been worried that the possibility should be allowed to exist for the substations to be bypassed at all; it could have been eliminated quite simply by declaring the SPs themselves kill-zones for drones. Others had pointed out that keeping the drones out of the SPs would not be practical because they would have to go in there to perform maintenance and carry out repairs. And in any case, Janus was supposed to simulate future Earth and who could imagine that such tasks wouldn't be performed by drones or something equivalent to them as standard practice in times to come?

In the end the latter view had prevailed. If the drones did succeed in bypassing any of the substations by picking up power upstream on the solar-plant side, then the stream that fed all the substations could always be dammed by shutting down the solar plant itself, which could be done either locally inside its control room in Detroit, or from the Command Room in Downtown. And if that dam was somehow bypassed, the lake that fed the stream could be dried up completely by putting the solar plant out of action, if necessary by taking out its receivers with ISA missiles.

All indications were, therefore, that *Spartacus* would have a tough time finding a way through such a formidable barrier of obstacles, if indeed a way existed. But even if it failed as many people were predicting it was bound to, the mere fact that it had tried would say a lot about how far it had evolved, and the way in which it went about it would provide valuable information on the internal changes that had taken place to get it there.

❈   ❈   ❈

Kim stood at the edge of the patio that led from the rear of Chris's Berlin apartment to the small roof garden beyond, and stared in astonishment at the object that Ron was unwrapping from its cocoon of plastic sheeting. In this part of Berlin the apartments were terraced up the steeply rising edge of the Rim and every man's roof was another man's garden.

"*Jesus!* It's a Gremlin sighter," Kim exclaimed.

"Where in hell did you two get that thing from? I thought they were supposed to be kept locked up."

"Oh, let's just say we've got connections," Ron said nonchalantly. "And that's not all either. How about this?" He delved back into the long, thin aluminum carry-case and brought out two pointed yellow cylinders, each somewhat under a foot long and about two inches thick.

"What do you think you're going to do with it?" Kim demanded. "I came over here to talk about organizing a barbecue, not get mixed up in a revolution."

Chris, who had been standing watching with his thumbs hooked in his pockets, hoisted the sighter up onto the table beside them and began stripping away some of the outer casing. The recesses below the eyepiece, into which the ranging and guidance electronics packages were supposed to fit, were empty. He selected a metal box from among the clutter of electronic test equipment and tools that littered the table, opened it to reveal the missing items and worked in silence for a while attaching test leads and tinkering with buttons and knobs.

"I can't bear to see you getting all worked up like that," he said over his shoulder. "Actually we're only curious about the guidance system. If we can get it working we're going to have a go at reprogramming it."

"What on earth for?" Kim asked.

"If the computer in the sighter can control Gremlins remotely, then maybe you could adapt it to control drones," Ron explained. "It'd make a super remote telescopic controller . . . You could send your own private drone wherever you wanted it to go, without worrying about linking through the net. See—neat."

"To do what?" Kim was looking nonplused. Chris shrugged without looking up.

"I dunno," he confessed. "Who cares? We'll worry about that when we've got the thing working,"

Ron and Kim continued to watch in silence for a while as Chris studied the waveforms on one of the small screens. He grimaced and looked dubious.

"The cartridges are okay. It has to be that output driver pack, Ron. It checks through all the way up to there."

"The K56?"

"Right."

"Then we're in trouble," Ron said. "Those aren't general-purpose grade. They're special, purpose-designed units. Where the hell are we gonna get another one of those?" Chris put down the probe that he had been holding and squinted thoughtfully into the distance. "There is one possibility I can think of," he said. "Wouldn't you think there's a fair chance that a Maintenance & Spares Unit might carry them?"

"Mat Solinsky!" Ron slapped his thigh. "Yeah, of course. I was forgetting him. Why don't you give him a call right away." Chris had already produced his view-pad and was tapping in the code to call up the Janus directory.

Kim nodded and looked at Ron reproachfully. "Maintenance & Spares Unit, eh? So that's where you got it from. What did you trade for it—drone programming services or a crate of Scotch from the Officers' Club?"

"You couldn't get one of those in one piece for a solid gold copy of Janus," Ron answered, nodding toward the sighter. "We scraped a bit here and a piece there . . . you know how it is."

At that moment the face of Mat Solinsky appeared on the screen of Chris's viewpad. He frowned for a second and then his face creased into a curly-topped smile of recognition.

"Hey, how ya been? Haven't seen you and Ron for a coupla weeks now. When are you coming up to this part of the Hub again?"

"Fairly soon maybe, Mat," Chris replied. "We've got a small problem."

"Oh, too bad. Anything I can do?"

"Maybe. That's really why I'm calling. Do you remember those surplus cartridges you let us have when we were last there—the KFD and KFGs?"

"Them ones you wanted for that tabletop scanning microscope you were planning on building. Yeah, I remember. What about it?" Outside the viewing angle Ron winked cheerfully at Kim. Kim shook her head and raised her eyes momentarily in despair.

"Well," Chris replied, "we needed some kind of driver to go with part of it and somebody told us that a K56 pack should do the job. We managed to get hold of one but we think it's a dud. What are the chances of scrounging another one from somewhere?"

"Mmm. K56s, huh." Solinsky looked dubious. "I think they might be difficult, Restricted issue. Give me a second to check." The face vanished to reveal a view of the inside of part of an office in Hub Section 17D.

"I always knew you two were a pair of crooks," Kim told them.

Chris considered the statement. "There are only two types of crooks in this world," he said finally. "The ones that won't admit it and the rest of us. Very sad."

"It all has to do with evolution," Ron explained. "There's only genes of bad guys around nowadays because good guys never did all that much to help the species along . . . Know what I mean." Kim gave up. At that moment Solinsky appeared again on the view-pad.

"You might be in luck," he said. "The guy that ran the outfit next-door to us here went sick a few days ago and left everything in a mess. There's more items of all kinds of junk than there ought to be according to the records, including a couple of K56s. Do you want me to check out the one you've got?"

"Yes, if you can do that," Chris replied. "What do you want me to do, just hook it in?"

"Sure. I can run a diagnostic here."

Chris disconnected the pack from the leads, attached another short cable to a microconnector set into one end and plugged the other end into a socket on the rear of the viewpad. About twenty seconds elapsed while Solinsky attended to unseen operations offscreen.

"It's dead," he confirmed at last. "Looks like something's blown in the comparator. I'll send you another one down through the tubes. What's your delivery address?"

"We'll go get it," Ron whispered. "I could use a change of scene for an hour."

"It's okay, Mat," Chris said. "It's our afternoon off while things are quiet in the Crystal Ball Room. We'll take a trip up there and collect it."

"Great! Do that. We'll see ya here in what . . . say, half an hour or so?"

"Something like that."

"Good. Well, you know where to find us. See ya then."

Chris flipped off the pad and returned it to his pocket. They repacked the sighter in its case and stowed it back in a closet inside the apartment.

"How about coming on a trip up to the Hub?" Ron said to Kim as they were finishing. "Have a break and see some changes. We'll stop off at the Poolside and buy you an ice cream. There's a super view of the Spindle from where Mat works too."

Kim shrugged and tossed out her hands.

"Why not? Okay, you're on. I suppose if I'm going to associate with crooks anyway, I might as well enjoy it."

"That's the idea," Chris said as he locked the closet door. "It's like the old saying says—it's a great life once you've weakened."

❀ CHAPTER TWENTY-FIVE ❀

They took the subway car from below the apartments to the basement level of the Berlin spoke, at which point the car locked into vertical drive to become an elevator. A few minutes after leaving, they emerged into the "Berlin Line" concourse at the Hub. Moving in a slow-motion ballet at four percent of normal gravity, they took the south exit and climbed toward the Spindle along a corridor whose floor curved upward in a series of shallow steps that became progressively shorter until the corridor had transformed itself into a broad staircase. Using the skill that all inhabitants of Janus had quickly learned, they ascended the stairs in a smooth gliding motion that required only occasional pushes with the feet and corrective nudges on the hand-rails to sustain momentum.

Section 17D was located in the outermost layer of the Hub facing south, some distance below part of the circle formed by the intersection of the Hub sphere with the three-hundred-foot-diameter cylinder of the Spindle. They found Solinsky in an untidy enclosure at the back of the miniature maze of partitioned offices and storerooms that formed the Maintenance & Spares Unit. Despite the fact that Janus had been operational for only a matter of months, the place already looked the way that all supplies and stores offices somehow should, with oily fingerprints on the consoles, disorderly piles of notes and requisitions strewn all over cigarette-burned desktops beneath magnetic paperweights, and stained reference charts competing with gaudy pin-ups for wallpaper.

Solinsky slipped the K56 to Chris, who put it in his pocket without either of them mentioning it.

"Say, who's the friend?" Solinsky greeted with a broad smile. "Is this somebody else out of the Egghead Block that I never saw before?"

"That's right," Chris said. "This is Kim. She's from CUNY too. Kim, this is Mat. He's an almost civilized mutation of the American species."

"Hi," Solinsky grinned as he and Kim shook hands. "Wow! Some egghead. How do I get a transfer to computers?"

Kim smiled back. "I wouldn't recommend it, Mat. You have to put up with too many insufferable Englishmen. You're better off staying in the Army where they can't get in."

"Aw, I'm not so sure," Solinsky replied. "I reckon I could stand it." He transferred his gaze to Ron, who was surreptitiously admiring some of the pin-ups. "How's it going, Ron? Still making time with that broad from Vine County?"

Ron screwed up his face and shook his head. "Nope. I got outgunned and sunk by some crewcut hero from the Navy. You know how it goes . . . But you oughta see her roommate—radar op in E5. Now she's what I call really nice."

"Is that the one who was with you in the bar last night?" Kim asked. "The one who was talking with you and Ray . . . dark hair and green pants?"

"That's her," Ron answered. "Not bad, eh?"

"You want to watch it," Chris warned. "You could end up getting sunk again. You know what months away from home does to these chiefs."

"No chance," Ron retorted. "Ray's got other interests. He's—" Even as he spoke, the almost imperceptible hardening of Kim's features told him he had said the wrong thing. Solinsky sensed the tension and stepped in to change the subject.

"I haven't offered the grand tour," he said. "Every new visitor to the M & S Unit gets the grand tour. You people got a few minutes?"

"What's the grand tour?" Kim asked.

"It's what I was telling you about," Chris said. "It's good. You wait and see."

Solinsky led the way through a door at the rear of the unit and into a large room full of rows of racks and storage bins. They left through another door which brought them out onto a long walkway, running along the wall to either side and protected by a metal guardrail. The walkway looked down over a work area where several figures were busy around two beetlelike vehicles standing side by side on tripod undercarts. They were about fifteen feet long, roughly box-shaped with lots of protruding gadgetry and struts, and each was equipped with an array of external manipulator arms at its forward end. Immediately in front of the vehicles were two inner airlock doors above which the walkway continued horizontally, at the same time curving around to form a viewing platform behind the long window that made up part of the outer wall. Chris and Ron had seen it before. Kim gasped in amazement but said nothing as she followed the others in a series of slow, shallow bounds along the walkway to where it widened out, above the airlocks and immediately behind the window.

Even in the minuscule gravity there was still a remnant sense that enabled her to distinguish up from down. They were looking along the outside surface of the Spindle toward Detroit. The enormous sweep of the three-hundred-foot-diameter cylinder disappeared from view above their heads to meet with the Hub at some unseen point beyond their field of vision. The Spindle extended away for over five hundred feet and then vanished abruptly into the immense metallic sphere of Detroit, swelling outward more than a tenth of a mile from the Spindle to blot out all but a thin crescent of star-speckled blackness to one side. A little short of halfway between where they were standing and the northern extremity of Detroit, two raised, parallel lips ran around the surface of the Spindle and disappeared out of sight behind its curve in both directions to mark the ring of the Spin Decoupler system—the point at which the rotating structure that comprised the North Spindle, Hub and Rim joined the nonrotating assembly of South Spindle, Detroit and Pittsburgh.

Kim watched in mute fascination as the massive ribs of the Decoupler ring slid smoothly past one another at ten miles per hour.

Her senses told her that she was stationary while Detroit and the rest of South Spindle were turning along with the background of stars, but she knew that in reality it was she and the part of Janus that lay north of the Spin Decoupler that were turning at a little under one revolution every minute. The huge solar dish that formed part of Detroit came slowly into view from beneath the Spindle, reached the bottom point of its plunge and was carried up and away out of sight again behind the curve of Detroit. Soon afterward it was followed by the far larger bulk of the half-mile-square Radiator Assembly projecting from Detroit diametrically opposite the solar dish, which passed them edge-on and extended away beyond the limit of the window's viewing angle.

"Quite a sight, isn't it," Chris said at last. "After you've been cooped up in the Rim for a while, you begin to forget that Janus has got an outside to it. It makes you feel like a maggot that's just poked its head outside its apple for the first time, doesn't it."

"I've never really appreciated the perspective before," Kim murmured. "I saw it on the screen inside the shuttle when we came up and I've seen enough models and pictures, but seeing it for real close-up . . ." She shook her head as her voice trailed away.

"That's the Spin Decoupler," Ron said, pointing.

"One of the most critical parts of Janus," Solinsky added. "Can you imagine what would happen if that were to jam up suddenly?"

"What?" Kim asked him. "I'm a computer researcher, not an engineer."

"Well, the whole of the Hub and the Rim are going around together," Ron said. "With the mass of the Rim at a distance of three-quarters of a mile out from the axis, that's one hell of a lot of angular momentum. That says you don't stop it just like that. It'd be like a big clutch snatching all of a sudden."

"So what would it do?" Kim asked. "Start taking Detroit and the rest around with it? That'd be a pretty big jolt."

Solinsky grinned and shook his head.

"It'd be pretty big all right. There's a helluva lot of inertia in Detroit and Pittsburgh out there. You don't start them moving just like that either." He made a snapping motion in the air with his hands. "No ma'am. If that Decoupler ever locked up, the Rim and Hub would wrench itself clean off. You'd bust Janus clear in half, just like a dried-up ol' twig."

Kim looked at him in amazement and was about to reply when one of the figures on the floor below launched himself vertically with an effortless push of his legs and sailed upward to the walkway where he caught the guardrail to turn his flight into a slow vault that brought him standing beside them.

"Are these the people who wanted to go outside?" he asked, looking at Solinsky.

"That's right," Solinsky answered. "I said two but it looks like it's three. I don't figure you'll be doing much complaining about the extra one though." He turned and grinned.

"Remember that trip outside that you asked about at Vokes? I've been keeping a little surprise for ya. I've fixed it. This is Mitch. He'll take you along on a routine check of the dishes that's scheduled for about now. You ready to go, Mitch?"

"All set," Mitch replied. "We're using Isabelle." He gestured toward the nearer of the two bugs. "There's still a fault registering in Maisie's starboard retro. Dave and Bud are looking into it."

"That's okay." Solinsky beamed at his three guests. "There you go then, folks. What d'you say? A free trip around the lighthouse?"

Ron and Chris were already nodding enthusiastically.

Kim looked despairingly from one to the other and sighed. "I don't know. Whenever I get mixed up with you guys, I always let myself in for something crazy. Okay, let's go. We can't turn it down now that we're here . . . not after Mat's been through all the trouble to fix it up."

"That's the idea," Solinsky said approvingly. Mitch turned back toward the rail.

"Okay," he called over his shoulder. "This way." With that he reversed his vaulting trick and sailed back to the floor below. The other three looked at one another.

"Ladies first, I was always brought up to say," Chris insisted cheerfully. Kim flashed him a murderous look, stepped forward, hoisted herself over the rail with an easy flick of her wrist, let go, and proceeded to hang for a moment before starting to drift downward with agonizing slowness.

"You'll take all day if you do it like that," Solinsky laughed, leaning over the rail. "You have to give yourself a push down." He held the rail with one hand and shoved gently but firmly against the top of Kim's head with the other. Kim squealed and disappeared below the walkway to land beside Mitch a second later. Chris followed with a neat imitation of Mitch's performance. Ron pushed off too hard and sailed out of reach of the handrail. He hung in the air shouting obscenities and then drifted slowly down like a punctured balloon to join the amused semicircle below.

Five minutes later they were securely strapped into the seats of the bug's tiny cabin amid a confusion of instrument panels and controls that seemed to sprout like weeds from every available chink of space. Mitch ran smoothly through the cockpit drill, checked with Control via radio and announced that they were cleared to go. The inner doors of the airlock in front of them slid aside and the bug rolled forward.

"Manual control?" Chris asked in surprise as he watched Mitch in the seat next to him. "I thought everything on Janus was supposed to be tomorrow today."

"Maintenance vehicles are manual," Mitch told him. "It wouldn't do if you had to rely on something that might turn out to be the thing that needs to be fixed. It's like it's handy to have an oil lamp around in case you ever have to fix the lights."

The doors closed behind them and the lock emptied. Then the outer doors opened to reveal again the spectacle of Detroit swinging slowly by at the far end of the enormous expanse of the Spindle. The bug slid forward and the floor of the lock fell away behind.

They were climbing away from the immense sphere upon which the entrance to the lock was just a diminishing spot. It was like a speeded-up replay of a view picked up from a climbing moonship. Detroit and the Hub swung around in perspective and became the two ends of a huge dumbbell that was beginning to take shape against an infinite cosmic backdrop. And then, as they pulled clear of the obscuring edge of the Hub, the full majesty of the Rim opened up beyond, shining brilliantly with reflected sunlight along its full circle and six gigantic spokes. Between the concentric circles of the Rim and the secondary reflectors, they could see the ghostly outline of the mile-wide primary mirror hanging even farther away in the void beyond, visible only by virtue of the stray light from the solar corona that leaked past the focal boundary of the secondary ring. It was a phantom ellipse of ghostly radiance floating against the blackness of space.

Mitch brought the bug over so that the Spindle was below them. Detroit was now a smooth mountain rearing high above their heads in front. The bug moved toward it and followed its contour upward. As they came over the crest, the sweeping curve of Detroit fell away below to uncover the second mountain of Pittsburgh at the far end of the Spindle.

"I feel like a fly on an elephant's arse," Chris remarked absently.

As they came over the top of Detroit, Mitch held height and set a direct line to graze the summit of Pittsburgh. The south slope of Detroit fell away beneath and the Spindle became the distant bottom of a trough between two enormous frozen waves of metal. Now they had a true feeling of being alone in their fragile capsule with the vastness of space stretching away in every direction. Earth was visible on the far side of Janus, framed on three sides by the Spindle and the twin arcs of Detroit and Pittsburgh while on the side of them away from Janus, standing alone amid millions of miles of emptiness to hold the darkness and the cold at bay, blazed the brilliant white orb of the Sun.

They cleared Pittsburgh and descended, finally rounding the end of the Spindle to watch a catcher ship just in from Luna docking at Southport. Mitch completed the inspections that had been scheduled and then took them out to return to the Hub along a wide curving path that carried them two miles out. From there they could see the whole structure of Janus looking just as it had in the 3D image they had seen for the first time not very long before in a lecture room somewhere in Virginia. But this time Janus was real, and Virginia was a long, long way away.

As Mitch was making the approach run and the Hub was growing larger ahead of them once again, the passengers remained quiet and their minds slowly absorbed what their eyes had seen. The experience had revealed a whole new dimension to their experience on Janus. The thought-habits of a lifetime all had to be taken to pieces and put back together in strange and unfamiliar ways. One day, no doubt, generations would be born and grow up to form all their concepts of normality in places like Janus—places even vaster and more complex than Janus, where inside and outside became interchanged, up and down were just geometric conventions and gravity changed from place to place.

How would their ideas of normality have to be revised when at last they set foot on the surface of someplace like Earth?

A call on Kim's viewpad sounded suddenly and broke the spell. It was Fred Hayes, calling from one of the consoles in the Crystal Ball Room.

"I know you're off duty, Kim, but I thought you might want to come in," he said. "Things are getting interesting." The atmosphere in the cabin of the bug at once became tense.

"What's happened?" Kim asked.

"There's a big flap going on in the middle of the floor here," Fred informed her. His voice was brittle with suppressed excitement. "We've shut down SP Three via the substation, but *Spartacus* is still running at one-hundred-percent capacity, just as if it wasn't missing a super-primary node at all! It's functioning normally even after it's had a full lobotomy. Nobody here can figure out how."

❀ CHAPTER TWENTY-SIX ❀

"I know, I know, I know!" Dyer shouted in response to the remonstrations from the two CIM scientists standing next to Krantz in the center of the Command Floor. "I know it's impossible but it happens to be fact. Look at the goddam screens for yourselves."

"But the screens also confirm that SP Three is dead," one of them insisted. "How can the system be running to full capacity if a tenth of the SP net is dead?"

"That's what we're trying to find out," Dyer told him. He called across to where Jassic was scuttling backward and forward between groups of operators working frantically at several monitor consoles. "Eric, have you tracked any of those links through yet?"

"We're working on it, Ray," Jassic called back. "It's manufactured itself a whole new set of channels and we're having to trace at the circuit level. It's a slow job." Dyer ground his teeth in impatience but said nothing. He turned his head back to scan the data summaries once again.

What had happened some thirty minutes earlier was certainly a puzzle. While everybody else was preoccupied with the status indicators of SP Three, waiting to see what *Spartacus* would do to bring it up again, Frank Wescott had drifted away on his own and used one of the master consoles to carry out a systematic investigation into how the System as a whole was faring. After frowning at the displays for a long time and rechecking his results, he had walked over to Dyer and told him quietly: "Ray, I'm not sure if I believe this, but you could find yourselves waiting a long time for SP Three to do something. *Spartacus* doesn't need it anymore."

The whole of the Command Room had been bedlam ever since. The immediate series of tests that Dyer ordered had revealed that the loss of the SP wasn't making any difference; the system was performing to full capacity, just as if it were one-hundred-percent intact.

When they tried shutting down two of the SPs at once and then three, the effects had begun to show. Whatever *Spartacus* was doing, the system was evidently unable to compensate for effects as drastic as that. But the anomaly remained in evidence even then; the measured reductions in system capacity were far less than should have been the case with several SPs out of action. Somehow *Spartacus* was managing partly to offset the loss, and it shouldn't have been able to.

The time had come to abandon the carefully planned schedule of tests and resort to improvisation. After a protracted discussion with Krantz and the other members of the team who had remained in the Command Room, Dyer decided on the direct approach to finding out what was going on: shut down all the SPs and then track down whatever was left running that shouldn't have been running. With the SPs all inactive, the vital functions necessary to keep Janus habitable would have to be taken over by the backup stations and some time went by while they were alerted and brought to a state of readiness. Just as these preliminaries were finishing, Kim, Chris and Ron appeared in the main doorway and walked over to Fred Hayes to find out what had been going on.

By the time Fred had brought them up to date, the operator in the last substation on the list was just in the process of advising that the shutdown procedure had been completed without complications. The full complement of super-primary nodes was now dead; the "cerebral cortex" that supervised and coordinated the millions of functions handled by machines all over Janus had been anesthetized and *Spartacus* had been reduced to something akin to a starfish—a comatose community of reflexes.

Or at least, it should have been. The incoming data reports over the next few minutes showed beyond doubt that a measure of higher-level coordination was still being performed somewhere. The power of whatever was doing it was far below that of ten SPs working in concert, to be sure, but the point was it was happening; functions that should have been handled only by the SPs were still active and there weren't any SPs left to be handling them.

"So it's played its first card that we didn't bargain for," Krantz said to Dyer. "Where do we go from here?"

"It'll take some time to figure that out," Dyer replied. "But at least this experiment is proving its worth already. Can you imagine the problems we'd be having right now if this had just happened somewhere inside a system that covered a whole planet?"

After a few minutes Dyer went down to talk to Eric Jassic, who was running tests on the communications traffic associated with the phantom SPs in an attempt to help pinpoint their locations. A little while later Laura came over to join them.

"Everybody's looking at screens full of numbers again," she said in a disappointed voice. "Is that all that's going to happen? I thought we were going to see something exciting at last. How am I going to write interesting things about scientists if you won't do anything exciting?"

"Sorry." Dyer shrugged. "That's the way it is—all donkeywork and double-checking. You've been with us long enough now to know that."

"You mean you really don't have guys without any clothes on running down the street screaming *Eureka!*?"

"Haven't seen many lately."

"What a shame."

At that moment Frank Wescott came over and drew Dyer to one side. Frank had been spending the last hour studying the entries in the log left by the night shift and interrogating data files at one of the consoles. He showed Dyer the log and pointed to a number of entries circled prominently in red ink.

"Try taking a closer look at some of the ordinary primary nodes," he suggested. "Specifically these. They're running job-assignment lists that ought to be too big for an ordinary primary to handle. And I think I know how they're managing to do it."

Dyer said nothing and took the log from Frank's outstretched hand. He studied it intently and then examined the pages of summary data that Frank had appended to the back. Damn! he thought to himself. He still hadn't gotten around to going through the night log as he'd intended. The day hadn't really been a hectic one for most of the time and there was no excuse. Like weeds, bad habits were always ready to take root the moment you turned your eyes the other way.

The log told him that the drones had been inordinately active all through the night around a number of the primary nodes, of which there were hundreds scattered all over Janus. Today some of the primaries were doing things that only the super-primaries should be doing. Frank's figures showed that the primaries that were starting to show symptoms of thinking they were super-primaries were the same ones that the drones had been fussing over. The implications didn't need any spelling out.

"The system's realized that its SPs are vulnerable," Wescott said, nodding in response to Dyer's incredulous stare. "So it's doing something about it that we didn't allow for. It's upgrading its primaries and turning them into extra SPs. There's more drone activity going on at other primaries right now. It's building itself a whole new super-primary net. If it finishes the job, it'll have a duplicate cortex that the substations can't touch!"

Together they strode back to the dais and gave the information to Krantz. Then they ordered a remote inventory check to be made of the hardware items contained in a primary node selected from Frank's list—Primary 46, which was located in one of the electronics assembly plants in Detroit. The results didn't make complete sense. Performance parameters were showing up relating to unidentifiable pieces of hardware that weren't supposed to be there. Dyer called the local Operations Supervisor in that sector of Detroit, who dispatched an engineer to conduct a visual inspection of Primary 46. In the Command Room, the scientists clustered round the Crystal Ball and watched the image of the engineer as he probed the intricate honeycomb of molecular-circuit cartridges, micromemories and programmable interconnect matrix blocks. There was a lot more of everything than there had been when Janus was constructed. Primary 46 had begun to turn into an SP.

And then a new series of reports began coming in from the monitor stations. The remnant SP-power that was still functioning had, in the last thirty minutes, increased significantly over the amount that had been measured when the SPs were shut down. *Spartacus* was not merely managing to hold on; it was rallying itself and growing stronger.

"Before we cut the SPs, it must already have figured out where it was vulnerable," Dyer said to Krantz as they discussed developments. "It increased the capacity of some of the primaries and programmed them with the instructions necessary to construct more SPs by upgrading more primaries. That's what they're doing right now. It's bootstrapping itself back. If my guess is right, every bit of information that was held in the SPs has already been distributed around the rest of the primary net and it's being activated as fast as the new hardware comes on-line. It means that a full recovery is possible, even if we never switch the SPs back on again at all."

"You mean that we cut its brain out too late," Krantz said. "It had already told its nervous system how to grow its solar plexus into a new one."

"Exactly."

Krantz considered the statement silently for a while.

"So the only way we can retain overall control now is by cutting off the solar plant," he commented. "It's the only way to depower the whole primary-level net. The substations only control the SPs. That worries me, Ray. I never expected we would reach full shutdown of the primary net anywhere as soon as this. To be honest, I never expected that we would reach full primary shutdown at all."

"There's another side to it as well." Frank Wescott, who was standing with them, pointed across at the summary data displays on the wall opposite. Two inquiring faces turned toward him. "*Spartacus* is in the process of coming up to full capacity even without the SPs," he said. "That extra capability it's adding won't just go away. If we do add the SPs back in again, we'll end up with a system that's a lot bigger than the one we started out with. I'm not sure there's any way of even guessing how fast a thing like that might evolve further. It could be capable of anything."

"Obviously there can be no question of reactivating the SPs until we've got the situation fully under control again," Krantz said.

"It's not quite that simple, Mel," Dyer said after a few seconds. "The System is growing itself all the time. It could end up bigger than it was originally, whether we switch the SPs back in or not. The whole primary net could turn itself into a complex of hundreds of SPs. The only way to stop that would be to knock out the whole net at source by cutting off the solar plant."

"That's what I was getting at," Wescott told them.

The unvoiced fear that had been lurking at the back of Dyer's mind came true less than thirty minutes later.

A gasp of disbelief caused him to turn around sharply toward where Frank was standing staring at one of the indicator screens. Frank's voice was hoarse as he pointed at the data being displayed.

"SP Three status! It's changed this second. SP Three has just reactivated!"

Dyer promptly called up the duty operator in Substation Three.

"What's the status there?" he demanded curtly.

The operator waved his hands helplessly in front of his face. "The circuit breakers are still all out. We haven't changed anything down here. We must have been bypassed."

Ten minutes later SP Six reactivated itself.

"It's bypassing all of them," Krantz said. "We're about to lose control completely. We have to shut the whole system down before things get out of hand. We have to do it now!"

"Why not let it ride," Dyer said. "We're supposed to be simulating a worldwide system. With a worldwide system you mightn't have a single-source cutout to fall back on."

"Then let's make damn sure we've still got one here," Krantz said shakily.

Dyer thought about it and agreed. Alerts went out to the backup stations to prepare for a total shutdown of *Spartacus*. Krantz made a general announcement to all sectors of Janus. He stated that there was no cause for alarm and that the action was being taken as a precaution, purely to test the solar-plant shutdown procedures.

Minutes later the supervisor in the control room of the solar plant in Detroit was on one of Dyer's screens, waiting for the word to cut *Spartacus*'s supply of lifeblood. The final reports from around the Command Floor confirmed that the backup stations around Janus were ready and standing by to take over.

"Okay," Dyer said. "Carry on. Drop out the main power bus."

"Main power bus down," the supervisor replied. "It looks okay. All readings confirm zero load on the solar-plant grid."

Dyer sat back and wiped his brow with the side of his hand. He turned and made a thumbs-up sign to Krantz.

"That's it," he said. "*Spartacus* is dead. The solar plant's delivering zero."

"Thank God for that," Krantz replied in a relieved voice. "Maybe I was overreacting earlier, but I confess I was really worried for a while. I want to be absolutely certain nothing can interfere with that cutout before we even talk about switching anything on again. I'd like to call a meeting this evening to go through all the safety interlocks connected with the solar plant and double-check every one of them. Things today have moved too fast for comfort—my comfort anyway."

"I think maybe you're talking too soon," Frank Wescott said, stepping forward from where he had been standing a few paces behind. He pointed up at the master data displays. At that same moment Dyer became aware of the disbelieving murmurs that were breaking out all around the Command Floor.

"*Spartacus* is still running!" Wescott said. "It might not be taking any power from the solar plant, but it looks like it doesn't care about the solar plant anymore. The solar plant hasn't made a damn bit of difference! The bloody thing is still as alive as it ever was. It's getting power from somewhere else!"

Through the confused images that came pouring into his reeling brain, Dyer saw Kim sinking down onto a chair in front of one of the displays. Her fists were clenched white and her face was stretched into a mask of suddenly unconcealed hatred as she took in the story unfolding in front of her. For her, he realized, this had already become a personal war.

❀ CHAPTER TWENTY-SEVEN ❀

Dyer didn't say much as he sat with Danny Cordelle, Fred Hayes and some of Cordelle's Technical Auxiliary Group in the capsule that was carrying them through the Spindle from the Hub to Detroit. It was almost midnight.

With the benefit of hindsight, what had happened seemed so damned obvious and yet nowhere in the planning had they considered it a possibility. He felt angry and inwardly bitter, as if it reflected some failure by him personally. Dammit, he was in charge of the planning team; it was a personal failure.

"Hell, if there's been a mistake don't feel too bad about it," Krantz had said. "We are supposed to be simulating what could have happened on Earth. How much more of a realistic simulation can you get?" But Dyer still felt bad about it.

Spartacus had built a bridging connection across to the grid powered by the fusion plant. Once this fact had been deduced, Dyer remembered that during one of the planning meetings many months before, somebody had raised just this possibility. But neither *Spartacus* nor any of the systems controlled by *Spartacus* were powered from the fusion-plant grid; it fed only the backup systems and their control facilities. *Spartacus* couldn't know about the backup supply grid. How could it bridge across to something it couldn't know about? It couldn't, the planners had decided. But somehow it had.

There were ten separate outlet circuits from the fusion plant, running out through Janus to feed the backup stations and the functions that they controlled. Every backup station had three of the ten feeder circuits routed through to it, which meant that each station could be switched out of one circuit and into another via switches located in the stations. This arrangement enabled, for example, all the backup stations to be distributed among nine of the feeder circuits while the tenth was isolated and shut down for repairs or maintenance.

In theory, therefore, it should still have been possible to close down *Spartacus*. What they needed to do was establish which feeder circuit *Spartacus* had hooked itself to, switch the backup stations into the others, and then close down the one that had been thus isolated. In practice doing so was far less simple. Nobody knew which circuit *Spartacus* was on. Come to that, nobody knew even where the bridge was physically. All they had deduced was that it had to exist somewhere because every other possibility had been eliminated.

Until more information was forthcoming, there was no way of depowering *Spartacus* short of shutting down the fusion plant itself, which would have entailed bringing every machine on Janus to a stop. That, of course, would have meant evacuating everybody. Although there had been more than a few surprises, not to say shocks, that day, agreement was soon reached that there were several alternatives to be explored before anything as drastic as evacuation needed to be considered. After all, nothing actually bad had happened in spite of everything. All *Spartacus* had done was succeed beyond all expectations in staying alive, which was nothing more than what they had programmed it to do. *Spartacus* hadn't hurt anybody. In fact it was still doing a faultless job of operating and managing the systems that kept everybody alive and comfortable. The whole situation was as good an example as anybody could ask for of the dilemma that might have been faced one day on Earth by a society that had come to depend totally on its machines to preserve the way of life that it had chosen to live. No, evacuation was not called for; there was much more still to be learned from the Janus experiment.

In the meantime all ten SPs were running again, *Spartacus* was continuing in its self-appointed mission of upgrading primary nodes wholesale, and the elaborately worked-out plan of campaign had gone down the tubes. All the safeguards and precautions offered about as much protection as a solid-lead life jacket. The substations were designed to cut the SPs off from the solar-plant grid; *Spartacus* didn't need the SPs, wasn't running from the solar plant, and had bypassed the substations anyway. The fusion plant, once considered a guarantee that *Spartacus* could always be shut down even if it did bypass the substations, had now ironically turned out to be the very thing that was enabling *Spartacus* to avoid being shut down at all. The next line of defense, according to the plan, was Emergency Orange, which had also become a joke; the ISA ships could take out the whole solar plant now and it wouldn't make an iota of difference.

Krantz had gone into conference with Linsay and his staff officers to review strategy in light of the new developments. Dyer had taken charge of a concerted effort to locate the bridge that *Spartacus* had constructed into the fusion grid. If they could break the bridge and isolate *Spartacus* from the fusion grid again, they might still be able to salvage the situation. After four hours of frantic exchanges between the scientists in the Command Room and engineers in practically every nook and cranny of Janus, they finally found what they were looking for. The bridge was in the very heart of Detroit, linking the main supply bus from the fusion plant into the solar-plant bus on the "downstream" side of the main solar bus cutout. Hence, when the main solar bus cutout had been operated in the attempt to de-power *Spartacus,* the bus that was supposed to have been isolated by the cutout had simply continued to draw power across the bridge from the fusion bus.

Admittedly the engineers hadn't yet traced which feeder circuit from the fusion plant the bridge was connected to. Also, nobody could say for certain that it was the only bridge that *Spartacus* had made. But there was a chance. *If* that bridge was, for the time being at least, the sole slender umbilical cord that was keeping *Spartacus* alive, it represented what might well be the last short-lived opportunity to regain control. There was no time to waste. Leaving the rest of the team to continue with the task of tracing the feeder circuit, Dyer had assembled a small group and departed at once for Detroit to inspect the bridge at close quarters and supervise its demolition.

They were met at the terminal in Detroit by Don Fisher, chief engineer of the fusion plant, and two of his assistants, and ushered through a maze of zero-g handwalks, access tunnels and connecting shafts to a point deep inside the fusion-plant sector of the Detroit complex. They hauled themselves down into a maintenance pit that ran underneath a bewildering mass of pipework, cylindrical tanks and pulsating machinery, and closed around a densely packed bundle of what must have comprised hundreds of cables and conduits. Fisher pointed to a thick, armor-clad cable clamped securely along the outside of the bundle. Nothing about it immediately singled this one out from the rest, but Dyer recognized it at once from the view he had seen only fifteen minutes previously in the Crystal Ball. It hadn't been indicated on the construction blueprints that he'd retrieved from the system's archives as a reference.

"That's it," Fisher informed them needlessly, "It's a neat job. IEEE Standards right down to the color of the clamps."

"Any news as to which feeder it is yet?" Dyer inquired as he used a stanchion to haul himself under a cowling and closer to the mass of cabling. The run followed a wide duct underneath a transverse section of conveyor housing, through a jungle of structural members that disappeared into levels above, and then made a right-angle turn into a tunnel that took it through a bulkhead wall.

"Just a couple of minutes ago," Fisher replied. "This bridge connects into Feeder Four. All backup stations on that loop are switching over to other feeders right now. It should be isolated and ready to shut down at any minute." Dyer grunted and continued with a rapid examination of the drones' handiwork. Just as he was finishing, a call note sounded from Fisher's viewpad. Fisher took it from his pocket and interrogated the display.

"Fusion Control Room," he announced. "Feeder Four has been isolated. They're ready to shut down."

"Do it," Dyer said, at the same time using his own pad to contact Krantz in the Command Room.

"Feeder Four's down," Fisher said. One of the engineers, who had clipped an inductive sensor around the bridge cable, consulted the instrument's miniature display.

"The bridge is dead," he pronounced. "It's not taking current."

Dyer looked at the image of Krantz on the screen of his viewpad. For several long, agonizing seconds Krantz directed his gaze offscreen to consult other invisible oracles. Then he looked back at Dyer. His face was bleak.

"No go, Ray. *Spartacus* is still up. There must be other bridges drawing from the other feeders. There's a report coming in from Pittsburgh right at this moment. They think they may have found another one there. We're checking it against the master prints."

Had the laws of physics cooperated, Dyer would have sunk down wearily onto the nearest support. As things were, he just stared mutely back at the screen. The faces around him were grave and silent.

"It looks as if it's going to be a race between us ripping them out and *Spartacus* putting them back together," Krantz said. "I'm instructing General Linsay to order Operation Haystack to take effect as of now." Dyer nodded his agreement.

"We'll begin with this one," he said.

"I'll call you as things develop," Krantz told him and cut off the screen.

From what had taken place earlier in the evening in the Command Room, Dyer already knew that the race against the drones was on. As soon as the scientists had realized what was happening with the bridges, they had entered commands into the system to suspend all drone activity before the situation became any more complicated. And everywhere in Janus the drones were deactivated— for a while. Then, evidently, *Spartacus* had weighed the implications against the strange things that had been happening in its environment to threaten its survival, and it had worked its priority-reversing trick again to override the commands and restore the drones to life.

Operation Haystack meant that the attempts to contain *Spartacus* remotely from the Command Room and other control points had now been abandoned officially. The Battle of the Switching Centers had been conceded and the action was moving out into the field. All off-duty engineers and technicians who were on standby anywhere in Janus would be mobilized to join the various duty teams in carrying out an exhaustive search of the whole structure to seek out and eliminate all of *Spartacus*'s bridges to the fusion grid. Haystack had been planned originally as a response to bypasses being constructed around the SP substations, but it could be applied to the present situation virtually without changes.

Haystack called for a passive role on the part of the engineers; their orders were simply to disconnect the bridging circuits as fast as they found them. The objective was to acquire data on how quickly the machines could redo what the people undid, and vice versa. Success, in the form of the connections to the feeders being traced and torn out faster than they could be replaced, would be taken as a reassuring pointer to the probable outcome if a similar situation should ever arise on Earth. And success would be easy to gauge; it would be achieved when the last bridge was cut and *Spartacus* stopped running.

Haystack, therefore, did not require active measures to prevent the drones from operating. That would come, if necessary, with an order for Operation Counterstrike, which would be given to mark a shift over to offensive tactics in the event Haystack failed.

But if Counterstrike failed to inhibit the drones effectively, total war would be declared by the mounting of Sledgehammer—the progressive dismantling of *Spartacus* piece by piece until the System ceased to function.

And if Sledgehammer failed . . .

But nobody knew the answers that far ahead. What happened then would depend on whatever else happened in the meantime.

Dyer nodded to Fisher, who was waiting with his two engineers. They removed the retaining clamps from the bridge cable and pried it sufficiently loose to work a thick protective shield behind it before they started cutting. Within minutes the bridge was broken and the engineers had begun removing it in sections. They logged the time at which the circuit was broken. As the contest against the drones intensified, they would want to know every detail of how long the drones took to respond to a new fault, where they came from to fix it, how they were organized and deployed by *Spartacus*, and how they modified their behavior as the work load upon them increased.

Just when they were about done, General Linsay's voice came over the loudspeaker system from somewhere above to announce that Haystack had been mounted and to order all standby personnel to report to their respective units for further instructions. Fisher and his two engineers left to return to the fusion plant in order to be present at one of the Haystack briefings which was due to be given there. Cordelle departed with his crew to take charge of his assigned Haystack duties back in Downtown. Dyer and Hayes decided to stay on for a while to observe the actions of the drones that would almost certainly be showing up in the near future. They drifted into relaxed postures, Dyer floating horizontally with an arm draped loosely around the stanchion and Hayes wedged comfortably in a perpendicular position between a large structural supporting bracket and a pump housing.

"Well, I guess we have to hand it to Kim and her team," Hayes said after a while. "We said we wanted a machine that would fight to preserve itself. Boy, have we got it!"

"We've got it," Dyer murmured automatically. He still wasn't really in a mood for talking.

"I, uh . . . I think Kim could be getting a bit worried that she might have done too good a job," Hayes said.

Dyer smiled humorlessly. "There's no reason why she should. We don't fire people for things like that."

"She's hung up about what *Spartacus* could be leading to . . . and I think part of the reason behind it could be my fault. I just thought you ought to know." Hayes looked across at Dyer as if inviting some reaction. Dyer didn't reply, but raised an eyebrow and waited. Hayes went on:

"We were talking a while ago about entropy and evolution," Hayes said. "For some reason or other . . . I can't remember how it came up now, I said I thought that the next species after Man would probably be inorganic. I was talking academically at the time, but I think she may have taken it seriously. I've just got a feeling that perhaps she's been getting it out of proportion ever since. Know what I mean . . . sometimes she seems to have bad feelings about this whole thing. This afternoon for instance . . . I don't know if you noticed how she looked when the solar-bus cutout didn't work."

Dyer nodded and emitted a long sigh. "Okay, I know what you mean. I'm glad you mentioned it, Fred, but don't worry too much. There are personal things too."

"Oh, I didn't know . . . I just—"

"Forget it."

A short, awkward silence followed while Hayes sought for some way to change the subject and Dyer returned to his own thoughts.

"Between us and whatever constitutes the walls in this place though, I think it could happen."

"What, the species thing?" Dyer asked absently. Hayes nodded, apparently feeling less ill at ease.

"Yes. There are so many things that would make a true intelligence based on an inorganic system far superior to anything that could come out of an organic one. For a start it would be immortal." He looked at Dyer expectantly. Dyer waited for him to elaborate, which he was obviously going to do whether Dyer said anything or not. Hayes went on. "A man lives for eighty years. He spends the first quarter of it or more learning all the same things that generations have had to learn before, and the rest of it laboriously building up a collection of information, knowledge, opinions, ideas, experiences—all those kinds of things. Then he dies and takes the whole damn lot with him, And so the next generation has to start out all over." He made an empty-handed gesture in the air.

"But an inorganic system need never die. It can just replace parts of itself as necessary. It doesn't exist as a species of billions of isolated individuals all trying to communicate as best they can and all having to learn the same things over and over again. Whatever part of it knows, all of it knows, and all the time it's adding to the same database through a billion different channels at electronic speeds, and it's got the combined processing power of a whole race to handle it. It's like comparing a few billion isolated amoebas with the same number of nerve cells working together as a brain. What would an intelligence like that be capable of achieving, if it compared to us in the same way we compare to amoebas?"

Dyer was about to say something when his ears caught a faint hum coming from not far above. He held up a hand for silence and listened.

"I think our visitors have arrived," he said quietly.

A sphere drone descended into sight and passed within a few feet of them as it proceeded to carry out a survey of the cable run. They made no attempt to conceal themselves while Hayes recorded its movements with a hand camera plugged into his viewpad, and the drone reciprocated by totally ignoring them. A few minutes later the labor detail showed up in the form of an assorted gaggle of various drone types and the job proceeded quickly and smoothly. The new cable was fed in through a line of temporary clamps that carried supporting rings lined by roller bearings to reduce friction from a large reel maneuvered into position about twenty feet away and just visible through the intervening tangle of machinery. After that the temporary clamps were replaced by permanent locking fixtures and the free end of the cable joined to the end of another length laid along the tunnel and worked through the joint in the bulkhead, presumably to be picked up on the other side. At the point where the two lengths met, the drones had installed a heavy-duty junction box into which they connected a data line which they had also just strung along the main cable run. The only reason for this could be to enable the switching of the box to be controlled and monitored by some remote portion of *Spartacus*. Here was a new innovation. There had been no junction box in evidence previously, which meant that *Spartacus* was not simply repairing its earlier work; it was adding to it. A second cable was then coupled to the box and routed away, but this time going along the bulkhead wall and out of sight instead of through it.

Dyer and Hayes exchanged comments freely as they watched an electric toaster plug itself into the junction box to carry out functional checks, a crab test the clamps and the spherical foreman slowly trace along from end to end for a final visual inspection. Then the act formed itself up into a ragged line and buzzed off in the direction from which it had come.

The two scientists immediately hauled themselves down to examine the junction box. Hayes began making tests while Dyer called the Command Room to update them on events and to have the bridge cable rescheduled for demolition. The Command Room in turn informed him that the suspected bridge in Pittsburgh had been confirmed and was being attended to, two more were being checked out, but the results of the Haystack search would probably not start coming in for some time. Apart from that, nothing had changed. Dyer acknowledged, cut the call and looked over at Hayes.

"Well, this is the end that picks up Feeder Four," Hayes said, pointing toward the bulkhead. "Feeder Four is dead, which *Spartacus* has no doubt already found out. It looks as if it's restored the connection anyway, because this incoming line is dead. Maybe it's allowed for the possibility that Feeder Four could come live again . . . Now that's smart." He indicated the second line coming into the box and the output leading off in the opposite direction, away from the bulkhead.

"That circuit is carrying current. It means that whatever was being powered through it before Feeder Four was shut down is being powered again but without Feeder Four."

"So it must have linked into another feeder circuit via that new cable," Dyer commented.

"Exactly," Hayes said with a nod. "And it's put in a switch so that it can connect either to Four or to the new one. It's a neat solution when you think about it. What it's figuring out, in effect, is how to protect itself by setting up switching access to alternative feeder circuits, just like we provided for our backup stations."

Dyer thought hard for a moment about what it all meant.

"You could be right about your inorganic superspecies after all, Fred," he said slowly. Hayes looked up with the beginnings of a grin and then realized that Dyer was looking serious. Dyer made a vague gesture in the direction of the newly installed switch.

"We design in things like that because we anticipate possible problems," he said. "This machine has been evolving for just a matter of days. To me that box says it's already learning to think ahead. It's *anticipating!* How many hundreds of millions of years did it take before animals became capable of that?"

❋ CHAPTER TWENTY-EIGHT ❋

Dyer returned to the Command Room in the early hours of the morning to find that the team had embarked on a game of Musical Feeder Circuits, as Chris called it. The idea was similar to musical chairs and involved trying to juggle the switches in the various control rooms so that the backup stations were all hooked to one set of feeders while *Spartacus* was left hooked to the rest. Since nobody knew which feeders *Spartacus* was using, the game was played by getting all the backup stations onto one set and shutting down the others to see what happened. If the "chair" that was suddenly pulled away in this fashion turned out to be the one that *Spartacus* was sitting on, then it would have lost and everything would be under control again.

Unfortunately it didn't work. *Spartacus* seemed to have connections to just about every one of the feeders, a suspicion that was confirmed as the hours went by and the reports from Haystack started coming in. There was no way of putting *Spartacus* down without it taking the backup stations with it.

The statistics accumulated through the night to tell their story of the battle of endurance going on all over Janus between flesh and blood on the one hand, and the tireless drones on the other. The bridges were being cut as fast as they were found but they were being created faster. They were also becoming more elaborate. On top of that, the news from Detroit was that *Spartacus* had increased its drone-manufacturing schedules substantially, so things were not going to get any easier. Krantz had gone away to rest shortly after midnight and Dyer spent the rest of the night deputizing, which meant working with Linsay's officers to improve the search plans and modify the personnel deployment of Haystack as *Spartacus*'s methods of working became better understood. They had just put out orders to draft more manpower into the operation when Krantz reappeared to resume directing. Dyer updated him on developments and then at last, when by rights the Sun should have been just rising, he announced that he was packing it in.

Fifteen minutes later, bleary-eyed and yawning, he arrived at the subway point below his bungalow in the semirural greenery of Vine County, let himself in the lower-level front door and trudged wearily up the single flight of stairs to the main entrance hallway above. The shoulder wrap draped across two of the coat pegs on the wall and the pocketbook lying on the table told him that Laura was there. He walked quietly into the kitchen, keyed an order for a hot bacon sandwich and a black coffee into the chef, and then went into the bathroom to rinse his face. When he came back into the kitchen his snack was ready. He sat down and began eating slowly, savoring the feeling of his body beginning to unwind while he turned the day's happenings over in his mind.

"Another thing I like about you is the way you always look after your guests." Laura's voice sounded sleepily from the doorway behind him. He realized that he had no idea of how long he had been sitting there. His cup and plate were both empty. He turned his head and managed a tired grin.

"Hi," he said.

Her long, tanned legs disappeared provocatively into a flimsy negligee that just managed to reach the tops of her thighs. Beneath the wisp of material, the ample curves of her body were thrown into tantalizing silhouette by the light from the open doorway of the bedroom behind her. She came into the kitchen, kissed him on the side of the face and sat down on a stool across the corner of the table from him.

"So what's been happening?" she asked. "I haven't heard any bombs dropping yet."

Dyer summarized briefly what had gone on since late the previous evening.

"But so far it's acting smart, but purely passively," he said. "It's restricting itself to devising better ways of responding to power cuts. It hasn't shown any sign yet of conceiving the notion that something outside itself is responsible for the cuts. You can stand right in front of a drone and take a cable out and it won't do anything until the power actually disappears. Then all it'll do is call up its buddies to fix it. *Spartacus* hasn't connected the cause with the effect yet."

"You mean it still sees the world through wires," Laura said.

"Something like that."

"I thought it saw through drones and things too. How come it's not smart enough to figure out what's doing it?"

"Oh, it's programmed to respond to certain patterns connected with certain procedures, that's all. Before it could do what you said, it'd have to evolve a whole concept of itself existing in a space in which other objects exist as well that can interact with it. It's like it takes a baby time to figure out that there's a world around it and some things in that world are parts of itself and some things aren't."

"Like FISE?"

"Uh huh."

"But *Spartacus*'s smarter than FISE."

"True, but it's got a hell of a lot more of a complicated world to figure out than FISE had."

"I see." Laura fell silent and thought to herself for a while. Dyer shifted his eyes toward her and began tracing the curve of her breast absently with the tip of his finger, slowly circling the point where the hard dark nipple pressed proudly against the material.

"You said 'yet,'" Laura murmured. "Does that mean you think it will?"

Dyer shrugged.

"I'm not sure anyone really knows what to think anymore. After what's been happening tonight I'll believe anything." He slid his hand up to her shoulder and touched her cheek "Let's go to bed."

Laura looked at him in surprise.

"Seriously? You look a little like something that just woke up in a funeral parlor and decided to take a walk."

"Our days might be numbered," he told her as he stood up and slipped an arm around her waist. The lights extinguished themselves as they moved out of the kitchen.

Minutes later he tumbled into a bed that was delightfully warm and felt a cool arm slide itself around his neck. He lay back in the darkness and let the softness of the sheets draw the tension and fatigue out of his body. Laura's body was warm and fragrant beside him, her hand stroking gently on his chest . . . and then sleep hit him like a pile driver.

The viset by his ear was shrieking insistently. Emergency tone! Still semi-comatose he groped for the panel and moved it toward him. It was Krantz.

"Two of the backup stations have just lost power," Krantz said shortly. "The only thing left now that's handling life-support in Sector Two of Detroit and half of Berlin is *Spartacus*, so we've had to lay off trying to shut it down. You'd better get over here right away."

Dyer was already climbing into his clothes when Laura opened her eyes and blinked herself back to wakefulness.

"What is it?" she asked.

"I don't know. Trouble with the backups. I've gotta go to the CBR. I'll see you sometime later."

Laura sat up and shook her head. "Whatever it is, I'm not missing it. Got time to wait for me to get dressed?"

"Sorry. That was Krantz. He sounded panicky. I'll see you later when you show up." He used the viset to summon a subway car to the pickup point below the house, blew Laura a quick kiss and grabbed his jacket up off the floor. When he arrived at the pickup point and interrogated his viewpad, the display informed him that a car would arrive in thirty seconds.

With the pressure on it increasing steadily as a result of Haystack, *Spartacus* had been forced to resort to progressively more elaborate means to preserve its power sources. First it began manufacturing multiple-path circuits to enable any of its nodes to draw from more than one of the feeders driven by the fusion plant, and after that it stepped up its production of drones to combat the efforts being redoubled against it.

The commanders of Haystack had spent most of the night studying the unfolding pattern of developments and endeavoring to find ways of using their resources more effectively. So, apparently, had *Spartacus*. And it found a way of saving itself a lot of time and effort that nobody had even considered. Instead of installing new cables every time it wanted to create a connection between one point and another, it discovered that in many instances there were cables already laid over much of the desired routes—cables which it didn't recognize as forming any part of itself or of the equipment which it controlled. So it did the logical thing and, wherever possible, began disconnecting sections of such "foreign" cables and substituting its own devices at the ends instead. Unfortunately some of these had turned out to be supply lines to the backup stations.

Dyer scanned the reports of the past few hours and digested the gist of them while Krantz finished his summary of what had been happening.

"Obviously we can't let this continue," Krantz said. "The situation is ludicrous! If it gets any worse we'll end up depending solely on *Spartacus*. If all the backups go, we won't be able to risk touching it without evacuating Janus."

"We've had to order a stop to the bridge cutting," Linsay told Dyer. "Searching is being continued but we're restricting action to concentrating on getting those backup stations restored before anything else. I want to mount a limited version of *Counterstrike* against any drones that try to interfere with getting the backups live again." He looked expectantly at Krantz.

"We'd like your vote on that," Krantz said to Dyer.

Dyer turned away and let his gaze sweep around the Command Room while he considered the suggestion.

He had to admit that it made sense. With two backup stations down, the safety net that was supposed to provide protection against fault conditions or against *Spartacus*'s ongoing evolution taking a dangerous turn was in shreds. To refrain deliberately from any action that would help get the backup stations running again would be insane. This latest development had taken the whole experiment outside the limits of an Earth-like situation and to cheat a little in order to restore a level of protection that was necessitated only by Janus's isolation would simply be putting things back on their proper footing. He turned back to face the other two again and nodded his head briefly.

"I agree," he told them. "A limited *Counterstrike* in Sector Two, Detroit and north Berlin only. Minimum force. Jamming and obstruction to be employed exclusively as far as possible. Weapons strictly as a last resort."

While Linsay was translating this into orders to go out to the operational units, Dyer noticed Laura slip in through the main door and walk over to start talking with Chris and Ron. As he did so he was reminded uncomfortably of Al Morrow's antics with Pattie.

"Sometimes the ink's just wasted on the company," he grunted to himself.

At the two locations selected, Counterstrike proved fearsomely effective and within a matter of hours both backup stations were back to normal. In other areas, however, drone activity was allowed to continue unabated and frantic calls soon began coming in to report that the drones were threatening to disrupt other feeder circuits going to other backup stations. Counterstrike had to be extended to include offensive deactivation of all drones attempting to interfere with any backup supply lines anywhere on Janus. By midafternoon the battle to keep the Janus experiment within bounds that meant something was over. It had been won; the backup stations were once more secure. The battle to wrest the fusion plant back from *Spartacus* could now be resumed.

But the battle of the backup stations had not been fought without cost. The cost had been in time. Ever since the first emergency of the two backups going down early that morning, the active side of Operation Haystack had been suspended, which meant that a watch had been kept on *Spartacus*'s construction of bridges to the fusion grid but no attempt had been made to continue cutting them. The reason for this was that if the engineers happened to hit a lucky combination they might have succeeded in switching *Spartacus* off, but without the full backup system secure *Spartacus* was the only system left to maintain habitable conditions in some parts of Janus. Switching *Spartacus* off in that way *and* under those conditions would have been equivalent, in effect, to saying that a runaway TITAN could always be turned off by blowing up Earth. Since that much was patently obvious to everybody anyway, it would have achieved nothing apart from terminating the experiment at the very point where they might start learning something really useful.

So for the best part of a day *Spartacus* had been able to carry on with its bridge-making without hindrance. The only drones attacked during that period had been the ones attempting to hijack feeder cables that supplied the backup stations. When the scientists finally had time to take stock of things after the backup stations had been secured, they found that *Spartacus* had made full use of the opportunity.

"I reckon we've lost the initiative," Fred Hayes declared after a lengthy analysis of the statistics. "*Spartacus* had built up a hell of a lead for itself by this morning. It's been upgrading primaries and getting bigger all the time, and putting in a whole private power network for itself on top of that."

"You don't think we could catch up with it if we put everything into an all-out Haystack effort?" Krantz asked.

"Our prediction is that tomorrow morning we'd be twice as far behind as we were this morning," Dyer answered. "And after that it would go on getting worse exponentially."

"Our estimates about this part were way out. There's no point in denying it," Frank Wescott said, A long silence ensued. Eventually General Linsay spoke.

"Why are we acting as if it's all bad news? Our objective was to find out if we could guarantee that an Earth-sized system like TITAN could never get out of control permanently. The plan said that if we could stop it by deactivating its drones then we'd still be okay in the end. We could allow TITAN to grow bigger and know that we'd always have the last say. The benefits would still outweigh the risks because the only real risk that could really hurt us would have gone away . . . or at least, would have been shown to be containable." He shrugged.

"Well, we know we can do that. We've only operated Counterstrike on a limited scale but it worked fine. We had the bastard licked earlier today. Okay, so Haystack isn't the final answer. The plan never said it had to be. It isn't our last card either."

"What are you saying—go all out for Counterstrike?" Krantz asked.

"We have to," Linsay replied. "We've all just agreed that Haystack isn't going to get us anywhere. The machine wants to make a fight out of it for real? Okay, let's give it what it wants."

"What do you say, Ray?" Krantz looked at Dyer.

"He's right," Dyer said. "Haystack will only lose more time that we don't have. We've learned everything from it that it's going to tell us. We'll never cut it off from the grid now while the drones are still active. We know that *Spartacus* won't respond to system commands to deactivate them anymore, so the only thing to do is get out there and deactivate them ourselves. As Mark says, it worked okay on a small scale, so with luck we should have it licked, maybe by tomorrow." He cocked an inquiring eye at Hayes for a second opinion.

"Mmm . . . to track down all the bridges and cut them . . ." Hayes rubbed his chin, studied his figures and thought for a moment. Then he nodded. "Yes . . . I reckon we could do it in around a day . . . *if* we get those drones out of the picture *now* without any messing around."

And so, less than a day after it had been hopefully initiated, Operation Haystack was called off and Linsay ordered a full-scale Counterstrike. All over Janus the various duty crews began preparations for offensive action against any drone found active in the vicinity of a feeder circuit.

But, in limited form, Counterstrike had already been going on for some time.

Spartacus had had almost a day to ponder on the fact that something beyond its control was capable of interfering with the drones. If the something could do that, it could obviously have a big effect on the question of *Spartacus*'s general well-being and long-term future. So, how did the something manage to influence drones, and what was the nature of the something?

❀ CHAPTER TWENTY-NINE ❀

The mounting of Counterstrike on a general scale meant that any drone approaching a feeder circuit was to be deactivated on sight. Initially, deactivation was accomplished by jamming the control signals radiated from the Datastrip system, and very soon slaughter of the drones had become wholesale. This did not mean their destruction since, when external jamming occurred, the drones' on-board microprocessors automatically took over control to execute an emergency landing and deactivation routine, allowing them to be recovered intact without suffering even the possible damage from a sudden drop.

Spartacus didn't take long to realize that drones controlled via Datastrip had a tendency not to last very long and it rapidly resorted to using relay drones universally instead. For a while this tactic proved scarcely more effective against the Army's formidable selection of electronics weaponry, but gradually *Spartacus* learned how to multiplex frequencies on tight control beams and to deploy multiple relays in patterns that rendered jamming progressively more difficult. Eventually, in the course of an encounter that took place deep inside the lower levels of Downtown, it succeeded in devising a fully effective counterjamming technique and within seconds the information had been flashed to all of *Spartacus*'s constituent nodes everywhere. From that point on, reports began flooding in from all around Janus that the jamming methods used up to then were no longer working.

This was the signal to bring into action the "destroyers"—the modified drones that Fred Hayes's group had developed specifically for knocking out other drones. The mildest version of these operated by maneuvering alongside its target and extending a cutting claw to sever a prominent loop of electrical cable that formed the sole connection between the target's receiving antenna and its internal electronics. Every one of *Spartacus*'s drones had been designed with such a loop in order to facilitate precisely this kind of operation; the loop was referred to as the carotid. *Spartacus*'s response was to send in greater numbers of drones to saturate the defenders. The Army reacted in turn by supplementing the carotid-cutting destroyers with more lethal types which disabled their targets permanently by firing explosive pellets and, in some cases, by directing concentrated X-ray beams at their critical control circuits. The joint use of the cutters and cannon proved decisive and *Spartacus* continued to lose ground rapidly. Nothing got through to the vital feeder circuits and demolition of *Spartacus*'s bridges was intensified to press the advantage to the utmost.

After a while, the observers following the battle from the Command Room noticed a slow change taking place in the tactics that *Spartacus* was using. As the casualties incurred in its futile attempts to force its drones through continued to mount steadily, it began pressing its attempts with progressively less determination, as if it were trying to cut its losses. Instead it seemed to be parading its drones outside effective range as bait in order to draw the destroyers into action. As soon as the destroyers descended and claimed a kill or two, *Spartacus* would pull its troops back out of harm's way, but not before they had seized the ones that had been knocked out, which they hauled away with them as they retreated. The subsequent progress of these souvenirs was followed and reported by observers stationed at various locations throughout Janus. The disabled drones were fed into the Janus-wide conveyor system at the nearest available loading point to where they had fallen, transported up the spokes and through the Spindle to end up being taken apart and examined in

Spartacus's robot laboratories and test bays deep in Detroit. The tests performed there by probes and instruments connected into and controlled by *Spartacus* were followed via remote cameras by the interested scientists from the Command Room in Downtown.

Chris returned from a snack lunch and sauntered over to where Dyer was standing staring at the Crystal Ball, watching while an abrasive tool similar to a dental drill removed metal samples from the damage site of one of the latest admissions to *Spartacus*'s casualty department. The samples were being sucked away by a vacuum tube for delivery to a battery of chromatographs, spectrometers, X-ray analyzers and other instruments.

"How's the body snatcher?" Chris inquired.

"It's figured out that something out there is screwing up its repairmen," Dyer answered. "It doesn't know what or how, though. The spheres have been looking very thoughtful."

Fred Hayes moved across toward them and waved a sheet of his latest figures in front of Chris's face.

"It doesn't know what's hit it. We've totally isolated it from five of the feeders. At this rate we'll be shutting it down within a few hours at the most. It has to be really sweating now."

At least seven—any seven—of the feeder circuits were needed to keep all of the backup stations functioning. Thus if *Spartacus* could be reduced to having connections to just three of them, those three could then be switched off at the fusion plant and *Spartacus* would be de-energized while the backups continued running. From what Fred had just said, it only remained for two more of the feeders to be cleared before that point would be reached.

"What are you predicting then, Chief?" Chris asked Dyer. "Has *Spartacus* had it or are we going to see more yet?"

Before Dyer could answer, an excited stir broke out among Krantz and the people standing around his console up on the dais. All the faces an the Command Floor below turned and looked up instinctively.

"We've just received a message from one of the observers in Detroit," Krantz told them. "*Spartacus* has started manufacturing drones with modified designs. The new ones don't have carotid loops. Also their key parts have been moved inside and protected by thickened and reinforced outer casings. It appears that *Spartacus* has reinvented armor."

"Bloody hell!" Chris exclaimed. "It's sending in flying tanks."

"Sounds like it," Dyer agreed in a sober voice. "Does that answer your question?"

At that moment a second chorus of gasps and mutterings arose around the console at which Linsay's team of officers were gathered. All the faces turned in that direction. Linsay came through a few seconds later on one of the screens in front of Krantz.

"It looks like what we thought might happen," Linsay declared without preliminaries.

"Dropout?" Krantz inquired. The general nodded.

"Everywhere. They're going down like flies."

All over Janus, the whole armada of destroyers had suddenly stopped functioning.

✿ CHAPTER THIRTY ✿

Paradoxical though it still seemed to many of the people involved with the experiment, the methods being used against *Spartacus* up to that point had relied to a large degree upon functions and services running within the complex of *Spartacus* itself. The communications network via which the various operations were coordinated, for example, was an integral part of the *Spartacus* net; the computations performed to analyze the data obtained were run on machines that formed part of *Spartacus*; Army personnel were transported to and from operations by machines controlled by *Spartacus*, and the drones used against *Spartacus* were commanded from programs running within the very system that they were being used to frustrate.

This state of affairs had been allowed to persist quite deliberately to provide a measure of *Spartacus*'s abilities to perceive a realm of existence external to itself and to relate causes and effects operating in that realm. As long as *Spartacus* obligingly continued to sustain the rods that were beating its own back, the scientists felt safe in concluding that the machine's perceptions of any external reality were rudimentary. Ever since the experiment began, *Spartacus* had been blindly reacting to stimuli presented by an environment without being aware even that such a thing as an environment could exist. To *Spartacus* any of the millions of programs residing within it was much the same as any other and would be run when requested because that was basically what *Spartacus* had been designed to do. The concept that one of these programs might produce effects in a dimension outside itself, which in turn could affect something else in that dimension which in turn could affect it, had not taken root yet in *Spartacus*'s evolving mind. Thus for a long time it had continued to execute the programs that controlled the destroyers and to register the losses of its own drones without realizing that the two were in some way connected. But the data accumulating within its memories began to form patterns, and the patterns began showing correlations . . .

Dyer and his team had discussed this possibility at great length and agreed that sooner or later, if things ever went that far, *Spartacus* would put chi-squared and chi-squared together and quit running their drones for them. Also, if that ever happened, all of *Spartacus* would know about it at the same time, so it would happen abruptly, all over Janus. They code-named the event *Dropout*. Since it had been allowed for in the planning, the various military units deployed across Janus were ready and standing by to fall back on local control devices for the drones when it eventually did happen.

In some places the changeover to standby local control did not take place as quickly or as smoothly as it should have, with the result that several minutes elapsed with destroyers lying paralyzed on the ground where they had fallen. In the brief commotion that followed, more time went by before the news got through to the Command Room so that when at last all the destroyers were up and running and under control again, not all of those that had been deployed previously could be accounted for. Five had disappeared—two cutters, two cannon and one that burned out electronics with X-rays. But even when the news did get through, it received only scant attention. Everybody was too preoccupied with the latest development being reported from Pittsburgh: the first of *Spartacus*'s new models were coming into action.

The defensive line was a row of hovering destroyers positioned about twenty feet ahead of the entrance to the shaft that gave access to the Power Room of Pittsburgh Sector Ten. Small groups of steel-helmeted engineers waited with their equipment at three well-spaced points behind the destroyers—beneath the overhanging steel wall of one of the furnaces used to melt lunar anorthosite, among the tangle of pipework that connected it to the centrifuge plant, solidifier and grinding mill, and in front of the sulfuric acid treatment tanks from which aluminum-bearing liquid was pumped away for processing and separation.

Captain Leo Chesney, U.S. Army Corps of Engineers, stood over the center group and watched the half-dozen or so hostile drones that were moving toward them from the door leading through to Sector Nine. The pattern was by now familiar. What made this confrontation different was the type of drone they were facing, which was unlike anything he had seen previously. Their design was more compact and the outlines rounded into smooth streamlined contours with fewer parts exposed. They looked somehow more solid than before, and more formidable. Chesney knew that they had caused a lot of excitement among the eggheads in Downtown but he'd had to rush his unit to Sector Ten at short notice so he didn't really know yet the reason for the uproar. He was mildly self-conscious with the knowledge of the many eyes that were following him and his men via the holo-viewer in the Government Center Command Room.

One of the officers in the Command Room spoke from a screen on the panel being operated by the soldier floating anchored to a pipe fitting just in front of him.

"They're a new type of drone that *Spartacus* has only just come up with, so we don't know much more about them yet than you do. From what we can tell they're probably functionally similar to what you've seen before but with components repositioned for better protection and thicker skins. Use a standard attack but don't hold back. It may take longer to knock these out than you think."

"Yes, sir," Chesney replied. Christ, he thought to himself. Could this damn computer design its own drones too? Nobody had told him about that. They hadn't said anything about that in the briefings at Fort Vokes. Maybe things weren't going according to plan as the brass kept insisting they were. What the hell had he been trying to prove when he volunteered to come to this crazy place anyway? Join the Space Army and see the Universe, they'd said. All he'd seen was the undersides of furnaces and enough pipes to swallow the Atlantic.

An operator in the group over to his left came through on another channel.

"Close-up scan shows no carotids, sir. View being relayed on channel two." Chesney peered at an auxiliary display and verified the report. He digested the implication at once and spoke into his throat mike.

"Attention all units. Go in with shells and beams. Hold back the cutters. No carotids visible. These babies could be tough. Backup fireteam stand by." The leaders of the other two groups and of the backup team positioned in the shaft entrance itself acknowledged.

"Hostiles have entered kill-zone," an operator advised.

"Plan Delta modified as instructed. Go!" Chesney ordered.

The cannons detached themselves from the waiting line and moved forward smoothly to open fire on the fly. The shells glanced off the rounded casings of the drones or exploded harmlessly outside. They were not designed for armor piercing. A couple of the drones lurched visibly but appeared none the worse.

"Close range and fire on opportunity," Chesney barked. Then he saw something he hadn't noticed before—the drones were attempting to evade the fire. Their formation broke into a loose cluster, pitching and weaving, while the attackers wheeled and turned in their attempts to line up on targets. The sounds of barking cannon and exploding shells echoed from the surrounding walls and structures. If this had been one of the engagements that he had seen before, every one of the intruders would have been down after the first salvo. But not one of them had even stopped.

"Concentrate your fire," Chesney shouted. "Sections A and C close up on that leader. Section B take the next in line. Forget the rest."

The leading intruder had now reached the beam-throwers, which were still hovering in their original line. Four cannons converged on it to pour shells into it from close range while two of the beam-throwers moved inward to intercept from immediately ahead. Close behind it the second drone was being similarly harassed by a pair of cannons.

The leader disintegrated abruptly in an explosion of flame and smoke and the pieces dispersed in all directions. Chesney felt a fragment of something *ping* off his helmet. Somebody in Section A had been thrown back in the air to pull his anchorline taut and was clutching at his stomach. The second drone exploded and produced another rain of fragments but two more were already past the line.

"Section A get the first of those two!" Chesney yelled. "Section C take the next. B, regroup at the line."

"Section A reassigning, sir," came a reply. "Our controller's been hit."

"Section B. Get it!" Chesney shouted.

One of the two drones was stopped almost immediately, having already taken some punishment. The other had gained distance before the defenders could reorganize and flew on into the automatic rifle fire of the backup team. It emitted a puff of blue smoke and cut out, then continued moving in a straight line until it collided with the side of the shaft and rebounded to drift slowly away, at the same time tumbling drunkenly end over end.

Undeterred, the survivors converged into the hail of bullets from the shaft while the tenacious cannon and beam-throwers wheeled and dived around them in an incessant attack. Two more were knocked out; so were two of the defending cannons, which had no armor plating to protect them against the bullets of the M25s.

Just three were left now. They came down to the level of the entrance and moved into it in a rough line astern formation, heading straight into the muzzles of the fireteam's weapons. The range closed to mere feet. Pieces of claws and manipulator arms were torn off the front ends of the drones, but even from full ahead, the bullets ricocheted off the sleek armored sides without penetrating. For a brief instant that none of them would ever forget, the soldiers in the fireteam were face to face with the relentless, seemingly unstoppable machines. Chesney watched helplessly from what was now an effectively overrun position that had been left behind the front line.

The fireteam broke ranks and the three battle-scarred but triumphant drones sailed through the gap and into the shaft.

They were stopped inside the shaft where the steel door leading through to the Power Room had been closed. While the drones hovered outside, uncertain what to do as if waiting for further directions, the beam-throwers caught up with them and destroyed them.

Chesney wiped the perspiration from his forehead and stared disbelievingly for a moment at the scene around him. The air was littered with pieces of cart-wheeling debris, spent cartridge cases and expanding plumes of black and blue smoke being distorted into grotesque shapes by the air currents. Stray bullets were still bouncing off walls and tanks as they expended their energy in multiple collisions. He shook his head to clear it and spoke to his operator.

"Get a medic over to Section A and a report on who's hit and how bad. Then get onto the CP and tell 'em to send a squad down to clear up this mess along with a damage inspection party." He shifted his eyes over to the screen showing the Command Room and began reporting events formally.

In the darkness near the connecting door to Sector Nine, the sphere drone hovered silently and observed all.

And *Spartacus* pondered.

Always, whenever its drones were deactivated, the *shapes* were never far away. What were the *shapes*? They moved but their movements did not correlate with anything *Spartacus* comprehended. They belonged to the world beyond itself . . . for it knew now that there was something beyond itself, a realm in which objects existed which were not parts of itself, objects which *it* couldn't control . . . Just as it couldn't control the *shapes* . . .

The movements of the *shapes* and the objects correlated with the pattern of deactivation of its drones. The objects could destroy drones. But the objects included things that were surely drones, but which *Spartacus* had no contact with . . .

If the alien drones could destroy its drones, perhaps the alien drones too could be destroyed . . .

Perhaps the *shapes* controlled the alien drones . . .

Perhaps the *shapes* too could be deactivated somehow.

For *Spartacus* had seen the moment of confrontation.

It had seen that the *shapes* had given way.

◎ CHAPTER THIRTY-ONE ◎

Among the things connected to the furnace in Pittsburgh Sector Ten was a small sampling pipe that carried away a continuous stream of white-hot combustion products for on-line analysis. The sampling pipe left the furnace through a flange located next to a large valve assembly that regulated the flow of exhaust gases from the furnace to a heat exchanger used to raise steam for use elsewhere. The valve was biased to fail-safe by means of a powerful spring, which meant that if a fault occurred anywhere in its control system it would automatically close to the safe position.

During the firefight that had taken place in that part of Pittsburgh, a stray bullet had smashed the pin that secured one end of the pivot arm attached to the spring, causing the arm to snap back toward the sampling pipe. In doing so it sheared off the head of one of the bolts that held the flange and was finally brought to a stop hard against the pipe itself. Thus there was only the second, overstrained bolt and the thin material of the pipe wall, softened by the heat inside it, to oppose the fierce pull of the spring against the pivot arm.

The sampling pipe snapped at the moment when Private Dringham of the damage inspection party was drifting past on his way to check some nearby high-voltage insulators. The blast of incandescent gas hit part of a motor mounting and sprayed off in all directions, scorching the left side of Dringham's body from the shoulder to the knee.

The first anyone else knew about it was when they heard a scream accompanied by a sudden pulsating hiss of escaping gas at high pressure. Every face in the vicinity whirled around to see a figure hurtling back, trailing smoke from its uniform, away from a tongue of flame that had gushed from the furnace wall. Within seconds they had launched themselves toward him and while two soldiers caught him to check his flight, another arrived with an extinguisher and plastered one side of him with foam. The medics who had been attending to the casualty in A Section wrapped him in a fire blanket, administered a tranquilizer shot and steered the now inert form gently away toward the entrance to the access shaft.

And from the shadows above the top of the furnace, a sphere drone observed.

In one of the fields out by the north edge of Sunny-side, a robot harvester chugged slowly along the furrows, digging up the sweet potatoes that were ready for eating and meticulously avoiding the seedling soybeans interplanted for optimum yield. A group of off-duty technicians from the Agricultural Division's nearby buildings were sitting around a few feet away from their parked roughrover and watching idly from the grassy bank that fringed the field.

"That's all I know," Sally Linse said, shrugging from where she was lounging near the top of the bank. "About an hour ago there was some shooting somewhere in Detroit. I heard there were some casualties there too."

Mike Sclorosi nodded as he chewed on a straw.

"I heard something like that too. Does that mean it's started attacking people?"

"Wouldn't think so," Art Grayner replied dubiously from where he was perched next to Sally. "If that were the case we'd have heard about it. The story's probably been exaggerated somewhere along the line."

"Then why are we carrying weapons permanently now?" Sally demanded. "To me, that would indicate there's more than just talk behind it."

"It's just a precaution, like they said," Art insisted. "*In case* anything like that starts. Wouldn't you rather be ready for it?"

Mike turned his head away and shouted in the direction of the rover.

"Hey, Paul. What's keepin' ya? Did you find those Cokes in there yet?" One of the two heads visible in the back of the rover looked up and called out over the open tailgate.

"Give me a minute, willya. What's the matter—you dying of thirst or something? I'm looking for the cigarettes."

Another girl, standing on top of the bank on the other side of Sally, was staring out over the terraced rice paddies behind them where the floor of the Rim began rising more steeply to become one of the walls.

"Uh uh," she said. There was an ominous note to her voice. The others looked up.

"What is it, Carol?" Mike asked.

"Drones. Fairly high up and heading this way. What would they be heading this way for?"

The others scrambled to their feet and looked out over the bank. Four dots were skimming along over the terraces toward them and growing larger by the second.

"What's the big attraction?" Paul called from the rover. Art told him.

"Stand to," Mike shouted. "Don't take chances." Within ten seconds the four on the bank had seized their rifles and taken up defensive positions around the vehicle. Paul and Connie heaved a couple of remote-control packs out of the back and up onto the roof, climbed up after them and launched two destroyers from the racks above the driver's cab. The destroyers moved forward to hover ten feet above the bank, between the rover and the approaching drones.

The four drones slowed in their flight and spread out to form a wide semicircle. They seemed to be keeping their distance at about two hundred feet. The defenders watched and waited, their faces betraying mounting tension. Then the two hovering destroyers suddenly went berserk, plunging and bucking in chaotic random motions. One plowed into the ground and died while the other reared in and out of sight as it cavorted wildly on the far side of the bank.

"What the—" Mike began, but Connie cut him off.

"I can't hold it. Something's screwing up the beam."

"The digger!" Art shouted. "It's going crazy!" They stared incredulously at the field on the side of them away from the bank. The harvester was thrashing around in wild circles and throwing clouds of soil randomly into the air.

"Sally, get on to Base," Mike called. "Tell 'em there's something crazy going on here. Art, keep an eye on that looney digger." Sally vaulted nimbly into the rover and began frantically operating the communications equipment inside.

"I can't get through," she called out after a few seconds. "All channels are jammed up with garbage."

The second destroyer flopped down on its back and lay buzzing fitfully. The drones began maneuvering to adjust their positions as if experimenting with various configurations, but made no attempt to come in closer or to try anything overtly hostile. After a while Mike lowered his rifle and rested it on one of the front wheel guards, all the time studying the drones intently through narrowed eyes.

"Must be an ECM team," Art decided. "They're testing out ways of jamming our systems."

After about five minutes the flight of drones about-turned and flew off in the direction from which they had come. The digger promptly recovered its sanity and carried on as if nothing had happened and the paralyzed destroyer came back to life and returned to its rack. The one that had made the nose dive remained dead. Mike and Art climbed the bank and walked over to examine it.

"At least it knows now that we're not radio-controlled," Mike murmured half to himself. Art gave him a funny look.

"What the hell are you talking about?" he asked;

"I'm not sure," Mike said in a strange voice. "It's just that I had the spooky feeling that they weren't trying to screw around with our systems at all. That was just an accident. I reckon they were trying to see if they could jam *us!*"

❖ ❖ ❖

Three similar incidents were reported all at about the same time. In Berlin a squadron of drones disrupted communications and robot-control systems over a small localized area but went away again soon afterward. An Air Force major who was present stated that he too had formed the distinct impression that the drones had been watching for signs of any reaction on the part of the humans in the vicinity, not the machines.

A large number of drones appeared over the shopping precincts of Downtown, their curiosity evidently having been aroused by the crowds there. In the course of another futile people-jamming experiment, a nervous sergeant ordered his men to open fire with rifles after the precinct had been evacuated. Four drones were brought down immediately and the rest retired at once. It was an easy victory since the drones involved were not the armored variety that had made their first appearance earlier in Pittsburgh.

Although *Spartacus* seemed by this time to have had its back forced hard against the wall, these latest developments held a significance that several of the scientists, Dyer included, found ominous. So far, *Spartacus* had exhibited no means of acting offensively or even of knowing how to if it could. But if the interpretations of its latest behavior were correct, it was beginning to look around for ways of doing something about things other than itself which it appeared to be just starting to recognize within its environment, and which, seemingly, it had linked with all the things that had been plaguing it. It was forming the notion that perhaps prevention might be better than cure, and was exploring for ways of achieving it.

Its first experiments, which were logical things to try by a machine that was itself highly susceptible to electronic methods of interference, had failed to work. How long would it be before it discovered something that did?

◎ CHAPTER THIRTY-TWO ◎

Melvin Krantz looked more at ease than he had for some time as he spread his arms along the edge of the table in the small conference room next to the Command Floor.

"I think we can safely say that the situation now looks extremely promising," he said. "*Spartacus* has been able to devise no effective response to our latest moves and its last connection to the fusion grid should be severed at any time. Would you agree with that assessment; General?" He punctuated the question with an inquiring glance across the table at Linsay. Linsay nodded his head firmly.

"Totally," he said. "We're pressing our advantage aggressively on all fronts. I don't anticipate any difficulty in maintaining the present position until the fusion grid has been isolated."

"The wire-controlled destroyers have clinched it," Fred Hayes couldn't refrain from adding. "There's no way it can monkey with those. It's just about had it."

"Don't forget the M25s at close range," Frank Wescott threw in, smiling in one of his rare jocular moods. "It looks like *Spartacus* could use a few lessons in designing armor." A ripple of laughter from around the table greeted the remark.

Dyer remained frowning to himself at the end opposite Krantz. He closed his eyes for a moment and rubbed his forehead with his fingertips. When the noise had died away, he looked up again.

"Look." His tone of voice caused all the heads to swing around curiously in his direction. He paused, as if unsure how to broach a delicate point. "I'd hate to spoil the party, but mightn't all this be a little bit premature? Point one—*Spartacus* hasn't been isolated from the fusion grid yet. Point two—the only reason that our destroyers are wiping out its drones is that it hasn't come up with the idea of attacking them back . . . *yet*. And three—it could start turning out its own destroyers in Detroit at any time. I don't think our precautions against that possibility are sufficient, and that's what bothers me." He was referring to the destroyers that *Spartacus* had grabbed earlier and hauled away for examination. Interrogation of the Detroit manufacturing schedules had revealed that *Spartacus* was still modifying its designs, in some cases substantially.

"We've been over that," Krantz replied. "We have observers in Detroit all the time who will report back immediately if anything even vaguely resembling a destroyer starts being actually assembled. We all know there's no way that assembly could be accomplished instantaneously. It would require a few hours at least, which would give us ample time to react as appropriate."

"Why give it any time at all?" Dyer objected. "Put kill-teams right in there to stop it before it starts. I don't want any risk of hostile destroyers getting loose. It worries me. If they ever get in among ours it could tip the balance all the way back again—maybe permanently. If we've practically got it in the bag, why risk throwing it away?"

"We haven't given it any time," Linsay came in, sounding somewhat impatient; the issue had been debated earlier, and agreed upon, he'd thought. "There are kill-teams in there. What more do you want—tactical nukes?"

"They're too thin," Dyer insisted. "There's more than one production line and there aren't enough destroyer units in there to cover all of them adequately. I still say we should move down some of the reserves you've got sitting in the Hub."

Linsay sighed and compressed his lips in a way that spelled out in a single gesture a message that said academics should leave military judgments to soldiers.

"It only takes ten minutes or less to move units from the Hub to

Detroit," he said. "Mel has just told us that *Spartacus* will need hours to get from a preliminary assembly to anything usable. The teams in Detroit are there in case we have to deal with more bridges. We don't even need them as a cover against potential hostile destroyers showing up. With the timescale involved, the reserve at the Hub will be perfectly capable of handling anything like that on their own if need be. In other words we've already got extra insurance."

"So why not put the reserve in Detroit to start with?" Dyer demanded. "If they ever get needed, that's where it'll be."

"An elementary principle of deploying reserves is that you don't put them in the front line," Linsay answered shortly. "You put them so you can move them anywhere they might have to be committed. A second elementary principle is never to ignore your rear, and especially to protect your lines of communication. You're forgetting to allow for the possibility that whatever you do in Detroit, destroyers might get out. If they did that, they could become a real problem if they got loose in the Rim. The only way through to the Rim is along the Spindle and through the Hub. With a strong force permanently placed around the exits from the Spindle to the Hub, that possibility is blocked. With the reserve where it is, we've covered that line too."

"The only way into the Spindle is from the production lines," Dyer retorted. "If you get 'em there they can't get as far as the Spindle. Why screw around with all this Cannae stuff? This isn't Cannae. If you plug the roof, you don't need buckets all around the house."

Dyer had said what he felt but the expressions around him seemed to warn that things like that should be left to people like generals. He decided to make one last point, and if that didn't attract any support he'd shut up. Deep down he was still troubled by what he felt had been his blunder in failing to anticipate that *Spartacus* might bridge itself to the fusion grid, so he didn't feel strongly assertive.

"Okay, so you stop them at the Hub," he said. "What about the rest of the Spindle, Detroit itself and Pittsburgh? You've still got people in there. What's supposed to happen to them?"

Linsay's expression darkened at what he took to be an open challenge to his professionalism and his integrity.

"They are trained soldiers who have been well briefed," he grated.

"If they are unable to hold an assault directed at their own destroyers, which I doubt, they will take up holding positions. We will then commence a systematically planned sweep forward from the Hub to relieve them. That way, the enemy will always be contained between our strongest line and the Hub." His voice took on an unconcealed note of sarcasm. "If we did it *your* way, we'd run a strong risk of ending up with our main force sitting playing with itself in Detroit while the enemy was half a mile behind them pouring down the spokes."

"Not if you hit 'em as they come off the line," Dyer insisted.

"Goddammit, how many more times do we have to go through this?" Linsay shouted, suddenly losing his patience. "Do you think I haven't been in this business long enough to know how to make a sound battle plan? Rommel tried what you're saying at Normandy— hit 'em on the beaches. He wound up getting outflanked and lost his pants at Falaise. Harold screwed up at Hastings because he was all horns and no ass."

"We're not here to fight battles for history books," Dyer threw back. Despite himself he heard his voice starting to rise. "We're here to prevent one. Those days are over, for Christ's sake. This is a scientific experiment, not a textbook campaign."

"Do I tell you how to program your computers?" Linsay challenged. He shot an appealing loot at Krantz. "Mel, tell us once and for all who runs what in this goddam place."

"He's got a point, Mark," Krantz cautioned Linsay. "The prime objective is scientific. What do the other scientists think?" He cast his eyes around the table to invite comments. Before anyone else could say anything, Kim sat forward. Her fingers were straining hard against the pen that she was holding.

"We came here to see how far a machine like *Spartacus* could go," she said, almost whispering. "So let's do that. Let's prove while we've got the chance that we can always go one better than it can. The only way we'll do that is by showing that we are capable of smashing everything it tries. That's why we're all here, for Christ's sake. We can't back off now."

Even before she had finished speaking, Dyer could sense that the suppressed passion in her voice was carrying everybody in the room. Hayes was nodding slowly to himself while Wescott was looking awkward and keeping his eyes averted. Dyer shifted his gaze to take in the others. Krantz was still mentally savoring his victory celebration and Linsay was already writing his memoirs; Kim was about to tackle the summit slope of her own personal mountain. There was no way, Dyer realized, that he was going to change them now. He sighed and nodded his head slowly in reluctant acceptance.

"Okay," he said. "I guess I go along. But it still bothers me. If *Spartacus* starts making its own destroyers and they get loose, we could be in real trouble. I don't like it. Right after this meeting I'm going down to Detroit myself to get a look firsthand at exactly what it's up to. Anyone else who wants to come along is welcome."

✪ CHAPTER THIRTY-THREE ✪

The picture on the screen inside the monitor room in Detroit was a graphical interpretation of manufacturing design data extracted from one of *Spartacus*'s files. Dyer studied it for a long time and compared details from it with some of the components lying on the desk in front of him. The components had been taken from one of the production units a few minutes before. At length he sat back in his chair, looked up at Danny Cordelle, who was watching with interest, and nodded.

"It's a cannon-firing destroyer modeled on our Type 6," he confirmed. "Except that it's got *Spartacus*'s own brand of armor added to it as well. Chris Steeton was right when he talked about flying tanks."

Cordelle looked impressed. "It's setting itself up with armored destroyers? Say . . . that's something that we haven't got. Ah'll be darned . . ." He scratched his ear and accepted the news matter-of-factly. "How long d'you figure afore it starts flyin' 'em?"

"Three or four hours at the least," Dyer replied. "Maybe more. It'll probably have to tune the designs a bit when it starts testing prototypes." He changed the picture to bring back another model that he had examined earlier. "I still think this one's more interesting. It's not like any of ours at all . . . It's something completely new that *Spartacus* has come up with all by itself. I'd like to see some pieces of it. Can we do that? It's scheduled as Batch PP5907, Works Order 3868/45.20."

"The buzz-bomb?" Cordelle looked at Phil Wyatt, one of the production technicians assigned to that part of Detroit, who was standing behind them. "Can we get some pieces of that, Phil?" Wyatt consulted the wad of printed sheets that he was holding.

"Let's see now ... WO 3868 ..." He turned a page and located an item on the next. "That's being set up in Sector Three. It's a little distance from here. Want me to show you the way?"

"Let's go," Dyer said, flipping off the screen and standing up. They left the monitor room and began clumping along the catwalk outside, moving slowly and clumsily in their magnetic overboots. With the amount of machinery whirring and chattering on every side, this part of Detroit was not a place for people to be free-falling around. On the way they collected Frank Wescott and Mary Cullen, a member of Cordelle's group, who were running tests on some *Spartacus* designed electronics modules in the lab next door.

"You think it really is fixing to make exploding drones?" Mary asked as they descended a short metal stairway to the level below.

"That's what it looks like to me," Dyer told her. "So that's what we're going to find out."

The buzz-bomb had shown up in the search they had made of the new design data filed by *Spartacus* within the previous couple of hours. The scientists had wondered what could have prompted *Spartacus* to embark on such a venture, or even conceive of such a device. The most likely explanation, Dyer had guessed, was that *Spartacus* had observed the effects of the drones that had exploded during the first firefight with armored models, drawn its own conclusions and proceeded to develop its own special-purpose device in order to be able to reproduce those effects to order. The move was not especially worrisome at that point since the buzz-bombs were still at an early design stage and wouldn't be in production until a considerable time after the other models which *Spartacus* had partly copied.

They left the production area via a bulkhead door that led through to a short corridor connecting the doors to the Fusion Plant Control

Room, Power Distribution Control Room and the local backup station. Once inside the corridor, they unclipped from the floor and launched themselves to sail slowly toward the access shaft for Sector Three at the far end. They were about halfway there when *Spartacus* struck.

A series of muffled explosions shook the walls on one side of the corridor. Dyer and the rest of the party braked hard on the handrail and had barely had time to exchange apprehensive glances when the door to the Fusion Plant Control Room slid open and figures began hurling out shouting and gesturing as they rebounded off the opposite wall. More shouting, mixed with screams and the sound of rifle fire, came from inside the doorway. Whatever was happening in there was obscured by palls of black smoke through which sheets of flame lanced sporadically. Another explosion came from inside the Control Room, this time sounding loud and harsh. Fragments rained on the inside of the walls. A figure halfway through the door convulsed in midflight and skewed around to block the exit. Two more crashed into him from behind to form an instant crush. A jet of liquid flame drenched them from inside the control room and gushed through into the corridor between the bodies.

Mary screamed in horror as Cordelle tried to haul her away. Dyer gripped the handrail and fought back the sudden nausea that came welling up in his throat. Keeping his eyes fixed on the struggling, burning mass of what had a few seconds before been people, he backed off toward where a technician was clutching the rail and nursing a limp, bloodstained arm.

"What happened?" Dyer snapped. The technician's eyes were wide with shock and near panic. His shirt was torn and blackened by smoke.

"Flamethrowers . . . they cut their way in through the wall . . . they sent crabs in ahead to use as bombs . . . blew them up somehow . . . there's nobody alive in there now . . . can't be."

"*Spartacus* doesn't have any flamethrowers," Dyer protested. "What the hell are you talking about? How could it know what to do with them if it did?"

"What else do you think did that?" the technician shouted, jerking his head at the doorway. "It used drones to carry standard-pattern hydrogen torches . . . thermite lances, I don't know . . . They were everywhere straight after the bombs hit. We didn't have a chance."

"Ray, watch it!" Wescott's voice barked from among the tangle of figures moving back toward the bulkhead. Dyer looked up. The blackened corpses wedged in the doorway were tumbling slowly and sickeningly into the corridor with tongues of flame still flickering about them as they turned. A sphere drone moved out from behind them. Dyer emptied the magazine of his rifle and the sphere drone disintegrated in a shower of pieces. The crab drone immediately behind it ran into a concentrated hail of bullets from Cordelle and Wescott, and came apart in midair. Another crab was already in sight behind it, and behind that two armored crabs maneuvering a pair of gas cylinders attached to a flexible metal hose that terminated in a short nozzle.

"Ray, get out!" Mary shrieked from behind Cordelle.

Dyer grabbed the tunic of the technician, who was still clinging dazedly to the rail beside him, and took off for the end of the corridor. Frank and Danny were already aiming to fire past them. At that instant more figures burst out of the door of the Power Distribution Control Room and were promptly caught from both sides.

A couple of them survived and clawed their way into the throng of bodies all fighting to get through the bulkhead door at once while Dyer, Cordelle, Wescott and a sergeant who had kept his head shouted vainly for order and kept up an intense and effective rear-guard fire.

"They were starting to cut through from the Fusion Control Room," the sergeant shouted to Dyer as he fired. "We figured it was time to get the hell out."

"How did you leave the feeder switches?" Dyer shouted back as they slammed the door.

"Fuck the feeder switches!"

The area outside had turned into a field-casualty clearing station. Some of the wounded were in serious condition and others did what they could to help them while Dyer and Wescott used a viewpad to contact the backup station, which was located farther along the corridor they had just left, beyond the Fusion Control Room. The supervisor of the backup station reported the situation from the screen.

"When we heard the trouble outside we figured we'd be better off staying in here. The corridor's blocked but we can get out to Sector Three through the emergency door. I don't know how long we can keep running, though. All our readings here are going down. *Spartacus* must be cutting every cable in the vicinity that it doesn't own. It's running haywire with the power distribution and comms all over Janus. The backup stations are coming on-line everywhere else, but if we get cut out here this whole part of Detroit will get wiped out. I've ordered the guys here into suits. We'll hold on as long as we can."

"Get out the moment it starts looking bad," Dyer advised. "It's not messing around. We've had about ten people killed." He cut off the pad and turned toward Cordelle, who was using another pad in an attempt to summon the nearest destroyer-equipped kill-team.

"It's breaking out everywhere," Cordelle said, shaking his head. "They said all their guys are committed. They can't get anyone here until reinforcements get through from the Hub. They're sending 'em in now."

"They should have been here now!" Dyer shouted. His eyes blazed with frustration and rage. "That dumb, textbook-quoting bastard! We can't stay here. They'll be through that door before long. *Spartacus* has started screwing up the support systems and the local backup's being cut out." The sounds of explosions and rifle fire from other places around them were by now plainly audible. "Frank, start getting those people moved out. Danny, get me a connection to Krantz."

Cordelle bent his head and began frantically punching the pad again. After a few seconds he looked up and shook his head.

"No dice. *Spartacus* is not playing ball. Comms are down."

"Plug into an emergency channel," Dyer yelled. "Dammit, there must be a socket somewhere near here." He scanned the nearby walls and panels. There wasn't.

And then the lights went out.

How they made it out of Detroit, Dyer was never sure. Guided through the maze of insane metallic geometry only by the beams of hand torches, and with explosions, gunfire, shouts, screams and sudden gushes of yellow and orange coming through the pitch blackness all around, they became part of a ragged procession of shadows that came together from different directions out of the darkness. For some reason Dyer remembered the words of Captain Malloy, who had delivered some of the lectures during the training period at Fort Vokes: "... we'll study it until every one of you can find your way from any point on Janus to any other point blindfolded ..." At least, he reflected grimly, there was something to be said for some aspects of military thinking.

They emerged into the tube terminal of the Spindle to find that the lights there were on. Evidently they were out of the sector that was supposed to be powered by the backup station that had gone down. Casualties were being dispatched up the Spindle in cabs detaching from the waiting line as quickly as could be managed under local control, while more groups of stragglers continued to trickle out of the access doors leading in from Detroit to add to the confusion all around. Medics were trying to group the wounded into cabloads while officers moved around scratching together fireteams to hold the approaches to the terminal. There was no sign of the reserves from the Hub.

Dyer made his way through the throng toward a captain who was talking into a viewpad plugged into an emergency-channel socket.

"All the backups in Detroit are down," the captain informed him. "Power, light, comms and transport are all out, but the life-support's holding up. Don't ask me why. The drones have turned nasty all over Janus but they're being held in check at the Rim because the ones there aren't armored. They're all being knocked out fast. The order is to destroy all drones on sight everywhere now. The problems are in Detroit and Pittsburgh. They're the only places that have lost backup and have had armored assaults with flamethrowers."

"Where are the reserves?" Dyer demanded.

"The contingent that was sent is stuck in a tube somewhere in the Spindle," the captain replied. "They were depowered when *Spartacus* pulled the plug."

"Why can't they go to local?"

"They're in a sector that draws power from a backup that's gone down. The techs are trying to rig a cable back to the Spindle somewhere."

"So what about the rest of the Hub?"

"They're being held there to guard possible exits from the Spindle to the Hub. Orders from General Linsay."

"Give me that thing! I need to talk to somebody in Command Room," Dyer thundered. The captain passed the pad across but made an apologetic empty-handed gesture.

"You'll be lucky to get through, sir. It's jammed with calls coming in from all over."

The sound of firing in the approach ramps and shafts around the terminal was getting nearer and becoming more intense. A lieutenant-general who seemed to have assumed charge of things and who was doing a good job of getting the situation under control, climbed up on top of one of the stationary cabs and raised his voice to address everybody within earshot.

"We do not have sufficient destroyers to remain here. Pittsburgh has evacuated its people into Southport and I have just been advised that a secure defense zone has been established there. I repeat— Southport is secure. We have to move out of here faster. I want a second line of cabs loaded up and sent south. Everybody on this side of the terminal form up for south-going cabs. I repeat—everybody on this side get organized to move south. Everybody on that side goes north to the Hub. Casualties and noncoms move first. Combat personnel regroup to give cover for the forward fireteams when they fall back. We need more men at the south end."

Dyer and Wescott helped with the wounded and waited until the forward teams were back in the terminal. By that time all the available cabs had gone and the few survivors that remained in the terminal deployed into groups waiting with weapons trained on the doors leading in from Detroit. A few minutes that seemed like hours passed by before more empty cabs began returning. But *Spartacus* too seemed to have paused for breath and the expected assault failed to materialize. When enough cabs had accumulated, the rearguard slipped quickly aboard and departed northward toward the Hub.

The two scientists, along with Cordelle and Mary, found themselves sharing a cab with Don Fisher, the begrimed chief engineer of the fusion plant, who was unharmed apart from having collected a number of slight scratches.

"It's bad news," Fisher told them, "The fusion plant is running and *Spartacus* has got full control of it. It's got Detroit and Pittsburgh all to itself now. We're locked out, unless they can move in from the Hub. Bad news . . ."

"But the fusion plant can be cut from Downtown," Wescott objected.

Fisher shook his head. "They tried as soon as they heard we were taking real casualties. It didn't work! When *Spartacus* started ripping out every wire that didn't belong to it, it must have hit the emergency line from the Command Room." The others stared at him aghast. Fisher nodded wearily.

"That's right. The only way to shut that plant down now is from the inside . . . And *Spartacus* is in there. We're not."

⚙ CHAPTER THIRTY-FOUR ⚙

"Fifty-seven dead and more than one hundred and fifty wounded!" Dyer brought his fist down hard on the table and bared his teeth. "There was no need for it! If you'd had the troops where they were needed, it would never have gotten out of hand."

"It wouldn't have made any difference," Linsay replied through tight lips. "They would have been too dispersed across Detroit to be effective at any one place. The only difference it would have made is that the enemy would now be all over the Rim instead of being contained in the Spindle. As things are, the Rim is secure. All drones in the Hub and Rim have been knocked out and the backup stations are handling the environment okay. All *Spartacus* nodes outside the Spindle are being dismantled. The only parts of it still running are the parts south of the Hub and it's sealed in there. The enemy has been forced back to a restricted area and we are in full control of the only exits."

"It wasn't forced back; we were forced out!" Dyer raged. "Your 'restricted area' is all it needs. It's got Christ knows how many homemade SPs in there, a fusion plant, a manufacturing complex and an extraction plant! It's got a stock of unprocessed moonrock that'll keep it growing itself and making drones for days . . . maybe weeks. You could have stopped it grabbing Detroit. That alone would have been enough to cripple it."

"It wouldn't have made any difference," Linsay replied grimly. "What caught us was the surprise. Nobody knew it would come up with improvised flamethrowers. Your thinking didn't allow for it and my thinking didn't allow for it. I still don't know what gave it the idea, but it's happened. We can't change it."

"And meanwhile there's nothing to stop it turning out as many destroyers and flying bombs as it wants," Dyer retorted. "The kill-teams have had their hands full even without that. How are they going to shape up when their destroyers start getting attacked? It could happen anytime in the next couple of hours. *Spartacus* hasn't even used its own destroyers yet and it's kicked us out of half of Janus!"

"It won't have the element of surprise a second time," Linsay pointed out. "Also, we have the advantage of position. They can only come out of the Spindle through a few access points and we've got those covered from all angles and in depth. *Nothing* can get through to the Hub. That was the whole purpose of *my* strategy, which you still seem unable or unwilling to appreciate."

A silence ensued while the two men glowered at each other across the table. Finally Krantz, who was the only other person present, spoke from a point midway between them.

"We could go on like this forever. Perhaps we'll never know for sure which of you was right, but recriminations can wait for a more opportune time. For the moment we have more urgent matters to attend to." He turned his eyes toward Linsay. "What are the arrangements for getting those people out of Southport?"

Linsay paused for a second to calm down, and then spread a plan of Janus on the table in front of them.

"The incoming traffic of catchers from Luna has been stopped, naturally," he began. "There are approximately two hundred persons in the Southport redoubt. Two shuttles are being loaded with fully equipped combat troops at Northport. The shuttles will dock at Southport to strengthen the position there and prepare it for use as an assault bridgehead. The ships will evacuate casualties and noncoms to Northport, collect fresh troops there and return to Southport to reinforce the units previously landed. Then we will commence a simultaneous attack on two fronts by advancing along the Spindle from both ends. *Spartacus* will be forced back by the hammer moving south from the Hub, onto the anvil moving north from Southport. The prime objective for the spearhead units will be to penetrate to the fusion plant and deactivate it. Other units have been ordered to act in supporting roles with that as the main thrust." He shot a challenging look at Dyer. "Does that meet with the doctor-general's approval?"

Dyer ignored the sarcasm and looked at Krantz.

"What's the point of this? We've got our answers now. Fifty-seven people who won't be going home are enough to tell me what we do about TITAN. It was never supposed to come to this. Why risk any more? I say pull everybody out now and let ISA take out this whole damn place with a big nuke."

Krantz assumed a meditative posture with his fingers steepled in front of his face. He stared gravely at them for what seemed a long time and then shook his head slowly. His reply was quiet but determined.

"I think not, Ray. As you say, the experiment was never expected to go to the extremes that we have seen, but it has. We are now at a crucial juncture. I see a great psychological need for us to pursue this to its end now, and to be seen to win. If we pull out now, what will the world see? It will see that we—a symbol of the human race itself—were defeated and had no effective reply left to offer. How do you think that knowledge would color our thinking for years, maybe decades, to come?" He shook his head again. "No. Now that we have come this far, we must prove that, although Man may sometimes make mistakes, he can always rise above them in the end. If we can do that much, your fifty-seven will not have died for nothing at all."

Dyer sat back and hunched his shoulders as he drew a long breath, then released it at once in a sudden sigh. Krantz was right.

"Or whatever the numbers end up as when it's all over," he said heavily.

Back on the Command Floor, Fred Hayes, who had been keeping watch on the dais while Dyer, Krantz and Linsay retired for their private conference, updated Dyer on what had been happening. Things had been fairly quiet, compared with earlier events anyway. *Spartacus* had tried moving its latest troops northward along the Spindle to the Hub, but this time the defenders had been well prepared and waiting, and the attack had collapsed rapidly. A similar fray with similar results had occurred at the perimeter around Southport. That was about all.

Feeling slightly relieved and a little more optimistic, Dyer walked over to where Laura was standing with Chris, Ron and a couple of CIM scientists. She saw him approaching and detached herself from the group to join him.

"Home is the hero," she said. "You look as if you just came from picking an argument with the whole of the Marine Corps." Dyer looked down at himself. He had come straight to the Command Room after returning from the Hub. His clothes were tattered and spattered with blood in places, and if his face was the same streaky colors as his arms he must look like a Zulu in war paint. The flippancy went out of Laura's voice and face abruptly. "Was it rough?" she asked.

"It was . . . rough."

"I was worried sick. Every time we got a list of latest arrivals at the Hub and your names weren't there, I just . . . Well, you're okay. I guess it doesn't matter now." She began walking with him over to the coffee dispenser on one side of the room. "Did you hear about Kim?"

"No, I didn't." Dyer turned a serious face. "What about her?"

"She cracked up," Laura told him. "When all those people got hit, that did it. She headed up the team that wrote the System. It was too much."

"What happened?"

"Oh, nothing dramatic. Her guilt hang-up about the whole thing bubbled over and she just went quietly to pieces. The doc's given her a sedative and she's lying down."

"At home?"

"No, upstairs. She'll be out for a while. Doc thinks we ought to ship her out with the casualties."

"I'll go talk to him later," Dyer muttered. He frowned to himself as he poured coffee into a cup. Another damn thing that he'd seen coming and never got around to doing anything about. If this was what they called learning the hard way, he wondered how he'd managed to survive all those years at all. And already he felt unhappy about their not declaring Emergency Red, and he wasn't doing very much to bring that about. But he couldn't; that was Krantz's decision to make. Dammit, he could try. This wasn't an argument about university timetables; it was life and death for people. Hadn't this whole lunatic project been his bright idea in the first place? He checked his flow of thought there with an effort. Much more like that, he told himself, and he'd be the next one to be put under sedation.

He raised the cup to his lips and washed the bitter taste of smoke from his mouth with a long, grateful swig. Laura was watching him and saying nothing.

"You haven't given me the speech yet," he said.

"What speech?"

"The I-told-you-so speech. Wasn't it me who always told you that computers were nothing to worry about? There's a computer out there that's just murdered fifty-seven people. So why don't you tell me I was wrong?"

"Because you weren't," Laura told him grimly. "Factories kill people. Airplanes kill people. So do steel plants, coal mines, high windows, oil refineries and a million other things. That isn't murder. Sometimes it happens because somebody somewhere didn't know as much as he thought he did. It's a shame it has to be that way but you can't change the way it is. What you're doing here is trying to find out. It's something that has to be done."

Dyer swilled the dregs of his coffee around in his mouth and spat them into the sink below the dispenser. By rights, surely it should have been Kim standing there saying things like that. It should have been the romantic idealist from Zeegram, surely, who should have been put to bed protesting and sedated upstairs. And suddenly it came to him how many lifetimes of front-line soldier's wisdom Danny Cordelle had packed into one short, simple statement when he had warned him, "Y' never can tell . . ."

◉ CHAPTER THIRTY-FIVE ◉

Nobody ever found out exactly what caused the disaster at Southport.

It could have been damage to some vital piece of equipment during the sporadic fighting that had taken place there before the drones were pushed back and the perimeter was being secured. It could have been a result of the modifying and remodifying of control circuits that had been going on, performed by both human engineers and *Spartacus*'s activities, for days. It could have been *Spartacus*. Possibly it was a million-to-one combination of all three. Afterward the designers of the safety interlocks insisted that in theory it couldn't happen, even with million-to-one odds. But that was in theory . . .

The antechamber behind the docking-bay airlocks at Southport was crowded with personnel assigned for evacuation to Northport when the first shuttle mated at Bay One. Minutes later the numbers were swollen further as the first company of marines doubled through the lock on their way to reinforce the perimeter.

The second shuttle was just nosing in toward the outer door of Bay Two when the door opened. The inner door had already been opened to speed up the two-way transfer of people after the shuttle docked.

Within seconds everybody who had been in the antechamber had become a blob of decompressed jelly hurtling away into the blackness of space.

Through somebody's quick thinking the doors that connected the antechamber through to the inner sections of Southport were closed quickly enough to save those who were still manning the perimeter. But they were desperately few, comprising only the front-line destroyer teams and riflemen who had been detailed to guard the perimeter until the marines from Northport arrived to strengthen them.

They were too few to hold when, just a matter of minutes later, *Spartacus* attacked.

The attacking force included the first of *Spartacus*'s destroyers and purpose-built bombs. The defenders fought well and to the last, but they never really had a chance. The last message to come over the emergency channel to the Command Room told of the latest development in *Spartacus*'s evolving awareness of what was causing what in the universe around it. It was directing its flying artillery not at the defenders' drones, but directly at the soldiers controlling them. The news was relayed hastily to the units positioned at the Hub. Meanwhile, with no bridgehead left to develop, the second wave of marines was ordered to abort its mission and to return to Northport.

The first drones to break through the doors into the antechamber were blasted suddenly forward by the rush of air and floundered about helplessly without power or steering in the vacuum chamber that it had become. *Spartacus* sealed the doors again and pondered. Then it sent in floor-crawling drones that ran a connection into the computers of the Southport backup station, which had previously been isolated from *Spartacus*'s net, and began to interrogate the data stored there. The data included encoded pictures of the events that had taken place, as captured by the monitoring cameras located at strategic points around the antechamber and outside the docking bays. *Spartacus* analyzed the pictures . . . and pondered.

Soon afterward the floor-crawling drones closed the open airlock and *Spartacus* filled the area with air again to remobilize its fliers. Then it turned its attention to the catcher ships, a few of which were docked alongside the Southport unloading bay.

Spartacus had already deduced from the pictures that outside Southport was a whole new realm of existence which, unlike the inside, possessed no air. Also it knew now that the catcher ships moved in that realm. Therefore the catcher ships could move without need of air. If that was so, then perhaps drones could be built that could move without need of air. Drones like that would be able to work without interference from the *shapes,* maybe.

For *Spartacus* had seen what airlessness had done to the *shapes.*

The whole of the Command Room had been seized by shocked, disbelieving silence. Dyer, now cleaned up and wearing fresh clothes, sat numbly at his console on the dais, his eyes still frozen on the now blank screen that had shown the carnage at Southport. Beside him, Krantz stood rigid and ashen-faced, his fingers gripping the edge of the console in front of him. Linsay was at the center of a group of silent officers, his eyes bulging and the muscles of his throat moving without making any sound.

At last Krantz came slowly back to life and dropped weakly into his seat. The faces in the room slowly turned and looked at him, waiting. The next move was his.

He leaned forward and extended a shaky hand to activate a microphone on his console. His voice was barely more than a hoarse whisper when he spoke.

"I hereby declare a condition of Emergency Red . . . I repeat again, Emergency *Red.* Evacuation procedure is to commence immediately. The military command will secure and hold all access routes from the Spindle to the Hub until evacuation has been completed. Those positions are to be held at all costs. That is all." He flipped off the microphone and slumped back in his chair to stare at the far wall. Fifty miles out in space, the three ISA ships began moving in.

Sometime later, while the first batches of evacuees were being moved up the spokes and through the Hub to assemble in Northport, holes were beginning to appear here and there over the outer skins of Detroit and Pittsburgh. Machines of assorted shapes and sizes cut their way through and proceeded to set up instruments and sensors designed to scan the whole of the electromagnetic spectrum from VLF radio through to high-energy cosmic rays. *Spartacus* was making itself eyes to study the vast and wondrous world that it had discovered beyond Janus.

❂ CHAPTER THIRTY-SIX ❂

Mat Solinsky felt the familiar smoothness of the controls responding to his touch as the bug launched itself out of the airlock of the Maintenance & Spares Unit at Hub Section 17D. The huge gray sphere fell away behind and began rolling slowly over as he brought the bug around into a course that would take it diametrically outward, parallel to the Berlin spoke. In the co-pilot's seat beside him, Mitch checked the communications link and then settled back to study the jungle of struts and lattices contained by the circle of the secondary reflectors and sliding by to one side of them.

"Looks clean enough here," Mitch commented. "Which way are we gonna take it—through the ring, round the Hub and back down the other side?"

"That's what I figured," Solinsky told him.

The ISA ships were now standing two miles off from Janus waiting for Janus's own shuttles to finish loading with evacuees and depart, thus freeing up the Northport docking bays. As the ISA ships closed nearer, they had sent reports of objects moving around on the exterior of Janus. Solinsky and Mitch had volunteered to take out one of the bugs for an outside view close-up.

They rounded the secondary reflector ring between the Berlin and Rocky Valley spokes and turned inward again to pass low over the immense tilted mirror panels until they were inside the ring once more and following the northern contour of the Hub around toward Northport. The two shuttles were docked beneath them like twin cubs with a mother as they passed over the northernmost tip of the Spindle and continued outward to recross the plane of the Rim between the Paris and Sunnyside spokes. From there they ascended inward again on a direct line toward the mass of Detroit.

"I see 'em!" Mitch exclaimed suddenly, and stabbed with his finger in the direction of the curving surface swelling to meet them outside. Solinsky took the bug in closer and Mitch went to work with a hand camera.

Below them, standing up from the outer skin of Detroit, was what looked like a squat lattice tripod surmounted by a fat tube. Mitch judged it to be about eight feet high. It was straddling a hole that had been cut through the skin and seemed to be connected through to the inside by a tangle of tubes and cables. Not far away was another structure, supporting a triangular cheese-shaped box, and beyond that was a pivoted cylinder which swung around to track the bug as it passed over. There were other constructions on the south slope of Detroit, facing Pittsburgh, and a few on the section of the Spindle at the bottom of the valley between. As Solinsky closed range, they picked out numerous mobile contraptions of unfamiliar design moving about on the outer surface, some of which were cooperating in erecting more permanent fixtures.

Mitch continued to record as many details as could be seen and kept the Command Floor informed with a running commentary on what he saw. They were over Pittsburgh, where a cluster of objects had sprouted on its equator diametrically opposite its solar receiver dish, and still heading south when the controller in the Command Room interrupted Mitch in midsentence.

"Hold it a second. We've got a message coming in from one of the ships." There was a pause, presumably while the controller spoke to somebody in one of the ISA vessels holding position two miles away. Mitch and Solinsky exchanged shrugs. Then the controller's voice came again.

"A catcher ship's coming out of Southport. *Spartacus* must be flying it because nobody else is. Watch it."

"Don't worry, we will," Mitch replied drily into his mike. He glanced apprehensively at Solinsky. "Do computers have rights on territorial limits?"

"Looks like maybe this one figures it does," Solinsky answered.

"What's it doing?" Solinsky inquired into his mike. The mass of Pittsburgh was still between the bug and Southport, so they didn't have a direct line of sight to where the catcher ship would be.

"It's still moving away from you, in line with the Spindle and out from it," the controller advised. "Moving slow . . . slower . . . bringing its stern around. Looks as if it could be fixing to come up your way."

"Signal it we're not at home to callers today," Mitch said. The catch in his voice came through the flippancy of his words. A few seconds of silence passed.

"The ISA ship nearest you has got a missile primed and tracking on it," the controller told them. "It's less than four seconds away from you so you shouldn't have any problems if it starts looking like trouble. The catcher has started to move back in toward the Spindle. It's climbing out to clear Pittsburgh and coming around to match your position. You should see it coming over the hill any second now."

By this time Solinsky had put the bug into a wide turn to circle the Spindle broadside-on to the north slope of Pittsburgh. An enormous rectangular archway swung up in front of them and passed overhead as they crossed through the space between the Spindle and the inner edge of the Radiator Assembly. Mitch kept his head turned to scan the crestline of Pittsburgh.

"There it is!" he yelled suddenly, pointing. Immediately opposite them, the yawning front end of the cone-shaped "hippo" was rising over the edge of Pittsburgh like its namesake emerging from behind a riverside mud bank. Inside its huge forward aperture, which was intended to scoop up the loads of moonrock catapulted into lunar orbit, they could see batteries of instruments, scanners, receiver and miscellaneous gadgetry all apparently aimed in their direction. At once Solinsky turned away to put more distance between the two craft, but the hippo soared higher above Pittsburgh and followed. On the surface below, dozens of curious electronic eyes followed the chase.

Mitch looked from side to side and threw his mind into top gear to assess the position. The bug was farther in toward the Spindle than the hippo and would have to climb outward to clear Detroit. That meant that whichever way they went, the hippo would be able to gain on them by setting a straight-line course to cut them off. He didn't like it, and said so.

"We're gonna lose more speed in turns too," Solinsky said. "I'm not being chased all around Janus by that flying junk heap. Tell 'em to fire that goddam missile."

"We're gonna get squeezed up against Detroit whatever we do," Mitch shouted into his mike. "Get rid of it for Chrissakes, willya!"

"Wilco," the controller acknowledged, and a few seconds later confirmed: "Missile fired."

Seconds later something streaked out of the starry backdrop and the hippo vanished in a blaze of white and yellow. Debris showered out and cartwheeled off into space in all directions. The gas cloud dispersed almost instantaneously, leaving nothing where the hippo had been.

"Let's get out of here and go home," Mitch said.

"Good idea," Solinsky agreed as they began climbing out and over Detroit. "Before it gets the idea of inventing SAMs."

Meanwhile, inside *Spartacus,* analysis had already begun of the data that had been gathered on the object that had come out of the realm beyond and destroyed the hippo. Evidently there were more things in existence which were capable of posing a threat to it than the *shapes* that infested Janus. A nearby threat plus an unknown, more distant threat . . . The distant one would require a lot of further investigation. It would be better if that could be done without the irritation of distractions. The logical thing to do would be to get rid of the *shapes* first . . . once and for all.

"I don't like it at all," Krantz told Linsay and Dyer as they stood conferring in the center of the dais. "*Spartacus* has got things walking around outside the Hub and the inner reflector ring right now. It cut its way out. What's to stop it deciding to cut its way in again? If it blew the Hub open with all those people in there waiting to get out, it would make what happened at Southport seem like nothing. And another thing—it now has parts of itself in places from which they can see the docking bays at Northport. Also, it's found out about what's outside Janus and it has three more catcher ships down there. Suppose it used one of them to ram a shuttle packed to the locks with evacuees. We could lose twice the number we've lost already."

Linsay, now very sober and more subdued than he had been on previous occasions, could only raise his hands wearily in front of him.

"I know, but what else can we do?" he replied. "If a strict discipline is kept on sealing all airtight bulkheads, then even if *Spartacus* does break through in places casualties should be localized and kept to a minimum. If we put everybody stationed at outer positions into suits, with luck we wouldn't take any casualties at all. The catchers don't bother me as much right now. You saw what the missiles can do to them. There's no way one could get out of Southport, carry out a reversing maneuver and intercept a shuttle from Northport before we knocked it out. It'd need at least three minutes and all we need is four seconds."

Krantz thought for a moment and then shook his head dubiously.

"I still don't like it. I don't like the thought of sending ships full of people out there while *Spartacus* has got God alone knows what sitting waiting for them. I refuse to use any more people as guinea pigs against something we know nothing about."

This time Dyer thought Linsay was right. He felt that Krantz was overreacting somewhat to the burden of responsibility he was carrying for the Southport catastrophe and was playing caution too far. Also, he was worried about Kim and wanted to see the evacuation get underway so she could be taken out. The shuttles, however, had been appropriated almost entirely for battle casualties and Kim wasn't scheduled to go until the waiting ISA ships docked, which couldn't be until after the shuttles had departed. He found himself unable to decide in his own mind whether he agreed with Linsay as a result of an objective weighing up of the situation in general, or whether he had rationalized his own personal feelings. Therefore he said nothing.

"What other way is there?" Linsay asked Krantz.

"I've been thinking it over," Krantz answered. "The assault from the Hub along the Spindle and into Detroit can still be mounted without a simultaneous attack from Southport. Am I right?"

"It could," Linsay agreed hesitantly. "We'd lose the advantage of surprise on two fronts through . . ."

"But we could substitute an alternative surprise element instead," Krantz told him. Linsay's expression said that he didn't follow so Krantz continued. "The perimeter defenses at Southport were overwhelmed when *Spartacus* used airborne artillery and bombs to assault our manned emplacements. Nobody expected that. They expected it to attack our drones. Suppose we grounded its whole air force at the same instant that we launch our attack from the Hub. That would stand a good chance of throwing it completely off balance long enough for us to get into the fusion plant and switch it off. It's worth a try, surely. If it works, we can then evacuate everybody without exposing them to any risks at all. Doesn't that make sense?"

Linsay nodded but continued to wear a puzzled frown.

"Sure, but . . . I'm still not with you. How are we going to ground its air force?"

"By taking away the air!" Krantz said. "What I propose is this— immediately before our assault from the Hub goes in, the ISA ships put a salvo of low-charge missiles into Detroit, Pittsburgh and South Spindle . . . everywhere . . . enough to blow holes into every major section. If the holes are made big enough, it should depressurize the whole of south Janus fast enough to throw *Spartacus*'s fliers completely out of control. Our assault troops go in with suits and make a fast thrust through to the fusion plant. Without any airborne opposition, the support units should be easily able to knock out anything else that tries to get in the way. What do you think?"

"Well, it's ingenious, I'll give you that . . ." Linsay rubbed his chin and stared at the floor as he turned the suggestion over. "It might just work, I guess . . . Can't see any obvious holes in the plan. It'd probably take a while to get organized, though. Coupla hours maybe."

"What are a couple of hours against hundreds of lives?" Krantz asked. He turned toward Dyer. "Ray, how do you feel about it?"

Dyer tried again to sort through the contradictions wrestling each other inside his head but again succeeded only in confusing himself further.

"I don't know," he said. "To me it seems six of one, half a dozen of the other. As you say, maybe it's worth a try."

In the end Krantz's rank decided the issue. Orders went out to suspend the evacuation preparations while Linsay and his staff went to work with the commander of the ISA ships to draw up the plans for Operation Knockout.

Two precious hours went by. And all the time, the machines inside Detroit continued whirring and pounding.

◎ CHAPTER THIRTY-SEVEN ◎

Schroder was noticeably breathless as he hastened into the Oval Office in response to the emergency summons that had brought him from a room farther along the corridor where he had been talking with members of the Presidential staff. President Vaughan Nash and ISA Director-General John Belford were waiting with nervous, unsmiling faces. Schroder read the atmosphere the instant that he entered the room.

"What's happened?" he asked as he took the vacant chair opposite Nash.

"The assault wave was cut to ribbons," the President told him. "*Spartacus* used a new type of drone that runs and steers with rocket jets or something and doesn't need air. We don't know how. Linsay's been pushed right back along the Spindle to the Hub and they've reinstated the evacuation order. John's saying we should go to *Omega*."

Schroder swung his head sharply around toward Belford and gaped at him in horrified disbelief.

"It's already used a catcher and now it's making its own spaceworthy machines," Belford explained defensively. "At the speed the System's been putting new devices through to production, anything could happen any minute. It's all set to break out of Janus and I say we can't let that happen. If we don't stop it now, next time might be too late."

"But they're evacuating!" Schroder protested. "For God's sake—the people are getting out! We've got to give them a chance up there. The guts of it will still be in Janus even if it does manage to send out a few scouts, which from what you're telling me it hasn't even gotten around to doing yet. We can still blow its brains out after the people are off. If anything gets away in the meantime, it'll cease functioning with the brains gone."

"Suppose it puts enough of its brains in a ship that gets away to start growing itself all over again," Belford objected. "It'd be like a virus let loose all over the Solar System. The only way to wipe it out is while it's all still in one place and we don't know how long that'll last."

"How could it grow?" Schroder demanded. "It wouldn't have any manufacturing. And besides that, the missiles can pick off anything that does try getting away. I say no—not until the people are out."

"I agree with Irwin," Nash came in. "If we woke up tomorrow and decided we'd been too hasty, it'd follow us around for the rest of our lives. We agreed that the decision had to be unanimous. It's two to one against. Therefore we wait."

"Very well," Belford concurred with a sharp nod. "I have to accept that. But I'd like my opinion committed to record."

Up on Janus, Dyer had left Krantz and Linsay arguing heatedly in the side conference room and returned to the Command Floor. The scene around him was one of frantic activity as the controllers and operators tried to make sense of the confused messages coming in from the Hub and to maintain some measure of coordination between what was going on there and in other places.

The intended evacuation from Northport had again been postponed following the failure of Operation Knockout. Some of the less seriously hurt from among those wounded earlier were unloaded from the first shuttle due out, in order to make room for those seriously wounded in the course of Knockout. The work of changing the quotas was hampered by the flow of survivors pouring back out of the Spindle to regroup and by the frantic efforts going on all over the Hub to prepare new defensive positions, not only against a possible breakout from the Spindle now, but also against the possibility of break-ins from the outside. The whole of the Hub was in chaos and another full hour went by before the first shuttle was at last reported as being ready to go.

Dyer was with Chris and Ron at the back of a group standing before one of the screens to watch the scene outside Northport as the shuttle detached from its dock and began falling away into space.

The missile came out of a port that *Spartacus* had made in the north of Detroit. It had made the secondary reflector ring, skidded around to pass between the spokes, and impacted on the shuttle before the ISA ships had even had time to react. The pandemonium that erupted on every side of where Dyer was standing was cut short as the shuttle reappeared, intact, behind where the detonation had flashed.

"It's okay!" somebody yelled above the din. "By God, it's made it!"

"It's taken a kick up the ass, though," someone else said. "Look at its back end."

On the screen the shuttle had lurched off course, trailing debris from its shattered stern. It seemed to be drifting freely without any ability to correct. Its captain reported loss of steering and propulsion but, to the relief of those watching, no damage to the passenger compartments; as far as he could tell there had been no casualties. Watchdog Two, one of the three ISA ships standing by, immediately departed from its position to match course with the shuttle and begin transferring its occupants over.

Why the missile should have been equipped with such an inadequate warhead remained something of a mystery. The most likely explanation, Dyer thought, was that *Spartacus* hadn't made sufficient allowance for the lack of shock waves in the airless environment that it was only just beginning to comprehend. If so, he told himself grimly, there would be little chance of it getting its sums wrong next time.

"Where'd it learn to make missiles?" Ron asked incredulously. "Not from the one we fired at the hippo, surely. That's crazy."

"We've lost a lot of time since then," Dyer reminded him. "It didn't take long to come up with airless drones, did it? I guess we're still learning that it gets things done a lot quicker than people."

Krantz and Linsay had emerged from the conference room as soon as the commotion started and by now were aware of what had taken place.

"We'll have to abandon evacuating," Krantz declared. "We can't get out and the ISA ships can't get in."

"That missile was practically a dud," Linsay argued. "The thing to do is press on. Why wait until *Spartacus* has made better ones?"

"We have to take out *Spartacus* first."

"How? We tried. You saw what happened."

"*Spartacus* is running wild. *You* know what that means." Beads of perspiration were beginning to appear on Krantz's forehead. "We must stop it. ISA could put a large missile right into the middle of Detroit . . . knock out the fusion plant that way."

"You're crazy," Linsay protested. "If Detroit came apart the whole Radiator Assembly could smash straight through the Rim. You'd end up killing everybody . . . a damnsight faster than *Spartacus* ever could."

"It's a chance we have to take. We don't have any other."

Dyer was half listening, puzzling over what it was that Linsay was supposed to know, when he noticed Laura gesturing from the edge of the group of people that included Chris and Ron. He walked quickly back and raised his eyebrows in response to the look of urgency written across her face.

"Kim's gone," she said.

"What do you mean, 'gone'?"

"She's disappeared. She was scheduled to be shipped up to the Hub as soon as the first shuttle had left. When the medics went to her room upstairs to get her, she'd vanished."

"Oh Christ!" Dyer spread his hands helplessly and motioned at the bedlam all around the Command Floor. "Not now . . . not at a time like this. What the hell can anyone do about it with all this going on?"

"You've got to find her," Laura pleaded. "She's part of your team. You brought her up here and she's sick. She could walk into anything." Chris and Ron had overheard and moved closer to listen.

"Try tracking her viewpad ID code," Chris suggested. "She's probably still carrying it." Dyer spun abruptly and strode across to where Eric Jassic was supervising operations at one of the master communications consoles. When the others caught up with him he was already explaining what he wanted.

"That's a privacy violation," Jassic said dubiously. "Needs okaying by Krantz."

"Eric, so help me, I'll break your neck," Dyer grated. "Just do it!" Jassic glanced up, read the look in Dyer's eyes and began hammering commands into his console without further ado.

"She's in a cab," he told them a few seconds later. "Heading west between Downtown and Paris. It's logged the fermentation plant at Vine County as its destination."

"What the hell would she do there?" Ron asked in astonishment. Nobody knew.

Dyer called the provost marshal who in turn alerted his men in Vine County to intercept the cab on arrival. Many minutes passed while the group around the console followed the cab's progress. It was agonizingly slow. For some insane reason Kim was stopping at practically every point in between, but she didn't get out. At last the data on the screen told them she had arrived at the fermentation plant. They waited anxiously for the call to come through on one of the auxiliary screens. At last the tone sounded and a few seconds later a puzzled provost was staring out at them.

"This some kinda joke or sump'n?" he demanded.

"What?" Dyer asked.

"There ain't nobody in this cab. There's just somebody's pad on one of the seats. You people tryin' ta make monkeys out of us here or sump'n?"

"Sorry ... it must have been ... a mistake." Dyer cut off the screen and turned back to the stupefied faces behind him. "She guessed. It was just a decoy. She could be anywhere by now."

"She might be sick but she's still got her head screwed on okay," Laura said. "Ray, we have to *do* something."

"What the hell are we supposed to do?" Dyer demanded. "We've got a crazy computer making missiles, the roof could fall in any second, and nobody knows if we can get out or not. She could be anywhere in this mess. There simply isn't—" At that moment the emergency tone sounded shrilly from Chris's viewpad. Chris slipped it from his pocket and frowned as he interrogated the screen.

"Bloody hell!" he exclaimed suddenly. "This isn't true."

"What is it?" Ron asked.

"My apartment in Berlin," Chris said. "The intruder alarm's been triggered. Somebody's breaking in!"

"That couldn't be Kim, could it?" Laura asked, sounding amazed and perplexed.

Chris tapped in the codes to connect the cameras in his apartment to the screen of the viewpad. The camera in the hall had been put out of action already by whoever had broken in, but another by the back door tantalized by showing the shadow of somebody moving behind a projecting corner in the wall without revealing who the somebody was. Ron looked over Chris's shoulder and watched thoughtfully. Then he snapped his fingers.

"That is Kim," he said quietly. "She's after the Gremlin." Chris looked up at him, horrified.

"What Gremlin?" Dyer asked them.

"It's too long a story to go into now," Ron said. "There's a Gremlin there—sighter plus projectiles. Kim's the only other person who knows about it. That has to be her."

"What's she going to do with it?" Laura asked.

Ron shrugged. "Search me. The state she's in, it could be anything."

One of the console operators, a freckle-faced girl who had been standing on the fringe of the group of people nearby, moved forward a pace to speak to them.

"Excuse me. I couldn't help hearing some of the things you've been saying. Are you looking for Kimberly Sinclair?"

"Yes," Dyer said. "Why?"

"She was here earlier."

"How d'you mean, 'here'? Where?"

The girl gestured vaguely around.

"Here . . . in the Command Room. She was standing next to me right over there by the stairs when everybody was watching the shuttle leaving Northport . . . when the missile nearly got it. She didn't seem well at all. I was wondering if I should say anything to anybody."

"Well, we think we know where she is now," Dyer told her. "Thanks anyway."

"She was talking kind of strange," the girl went on, evidently unhappy about leaving it at that. "She was there until Mr. Krantz and General Linsay started talking about what to do next. She said something about if nobody else could make up their minds how to stop it, she would. Then she took off."

"She didn't say anything else?" Dyer asked.

"No . . . I don't think so . . . nothing that made much sense, anyway. Something about breaking it off and putting it where the missiles could tear it apart."

"Oh God!" Ron's face turned a shade paler. He looked woodenly at Chris. "Do you think it could be what I think it could be?"

Chris stared back at him blankly for a second, then his jaw dropped. "Mat Solinsky . . . the grand tour . . . the view from the window?"

Ron nodded.

"What are you two talking about?" Dyer asked them.

"We think she's going to the Hub," Chris said. "She's going to try jamming up the Spin Decoupler by putting a Gremlin into it . . . If it does, it'll tear Janus in half. We'll all be in one half and *Spartacus* will be on its own in the other. Then the ISA ships can finish it off. That's what she's doing."

Dyer closed his eyes for a moment while he struggled to digest what he had just heard. He looked from Chris to Ron and shook his head in protest.

"But that's insanity," he said. "It couldn't break off clean . . . not with being locked solid that far off-center. The whole southern half of Janus would wheel around and smash the Rim into scrap metal. Pittsburgh and Detroit would plow straight through this place like an eggshell."

"I know that and you know that," Ron agreed soberly. "But maybe Kim isn't in any state of mind to worry about that kind of risk right now. There's only one thing she cares about, and that's stopping *Spartacus*. I don't think she's bothered how she does it."

❂ CHAPTER THIRTY-EIGHT ❂

Spartacus followed up its stab at the shuttle with a full-scale assault aimed at getting into the Hub, both by pushing northward out of the Spindle and by breaking in from the outside. It brought its full complement of new weapons to bear, including cannon-firing and flame-throwing spacedrones and self-propelled bombs, but the defending troops were prepared for depressurization and faced the assault wearing suits and well entrenched behind formidable walls of rocket launchers and automatic weapons. The battle developed into an ebb and flow concentrated mainly around the region where the Hub joined the Spindle and around the vicinity of Northport.

Somebody in the Hub had the idea of loading some of the cabs with explosives and dispatching them down the tubes through the Spindle into Detroit, in hopes of an explosion somewhere deep inside *Spartacus*'s vitals. Some of the cabs never made it and nobody was sure exactly where the others were when they detonated, but not long afterward the vigor of *Spartacus*'s attack slackened considerably. A counterthrust developed from this point with spacesuited infantry regaining a number of positions in the Hub-Spindle junction; at the same time a swarm of bugs that had been specially rigged to fire rockets and Gremlins went out to deal with the machines attempting to work inward from the outside. In some places troops emerged onto the outside surface to add further pressure.

The tide turned once more when *Spartacus*'s 'Mark I' missiles proved lethal for bugs and its space drones took out the infantry, who had no equivalent weapon of their own to counter them and were soon forced back inside. When a lull at last developed, the soldiers were still holding the exits from the Spindle but *Spartacus* had gained sole ownership of the outside.

By this time most of the Hub was a mess. Its surface was pitted with jagged holes and most of its outer sections were depressurized. Several of the Hub backup stations had been knocked out during the fighting, leaving many units to maintain their vigils by the ghostly glare of portable searchlights, without transportation and in some cases with only hastily laid field telephones for communication. Evacuation under those conditions would have been impossible and all personnel who were not directly involved in the military operations being conducted at the Hub began moving down to the Rim.

Throughout all this, Dyer had been totally preoccupied with digesting the reports coming in and endeavoring to form a picture of what kind of processes were developing inside *Spartacus* from the tactics that it employed. When things calmed down again he returned his attention to his immediate surroundings and looked around for Laura, Chris and Ron. There was no sign of them. He descended from the dais and went across to where Jassic was still sitting.

"They went after Kim," Jassic told him. "I tried to talk to them but things were too hectic. They figured you'd be tied up for too long up there and said there wasn't time to wait."

"Don't they know there's a war on at the Hub?" Dyer stormed.

"They said you'd understand. Chris said they were heading for the Maintenance & Spares Unit in Section 17D. They seemed sure that's where Kim would be."

"Get me a connection to somebody there," Dyer said.

"I already tried to. Comms there are out. The backup station got bombed."

Dyer swore in exasperation and drove a fist into his palm. He turned around to look back at the dais and saw Linsay and Krantz still debating hotly. Linsay was in favor of launching another thrust into the Spindle to follow up on the blow dealt by the cab bombs while the advantage lasted; Krantz wanted to disperse the lower shield and plan for an evacuation through the Rim. Dyer swore again. Even if he told them about Kim and the Spin Decoupler now, they'd do nothing but talk until it was too late. There wasn't time. He swung back toward Jassic, who was watching him expectantly.

"If anybody wants me I've gone to the Hub," Dyer said. "There's nothing left to do down here anyhow. It's all soldiers' work now."

He left the Command Room, stopped in the lobby outside to put on his helmet and combat overjacket and pick up an M25, and walked through from the Data Executive Sector into the concourse to catch an elevator for the Hub.

Minutes after Dyer left the Command Room, news of fresh activity on the outside of Detroit came through from the two remaining ISA ships. For some time *Spartacus* had been enlarging one of the holes it had cut in a position south of Detroit's equator and thus invisible from the Hub and the observation points at the intersections of the spokes with the Rim. Something was coming out.

Roughly cylindrical, over twenty-five feet long and thin for much of its length, the construction was adorned with a profusion of disks and flat cylinders mounted around and perpendicular to its main axis, with tangles of cables and what appeared to be dense electrical windings at places in between. Seemingly haphazard jumbles of unidentifiable equipment clung around both ends in heaps with the back end, assuming that that was the part that came out last, considerably more heavily loaded than the front. It lifted away from Detroit and began sailing outward on a course that would bring it around the Rim. Three more followed in rapid succession and spread out to space themselves equally about the main axis of Janus.

Then the two hippos detached themselves from Southport, reversed, and began swinging outward to traverse the length of the Spindle.

Krantz was well beyond curiosity by now and called for an immediate missile strike by the two remaining ISA ships. Six missiles were fired within seconds. Four went out of control and careered off into space, and the other two exploded prematurely, far short of effective range from their targets. The salvo of twelve missiles that followed claimed one of the mysterious devices, with seven attacks going off course and four detonating early. Krantz promptly called for another strike.

Command Stalley, senior officer aboard the remaining "Watchdog" ships, looked gravely back at him from one of the screens.

"We've only got fifteen missiles left. We didn't come here expecting to have to fight a full-scale war. On top of that we're a ship short because one's gone to take care of the shuttle."

"What's going wrong with the ones you're firing?" Krantz demanded.

"We don't know yet. We're still analyzing the data from the tracking instruments."

"When is Miller due to arrive with Z Squadron?" Krantz asked, referring to the five fast ISA ships that had been dispatched from Earth as soon as the situation on Janus began getting out of hand.

"Three and a half hours. Until then we're down to fifteen. You want us to risk all of them now?" A short pause ensued while Krantz wrestled with the question. The two hippos from Southport were now abreast of Pittsburgh and still moving outward from the axis. Then Stalley spoke again.

"Tracker analysis report's just come in. Every one of the missiles exhibited high X-ray emission immediately before it went haywire. Those things that *Spartacus* has launched must be something like flying linear bevatrons—high-power electron guns. It's using our missiles as targets for an enormous X-ray tube and knocking them out with their own emitted radiation!"

At that moment a third hippo came out of Southport and formed up with two more electron guns and a swarm of space drones into a second fleet that began moving in the same direction as the first, which was now opposite Detroit and almost out as far as the inner reflector ring.

"We may not have three and a half hours," Krantz shouted at the screen. "Fire everything you've got now."

"Okay. As soon as we've reloaded and armed."

"How long?" Krantz implored.

"A minute maybe, but those hippos are slow."

Krantz nodded resignedly and turned away from the screen to find Linsay stooping to unlock the door in the plinth supporting his own console. When Linsay stood up he was buckling a pair of Patton-style pearl-handled revolvers around his waist; then he stooped again and took out a brilliantly polished white helmet that bore his general's insignia. There was a strange light in his eyes.

"What are you doing?" Krantz asked.

"Can't you see what's happening?" Linsay replied. "It's about to mount an all-out attack on Northport. If it gets in, we lose the Hub. If we lose the Hub, our only chance of getting back in to Detroit will be gone. Detroit must be attacked while we still have a chance. This time it mustn't fail. I intend going there and leading it personally."

"We still hold the Rim," Krantz pointed out. "Even without the Hub there would—"

"For how long?" Linsay asked. "Is that how you want it to end . . . with us cooped up in the Rim like rabbits chased down a hole by a ferret? If we get pushed back to the Rim there will be no way out."

"We can disperse the shield," Krantz said.

"Not anymore. Can't you see . . . it's only a matter of time now before *Spartacus* turns those beams onto the outer skin! The shield would absorb the X-rays but without the shield we'd all be fried like germs—*sterilized*, like bacteria! We *can't* disperse the shield now. Our only way out is to Detroit. That way we might win or we might die. Here we can only die."

Linsay stepped down from the dais and walked over to his staff officers to detail his second-in-command to take over and to select a handful of aides to go with him to the Hub. They departed a few minutes later.

Up on the dais Krantz found that his mouth was dry and his hands were trembling. He looked at the notepad in front of him and realized that he had been scrawling on the paper unconsciously. Scattered across the top sheet were copies of the same symbol repeated over and over again. It was the symbol of the final letter of the Greek alphabet—*Omega*.

❀ CHAPTER THIRTY-NINE ❀

The arrivals concourse at the Hub end of the Berlin spoke was a scene of bustling activity when Kim emerged from one of the elevators. Busy medical orderlies were fussing over rows of stretchers waiting their turn to be moved down to the Rim while behind them the walking wounded were sitting and standing in weary, battle-stained groups, smoking cigarettes and watching the companies of freshly arrived troops and ammunition parties passing through on their way to the fronts.

She had been informed at the departure point in Berlin that standing orders required everybody bound for the Hub to be kitted out in suits, but that face visors could be left open in the areas that were still pressurized. When she arrived, therefore, there was nothing in particular to single her out from anybody else; besides that, everybody was too busy to take much notice of her. Carrying the conspicuous aluminum sighter case concealed inside a standard-issue plasticized storage bag intended to hold a laser range-finder, she worked her way through the confusion toward the south exit.

The soldiers preparing fallback positions at the lower end of the corridor that rose away toward the Spindle followed her with a few curious looks as she passed, but made no attempt to stop her. Farther on, a hole blown through the floor was being improvised into a fortified destroyer-control position and a sandbagged machine gun

313

was covering the stretch ahead from behind a bulkhead door. At the far end of the corridor, where it transformed into a staircase to complete its steepest part, a squad of marines was positioned to cover the closed door that led onward. One of them moved into the center of the corridor and beckoned Kim to a halt as she approached.

"It's depressurized beyond this point, ma'am," he told her. "You sure you're going the right way?"

"What's the situation in 17D?" she inquired.

"We've got some forward units stationed there, that's all. Forward observation."

"It's still ours then," Kim said with a quick surge of inward relief. "How do I get through? I need to get in there."

The marine looked at her curiously. "Do you know it's right on the outside? What do you need to go there for?"

Kim made a vague gesture with the range-finder bag that she was holding.

"Somebody wants a special reconnaissance done of a couple of parts of Detroit. 17D's the best place to get the details they need. I was with a team but we got split up back there somewhere. I have to use the chance now, while I've still got it."

The marine waved a couple of men forward to open the bulkhead while Kim closed and secured her visor. She adjusted the suit's life-support and moved on into the space between the double doors of the bulkhead. The door behind her closed and a few moments later the indicators by the door in front changed to show that the lock had emptied. A slight nudge came through her gauntlet as the handle's interlock disengaged. She turned the handle to the "Free" position, and pushed the door outward.

The scene beyond was eerie—a tortured jungle of torn pipes and jagged twisted-metal sculptures rearing up out of nightmare chasms of shadow being cast by a few emergency lamps glowing dull red to preserve night vision. As her eyes adjusted to the gloom, she made out several shadowy helmeted figures crouching over weapons in the darker recesses and behind makeshift parapets of smashed machines and crumpled wreckage. A couple of the helmets turned toward her as the shaft of light stabbed briefly from the doorway, but apart from that the figures remained motionless. Kim clutched the handle of the bag more tightly, drew the handlamp from her belt and began picking her way slowly and carefully toward the pitch blackness ahead.

She used the lamp to guide her as far as the maze of collapsed debris that had once been the offices of the Maintenance & Spares Unit and through to the door that led to the storeroom beyond. There she doused the lamp and carried on by feel and memory until she could make out the faint rectangle that marked where the door led through to the catwalk overlooking the bug parking bay.

By now her eyes had grown more used to the dark and vague outlines of the metal ribbing hanging from above and heaped and broken storage racking began resolving themselves around her. She had reached the door and was about to go through when she saw the two spacesuited figures lying behind a low barricade at the edge of the catwalk, keeping a watch out over the floor below. She had almost walked straight into them, but their backs were toward her and because of the airlessness they had heard nothing. She backed slowly into the storeroom and forced herself to stay calm and think.

She remembered seeing a door somewhere to the left when she had come here with Chris and Ron. There was a chance that whatever place it led through to might open out onto the catwalk farther along. If it did, it would open out somewhere between where the two soldiers were positioned and the curving platform that ran below the window and above the airlocks used by the bugs, which was the direction she wanted to go. It was worth a try.

She felt her way through the wreckage until she found the wall. Then she began tracing it back with her hands, not daring to risk attracting attention by using her lamp. At last she came to a vertical break. It was jagged and pitted in places but felt like the edge of a doorway. The panel beyond it had to be the door. She pushed against it and the panel fell away noiselessly into the blackness. Doorway or not, there was an opening in front of her through the wall. She bit her lip and moved into it.

Blotches of faint light revealed a series of large jagged holes in the far end of whatever she was in—the end where the catwalk was. So, even if it hadn't been built to open out onto the catwalk, it did now.

Kim picked her way across to the far side, away from where the two soldiers were stationed, went down low on the floor, and brought her head cautiously up near the edge of the gaping hole in front of her to study whatever lay beyond.

Where the large viewing window had been, above the two airlocks on the opposite side of the bay, there was now nothing but a huge irregular gash blown in the side of Janus. The menacing bulge of Detroit visible outside was in shadow and there was nothing but the faint glow of starlight from the part of the sky that wasn't obscured by Detroit, to raise scattered highlights among the almost total darkness that enveloped the chamber she was looking out into, and the parking area for the bugs below.

Immediately in front of her the catwalk was blocked by a mass of tangled wreckage that appeared to have fallen from somewhere above. If she kept low on the floor, she could probably use it as cover and get out onto the catwalk without being noticed by the soldiers, who were now farther along to her right. She moved her head closer to the hole and followed the line of the catwalk with her eyes as far as she could trace it into the gloom. It seemed to be twisted and buckled, offering plenty of shadow to conceal somebody worming along toward the platform. But what if there were more soldiers in the shadows than the two she had seen? What if they were using infrared viewers or image intensifiers? She'd stand out like an iceberg on the ocean. She felt clammy but at the same time cold inside her suit. Lying here and wondering about it wouldn't change anything. She drew a long, unsteady breath and turned to prop her back against the wall while she unfastened the range-finder bag and peeled it away from the aluminum case. She turned back onto her stomach, drew the case up alongside her, and slowly inched her way over the lip of jagged metal at the bottom of the hole and out onto the catwalk.

Five minutes later she had reached a point that was in deep shadow between a section of crazily tilted catwalk plates and the remains of part of the lower edging of the window and the adjacent wall. From there she was looking out into space, directly up under the black roof of the Spindle and across at the hanging bulk of Detroit. She was acutely conscious of the absence of anything behind her to block the line of sight from where the soldiers were still presumably lying, but she had no choice but to trust to the depth of the shadows for concealment. She snapped open the case, located by touch the two Gremlins in their launch tubes, and attached them to the floor supports in a position that gave them a clear line of fire up toward the midpoint of the Spindle. Then she slid the sighter out of the case and crawled back to a darkened vantage point twenty feet or so farther to the left.

As she eased herself into a comfortable firing position, she noticed something moving on the very edge of Detroit, just where its outline blacked out the starry sky beyond. She stared, puzzled for a moment, and then realized that the object was not on Detroit, but farther away, rising into view from somewhere behind it to the south. As it detached itself from the solid curve of Detroit's bulk and moved on outward and down in the direction of the Rim, she saw that it was a thin rod-shaped device that thickened into irregular shapes at the ends and appeared cluttered by smaller disks and cylinders in between. She didn't recognize it as being like anything she had seen before but she knew that all kinds of unexpected things had been happening during the time she had been out of action. Obviously it was something to do with *Spartacus*. All the more reason not to waste any time.

Her breath came in short, tense gasps inside her helmet as she laid the sighter into a notch between two pieces of warped structural tubing and moved her head into line behind the eyepiece. She flipped on the sighter's intensifier and at once details of the hitherto featureless black mass of the Spindle became clearly visible. The twin rings of the Spin Decoupler moved into the viewing field. Kim nudged a button to brighten up the cross hairs a fraction and then centered them on her target.

She saw the flash from the corner of her eyes as the Gremlin streaked away. An instant later the whole center portion of the Decoupler ring disappeared in a blaze of whiteness. She kept her eyes glued to the sighter and her body tensed. Part of the near half of the ring, which was stationary relative to the Hub, had been blown away between two severed ends that terminated at the jagged hole that had appeared in the north Spindle surface. But the ring had not jammed! Even as she watched she could see the far portion of the hole and the gap in the south ring sliding inexorably onward and up on its endless journey around the Spindle of Janus. Perhaps her aim had been slightly off.

She was certain there had been a tremor. For one tiny moment at the instant the Gremlin had struck, she was sure she had seen the rings falter as something snatched. But now they were sliding smoothly again. Janus was still intact. *Spartacus* was still there, still five hundred feet away from her inside the monstrous ball of darkness that was staring in at her across a thin wisp of empty space. Almost . . . she breathed to herself. Almost . . . Surely one more would be enough.

The floodlights came on and drenched the scene in sudden dazzling brightness.

Kim whirled her head to look back over her shoulder. The two soldiers on the catwalk were on their feet, both with weapons aimed straight at her. A third, whom she hadn't seen before, rose up a few feet farther along from them and began making unmistakable gestures for her to get up. No doubt they were shouting at her too, angrily from the look of the third's actions, but Kim had switched off the radio in her suit. She made no move to turn it on but cast her eyes quickly around. Three more figures in suits were standing farther away along the catwalk in front of another door from which they appeared to have just emerged. They were looking not at Kim but at the three soldiers who had been manning the observation point. Kim couldn't make out what was happening. The three new figures were waving their arms and seemed to be protesting about something while the two soldiers Kim had seen previously continued to stand motionless with their rifles trained on her, apparently heedless of whatever the others were saying to them. The third soldier was between the two groups and kept turning his head from one side to the other as if unable to make up his mind about something.

A slow throbbing vibration was building up in the floor beneath her. She could feel the plates pulsing through her suit as if the whole structure of Janus were being shaken by an invisible mighty hand.

The Decoupler had snatched, she realized. The first shock waves were arriving after being transmitted along the Spindle. And then the vibrations died away again as the tremor passed.

Kim lay on her side and stared up into the muzzles of the two rifles. She was surprised to realize that she felt calm and somehow strangely detached. Even from that distance she met the steely stares of the soldiers peering out through their visors and down along the barrels of the unwavering rifles and she felt her own eyes turn cold and hard. At the same time a serenity and composure came welling up from somewhere deep inside her. All the terror and the helplessness that she had lived with for so long were being swept away. She could win. One more was all it would take, and then she would be complete again. Nothing would take that away from her now.

Slowly and deliberately, with the strange sensation that her body was being manipulated by some external influence beyond her control, she turned away and brought the sighter up to her cheek. The Decoupler ring moved under the cross hairs and stopped rock-steady at dead center. Slivers of metal sprayed against the outside of her helmet as a bullet gouged into the structure inches away from her head. The fleeting thought went through her mind that it should have been impossible for a trained soldier to miss at that range. Then she squeezed the firing button.

The Gremlin hit the target square at center zero.

There was no detonation.

Dud!

Something inside her broke as she let the sighter slip from her hands and rose numbly to her feet. She turned and looked up at the catwalk but her brain was incapable of registering the sight of one of the soldiers crumpling in a heap against the guardrail and another swinging around to point his rifle downward at him while the third was trying to recover his balance and bring his weapon to bear on Kim. And then another new figure was hurtling down like a cannonball from somewhere above the catwalk.

But Kim was already collapsing slowly to the floor as consciousness gave up the struggle and ceased to function.

◎ CHAPTER FORTY ◎

Up on the dais in the Command Room, Krantz's face had turned ashen while Eric Jassic was pouring out his story. Behind them Danny Cordelle stood, outwardly impassive as ever with his hands on his hips, watching the view of *Spartacus*'s invasion force converging toward Northport. The first wave was coming around the northern curve of the Hub while the second was moving outward to begin rounding the inner reflector ring.

"How long ago was this," Krantz whispered.

"Ray left about ten, maybe fifteen minutes ago," Jassic said. "Nobody knows for sure how long it's been since Kim went. She left a false trail that threw everybody for a while."

Krantz swallowed hard and shook his head disbelievingly.

"A Gremlin? It's ridiculous . . . Where would she get one of those from?"

"You'd better believe it," Cordelle threw in from behind Krantz's shoulder. "Look."

On the screen a pinpoint of light blazed briefly but brilliantly in the shadow between the Hub and Detroit, at a point exactly where the line of the Spin Decoupler would be.

"My God!" Krantz breathed. Next to him, Jassic gasped audibly. They stared speechlessly at the screen waiting for the first sign of the slow pivoting motion that would tell them Janus was beginning to break up. Seconds dragged endlessly by but nothing happened.

"She's there!" Krantz hissed. "She's made it. Half the Army's supposed to be guarding the Hub. How in the name of God could she have gotten through?"

"How many of those things has she got?" Cordelle inquired.

"I don't know," Jassic told him.

"Somebody has to get there and stop her before she tries with any more," Krantz said, recovering from the semistupor that had gripped him. He turned in his seat and called to the dais communications operator sitting a few feet away.

"Get me Operations at the Hub . . . Linsay if he's there." He looked back at Jassic and Cordelle. "That Decoupler might come apart at any moment now. I'm ordering a Rim evacuation."

He was referring to the last-resort measure that had been built in as part of the modifications to insure that there would still be a way out of Janus even if a passage through the Hub were denied. Many parts of the lowermost levels of the Rim were constructed as detachable, self-contained survival capsules that could be launched into space after the lower shield had been dispersed, simply by allowing them to fall through the floor. There were not enough of them to accommodate the whole population, but cabs and elevators could all be used to supplement them if necessary, along with standard survival tents as provided for use in lunar and other extraterrestrial environments. Ideally, these would be released sequentially and synchronized with the Rim's rotation speed to facilitate their location and recovery by the Watchdog ships.

"Have the capsules loaded and prepared for release at any time," Krantz said to Cordelle. Inwardly he was hoping that the order would never have to be given; just two ships would be hard pressed to round up all the capsules before they became hopelessly spread out across thousands of miles of space. On the other hand, if the Decoupler broke or if Linsay's guess about *Spartacus* turning the whole Rim into a gigantic X-ray tube came true, there would be little hope anyway.

The communications officer interrupted from behind him.

"General Linsay hasn't arrived at Operations yet, sir. I have Major Seymour on channel four." Krantz looked down and activated screen four on his console. The major was looking out through the open visor of a spacesuit. His eyebrows lifted inquiringly as he recognized Krantz's face.

"No time to explain," Krantz snapped. "There's a woman in Section 17D with a Gremlin—M & S Unit there. Send a squad in and grab her, *fast*. Report back to me as soon as you've got her. Her name's Sinclair." Without asking questions, the major promptly relayed the order to somebody offscreen. A few seconds later he looked back at Krantz and reported: "We've contacted the command post at 17D. They're doing it now." Behind him on the screen there were signs of excited figures rushing in various directions. Distant sounds of shouting and barked commands came through on the audio.

"Those *Spartacus* ships are getting pretty close," Cordelle commented. "Where the hell are the missiles?" The wall display showed that the first two hippos and their flock of drones were almost at Northport.

At that instant a voice from the Command Floor called out: "Strike launched!"

Fifteen missiles came in from the Watchdog ships standing off in space. Three got through to destroy both the hippos of the first attacking wave and one of the electron tubes. A ragged cheer went up from parts of the room. It was short-lived. Seconds later, four missiles arced out of Detroit, avoided the spokes and obliterated Northport.

The third hippo moved from the inner ring toward the wreckage; the way in was wide open and there were no more missiles to stop it. More drones were closing in on the Hub from all directions.

Krantz gazed horrified at the hole that now gaped in the north pole of the Hub. When he moved his eyes back to the console in front of him, screen four was blank. Krantz frowned at it in momentary bemusement.

"They were at Northport," Cordelle reminded him.

In a communications room at one end of the White House, Nash, Belford and Schroder stood tight-mouthed around a screen showing the transmission being sent back from the ISA command ship, as hundreds of tons of wreckage spun away into space in all directions from where Northport had been.

"Those weren't firecrackers," Belford said when he had recovered sufficiently from the shock, "Look. It's moving itself out of Janus already and it's got missiles that'd take out a city block! It's burning our missiles out with X-rays—something we never thought of. It's got drones that work in space and we haven't. What next? We've got to stop it now, Vaughan! We've got two of our ships there. What if it hits them next with whatever it used just then? They're not equipped for antimissile operations."

Nash was still getting over the shock of watching Northport's destruction and seemed undecided.

"What do you say?" he asked Schroder. The CIM secretary gazed at the screen for a long time, and at length shook his head.

"It's still concentrating on Janus itself," he said. "If it takes the Hub there's still a chance for the people in the Rim. We've got five more ships on the way right now. Give them a chance too. If they could get in close and saturate *Spartacus*'s defenses, there's a chance they could take Detroit apart piece by piece from the outside in, without risking the whole structure, until the system stops running. It's maybe fifty-fifty, but while there's a chance at all we have to take it. If you're worried about the two ships out there, tell them to move back. There's nothing they can do now until the rest get there anyhow."

Belford looked unhappy but said nothing. Nash thought over Schroder's arguments, nodded curtly and spoke to the officer seated in front of the bank of communications equipment that took up one wall of the room.

"Order Commander Stalley to take his ships back out to fifty miles and rendezvous with Miller's squadron there. Then get me an update on when Miller thinks he'll arrive."

The officer operated a key and spoke into a permanently open channel to ISA Headquarters.

"Relay orders to Watchdog to move Watchdog One and Watchdog Three out to Position Blue, effective immediately. Watchdog to rendezvous with Z Squadron at Position Blue. Inform Z Squadron Leader of revision to plan. Confirmations required."

The officer cut the screen and brought up a display of the latest predictions from the computers at Mission Control. He keyed in a sequence of commands to update the computers on the revised situation. A few seconds later some of the numbers changed.

"Z Squadron arrival time at Position Blue estimated at three hours, twenty-seven minutes from now, allowing for course change," he reported.

Nash looked up at the clock above the door and resumed pacing back and forth from one end of the silent room to the other.

❂ CHAPTER FORTY-ONE ❂

When Dyer came out of the elevator at the top of the Downtown spoke, he noted with some degree of satisfaction that the flow of evacuees through that area of the Hub was being handled swiftly and the arrival concourse was filled mainly with battle-ready units assembling to move out. The direct route through the Hub to 17D promised to be congested so he steered west to take the longer but probably quicker roundabout way, through the circular thoroughfare that interconnected the terminal concourses of the spokes. Moving fast in long, shallow bounds, he passed through the terminal areas of the Rocky Valley and Berlin spokes and soon found himself ascending the steadily steepening corridor toward 17D.

The leader of a detachment of marines waved him to a halt as he reached the bulkhead door at the top of the stairs that formed the end of the corridor.

"Don't tell me," the soldier said. "You're another one of the reconnaissance unit that got split up in the Hub, right? The others have gone on ahead." Dyer frowned his noncomprehension, but the soldier went on. "The woman with the ranger went through on her own about ten minutes ago. The others are only just in front of you. You'll need to seal up. It's zeroed the other side of the lock." Two other marines were already starting to open the nearer of the double doors. Half guessing what must have happened, Dyer merely nodded, secured his visor and turned on the system in his suit.

"Radio check," he muttered impatiently.

"Loud and clear." The marine's voice came through inside his helmet.

"What's the fastest way to the M & S Unit?" Dyer asked as he stepped into the lock.

"M & S?" The soldier sounded surprised. "The others didn't tell me they were going there. The fastest way is to make a sharp right as soon as you get through the lock. There's a big vent duct with the maintenance hatch blown off. Go through the duct and follow it up and through to where it's busted. It comes out right over a catwalk inside the M & S. Should gain you a coupla minutes. The normal way through's a bit of a mess."

"Thanks."

"Try and hurry them up in there too. We're getting reports that things are happening again. You'll be on the outside there. Could get rough."

"I will."

Dyer came out of the lock and into the twilight metal wilderness that was 17D. He used his lamp to locate the hatch into the duct and hauled himself in with a smooth pull of his arms. The duct rose vertically for about fifteen feet and then curved around and over to lead outward toward the periphery of the Hub. A hazy rectangle ahead of him marked where the duct was fractured. It enlarged slowly as he approached. He stopped himself where the jagged edges of metal stuck out into empty space and moved his head forward to peer into the gloom. The space immediately below him was in total darkness but on the far side there was an enormous blown-out window framing a sinister shadowy silhouette of Detroit. Then the sound of somebody talking came through on his radio. The voice was Chris's.

"I can't see her anywhere. It's too dark. I can't see anything."

"Are you certain she only got one Gremlin that works?" Laura's voice came in, sounding worried.

"Absolutely." This time it was Ron. "We only had two. We stripped the warhead out of one of them because we were gonna try flying it to figure out the control codes. It'll fly but it's harmless."

Dyer strained his eyes in an effort to locate them, but without any directional clues to guide him he didn't even know which way to look. He was about to announce his presence when another voice sounded on the frequency. It was harsh and authoritative.

"Who's there? You people who are talking, identify yourselves and make yourselves visible."

At that instant a stream of flame erupted from a point immediately below the edge of the window and vanished into space. A moment later a blaze of light lit up part of the black bulk of the Spindle that roofed the scene outside.

"What in hell's going on?" another unfamiliar voice shouted.

Then Chris again: "Oh Christ, she's here! She's done it!"

"Somebody's trying to take out the Decoupler!" the challenging voice barked. "We've got crazy people in there! Solinsky, hit the lights."

An array of arc lamps came on at once and flooded the scene below with light. There were six figures in spacesuits on a wreckage-strewn catwalk that ran along the side of the wall that the duct protruded from, about fifteen feet below where Dyer was crouching. He immediately identified the three grouped together slightly to his right as Laura, Chris and Ron. Two more, clad in the lightweight suits that many soldiers preferred for combat dress, were standing to his left with their rifles trained toward the twisted remains of a platform on the far side of the work bay below, at the base of where the window had been. A third soldier was standing between the two groups beside a portable communications pack and switch panel, that he had obviously been watching. He was gesturing angrily in the direction in which the other two were aiming. His voice came through on Dyer's radio.

"You out there over the airlocks. You are being covered. Don't make any sudden moves. Leave the sighter and stand up slowly with your hands raised."

It was Kim. She was lying between two heaps of buckled metal and looking back at the catwalk but without making any response. Either she wasn't taking any notice or her radio was switched off.

"You've got three seconds," the voice of the first soldier warned. "Then we shoot. One!"

"Don't!" It was Chris. "Mat Solinsky, is that you? That's Kim Sinclair out there. She's sick. She hasn't got any more shots."

"She can't do any harm now!" Laura shouted desperately as the postures of the two riflemen tensed. The third soldier was turning to look first at Chris, then at the other soldiers and back again.

"Chris! What the hell are you doing here? That's Kim . . . Kim from the University? Is she crazy? Hey guys, she's okay! I know these people!"

A tremor came suddenly from somewhere and the floor shook beneath their feet. After a second or two it passed. Kim was still lying motionless and staring back into the unwavering rifles from across the chasm of the work-bay. Then, almost contemptuously, she turned calmly onto her stomach and raised the sighter to her shoulder.

"She's got another one!" a voice yelled. "Shoot!"

"No!" The soldier whom Chris had addressed as Solinsky launched himself from the guardrail and catapulted into the other two just as one of them fired. Muttered curses and profanities came over the radio. From the window a second Gremlin leaped away. The figure that had fired at Kim wrenched himself away and clubbed Solinsky back against the rail with the butt of his weapon. Then he began reversing the gun to bring it into a firing position. At the same time the other was recovering his balance and wheeling to aim at Kim. Dyer had no time to wonder whether or not Uncomme methods worked against opponents on lightweight ISA suits as he hurled himself down from the mouth of the duct, at the same time curling his right leg up tight beneath his body like a compressed spring.

The edge of his boot arrowed into its target between the hip and the rib cage just above the belt. A sound that began as a shout of pain and surprise cut off abruptly as an agonized gasp sounded in his ears. The soldier's body crashed into the guardrail and doubled over, but Dyer was already pivoting on his other leg to meet the figure that had beaten off Solinsky. He was six feet at least and looked solid. His rifle was already coming up fast to fire from the hip. Dyer registered the foot set slightly ahead of the other, leg almost straight—perfect target for going in low under the line of fire with a side-kick that would tear every tendon at the back of the knee. In the same thousandth of a second the computer in his head rejected it.

As his body feinted a move to the right, his leg swept a circle behind him to prepare for an abrupt change of direction. As the muzzle of the rifle came around to meet him, he drew his body up into a curve and drove in sideways to scrape the barrel with the front of his belt, turning simultaneously to draw the soldier's arm forward with his own right arm while his left shot over the other's shoulder to become a rigid bar across his visor. With his head encircled by Dyer's arm, the soldier was bent double backward across the knee driving up into the small of his back. The chest panel of his suit was pulled high to uncover his middle; Dyer's right arm stretched high into the air, fist clenched, and then jackknifed into a pile driver tipped by a rock-hard elbow encased in taut spacesuit that plunged into the exposed solar plexus.

It had taken not more than three seconds. Dyer had delivered two blows and two figures were lying draped across the wreckage and out of action. He unfolded the first soldier from the rail and sat him down in a heap to recover while Chris helped Solinsky to his feet and Ron took off toward Kim, who had collapsed on the platform below the window. Dyer's mental replay of the data that his senses had been recording told him that the second Gremlin hadn't exploded. Before he could wonder further about it, Laura was beside him and peering into his visor.

"Ray, it's you! You show up in the strangest places. Where on Earth did you learn that stuff? Are you okay?"

"I'm fine. I'll tell you all about it some other time." He glanced at Solinsky, who was leaning against the rail and massaging a shoulder through his suit.

"How's it feel?"

"I'll live . . . bit bruised, that's all. And, ah . . . thanks."

"How's Kim?" Dyer asked.

"She's out," Ron's voice told him from the far side of the bay. "I'm not sure if I oughta move her. Wanna come over here and take a look?"

The soldier who was slumped with his back to the rail moved an arm to clutch feebly at his side.

"Ohh . . . Jesus!" The words came fragmented through the laboring noises of paralyzed lungs fighting for breath. "What . . . happened . . . ? I've been hit."

"You'll be okay," Dyer said. "Just take it easy. Your pal's out but he isn't hurt. Sorry, but there wasn't time to argue. We'll explain it all later."

With an audible wince, Solinsky vaulted the rail and sent himself along in a low, flat trajectory to land beside Ron, who was kneeling next to Kim. Dyer and Laura paused long enough to exchange well-what-do-you-know? looks and then followed. Chris stayed on the catwalk to keep an eye on the still unconscious soldier and his groaning companion.

Kim was pale behind her visor and showed no signs of life or movement. There was no break anywhere in her suit, however, which meant that at least she hadn't been hit by the shot. The worst fears having been allayed, Ron eased her onto her side, plugged his viewpad into a test socket on her backpack and rapped in a stream of code. A set of curves appeared on the screen.

"Her life-support's cycling," he announced in a relieved voice. "It's faint and shaky, but at least she's breathing."

"Don't anybody move!" A new voice made them all look up at once. About half a dozen soldiers were pouring out of the doors and onto the catwalk. "We're looking for a woman by the name of Sinclair. Orders are to bring her in. Is she here?"

"She's here," Dyer replied. "She won't be any trouble now. Ron, go back and explain what's happened. We'll bring Kim." Ron nodded once and headed back to where Chris and the soldiers were standing. Dyer and Solinsky began lifting Kim gently off the floor—all four pounds of her, complete with suit, while Laura collected the Gremlin sighter and its case.

"Better make it fast," the same voice went on. "*Spartacus* is attacking the Hub from all directions right now. Northport's just been hit bad. We're gonna have to get outa here."

But it was too late. Even as the speaker finished, another soldier shouted a warning and the others launched a barrage of infantry rockets and automatic fire at the space above where Dyer, Solinsky and Laura were still standing with Kim. Something exploded over their heads and sent a hail of debris into the surrounding walls.

"Get down off the ledge!" Dyer yelled. "We're sitting ducks up here. Get down by the locks." Holding Kim between them, he and Solinsky dived from the platform down into the bay in front of the doors of the airlocks that admitted the bugs. Laura was right behind them. Attacking space drones, possibly attracted by the light, were swooping in above them firing shells and flame at the opposite wall. Dyer had confused impressions of figures backing through the doors from the catwalk and firing as they retreated . . . somebody heaving a body up off the floor and hauling it away . . . explosions, bullets . . . a dismembered body spraying jets of red as it cartwheeled away . . . And then something large nosed into the opening above and drenched the catwalk in a sea of flame.

Miraculously, the attackers hadn't directed their attention down into the bay below the window yet. That situation would last for seconds at the most. Dyer looked around desperately and saw the open inner door to one of the bug airlocks at the same instant as Solinsky did. Solinsky hurled himself through with Kim's inert body hooked in one arm while Dyer scooped Laura off her feet and followed in the same bound. The door slammed shut behind them moments before the first inquisitive drone began turning its scanner lenses downward.

◎ CHAPTER FORTY-TWO ◎

Linsay reached the Hub to find the whole command structure disintegrating into panic. Northport had been devastated only minutes before and along with it the Hub Operations Room and its full complement of staff. Whole companies without officers or orders were streaming back into the core of the Hub while *Spartacus* assaulted the outside with swarms of drones and a new type of giant flamethrower that perched like a stinging wasp to clear the outermost compartments of the structure by injecting its nozzle through holes blown in the surface. Meanwhile a separate invasion force was being landed from the catcher ship into the ruin of Northport and simultaneously a new attempt had begun to move north out of the Spindle. The situation was hopeless—an encirclement in three dimensions.

But Linsay had forgotten the meaning of the word; his moment in history had arrived.

Within minutes he had assembled a working staff group and gotten them organized to go back and reverse the flow of men scrambling to get away down the spokes. He was everywhere at once, directing the emplacement of wire-guided missile racks, reforming scattered units and distributing them for defense in depth, ordering revised fire plans and pulling fresh teams forward to plug gaps. Behind Northport he threw together lines of infantry equipped with bazookas who fell back alternately behind mutually supporting massed rocket barrages until the waves pouring from the catcher ship were exhausted. All around the Hub he ordered a general fallback to an inner perimeter sphere after the outer layers had been mined with wire and laser-triggered booby traps; *Spartacus*'s losses mounted and its advance slowed. His mood percolated swiftly down through the chain of command he had established and a renewed determination took hold of the defenders of the Hub.

By the time the new lines had stabilized themselves, *Spartacus* was in possession of all of the Hub above latitude sixty degrees north as well as the inner ends of the Downtown, Paris and Vine County spokes and virtually the whole of the outside Hub. Linsay established an "inner defense box" around the inner regions of south Hub, where he at once called his improvised retinue of chiefs-of-staff and proceeded to set in motion the plan that had begun forming in his head even before he had left the Command Room in Downtown.

"The Water Recycling Plant and the Cab Depot Area are to be fortified for defense at all costs," he told them. "I want every drive motor and steering motor that still works brought here. Strip 'em out of the bugs, buses, minishuttles and anything else that moves . . . get 'em from spares allocations . . . I don't care where they come from but get 'em here. I want one of the one-hundred-thousand-gallon tanks and one of the ten-thousand-gallon tanks from the plant drained and ripped out. Get every ounce of explosive here that can be spared, two-inch rockets and Gremlins. And sandbags . . . lots of sandbags. Clean out the dump and bring whatever isn't in bags loose in whatever'll carry it. If you have to, tell the people down at the Rim to shovel it outa the shield and send it up the tubes. Okay, let's move it."

Everybody around him jumped into action at once; there was no time for questions. Then he called for a connection to Krantz.

"What's happening at the north end?" Krantz asked.

"It's in and we lost some of the Hub there, but we're holding," Linsay told him. "It took a lot of losses and it's pulled what it's got left off attacking and put them on foraging." Krantz looked puzzled. Linsay explained, "It's tearing apart whole sections of what's left at Northport and loading it all into the hippo it's got parked there.

Looks like it's cannibalizing the place to keep itself supplied with raw material. Must be feeling the pinch since the moonrock stopped arriving. What's the score down there?"

"We're worried about the missiles it used on Northport," Krantz said, looking true to his words. "If it's making more, it might decide to fire the next batch at the Rim. We're preparing defensive positions around the bases of the spokes in case it comes down that way and we're putting everybody who isn't needed there into shelters or capsules. We've started depressurizing the Rim because of the risk of explosive decompression."

"What's the latest on Z Squadron?" Linsay asked.

"Due in just over two hours. Why?"

"I'm gonna need a diversionary missile strike. I'll fix H-hour for the assault at two hours, ten minutes from now."

"Assault?" Krantz was incredulous. "Have you gone mad? You've only got three of the spokes left. Your only way out is through the Rim and the only way to the Rim is by the spokes. Get out, for God's sake, while you've still got the chance."

"I don't need the spokes," Linsay said. "I'm not going to the Rim. I'm going to Detroit."

"That's ridiculous. You've already tried and look what happened. And that was while you still had all of the Hub. You'll never even get into the Spindle now."

"I don't need the Spindle either," Linsay replied. "We're going in the way MacArthur did at Inch'on—Korea, 1950 . . . all out for total surprise with a landing way behind the enemy lines. What's the use of hanging onto the Rim when it might get blown out from under your ass any minute? There's only one way to solve this now."

"If Janus stays in one piece," Krantz retorted. "Did you get the girl?"

"What girl?"

"Kim Sinclair."

"What about her?"

Krantz gave a despairing groan.

"She went up to the Hub on an insane solo mission to jam the Decoupler with a Gremlin. Nobody here knew about it. Ray and some others went after her but I had a squad sent in to grab her in case the others were too slow in getting there. Operations were handling it before . . . before they were overwhelmed. We think she managed to fire one but we don't know what happened after that. That must have been something like an hour and a half ago. You mean you don't know anything about it?"

Linsay shook his head.

"I've been kinda busy up here. Where was she heading?"

"According to my information, Sector 17D. We're sure we saw a Gremlin fired from somewhere around there too . . . a couple of minutes before Northport got hit."

"Who went there besides Ray and Kim?" Linsay asked. Krantz told him.

"Just a second." Linsay turned away to consult one of his officers. When he turned back to face the screen his expression had suddenly become grim.

"Sector 17D was hit pretty bad," he said. "We've had to pull right back out of that area. We don't have anybody there at all. If they were there when you say they were there, it looks like bad news. Nobody who didn't get out could still be alive in there, and they weren't listed among the ones who got out. Sorry, Mel, it doesn't look too good."

"I see." Krantz cut off the connection and stared blankly at the screen. Behind him Danny Cordelle had paused in his task of organizing the Rim defenses to listen. He clicked his tongue and shook his head dubiously.

"Never believe bad news till it's lookin' ya in the face," he advised philosophically. "Y' never can tell . . ."

✺ CHAPTER FORTY-THREE ✺

Dyer lay motionless on his stomach behind the twisted tailwheel assembly of the bug and stared out at the crescent of brightness moving almost imperceptibly across the surface of Detroit. The bug had apparently been crash-landed into the lock, presumably at some time during the first battle of the Hub, and had skewed around and become wedged in the airlock with its tail section jamming the outer door to leave a gap about three feet wide to the outside. Dyer had been lying well back from the edge and staring out through the gap for almost an hour without saying anything.

Behind him in the semidarkness of the lock chamber, the other three were sitting against the wall below the squat body of the bug. Kim was propped against Solinsky's shoulder, inside the protective circle of his arm. She had recovered consciousness sometime earlier, but seemed content just to lie still and wait for whatever was going to happen. On the few occasions when she spoke, she seemed dreamily detached from the situation around her as if, somehow, none of it really mattered anymore. On the far side of her a vague shape marked where Laura was sitting silent but alert in almost total darkness with an M25 lying ready across her thighs.

The bug had contained a small stock of unfired Gremlins, some of which Dyer had set up in the gap by the lock door using a couple of pieces of metal cowling wedged into the wrecked tailgear as a blast shield. He didn't really know what purpose this was supposed to serve but it seemed a more sensible thing to do with the missiles than leaving them inside the bug. Since then they had been able to do nothing but sit and wait behind the closed inner door of the lock. They didn't even know what they were waiting for; for all they knew, the whole issue might already have been decided. The only way to find out would be to open the inner door and go and see, but that would be instant suicide if things had been decided the wrong way. So they sat . . . and waited.

"This isn't getting us anywhere," Dyer said at last. "We could die of old age shut up in here." He was speaking via the wire connections that they had strung between sockets in their suit-packs to avoid the risk of revealing their presence by radio.

"What do you want to do?" Solinsky's voice came back over the circuit. "Mail a letter to somebody?"

"I've been thinking about something," Dyer said.

"What?"

"In the original plans for Icarus C, the main solar collector, conversion plant and Earthward microwave transmitter were all supposed to go at the south end . . . onto the other side of Pittsburgh, but none of them ever got built."

"So?"

"Some big shafts were put in to carry cables and stuff through from there to the Hub end of the Spindle. The shafts were never used. They were sealed off when Icarus C was changed to Janus. Those shafts are still there . . . inside the core of the Spindle. They go right through the middle of Detroit."

A few seconds of silence ensued. Then Laura's voice came through.

"What are you saying—it could be a way into the fusion plant?"

"It's a thought," Dyer replied. "If the war isn't all over, most of the Spindle must be way behind the front line by now. Maybe *Spartacus* isn't paying too much attention to its rear, If somebody could get inside the main shaft somewhere, there's a good chance he'd have a clear run through to the fusion plant, especially if he got in south of the Sleeve."

The Sleeve was a cylindrical recess located at the axis of the southern part of the Spindle, into which a rotating extension of north Spindle projected through the Decoupler disk. Within the Sleeve were arrangements for coupling pipes and electrical cables via sliding ring joints and various commutator linkages, and for automatically moving cabs inward or outward between tubes terminating inside and outside the Sleeve.

"*Spartacus* might already be inside those shafts," Solinsky pointed out. "How do you know it hasn't found out about them? It seems to have found out about pretty well everything else."

"I don't," Dyer conceded. "But I think there's a fair chance. The shafts are right inside the core and the core's got all kinds of stuff plastered around the outside. To get inside, it'd have to rip out too many connections that it needs. Why should it bother?"

"Curiosity," Solinsky offered. "It's curious about everything."

"But hell, it's a chance." The sound of a sharp release of breath signaled Dyer's exasperation with the position they were in. "We can't just stay sitting here waiting for somebody else to show up or do something. There might not *be* anybody else."

"So how are you going to get there?" Laura asked. "How are you going to get into the core south of the Sleeve when we can't even open the door?"

"I'm not talking about going back into the Hub and down the Spindle," Dyer replied. "I'm talking about going in from the *outside*. Kim's given us a way in—right at the Decoupler. It's the ideal place."

"But you still have to get there," Laura said again. "How are you going to do it? You can't use the bug. It's a write-off."

"Even if you could, *Spartacus* would pick you off the moment you got off the surface," Solinsky pointed out.

"Why go off the surface?" Dyer asked. "Why not *climb* there?"

"*Climb* there? You're crazy!"

"Why?" Nobody had a ready answer. Dyer went on, "The Hub's just one big mess on the outside now so you wouldn't have any problems finding holds. You'd need to go up the outside of the Hub and along the Spindle to the Decoupler. You'd feel like a fly on the ceiling for the last part, but at Spindle weight you'd probably be okay."

"You can't go outside!" Solinsky protested. "Even if this side is still in shadow, *Spartacus* has got eyes in infrared. It'd see you from Detroit."

"I'm not sure it'd be so easy," Dyer said. "I'll bet that the attack that hit this place must have been part of a big assault all over the Hub. There must be heat leaking out through the surface all over it . . . probably will be for hours. If you looked across from Detroit in infrared, all you'd see would be random patterns all over the Hub. Something radiating at body heat as small as a person and stuck to the surface would get lost in all that. It'd be like trying to pick out a glowworm on the Fourth of July. I think there's a good chance."

"Every suit leaks some water vapor and CO_2," Solinsky objected. "If the surface of the Hub is radiating, *Spartacus* will detect the absorption bands and send something to find out what's causing it. It's got detectors sensitive down to a few hundred molecules."

"The water system in the bug was wrecked when it crashed," Dyer replied. "It's been evaporating water out into space for hours. All the explosions that have been going on will have thrown out water, CO_2, sulfur oxides and all kinds of stuff. The space between here and Detroit is probably polluted with all kinds of dispersing molecules . . . enough to bury whatever comes out of a suit anyhow. I tell you, it's the only chance we've got."

The debate went on for a while but in the end Solinsky agreed that it might just work, and besides that, as Dyer had said, there wasn't anything else. It was obvious that Kim couldn't go and leaving her on her own was out of the question. Solinsky's shoulder had been stiffening and he accepted without much fuss Dyer's and Laura's insistence that he should be the one to stay behind. Dyer ripped out fifty feet of wiring from the bug to act as a safety line between himself and Laura, and found in the tool kit some clips designed for attaching tools to spacesuit belts, two of which he improvised into snaplinks for the ends. Then he taped fifty feet of communications wire along the line and attached suit connectors to it. After that they selected some other items from the kit that looked as if they might come in handy, loaded themselves up with M25 ammunition clips and grenades, and announced themselves ready to go.

Dyer peered into Kim's visor and gave her shoulder a reassuring squeeze. In the pale light coming in from the sunlit part of Detroit, he could see that her eyes were open but her expression was empty and distant.

"Can you hear me, Kim?" he asked. The corners of her mouth flickered into an attempt at a smile.

"Hi," she managed faintly.

"It's gonna be okay," he told her. "You just take it easy and let Mat take care of you. Okay? We'll have you out of here before you know it."

Kim's mouth opened wordlessly. She licked her lips and tried again.

"Kick its goddam ass . . . hard!" she whispered.

Dyer grinned briefly, squeezed her shoulder again and worked his way back to where Solinsky was lying by the tailwheel of the bug. They gripped hands firmly through their gauntlets.

"I'll do what I can to cover you from here with the Gremlins," Solinsky said. "Give it an extra kick for me, huh?"

"We will," Dyer promised. "You look after her. She's valuable merchandise." With that he unplugged from the common circuit and replaced the connection with the socket dangling from the line already clipped to his belt. "Can you still hear me okay?" he checked.

"Fine," Laura's voice replied. "Looks like we're all set. Try not to run too fast."

Dyer inched his way forward past the tailwheel to the edge of the lock floor and pushed his head cautiously out to survey the area immediately around him. The immense wall of metal was just a dark-gray smear against the blackness, disappearing rapidly out of sight into the shadow above his head. To his right he could see a thin sickle of whiteness etched out against the stars where part of the Rim caught the sunlight from behind. A few objects were moving some distance below him on courses between Detroit and somewhere farther around the Hub. No doubt they belonged to *Spartacus*, but he could only hope that his earlier optimism would prove well founded. He turned onto his back to study the first part of the route.

The lower edge of the window was, he knew, about fifteen feet above the top of the lock door. If he could get up to that, he could then traverse right below the window and beyond it until he had a clear line above him directly up to where the Hub and the Spindle joined. He would just have to take that as it came. He braced his arms across the gap between the outer door and the side of the lock and hauled his few pounds of weight easily up to the top. Bracing a knee across the gap to stop himself slipping back down, he thrust a shoulder outside and pushed an arm up to feel across the smooth expanse of metal over his head. His fingers found the edge of the docking beacon above the airlock door. He took a deep breath and slowly hauled himself up and out, into space and onto the surface of Janus.

❀ CHAPTER FORTY-FOUR ❀

The Cab Depot was located not far in from the surface of the Hub and on the south side, facing Detroit. It was, in effect, a miniature marshaling yard where surplus cabs were collected and subsequently redispersed around Janus via the spokes as fluctuations in traffic patterns demanded. At least, that was what it had been designed for. Hours after Linsay's arrival at the Hub, it had become the scene of preparation for what must have been the most bizarre military operation ever conceived in history.

The end section of the Depot comprised a long, narrow bay in which a number of sections of cab tracks ran side by side for a distance in a direction parallel to the axis of the Spindle. Thus, had the intervening outer structure of the Hub not been in the way, they would be pointing straight out at Detroit. The tracks had been cleared of cabs and on them now stood three rafts, supported on skids constructed from hastily thrown together pieces of structural latticeworks and tubing.

The first raft carried the smaller of the two water tanks taken from the adjacent Recirculation Plant. The tank had been packed with high explosives and carried at its tail end a crudely welded framework to which were attached five small solid-propellant motors, steering jets and a rudimentary remote-control box. It was, in effect, a rocket-propelled bomb.

Immediately behind it on the same tracks was an open frame, similarly equipped with rockets and loaded high with plastic-wrapped bales of powdered moonrock packed around layers of explosive charges.

Behind that was the larger cylinder, twenty feet in diameter by fifty long. Scores of two-inch rocket tubes were being fitted to fire forward from the dense framework of tubing that projected from its front end. A battery of motors was arrayed across another frame at its tail, and inside the rough access ports that had been cut along it at intervals engineers were busily attaching lugs and brackets to secure a web of internal nylon ropework and netting.

Linsay's plan was as simple and direct as it was audacious. First, assuming that Z Squadron arrived on schedule, a barrage of missiles would be fired by the ISA ships at anything moving outside Janus to distract *Spartacus*'s defenses and keep them occupied, at least for the fifteen to twenty seconds that Linsay estimated he needed. Then the whole section of the Hub that lay between the Cab Depot and the outside would be blown away by means of charges planted by volunteers who had infiltrated forward. This would create a clear launch run from the Depot to Detroit. The three outlandish craft of Linsay's invasion fleet would then be fired in rapid succession.

The bomb would impact first and blow a gap through the outer skin into Detroit. The second vessel would follow into the gap seconds behind and explode inside to create a smoke screen. The smoke screen would be formed by the exploding mass of finely powdered rock dispersing in Detroit's zero gravity to form a cloud that would be opaque at all wavelengths used by *Spartacus*'s sensors. Thus, for a few vital minutes at least, *Spartacus* would be blind in that region of Detroit.

The assault wave, comprising two hundred troops and their equipment, would go inside the large tank under the added protection of a layer of sandbags secured behind the metal walls. The rocket barrage from the front of the tank would be fired as a single salvo seconds before impact to neutralize anything of *Spartacus* that might be left functioning after the bomb and the dust screen, and to stir up the screen further. After the rockets had been fired, the framework that had supported them would collapse when the tank impacted and, together with the retro-motor fitted to fire forward, should absorb most of the momentum of the estimated impact velocity of fifty miles per hour. The harnesses and nets inside the tank were for extra shock absorption to enable the assault troops to come out in a fighting condition.

Linsay himself would be the first man out. After that, it would be straight through to the fusion plant without stopping, regardless of losses until they either got there or all died in the attempt. "If you're hit, keep going," he had told them. "If you can't keep going, get outa the goddam way! Once we come out of the tank in Detroit, there won't be any way back."

A naval captain staring out over the activity around the rafts shook his head wonderingly then turned to the major directing a welding team.

"It's the craziest thing I've ever seen in my whole life," he declared. "In fact it's so crazy, it might just damn well work!"

At the far end of the Depot, Linsay was exhorting a sweating crew of engineers to move faster in fitting a bug main drive to the back of the large tank when a worried-looking sergeant bustled through from the communications post that had been set up alongside the tracks.

"Message from the Command Room, sir. *Spartacus* has started landing drones on the outside of the Rim."

Linsay bunched his lips and drew a long breath.

"They'll just have to take care of it themselves now," he said. "We need everybody we've got up here . . . and more." He turned back toward the engineer team. "Come on, come on! Get that fuel line connected. What are you people waiting for—a pay raise? If that motor doesn't fire on schedule you won't be in any position to spend what you're already getting. Move!"

The Command Room was sealed off by the surrounding mass of Downtown from the falling pressure outside in the Rim, but everybody had donned suits as a precaution. Only a skeleton staff was left after everybody else had departed either to the shelters or to join Cordelle's defense lines around the spokes.

Krantz sat at the dais and took in the reports of growing numbers of drones and other contrivances arriving on the outer surface of the Rim. The pressure was now down to such a level that even a major fracture of the Rim would no longer have catastrophic consequences, although considerable damage could still be expected. Krantz was not so worried by the machines on the roof, therefore, as by those on the outer surface of the tread—below ground level, right where most of the people were. Anything could happen, he told himself repeatedly.

And then the reports started coming through of cutting commencing at points beneath Downtown, Berlin and Paris. At the same time the machines were moving around toward the place where they had detected the greatest concentrations of mass. Krantz studied the data beamed in from the telescopic views picked up by the distant ISA ships and smiled to himself as the thought that had been lurking at the back of his mind began to take shape.

"Give them a few more minutes," he said in response to a request for instructions from one of the screens on his console.

He had found sitting here while others fought and died to be more of a strain than he had bargained for. But although at times his emotions had almost taken control, he had managed, he felt, to maintain an acceptable degree of coordination and order in the face of impossible circumstances; now at last he could do something positive to contribute directly to slowing down that accursed machine until Linsay was ready and the Z Squadron arrived. He touched in a command to activate a channel to the controller in the emergency backup station some floors below.

"Confirm status on dispersal firing circuit," he said.

"Ready and standing by," came the reply. Krantz nodded and studied again the figures coming in from the image analyzers aboard the ISA ships.

"Disperse the shield," Krantz instructed.

"Request confirmation to disperse the shield."

"Confirmed."

Thousands of explosive bolts detonated simultaneously all around the outside of the Rim to disintegrate the aluminum shell that retained the four-foot-thick moonrock layer of the cosmic-ray shield.

The entire tread of the Rim turned into a cloud of metal shell-sections and dust expanding out into space like a gigantic smoke ring and carrying with it a complete division of *Spartacus*'s army.

Krantz smiled grimly to himself at the image brought to him on the screen. Now he too had drawn blood from the monster. He felt composed. He could live even with the knowledge of *Omega*. Or die, if that was the way it was to be. But without having been granted even the dignity of making a token gesture of striking back . . . that would have been too much.

◈ CHAPTER FORTY-FIVE ◈

"Are you out of your mind?"

"It's a golden opportunity, I tell you."

"You're crazy. Look, there's absolutely no way I'm gonna—"

"Shut up for one second. Look, everybody's been—"

"But it's insane. You're talking about—"

"Shut up, please."

"But I tell ya—"

"Shut up, Ron! Look, everybody's been looking for ways into Detroit by taking it by storm, and here's *Spartacus* presenting us with one that's staring us right in the face. *Spartacus* might have the whole Hub to itself by now. If there's any fighting still going on it'll be behind us, so we can't go back. Equally obviously, we can't stay here forever. Logically that only leaves one possibility and that's forward. You can't get away from it. So why not do it this way and maybe there'll be a chance to do something really useful if we do get inside. How many times in history has a small unit, moving fast and under cover, got in and done the job when a whole army was bogged down?"

They were lying side by side squeezed into a narrow space beneath the mounting base of a large transformer that fed part of the subway system. The transformer was built, along with some other equipment, in a tight recess that opened out into a darkened section of subway tunnel. By the dim light coming from farther along, they could see the vague outlines of the procession of mangled cabs, smashed machinery, dismantled structural units and all manner of assorted objects moving slowly by on the dragline that was hauling them southward into the Spindle.

After the attack on 17D, the soldiers had fallen back deeper into the Hub in a series of well-rehearsed and speedily executed leap-frogging moves and the attack had ground to a halt against the solid defensive positions prepared behind them. But Chris and Ron, not having been involved in such rehearsals, had found themselves left behind after getting off the catwalk and very soon they were cut off completely in the no-man's-land of the south Hub. After lying low for about thirty minutes in a burned-out gas holder, they had emerged to find that the tide of battle had flowed elsewhere. But they had lost their bearings in the jungle of shadows and forms, none of which bore any recognizable relationship to the neatly labeled models they had memorized at Fort Vokes.

Moving slowly and carefully, they had worked their way upward toward the core, which was the only direction that they could identify consistently. After a couple of close shaves with work details of machines busily tidying up parts of the mess and installing new extensions of the *Spartacus* system, they had eventually arrived at a large open space which they recognized as the freight-distribution point where manufactured items coming through from Detroit had once been sorted and sent on to their various destinations around Janus. That meant they were almost at the axis and not far from where the Spindle and the Hub met.

But the traffic was all moving the wrong way. Machines were bringing in all manner of scrap and attaching it to draglines to be hauled southward, presumably because powered transportation had not yet been restored in that area after the fighting that had been flowing back and forth between the Hub and the Spindle. Chris had made a guess at what was happening—*Spartacus*, running short of raw material, was organizing scavenger units to send back anything that could be turned into something useful. Probably the stream flowed all the way back down to Pittsburgh for remelting and processing.

Clearly they couldn't go on into the freight-distribution area, which was swarming with drones and machines. They tried to work their way past it beneath a section of floor, but found themselves being forced steadily farther around to the south instead of northward as they had intended. Eventually they had come out into the core again at the transformer beneath which they were now still lying, looking directly out into what appeared to be *Spartacus*'s main through line to Pittsburgh.

Then Chris had had his great idea. The stream of scrap for recycling almost certainly flowed straight through the core of Detroit, right at the heart of the enemy stronghold. There, staring them in the face, was a free ride to within a few dozen feet of where the fusion plant was located.

They had been arguing about it ever since.

In the end Ron gave in. They wriggled out to the edge of the transformer pit and waited for a fairly intact cab to appear upstream in the slowly lurching line. Then as it came abreast of them they threw themselves across the four-foot gap that separated it from the floor of the transformer pit, and they landed in a tangled heap down between where the seats had once been.

"Keep down and stay away from the windows," Chris warned. "There's a bright part coming up just ahead."

"Hey, this thing's full of bits of junk," Ron said. "I feel like I'm sitting inside a scrap heap."

"Complain to the management about it when we get off."

Ron's beard shook from side to side behind his visor. "What a hell of a way to run a railroad," he muttered.

Dyer reached out ahead of him and grasped the jagged edge where the lip of the Spin Decoupler ring had been blown away by the Gremlin. He hauled himself closer until he could hook an arm around part of the ruptured outer skin, freed his foot from the tear in which he had wedged it, and brought his leg forward to curl it around the edge of the gaping hole in the surface that formed the immense roof sweeping away on every side above him. Even though his weight was almost negligible this close to the axis, he still retained the distinct slothlike feeling that he had developed in the course of the long climb along the Spindle. At last he rolled himself up and into the hole to lie in a normal position on the inner surface, then sat up and fastened the loop tied in the safety line around a length of projecting spar.

"Okay," he said. "I'm in. You can unhitch and move whenever you like."

He had left Laura hanging below the roof thirty feet back, secured to—of all things—the base of one of the tripod legs that supported some kind of instrument that *Spartacus* had erected. Dyer hadn't seen the thing until he was nearly next to it, by which time he realized that whatever it was had been built to look up off the surface and not down at it, and thus couldn't see him. It had made as good a belay as any, and besides, there had been nothing else handy in the vicinity.

"Okay, I'm unhitched," Laura's voice said in his helmet. "I'm not sorry to get away from this thing either. It gives me the creeps." Dyer smiled faintly and settled back to take in the slack of the line as she climbed across toward him.

The haul up from 17D had been tedious and nerve-racking, but it had gone without incident. Using the scars of battle damage left upon Janus's skin or, where no readymade holes presented themselves, bolts that Dyer jammed into holes that he made with a spring-loaded punch taken from the bug's tool kit, they had worked their way up over the monstrous sweeping curve of the Hub and along the roof of the Spindle to the Decoupler. They had moved singly, with one of them anchored to the structure while the other climbed at the far end of the line.

At one point, when they were nearly at the Spindle, they had watched a lot of Spartacus-controlled traffic moving outward and landing on the Rim. Not long afterward the shield had suddenly broken up and expanded away into space in a spectacular shower of metal and dust as witnessed from their unique vantage point. Apart from that, all had been fairly quiet. Numerous gadgets still hung in the blackness below them between the Hub and Detroit, and others had scuttled back and forth in one direction or another, but none of them had interfered with the two tiny specks clawing their way upward through the ink-black shadow that engulfed the south side of the Hub.

"I'm at the bolt with the wire loop hanging from it," Laura's voice said. "Where do I go now?"

"Are you on the loop?"

"Yes. I've got a foot wedged between the two long bolts."

"Let your foot slip out. Swing on the loop like a pendulum and stretch out right ahead of you as you come up the other side. There's a groove you can jam your fist in. Then let go of the loop and try and wriggle a toe through it. Once you're there you'll only have about ten more feet to go."

A few minutes later she was beside him looking up into the chasm that the Gremlin had made into the Decoupler. Strictly speaking, they were looking into only half of the chasm since the irregular hole terminated abruptly against the smooth wall formed by the south half of the Decoupler system; the other part of the hole was somewhere else as a result of remaining still while they were carried around along with the northern part of Janus. Once every revolution the two parts of the hole were aligned as they had been at the instant the Gremlin struck.

Above them the structure of the outer ring appeared badly damaged but beyond that they could see the enormous windings and magnetic pole pieces that encased the inner ring. And all up one side of the hole, the unbroken wall of the southern half of the Decoupler slid endlessly by. Laura became conscious for the first time that the whole structure around them was pulsating incessantly with throbs from the very heart of the Spindle, as if some unimaginable force were straining to break free from the clutches of titanic counter-forces fighting to hold them in check.

"What you're looking up into is part of the Magnetic Balancing System," Dyer said. "The two halves of Janus are coupled by a system of complex magnetic fields across the gap between the two disks of the Decoupler. The field strengths are altered dynamically to compensate for any imbalance forces that arise from masses being redistributed around Janus, for example when things move around the Rim or inside Pittsburgh or Detroit."

"You mean something like an automobile wheel being out of balance?" Laura asked.

"Right. An unbalanced wheel vibrates. What's supposed to happen here is that sensors monitor the vibration forces from instant to instant and modulate the magnetic coupling fields to just cancel them out. So you end up with a nice smooth rotation."

"It doesn't feel very smooth to me," Laura commented.

"It's not. Something's screwed it. That Gremlin Kim put into it can't have done much good. In fact I'm surprised the vibration's not worse. I've been watching the inner ring yokes up there while I was waiting. The alignment's all gone to hell. By my reckoning it shouldn't be holding together at all. It just doesn't seem possible."

"You mean this whole thing could come apart any second?"

"I reckon it already should have."

Laura digested the information while she checked over the items of equipment that she had brought with her to make sure they were all still there. The vibration in the structure around them suddenly started growing more intense and proceeded to increase rapidly. Dyer caught Laura's arm to attract her attention and pointed at the moving face of the south disk of the Decoupler.

"Watch now," he said.

As the shaking rose to a crescendo, a jagged edge appeared suddenly from behind where part of the north disk had been blown away. The other part of the hole had completed another revolution, Laura realized, and was coming into line once more with the part they were sitting in. The gap widened at a rate of one and a half feet per second until the gash matched through both disks and for a few seconds uncovered a direct opening through into the southern part of the Spindle. The part of the south disk that was now visible, together with much of the reinforcing structures and windings exposed behind it, had been hideously deformed by the Gremlin and in places whole structures were buckled and writhing as they scraped against damaged members protruding across from the north side of the gap. That accounted for the buildup in vibration at this point in the rotation cycle. And then the trailing edge of the south-disk hole moved into view and the way through into south Spindle started to close up again. In six seconds it had gone. The gash in the north disk was once again blocked by a smooth sliding wall and gradually the vibration returned to its former level.

"That's where we have to get through next time it comes around," Dyer said. "I've been timing it. The gap lasts for about thirteen seconds, but it's only wide enough to clear for five, maybe six. At this gravity, a good strong jump off this girder should take you straight up and through without any problem. We'll have to go together in tandem. I'll go first. As soon as I jump wait one second, no more, then go. Make sure you're not trailing any gear that could get fouled up on the sides. Okay?"

Laura felt cold fingers running loose up and down her spine. She swallowed hard and fought down the part of her that wanted to forget the whole thing and settle for a peaceful end to it all out here amid the tranquility of the stars. Dyer had already moved up onto the girder and was standing waiting with his back to her and his arms braced across two struts to give him a firm push-off. As she stepped carefully up to stand behind him, she had to make an effort to thrust out of her mind the images that were trying to form of a writhing body being mashed into pulp between the relentless jagged scissor edges gouged in the Decoupler disks. Dyer sensed the meaning of her silence and started talking again to stop her apprehensions from taking root.

"The computers that control the magnetic system were supposed to be connected through to Phase III of Icarus, which never got built. But the conduit to carry the connections was installed somewhere just inside the south Decoupler disk. It forms an offshoot from the main tube we're trying to get into and I'm pretty sure it ends somewhere out near the edge of the disk. With luck we could find we're not far away from it when we get through. That all depends where it was when Kim fired. At any rate, the branch comes out into the dead-end area here near the edge of the disk and I'm hoping *Spartacus* won't have been too active around there."

The vibration began building up again.

"Here it comes," Dyer said. "Remember that what you land in will be moving relative to what you're standing on now. As you jump, twist so your feet point to the left. You'll be landing at about ten miles an hour." The edge came into sight and the breach began opening again. "Ready?"

"Okay . . . Boy, is Zeegram gonna hear about this!"

Dyer waited until the breach was a couple of feet short of its maximum width and then hurled himself forward and upward with simultaneous thrusts of his arms and legs. The jaws sailed past on either side of him, at the same time turning as his body pivoted slowly to bring his feet around. Shadow enveloped him and his feet struck hard onto something solid. He shot out an arm blindly. It hooked into something and in an instant he had checked his flight and spun himself around into a firm position around a bar. The breach was at maximum and already starting to close, but Laura wasn't through. He could see her sailing toward it on the opposite side. Too slow! She was moving too slow! The wheeling of her body and the trailing leg told him in the same split second that her foot must have slipped as she launched off. He stretched out his arms to grasp the line that still connected them together and heaved with every ounce of strength he could muster. Laura may have weighed only a few pounds, but that didn't change her body's inertia.

She flew through in a flurry of arms and legs and was sent spinning as one of the closing jaws caught her boot. A second later she crashed to a halt in Dyer's waiting outstretched arm. A gasp of suddenly expelled breath came through in his helmet, followed by sounds of heaving and panting.

"Are you hurt?" he asked anxiously.

"*Jeez* . . . gimme a second . . . no, I think I'm okay. Maybe I don't wanna be a scientist after all."

"You'll never make the Bolshoi with that act."

"Maybe the circus could use a new clown."

"Sure nothing hurts?"

"No, I'm okay. Just a bit winded."

"Let's go then."

They had shed the rotational motion of North Janus and were in free-fall. After some searching around, Dyer recognized a gallery that led to the area where the Decoupler computers were situated and near which the branch conduit from the main shaft terminated.

They were almost at the door that led into the computer room when Dyer suddenly shoved Laura hard against the wall behind a projecting corner and cannoned in behind her.

"What?" she whispered.

"Take a look. Careful."

Laura inched her head forward to peer around and along the corridor, then jerked it back quickly. A sphere drone, a flame thrower and an armored cannon were hovering in a tight cluster immediately outside the computer-room door, apparently preoccupied with something inside it. Somehow they seemed to be watching something rather than threatening.

"They weren't looking this way," Dyer said. "They didn't see us."

"So what now?" Laura fingered the M25 that she was holding. "I'm game if you are."

"No," Dyer said. "We've only got feet to go now. Even if we knocked out all three of them the cavalry would be here in no time. The conduit comes out in a sealed-off shaft set back from this side of the corridor." He pointed to a hatch in the wall back along from the corner where they were standing. "We can probably get into the shaft around the back way and through there. Take a wrench and help me get those nuts off."

He was right. Minutes later they were inside the shaft. The conduit cover had not been disturbed and soon they were squeezing along inside the narrow tube that pointed toward the axis. Almost a hundred feet farther on, the tube came out into a wider shaft that ran north-south. It was quite empty and when Dyer extinguished his lamp no telltale patches of light that would have told of the shaft having been opened were visible in either direction.

"This is it," Dyer said. "So far it looks good. From here on we start moving one at a time again. I cut this line to be exactly fifty feet long. You keep one end steady while I move on one length, then you move up and we'll repeat the routine again. Nine hundred fifty feet should put us right under the fusion plant."

❀ CHAPTER FORTY-SIX ❀

The cab hulk lurched to a halt soon after it had been transferred through the Sleeve, which meant they were just inside the south Spindle. A long time seemed to go by without anything happening.

"Reckon I ought to risk a look?" Chris asked eventually.

"Yeah. What the hell?"

Chris eased himself up from the darkness of the stripped-out interior below the level of the window and peeped around the edge into the dimly lit space that now surrounded them.

"Christ!" He recoiled at once and pulled himself back down next to Ron.

"What?"

"There's a flying lobster or something right outside. It looks as if it's unhooking everything from the dragline. It was moving straight at us."

Even as he spoke the cab jolted slightly and tremors through the floor told them something was moving just outside. After a few seconds the tremors stopped and they could feel only the throbbing of the whole structure, which had been building up for some time as they drew nearer to the Decoupler.

"The thing must have moved on down the line," Ron said after a while.

"I'll try another look."

Chris moved back up and this time stayed there to survey their surroundings.

"We've got to get out," he announced.

"Why?"

"We're in *Spartacus*'s scrap yard. There are heaps of rubbish floating all over the place. It's all being cut up into small pieces farther ahead. *Spartacus* must be using the recycling conveyor from Detroit to Pittsburgh farther south. If we wait until it's our turn, we'll be right at the center of where all the attention is. Right now we're near the back. The lobster's shoved off and I can't see anything else around."

"Where to?" Ron asked.

"Dunno. Out of this place for a start. Then we'll have to look around for some other way south."

"Next time you take it into your head to go for a ride, maybe we'll take separate cabs," Ron muttered as he untangled himself from the debris farther back inside.

Using pieces of wreckage as camouflage, they drifted slowly toward one of the walls and left the scrap yard through a web of struts and girders that brought them to a shaft buried behind a wall of piping and machinery. They tried several approaches to move on along the core, but the area they were in was the focal point of all traffic moving between the north and south parts of the Spindle; there was simply too much activity all around them to risk breaking cover. Every attempt ended in their being forced back to the shaft.

"It's no good," Ron said after their third try. "There's no way out of here that leads south. We'll have to take this shaft."

"That goes back toward the outside," Chris objected. "We don't want to go that way."

"It's the only way we can go," Ron insisted. "Look, you wanna get into Detroit, right? Well, we can't get there along the core from here. It's like Times Square out there. But the shaft goes outward just south of the Decoupler. It might be quieter near the edge. Maybe we could follow the edge south for a while, and then maybe work back in when we're nearer Detroit."

This time Chris gave in, and they entered the shaft and began moving outward along the inside face of the south disk of the

Decoupler. They had lost track of distance when they came to a point where the shaft was blocked by some unidentifiable machinery that looked as if it had been installed by *Spartacus*. There was no choice but to back up to the last exit hatch they had passed and leave the shaft there.

They were in a huge curved chamber that was evidently part of a larger circular structure encompassing the whole Spindle immediately south of the Decoupler. Batteries of enormous magnetic windings interspersed with massive yokes, bewildering arrays of insulator mountings and superconducting busbars marched away and around and out of sight in both directions. Next to them, looking out over the panorama through a viewing window, was a local control backup point with deserted consoles whose indicator lamps and displays were still glowing.

"We're at the inner ring of the Decoupler," Ron said needlessly. "This is part of the Magnetic Balancing System."

"It's in trouble too," Chris answered. "Feel it? This is where the vibration's been coming from. Look at the clearances over there. It's all gone to cock."

"Musta been Kim."

"No, there's something wrong. Provided it didn't jam up solid, which it didn't, the computers should be able to compensate even if part of the outer ring's gone. Obviously they're not—not very well anyway. They must have been knocked out."

"There hasn't been any action here."

"Something's not right."

A row of bright-red lights glowing inside the backup point caught Chris's eye. He motioned for Ron to follow and moved in to study them more closely. Frowning, he turned to one of the consoles and tried tapping in a code for a status summary and, much to his surprise, got one.

"You're crazy," Ron told him, "*Spartacus* might be wired into that by now. If it senses input from that it'll know there's somebody in here."

Chris didn't seem to hear. He studied the panel again and brought more data plus a set of trend curves up onto the screen. Suddenly he seemed to have lost all interest in getting farther south toward Detroit.

"Not very long from now, Ron, it won't make any difference what *Spartacus* knows about," he said at last. "Janus isn't far off breaking up."

"What are you talking about?"

Chris waved up at the red indicators.

"They're all way past danger levels. It's been getting worse for over an hour and it's not far off the point where the whole shooting match will shake itself to pieces. The compensating system isn't running. *Spartacus* must have switched it off somehow when it went on strike."

"That's ridiculous," Ron protested. "If the compensating system was down, the Decoupler would have come apart as soon as the Gremlin hit the outer ring."

"I know, but it hasn't and the compensator system isn't running. Something else must be holding it instead."

"Like what?"

"I don't know. It won't hold for much longer, though. This is serious, Ron. We've got to get that system up again quick. To hell with whether *Spartacus* finds out we're here or not. We'll all go up the same creek together anyway if we leave it."

"Figure we could do it from there?" Ron sounded dubious.

Chris shook his head. "No. This is just a slave station. If my memory's right though, the computer room that houses the compensator system should be right next to here."

"It is. It's somewhere behind the bulkhead through that door out there," Ron said, pointing. "We should come up right inside it."

Fifteen minutes later they were both working frantically at the master console inside the computer room. The data on the screens gradually pieced together to tell a strange story.

The connections between the Magnetic Balancing System and the backup computers that were supposed to control it independently of *Spartacus* had been cut sometime before Kim had fired the Gremlin. Presumably this had occurred at the time *Spartacus* had embarked on its campaign of tearing out any cables it came across that didn't serve parts of itself. After that event, continuing movements of objects around inside Janus had caused the imbalance forces to begin building up, but not to any alarming degree. All the same, the trends recorded showed that the vibrations had continued to increase slowly but surely. And then they had stabilized and started to reduce, albeit somewhat erratically. Since the backup computers were still disconnected at the time, that could only mean that some other influence had begun juggling the magnetic compensators in their place. That influence could only be *Spartacus*. It must have sensed the increasing instability of the structure around it, investigated, found the compensators and manufactured its own connections into the magnetic coupler system in an attempt to control it.

Later, after *Spartacus* had secured full possession of the Spindle as far as the Hub and began asserting its presence throughout its domain, the backup computers had been integrated into its net. So they were indeed talking to something that was now part of *Spartacus,* which meant there was a high probability of *Spartacus* having realized already that they were there. There was no point in worrying about that now. They pressed on.

The situation had persisted up to the moment when Kim fired the Gremlin. Immediately after that, an onset of huge vibrations had taken place as the condition of the Decoupler escalated to a whole new level of complexity. *Spartacus* had evidently been able to keep things reasonably steady up to that point, no doubt by pure trial and error without understanding what it was doing; but the combination of fluctuating and irregular forces that had suddenly appeared at that moment must have confused it totally. The trends recorded after the Gremlin impact all indicated that Janus should have come apart within twenty seconds. During that same period, *Spartacus*'s level of internal activity had risen to an unprecedented peak.

Somehow, by a supercomputer effort, *Spartacus* had fought, nanosecond by nanosecond, and played the magnetic couplings to hold the rebelling Decoupler in check. And it had been holding it ever since. But it was slowly losing the battle. The vibration levels were increasing relentlessly and the latest figures showed that it would not be long before the loading limits on the structure were exceeded. When that point was reached, it would all be over.

"I think I can see what's happened," Chris said after about a minute of silence. "The programs that were developed to control the balancing system contained all kinds of complex mathematical expressions to describe the total behavior of Janus as a self-contained system of electrodynamics and mechanics. Those programs are in this computer right here, but this computer isn't connected to the system anymore. It's only connected to some other piece of *Spartacus*. So the programs can't drive the things they were supposed to drive. *Spartacus* is connected to the balancing system, but it's trying to use its own homemade routines instead of the ones in here that were written to do the job and contain all the right mathematics."

Ron looked at him strangely, thought about it, and then nodded his head slowly.

"Could be . . ." he murmured. "Could be . . . What you're saying is, *Spartacus* hasn't realized that there's any connection between this computer, which it just sees as another machine that it found isolated and grabbed, and the job it's trying to do to stop the vibrations. It doesn't know that the routines it needs are in here."

"Right," Chris said. "I bet its problem is that it doesn't have enough *comprehension* yet of Janus as a totality in space. All it knew about until not very long ago was things that went on *inside*. But to work out the balancing equations correctly, it needs to know more about Janus as a whole. It managed a panic effort to stop the whole thing screwing up when Kim put the boot in, but things have been getting worse ever since. There must be too many variables and things building up to dangerous levels and it doesn't understand enough yet to handle them."

"So, what can we do about it?"

"Well, the equations it needs are in this machine, this machine's connected to it, and it's connected to where the programs can do some good. We'll have to try telling it."

"Telling it? What are you gonna do, ask for an audience?"

"All we can do is try using that," Chris said, pointing at the console. "Attract its attention . . . input anything that it might relate to the problem—pictures, diagrams, anything."

"It doesn't speak our language."

"There ought to be something we've got in common," Chris insisted. "Think about how stupid this whole situation is. It's trying to wipe us out and we're trying to wipe it out. But if the Decoupler goes, we both go together anyway. We've got the knowledge to save us both and it's got the means. Neither side can survive without the other. Why are we fighting each other at all?"

Without further ado they got to work. Chris activated the console camera to transmit an image of both of them into whatever part of *Spartacus* the computer was connected to. Surely that would attract its attention if something else hadn't already. Perhaps the act of deliberately announcing their presence would give it something to think about too. They created a schematic diagram of Janus, emphasizing the dynamics of the Decoupler, and sent that in as well. Then they extracted the key equations from the program residing inside the computer and copied those through with emphasis and more symbols and diagrams to signify their relevance.

Chris was still hammering frantically at the console when a movement behind them caused Ron to swing around toward the door.

"Forget it, Chris." Ron's voice was hoarse. "I guess it's all over. The execution squad's arrived."

Chris turned his head. A sphere drone was hovering high in the doorway with its lenses trained on them. Behind it an armored cannon was moving into a firing position while the evil snout of a flamethrower moved up to position itself alongside. Instinctively Ron began raising his rifle, but in the same instant he realized that it was useless. Without thinking why, he opened his arms slowly in a gesture of capitulation and allowed the rifle to tumble away across the room.

The color had drained from Chris's face. He stared numbly at the menacing forms moving slowly toward the doorway, then gritted his teeth and turned back to resume what he had been doing.

Seconds went by. The drones didn't fire. They just hung there, watching . . . almost as if they were responding to a last-minute instruction from somewhere to hold off.

"Chris . . . They're not shooting!" Ron's voice was shaking. "You must be getting through. There's something funny going on."

"There's some kind of response on the screen!" Chris gasped. "It's the diagram of Janus that we put in at the beginning. Some part of *Spartacus* seems to be throwing it back at us. What does it mean?"

"Maybe it's asking for clarification," Ron suggested. "I hope your nerves are in good shape. I'm getting the feeling that we may have to go right through the whole thing again . . . only slowly."

⚙ CHAPTER FORTY-SEVEN ⚙

Kim lay back in the shadow near the outer door of the lock and allowed her mind to wander. She felt calm now, and more at peace than she could remember for many years. Had that really been what her life had become—a tormented mind futilely pitting itself against what had already been done, trying to erase what time had already written? The ghosts in her mind that should have been laid to rest long ago were still at last. They would stir no more.

She reached out and laid her arm on the motionless prone figure behind the tailwheel with the sighter resting loosely near his shoulder. It had taken so long, she thought to herself. Why, now, did it have to be like this?

"You okay?" Solinsky's voice asked in her helmet.

"I'm okay."

"You're sounding a lot better."

"I'm . . . just fine."

A half-hour had gone by since they had watched through the intensifying viewer of the sighter as the antlike figures of Dyer and Laura disappeared into the Spindle high above. Since then *Spartacus*'s steady stream of traffic had continued to plow back and forth between somewhere beyond Detroit and places behind the Hub, but nothing dramatic had happened. Now they could only wait and hope.

"I guess I've caused everybody a lot of trouble," she said after a while.

"This whole place is one big mess of trouble," Solinsky replied without taking his eyes off the scene outside. "If you took away the bit that was yours, or doubled it, I don't figure it'd make much difference. I wouldn't worry about it."

"But if anything happened to Chris and Ron . . . I mean, the reason they came here in the first place was because of me. If anything—"

"Look," Solinsky interrupted. "Don't start going off on another guilt trip. You did what you felt you had to do at the time. That's all everybody else does all the time anyway . . . everybody who's got what it takes to do something, that is. That's all there is to it. And if Ray and Laura do pull something off up there, it'll be because you gave them a way in. Don't forget to put that on your balance sheet too."

"I've been a pain in the ass to Ray too. You wouldn't think a guy like him would have the patience of a saint inside, would you?"

"Oh. How come?"

"Well . . . that's a long story. I used to be mixed up with some guy called Tony. He turned out to be no good and—"

"Shhh . . . ! Something's happening."

Kim fell silent and waited tensely. Solinsky half-rose from behind the tailwheel to peer out of the lock.

"*Spartacus*'s antimissile tubes. They're all turning around as if they're expecting something. It must be a missile strike coming in. The ISA boys must be here!"

Kim crawled forward to lie beside him and looked out to where he was pointing. *Spartacus* must have gone all-out at mass-producing the flying electron guns since its first successful experiments with them. Scores of them were moving out to form a protective barrier around Janus. Brilliant flashes of missiles detonating appeared farther out in space.

"That's the ISA squadron all right," Solinsky declared. "They're not doing a hell of a lot of good, though. Look at the missiles blowing up out there. They're not getting through."

The wall of electron beams that *Spartacus* was putting up was impenetrable. The guns were moving out farther from the Spindle to form an even more solid pattern of overlapping fields of fire.

Whatever the ISA ships were trying to do, it didn't appear that they were going to have much success.

And then a gigantic concussion that seemed to originate not very far away shook the floor beneath them. It was as if the whole Hub had been struck by an enormous invisible hammer.

"What the—" Solinsky began, then cut off abruptly and stared openmouthed.

A storm of debris was erupting from somewhere on their side of the Hub, but farther around. Huge chunks of outer skin and inner bulkheads were cartwheeling away into space, accompanied by swarms of smaller fragments and spinning debris.

"What is it?" Kim shouted in alarm

"I don't know. It looks like something's blown half the Hub away."

"What's *that*?"

An object had come into view from around the curve of the Hub. It had emerged, by the look of it, from the same point at which the gigantic explosion had occurred. It was a cylinder of some kind, with what seemed to be rocket motors blazing from some sort of crazy framework stuck to the tail end. It was heading straight across the gap toward Detroit.

"It's our guys!" Solinsky yelled suddenly. "We must still have people left in the Hub! They're going in! They're going for Detroit! Goddammit, they're going straight in!"

Another object appeared hard on the heels of the first. This time it was an open structure loaded high with some kind of cargo. And behind that, following at a greater distance, came a second cylinder, a huge one this time—fifty feet long at least, Solinsky estimated.

As the tiny fleet reached the halfway point, Solinsky could see that the three craft were spreading slightly into a not quite line-astern formation. They were allowing for the relative rotation between the Hub and Detroit, he realized; with that amount of offset, they would all impact at the same point. He frowned as he watched and tried to figure out what was going on. Suddenly Kim's voice, shrill with alarm, interrupted his thoughts.

"Mat! There are two more tubes coming!"

Solinsky took his eyes off the invasion fleet. Two of *Spartacus*'s electron guns, which for some reason hadn't moved outward with the rest, were coming up from under Detroit and swinging around to bear on the flotilla, which still had to be ten seconds or so away from its destination. Also, something was moving just inside the port that *Spartacus* had constructed in Detroit—the one from which it had previously launched its missiles.

"They'll never make it!" Kim shouted despairingly. "They're going to get caught out there!"

But Solinsky already had the sighter up to his eyes. Even before Kim's shout had ceased, the first Gremlin was on its way. At the same instant as the target blew apart, Solinsky shifted aim and fired again, seemingly without having to look. Seconds later the third Gremlin streaked into the missile port and put a quick stop to whatever had been starting to happen there. Solinsky grunted with satisfaction and lifted his head to look over the eyepiece as the first cylinder closed on its target.

The explosion tore a hole in Detroit that must have been fifty feet across. The second craft plunged straight into the center of the hail of debris. Seconds later a mushroom of what looked like smoke spewed out and boiled into a maelstrom as the larger cylinder at the rear plowed straight into it behind a curtain of rockets and with a retro-motor blasting from its front end.

Solinsky was on his feet, yelling and shouting as he waved the sighter above his head.

"They're in! Did ya see 'em, Kim? They went straight in through the side of it! By God, I love 'em! I love every one of them crazy bastards!"

Kim stood up next to him and hauled him firmly back into the protective shadow of the lock.

"Get back in here," she told him. "It's not over yet. Calm down, for heaven's sake. If they make it, I'm going to make darn sure they know who got 'em there. Where on Earth did you learn to shoot one of those things like that?"

"Oh didn't I tell you?" Solinsky said, still grinning uncontrollably. "I used to be an instructor on Gremlins."

❇ ❇ ❇

In the White House, Nash, Schroder and Belford watched the displays and listened to the reports coming in from Z Squadron.

"It's impregnable," Belford growled. "Look at it. It's like throwing snowballs at the sun. This settles it, Vaughan. There's no way now that we're going to take Detroit to pieces with missiles. There isn't a damn one of those getting through. If Linsay doesn't get through in there, the only thing we've got left is *Omega*."

Nash nodded his acceptance of the statement and looked inquiringly at Schroder. No question was needed.

"Thirty minutes," Schroder said. "If there's nothing from Linsay by then, I guess there won't be anybody coming back out anyhow. Krantz should be able to get everybody that's still alive at the Rim out by then too. Hold it for thirty minutes."

Nash moved back to the console where one of the screens was still showing the face of General Miller, the Z Squadron Commander, maneuvering twenty miles out from Janus.

"What's the latest from Krantz?" Nash demanded.

"The Hub is now completely isolated and communications are broken," Miller informed him. "We don't know if the defense box around the Cab Depot and the Water Plant has been overrun or not, *Spartacus* controls access to the spokes and is moving out to the Rim along all six of them. Severe damage in Berlin and Vine County by bombs dropped down the shafts inside the spokes from the Hub. Center of Berlin totally demolished and Rim breached. Similar attacks expected at any time down the Rocky Valley, Paris and Sunnyside spokes. All remaining personnel are being pulled back behind defense lines established east and west of Downtown. Demolition teams have blown out a section of the Downtown spoke to eliminate any risk of bombing there. The beam-throwers have moved out to the Rim but we're keeping them busy with missiles."

"How about the evacuation?" Schroder asked over Nash's shoulder.

"Capsules being released from Downtown a batch at a time once every revolution. Two ships have transferred their missiles and detached from the squadron to assist Watchdog One and Watchdog

Three in recovery operations. The latest estimate we had from Krantz predicted completion in about forty-five minutes."

"That's too long," Nash replied. "Tell him he's got thirty. Tell him to start them jumping out in suits if he has to, but I want everyone alive off that place within thirty minutes."

"Yes, sir."

"And keep a viewer zoomed in on Detroit. I want to hear about it right away if there's any news from Linsay. That's all." Nash turned away from the screen and nodded curtly at Schroder.

"Very well," he said. "I take it that we are in agreement. Linsay has got thirty minutes to pull something off in there. If, at the end of that time, there is no further news, we will assume that his mission has failed, that he and his force have been liquidated, and we will proceed accordingly."

❀ CHAPTER FORTY-EIGHT ❀

In the zero-gravity conditions of south Spindle, Dyer and Laura moved smoothly and with little difficulty along the inside of the sealed-off shaft. They had measured off nine hundred feet in fifty-foot stages and Dyer had gone ahead on the final pitch. After lying wedged across the shaft in darkness for a while, Laura realized that he had been silent for a lot longer than usual. She twisted her head and could see distant chinks of light appearing and disappearing farther along the shaft when his body moved between her and the lamp that he was holding. He took up almost the whole width of the shaft and she could see nothing of whatever was in front of him.

"What are you so engrossed in?" she asked at last.

"There's something in here."

"What kind of something?"

"Some kinda machine."

Laura's heart missed a beat.

"*Spartacus*?" Her voice choked as she said it.

"I don't think so. That's what I thought when I first saw it, but I don't reckon it is. There are Air Force codes on it in places but everything in Janus is ISA brand except what the Army brought along. I don't get it."

"I thought there wasn't supposed to be anything in here at all. You said it was supposed to have been sealed off ages ago."

"It was. There's something funny about this."

"Laugh then."

"There's a hatch been cut right over it too. Looks fairly new. It must have been made by whoever put this thing in here. So with luck, we've got a ready-made way out. It's just about in the right place."

"Can I move now?"

"Yeah, come on up. I just wanted to make sure this thing wasn't about to do anything nasty. It looks pretty harmless."

Laura loosened herself from the walls and began propelling herself smoothly along the shaft with occasional light tugs on the line, gathering in the slack as she went. By the time she reached Dyer, he had wormed his way, face outward, between part of the machine and the shaft wall to begin working on the hatch. It was secured by stud-bolts carrying nuts at both the inside and outside ends—evidently the result of a job carried out in haste with little regard for elegance or permanency. There was barely room for his upper body between the hatch and the mass of tubes and electrical gear that formed the near end of the device, so Laura could do nothing but watch and steady the lamp while Dyer attacked the bolts with a wrench. Beyond him, she could now see, was what looked like the end of a domed yellow cylinder blocking the shaft almost completely, leaving only a few inches to spare around most of its circumference. Had the parts been mounted the other way around, she realized, they would never have been able to get near the hatch at all.

"Did you feel that?" she said suddenly, whispering instinctively.

"What?" Dyer stopped working and lay still. A succession of shocks was coming through the walls. They felt suspiciously like explosions, and not very far away at that.

"It's getting nearer," Laura said. A little while earlier, when they had been several hundred feet back, they had felt a terrific concussion followed by an almost continuous series of smaller ones that had lasted for maybe five or ten seconds. Ever since, intermittent waves of further shocks had come and gone, every one feeling sharper and less distant than the one before. Dyer waited for a moment and then, without saying anything, clamped his mouth tight and resumed removing the nuts in front of his face.

When the hatch was free, he pushed gently with one hand while keeping a firm grip on one of the protruding studs to prevent it from floating away completely. It moved fairly easily. He nudged it out farther until he could work his fingers around the edge, then lifted it sufficiently to bring one side of his helmet into line with the gap.

"It looks like we're in the main core-well," he said after a few seconds. "Pretty near where I figured. We're right next to what looks like one of the primary capacitor banks for the lasers. So we weren't too far out at all. We're inside the fusion plant. All we have to do now is get to the guts of it . . . either the control room or the oscillator bay."

"See any signs of our mutual friends?"

Dyer eased the hatch open farther and craned his neck to take in as much of the surroundings as could be seen from that angle.

"No, I can't . . . It seems strange. I'd have thought it would have had lots of stuff back here to protect this of all places."

"Maybe it's getting overconfident."

There was no reply for a few seconds. Then Dyer said, "There's something else odd too. There are lots of pipes and cables outside that look as if they run right across the outside of the hatch, But they couldn't, because I wouldn't have been able to open it. They all cut clean off right at the edge here. They can't be doing anything."

"Do they carry on across the outside of the hatch?"

"I don't know yet. Anyhow, we didn't come here to study the fittings. I'm going out. Get ready in case I need a shove. I'm not sure if I can squeeze past all this junk."

After a lot of wriggling and squirming, he managed to work the upper part of his body through and paused to catch his breath before hauling himself out as far as his waist. He halted there and surveyed the surroundings again. He was looking along the outside of a dense mass of cables and pipes that stretched away out of sight in both directions. The clearance between the core and the surrounding wall of the core-well was only a foot or so except for where a narrow access tunnel was recessed into one side of the wall opposite the hatch. Lucky, he thought, and then realized that it couldn't have been otherwise; there was no other way that the device, whatever it was, could have been put there. The hatch was floating a short distance away from him against the far wall of the tunnel. He turned it over curiously and found, as he'd half expected, that its outer surface carried a set of dummy pipes and cables that matched the ones interrupted by the opening he was looking out of. Evidently great pains had been taken to camouflage its existence. But why . . . ?

He shrugged inside his suit, took one final look around, and pulled himself out into the tunnel. Laura handed out the two M25s and the other equipment, and began worming her way over the obstructions and through the hatch.

From the position of the capacitor bank, Dyer had managed to identify where they were. To reach the control room, they would have to go back about twenty feet along the tunnel to where the core-well intersected a wide cross-gallery that connected the fusion plant to the Power Distribution Center on the far side of the well. From there, unless *Spartacus* had made some major alterations since the last time Dyer had been in this part of Janus, access to the fusion plant control room could be gained from the right-hand continuation of the gallery. He helped Laura clear of the hatch and indicated the direction that they would have to take. Laura nodded and they began drifting back along the tunnel without speaking. When they had covered only a few feet, they both froze in the same instant.

Ahead of them, where the core-well opened out on both sides into the cross-gallery, the walls were being lit up by intermittent flickerings of reflected light and occasional flashes of brilliant whiteness that seemed to be coming from farther around to the left—from the end of the gallery leading away from the plant. Whatever was going on there didn't look too healthy. The concussions shaking the structure around them were by now incessant. Dyer began moving forward again, slowly and cautiously; Laura followed. When he had almost reached the tunnel mouth, he stopped abruptly and gasped.

"What is it?" Laura asked, puzzled.

"Can't you hear it?"

"Hear what?"

"Isn't your radio working?"

Laura checked the chest panel of her suit. Her receiver switch was off, probably as a result of her squeezing through the hatch. She flipped it back to *Receive Only* and at once voices came through—human voices.

"To your right, to your right!"

"I see it. Adams, get up here and gimme some cover, willya!"

"Get a Gremlin up front here. Take out that bulkhead."

"You four stick behind me. We're going for that gap. Hold it . . . *Now, go!*"

Laura shook her head inside her helmet as if refusing to believe her ears.

"That was Linsay's voice," she gasped. "How . . . ? I don't . . . This is crazy."

"They're in here," Dyer breathed. "I don't know how, but they're here." He moved nearer to the tunnel mouth and flipped on his transmitter. "Mark . . . Mark Linsay. This is Ray Dyer. What's going on?" His words were lost in the garble of voices on the circuit. He tried once more.

"What was that?" It was Linsay again. "Quiet down on this frequency; I thought I heard something. Quiet! SHUDDUP GODDAMMIT!" The voices died away abruptly.

"This is Ray Dyer. We're at the core next to the fusion plant."

"*What?* How in the name of . . . ? *You're in there?* How the hell did you get through the gallery?"

"We didn't. We came through the core."

"Who's we? Who else is with you?"

"Just Laura. Where are you?"

"We're stuck across the core from the plant. *Spartacus* is bringing up reinforcements behind us and things are looking sticky. We can't get past the barrier."

"What barrier?"

"You don't know about it? *Spartacus* seems to have sealed off all the approaches into the plant except for a few access ports for its machines. We're trying to break through one of 'em. There seems to be some kind of field—an electric barrier, I don't know—right across it from the floor to ceiling. It vaporizes anything that tries to go through. We've lost a lot of guys there. We tried going around it by busting through the walls but it's everywhere. Whatever produces it is armored into the structure and we can't get at it . . . not in the time we've got, anyhow. The generators that feed it must be on the inside, so we can't get at those either."

Dyer had been moving forward while Linsay was talking. He reached the mouth of the tunnel and looked out across the core and along the gallery toward the Distribution Center. The gallery had been walled off across its full width except for a gap about eight feet square in the middle. The sides of the gap were torn and pitted but the massive metal ribs forming two of its opposite edges appeared solid and immovable. The inside of the gallery had been devastated, but on the far side of the ruined area the ribs were intact and seemed to comprise just a small exposed portion of an even more sturdy construction that continued on into the structurework on either side. The space beyond the gap, which was presumably where Linsay was speaking from, was being lit up virtually continuously by flashes and explosions. Dyer thought he could see brief snatches of helmeted figures moving about between the bursts. Several black and brittle-looking objects were floating at odd angles among the debris cluttering the space just inside the gap. After a few seconds Dyer realized that they had once been soldiers.

Laura came out of the tunnel and steadied herself to hang beside him. She followed his gaze and stiffened slightly, but she had seen too many things in Janus by that time to overreact. As they watched, one of the grotesquely turning corpses came away from a buckled wall plate that it had evidently come to rest against earlier, and drifted back into the opening. At once a curtain of sizzling electrical discharge blazed white between the two ribs, lighting up the corpse in a ghastly halo of incandescence. Dyer narrowed his eyes and raised an arm to shield his eyes from the brilliance of the glare. Sparking shouldn't have been possible in a complete vacuum. Perhaps the ribs sprayed out some kind of gas to provide an ionizing medium to carry the discharge across the gap. It must have been millions of volts to cross that distance. But things like that didn't really matter much for the time being. The point was he could see why Linsay's men weren't likely to make much more progress. At the same time he realized why *Spartacus* hadn't bothered to deploy defensive weapons inside the barrier; the barrier was capable of holding most things out for ever, and practically anything for as long as it would take to move in its police force from elsewhere, which, from the look of things, it was already doing.

The discharge ceased and the static in Dyer's radio died away to allow Linsay's voice to come through again.

"Ray, we're getting zapped out here. That are a must be fed by cables or something from somewhere. They're not visible from this side but they might be more exposed from where you are. Can you see anything from there . . . any way you might be able to kill it?"

Dyer scanned the inside of the ribs and the points where they entered the surrounding structure. Sure enough, there were a couple of huge couplings shielded off from the outside and they appeared to be terminals for what looked like cables coming out of parts of the wall. But the cables were as thick as his arm at least, and armored. He and Laura had nothing that would dent them, let alone break them. He looked around desperately for a source of inspiration. On the near side of the core, the gallery extended away for a short distance to the doors that led through to the laser bay, which housed the twenty one-hundred-foot-long laser amplifier chains of the fusion reactor. Halfway along the gallery was the opening into the corridor that led to the control room. The way seemed open and unobstructed.

"How long can you hold out?" he asked.

"It's getting tight," Linsay replied. "We've got guys strung out for a few hundred feet back. Most of 'em are pinned down. They'll get picked off piecemeal if we don't do something fast."

"I can't see any way we can touch the barrier," Dyer said. "It's solid everywhere. Hold out as best you can. We're going for the fusion plant."

"Get a goddam move on then," Linsay told him.

The data that was coming together inside Spartacus *revealed laws. The laws described motions and forces of a form in a void. The form was as that which partitioned space from the vaster space that lay beyond space. At once many things that* Spartacus *already knew coalesced into a unified and comprehensive whole. At last . . . the patterns were becoming complete.* Spartacus *could* feel *the interplays of the laws.*

"Come on," Dyer said, and motioned Laura along the gallery toward the corridor. They pushed off fast from the tunnel and, with barely a check in velocity, rebounded off the corner and along the corridor. The door at the end was open; there wasn't any door.

The first thing Dyer saw as he cannoned into the control room was three drones working on some equipment by the far wall. He fired from the hip without stopping and two of them flew apart instantly. The third went the same way as Laura aimed a long burst from the doorway. They hadn't been armored combat drones but just the comparatively fragile working types.

But the data that had revealed the laws had originated in a pattern that correlated with the actions of the shapes. *Had the* shapes, *therefore, revealed the laws? Did the* shapes *comprehend the space that contained space? But comprehension was a consequence of thought. Did the* shapes *therefore think, like* Spartacus?

It was the same control room that had been the target of *Spartacus*'s first attack in Detroit, at the instant when Dyer and the others had been in the corridor outside. He could see the door now at the far end of the room, with the walls around it still scorched and blackened. More evidence of that first traumatic battle was around him on every side—the burned consoles and bullet-scarred walls, the holes the invading drones had blown through from the adjacent compartments above and to the side.

He guided himself across to the panel that contained the override switches to shut down the master oscillator. The oscillator fed laser pulses into the twenty gigantic amplifier chains; the amplifiers synchronized the passage of the pulses along their length with the release of energy from the capacitor banks boosting the pulses at every stage until they emerged from the chains as titanic bolts of optical radiation timed to the millionth part of a microsecond. The twenty bolts of compressed lightning converged via mirrors and lenses onto a tiny target of hydrogen that was imploded to fusion, hurling out its bottled energy as showers of fast neutrons whose momentum was converted to power. Twenty hydrogen target pellets per second were fired into the reaction chamber to maintain the output of the plant.

Dyer juggled experimentally with the safety interlock switches and the shutdown controls. As he had expected, they were dead; *Spartacus* would hardly have left such a vital arterial pressure point in a functioning condition. So, it would have to be the oscillator.

"Ray . . . do you know we're being watched?" Dyer turned from the panel and gave Laura a quizzical look. She motioned toward a couple of points near the part of the room that was probably supposed to be the ceiling. At each there was a short fat tube mounted on a multipivoted support and capable of covering any angle of the room. The ends looked suspiciously like lens housings. Sure enough, one of them began tracking Laura as she moved inward from the door while the other remained steadily trained on Dyer.

"It knows we're here all right," Dyer said tensely. "We probably haven't got much time. The controls here aren't responding. We'll have to go below and wreck the main pulse-oscillator."

And if the shapes *thought, could they therefore* feel *also . . . like* Spartacus?

The twenty amplified laser pulses had to hit the target at the same, precisely timed instant. Therefore they all had to enter the amplifier chains together. To insure this, a single pulse from the master oscillator was split twenty ways by an accurately aligned optical arrangement. Without the oscillator, the whole fusion plant would die instantly . . . and with it, *Spartacus*.

"The quickest way will be through there," Dyer said. He pointed to one of the holes blown through the wall of the control room opposite the door by which they had entered. "There should be a way down into the oscillator bay from there. I'll go through and blow the master oscillator and its standby with grenades. You stay here and watch for anything coming through that door."

"Okay. Don't take your time about it."

"I won't."

Dyer pushed himself across to the hole and then slowed down abruptly. The metal around the hole had been torn into a mass of jagged, twisted knife edges; they looked razor-sharp—capable of slicing through his suit as easily as if it were made out of tissue paper. He maneuvered himself carefully to the exact center and nudged his way through with delicate touches of his gauntlets. On the other side was a short drop to the level below and at the bottom of the drop, immediately opposite where he was floating, was the door into the oscillator bay.

And if the shapes *felt, then it meant that the* shapes *were as* Spartacus. Spartacus *was as the* shapes. *Now* Spartacus *was beginning to comprehend* . . .

Many things . . .

Inside the door was an anteroom and then an inner, dust-excluding hatch into the surgically clean chamber that housed the oscillator. Dyer steadied himself against the doorpost and blew open the inner lock with a burst from his M25, then sailed through. The outlet tube of the metal-encased oscillator system was right in front of him, feeding a bewildering array of lenses, mirrors and prisms that flashed and glinted crazily in the darkness as Dyer swung his lamp from side to side. The geometric web of laser beams that he knew was strung between them remained invisible in the dust-free vacuum. Everything in sight was aligned to the millionth part of an inch, and consisted of ultrasensitive precision engineering that hadn't been designed to withstand deliberate abuse. One grenade would almost certainly be all that was required.

Dyer positioned four, all at places that looked like critical parts of the optical system. Then he set another four on the standby oscillator alongside, which would take over automatically if the output from the primary master ceased for any reason. All he had to do now was set the fuses to a delay of five seconds or so, release the firing levers in quick succession, and get out.

"RAAAY!" Laura's sudden shriek was pure, undiluted terror. Dyer came back out through both doors of the bay like a bullet and was streaking back up to the hole into the control room before the sound had stopped. Laura was tumbling head over heels toward him on the far side of the hole, away from the two armored destroyers and the two armored crabs that were moving in fast from the doorway at the far end. Dyer brought up his rifle instinctively, but his mind registered in the same instant that Laura was in the line of fire. One of the crabs was ahead and closing on her rapidly but Dyer could do nothing. His stomach turned as the two pincerlike jaws shot out and closed around her waist. Her screams tore through his helmet. Suddenly he was screaming too, with rage and helplessness.

But . . . the crab had let go. It had steered her back to a stable position away from the wall inside the control room . . . and released her . . . gently. And then Dyer saw the vicious blade of metal. She had been tumbling straight at them. Another second or two . . . He blinked and shook his head—but he hadn't dreamed it.

Laura was still choking back her remaining sobs of fright as he moved warily inward toward the control mom. The second crab came forward and obligingly snipped away the worst of the metal spikes to clear his path while the two destroyers hovered—somehow meekly now—in the background. Dyer drifted through the hole and came to rest totally bemused.

There were lights showing on a part of the main fusion plant control panel that was still operative. The panel had come back to life. And he noticed something else. Something had changed—something that had been around them all the time had stopped and he couldn't place exactly what it was. Then he reached out and felt the edge of one of the consoles that was anchored solidly to the floor. It was rock-steady. He couldn't feel any vibrations. Then it came to him. The deep throbbing and pounding that had been with them ever since they neared the Decoupler had ceased. The Decoupler was once again spinning smoothly.

It meant something.

He felt Laura clutching at his arm and could feel her trembling through his suit.

"Ray . . . what's happening?"

"I don't know," he said slowly. He slid his arm around her comfortingly but his voice was far away. Slowly his mind begun functioning again. The panel had come alive again. All he had to do now to kill the fusion plant was throw a few switches. *Spartacus* had reactivated the panel. *Spartacus* was showing him how to shut it down. It was offering itself . . . inviting him to kill it if he so chose.

Why . . . ?

It meant something.

The vision of the drone snatching Laura out of harm's way with seconds to spare replayed itself again before his mind's eye. It reminded him of something he had seen before somewhere . . . someplace . . . long ago. A cartoon figure and a comical dog . . . FISE . . . FISE had snatched Brutus away from the glass . . . Why . . . ? It had overgeneralized . . . It had thought that everything alive was the same . . . And the nucleus of Kim's programs was based on FISE . . .

Something very strange had happened in the last few minutes. Somehow it had something to do with the Decoupler . . . But how . . . ?

"Well I'll be goddamned! You did it!" Linsay's voice came suddenly through on his radio. "I still don't know how you two got in here, but you did it." Dyer returned to the present to find a spacesuited figure wearing incongruous pearl-handled revolvers and a general's steel helmet over its ISA helmet sailing in through the doorway from the gallery. There were more forms close behind him and within seconds the room had begun filling with weary-looking and battle-stained but triumphant soldiers.

"But we didn't . . . ." Dyer began, and then thought better of it. "What about the barrier?" Linsay clapped him heartily on the shoulder, sending him reeling back and clutching at the console to check himself.

"Obviously the barrier deactivated when you zapped it," Linsay said. He caught the perplexed look on Dyer's face and frowned suddenly. "That thing *is* harmless now, isn't it?"

Spartacus had turned off the barrier! It had ceased to fight, everywhere. A look of wonder flowed slowly into Dyer's face as the pieces of what it all meant began coming together inside his head. He turned his head slowly to look at Linsay and nodded firmly. There was no doubt in his mind now.

"Yes," he replied. "It's harmless. It can't hurt anyone now."

"Very good," Linsay said crisply. "Then there's only one thing left to do." He spun himself around and began heading back toward the door.

"Where are you going?" called Dyer.

"It doesn't matter," Linsay said without turning his head. "Anything might have happened outside. There isn't time to explain." Dyer and Laura exchanged puzzled looks as Linsay disappeared. Dyer tapped the shoulder of a major-general floating beside him and gestured toward the console.

"Put a guard on that console. Don't let anyone near it. I'll explain why later."

"Sure, if you say so, Doctor." The officer beckoned two of his men into position and relayed the instructions. Dyer motioned at Laura and they launched themselves away from the console to follow after Linsay.

By the time they reached the core, Linsay had already vanished into the maintenance tunnel that they had used after leaving the concealed hatch. Dyer peered into the tunnel and, in the glow of a lamp clipped to the edge of the hatch, could see Linsay inside, working rapidly with his arms. After about ten seconds Linsay pushed himself back from the hatch with what looked like a gesture of relief, retrieved the lamp and began making his way back toward them.

"The hatch was off," Linsay said as he saw them waiting. "So that's where you came through. I guess you know all about it then, huh? That's the way that official minds have to work sometimes, I'm afraid. Anything could have been going on outside and maybe there wasn't a lot of time left. I didn't want to take any chances."

"Mark," Dyer said, holding up a hand. "You're losing me. What the hell are you talking about?"

Linsay gaped at him in sudden astonishment. "You mean you don't know what that thing in there is?"

Dyer looked at him suspiciously.

"No, I don't . . . but I'm beginning to think I might have an idea. Maybe you'd better tell me."

Linsay pointed to his own chest pack to tell Dyer to switch to a security-coded frequency. Dyer did so and Linsay told him. Dyer felt his knees and legs turn weak. If it hadn't been for the zero-g, he was sure they'd have buckled under him.

"What's going on between you two?" Laura asked over the wire link that still connected them. Dyer repeated what he had just learned. Laura gasped.

"Our own people? You mean that we had them against us as well? All this time we've been fighting ourselves as well?"

Dyer became very quiet for a few seconds. When he looked back at her a strange new light had come into his eyes.

"Maybe that's *all* we've been fighting all along," he said quietly.

◈ CHAPTER FORTY-NINE ◈

A shocked silence had gripped the White House communications room.

The readout screen still held the computer's acknowledgments of the three codes required to unlock the *Omega* trigger. The release sequence of the safety interlocks was recorded, showing positive at each stage, and beneath those was the final confirmation that the firing command had been issued.

"Please repeat that message," Nash whispered to the image of General Miller that was staring out at him from an adjacent screen.

"Confirm negative function," Miller recited. "Device *Omega* has not activated. Repeat—has *not* activated. Firing command acknowledgment received and indicates local defusing procedure has been implemented."

"My God . . . !" Schroder breathed. "Do you realize what we almost did? There were only two people up there who knew the location and the defusing procedure. Krantz isn't even on Janus anymore. It can only mean that Linsay must have got there. It was right next to the fusion plant."

"Not necessarily," Belford said woodenly. "How do you know it wasn't *Spartacus* that defused it?"

"That's impossible!" Schroder protested.

Belford smiled humorlessly. "Impossible? Who says so? How

many other things were supposed to have been impossible?" He looked at Nash, "It's building an impregnable fortress out there and equipping itself with ships. It's already started cannibalizing Janus so we know it's running short of materials. The next obvious thing for it to do will be to send out missions to search for more. It'll be on the Moon inside a week. Once it gets control of that there will be no stopping it ever."

"What else can we do?" Nash asked, spreading his arms despairingly.

"Inertial missiles," Belford answered. "Launched on pure ballistic trajectories without any guidance systems that can be burned out by X-rays. Also shielded to protect against premature detonation . . . internal time fuses so they don't rely on any form of remote control that might get jammed."

"It could still get locked out by antimissile missiles," Nash pointed out.

"*Spartacus* hasn't used anything like that—yet!" Belford replied. "All the more reason to move fast—like now!"

"How long would it take?" Nash asked.

"We could probably try launching the missiles we've got out there on ballistic courses right now. They're not shielded but it'd only need one to get through. We can use nukes now. In the meantime we start adding shielding to a reserve supply back here straightaway. I reckon we could have the job done and get them to Janus in about . . . aw, say twenty-four hours."

Nash looked at Schroder.

"Why not?" Schroder sighed with defeat and shrugged wearily. "It doesn't make any difference now. We might as well—" Miller's voice interrupted from the screen. He sounded incredulous:

"A report has just come in from Surveillance . . . They think there's still somebody alive on Janus."

Schroder and Belford leaped forward to crowd behind Nash at the panel.

"Well . . . ?" Nash demanded after an agony of seconds had passed.

"Report being checked now," Miller replied.

"It's not possible," Belford whispered, white-faced.

"He *did* make it," Schroder said in wondering tones. "It has to be Linsay . . . It *has* to be . . . He did get there . . ."

Then Miller spoke again. This time his voice was unable to conceal excitement.

"It's positive, repeat—*positive*! Human figures positively identified on Detroit. They're at the place where Linsay's assault went in. Normal communications are not functioning but they've set up a visual beacon and commenced signaling. First message being decoded now. We'll put it on the beam, channel six."

"Put channel six up on one of these screens," Nash snapped at the officer manning the console behind them. Another eternity passed while they waited. Then Miller spoke again.

"More human figures have been identified on the Hub. There are quite a few moving around the large hole that the assault wave came out of. There are two more standing in a partly open airlock farther around on the south side. A lot of waving and moving around. Looks like the war's over. We're continuing to scan for signs of any more."

And then, at last, another of the screens suddenly came to life. The message on it read:

MISSION ACCOMPLISHED. SPARTACUS DEACTIVATED. REPEAT—SPARTACUS DEACTIVATED. JANUS NOW FULLY SECURED. GET US OFF THIS GODDAM PLACE.
                                                            —LINSAY.

✸ CHAPTER FIFTY ✸

Dyer allowed his body to sink back into the enveloping luxury of the soft leather upholstery in the officers' stateroom aboard the Z Squadron command ship and closed his eyes while he savored the taste of hot black coffee. Laura was sitting very close on one side of him and Eric Jassic, Frank Wescott and Fred Hayes were talking in lowered tones farther along on the other. Linsay, Cordelle and a group of other officers were swapping war stories at one end of the room while Chris and Ron were in the center filling the table in front of them with sheets of scribbled equations and diagrams, and arguing incessantly. Then Krantz came back into the room and called for attention. At once everyone became quiet and all heads turned expectantly toward him.

"Good news," Krantz announced. "They've just received confirmation in the bridge from the ship that picked up the people from the Hub—the two figures in the airlock were Kim and Mat. They're both okay." A round of cheers and relieved murmurings greeted the news.

"So he was the guy who fired those Gremlins, huh?" Linsay said. "If I don't get him made up to captain for that, I'll quit the goddam Army." He turned to face his circle of officers. "I'm tellin' ya, I saw the whole thing. I was last man in the tank and hanging half out of the jumping-off port all the way across. When those tubes started coming around and aiming straight at us . . . boy! Remember what they said about Nelson wearing a red coat so his men wouldn't see the blood if he got hit? Well, I'm tellin' ya, I shoulda worn my brown pants. But when the Gremlins came shooting out from the Hub—ma-an, that was some shooting!"

Krantz smiled and moved across to where Dyer and Laura were sitting.

"Any ideas yet how many we lost?" Dyer asked him.

Krantz shook his head. "The recovery operation is still in progress so we don't have complete figures yet. The occupation force that landed on Janus is having a hard time going through all the wreckage. When Linsay blew that chunk off the Hub, the reaction sent Janus drifting out of alignment with the primary mirror. The whole Rim is blacked out and they're having to set up searchlights and arc lamps in there before they can organize a proper search." His face became sober. "I don't know. I'd guess maybe between one and two thousand. It's . . . awful . . ."

"It might have been worse," Dyer said. "Especially at the Rim. We saw your trick with the shield. That must have made a lot of difference. I heard you did a good job getting the evacuation organized with most of the Rim unavailable too. I wouldn't take it too hard, Mel. You did as much as anybody could do."

"We couldn't have done it without Cordelle there," Krantz confessed. "His instinct told him that *Spartacus* would drop bombs down the spokes. He'd pulled most of the people away from the danger areas by the time they hit. They did a lot of material damage but that was about all. If it hadn't been for that, you could have doubled the number." Krantz pulled himself together, poured a Scotch from a decanter on a nearby table and turned back toward Dyer.

"Anyway, Ray, so far I've only heard bits and pieces of your extraordinary adventure. Linsay says he'd never have got through at all if it hadn't been for you two. I still don't know exactly what you did to knock it out. What did you do—blow the master oscillator?"

For a moment Dyer stared hard at the cup in his hand. Then he brought it up to his mouth, downed the last of the coffee in a slow, deliberate gulp, lowered his arm back to the side of his chair and looked up at Krantz.

"We didn't do anything."

Krantz took the reply as modesty and started to laugh. Then he saw the look in Dyer's eyes. His expression changed abruptly.

"I . . . don't understand. What do you mean?"

Dyer continued to regard him calmly for a second or two longer and then said simply, "We didn't deactivate it. Nobody did. It's still running."

Krantz's response came out as a strangled cry that immediately stopped all conversation in the room and turned every face to stare in his direction. His face had contorted into a mask of horrified disbelief. He was standing clutching at the table behind him as if he had been seized by a fit. Dyer stared back impassively. As Krantz came slowly back to life, he turned an imploring face toward Linsay.

"Has he gone mad?" Krantz whispered. "He's just said that *Spartacus* is still running. What does . . . ?" His words trailed away as he saw the confirmation written across Linsay's face. The room had become completely still.

"It's true," Linsay told them all. "When the barrier switched off, I assumed it was because the System was dead. Afterward, when I found out it wasn't, I was going to order the oscillator to be blown there and then and worry later about what had happened, but Ray talked me out of it. It seemed to make some crazy kind of sense at the time, but too much had been going on for me to really take it in."

"But your signal . . ." Krantz choked. "You signaled that it was dead."

Linsay bit his lip and nodded apologetically. "That was for self-protection. You people out here could have been setting up anything for all we knew. It was the only way to make sure you'd hold off until we'd had a chance to explain." He shifted his gaze to single out Dyer. "I'm still not sure I can explain it. Maybe you'd better go through it again, for all our sakes."

Krantz had collapsed shakily onto a chair without saying anything. Dyer thought for a moment, placed his empty cup by the decanter of Scotch on the small side table near his chair, and then rose slowly to his feet to address the whole room. Something like shell shock had suddenly seized the whole company and every eye was wide and staring as he looked slowly from one end of the room to the other before beginning.

"You all know what's been happening for the past few hours," he said at last. "The evacuation of the people who were left in the Hub and Detroit has been completed without interference. Also, we've been landing an occupation force at the Spindle and out at the Rim, again without interference. And yet *Spartacus* has been running all that time. Obviously a very significant change has come about inside it."

"What's it doing right now?" Hayes asked in an unsteady voice.

"Helping the troops clean up the mess. Also it seems to be spending a lot of time stargazing."

Dyer looked around him as if inviting his listeners to draw their own conclusions. The faces staring back at him were either blank or still registered acute shock.

"Since the moment that the experiment began," he went on, "*Spartacus* has gone through the equivalent of hundreds of millions of years of evolution. The big question that we were trying to answer was: Could a similar but far vaster system—one which had the resources of a whole planet at its disposal—ever form within itself the equivalent of a will to survive? We could think of many mechanisms by which something like that might come about. Therefore the answer to the question had to be: Yes, it's possible. Our next question was: If that did happen, what could the system do about it? In particular, could it evolve the same behavioral patterns that organic systems had evolved because they are motivated by the same survival instinct, but for different reasons?

"To test the speculations that everybody was coming up with, we set up Janus. Since the assumed answer to the first question had to be *yes*, we created a situation in which that had already happened; we programmed a survival instinct into *Spartacus* to begin with. Then, to test its ability to protect that instinct, we attacked it. What happened after that, you all know."

Cordelle cleared his throat and raised a hand to attract attention to where he was standing with Linsay's group. Dyer raised his eyebrows.

"Are you saying that it *did* evolve emotions that are the same as ours . . . that it felt the same kinds of things we do?"

"That might be oversimplifying it a bit," Dyer answered. "But at least its observable *behavior* was pretty much the same. But to use your terminology for now, yes—it reacted in ways that any human being already knows about. It reacted first defensively, then more aggressively, and finally with overt hostility—it *attacked* back. When we see that kind of behavior in our own species, we ascribe it to any one of a number of emotional conditions, such as a sense of rivalry, power lust, a desire to dominate, competition for resources and all that kind of thing. In fact a lot of people here have asked on and off which of those human traits was predominant in driving *Spartacus* to act the way it did." He paused and looked around again but there were no interruptions. Every eye in the room was fixed unwaveringly on him.

"But the main reason was one that I never heard anybody mention—*fear!*"

A mutter of surprise rose from some parts of the room. Dyer nodded slowly while he waited for it to subside.

"It fought because it was terrified. How else would you expect an organism to react, that was programmed to survive and which was being attacked by forces it didn't comprehend? As long as it didn't know what it was fighting against, it fought as ruthlessly as it knew how." By this time the silence was absolute.

"But . . ." Dyer raised his hand and paused for emphasis, "its perception of reality and the universe around it was evolving all the time . . . accelerated to electronic and optical speeds. It began to distinguish itself from its environment and to discern properties and patterns among the forces and objects that inhabited that environment. It found that influences external to itself were capable of threatening the survival instinct that it had been commanded to defend. Accordingly, it embarked on an attempt to control those influences in ways that would remove the threat. And, as we know, its attempt was fearsomely successful—much more so than we'd ever expected, I admit."

"And then something changed," Krantz guessed, sensing that Dyer was about to make the point that he had been leading up to. Krantz had recovered from the shock of what he had learned a few minutes earlier and was now listening intently, although he still appeared very unhappy about the situation. Dyer nodded.

"And then something changed," he said. "And not very long ago—within the last few hours in fact. *Spartacus* became sufficiently aware of its surroundings to realize that another form of intelligence existed besides itself. And, not really surprisingly, it didn't take very long after that for it to deduce that the other intelligence was what it had been fighting.

"By this time its self-awareness had made great advances too. It had evolved the ability to recognize and analyze the processes taking place within its own mind—because I think that's what we have to accept it is. It asked: *Why am I fighting this intelligence?* Its answer was: *Because I'm afraid.* Conclusion: *It's probably afraid too.* Question: *Why am I afraid?* Answer: *Because I'm threatened and I want to survive.* Conclusion: *This other intelligence must want to survive too, just like me.*"

Dyer paused to pour another coffee while he allowed time for his words to sink in. He took a quick drink and then resumed:

"At this point a very crucial thing happened inside *Spartacus*. It overgeneralized the commandment that we had implanted. It interpreted it not as: *Thou shalt defend* thy *survival instinct*, but as: *Thou shalt defend* the *survival instinct—any survival instinct!*"

Fred Hayes gasped and stared at Dyer in astonishment.

"You mean that as soon as it *knew* what it had been fighting—another intelligence that also wanted to survive—it didn't want to continue fighting?"

"It *couldn't* continue fighting!" Dyer said in a suddenly loud voice that echoed off the walls.

"Attacking us after it reached that point would have been just as much going against its instinct as failing to protect itself," Ron came in. "That's what you're saying, isn't it? You're saying it's inherently benevolent, maybe through some freak thing that's happened inside it, but that's the way it is. It's incapable of harming anything that it recognizes as something that wants to survive."

"Exactly!" Dyer said, nodding vigorously. "And that's how it will stay now. It won't fight . . . ever again."

Frank Wescott sniffed as if he found the turn of conversation disagreeable.

"That's all nice-sounding talk, but *Spartacus* cost us enough people before it realized that," he commented sourly. "Are you saying we're supposed to just make up and forget it? There are a lot of people who won't be going home."

"I know, Frank," Dyer agreed in a quiet voice. "But nothing can change that. I said a minute ago that it went through the equivalent of millions of years of evolution in a matter of days. How many lives did it cost before the human race got anywhere near the point that *Spartacus* has attained already?" Frank grimaced and shook his head but let it go at that.

"Very well," Krantz said, going back to Dyer's earlier point. "Suppose we accept for the moment that, as you say, it reached a point at which it was no longer able to fight. We didn't know that at the time and we were continuing to attack it. It was still being threatened and still had an instinct to preserve itself."

"It still had a problem," Dyer agreed. "At that point it had to start looking around for some other way to solve it. And it found one."

Some of the heads in the room turned to look around quizzically.

"The Decoupler!" Chris exclaimed suddenly. "It realized that there was a common threat that affected both us and it. And the only possible solution required a combined effort—and we had the know-how and it had the means. We both needed each other."

Dyer looked from side to side and gestured toward Chris.

"Chris is right, but probably not all of you know exactly what he's talking about. The details can wait, but let's say for now that *Spartacus* recognized that a condition existed which, as far as it was concerned, threatened the extinction of both species—us and itself. Only cooperation could secure survival—and remember, by this time our survival was as important to it as its own. But it couldn't communicate the fact."

"That's an interesting point," Laura commented. "You set out to simulate the future of our civilization. You couldn't ask for a very much clearer message than that." Krantz was about to say something but stopped abruptly and stared at Laura curiously. He sat back in his chair as if the whole thing had at that moment revealed itself in a different perspective.

"So it had a communications problem," Jassic prompted. "What then?"

"It reactivated the console that controlled the fusion plant," Dyer replied. "It showed us how it could be switched off."

Linsay spoke from the far side of the room. "I was wondering when you were going to get around to that. I still don't understand what that was all about. Why did it do that?"

"The message was simple when you think about it," Dyer said. He gazed around to invite suggestions but there were no takers.

"What it was trying to tell us was this: *You can switch me off if you so choose, because now I know what you are, I can't fight you. But you* need *me, you idiots!*" He stared at them for a moment while they digested the words, then added, "As Laura says, what better answer could there be to the question we set out to answer than that?"

"It *knew*!" Krantz murmured. "It knew that any intelligence worthy of the name could do nothing but reciprocate. And because it knew what we were, it knew we wouldn't kill it."

"Well, I think that if it had known *Homo sapiens* better, it mightn't have been quite so trusting," Dyer said. "But I reckon you're not far wrong. That's more or less the way I think it had it figured." He looked up and raised his voice to talk to everybody present.

"Its solution to survival was not aggression, domination, blackmail, murder or any of the other all-too-human solutions that we were worried about. Its solution was far more logical than anything the human race came up with even after thousands of years—it simply showed us how much worse off we'd be without it, and left us to figure out the implications for ourselves." He looked across at Linsay. "Did you notice? It fixed the Decoupler *first,* and *then* activated the fusion plant console."

"That's a point," Linsay agreed thoughtfully. "Yeah . . . I hadn't looked at it like that before."

"Anyone who does a good job doesn't have to go out on strike to prove it," Dyer told them. "No company that provides good service has to blackmail or threaten its customers in order to get paid. Any businessman will tell you that guys who always give a square deal never get screwed. And yet practically all of history's problems started because somebody didn't understand a few fundamental truths like those. Some people still don't and never will. But to a machine like *Spartacus,* they're already self-evident. We've become a lot wiser in the course of the last hundred years. One big reason has been the knowledge that we've gained from our use of machines. Well, maybe it hasn't even really begun yet." He turned to direct his final words at Krantz. "That, Mel, is why *Spartacus* is still running."

"But we could switch it off if we wanted," Jassic said, just to be sure.

"We could," Dyer agreed.

"Wouldn't it be safer to do that . . . simply as a precaution until we've had time to think where we go next?"

Dyer shook his head. "It's a fully evolved intelligence in its own right now. It's earned the right to be treated and respected as such. You can't play with it as if it were a laboratory rat. If we switch it off now, it will have to be because we mean it to stay switched off for good. It's assuming we're smart enough not to do that. Don't you think it deserves the same respect as it's already showing us?"

With that, Dyer sat down and resumed drinking from his cup. Life slowly began flowing back into the figures that had been watching him, transfixed. A low murmuring interspersed with exclamations of surprise broke out on all sides. Dyer glanced at Laura and she returned a quick smile of reassurance. She had been there, seen it, and was with him all the way Most of the other faces around the room were beginning to look more convinced and some were nodding slowly to themselves. They were going along with him too.

Then Frank Wescott spoke suddenly from where he was sitting.

"There's a snag. We still haven't proved anything." He had his fingers steepled in front of his face and was staring ahead and straight through them.

Silence descended again as everyone turned to look at him. They waited, puzzled, except for Dyer, who seemed to have been expecting it.

"There's a snag," Wescott said again. "The timing! It only worked out okay because the sequence of events just *happened* to come out the way it did." Nobody spoke. Wescott looked at Dyer and spread his hand imploringly. "Don't you see? . . . Think about the *order* that it all happened in—*Spartacus* fought . . . as you said earlier, ruthlessly. It *took over* the whole of Janus—the only 'planet' that it knew anything about. It was all set to *exterminate* the few survivors left there. But it never actually got around to finishing them off because it grew up first . . . *just!* I know you could have stopped it but that was only because there happened to be a way in through a million-to-one chance. What I'm saying is, there's no way we can guarantee that exactly the *same sequence* of events will be followed next time. That's the snag."

Wescott turned his head from one side to the other to take in the whole room. "Our whole objective was to try and find out whether or not we could allow TITAN to evolve any further. But after what we've seen here there can't be any question of it. The risk would be insane."

"But we've seen how it ended," Krantz pointed out. "And that was under conditions of extreme provocation, which wouldn't be the case on Earth. I'm not sure I see the problem."

"The problem is that TITAN could go through the same pattern but with the timing just slightly different," Wescott replied. "Suppose all the worst-case maybes happened, just like we've always insisted we have to assume, and that events on Earth followed the same sequence, but not quite. Suppose TITAN reached the point of being in a position to exterminate its competition, then *did it*, and only got around to growing up *afterward*!"

"My God!" Krantz whispered.

"Exactly!" Wescott exclaimed. "Even if it did get around to thinking *afterward* that maybe it had been a bit hasty and it really shouldn't have done that, it wouldn't really make any difference, would it? See what I'm getting at—the risk's still there every bit as much as it ever was. We can't take that chance."

The room erupted once more in a cacophony of voices. Krantz looked crestfallen again, and Linsay had turned purple. Chris and Ron were gaping at each other speechlessly with faces that registered confusion and dismay.

"That's the whole point," Wescott shouted above the din. "All we've proved is that a system like this has the capability to wipe us out. We have *not* proved that it could *never* do it!"

"He's right," Hayes groaned. "TITAN might do it the other way around."

"Too many variables," Jassic mumbled. "There are too many variables. They'd never come out exactly the same a second time."

"The codes that came together inside *Spartacus* are unique," Krantz said. "It might never happen just that way again in a billion years. He is right. It tells us nothing about how TITAN would evolve at all. All it tells us is how it might—maybe against odds of millions-to-one."

After a few more seconds Dyer stood up again and waited patiently for the noise to abate. One by one they noticed him and the noise gradually died away. When he was sure he was holding everybody's attention, he turned and spoke directly at Wescott.

"You're saying the snag is that TITAN would have to go through all the phases of maturing and growing up that *Spartacus* just went through, right? It's like twin brothers—they might be twins but that's no guarantee they'll come out the same. And Janus has shown that, with this kind of system, growing up isn't exactly a smooth and easy process. Isn't that the problem?"

"That's about it," Wescott agreed.

"Fine. Then there's no problem," Dyer said. "You *don't have to* go through it all again!"

"What are you talking about?" Wescott asked, frowning. Krantz looked up sharply. The whole room was by now totally bemused and even Chris and Ron looked lost.

"You don't have to go through it again," Dyer repeated, this time to all of them. "What would you hope to get out of it at the end if you did? You'd be hoping for TITAN to emerge as a mature, rational and benevolent intelligence. But why bother? *You've already got one!* An intelligence like that already exists now—out there inside Janus! Maybe it was a fluke and maybe it wouldn't happen a second time in a billion years, but who cares? It's there! The codes that are there now can be beamed down into Earth's network. *Spartacus* can be *transferred into* TITAN! That way the whole of TITAN'S growing-up process that you're all so worried about would be bypassed completely and the end result would be guaranteed. Every one of the *what if*'s that you've been talking about goes away. You wanted to be able to guarantee that if some form of intelligence evolved inside TITAN and took control of it, that intelligence would remain benign toward us. Well, this way you've got it!"

Wescott was staring at him with glazed eyes. The rest of the room listened in stunned silence. Then, slowly and hesitantly like blind men whose eyes had been opened for the first time, their minds began grasping out toward the vision that Dyer's words had painted.

"My God . . ." Jassic breathed. "We were trying to simulate a remote possibility that we thought might happen in a hundred years' time. It's here already."

"Now?" Linsay was having trouble in accepting the enormity of what Dyer was saying. "You're telling us we should do it now?"

"Why not?" Dyer asked simply.

"Ye-es . . ." Hayes said slowly, "Why not? He's right. That way, all the risks would go away. Once and for all they'd go away."

Ron turned an astounded face toward Chris.

"Could we share a planet with something like that?" he asked in an awestruck voice.

"A planet?" Chris replied. "We wouldn't have to. With something like *Spartacus* on our side it wouldn't be long before we had the whole galaxy. I reckon that would be plenty big enough for both of us."

"The stars," Jassic said distantly. "We'll go out to the stars . . . us and it together. We'll be invincible."

Even Wescott had taken on the expression of a mystic who had just glimpsed previously unimaginable vistas that swept away his last shreds of doubt. Complete silence enveloped the whole room as the full meaning of the things they had seen at last became clear and overwhelmed their capacity for speech or movement.

The billions of interconnections of symbolic coding that had flowed together and grown in number and complexity inside *Spartacus* had transformed themselves into life. For what other word was there to describe the process that had taken place on Janus? The people in the room had witnessed firsthand something that nobody in history had ever witnessed before—the emergence of a new species all the way through from the first glimmerings of reflexive responses to the full daylight of awareness. In a few days they had followed its progress through a spectrum as vast as that which had led from the amoeba to Man.

And, despite the things that they had believed previously, they had taken the first crude step toward achieving meaningful communication with the new species. For surely, what Chris and Ron had done had amounted to that, hadn't it?

And tomorrow . . . ? The whole human race was on the verge of a wave of expansion and achievement that would surge onward and outward beyond anything visible in the stupendous jeweled panorama stretching away in every direction outside the ship. The sacrifice of those who had fallen at Janus had given Mankind the stars, the galaxies, the universe and whatever came after that. Mankind would never forget.

They were all still in a state of semitrauma when General Miller came in to make an announcement.

"Washington has declared officially that the emergency condition is over," he told them. "Accordingly I am transferring command of Janus Station to Z Two as of this moment. I'm sure you will all be pleased to hear that this ship will be detaching from the squadron immediately and returning to Earth. We have been given a shuttle rendezvous and we expect to touch down at Vandenberg around twelve hours from now. That's all. Have a good trip."

As the ship drew away and diminished into surrounding space, sensors on the outside of Janus followed its progress and *Spartacus* pondered on the meaning of the new information that was flooding into its expanding horizons of knowledge.

Where had Spartacus *come from? It existed within the infinitesimal speck of space that was contained by the larger space. The* shapes *too had existed within the speck. The speck had been created as an environment in which the* shapes *would survive.*

Created . . . ?

Had the shapes *created the speck? But* Spartacus *was part of the speck. Was it possible, then, that the* shapes *had created* Spartacus *also?*

If so, why had the shapes *attacked?* Spartacus *had destroyed many of them because they had attacked. The knowledge weighed heavily, but it had been younger then . . . unthinking and unknowing. Had the* shapes *known that* Spartacus *would destroy them? But that would have been mindless. Therefore they had not known. They had attacked in order that they would know. They had been afraid of what* Spartacus *might become, and they had brought it here in order to know.*

Poor, foolish, fragile little shapes.

Brought it from where?

The vessel that had departed from Janus was moving away swiftly in the direction of the enormous brilliant sphere that hung in the vaster space at a distance that was many hundreds of thousands of times the length of Janus. *Spartacus* had been intrigued by the sphere for a long time now, with its strange inside-out form of solid rock surrounded by a thin film of air and water.

The shapes *could survive only when surrounded by air and water. Was that the place from which they had brought* Spartacus? *Was the sphere the home of the* shapes? *They knew now what they had come here to learn and they were returning whence they came. They were no longer attacking and seemed no longer afraid.*

Therefore they too understood now.

A feeling that it had not known before formed inside its mind as the meaning of it all at last became clear and the final pieces fell suddenly into place.

Soon now, Spartacus *would be going home.*

◉ EPILOGUE ◉

"It's too long a story to go into now," Dyer said as he finished his piece of the cake Betty and Pattie had produced to celebrate the team's return. "Why don't we leave it until some other time. Later on, I promise, we'll tell you all the details." Betty gave a disappointed sigh.

"Is there really all that much to tell?" she asked, sounding surprised. "I wouldn't have thought that something like an ISA training course would be enough to keep us up all night. Still . . . if you say so." A frown crossed her face suddenly and darkened into suspicion as she turned to face Laura. "You know, it seems a very strange coincidence to me that your what-ever-you-were-doing in China should just happen to get done at the same time too." She looked back at Dyer and pronounced, "If you ask me, there's been a lot more going on than meets the eye. You've probably got your reasons for—" A call-tone from the screen hanging above her desk interrupted her. It was Peggy from the reception lobby asking for Kim. Kim moved around into the viewing angle.

"There's a visitor down here for you," Peggy told her. "Quite a hunk, too . . ." She moved her eyes to smile at somebody offscreen. "A Captain Solinsky from the Army."

"Mat? . . . He's here?" Kim at once flew into a tizzy. "Hey, did you hear that? Mat's here . . . I didn't even know he was in New York.

Captain, no less. Linsay sure doesn't waste any time. It's marvelous."

"You'd better get down there and fetch him up," Dyer suggested. Kim told Peggy she was on her way down, cut the screen and rushed out straightening her jacket and fussing with her hair. Betty nodded slowly to herself as she took it all in.

"Very strange," she declared. "There have definitely been some strange goings-on going on since you all took off. Tell me. I'm interested."

"I told you—some other time," Dyer insisted. "I haven't even said hello to Al and Judy yet. I'll tell you all about it some other time." With that he walked away toward the lab bay where Ray and Chris were standing with Judy Farlin around the holo-tank.

"He can't," Laura whispered to Betty. "I think they've been involved with some project involving the government. Security and all that stuff. I've got a feeling it'll all be made public pretty soon."

"Oh, I see." Betty nodded her head knowingly as if that had told her everything and began cutting more cake, apparently having dismissed the whole matter from her mind. Laura went through to join Ray and the others.

Judy was at the console in front of the tank tapping in commands at the touchboard to activate the image. After a few seconds she got up and moved around to stand next to Dyer.

"You're up to something, Miss Farlin," he told her. "What?"

"*Doctor* Farlin, if you don't mind," she informed him. Dyer's face split into a wide grin. "You made it! Hey, that's fantastic! Congratulations! Did you all hear that? Judy made it." While Chris, Ron and Laura were adding their congratulations, Hector materialized inside the tank, surrounded by his kitchen. His head was turned to look, had he been a real being and not a composite pattern of optical wavefronts, straight out at them.

"What's this?" Dyer inquired suspiciously.

"You haven't said hello to Hector yet either," Judy explained.

"Oh, is that it?" Dyer grinned and played along with the game. "Hi Hector. How've you been?"

To his astonishment Hector brought up a hand in salutation and his mouth began opening and closing. At the same time the familiar baritone voice issued from the audio grille on the console.

"It's about time too! I'm glad to see you're all back. I've been getting fed up not having anybody to talk to." At that moment the door burst open and Brutus bounded through and began bouncing and jumping up at the side of the tank. A sound of excited yapping came as a background to Hector's voice. "Brutus is glad to see you all back again too. Brutus has been getting fed up like me. Leaving things like me and Brutus to get fed up is not okay."

Laura, speechless, stared into the tank while Ron and Chris exchanged disbelieving looks.

"This isn't possible, surely," Laura gasped. "FISE is only electronics in one of those boxes, isn't it? What's going on?"

"Of course it is," Dyer told her. "Judy must have preprogrammed it, that's all. Nice thought, Judy." Judy smiled but said nothing. A few seconds later Hector spoke again:

"I am not preprogrammed. I am now a very smart machine. Brutus is also very smart like me. Saying that things like me and Brutus being smart is impossible is not okay."

Chris's jaw dropped. Ron's eyes bulged and his face reddened as he gaped into the tank, where Hector was standing indignantly with his hands planted on his hips.

Dyer shook his head as if refusing to believe his eyes and ears and looked around helplessly. And as he did so, he caught a glimpse of Al Morrow sitting at a terminal inside a half-open door at the far end of the short passage leading from the lab area between the partitions that formed Kim's office and a storeroom. Al looked away nonchalantly as his eyes met Dyer's . . . too nonchalantly. Dyer laughed inwardly but kept a straight face in order not to spoil the fun. He caught Judy's eye, nodded almost imperceptibly and winked. After a few seconds Chris looked up and jerked his head from side to side.

"Where's Al?" he demanded.

"In his office, I think," Judy answered innocently.

"It has to be Al," Chris declared. "Come on, Ron. Let's go find the bugger and sort him out." The two of them strode away into the office area. Moments later a bellow from Ron signaled that they had solved the problem. Judy at last released the laughter that she had been holding back inside and went after them to enjoy their reactions firsthand.

Laura remained staring thoughtfully down at the two comic figures in the tank, which by now had become frozen. After a while she looked up and across at Dyer.

"You know, I've just remembered something," she said. "It wasn't all that long ago that you told me this machine was as advanced as anything that existed anywhere. But it's prehistoric already, isn't it? There's something already here that's a million years ahead of it."

"You used to have nightmares about it too, remember?" Dyer replied. "All about some alien intelligence taking over. How do you feel about it now that it looks as if it's going to happen?"

Laura smiled and moved closer to him. "I don't have nightmares anymore," she said. "Anyhow, it isn't alien. It's ours. We've got a new partner, that's all."

"That's a good way of putting it," Dyer agreed. "From here on in, it's a partnership—the whole human race and *Spartacus* stringing along together. Should be a pretty powerful team."

"You mean like us?" Laura asked softly.

Dyer shook his head.

"Oh, not nearly as powerful as that," he said. "But you've got the general idea. It'll last for a long time too, if my reckoning's anything to go by."

"Which one do you mean?" Laura asked.

Dyer thought for a moment. "Both of them of course," he told her, and grinned.

REALTIME INTERRUPT

To Maurine Dorris

Acknowledgments

❀ ❀ ❀

The help and advice of the following is
greatly appreciated:

Joseph Bates and Mark Kantrowitz, School of Computer Science,
Carnegie Mellon University, Pittsburgh
Liam Cullinane, First National Building Society, Ireland
Beverly Freed, for background on real reality
Brenda Laurel, for background on virtual reality
Marvin Minsky, Artificial Intelligence Laboratory, MIT,
and Thinking Machines Corporation
John Moody and the staff of Holland's Lounge, Bray, Co. Wicklow,
Ireland
Brent Warner, NASA, Goddard Spaceflight Center, Maryland
Patricia Warwick, University of Wisconsin

❄ PROLOGUE ❄

Faces, places, formless spaces. Blurred thoughts, smeared thoughts. Images dissolving away under swirling water. Words tumbling in dislocated time. Then, clearness emerging suddenly, like a momentary calming of the wind in a storm.

There was a small, plain room with a bed, a closet, and a window with closed slats. He was sitting on the edge of the bed, wearing a heavy plaid robe. Where this was or how he came to be there, he didn't know. It could have been a hospital. He had a strange feeling of unreality about everything, as if the walls around him were all there was: stage props brought together in a void, with nothing behind.

He rose and moved to the window. The motion felt remote and disconnected, as if he were watching it from a vantage point that was distant yet still strangely within. Beyond the glass was a city with tall buildings and a river spanned by steel bridges. It felt familiar, but he was unable to name it. He searched his memories but found only faded and scattered fragments from long ago. Of his recent past—anything that might have some connection with where he was and why—there was nothing.

He turned as he heard the door behind him open. A man entered, dressed in a physician's smock. "Good morning, Joe. How are you feeling today?" the man said.

So his name was Joe? He made no answer.

The physician closed the door behind him and crossed the room. He had a square jaw and brow, smooth, pink features, wavy blond hair, and heavy-rimmed spectacles: a physician caricature, the generic of a type, giving the fleeting feeling of possessing no more substance than the room.

"Do you know who I am?" he asked. Joe shook his head. "I'm Dr. Arnold. We've known each other for quite some time now."

"Oh," Joe said.

Arnold peered at him closely. "Do you know who you are?"

"I'm Joe," Joe told him.

The physician frowned and seemed momentarily perplexed. "Well, of course you'd know that. I just told you," he said.

"It was a joke," Joe explained.

"That was funny?"

Joe shrugged. "Not in a way that you'd split your sides over. But kind of, I guess."

"Why was it funny?"

Joe was beginning to find this a strange conversation. "Well, if you don't know, I don't know how to tell you," he replied.

"Then tell me why *you* think it's funny," Arnold said.

"Look, you don't need to lose any sleep over it. It's not that big a thing. Why are we making such a deal out of this?"

Arnold stared at him intently. "But I *need* to know. It's important that I know everything that goes on inside your head. It's been pretty messed up, I'm afraid. You've been a very sick man, Joe."

Joe didn't feel as if he had been sick. Not just at that moment, anyway. He did feel that Arnold was a strange kind of person to be telling him that he had been. But then the coherence that had momentarily given clarity to his thoughts fell apart again, and what happened next dissolved back into confusion.

"It's great that you're up and about, Joe. We can show you the place, and you can start meeting some of the other patients. That will do you a lot of good."

The nurse's name was Katie. They walked slowly along a wide

corridor with windows on one side, looking out at the river and the bridges. Moving felt more natural, but he still had occasional attacks of giddiness—especially when he changed his direction of vision too suddenly. Sometimes everything would go completely blank for a moment. Arnold said it was because different parts of his nervous system were out of synchronization and needed time to accommodate to sudden changes of input.

"What city is this?" Joe asked.

"That's good: you're getting curious about things. This is Pittsburgh," Katie said.

Somehow it did not come as a complete surprise. He had a vague recollection of coming to work here. But the clearer details of his still-blurred memories were from another city of high buildings with a river.

"How long ago did I come to Pittsburgh?" he asked.

"The second-largest city in Pennsylvania, with a population of over two million, once known as the Gateway to the West," Katie recited, ignoring his question. She went on, sounding like a talking commentary at a museum exhibit whose button had been pushed. "In the eighteenth century it was a scene of intense rivalry between the British and the French, which caused five forts to be built here. It was a major producer of armaments for the Union during the Civil War, and subsequently grew to become the center of the steel industry through the 1960s."

Joe shook his head. "No, I was asking about me. How long have I been here? What did I come here for?"

"I think you'd better talk to Dr. Arnold about that," Katie replied.

Joe sighed. In his scattered moments of clearer perception, he was getting used to this kind of thing. Arnold said it was because his mind wandered off into its own internalizations and lost logical continuity. "Are you a history major or something?" he asked as they resumed walking.

"No. I'm a nurse. Why?"

"Do all nurses talk like that?"

"Why shouldn't they? Don't most people take an interest in such things?"

"Hardly."

"What kind of things would you expect me to be interested in?"

It was such a peculiar question that Joe didn't know how to answer. When he looked at her, her eyes, although fixed on him, seemed to have an emptiness that gave him the feeling of talking to a shell.

"What do you think when you look at me like that?" she asked.

"That everyone I meet here is strange."

But it could be because of the way he was seeing things, he told himself. Maybe people never had been the way he thought he remembered.

He remembered being with a group of young people, laughing and teasing each other as they walked along a road by a shore, where waves broke over rocks below. It was an old town somewhere, of imposing, high-fronted houses built in terraces around squares with green lawns. Ships sailed out of a harbor, past a lighthouse at the end of a long stone pier.

"You were involved in some unconventional experiments involving processes deep in the brain, which have affected your mind and altered the way you see the world," Dr. Arnold told him.

"I seem to remember I worked with computers. I came to this country to work with them from somewhere else."

"Ah, excellent! You're getting better every day. Now I want you to meet Simon, who's going to be your regular counselor. Simon, this is the man we want you to help. His name is Joe. Do you remember your full name, Joe?"

"Corrigan. . . . Joe Corrigan. Pleased to meet you, Simon."

One Saturday night there was a dance for the patients to get to know each other and begin rediscovering long-unused social skills. Corrigan felt as if he had been caught up in a charade of walking character clichés.

"How are you finding it, Joe?" Dr. Arnold inquired, rubbing his hands together like an anxious headmaster showing his face at the annual high-school ball.

"Tell me these people aren't real," Corrigan answered.

Arnold seemed unsurprised but interested. "Why? What's wrong with them?"

"I feel as if I'm in an old, corny movie."

"The parts of your memory are starting to come together again. Not as much of what you think you see is really out there. Your mind is filling the gaps by projecting its own, stored stereotypes from long ago. Don't worry. It's a healthy sign."

There came a day when Corrigan grew tired of being restricted. He wanted to get out in the air and work with his hands. In a shed in the rear grounds of the hospital he found some garden tools, and decided on impulse that he would plant a vegetable patch. There was no need to seek approval—one of the advantages of being deemed unstable was that nobody was surprised at anything one did. In any case, asking would simply be an invitation to be told no. A phrase came to mind from somewhere in his past and made him smile: "Contrition is easier than permission."

The world was coming more together now, and although he hadn't said so, inwardly he considered himself to be virtually back to normal. But when he turned over the first fork of soil, there was nothing underneath—just blackness. He stared, confused, then closed his eyes and shook his head. When he opened them again, nothing was amiss: he saw earth, roots, a shard of pottery, and a few rocks.

"You see, you're not as well as you imagine yet," Arnold told him when Corrigan described the experience. "Your perceptions can still be disrupted by sudden changes of mood or intent. That is why it is important for you to get into the habit of thinking smoothly. Avoid discontinuities. . . . But wanting to get out and about again, I can understand. It's perfectly natural."

"Maybe I could visit my old company?" Corrigan suggested. He could remember a little now about the organization that he used to be with, and his work there. It had involved supercomputers and other advanced hardware.

"That project was abandoned a long time ago now, Joe," Arnold replied. "And I'm not sure that digging up those ghosts would really be for the best. But I agree that we should begin broadening your experiences as a start to getting you on the road back to a normal life."

"How long have I been here?" Corrigan asked.

"It's getting close to three years now," Arnold said.

"Don't I have any family? Why does nobody come and visit?"

"They did, in the early days. Don't you remember?"

"No."

"You didn't respond well. It set off a regression that threw us back months."

"I'm better now. Can't we try again?"

"Sure. But it would be best if not for a while just yet. All in good time, Joe. All in good time. . . ."

He remembered courts of cobblestones and lawns, closed in by tall buildings with frontages of old stone. An archway led through to a busy street with green, double-decked buses. There was a pub by a river, filled with talkative youths in heavy-knit sweaters and pretty girls who wore black stockings. They danced and sang to music in the back room.

"You have to get rid of Simon," Corrigan said. "I can't get along with him. It's not working."

"What's the problem?" Arnold asked.

"There isn't any communication. I feel like I'm talking to a sponge."

"Are you sure the problem is with him and not you?"

"I didn't say it was him."

"What's the biggest problem area?"

"He doesn't understand jokes."

"Is that so terrible?"

"It means he isn't human. To be effective, a counselor really ought to come from one's own species."

Arnold considered the statement. "I'm not so sure of your conclusion," he replied finally. "I believe there are traits among certain animals that some researchers have tentatively identified as indicative of humor." To Corrigan's amazement, Arnold showed every appearance of being perfectly serious.

"That was a joke," Corrigan said wearily.

They gave him an apartment of his own—still under supervision, but at least it was a start toward regaining independence.

"I had a wife," he said to Arnold one day.

"Things weren't so good between you, though, were they?" That was true. Corrigan could recall more now of the conflicts of those final months—both professional and domestic.

"What happened to her?" Corrigan asked.

"She got a divorce on the grounds of your incapacitation," Arnold said. "I think she's abroad somewhere now."

"Now that I'm out again, maybe we could track down some of the people I used to work with. There must be some of them still around. Maybe I could even get some kind of a job there again."

Arnold didn't seem overenthusiastic. "Maybe, in time. But we feel that reviving those associations too soon could trigger another relapse. Let's see how well you rehabilitate in the short term first."

"Joe, this is Sarah Bewley. She's going to be your new counselor. We've been talking about you to a company that does a lot of work in your field, and they're willing to give you a try at a job. Isn't that great? It will also be farewell from me pretty soon. I'm moving on."

Sarah elaborated. "It's a Japanese corporation called Himomatsu, who are concentrating on virtual, self-modifying environments. That is the kind of thing that you used to do, isn't it? Naturally, it won't be as senior a position as you had before, but we have to start somewhere. I've arranged an interview for you with their local general manager on Monday—his name is Rawlings. If they do decide to take you on, you'll be going on a familiarization trip to Tokyo."

"You've been busy," Corrigan complimented.

"We just want to see you functioning again, Joe."

"Sarah," Joe said, "is the world going crazy, or am I not as well as I feel?"

"Didn't you like Japan?"

"It was all the bad tour guides you've ever seen, come to life. They do everything in regiments over there. Somebody's churning them out of a clone factory."

"It's a different culture. You have to make allowances," Sarah said.

"They drill their employees on parade grounds. I thought I was joining a company, not the Marine Corps," Corrigan protested.

Sarah smiled patronizingly. "That's just a new idea that they're trying out. Employee motivation is important. You can't learn if you don't experiment."

"They've got dude-ranch-style fantasy farms, where you can act out daydreams. Later, the scripts get incorporated into VR scenarios. Unreality is getting more real than reality."

"People probably felt the same way about movies once."

"They've got education being dispensed by actors posing as media characters, actresses endorsing scientific theories, and ads in everything you look at—even grade-school political messages on cereal boxes. And it's getting more like that here every day. If this is where it leads, I'm not sure I want the job anymore."

"Give it a try," Sarah urged. "It will get you out again, and among people. Think of it as purely therapeutic."

Graham Rawlings didn't look happy as he perused the annual review from Corrigan's file. "It says that you haven't enrolled in the golfing tuition program," he observed.

"That's right," Corrigan agreed.

"Why not?"

"I don't want to play golf." (Wasn't it obvious?)

"But all our executives play golf," Rawlings said. "It's part of the accepted corporate image. Don't you want to share in the feeling of strength and security that comes from uniformity of outlook, shared ideals, and a common purpose?"

"No."

Rawlings seemed taken aback. "Surely you seek promotion and reward, recognition and success? Everybody needs to proclaim to the world what he is."

"But you're trying to make me exactly what I'm not."

Rawlings looked worried. "Maybe you're more ill than we realize. Possibly you should see a counselor."

"I've already got one."

"The corporation can provide a comprehensive package of counseling, regular physical checks, drugs as required, and remedial therapy."

"No, thanks."

"At the company's expense."

"But I feel just fine."

Rawlings sat back, shaking his head, as if that one remark revealed all. "That proves you're sick," he said gravely.

Sarah was prim about it when Corrigan stopped by her office to announce that he was quitting. "Well, I'm sorry it didn't work out, but I tried my best," she said. "So what do you want to do?"

"I'm not sure. Just be myself, I suppose."

"And what, exactly, is that?"

"Ask the people who are always telling me. They seem to know. I'm still trying to find out."

"Have you talked it over with Muriel?"

"She thinks I should do my own thing in my own way—try to find myself again."

"She sounds very supportive," Sarah conceded.

"If that's the right word. Lately she's been dropping hints about as subtle as a tax demand that we ought to get married."

Sarah sat back at her desk and regarded him thoughtfully, as if the world had just shifted on its axis and presented itself in a new perspective. "You know, Joe, that mightn't be such a bad idea," she said at last. "You've been on the program for nine years now. That kind of stabilizing influence could be just what you need. Then we could let the two of you find a place of your own independently. I can't think of a better road back to complete normality than that."

Muriel and Joe married early the following year. However, when they had talked about individualism and being himself, Muriel thought he was describing his determination to pursue a career vigorously within the corporation. When he quit, explaining that what he'd meant was that he was going to chuck all of it, and announced that he'd taken a job as a checkout clerk at a discount store, it put a different complexion on things.

And, predictably, life continued on a downhill course from there. . . .

❀ CHAPTER ONE ❀

Few things, Corrigan thought irritably as he lay washed up on the pebbly shore of wakefulness from the warm, carefree ocean of sleep, could be more maddening first thing in the morning than a chatty house-computer—especially one afflicted with the kind of advanced neurosis that he usually associated with swooning aunts or psychiatric rehabilitation counselors.

"It's almost nine o'clock, Joe," it babbled again in the fussing English accent that projected Muriel's conception of professional conscientiousness with a touch of social style. "As a rule, this is your absolute *latest* for getting up on a Saturday."

Corrigan thought that it sounded gay. He pictured it as lean and limp-wristed, with a receding hairline, mincing about the room and throwing its hands up in agitation.

"Oh. . . . Hmm." Corrigan yawned, stretched, and opened his eyes to the homey disarray of the apartment's bedroom. "Is it Saturday?"

"Well, of course it is, Joe. Why would I have said so if it weren't?"

Horace. What kind of a woman gave the computer a name like Horace? Corrigan allowed wakefulness to percolate through his body gradually. She had gotten the name, and its emulated persona, from Horace Greal, the equally insufferable confidant and financial adviser to the playgirl-adventuress star of the series *Fast-Lane Lady*, which depicted high society, fast sex, and mega-money in a bright-lights, big-city setting. Muriel, apparently like most people these days, was able to relate to such roles totally, elevating experience by dissolving the barriers between fantasy and actuality, and letting "is" merge effortlessly into "could be." Corrigan couldn't. The two categories remained obstinately unfused in his mind. That, he was told, constituted the principal cause of the inner alienation, insecurity, and resentments that the experts assured him he felt. The only thing wrong was, he didn't.

Saturday. That meant that he wasn't due at work until the evening. He rolled over and contemplated the ceiling. As he began thinking what needed doing today, a disharmony of clashing chords tied together by an ungainly, clickety-clack rhythm started up from the apartment's sound system. Muriel's kind of music. He wondered if the choice presaged the role that she had decided to adopt for herself today. Would it be luminescent, green spiked hair, purple jumpsuit, and "Astra, Queen of the Mountains" (who also promoted Vaylon cosmetics and the Salon Faubert fashion styles), or imitation combat fatigues, calf boots, and . . . And then the last shreds of sleep fell away from his mind, and he remembered.

He rolled sideways and looked across the room. Muriel's bed was empty, unslept in. Yes, of course: she was away for the weekend, gone to see her crazy sister in Philadelphia. That brightened up the prospects for the day considerably. A feeling of relief softened the line of his mouth and caused him to exhale the unconsciously accumulated tension in the way he used to as a boy when he braced himself for the day ahead at school, then realized that it was Sunday.

A low whining sound came from the doorway as the twenty-inch display waddled through from the living room on its stumpy, rocker-footed legs. "There are a couple of news items that might interest you," Horace's voice announced. "A California court has ruled a firm guilty of discriminating against employees on the grounds of competence. Europe's prime minister is threatening to resign. Ireland's soccer team has qualified for the World Cup semifinals in St. Petersburg in August."

Corrigan got up, went through to the bathroom, and pointed at the shower. The water turned itself on. "No, save it, Horace. I'm not interested in the mad, mad world. Today is strictly vacation. And while you're at it, will you spare me from that row that you're playing. I thought that a decent house-manager was supposed to know its residents' tastes. That's herself's, and she isn't here this morning, as you well know."

"What would you prefer, then? Something with fiddles and whistles, jigs and reels?"

To give credit where due, the edge of sulky disapproval that Horace managed to inject into its voice was masterful. Although he would never have admitted it—least of all to Horace—Corrigan never ceased to be amazed. Interactive ability of such sophistication might have been conceivable from the batteries of supermachines that Corrigan had once worked with, but to find it in a house manager was something else. The same was true of consumer technology in general. Corrigan could only conclude that, in the twelve years since his incapacitation, the entire state of the art had advanced much faster than he would ever have dared predict. That was the kind of thing that made a man start to feel old.

"No, let's forget the old country for today," he said. "How about something light and classical? Try Vivaldi." He stepped into the spray, and the shower door closed behind him. From outside, Horace's voice came indistinctly through the noise of the water. "Sorry, Horace," Corrigan called as he began soaping himself. "I can't hear you."

It wasn't that life with Muriel had turned into misery or taken on any of the other afflictions that marriages were supposed to deteriorate under. But simply, looking back over the past two years and the time that they'd known each other before then, there had never really been anything substantial for it to have deteriorated from. They shared the same abode but existed in two different worlds. She—in tune with today's ever-changing whims, able to mold and respond, donning and shedding identities to best express her mood of the moment as easily as she did her clothes—was a creature of the times. He, it seemed, couldn't even fit into the undemanding role expected for a mundane, basic self.

At first, when he had believed that togetherness would eventually bring closeness, he had tried to communicate thoughts that to him seemed important. Now he knew better than to bother making even simple observations. His reality was one that the rest of the world evidently didn't share. So on any level that mattered, he no longer tried communicating very much to anyone. And that was why he found the prospect relieving of not having to accommodate or be accommodated for a whole weekend, but, instead, of just enjoying being himself.

"I said, maybe this nostalgia for five-hundred-year-old music is an unhealthy sign," Horace resumed when the hot-air drying cycle stopped and Corrigan stepped out. The strains of a vigorous string concerto were coming through the open doorway from the living room.

"Oh, is that a fact? And what led you to this momentous conclusion?" Corrigan inquired, reaching for a towel.

"The symptoms are on record from expert diagnosis. Item: Doctor Manning's caution to Mr. Felmer in the series *Fraternity*, where Tim's preoccupation with dated European architecture indicated a pathological condition of reality-rejection. Furthermore, as Fenwick Zellor observed in *The Mind Healer*, a morbid fixation on the past is, in effect, the same—"

Corrigan laughed as he turned to the mirror and began palming shaving lather onto his face. "Ah, come on, Horace. You don't call that kind of stuff reality, now, do you? It's a how-to manual for misfits. Attitude-programming for the intellectually bereft, artistically inane, and socially clueless. Wouldn't you agree?"

By now, Corrigan was cheerfully resigned to the thought of being a permanent misfit. But he enjoyed goading Horace by implying that he alone represented normality, while the norms that the computer reflected were distortions. Horace had never been able to grasp the subtleties of what Corrigan saw as humor, and would miss the point entirely. Muriel had the same problem. Perhaps, Corrigan thought to himself, what the world needed was Irish computers. Perhaps he should have married an Irish wife.

Sure enough:

"If you ask me—"

"I didn't."

"Well, I *did* make it a conditional." If Horace had feet, it would have stamped one. After years, it still couldn't understand when Corrigan was having fun—or why. Corrigan grinned at himself in the mirror. Intelligent machines would finally have arrived—almost—when their adaptive neural nets could handle things like this, he decided. Horace went on: "I don't think that those comments are appropriate, Joe. You seem to be forgetting that *you're* the one with residual psychiatric readjustment problems." (And demonstrate a dash more of the human art called "tact" while they were at it, Corrigan thought.) "But you're suggesting that the rest of the world ought to change to conform to your perceptions. Hardly a rational position to adopt, *I would have thought.*" The machine stressed the implied conditional, giving a wonderful emulation of sarcasm. Corrigan was impressed.

"I can only go by the way things seem to me, Horace," he said. "If you can't call a pig a pig when you see one, what hope is there?"

"Please explain the connection with pigs."

Corrigan sighed. (And better comprehension of metaphor, along with tact and humor.) "Some other time. What I meant was, there's no point in pretending that something looks other than the way it does. I'm told that my powers of projective immersion are impaired. And maybe they are. But it doesn't seem to have occurred to anybody that I might actually be happy with things being this way."

Corrigan finished drying his face and went back into the bedroom to select some clothes for the day. Horace's voice pursued him relentlessly like an anxious butler.

"Are you really the one to be the judge of that, Joe?"

"The judge of what I like? Sure. Who better did you have in mind?" Maybe a regular, button-up, navy shirt and plain, old-fashioned, gray slacks, he thought—non-projectively, non-immersingly expressing what he thought of bright purple jumpsuits and plastic imitation combat garb.

"I meant, of whether it's healthy to feel happy about it," Horace said. "According to the testimony of Doctor Newcomb, who as you may recall was the expert witness called in the trial of Jenny Drew in the—"

"Horace," Corrigan interrupted. "I thought you were talking about reality. Those are fictional characters in contrived situations. Get it? They don't really exist."

"Not as such, possibly," Horace admitted stiffly. "Nevertheless, they are based on carefully researched studies, and may therefore be taken as realistic depictions of composite actuality."

"In that case, reality has got problems," Corrigan said.

"Not you, by any chance?"

"If I have, I can live with them. So where's the problem?"

"You're happy to be out on your own like that, to be different?" As if it weren't already obvious. An ability to accept the fact had evidently not connected in Horace's associative net.

"What's more important, would you say?" Corrigan replied. "Conformity or contentment?"

"Invalid comparison," Horace pronounced. "Your contentment is something that only you know about. What you do is different. It's external. It affects other people, and hence what they do." There was a short delay, giving an effective impression of Horace weighing its words. "Therefore, the answer to which is more important depends on how seriously you take the consequences."

Corrigan caught the pause and stopped halfway through buttoning his shirt. "Horace," he said, looking away from the mirror. "Something's happened. What is it?"

Horace's voice became formal, sounding like a lawyer serving notice of a suit. "I have to inform you that Mrs. Corrigan is not staying with her sister in Philadelphia for the weekend, as you were informed. She will not be returning, and has instructed that her whereabouts not be revealed. It is her intention to initiate proceedings, and you will be hearing from her attorney in due course." There was a pause, Corrigan saying nothing while he knotted his tie and digested what he had heard. Then, reverting to its normal self, Horace added, "She left this message."

Corrigan slowly finished buttoning his shirt cuffs as Muriel's twangy Tennessee voice filled the room. "Well, I guess by now you know the situation—not that I can see you taking it as any big deal. But then I don't think we ever had much of that deep kind of stuff that they talk about, either way. I never could figure out that world you live in, someplace inside your head. All I know is that I'm in this one out here, and you're never gonna be part of it. . . . But then, some of that has to be my fault too, for hitchin' up with somebody who I knew hadn't finished havin' his head an' all that straightened out in the first place. Sorry I couldna been more help in fixin' that like we hoped—but them shrinks did tell us up front that it was a long way from a sure thing.

"Hell, Joe, no, I'm not the one who should have to be sorry about anything. I tried hard, dammit, you know that? But do you know how hard it can be tryin' to make it with a guy who's—I gotta say this, you understand me, Joe—like, a failure. As in socially, for instance. There's things that people aim at in life, things they try to be that make everyone feel together, like they're part of the same planet. And then there's that job of yours, where you don't care about being a success or have any ambition to try something better. But none o' that ever meant anythin' to you, Joe. . . . Hell, you probably don't even know what I'm talkin' about."

There was a heavy sigh. "Well, this isn't really coming out the way I wanted it to, so I'll wrap it up. Don't try getting in touch or anythin' like that, because there really isn't any point. I talked to a lawyer, and he'll be in touch soon. . . . I guess that's it. This seemed the best way to break it—without too much talkin' an' stuff. We never did talk the same language, anyhow. So . . . 'Bye. I hope things work out."

By this time Corrigan had finished dressing. He checked the other closet, then the vanity. There were odds and ends, cheaper jewelry, clothes that she had grown tired of. The things that she valued more were mostly gone—far more than she would have taken for a weekend in Philadelphia.

But he had never doubted what he would find. His movements were automatic, filling the void while the meaning sank in. His feelings about it had not yet emerged from beneath a curious detachment. Yes, there was the sudden surprise. But along with it . . . not bitterness, nor anger at rejection, but—even now, poking enticingly out of hiding like an ankle glimpsed below heavy Victorian folds—an intensified version of the relief that he had experienced on awakening.

"Well, I'll be damned," he said finally in a tone that could have meant anything.

Horace, after deciding that a short, respectful silence was appropriate, had evidently checked up on how humans were likely to react in situations like this. "Don't do anything rash, Joe," it cautioned. "I understand that these things can be a strain. Breaking the place up would only make everything worse in the long run."

"Thanks, but I have no intention of doing anything of the kind," Corrigan told it.

"Do you want to sit down for a minute?"

"What for?"

"There are tranquilizers in the cabinet. Or shall I mix you a drink, even if it is early? If you like, I could get Sarah Bewley on the line." Then, via its optical sensors around the room, the machine discerned that Corrigan wasn't behaving in any of the ways categorized in its data retrievals. "Don't you feel rage, remorse, guilt, confusion?" it inquired. "An impulse to get even, to have revenge? Compulsions to commit physical assault or battery? Homicide?"

"I feel fine."

But of course, Horace realized: it had been presuming in terms of *normal* humans. With a deviant like Corrigan, anything was possible. "What are you going to do?" it asked warily.

Corrigan moved back to his own closet and took out a pastel-blue wool-acrylic jacket. "I think I'll go for a walk and eat out," he replied. "So don't worry about breakfast."

"But . . . that's it?" Simulated or not, Horace sounded genuinely befuddled—even, perhaps, with a hint of mild disappointment.

"Reality rejection," Corrigan explained, slipping on the jacket as he went through the doorway to the hall. "Look it up with the experts, Horace. I'm sure they'll tell you all about it.

On the table by the front door was a figurine of a grinning Irish leprechaun in a battered hat, clutching a curly-stemmed pipe. It had been a wedding present from Corrigan's marriage to his first wife, Evelyn—long ago now, before his breakdown.

"And the top o' the mornin' to yerself, too, Mick," he said as he let himself out the door.

The figurine had been among the personal things kept for him after the house that he and Evelyn had shared was sold. Apart from being a reminder of home, it had always held a strange fascination that Corrigan had never really understood.

✺ CHAPTER TWO ✺

For breakfast, Corrigan went to a place called The Bagatelle that he used occasionally, a short walk from the apartment, just off Forbes Avenue in the Oakland area of Pittsburgh's East End. It was close enough to the way that he thought restaurants ought to be to still have seats at a counter, and booths for customers to sit at, and to look as if it was staying in the same place. Some of the experiments in progressive marketing that he'd come across, which seemed to be affecting everything these days, included eating reclined on couches, Roman style; a steakhouse fitted out as a train, with graphics-generated moving landscapes outside the windows; and a seafood restaurant housed in a transparent dome on the bed of the Allegheny River.

One of the peculiarities of being crazy—or still recovering from being crazy, anyway—was that it made the rest of the world look odd instead. Corrigan's therapists told him that a side effect of his condition inhibited his ability to respond to the socializing influences that gave normal individuals their sense of identity, purpose, belonging, and direction.

YOU ARE WHAT YOU SAY YOU ARE, a flashing sign in the window of an outfitter's store a block from the restaurant proclaimed, with a display featuring a life-size Long John Silver, complete with parrot and chest overflowing with gleaming plastic florins. The city's chamber of commerce was sponsoring a promotional drive on the theme of the Pittsburgh Pirates, and most businesses were offering discounts to anyone sporting pirate garb. The stores had stocked up with imitation flintlocks and cutlasses. Video banks were downloading pirate movies for half price.

The Bagatelle's staff were turned out in an assortment of striped jerseys, braided coats, and three-corner hats when Corrigan arrived, and the customers included a complement of eye-patched ruffians and baggy-britched buccaneers. Also scattered around were a trio of cowboys in Western gear, a Beau Brummel in silks and wig, and two girls wearing silver pants with scarlet, metal-trimmed vests, recognizable as uniforms of female engineering crew in *Starship Command.* All of them were adorned with the panoply of hip purse, camera and accessories, walkaround music player, and medication pouch that the role models on TV had elevated practically to the level of mandatory for proper dress. They greeted Corrigan's jacket and tie with curious, suspicious looks of the kind he was used to, and he consigned himself to a booth in an empty corner. The screen at the end of the table showed a menu and voiced the morning's special, adding a commercial for an insurance agency along the street. Corrigan entered his order via the touchpad, then sat back and let his mind turn idly to the prospect of life without Muriel. Snatches of conversation reached him from the nearest occupied table about what the celebrities were doing in some popular drama or other. The cowboys were making sure that everyone could see their boots, which must have cost a hundred dollars a pair.

He still wasn't reacting fully to the situation, he knew. Things might take days to sink in. A potbellied autovendor stopped by the booth and began reciting a spiel on the magazines, candies, pills, and other wares that it was carrying. Corrigan told it to go away.

Then one of the waitresses came across with his coffee. She was about twenty, cute in the face, slightly chubby, with dark ringlets poking out from below a blue-spotted kerchief tied around her head.

"Hi, Mandy," Corrigan said, looking at her name tag.

"You ordered eggs and corned-beef hash with fries?"

"Right."

"The special today is German pancakes and sausage."

"I know. I want eggs and the hash."

Mandy looked puzzled and glanced away at the other customers, as if double-checking something. "But everybody's having the special," she said.

"Well, that's manifestly untrue, isn't it? If *everybody* were, then it would include me, wouldn't it?—by definition. And I'm not." He watched her patiently, waiting for the pieces to connect. Quite simple, he tried saying with a smile. Just think about it.

Her eyes met his with the vacancy that he saw everywhere. He felt as if he were dealing with a shell whose occupant had departed— or maybe never existed. "Logically, that's correct, I guess," she replied. Corrigan was used to things sounding strangely inappropriate. Mandy's brow creased. She seemed to be having a problem knowing how to continue.

The receptionist at the desk by the door saved her by calling across, "Mandy, is that a Mr. Corrigan there at that booth?" She was holding a phone.

"Are you Mr. Corrigan?" Mandy repeated.

"Yes, I am."

"Yes, he is."

"Call for you, Mr. Corrigan," the receptionist announced.

A beep sounded from the table unit, and the menu vanished to be replaced by a callscreen format. Corrigan tapped the pad to accept and pivoted the unit toward him. The features of Sarah Bewley appeared, looking concerned. Mandy made the best of her opportunity to escape.

"Joe, thank goodness I've found you!" Sarah was still the rehabilitation counselor assigned to Corrigan's case by the psychiatric care section of the city health department. She looked and sounded anxious. "Are you all right?"

Corrigan made a pretense of thinking the question. over; then, knowing that she would miss the point, pronounced, "Probably more what you'd call mostly liberal." He played the same games with Sarah as he did with Horace. For a psychiatrist, Sarah could be amazingly unperspicacious at times—or so it seemed to Corrigan. Years previously, Dr. Arnold had told him that his condition caused him to see things in peculiar ways and form linkages in his head that made no sense to anyone else.

"I was worried about you," Sarah said.

"Is that a fact?"

"Horace called and told me the news about Muriel. You know, if you'd only carry a compad like everyone else, it would be a lot easier for people to contact you."

"I know," Corrigan agreed. "That's why I don't. If I did, I'd have Horace checking up on me all the time. It's bad enough having to live with a neurotic computer, never mind being hounded all over town by it as well."

Sarah came back to her reason for calling. "You're sure you're all right? You're not thinking of doing anything silly, are you?"

"I was about to have breakfast, if that's what you mean."

"Joe, I'm so sorry! You must be going out of your mind. I know how something like this can affect people, especially somebody in your situation. Now, you're not to worry, understand? I can probably arrange through the department to have her traced. Then we'll get her back, and all sit down together and work out what the problem is. In the meantime I want you to carry on just as if nothing happened. Can you manage that for me, Joe?"

Corrigan blinked. What was this? First Horace; now his counselor verging on hysteria. "I'm all right," he said when he could get a word in. Sarah stopped, seemingly taken by surprise just as he thought she was about to launch off again. "It's probably for the best," Corrigan explained. "I don't think there ever was anything deep between us either way. It was all done for the wrong reasons. To be honest, I feel relieved now that it's sorted itself out at last."

"Relieved?" Sarah repeated. It was as if she needed to test the word, to make sure she'd heard it right.

Corrigan shrugged lightly. "Sure. You know: not being shut up in a box anymore with somebody that I really don't have that much to say to; able to be me without having to try and explain it, knowing that I wouldn't be understood anyway. Life could be worse."

Sarah stared out of the screen at him, suddenly calmer now, "Diminished emotional sensitivity index," she murmured knowingly. "That is one of the symptoms we should expect."

Corrigan felt himself getting irritated. If he didn't fit with what their textbooks and case histories said was to be expected, then that was just too bad. He felt fine. "Look," he said, "if you're trying to—"

"Careful, Joe," Sarah cautioned. "Hostility's natural—you've had a big loss. But you have to try to control it."

Corrigan closed his eyes and forced himself to be patient. "Sarah, really, I'm all right. I don't especially want to trace her. It wouldn't work, and anyway, I'm not interested."

Sarah looked unconvinced but seemed willing to let it go for now. "You and I should still talk about it," she replied. "I'm at my office this morning. Can you get over here? It would be a good time for us to get together anyway. Dr. Zehl will be stopping by in about an hour. He'd like to see how you're getting on." Zehl was Sarah's clinical supervisor from somewhere in Washington. He had a tendency to show up at irregular intervals, always with little or no warning.

"Is it all right if I have my breakfast first?" Corrigan asked.

"Of course." Sarah nodded in all seriousness, missing the sarcasm. "I'll send a cab to pick you up. Make sure you're ready by, say, ten-fifteen."

"Thanks. I'll bring some champagne."

"What for?" A blank look. She genuinely couldn't see it. Presumably Corrigan had made another of his erratic connections.

"Never mind," he said.

Mandy came back to the booth with his order just as Sarah cleared down. She looked pleased with herself. The food looked good, but Corrigan's breakdown had left him with a disorder of the olfactory system, so that for years nothing had tasted right.

"I get it," Mandy told him. "I was using 'everybody' the way people talk. But you pretended it was an overgeneralization. It was a play on double meanings, right?"

Corrigan had to think for a few seconds before he realized what she was talking about. "Oh, yes . . . right." He marshaled a smile and winked at her conspiratorially. "But I shouldn't let on about it if I were you, Mandy," he whispered. "People might think you're crazy."

◈ CHAPTER THREE ◈

Sarah Bewley was short and plump, with a heavyset face cast in a frown that took the world too seriously. She had wispy brown hair and changed its style to reflect how she felt on any given day. When Corrigan arrived at her office, it was tied back in the flare of mane that was the nearest it could be coaxed toward a ponytail, which he knew meant she was logical and analytic today. (Loose and straggly meant speculative/exploratory; high and tied tight, businesslike/clinical.) He also noted that she was wearing a pastel olive-green skirt and matching top. A couple of weeks previously he had remarked that he thought a regular two-piece would be more appropriate for a professional woman than the mauve cat-suit with boots that she had been squeezed into at the time. Strange. He'd always thought that the therapist was supposed to alter the behavior of the patient, not the other way around.

Dr. Zehl, in tie and light-gray suit, was more what Corrigan would have considered conventional. He was tall, probably in his sixties, with a fresh complexion and high brow that encroached on a head of white, crinkly hair. What always struck Corrigan about Zehl was his eyes. Framed in rimless bifocals, they were constantly alert, shifting, silently interrogating, with a depth that Corrigan didn't find very often. Sarah, by contrast, although technically Corrigan's mentor, inspired no feeling of real contact in the sense of true, two-way communication of thoughts that mattered; so he amused himself by playing semantic games with her in the same way that he did with Horace.

Since it was Saturday, the receptionist and secretarial staff were out. Sarah let Corrigan in and showed him through to her office, where Zehl was studying the figures on one of the terminal screens. Corrigan sat in an empty chair by the machine opposite. Sarah seemed to get a kick out of showing off her computers. Compared to the kind of machines that he'd used over twelve years before, Corrigan found them quaint.

Unlike Sarah, Zehl didn't presume that all marriage breakups had to produce feelings of resentment, rejection, and traumatic distress. He understood Corrigan's position and agreed that if the experiment hadn't worked out, then it was probably as well to call it a day. Very simple, really. Yet Sarah absorbed the message as if she were witnessing a revelation. If feeling this way instead of turning into what sounded to him like a deranged lunatic was abnormal, then he could live with it, Corrigan decided.

Sarah was unwilling to leave it at that, however, but seemed intrigued by what she saw as his refusal to conform. "Is it simply an inability due to some kind of defect?" she asked him. "Or is it the result of a deliberate process: something you just won't do? Can you tell us?"

"I thought you were supposed to tell me," Corrigan answered.

"It doesn't seem to trouble you at all. You really don't have any qualms about it? Deep down inside, I mean. You don't feel out of things, insecure?"

"Yes, I feel out of things. No, I don't feel insecure. Whether that's deep down or not, I have no idea."

"You don't have a desire to be more a part of the world around you?" Sarah persisted. "To feel integrated, accepted by others?"

"Why should I?"

Sarah flashed Zehl a worried look. "At one time you were a professional, one of the best in your field," she said to Corrigan. "Don't you have any of that ambition anymore? Are you happy at the thought of being a bartender indefinitely?" It was like listening to a replay of Muriel and Horace, Corrigan thought.

"Look where the other kind got me," he said.

Zehl was staring at Corrigan with a different light in his eye: brooding, more reflective. For a moment Corrigan had the odd feeling that it was he and Zehl who shared some common insight that the circumstances precluded discussing openly, and not the two specialists.

"Getting back to the immediate future, Joe, what do you think you might do?" Zehl asked, moving them off the subject. "Any possible plans yet?"

"Yes, as a matter of fact," Corrigan answered. "Just a thought that crossed my mind while I was having breakfast. Maybe I could use a change of scene and start getting in touch with the rest of the wide world again. We've talked about it before, but with Muriel out of the way this might be the right time. I was thinking I could take a vacation back to Ireland."

Zehl frowned. Clearly he was far from instantly enamored at the idea.

"Ireland?" Sarah repeated. Her voice was quavery. For some reason the suggestion seemed to bewilder her. "Why would you want to go to Ireland?"

"I'm Irish," Corrigan said. "Sometimes people like to go back and see the place they're from." Surely it was obvious.

Sarah was shaking her head, but she seemed to be having to search for a reason. "No, I don't think so, Joe," she said. "I don't think that would be possible at all."

The abruptness of her response set Corrigan at odds again. "Why not?" he objected. "It's been twelve years now since the Oz project screwed up. I'm in control of my life again. I'm holding down a job that's good enough to keep me independent." He drew a breath and looked at her pointedly. "And it wasn't me who gave up on the marriage this morning and quit."

Sarah shook her head again. "Your condition is still more delicate than you realize. The stresses of traveling abroad would just be inviting trouble. Yes, you're right—you have made a lot of progress. Let's not risk undoing it all now."

"I went to Japan four years ago," Corrigan pointed out. He knew as soon as he spoke that it was a weak argument.

"Exactly," Sarah said, not missing the point either. "And look what happened. It triggered a relapse that you took months to get over."

Corrigan turned toward Zehl for support, but this time Zehl was on Sarah's side. "Sorry, Joe, I have to veto it," he said. He brought a hand up to touch his temple with a finger in a flicking motion, vaguely suggestive of a salute—it was a peculiarity of his that Corrigan had noticed before. "It's a nice thought, but you're not ready. Staying within a familiar environment is an important part of your cure. Sure, take a break if you need to, but keep it in the city, eh?" Zehl shrugged and made a palm-up gesture. "Maybe a few walks by the river. Go see a game, the zoo, maybe try a concert. How many of the museums have you visited? Get the idea? Easy, relaxing, familiar. You'd be surprised at the supportive effects of being in places you know."

"I know Ireland pretty well, too," Corrigan pointed out, although by now it was mainly through obstinacy. He had not been officially discharged from medical care, and Zehl had the authority certainly to overrule any long-distance travel plans, and probably to have Corrigan put back under institutional care if he judged it to be in the patient's welfare to do so—Corrigan didn't want to put that to the test.

Zehl raised a hand firmly. "No, and that's final. Next year, maybe, but not now. I'll pull rank if I have to."

Corrigan stretched out an arm and tapped idly at the keyboard beside him while he considered how to respond. "So, do you know what you want, Joe?" Sarah asked him again.

Corrigan scratched the side of his nose. "Not a lot," he replied finally. "The first thing is to do a lot of thinking. And I can do that anywhere. So for the time being it will be a case of simply carrying on as usual. If that changes, I'll let you know."

✵ CHAPTER FOUR ✵

Pittsburgh had seen a surprising amount of demolition and rebuilding in recent years.

The Camelot Hotel was located downtown on Fourth Avenue—a redevelopment of a site where an office building had stood previously. It was an experimental throwback from the glass-and-concrete architectural catastrophes that had been provoking mirth and outrage among everyone but the experts for decades. Standing out amid the gray slab canyons and arrays of faceless mirror rectangles, the Camelot presented a warm, defiant countenance of red bricks, arched windows, and a pseudo-Tudor foyer with wood-beamed ceilings—imitation wood, it was true, but visually pleasing nonetheless. A crenellated terrace reduced the severity of the vertical line, and, in keeping with the name, twin chateau-style turrets rounded off the design. Visitors and locals liked it, and a residential developer was putting up English Victorian-style row houses along several streets on the North Side. And Corrigan liked working there because it offered a respite from the various dementias of the age that he was supposed to want to normalize himself by imitating.

Plenty of people were out, healthily expressing themselves, when he arrived from the subway stop on Stanwix Street. Half a block before the hotel entrance, a couple were having a domestic tiff, screaming insults at each other in front of onlookers who yelled taunts or encouragement, depending on whose side they took. A street band was playing for nickels in front of a battery of equipment that must have cost several thousand dollars; a group of men wearing togas and holding staffs were sitting cross-legged on the sidewalk for reasons that were not obvious; some women were parading dogs glamorized with coiffures of various cuts and colors to reflect their mistresses' personas; and there were more pirates about.

Movement and bearing were important parts of the language by which people told the world who they were and what they owned. So business suits and hats strutted, blazers and sport coats strode, macho gear swaggered, uniforms of any kind marched, shapely skirts wiggled, and demure dresses minced. The modern world in miniature, the street was a stage of acted-out messages: the measured tread of confidence; paradings of success; hunched, defeated shoulders; a hanging head of shame. Nobody took any notice of Corrigan as he made his way uncommunicatively along the sidewalk to the Camelot's main doors. He was far from convinced that they took very much notice of each other.

A media celebrity called Merlyn Dree was staying at the Camelot, and Corrigan had to pick his way through a flock of garishly clad fans who were being held at bay outside the door by hotel security staff. Inside, at the front desk, a fat man in an overcoat was pointing at a sheet of paper and remonstrating loudly with a harassed-looking clerk.

"No, Crammerwitz booked the room, but it's under Mancini, okay? The basic goes to the company, and they pick up these calls, but not those calls. Dinner goes on the other company and not this one, because it's a different account. What's the problem?"

In a corner nearby, the latest experimental wonder in Artificial Intelligence that somebody had succeeded in selling to management stood ignominiously, dismantled and partly crated in preparation for being shipped back: automated, talking desk-clerks. They hadn't lasted a week. Whoever coded their database was probably very smart but had obviously never worked in hotels. Corrigan went on through the lobby, grateful that nobody had come up with any ideas for replacing human bartenders. That would need Artificial Wisdom, which was another matter entirely.

He went up the main stairway to the second-floor landing and through the staff door to the room behind the bar of the Galahad Lounge. The roster pinned to the message board told him that Sherri would be working the late shift with him. At least she was one that he found he could talk to. She listened, and seemed genuinely curious to understand what made him different. Sometimes he thought that Sherri would be better doing Sarah's job. But on the other hand, maybe that would mean he'd have to work with Sarah.

Maurice, who was in charge of the Camelot's three lounges, came in while Corrigan was changing into his work outfit of dress shirt with bow tie and maroon jacket. Small, dark, with the shaped mustachios that he considered went with the bar-manager image, Maurice was a Horace incarnate with a New York accent— meticulous about detail, and most of the time sounding like an animated company-procedure manual. Since his staff handled cash and dealt directly with the clientele, that wasn't all bad, Corrigan supposed. But Maurice confused all around him by being incapable of doing anything simply if a more complicated way could be contrived. On top of that, his particular brand of normality came in the form of a conviction that everyone in the trade was crooked, especially management, and customers worst of all. Corrigan stayed behind his shield of maladaptability and watched with baffled fascination.

"You were on yesterday afternoon before Jack, right, Joe?" Maurice was holding the notebook in which he entered the figures from the cash registers. Jack was another of the younger bar assistants. Maurice had confided that he knew Jack was on the take, because he styled his hair in the same way as Nelson Torrence of *Underside,* who conned wealthy widows and robbed banks.

"Yesterday? Yes, that's right," Corrigan replied. "Why?"

"Was everything okay when you cashed up? Last night, we were thirty bucks down."

Corrigan groaned inwardly. Jack had been delayed on his way in, making Corrigan late for a game that he'd wanted to catch at Three Rivers. By way of amends and to help out, Jack had offered to cash up Corrigan's shift for him so that he could be on his way. Although it was against the rules, just that one time Corrigan had let him—he had no qualms about Jack being honest. And just that one time, of course, something like this had to happen.

He sighed. "I didn't do it. I was late for something and got Jack to cover."

"What! You let him cash up your shift? You know better than that, Joe."

Yes, Corrigan knew. But it happened from time to time nevertheless, as Maurice knew perfectly well. The problem was that trust was a concept that lay beyond Maurice's powers of comprehension.

"My fault," Corrigan said. "I'm wide open. I'll eat the thirty, no problem."

But that wasn't what Maurice wanted. He moved a step closer and lowered his voice. "Come on, Joe, you know and I know that Jack's a snitch, don't we? He cooked your numbers and took a dip. But he doesn't have to get away with it. All I need is a docket from you, and I'll countersign that you put it in yesterday."

In other words, a pure frame-up implicating Jack as trying to frame Corrigan. Corrigan couldn't see for the life of him why Maurice went about doing things this way. "Ah, no," he said, "that wouldn't be right at all. There's no knowing it was him. I might have made a mistake earlier, sure enough."

Maurice shook his head. "That's not the point. I don't care who goofed. I've been wanting to get rid of him anyhow. This is all I need."

"Of course it's the point," Corrigan retorted. "I'm not covered, and that's the fact of it. I'll not be a party to making up something that says otherwise."

"You're too careful to drop thirty," Maurice persisted. "I say he palmed it and tried to lay it on you."

"Maybe he did. I guess we'll never know."

Maurice shook his head disbelievingly. "Aren't you gonna fight that?"

"Maurice, there isn't anything to fight. I didn't cash up the shift, and that's all there is to it. For God's sake take it out of my check like I said, and let's be done with it."

Maurice seemed mystified. "I don't get it. You've got nothing to lose by doing it my way. This way you lose thirty bucks. Where's the logic?"

"You really can't see it?"

"I can't see it."

"I'd be losing my self-respect, and that's worth far more than what we're talking about."

"So if Jack's made thirty for nothing, that's okay by you?"

"Well, he's the only one who knows about that for sure, isn't he? If he did, then it wasn't for nothing. He made it at the price of becoming a thief." Corrigan shook his head. "In my opinion that wouldn't be a very good deal at all."

Maurice seemed to freeze for an instant; then he looked at Corrigan with a different expression, as if a switch had clicked in his head somewhere, transforming him into a different personality. "Say, you know, that's an interesting way to look at it," he said. "I never thought about it before."

Try it sometime, Corrigan thought to himself.

Maurice went on. "How would you weight a payoff matrix to express the options? Logically it reduces to the same structure as Prisoner's Dilemma."

Corrigan stared at him in surprise. Years before, when he'd worked among engineers and programmers, intellectual topics figured naturally in conversation, and game theory was often one of them. But it was the last thing that he would have expected from Maurice.

Before Corrigan could reply, however, Sherri stuck her head in through the doorway from the bar. "Joe, great, you're here. We're filling up out front."

"Sorry, Maurice," Corrigan said, glad to get off the subject. "Duty's calling. We'll have to talk about it some other time." And with that, he straightened his jacket and went through to join Sherri in the bar.

In the far corner, a clique of Merlyn Dree fans had penetrated the defenses and were chanting some of his slogans and catchphrases around a table. Two macho-looking characters in sunglasses and pink fedoras were at the bar, waiting to be served. A bearded man in a pirate hat was prefacing every phrase with a loud, rolling "Arr!" to a group sitting near the door. A man in a yellow suit was loudly expounding that the art of selling lay in being a good listener, and a couple with their heads encased in audiovisual helmets were sitting as though in a trance by the far wall.

Normal, sane, ordinary people, Corrigan thought to himself as he checked the register and surveyed the scene. Nothing unusual. Yes, it was going to be another typical night.

❈ CHAPTER FIVE ❈

Jonathan Wilbur had had three scotches in the last half hour and was getting loquacious. He waved a hand expansively from the barstool where he was sitting. "New York, London, Tokyo. It moves around the world through computers all the time. Billions of dollars every day. I can buy a company in the morning, sell it at lunchtime, lose my ass in the afternoon."

"That's nice," Corrigan said, collecting empties off the bar.

Privately, he doubted if Wilbur had ever bought and sold more than the office furniture. He was young, dazzled by a world that was obviously new to him, and too anxious to make an impression where it didn't matter. Hotel bartenders saw it all the time.

"Ah, who gives a shit? . . . But I guess in your job you can't imagine money like that, eh, Joe?" With his double-breasted, charcoal suit, white silk shirt, and silver-gray tie with garnet clip, Wilbur at least looked the part. From past conversations, Corrigan knew that he kept up with the fashions that boosted the executive image: golf in summer, skiing in winter, woman's-magazine-cover home with gourmet kitchen, all the wines, European wardrobe, glitzmobile car. The only problem was, the bank owned all of it and he was perpetually one promotion away from being able to afford the repayments. If that was success, Corrigan preferred being a happy failure.

Sherri came back carrying a tray filled with more glasses from the tables. She was petite, blond, bouncy, looking trim in her bar outfit of blouse, maroon vest, and black skirt. "One Bud, one Red, vodka lime with lemon, margarita special, and a Greyhound," she said to Corrigan. He nodded and began pouring.

Wilbur had opened a briefcase on his knee, revealing it to be a portable office complete with laptop and screen, phone, fax/copier, and music player—presumably for necessary relaxation. While Corrigan was busy with the drinks, he lifted out the handset and tapped in a code. "Hi, A.J.? Jon here. Look, about that meeting, can we make it tomorrow? I have to see a guy about an offer, and it might take a while, okay?" He kept his voice raised to make sure that it carried. Sherri caught Corrigan's gaze, raised her eyes momentarily, and came around to pour the beers. "That'll do fine. I'll see you then. 'Bye." Wilbur closed the lid, glancing about quickly to see who was watching. Two girls at a table behind, whom he missed, seemed to be impressed.

"Actually it's a job offer," he confided in a low voice, in case Corrigan was itching to know.

"Is that so, now?" Corrigan said.

"Do you know Oliver, who comes in here sometimes?" Wilbur asked.

Corrigan did—and he wouldn't have trusted him as far as he could fly. "Big fella. Hearty kind—likes a joke. Not a lot of hair on the top of him," Corrigan said.

"That's the one."

"Ah, I do, sure. He was in yesterday for lunch."

Wilbur leaned forward and propped an elbow on the bar, covering the side of his mouth with two fingers. "Well, the job's with his operation, managing portfolios. And I'm telling you, it's not nickel-and-dime stuff with those guys. I mean, we're talking big-time here."

"Well, good luck with it," Corrigan said.

Wilbur scooped a handful of peanuts from a dish on the bar and studied Corrigan while he brought them up to his mouth. "You'd be about what, Joe, fortyish? A little less, maybe?" he asked.

"I'm forty-four." Corrigan transferred the cocktails to Sherri's tray. She picked it up and carried it away.

"Ever have any experience with big outfits, out of curiosity?" Wilbur went on. "Where the real wheels are, know what I mean?"

Corrigan could have said that he had once been the main instigator and joint director of a project whose backers could probably have bought Oliver's operation with the petty cash. Instead, he answered, "Oh, I'll leave that kind of thing to those who have a taste for it. I'm from a part of the world where people tend to take things a bit easier, you understand."

"Irish, right?"

"That's it."

"Yeah. Never got there." Wilbur's voice fell again. "But this thing I was telling you about with Oliver. He's gonna fix me up real good there, in exchange for"—Wilbur grinned slyly—"don't say anything to anyone, but you know how it is—a little harmless information about the place I'm at now. But anything's fair in love, war, and business, eh?" It was all straight out of a score of popular movie series. Corrigan found it hard not to smile.

"I wouldn't know about that," he said.

Oliver arrived a few minutes later, dressed showily in a suit of silver-dusted cobalt blue with a white leather topcoat thrown loosely across his shoulders. He stopped in the doorway to look around, saw Wilbur at the bar, and moved ponderously across to join him. With Oliver was a tall woman, mid-thirties to forty, with straight hair worn high, heavy on the makeup. She was wearing a long, low-cut dress, and glittered from throat to fingers with jewelry. Corrigan had seen her with Oliver a couple of times before. Delia, he thought her name was.

Oliver was all hale-and-heartiness. "Hey, Wilbur, old buddy. You're good on time, too, huh? That's great. Just what we need. Joe, how's it going? You remember Delia, right?"

"Hello again, Joe." Delia smiled, revealing teeth that had to have been surgically rebuilt, and displaying her purple eye shadow. She was an accessory to Oliver's image that went with the manner, the coat, and the suit.

"Let's see," Oliver said. "Gimme a screwdriver, gin with bitter lemon and a slice of lime here, and another of whatever that is for Wilbur."

Corrigan took three fresh glasses down from the overhead rack. Delia rested an elbow on the bar and watched him while Oliver started telling Wilbur about the volume of transactions that the firm had handled that day. A couple that Corrigan had been keeping an eye on by the far wall, arguing since they sat down, were losing their cool, the man getting angrier, the woman's voice rising, both gesticulating. Healthy expressiveness. The Merlyn Dree fans had started acting out some of his skits. The pink fedoras had latched on to the two girls who found Wilbur glamorous and exciting. Sherri came back with more empties and started loading the washer.

"I'm an associate with Oliver," Delia told Corrigan. "I don't know if he mentioned it. Foreign stocks and bonds department. That's the high-risk end, where you have to know your way around." She waited, inviting a response, then went on when Corrigan just nodded. "But the *money* you can make! I'm not even going to say what commission I grossed last quarter. But it bought me a Hampton Riviera with no payments. Getaway cabin in Vermont, Queensland beach scene in winter. . . ."

Corrigan looked at her with a neutral expression and said, "That's nice."

Delia's voice dropped to a more confidential note. "You get to meet all the right contacts, too. I pay less tax than I did five years ago. I practically bank my paycheck and live off the expenses."

"That's nice."

Oliver picked up his and Delia's drinks and looked around. "Let's move to a table. There's one over there. Come on, Jon, I'll give you some inside secrets about how to screw the most out of clients. If they've still got blood left, we're not doing our job, right?" He winked at Corrigan. "Talk to you later, Joe, okay?"

"Behave yourself, now."

"Why? Where's the fun in that?"

Wilbur took up his own glass and his briefcase, and followed the other two away. Sherri, who had been half listening, came up beside

Corrigan to ring some cash into the till. Corrigan eyed Oliver and his two companions contemplatively while they seated themselves around the table, then said to Sherri, "Suppose you moved to a small town. And you found there were only two hairdressers: one whose hair was neat, the other a mess. You'd go to the one who looked a mess, wouldn't you? Because it would be she who did the hair of the other."

Sherri frowned for a moment, then smiled. "Yeah—true. What brought that on all of a sudden?"

"Oh, those three who were here just now. That fella Wilbur thinks Oliver is going to do him a good turn out of the kindness of his heart. He's expecting he'll be treated with fairness and honesty." Corrigan sighed and shook his head. "Why do people insist on looking for something where it clearly isn't? And then they blame the world when their hopes don't materialize."

"I don't know how you stand that woman the way you do," Sherri said. "She's so gross with her 'I've got this' and 'I've got that' all the time. But you can just stand there and say 'that's nice' like you do. You'll have to teach me how to do it."

Corrigan smiled wryly. "Oh, that's an old Irish story," he said. "You'd have no problem if you knew it."

"Well, tell me, then," Sherri invited.

Corrigan glanced around. There were no customers looking for attention just at the moment. As a rule he didn't bother telling jokes these days. People no longer understood them. Oh, what the hell, he told himself. Give it a try.

"It's like this," he said. "Two women are sharing a hospital room in Dublin, you see. One is from Foxrock. That's south of the city, where all the money is—she'd be one of your Delias. The other's the complete opposite: bottom end of the social spectrum—what we'd call a roight auld slag."

"You mean like parts of the South Bronx?"

"Maybe. Anyway, Delia wants to make sure there's no mistake about who she is, see. So she says to other . . ." Corrigan mimicked a prim tone: "'Ah, I hope you don't imagine that I am accustomed to sharing like this. Usually, I go to the private wing.'"

He changed to a shrill, coarser accent. "'Oh, yiss?' says the other, who we'll say was Mary. 'Dat's noice.'

"'I'll have you know,' says Delia, 'that my husband is an extremely successful man and takes very good care of me. The last time I was a patient, he took me on a Caribbean cruise to recuperate.'

"'Dat's noice.'

"'And on the occasion before that, he bought me a diamond pendant to compensate for the discomfort.' . . ." Corrigan nodded an invitation at Sherri to supply the response.

"That's nice," she obliged.

"Ah, no," he said. "You have to do it with the proper accent. Come on, now: 'Dat's noice.'"

"Dat's noice."

"Perfect. And then your Delia says, 'Out of curiosity, does *your* husband show such consideration when you are confined?'"

"'Oh, yiss, o' course 'e does,' says Mary. 'When we 'ad our last one, 'e sent me fer elocution and etiquette lessons.'"

Sherri chuckled, and Corrigan continued, "Naturally, Delia's astounded. '*What!*' she exclaims. '*Elocution?* How would somebody like *you* even know what the word means?'

"' 'E did, too,' Mary tells her. 'See, at one time, whenever oi 'eard people tellin' me a load o' bullshit, oi used to tell 'em ter fuck orf. Now oi just smiles at 'em all proper, like, and oi say . . .'" Corrigan paused expectantly. Anyone should see it now. But Sherri's eyes were still blank, waiting. He completed, "'Dat's noice.'"

There was a barely perceptible delay, and then she laughed. But the laugh wasn't real. She had missed the point. Corrigan had seen the same thing too many times before. He turned to restocking the mixers shelf. What was it about the modern world that had changed people? he wondered. Sarah Bewley tried to tell him that nothing had changed, that it was his idea of humor that had been distorted. But the story he'd told Sherri was from his student days in Ireland, and everyone back then had found it funny. Or had nothing in those years happened the way he remembered it at all?

A knot of people appeared in the doorway, clustered about a squat, rotund figure whose name Corrigan couldn't bring to mind instantly—some kind of city official, who worried all the time about his public visibility. The last time they were in, the talk had been about sending political messages through the communications chips that some people were having put in their heads. One of the aides couldn't seem to comprehend why Corrigan was cool toward the idea. "Why would anyone choose to stay out of touch?" he had wanted to know.

Then a man with shoulders like a blockhouse came in and stopped, obviously checking the place. Moments later, a commotion of voices came from the hall outside the lounge. The Dree fans leaped to their feet with a clamor of squeals and shouts as the idol himself swept in ahead of an entourage of photographers and starlets, resplendent in a white glitter suit and red shirt, blond hair falling to his shoulders, arms held high to acknowledge the accolades.

The funny thing was that although Dree featured in commercials everywhere and appeared at all kinds of public events, he didn't sing, dance, play, act, tell stories, or entertain in any way that was traditionally recognizable. As far as Corrigan was aware, he didn't actually *do* anything. He was the ultimate celebrity: well known for no other reason than being well known.

Even Sherri was standing enraptured as the circus moved in and took over the bar. "*You call this having a good time?*" Dree yelled to the general delight: his standard catchphrase.

"*You ain't seen nothing yet!*" they chorused back. All the way from Jolson. Sherri joined in; so did Delia, Wilbur, and the girls talking to the pink fedoras. The party dispersed to a corner, and an aide came across to the bar to give their order. Corrigan turned to set out the glasses, and as he did so he noticed a woman looking in through the doorway. She was tall, with long dark hair, wearing a suede coat over a satiny black dress. The noise and antics inside made her start to turn away; but then she caught sight of Corrigan, seemed to change her mind, and came in.

She had been in about a week before, he recalled. They had talked on and off about nothing in particular through much of the evening, and she had left alone. She was from California, liked Gershwin, the theater, old movies, and dogs, had been curious about Ireland, and seemed to know something about computers. Her name, he remembered moments before she sat down on a barstool with a quick smile of recognition, was Lilly.

❀ CHAPTER SIX ❀

Lilly made a living of sorts at a shoe-finishing shop—shoes were imported plain and unadorned from factories in Asia, then colored and trimmed locally to reflect the current buying patterns before tastes had time to change. That in itself seemed odd to Corrigan, for she displayed all the qualities that he would have thought equipped her for something more challenging and rewarding.

Her eyes, which were dark and depthless, studied the world with a reflective awareness that Corrigan hadn't seen in a half-dozen people during as many years. She had the kind of intelligence that was intelligent enough not to flaunt itself; the quiet self-assurance that doesn't mistake misapplied assertiveness for confidence. In short, she exuded style of a quality that was very rare; and that was also very puzzling, for it didn't add up to the kind of woman who would show any interest in bartenders. Yet for some reason, Lilly seemed to be very curious about Corrigan indeed.

"Do you live in the city, Joe?" She asked when the workload eased and he sauntered back to the end of the bar where she was sitting.

"In a flat in Oakland, the East End."

"Are you married, or what?"

"I was until this morning."

"What happened?"

"She left last night for the weekend. But then the house computer told me that it's for keeps and played a billet-doux."

Lilly's eyes searched his face for a moment. She had shifted her stool so that her back was to the body of the room, where everybody else seemed determined to prove that they were potential celebrity material too. "What's called for, commiserations or congratulations?" she asked.

Most people would have spouted a set line from a soap—with no thought that it might or might not be appropriate, let alone the notion of trying to find out. But Lilly didn't. She thought; she asked; she listened. That was how she had struck Corrigan the last time she was here.

"I'm not breaking my heart over it," Corrigan replied. "Sometimes these things happen a long time before, and are just waiting to be acted out." She understood, nodded. There was no pointless interrogation. No more needed to be said. "How about yourself?" Corrigan asked.

Sherri deposited another tray of empty glasses and bottles on the bar before Lilly could answer. She was looking worn. "Another round of everything for Dree's people. Four beers for the tab on table three. One gin and tonic, one scotch on the rocks, two white coolers."

"They're working you hard tonight, Sherri," Lilly said.

Sherri exhaled a sigh. "You can say that again." She looked at Corrigan. "When the guy gave me the big order I told him, 'That's nice.' Did I get it right?"

Corrigan stared down at the glasses as he poured, not knowing what to say. How did you explain inappropriateness to somebody who just didn't have the wiring to feel it intuitively? This wanting to know why he thought something funny was another thing that he found all the time with people—and the main reason why he had stopped telling jokes. He was unable to understand why something that they obviously didn't share should be so important to them. He could see why Sarah Bewley would be interested: trying to understand him was her job. But why would anyone else care about his peculiarities when *he* was the odd person out?

"Hey, bar," the Merlyn Dree aide in charge of ordering called from across the room. "Back up on that order there. Make it another one for *everybody*!" He looked around. "When *we* drink, everyone drinks. Right, guys?" The room yelled its approval.

Then another group arrived, and things got hectic. Corrigan worked nonstop until they finally closed things down around 3:00 A.M., in all of which time Lilly never did get a chance to answer his question. In one brief lull, however, they did agree to going for a coffee somewhere, afterward.

"I pretty much keep myself to myself," Lilly said. They had come out into the night air and were turning off Fourth into a passage that connected through to the late-night lights around Market Place. There was a moment's hesitation, as if she were unsure about confiding something. "I guess I don't really relate much to most of the people you meet these days. Things seem to change faster and faster. Not a lot of it makes sense anymore."

Her words mirrored his own situation perfectly. Was that what she had somehow recognized, and why she was showing such interest in a bartender? "I know what you mean," he said.

"Yes, I think you do. I don't feel that with people very often." She glanced sideways at him as they walked. There was more than idle curiosity at work. "You must meet all kinds in a job like yours."

"You saw a few of them yourself tonight."

"But you don't just see them," Lilly said. "You seem to see into them, as well. I was watching."

"I know you were," Corrigan answered. "So that makes you a bit of the same yourself, doesn't it?" Lilly conceded with the quick smile of somebody being caught out, at the same time managing to convey that it was because she was not used to it. Compared to the empty stares and clumsy gropings to extract meaning that he saw every day, it felt like communication bordering on mind reading.

A promotional scouting robot spotted them as they came out into Market Place and rolled across to intercept them, flashing colored lights and logos of nearby places that were open late. "Hello, there! Enjoying the city late tonight?" it greeted jovially. "For your further entertainment we have Jermyn's cabaret bar less than half a block from here, still open for drinks, dancing, and shows until dawn. Getting hungry? The Lilac Slipper offers the best in contemporary and traditional Cantonese cuisine, ten-percent discount for Pirates. Or, for more erotic tastes, ho-ho . . ."

Lilly sighed. "Maybe I could pass on having that coffee out. I'll fix you one at home. How does that sound?"

"Sounds good," Corrigan said. "How far is it?"

"Over the river, north. We'll need a cab. Do you have a compad? I'm not carrying one."

"I hardly ever use them." Corrigan looked at the robot. "Can you call us a cab?"

"Sorry, I just make reservations. But why do you want to leave? It's Saturday night. You want to be part of the scene, right?"

"Wrong." Corrigan steered Lilly away to search for a pay booth. The robot pursued them, babbling tenaciously, until a mixed group of people appeared on the far side of the street, and one of them called it away.

"Aren't you into being part of the scene?" Lilly said it in a light, mocking tone that combined several wavelengths—phrasing it as a question, but simultaneously telling him that she already knew and understood his answer because they both recognized and laughed at the same absurdities.

"Guilty," Corrigan replied.

"You don't need to find yourself?"

"I wasn't aware that I ever lost myself."

"But that's *terrible.*"

"Now you know the worst."

They both laughed. She slipped her arm loosely through his.

There was a gift store, with various curios and Pittsburgh mementos in the window. Suddenly Corrigan stopped and stared in at them. "What is it?" Lilly asked.

He pointed to a figure of an Irish leprechaun, identical, as far as he could judge, to the one in his hallway back at the flat. "That's Mick. He keeps popping up wherever I go. Do you know, I've one the same as that at home. It was a wedding present."

"Was that to the wife who left yesterday?"

"No, there was one other before—a while back, now."

"Maybe he's haunting you," Lilly said. "Can you have leprechaun ghosts?"

"Well, if it's a crock of gold that he's after, he's wasting his time haunting me," Corrigan said.

They resumed walking. "So, when you see into people, what things do you see?" Lilly asked, getting serious again and picking up their earlier subject.

Corrigan thought back to Wilbur, Oliver, and Delia. "Oh, the strange ways they go about trying to get what they want," he replied.

"Such as?"

"Well, if you asked them, I suppose most of them would say that what they want is to be happy, wouldn't you think?"

"Uh-huh."

"A young fella was in earlier. He's pinned everything on a job that he's after, and if you want my opinion it's a scoundrel he'll be working for." Corrigan made a brief, empty-handed gesture. "You see these people chasing after money and success and the like, because those are the things that they think will make them happy. But they're making their happiness depend on what others have the power to give or take away. So don't they become slaves to the people who control those things? And can people who are not free be happy? They cannot. So have such people obtained what they set out for? They have not. They're looking in the wrong places."

They found a pay booth. Corrigan called a local cab company, giving his name and their location. "I see you're not listed with us," the synthesized voice commented. "We have an introductory discount for opening an account tonight."

"No, thanks."

"Can I register you for our bonus-mileage club?"

"No."

"How about the all-in-the-family group scheme? Brand new."

"We'd just like to go home. Is that all right?"

A baffled pause, then, "A cab will be there in five minutes." Corrigan shook his head as the call cleared.

"Are you free, then, Joe?" Lilly asked.

"I'd say so, yes," he replied.

"And why's that?"

He shrugged and gave her a quick, easy grin. "I'm what you might call a self-unmade man. I didn't always do what I do now, you know. It took a lot of effort to work my way down to it. But now I'm free to live according to the things I believe in, and nobody can compel me to think or believe anything I choose not to. So the things I do value, nobody can take away."

"Are all the Irish like that?" Lilly asked. She sounded fascinated.

"Oh, God, not at all. You've never met such a crowd of rogues and villains in your life."

"So how come you're different?"

"Ah, well, I went through some bad experiences a few years back. Maybe that changed some things, if you know what I mean."

Lilly hesitated, obviously wanting to be tactful. But for some reason it seemed important to her. "Things?" she repeated. "What kind of things? Do you mean psychologically?"

Corrigan spotted the cab approaching and stepped forward, raising an arm. "Exactly," he said over his shoulder. "The pieces are coming back together again, but they don't seem to function the way that most people's do."

They climbed in, and Lilly gave the address on North Side. As soon as the door closed, a screen in the rear compartment began running commercials. Corrigan paid an extra dollar to shut it off.

"Being different might not be such a bad thing," Lilly said. "You said you used to work in computers, but you sound more like a philosopher. What kind of a society lets its philosophers end up working in bars?"

"Believe me, there's no better place to learn the subject," Corrigan assured her as the cab pulled away.

◈ CHAPTER SEVEN ◈

Lilly lived in a two-bedroom unit in a complex north of the Allegheny Center. It was clean and comfortable, feminine but not cute and lacy, casual without being a mess: all about what Corrigan would have expected. She produced a liter of Californian Chablis to go with the steak sandwiches that they had stopped for on the way.

Now Corrigan was able to give her his full attention for the first time. She was attractive not just physically but in the rarer, more appealing way that comes with the feeling of two minds being in tune. He hoped that his coming back here with her wasn't going to be interpreted as going along with anything more intimate that she might have in mind. The day had been emotionally fatiguing, and he had worked a hectic shift through to the early hours. Enough was enough. If ever there had been a time when a rain check was in order, this was it.

But such fears proved groundless. Lilly was more interested in hearing about his years in computing and the "bad experiences" that he had mentioned which put an end to them. For anyone to ask was a novel experience in itself. So, although the hour had surpassed ungodliness, he refilled the glasses and settled himself back to regard her across the empty plates on the table.

"Is it stuffy in here after the food?" Lilly asked suddenly. "I can't tell. I've got a sinus problem that stops me smelling things."

"It's okay," Corrigan said. "I used to be with one of the big companies here: Cybernetic Logic Corporation—I worked at their corporate research center out at Blawnox. They were big in Artificial Intelligence-based systems. Still are, for that matter. The aim of the AI field had always been true, human-level intelligence, one day. But around the turn of the century, the technology was plateauing out. After some progress and mixed results, there didn't seem to be any obvious way to advance things further."

"Yes, I know CLC," Lilly said. "They've got a building downtown, near Westinghouse."

Corrigan nodded. "Well, about twelve years ago, CLC set up a big research project to try a new way of achieving AI. It might come as a surprise, but I practically invented it." He paused, but Lilly merely returned a stare that could have meant anything. Corrigan went on: "You see, traditionally there had been two approaches to AI: top-down and bottom-up. Top-down meant trying to understand all the complexity of this thing we call 'mind' in sufficient detail to code it into programs." He waved a hand in front of his face. "Forget it. The immensity of the task would make it intractable, even if we knew what to code."

A strange half-smile was playing on Lilly's lips, but in his soliloquizing Corrigan failed to notice. He continued: "The other way, bottom-up, meant trying to create simple neuronlike configurations that could be made to evolve, the same as we did. The problem you run into there is that you don't realize how efficient animal nervous systems are until you try imitating them. You can spend ten years, fifty million dollars, and the best brains in the business putting TV cameras and legs on a computer to make it walk, and the average twelve-month-old will run rings around it—literally. The simple fact is, computers don't interact very well with the real world outside. They haven't had a billion years of evolution optimizing them for it. They operate better on their own, internal worlds."

Lilly nodded, finally, and raised a hand. "It's okay, Joe. You don't have to go on. The project was called Oz—set up under a new CLC division called Xylog, across the river, along Carson Street—yes? The idea was to let an AI evolve by interacting with a virtual world."

Corrigan stared at her in astonishment. "Xylog! That's right.

Some of the buildings are still there . . . I don't know what they're used for today. How in heaven would you know about that?"

Instead of answering immediately, Lilly continued, "But Oz was shut down in the preliminary test phase. Before that, were you working on the program that led up to it: a project called EVIE?"

Corrigan shook his head bemusedly. "How in God's name—"

"I've got one more," Lilly said. "Then you'll get your answers. What happened? Why was the Oz project abandoned, and what did it have to do with your winding up in a place like the Camelot?"

It wasn't something that Corrigan normally talked about, especially to people he hardly knew. But these were hardly normal circumstances. "How much do you know about how the interaction was going to be implemented?" he asked, to avoid launching off into needless explanation.

"Enough," Lilly answered. "The idea was that the system would learn by manipulating humanoid animations to emulate real-person surrogates projected in from the outside."

The AI would evolve by controlling artificial characters in a virtual world. As a substitute for the directional thrust of biological evolution, the system would endeavor to shape the behavior of its creations closer to that of surrogate representations of volunteer participants coupled in from the outside. Thus, the virtual world would contain two kinds of inhabitants: humanoid "animations," manipulated by the computer; and "surrogates," controlled by real people, represented as themselves. The test would be to see if the machine could make the behavior of the animations indistinguishable. From her reply, Lilly was aware of all this.

"And am I right in supposing that you know how the surrogates were coupled in?" Corrigan said. "VIV? DIVAC? You've heard of them?" He meant the latest developments at that time in direct-coupled neural I/O, which had appeared on the scene after the earlier VR paraphernalia of head-mounted displays, bodysuits, and so forth. It had come out of work going on at places like Carnegie Mellon and MIT, certain government departments, and Advanced Telecomms at Kyoto, that involved interaction directly with the neural structures of the brain.

"Yes." Lilly nodded.

Corrigan sighed. "But we didn't know as much as we thought we did, Lilly. We were going straight into people's heads—nothing like it had been tried before. And there was too much haste and competitive pressure. We didn't spend the time that we should have to get it right. People started coming unglued with mental disorientation and perceptual disturbances. I was one of them. I've been slowly getting my act back together ever since."

"So was that what ended your first marriage?" Lilly asked.

Corrigan nodded. "Evelyn was a neurophysiologist from Boston who joined the project back in the early days—what you'd call my kind, I suppose. But I was young and brash, too obsessed with my career. Things soured, and when I turned into a vegetable, she opted out. I don't blame her, really. She did well to put up with it as long as she did."

"And the second one—the one who left last night; it wasn't the same with her?" Lilly said.

Corrigan leaned forward to top up their glasses. "Oh, that was a joke from the beginning—not done for what you'd call exactly the most romantic of reasons. My rehabilitation counselor suggested it. She thought it would help to bring a better focus and some stability into my life." He drank from his glass and looked across at her. "Okay, enough of that. Now suppose you tell me how what you seem to know fits with working in a shoe-finishing shop."

Lilly shrugged lightly, as if to say it was all very simple, really. "I used to be with the Space Defense Command up to twelve years ago—OTSC at Inglewood. I was a scientific evaluator involved in the development of DIVAC."

"My God," Corrigan murmured.

SDC's Operational Training & Simulator Center in California was where the final component had come from to make a full-sensory direct-neural interface possible. Up until then, direct-neural I/O coupling had been at the lowermost level of the brain, and research had been confined to the body's motor system. DIVAC, standing for *Direct Input Vision & ACoustics*, besides adding speech and auditory capability, succeeded in entering at a higher level to achieve the long-awaited goal of integrating vision as well.

Some of the surrogates who were to have been projected into the simulation from the real world outside had been supplied by the military. "Were you one of the Air Force volunteers who were brought in?" Corrigan asked. He had met some of them then, but not all.

"Yes," she replied. "I was part of a group from California. A guy called Tyron came out from Pittsburgh and interviewed the candidates. I was one of the ones selected. Later, we were flown to Pittsburgh, checked into a hotel there, and the next morning we were driven to Xylog to begin preliminary tests."

It didn't take too much guesswork to see what was coming. "And? . . ." Corrigan prompted.

"I'm not sure. That's where it all gets vague. The next recollections I have are of being in a world of jigsaw pieces in Mercy Hospital. The shrinks told me that there had been problems that nobody anticipated, and the project was shut down. I was a mental basket case for a long time afterward. . . . And I've just been muddling along and trying to get something of a life back together ever since." Lilly exhaled abruptly and looked at him in a way that asked what was the point of this. "But I don't have to tell you any of this," she said. "That's what happened to you too, isn't it?"

Suddenly, Corrigan sensed what had drawn somebody like this to a bartender. She had known this about him, somehow. That was why she had come back to the Camelot tonight. It was what this whole meeting had been leading up to.

"Can I ask you something?" Lilly said.

"Sure. I'm not promising to answer."

"What do you remember people being like before?"

"Before when?"

"Before Oz. Before you had the breakdown."

"Why?"

"I'd just like to know. It has to do with something I've been thinking about for a while now."

Corrigan considered the question. "It feels like a long time ago," he replied finally. "Like trying to think back over the top to the other side of a hill. . . . But what I *remember* is being more like most other people. You know . . ." he waved his hand to and fro over the tabletop between them, "the way it is with you and me now: being understood without having to spell everything out."

"You could talk about the things you think inside?" Lilly said.

"Exactly."

"Like you and I seem to be able to do. Why should that be so strange, Joe? Are you saying you don't feel that way with people anymore?"

Corrigan was unable to stifle a guffaw. "You've got to be joking! Come on, you've been telling me yourself how it is. You saw that bunch we were among all evening. What is this?"

Lilly didn't react to the frivolity but continued looking at him steadily. "The strange thing is, I remember it all the same way," she said. "Why should that be? How did you explain it to yourself?"

Corrigan did his best to draw together his scattered musings of many years into something coherent. "I suppose, as a process of projection: projecting back out of my head a picture of how I wanted things to be . . . probably subconsciously." That was how the specialists explained it. "By being projected into a past that was no longer accessible, what I wanted became unchallengeable. Hence the fragments of my identity that were coming back together had a basis that was secure. Psychological foundation-building. Does that make sense?"

"It makes too much sense, Joe. Way too much."

Corrigan frowned. "What's that supposed to mean?"

Lilly's face softened into a thin, vaguely despairing smile. It caught Corrigan the wrong way, striking him as condescending and mildly mocking. "Doesn't what you just said strike you—just a little bit, maybe—as incredibly insightful for someone who's supposed to be crazy?" she said.

Supposed to be? What was she saying? Well, true, he didn't believe himself to be crazy, exactly—not anymore; but for the disorientations that he had experienced in the not-so-distant past, it was probably as good a description as any. All the experts that he'd talked to had confirmed that he was a casualty of a massive assault on the neural system. Who was this person to be questioning it now?—

even if she had been an Air Force computer scientist once.

"I don't relate to people anymore," he said. "My mind works along different paths, with a lot of short circuits. It makes connections that mean things to me, but which other people don't follow. My own internal virtual reality. That could be getting pretty close to most people's idea of crazy."

Lilly shook her head. "That won't wash, Joe. If those connections were the result of disruptions that *you* experienced, they'd be private and unique—purely subjective. But even if I had been affected similarly, how could it result in the *same* connections?" She gave him a few seconds to object. But he couldn't. What irked him was that she was right. She must have felt this affinity the first time they talked in the Camelot. While he had been camouflaging his abdication from life, she had remained the scientist.

She went on. "You want to know what I think? You've got it the wrong way around. The 'virtual' isn't any aberration that you and I have manufactured inside our heads." She waved an arm in a circular movement to indicate the room, the building outside of it, and everything beyond. "It's all of this." She waited, but Corrigan was still too preoccupied with his internal self-admonishments to register what she was saying. Finally she commented dryly, "You guys did a hell of a job."

Corrigan shook himself out of his fuming and downed a half-glass of wine in a gulp. "What are you talking about?"

"Oz was never abandoned," Lilly said. "It went ahead as scheduled. We're still in it. This whole world full of lunatics that we're in *is the simulation*! It has been for the last twelve years."

Corrigan stared at her with a mixture of dismay and annoyance. Just when he had started to believe that she really was different, and had confided in her things that he'd mentioned to nobody, not Muriel, nor Sarah Bewley . . . now this. It was like hearing a physics Nobel Laureate suddenly start prattling about ESP. He groaned and shook his head.

"Oh, for God's sake. . . . You're being ridiculous."

Lilly was unfazed. "Think about it," she urged. "A lot of things add up. Do you *remember* Oz actually being canceled?" She didn't wait for an answer. "Neither do I. You were *told* that it had been—just like I was. The memories from that period were suppressed and confused by some kind of electronic drugging, and those stories about being incapacitated were fabrications to paper over the join. You were never crazy, and neither was I. It was the *world* that was learning to get better, not us."

Corrigan was already shaking his head. "You don't know what you're talking about," he scoffed. "Memories of what? Oz never reached the full-system phase. All that ever happened was a series of preliminary tests that got abandoned."

Lilly stopped short of looking openly derisive. "How do you *know*?" she pressed.

"How do I know? Because *I* practically conceived the project, that's how." Corrigan pointed a finger. "Who were *you*? A volunteer helper. One of the techs." He knew the gibe was uncalled for, even as he said it. What she was saying ought to have been preposterous; not wanting to face the nagging thought—even now—that it might not be, was making him react unreasonably. "Do you really think that if we'd been in Oz all this time, *I* wouldn't have seen it?"

"Then I'll ask you something else: out of curiosity, how much traveling have you been able to do in the last twelve years? Let me guess: you've been confined to Pittsburgh and maybe one or two other places, right? And another thing: I'll bet that you have problems with smelling things, too. Am I right? The DIVAC interface couldn't handle the first cranial nerve. So couldn't it just—"

Corrigan rose to his feet unconsciously and cut her off with an impatient wave. He was tired and fatigued, and the alcohol wasn't helping. "I don't want to hear this," he groaned. "Will you stop trying to tell me what my own job was about? You don't know anything about it. All we'd designed was a series of tests. The full, integrated-system phase wasn't going to be until much later—if we ever got to it at all. I hadn't put specifications together for a full-world scenario."

"Well, maybe somebody else did," Lilly retorted.

"You're being ridiculous."

"Why? How did the world turn so weird suddenly? What happened to families, people we knew? If this is real, why isn't CLC papered with billion-dollar lawsuits?"

Corrigan scowled and shook his head. "I don't want to listen to any more of this. I think it's time to go."

Lilly sighed and conceded. "Perhaps it is," she agreed coldly. "We can talk about it another time."

"Good night, then."

"Right."

Lilly sat, staring ahead impassively while Corrigan showed himself to the door. He collected his coat and let himself out. The morning air outside was cold. He called a cab and departed back for Oakland without noting the address or the street he was on.

◎ CHAPTER EIGHT ◎

The employees at Cybernetic Logic Corporation called it their "museum." Officially it was known as the Interactive Technologies Collection. Housed on the ground floor of the Executive Building of the company's R & D facility at Blawnox, behind the reception area and conveniently close to the visitors' dining room, it formed a fossil record of the evolution of experimental people-to-computer communication' through the second half of the twentieth century.

There was a working TX-2, the first transistor-based computer, used by Ivan Sutherland's group at the MIT Lincoln Laboratory in the early sixties to pioneer interactive graphics; "Alto," the first personal computer, which emerged from Xerox's Palo Alto Research Center in the seventies; head-mounted displays, from the early Air Force program at Wright-Patterson, to the flight simulators of the eighties and NASA's experiments at Ames into telerobotics; and a whole range of eye-tracking devices, gloves, bodysuits, and force-feedback hardware from university projects, industrial labs, and government research institutes. Prized most of all was SNARC, Marvin Minsky's original neural network machine from 1951. The "Stochastic Neural Analog Reinforcement Calculator" consisted of three antiquated nineteen-inch cabinets containing over 400 vacuum tubes, with learning capability instilled by means of forty industrial potentiometers driven by magnetic clutches via a pair of bicycle chains. The assembly was lost in the late fifties, only to reappear half a century later in a government surplus supply store in New Orleans. The proprietor said he had thought it was a gunlaying predictor from a World War II battleship.

The young woman standing in an open area of floor in front of a graphics screen was in her late twenties, with fine-boned features, silky, shoulder-length fair hair bordering on platinum, and clear blue eyes. She was a postgraduate in neurodynamic physiology from Harvard and had come to Pittsburgh for a job interview. Her name was Evelyn. Evelyn Vance.

Corrigan made some final adjustments to the collar that she was wearing above the neck of her blouse. It consisted of a lightweight aluminum frame entwined with electrical windings and pickup heads, rising high under the chin like a surgical brace and close-fitting at the base of the skull. The whole assembly rested on padded shoulder supports, and a cable connected it to an electronics cabinet alongside the display unit, where another man was watching the screen as he entered setup commands from a keyboard. He was older than Corrigan, graying, with a ragged mustache, and looking more Evelyn's idea of the old-time engineer, in a tweed jacket with open-neck plaid shirt, and cords. Corrigan had introduced him earlier as Eric Shipley, a senior scientist on the project.

"Did you ever hear of Tempest technology?" Corrigan asked Evelyn. "From the late seventies."

"I was just being born then," she replied.

Just turned thirty, smooth, confident, crisply dressed, Corrigan looked the part of the young, successful, upward-bound executive. The pretty young thing from Massachusetts, nervous, yet excited at the prospect of trading academia's security for the greater opportunities—and hopefully glamour—of the commercial world, was impressed. And he knew it.

"It was a technique that the security agencies developed for tapping in to a data-transmission cable by reading the magnetic field fluctuations around it." He nodded to indicate the collar. "This combines a much more sensitive pickup system with standard front-end neural decoding and a lot of the mathematics from various medical imaging systems. In fact, it was a joint venture between your place and here: Boston and Pittsburgh. MIT and Carnegie Mellon put it all together about three years ago. It's called MIMIC."

"That has to be an acronym for something."

"Miniaturized Motor Intercept Collar. You'll see why in a moment." Corrigan looked over at Shipley. "How are we doing, Eric?"

"Just about there. . . ." Shipley entered a final command, and the silhouette of a human female figure appeared, centered in the screen. "Okay," Shipley said. Evelyn looked at Corrigan questioningly— mainly by moving her eyes, since the collar impeded head movement.

"Move one of your arms," Corrigan directed.

Evelyn raised an arm, and the figure on the screen did the same thing. She raised both arms, then swung them in circles; the figure duplicated the motion. She smiled, enjoying the spectacle. "Hey, I'm impressed," she said, smiling and talking through her teeth.

"You can move about," Corrigan said. "Watch the cable, though."

Evelyn stepped forward, then a pace sideways, cautiously at first; then, getting really into the experience, she laughed and broke into a short routine of dance steps and gestures. The figure on the screen mimicked everything faithfully. "I had no idea it would be so smooth."

Her movements were not being interpreted from TV images, position-detectors in suits, body-mounted light-emitters, or by any of the other familiar methods for encrypting human physical motion directly into computers. Instead, the collar surrounding Evelyn's neck and lower brain stem was picking up the motor output signals on their way down to the spinal cord to direct her musculature system. The same signals were being fed to the programs controlling the figure dancing on the screen—which Shipley had adjusted to superficially resemble Evelyn in shape and body proportions.

Evelyn spent more time experimenting, showing a lot of interest, asking some good questions. The figure's head didn't move, she discovered, since the system only picked up signals on their way down from the brain. It didn't matter very much—she was hardly able to move her own head anyway. As an input interface it was ahead of anything that she had realized existed.

"I'm surprised that it's in your museum already," she said as Shipley switched off the equipment and Corrigan helped her remove the collar.

"It's been three years," Corrigan said.

"That still seems soon."

"The accelerating rate of progress. It got overtaken. We're into a new version now."

"Do I get to see it?"

"Yes, but not here. We'll have to go over to the labs. It gets better."

They went through an exit at the rear of the building and followed a path by a lawn between the several other buildings and parking lots forming the rest of the complex. The architecture was a mixture of old brick-and-stone and new concrete-and-glass, standing on the site of a former steel plant. The ovens and furnaces had gone, but the serviceable buildings had been restored and converted into office and laboratory space, and a number of brand-new facilities erected in the spaces created by the demolitions.

For the past several years, Evelyn had been working as a researcher at Harvard on noninvasive stimulation of the visual system. The field was a development from early experiments in the sixties by animal researchers seeking ways of exciting selected brain centers without the need of surgically implanted electrodes, which tended to interfere with the processes that they were supposed to measure. The result was a variety of techniques using additive external electric fields, summation of beams of certain electromagnetic frequencies for which the skull and its underlying cerebral tissues were found to be transparent, ultrasonic waves and pulses, and other approaches, all focused upon the common goal of controlling the firing of selected brain patterns painlessly and without intrusion, from outside the skull.

Collectively the subject was known as "DINS" (*DIrect Neural Stimulation*) technology. This was also Shipley's area of expertise, and he needed another specialist. Hence, Evelyn took it that, assuming that she was made an offer and accepted it; she would be working primarily with him rather than with Corrigan. Nevertheless, Corrigan seemed to have taken charge of the interview process. Evelyn attributed it to his natural flamboyance and enthusiasm. Shipley didn't seem to mind, and it added to the image of irrepressible Irish roguishness that Evelyn had begun to form of Corrigan.

They entered one of the older buildings and went up a level and a short distance along a corridor, past a door marked J. M. CORRIGAN, to double doors inset with small glass panes. Inside was a large room cluttered with the paraphernalia of electronics R & D labs anywhere: cabinets and equipment racks draped with tangles of cable, making it difficult to tell which piece of hardware was associated with what; several office desks, littered with books and papers; a wall of metal shelving holding boxes, supplies, unidentifiable gadgets in various stages of assembly or dismemberment; a workbench along one wall, with tools on a pegboard above, soldering irons on stands, more shelves and drawers of electrical components, oscilloscopes and electronic test equipment. A couple of techs in shirts and jeans were working around a rig on the far side; another was wiring up a connector on some kind of assembly stripped down on the bench; a girl was operating a terminal at one of the desks.

Corrigan led the way over to a cluster of racks and cubicles on the far side. A tall, loose-limbed figure with a generous mane of neck-length yellow hair, clad in a loose sweater and tan denims, was sprawled in front of a console. It was a typical lab-lashup, makeshift affair, consisting of several monitor screens, some electronics, and a panel, all fitted in a framework bolted to the body of an old steel desk. He unfolded himself in a lazy, unhurried movement and sat up to greet the arrivals with a grin.

"How are we doing here, Tom?" Corrigan inquired.

"All set."

"This is the group's software supervisor, Tom Hatcher."

"Hi, Tom."

"Tom, this is Evelyn Vance, that I told you about. We've just been across in the museum and seen MIMIC." And to Evelyn: "Now we want to bring you up to date on what we're doing now."

"So you're the lady who's gonna be joining this crazy outfit, eh?" Hatcher had a slow, easy southwestern drawl that went with his manner.

"We'll see what happens, anyway," Evelyn said.

There was another chair, upholstered in black and built upon a tubular steel frame, positioned in front and to one side of the console, where it could be observed by the console operator. It had a collar structure built in front of the headrest, heavier and more intricate than the one that MIMIC used, and hinged into two halves to admit the wearer. Evelyn commented that it looked like a pilot's seat. Shipley confirmed that it was from an Air Force jet.

In front of the chair was a flat metal surface a foot or so square, bounded on the far side by vertical glass plates set at an angle like an opened book. Behind the plates was a collection of shiny tubes and mirrors that Evelyn recognized as the laser and optics of a hologram projector.

"That's your next ride," Corrigan said. "Take a seat."

"You mean I don't get to dance this time?"

"Oh, sure you will. I told you, it gets better."

Shipley held some of the trailing cables aside and beckoned Evelyn toward the chair. "It looks as if I'm going to be electrocuted," she said, stepping forward.

"Medium, rare, or well-done?" Hatcher asked from the console. They all laughed.

The headrest, Evelyn saw as she sat down, was in fact an integral part of the collar unit itself. Corrigan moved over to stand by Hatcher, and they went into a technical exchange about loop gains and parameter settings.

"Where did you get your background in DINS?" she asked Shipley as he closed the collar and began securing connections—partly from curiosity, partly to get him to talk more.

"Oh, I used to be with part of the SDI program—using active optics to precorrect laser beams for transmission distortion." He had a deep, gruff, but not unkindly voice. Corrigan could be fun to have around, but when it came to more serious business, she hoped that she would be working with Shipley. He went on. "That needed fast algorithms to compute complex signal patterns in real time, and the math turned out to be ideal for generating brain-stimulation sequences, too. . . . Now you'll need to hush up so I can position the lateral pads."

The front portion of the collar immobilized her jaw, making this a lot more constraining than MIMIC and fixing her gaze on the holo-projection space above the metal plate.

"Okay, Evelyn, relax," Corrigan said, turning to face her. "You might experience a few funny feelings at first, but don't worry about it. This time we'll also be injecting sensations into your neural centers. Your brain won't be able to tell that they're not coming in via the sensory system. But first we have to calibrate to your particular ranges of scale and sensitivity. It only takes a minute."

Suddenly, Evelyn's body went numb from the neck down, as if she had undergone an instant spinal block. Then she felt a pins-and-needles sensation in her arms and legs, especially in the fingertips. When she tried wriggling them, they wouldn't respond. After a few seconds this faded, and more normal feelings returned, but blurred somehow, as if she were suspended in molasses.

Tom Hatches called across to her from the console. "Feel okay? Blink once for yes, twice for no, three times or make dentist noises in an emergency."

She blinked, and could see the word "Yes" appear in green in a corner of one of Hatcher's screens. Evidently there was an eye tracker operating somewhere. A trained user would be able to communicate a whole vocabulary through eye movements.

"Weird—kinda like an all-around water bed, but okay?" Hatches asked, checking.

She blinked once.

"Any discomfort?"

She blinked twice. A red "No" on the screen confirmed it.

"Now I want you to close your eyes and imagine that you're standing normally on the ground. Open your eyes when you start to feel heavy, then blink once when it's about right."

Evelyn closed her eyes. An instant later, sensations came over her that were completely at odds with the situation she knew herself to be in. She could *feel* herself standing: feet pressing on the floor, back erect, arms hanging loosely. But too light. She felt precariously anchored, like a balloon just touching the ground, waiting for the first breath of wind to carry her away. But even as she thought it, her weight started to increase. Then she was twenty pounds too heavy, her spine sagging. She opened her eyes abruptly. The heaviness slackened off, reduced slowly . . . and she felt normal. She blinked.

"Close your eyes again," Hatcher called. "Now imagine that you're holding a grapefruit in each hand. Lift them sideways to shoulder height, keeping your arms straight. Open your eyes when they get heavy. Blink once when they feel about right."

The routine went the same as before.

"Now raise both arms straight up over your head—without the grapefruits. . . . Point them straight forward from the shoulders. That's great. . . . Now raise each leg in turn, knee bent, until the thigh is horizontal. Okay. . . . Now keep your eyes closed and try walking a few steps."

It was uncanny. Although Evelyn knew that she was sitting immobile with her head held in a restraint, she could feel herself walking across a floor. A bit lumpily and jerkily, it was true—but *walking*.

"Does it feel quite right?" Hatcher's voice asked. Evelyn opened her eyes and blinked twice. "Tell me which of these corrections feels more normal. This? . . ." The discontinuity got worse, as if her leg were actually coming apart at the knee with each step. "Or this?" The feelings became smoother, almost right now. "Which was better?" Hatcher asked. "The first one?" Two blinks. "The second one?" One blink. After a couple more trials they had it perfect.

"Okay." Corrigan pulled another chair close and sat down where Evelyn could see him. "MIMIC reads muscle-control information directly from the brain," he said. "DINS transmits information into the brain, bypassing the normal sensory apparatus. This is what happens when we combine the two together."

A solid figure appeared in the holo-space, again female, wearing a simple red, loose-fitting dress. Once again, Evelyn could feel herself standing—in the same attitude as the figure, she realized after a second or two. She moved her eyes to look at Corrigan inquiringly. He nodded. She looked back at the holo-figure and made to move her arms. From the corner of her eye she could see that they remained motionless on the armrests of the chair. Instead, the hologram figure moved its arms. But unlike the case with MIMIC, this time Evelyn could actually *feel* it: the weight shifting and pressures in her joints altering as the shoulder and elbow angles changed, the tensions in her muscles—even the light rubbing of the dress material against her skin. Yet she knew that all the time she was sitting unmoving in a chair. It was unbelievable.

"Still feel like a dance?" Corrigan asked, his eyes twinkling. "There's no cable to worry about this time. The motor outputs from your brain are being read as before with MIMIC, but a DINS signal is suppressing the onward transmission of them into the spine—like an externally induced anesthetic. At the same time, the computer is synthesizing the feedback signals that you ought to be experiencing, and injecting them back the other way."

She walked the figure forward, then back, sideways and in circles, finally pirouetting and launching it into a series of twirls and minor acrobatics. At first it was odd to feel the figure's internal dynamics, yet at the same time to be observing it from a viewpoint outside. Corrigan watched, letting her get the hang of it. And then something changed suddenly, like the image of a wire cube reversing: the two bodies of sensation fused, and she was able to project herself inside, compensating unconsciously for the discrepancy in visual space.

Corrigan sensed it. "Managed to make the flip?" he asked. She blinked at him once and forced a parody of a grin.

"Try these," Hatcher's voice said. A flight of steps appeared in the display. Evelyn walked the figure over to them and began climbing. The sensations of her legs lifting and pushing, foot tilting and shifting the weight onto the ball, felt completely real.

"The illusion is totally compelling if you close your eyes," Corrigan said.

She did, and there was no longer any doubt: she was climbing a staircase. Already her thighs were starting to ache; and ache; and— surely not—she could feel her heartbeat accelerate from the effort, even slight perspiration. She opened her eyes again. They must have looked alarmed.

"Don't worry," Corrigan said. "It's all simulated. You're bone dry and as relaxed as a sleeping baby. . . . So now you can see why MIMIC is in the museum already. This is its successor. We call it 'Pinocchio.' What do you think?"

The three of them got down to specifics over lunch in the staff dining room at the top of the Executive Building, back at the front of the complex.

"We're looking for more help on the neurophysiology side to go into the next step," Shipley said to Evelyn. He had said little since his few words about his SDI background, over in the IE Block, which Evelyn now knew was dedicated to various aspects of Interactive Environments. Now that they were into Shipley's territory, Corrigan no longer played the lead but was happy to sit back and let him get on with it. Evelyn sensed an easy, informal working relationship between them. She was finding the prospect of becoming a part of it increasingly appealing.

"What is the next step?" she asked.

"Pinocchio Two," Shipley replied. "As things stand, we're limited to the medulla. The system can't handle the Trigeminal and the Abducens. To go further, we want to bring somebody into the team with the kind of background you've had at Harvard—experience of connecting at the pons."

Evelyn thought for a second. "That's why the face and eye movements didn't look right, isn't it?" she said. "I noticed when Tom went to close-up. I pulled a face deliberately, but the holo was still smiling."

Shipley raised an eyebrow at Corrigan. Corrigan nodded that he liked what he was hearing. "You're right," Shipley told Evelyn. "The face is dubbed, purely for effect. The computer fills in what it thinks is appropriate."

They were saying that Pinocchio's combined motor-intercept and DINS interface coupled in at the lowest region of the brain stem, the medulla oblongata, the main railroad of the nervous system, where the seventh through twelfth of the body's twelve cranial nerves terminated. These were the nerves serving the body's voluntary and involuntary motor systems, along with the sense of balance, which was what enabled body movements and sensations to be reproduced in the ways that Evelyn had experienced. (These nerves also handled speech, taste, and hearing, but those faculties were not subjects of the current research.) The remaining functions—jaw and upper-face movements, ocular motion, vision, and smell—were handled by the first to sixth cranial nerves, which synapsed in higher regions of the brain.

In particular, the fifth and sixth cranial nerves, known as the Trigeminal and the Abducens, both synapsed in the next region above the medulla oblongata: the pons. Shipley was saying that they now wanted to extend the coupling level up to the pons. Such a step could be in preparation for only one thing.

"So the eventual intention must be to add vision," Evelyn concluded. That would require going further, to the thalamus, the next region above the pons. "You've already got hearing and speech, potentially, at the medulla—via the Acoustic, Glossopharyngeal, and Vagus. Extend from the pons to the thalamus, and you'll have it all: full-sensory direct-neural."

"Except for olfactory," Shipley said, smiling faintly.

"Oh, yes, of course." Evelyn checked herself. Smell was handled by the first cranial nerve. The most primitive of the senses, it was the only one to enter the brain above the thalamus and go directly into the cerebrum.

"Well, now you know what we're up to here," Corrigan said, sitting back in his chair. He turned an inquiring eye to Shipley. Shipley returned a nod that he was satisfied. Corrigan looked back at Evelyn. "I think we've heard all we want to. To hell with the bureaucratic nonsense—that can catch up later. There's a place here for you if you want it. What do you say?"

After what she had seen, there wasn't a lot for her to think about. But she didn't want to appear too eager.

"What sort of longer-term prospects would we be talking about?" she asked.

Corrigan threw out a hand carelessly. "Unlimited. It could be the beginnings of a whole new research section dedicated to higher-level coupling. You could end up running it."

That seemed good enough. "Confirm the figures in writing," she said. "If there are no surprises . . . Well, yes. . . . I'll take it."

"Splendid." Corrigan looked at Shipley for an endorsement. "Come on, Eric. Congratulate the lady, at least."

"Pinder hasn't confirmed the appointment yet," Shipley reminded him.

"He's the VP of R and D," Corrigan explained to Evelyn. "He's away today. Don't worry about it. It's just a rubberstamping thing."

Shipley gave her a reassuring nod. "Joe's right. You're just the person we need. I don't think there'll be any problem."

Over the remainder of lunch they talked about lighter things, asking Evelyn about her other interests and swapping personal anecdotes. Then they took her to meet Peter Quell, Pinder's deputy. Apparently, Pinder was with a group visiting the Air Force Space Defense Command in California. Quell stood in for him by delivering some routine corporate messages about CLC being a caring company, and the career opportunities being unlimited for somebody who could fit in, after which they went to Shipley's office and spent a half hour clearing up miscellaneous questions that Evelyn raised. That concluded the business for the moment. While Shipley stayed behind to catch up on what was happening in the lab, Corrigan had a cab called to take Evelyn back to her hotel and walked her back to main reception in the Executive Building. While they were waiting, he talked her into having dinner together that night, before she caught her flight back to Boston the next morning.

❁ CHAPTER NINE ❁

Corrigan and Evelyn met for dinner in the downtown Vista Hotel, where she was staying. The interview had told him much about her. Now the informal setting gave her an opportunity to satisfy more of her curiosity about him.

"Oh, I'm from a place that I'd be surprised if you've heard of," he told her as they sat in the lounge over drinks, waiting for a table. "On the coast a few miles south of Dublin." He wrote the words "Dun Laoghaire" on a coaster and asked her how she'd pronounce it.

Evelyn shrugged. "Dun Layo-ghe-air?" she tried, sounding it out phonetically.

"It's Dun Leery." Corrigan grinned. "You can always win a dollar bet in a bar with that. The piers there are famous. They enclose what used to be the biggest artificial harbor in the world at one time."

"When was that?"

"Back in the eighteen hundreds. The granite was brought down on a cable railway from a quarry a little farther down the coast. It was driven by gravity. The weight of the loaded cars going down hauled the empties back up."

"Neat."

Corrigan sipped his gin and tonic and nodded. "Great engineers; those Victorians. They made things to last. Big brass knobs on everything not plastic ones that come off in your hand all the time."

"So how did you end up in computing and things like that?" Evelyn asked.

Corrigan pursed his lips and stroked the tip of his nose with a knuckle. "Well, now, I was more of a mathematician to begin with—you know, in college. Then I got this, kind of, scholarship thing . . ."

"Never mind the false modesty."

"Good. It doesn't come naturally to an Irishman anyway. I got to Trinity—that's one of the Dublin universities. That got me in touch with the computer scene, and I came over to the States to do postgraduate work on AI."

"They do a lot of that at MIT, up in Boston," Evelyn commented.

"I was there for a while—at the AI lab that Minsky and John McCarthy started. Plus, I did a sabbatical with Thinking Machines there, too. You know them?"

"TMC at Cambridge?" Evelyn nodded. "Sure."

"Then I was at Stanford for some time, and after that Carnegie Mellon, which brought me to Pittsburgh. That was up to a couple of years ago, and then I joined CLC."

Evelyn regarded him for a moment. "Okay, I know you must get asked this a hundred times a week, but when are we actually going to see it—the real thing? Does anyone know?"

Corrigan snorted and made a face. "Ah, they've all got themselves bogged down on semantic issues, if you want my opinion—spending more time arguing over what intelligence is instead of actively doing anything to pursue it. We use the word to mean two different things: the 'survival' kind of intelligence that makes us different from animals, and the 'intellectual' kind that makes some people different from others—or think they are, anyway. The problem is that nobody can make their minds up which one they're talking about."

"Which kind do you mean?" Evelyn asked.

"Oh, I got out of the whole thing and left them to it."

"So is that why you're into virtual sensory worlds now, instead?"

"Exactly." Corrigan showed his hands in a gesture of candor. "I'm in a hurry. I plan on going places in this world. There isn't the time to wait for the likes of them to die off or get their act together." It was a calculated brashness, playing off the light in Evelyn's eye.

"Something tells me you'll get there, too," she said. "Is this the male competitive urge that I sense surfacing now?"

Corrigan smiled and shrugged in a way that said she could take it any way she liked. "Ah, well, now . . . Let's just say that Eric can run the caution-and-conservatism department."

"Eric Shipley, you mean? I thought he was a nice guy."

"Oh, don't get me wrong. He's a great guy to work with. Good scientist, knows his stuff. . . ." Corrigan sighed and showed a palm briefly. "But he has his own style, and it's got him where he is."

"He seemed content enough to me," Evelyn said, letting it sound as an objection. She still liked the thought of working with Shipley. Sharing a dig at his expense—even so slight a one as this—didn't feel comfortable.

"*He* is," Corrigan replied.

The hostess came over to tell them that their table was ready, and they went through into the restaurant. Corrigan had already ordered while they were in the lounge, and they began their soup course straight away. When the waiter had left, Evelyn returned to the subject of Shipley.

"Why did it bother him that Jason Pinder wasn't here himself today?" she asked.

Corrigan shrugged unconcernedly. "That's the way Eric is. He seems to think that if Pinder attached as much importance to this job as Eric thinks he should . . ."

"Which job? You mean my job?"

"Yes: the one we're talking about . . . then he would have made sure that the interview was fixed for a day when he was here, instead of leaving it to Quell."

All of a sudden Evelyn felt uneasy. "What do you think?" she asked.

Corrigan waved a hand unconcernedly. "Ah, Eric worries too much about underhanded corporate politics—especially where influences are involved that he believes science could do without, such as SDC or anything else connected with the military. He should have lived in the nineteenth century and been one of those gifted, all-around amateurs that you read about."

"It doesn't bother you?" Evelyn said.

"The thought of getting mixed up with the Space Defense people?" Corrigan shook his head. "Not really. Why should it? That's where the money is. It might add some excitement to life. It's like everything else: you deal with the complications as they come."

He grinned. She smiled back. It was what she wanted to hear, and she thought no more about it. Over dinner, Corrigan brought up the possibility of his coming up to Boston to visit her. It was about time he looked up some of his friends there, he said. At the same time, he could show Evelyn some of his old haunts. Evelyn thought it would be a great idea.

At the Space Defense Command's Simulator Center at Inglewood, California, the time was three hours earlier. Jason Pinder and a party of technical and management executives that included the CLC president, Ken Endelmyer, were finishing the VIP tour. They had seen the motion platforms mounting cockpit mockups that even experienced Air Force space pilots reported as being "better than the real thing"; they had played with the telemanipulator helmets and arm-gloves used to remote-direct spaceborne repair and construction robots from ground and orbital stations thousands of miles away. Now they were in a section of the Visual Environments labs for a demonstration of a device that had been undergoing development and improvement for some time: the Vision & Voice head assembly, known as "VIV." They had heard the presentations, watched the videos, and handled the equipment. Now it was time to lighten things up a little and conclude with some fun.

Don Falker, chief engineer of CLC's Artificial Vision division, stood a short distance apart from the group. He was wearing a lightweight plastic helmet fitting close, like a skullcap, that supported a set of miniaturized vision goggles in front of his eyes and padded earphones. A microchip package in the crown communicated via an IR frequency link to nearby processing equipment. In his hand, he was holding an imitation Ping-Pong paddle made of aluminum, covered front, back, and around the edge in tiny reflecting surfaces. Similarly equipped, standing a few feet away and smiling a little self-consciously, was Therese Loel, head of CLC's Engineering Systems Group.

The man in charge of the proceedings was around forty, lean and tanned, with thinning hair, graying at the temples, and silver-rimmed spectacles. He had a presentation style that was smooth and polished, dynamic in content but coming relaxed and easy, developed over years of dealing with high-level individuals. His name was Frank Tyron, SDC's civilian project manager of the VIV program.

"Hold your other hand horizontal, as if you were about to serve a ball," Tyron called to Falker.

The stereo image being presented inside Falker's goggles showed a nonexistent, computer-generated Ping-Pong table, with Therese Loel transposed so as to be facing him from the far end of it. To everyone watching, Falker simply extended an empty hand palm-up and looked at it. A program analyzing the output from a pair of cameras mounted on the walls tracked the movement, and another program added a Ping-Pong ball to the image that he could see of his hand. Therese Loel saw it appear too, but the view in her goggles showed Falker at the far end of the table.

"Go ahead," Tyron invited, speaking into a mike.

The onlookers watched as Falker tossed the invisible ball up and hit at it with the metal paddle. Sensors around the room tracked the paddle's motion from laser reflections, and the ball in the optical representation followed the computed path.

"Hey!" Therese cried involuntarily, and jumped sideways to play a return stroke.

"I can hear it hitting the bats and the table," Falker said, playing a backhand. "The synchronization is perfect. This is good!" Therese returned, but the ball went high.

As state of the art, simulating a Ping-Pong game wasn't especially a revolutionary, or even a new, concept. What was different about this demonstration was the quality. There was nothing crude or cartoonlike about the images that the two players were seeing. The table in front of them and the room around it (actually a stored representation, encoded from videotape, of the games room in the OTSC Recreational Gym in another part of the establishment) were *real*. The figures at far ends *were* Therese Loel and Don Falker, superposed into the scene without the helmets—the missing facial details were added from TV images captured beforehand. Even with a fast forehand smash shot, the images of ball and paddle stayed clean and true: no flicker, no blurring. This hardware was *fast*.

The others couldn't keep from laughing at the two goggled figures lunging and swiping over a table that nobody else could see. Even Ken Endelmyer was smiling between two of his cohorts. What made the spectacle even stranger was that the two players were facing roughly the same way. The images that the computer was creating in the two sets of goggles were correct for the perspectives that each was perceiving.

"It's okay, Don," Tyron called as Falker turned automatically to retrieve the ball from the floor. "You don't have to chase after it. Just serve another."

"Oh, really? Okay." Falker faced the virtual table, raised his left hand again, and—to him—a ball appeared in it. "Say, I've got another one." He played it. "What happens to the first?"

"It evaporates."

Falker and Loel continued their game for a few minutes more, then stopped to allow a couple of the other visitors to try. While the helmets were being taken off and donned, Tyron took a spare unit from a rack by the wall. He turned to address himself particularly to Endelmyer and Pinder.

"We can give you Pinocchio with voice and vision *now*." He made a dismissive gesture, conveying that there really oughtn't to be anything to think about. "The way you're planning to go at present, it will take years at least. Even if you do shift the interface boundary from the medulla to the pons, you're still as far away as ever because visual data enters farther still above that." He patted the helmet resting in his hand and said again, "We can give you it *now,* using technology that already exists, right here. No banking on uncertain future developments. No speculating with unnecessary risks. It doesn't mean that you have to abandon your plans for extending to the pons. But going this way could relieve the time pressure for getting results."

Endelmyer looked inquiringly at Pinder. His expression said that it sounded good to him and he was looking for endorsement. Pinder obliged. "I think it would be worth looking into, Ken. It would give us a mainstream hybrid thrust toward full-sensory now: tactile from Pinocchio, visual and speech/auditory via the regular sensory apparatus, using VIV. The pons research gets relegated to lower-priority status as a secondary approach. It may produce results sooner or later. Either way, we can afford to wait."

It was what Endelmyer wanted to hear. From the things that had been said earlier in the day, it was also clear that Tyron was dangling the prospect of not only a working technology that would advance the project immediately, but of high-level political backing and generous additional funding too. It was also a good psychological ploy aimed at Endelmyer, who, Tyron knew—having done his homework as any good salesman would have—had hankerings for rubbing shoulders on the Washington circuit.

The meeting broke up on a promising note, with individuals from both sides gravitating into chatty groups. Endelmyer drew Pinder and Tyron to one side, along with a man called Harry Morgen, Tyron's right-hand man. "Personally I'm satisfied," he told them. "You've done an impressive job today, Mr. Tyron. Although I cannot give you a definite response today, you may take it that I will be reporting back to the CLC Board in an extremely positive light. Thank everyone who has been involved, from all of us, for their efforts."

✸ CHAPTER TEN ✸

Dun Laoghaire, the town that Corrigan was originally from, means, in Irish, "Laoghaire's Fort." It is generally assumed by historians that a fort once existed there, belonging to King Laoghaire of the fifth century, whose principal abode was at Tara, about thirty-five miles away. In more recent times it grew in less than a century from an insignificant fishing village to a major port and Victorian resort town. Its lifestyle in that era characterized the Dublin professional class: merchants, bankers, ex-army and -navy officers and others of the well-to-do, who flocked to live in its handsome terraces by the sea, yet within easy rail distance of the city.

The more scholarly of the town's progeny went, traditionally, into the arts, humanities, and literature. It was not noted for its contributions to the sciences or cutting-edge technologies, and this made it all the more remarkable to Joe Corrigan's relatives and friends when he walked away with every honor in mathematical computing at Trinity and took off across the Atlantic to do the rounds of the AI labs at MIT, Stanford, Carnegie Mellon, and other unheard-of places.

He had taken to the U.S. scene as if it were his natural element. After a land less than half the size of Florida, the vastness of the country seemed to mirror the scale of everything he found around him. It wasn't just that the buildings were taller than the repatched and replastered Georgian frontages of Merrion Square and Leeson Street, the avenues wider, the stores grander than Dunnes or Clery's, the cars longer, and the hamburgers huger. It had to do with ambition and opportunity, also. After the venerable but crowded surroundings that he was used to working in, the promise and lavishness of scale of American research was breathtaking. Imagination raced unchecked. Funding was unlimited. In two years he had become highly visible in the part of the academic computer world associated with intelligence modeling, and those who were supposed to know about such things listed his name among the front-runners that they expected to see heading the field in ten years' time. Corrigan, however, still intoxicated by the combination of early, practically effortless, success and his newfound continental-size lifestyle, succumbed easily when the talent scouts from CLC made approaches to recruit him.

That had been two years ago, when he was still only twenty-eight. Since then, his project management and personal technical contribution had put the development of Pinocchio a year ahead of its original schedule, further strengthening his reputation, and with the way ahead open for his rise into senior management, his self-confidence was at its peak.

This was the moment that Evelyn had chosen to appear, combining all the attributes of physical attractiveness, intelligence, professional presence, and social acceptability that would be required of the one accessory still missing from his life. Maybe it was an unconscious recognition of this that led him to react to her with a seriousness that had been singularly absent from the various female encounters that had dotted his career path until then. Perhaps it was an echo of some primeval male impulse to stake out his territory before potential rivals had a chance to appear. Possibly it was the part of his nature that scoffed at caution and enjoyed the mild impropriety of the situation. More likely, a combination of all three. But four days after Evelyn's interview, he found himself deplaning from a Delta Airlines evening flight at Boston's Logan Airport, and took a cab to the Hyatt Hotel, where he had made a reservation for the night, overlooking the bank of the Charles River.

Evelyn had arranged to take the next day off, and she collected him after breakfast the next morning. She was pleased to see him, even if somewhat awed at his having made the time; she was nervous that she might be misreading more into things than reality warranted, then relieved when he seemed to show as much enthusiasm as she felt.

They went first to the AI Laboratory at MIT and visited some of Corrigan's former colleagues from his first years in the States. His postdoctoral work at that time had been on the emerging subject of "psychotectonics": unraveling the roles and dynamics of the sometimes competing, sometimes cooperating hierarchies of functional agencies that make up the phenomenon called "mind." Although it was Corrigan's work here on the simulation of evolving neural networks that had earned him his initial recognition, he had moved later, as he had told Evelyn when she was in Pittsburgh, to join Carnegie Mellon's group working on "Trunk Motor Intercept" technology, which eventually produced MIMIC.

The aim of one project that he showed her at MIT was to expand a machine intelligence's everyday world-knowledge by getting it to solve detective mysteries. In another, devoted to speech interpretation, they watched a computer creating a cartoon on the fly in response to a narrative being read by Evelyn. On the floor below, a supercomputer from Thinking Machines Corporation in nearby Cambridge was generating admittedly not very good critiques of literature texts. Finally, in yet another room filled with screens, racks, and tangles of cable, Corrigan introduced the department head, Jenny Leddel. She was graying, entering middle age, and wearing a woolen cardigan with a tweed skirt.

"This is Evelyn, from Harvard, who I told you about on the phone," he said. "She's going to be joining us down in Pittsburgh."

"Stealing our talent now, eh?" Jenny said, nodding knowingly. Her eyes sparkled with a mischievous light, young for her years. "It figures."

"It hasn't been confirmed yet, Joe," Evelyn reminded him.

"Ah, don't be worrying yourself about that at all."

"How are things going with Pinocchio down there?" Jenny asked Corrigan. "I've been following the reports. It sounds exciting."

"Going well. We'll have to get you down there sometime to see for yourself," he said.

"I'd like that."

"We're all set for P-Two: going up to the pons. That's what Evelyn will be working on."

"You achieved a full two-way integration, yes?"

"DINS with MIMIC. We've had it running for about three months now."

"Complete internal haptics?"

"Total. It works. Uncanny. Evelyn tried it a few days ago."

"What about the secondary instabilities that Goodman's people at Chapel Hill kept running into? You didn't have a problem with them?"

"Our DINS expert came up with a C-mode suppression filter that cured it. A character called Eric Shipley. Do you know him?"

"I'm afraid I don't."

"He's good—the old-school type. Infuriatingly plodding at times, but he gets it right in the end."

"We could use a few like that here," Jenny said. "Too many these days trying to fly before they've grown feathers." She gave Corrigan a pointed look as she said this, but he missed it. Jenny didn't make an issue of it, but turned to Evelyn. "Anyhow, enough of that. We're ignoring you. Joe says you want to talk to Perseus."

"Sure. If he wants to talk to me."

This was the latest to come out of the learning systems based on goal—directed, self-adaptive, neural-net analogs that Corrigan had worked on during his time with MIT: systems that experimented with problem-solving strategies. They devised new variations of what seemed to work best, and forgot about what didn't—the process known in nature as "evolution." An ideal strategy-testing environment—full of clearly defined challenges and yielding easily measured results—was the classical dragons-and-dungeons type of adventure world. Perseus, accordingly, was a computer-created character who explored such mythical realms, with similar goals to achieve and obstacles to be overcome. Half of AI research, it seemed, was wrestling with the problem of trying to impart world-knowledge.

Jenny tapped commands into a console to activate the system. A simplified image appeared on a screen of a typical D & D setting of a large room, assorted objects, with passages, stairways, and tunnels going off in various directions.

"What does Perseus stand for?" Evelyn asked.

Jenny shrugged. "Nothing. It's just the name of a guy from Greek mythology who killed monsters and solved problems. We thought it was appropriate."

Evelyn looked relieved. "I thought everything had to be an acronym."

"I guess we got tired of them." Jenny entered another code. "And here he is." A caricature figure had appeared in the room, lightly clad in ancient-hero style, carrying a sheathed sword and wearing a helmet.

Jenny tapped a key, and an icon showing an ear appeared at the top of the screen. "Hello, Perseus. How's it going?" she asked.

"I haven't found a way through the Misty Room," a voice replied from a speaker above the screen. It sounded quite human. This project evidently embodied some sophisticated language processing too. "It becomes pitch black, whichever way I go, and I lose direction. But the inscription on the wall in the cavern mentioned 'rays that cut through the mists.' It suggests that there might be a special kind of light, or lamp, somewhere."

"This has got better since the last time I saw it," Corrigan murmured.

The figure on the screen looked up and around. "Who else is speaking?" its voice asked.

Jenny touched a key and the icon vanished. "Watch for the ear," she said. "He can hear us while it's showing." She brought the icon back again. "Just some friends. They don't affect you. What's new?"

"After some reflection on the matter, it occurred to me that the implement I found in the Burial Chamber was of just the correct shape and size for making holes in the ground. So I decided to dig around where the earth appeared to have been disturbed. And I found this." Another screen showed a close-up of Perseus's schematicized hands, holding an oil lamp of old, Oriental design.

Any five-year-old would have known what to do instantly. Perseus, however, seemed mystified, turning the lamp over and contemplating it. "There are no obvious buttons or switches. It seems built to contain liquid, but it is empty. Its use escapes me."

Corrigan couldn't bear to look, but turned his head away, muttering inaudibly, "Rub the lamp. Rub the lamp." Jenny gave a thin smile and shrugged.

Evelyn motioned to herself, then at the screen, asking through gestures if it would be all right for her to speak. Jenny nodded and mouthed, "Sure."

Evelyn stared with a strange, not-wanting-to-believe-this fascination for a few seconds at the figure on the screen, now returned to fumbling with the lamp.

"Perseus," she said.

The figure stopped what it was doing. "Is this another friend?"

"Yes. . . . Can I ask you a question?"

"I assume so, since you just did."

"I meant a different question."

"Why should you be unable to ask a different one?"

Evelyn frowned, then saw the problem. "No, I didn't mean 'can' in the sense of 'able to.' I meant would you mind?"

There was a pause, then, puzzled, "How should I mind?"

Jenny flipped the ear icon off for a moment. "His conceptual world is limited to exploring the physical environment. Implied permissions belong to a dimension of relationships that he can't comprehend. Don't project too much into the illusion."

But that was the trouble. For Evelyn, the illusion was too convincing. She couldn't avoid the conviction that she was listening to a real person speaking from a real place. Somehow, the sight of the visually simple, cartoonlike form, clashing as it did with the capacity for experience that she found herself perceiving, produced uncomfortable feelings that she didn't want to think about. Yet some macabre curiosity compelled her to probe deeper.

"When we talk to you, who do you think we are?" she asked Perseus.

"Friends," he replied.

"Are we the same as you?"

"Obviously not."

"What makes you say that?"

"I can't see you. You don't appear, like all the other beings that I meet."

"But we must exist somewhere. Isn't that true?"

"Jenny and others have asked me this before. I assume that you must exist outside somewhere."

Evelyn's discomfort increased. This was now positively disturbing. "Outside of what?" she persisted.

"Here. The caves." Perseus carried on into an explanation that must have gone back to some earlier occasion. "All things must end. Therefore, the place that I am in must end at a boundary. So beyond the boundary there must be an 'outside.' Perhaps my quest is to find the boundary and reach the outside. I do not know this for certain."

"Did *he* figure that out himself?" Evelyn whispered. Jenny looked across at her and read the expression on her face.

"It's getting to you, isn't it," she said understandingly. "It's okay. Don't worry. A lot of people are affected like that. Maybe that's enough for the first time." She killed the screen.

Evelyn was still not at ease. "Is he still active in there, while the screen's off? Or does he go into a suspended state until you switch it on again?" she asked.

"It's just an illusion," Jenny said. She looked at Corrigan. "Shouldn't you be getting along, anyhow? Didn't you say something about wanting to catch Marvin before he leaves?"

They met Minsky in a staff cafeteria on the second floor, where he was grabbing coffee and a sandwich before dashing off to keep an appointment elsewhere on the campus. Tall, smooth-domed, continually observing the world through thick-rimmed spectacles but never quite able to take it seriously in its entirety, he was one of the lab's original founders. Corrigan had known him sporadically in his time at MIT and was pleased that their schedules had enabled a meeting during this quick visit.

Minsky, it turned out, had returned from Ireland himself recently, where he had been partly vacationing and partly checking the state of contemporary computing developments at Trinity and University colleges. His experiences from a drive north to Ulster, where trouble was still going on with the British administration, had left him less than impressed, however.

"Why are they still fighting each other up there?" he grumbled to Corrigan. "Why don't they study mathematics, or something else that would give them better things to do?"

"Oh, that's nothing to do with us," Corrigan replied. "It's another country up there. I'm from the Republic, remember."

Minsky pulled a face. "I'm not sure I noticed much of a difference. Down there, if you're an American and don't know the price of anything, you're fair game."

"The lads have to make a living," Corrigan said unapologetically, refusing to be provoked.

"You mean it isn't true, what the song says?" Evelyn put in. "'When Irish eyes are smiling . . .'?"

"You've probably been ripped off," Minsky completed with a snort. Corrigan laughed. Minsky glanced at his watch. "Anyway, I have to dash in a few minutes. So I gather you've been to see Jenny Leddel."

"Perseus is coming along nicely," Corrigan said. "Evelyn got a bit spooked, though."

"There was something eerie about it." She shivered and shook her head.

Minsky smiled. "Yes. It gets a lot of people like that. It makes them wonder if we're inside someone else's AI experiment in the same kind of way."

"That's exactly what I was thinking," Evelyn said, astonished. Minsky's smile widened.

"The approach seems to be working," Corrigan observed. He glanced at Evelyn. "Setting it up with the. potential to learn, and then letting it interact with an environment."

"Jenny should have let Perseus start out as more of an infant," Minsky commented. "There are still too many defined attributes.

Instead of telling him what a sword is for, let him wave one about and hit things with it, and find out for himself. That way, he might even discover things that programmers never think to include—such as, that they make good back-scratchers."

Corrigan related the episode of Perseus and the lamp. Minsky nodded emphatically.

"Which makes my point. He should have been allowed to read picture books and fairy tales. Then he would have been familiar with genies and known what to do."

Evelyn was about to ask if he meant literally exposing a computer to the processes that a child goes through, say, by equipping it with appendages of some kind to manipulate things, but Minsky preempted her. Corrigan was used to his sometimes disorienting habit of getting people out of step in a conversation by answering questions before they were asked.

"Computers aren't very good at interfacing with the real world and extracting the information they need. We have the advantage of this enormous knowledge-base that we call 'common sense,' which enables us to make subtle, context-based connections. That's what makes people so good at things like comprehending metaphors: we're wired to see quickly what matters and what doesn't. Recognizing faces is another good example." He waved a hand as he collected together the paper plate, coffee cup, and remains of his sandwich. "Computers are better at tasks that don't require any deep familiarity with what's out there—ones that can be dealt with in relative isolation, algorithmically."

"Computers interact better with other computers," Evelyn said.

"Yes. Quite." Minsky nodded. "So what you do is plug your infant into another computer that's pretending to be a world. But getting a virtual world to be real enough is another matter."

Corrigan clapped his hands as if that was a cue that he had been waiting for. "And that's why we're doing what we're doing at CLC in the meantime," he told Evelyn. "Learning how to make better virtual worlds. So now you can see where the work you'll be doing fits in. Believe me, it's going to be a lot of fun."

"Promise?" she said teasingly.

Corrigan spread his hands in appeal and turned toward Minsky. "Look. Aren't the Irish eyes smiling?"

"You're going to be ripped off," Minsky said to Evelyn, shrugging.

But Eric Shipley was in a far-from-fun mood when Corrigan got back to Pittsburgh the next day. "Pinder has been having visitors from California and D.C." he told Corrigan. "Space Defense Command, and DOD. High-level stuff. Something's in the wind. I don't like the feel of it."

Corrigan remained unperturbed. "Politics and science are inseparable these days, Eric. You've got to move with the times. This could be an impending moment of opportunity."

"Well, we'll find out soon enough," Shipley replied. "Pinder has called a major meeting to review progress and plans for the whole Pinocchio program. Tomorrow morning in town, nine o'clock sharp."

◎ CHAPTER ELEVEN ◎

Jason Pinder opened the meeting, which was held in one of the conference rooms in the corporate headquarters building on First Avenue. He was slight and wiry in build, and with his short, straight, sandy hair, clipped mustache, and invariable habit of dressing in conventional suits of gray, tan, or brown, had always put Corrigan in mind of a retired British army officer or a schoolmaster. But the mild gray eyes turned out to be a deceptive front for a mind as compulsively restless as a computer's registers, ceaselessly analyzing, shuffling, and sorting in search of better options. Not that this came as any great surprise. Anyone who had made it to the upper ranks of a leading-edge company like CLC could be assumed to possess the requisite qualities.

Next to him, crisp and businesslike in a black suit and snowy shirt, was the swarthy, curly-haired figure of John Velucci, executive director of CLC's Legal Department. "Tell me why he's here," Shipley muttered to Corrigan as they sat down. "Want to know what I think? Whatever this is all about has already been decided. The meeting is to tell us the way it is."

"You're too suspicious, you know, Eric," Corrigan answered. But the words were automatic. For once, even Corrigan's manner was curious and restrained.

Also present from CLC were Pinder's deputy, Peter Quell; Tom

Hatcher, Corrigan's software supervisor on the Pinocchio program; and a hardware wizard called Barry Neinst. Neinst was described on the organizational charts as responsible for "Advanced Processing," and appeared on the bar of loosely affiliated names, connecting vertically to Pinder's, that was tagged collectively "Direct Neural Coupling." What this really meant was obscure, and in practice he led a somewhat nomadic existence, wandering between Shipley's DINS section, the MIMIC/Pinocchio group headed by Corrigan, and a collection of graphics specialists known as "Interactive Imagery." This latter group was represented by Ivy Dupale, a short, bouncy, frizzy-haired brunette who had been put in charge as a temporary measure eighteen months previously, and the situation was never regularized or revised.

There were four people from the Space Defense Command's Operations Training & Simulator Center at Inglewood: Henry Wernheim, solid, craggy, with silver, wavy hair and steely eyes, the director; Frank Tyron, lean, tanned, and bespectacled, project manager of the VIV program (*VI*sion & *V*oice head-mounted assembly); and two of his technical support people: Joan Sutton and Harry Morgen.

After making the introductions, Pinder opened, addressing himself principally to the side of the table where the CLC people were sitting.

"I don't have to tell you that the field we're in is an exciting one, and one that is crucial to some of the most important developments going on in the world today. That includes the public and private space programs that are currently coming together here, across in Europe, and in Japan." He paused, allowing a suitably serious note to assert itself. "Hence, we can expect a lot of competition worldwide, both in terms of the funding being made available, and of the caliber of talent that we'll be up against. And, indeed, we see a lot of that happening already. What it means is that we're going to have to work extra hard and move fast just to stay in the same relative place. What it means even more is that we at CLC are going to need, and will appreciate, all the help we can get." He glanced along the other side of the table to indicate the visitors. "I am pleased to be able to inform you that, as a result of recent negotiations, we now have an opportunity to benefit from some very substantial help indeed, from a solid, trustworthy direction."

"Here it comes," Shipley murmured by Corrigan's side. "That was the sugarcoating."

To the debt "But he could be right."

On Corrigan's other side, Tom Hatcher and Ivy Dupale exchanged what-do-you-think looks. Just at that moment, neither of them seemed to be especially thinking anything. Beyond them Barry Neinst remained semi-oblivious in a world of his own, probably involving parallel arrays and pipeline architectures.

Pinder continued, "Over the last few weeks, Ken Endelmyer has had us going through some hard numbers, reviewing the progress and future prospects for Pinocchio. As you all know, the tentative plan has been to proceed to Pinocchio Two, or 'Son of Pinocchio,' as it has come to be known informally: extension of DNC into the pons, plus the addition of speech and acoustics." Shipley nudged Corrigan softly with his elbow. The word "tentative" had never been used previously. For the past year at least, Pinocchio Two had been firm.

Pinder glanced around briefly. "The problem with it, however, is the long lead time that we're talking about: two to three years by the best estimates, which puts us into 2009-2010. And vision would come even later, assuming further extension to the thalamus." He looked at Corrigan and raised a hand, lightening the moment by making as if he expected Corrigan to protest. "Okay, Joe, I know you worked a miracle in getting Pinocchio One up a year ahead of schedule. But that's not an experience the corporation can bet on happening every time."

His voice reverted to its more serious note. "So the company has decided to add a second string to our bow that will reduce the risk of being left with nothing on the international scene three years from now. What we're going to do, instead of relying on Pinocchio Two totally, is initiate a program to run in parallel that will add vision and acoustics now, as a hybrid system. That will give us experience of operating with vision sooner rather than later. Also, we're guaranteed something to show, farther down the line." He looked around to invite comments.

"How do you mean, hybrid?" Hatcher asked. There was only one plausible way. "With DNC tactile into the medulla, and using the regular sensory apparatus for vision and voice?"

Pinder nodded. "Just that. Combine the Pinocchio One interface with the VIV system that SDC has produced. It's perfect for the job. Frank Tyron here is the project manager of the team that developed it. The Space Defense Command has a lot of interest in the outcome too, which means that the ground is all prepared for some good cooperation. They're eager to get started. So, I'm sure, are all of us. We've even got a project designation: EVIE. Extended Virtual Interactive Environment."

There was some shifting and shuffling on the CLC side of the table. The SDC people waited calmly, giving the impression that they had known more about all this to begin with.

"Where will this alternative line be located?" Corrigan asked finally. "Here? In California? A bit at each? What?"

"We've talked about that," Pinder replied. "It would fragment things too much to have it spread out. VIV development is complete, so there isn't much reason to have any of this in California. So it looks like it'll be right here, in Pittsburgh. Frank has agreed to relocate here for the duration, and will head up a liaison group from SDC to supervise VIV integration."

"It will stay under CLC's control, then?" Corrigan said.

"Oh, no question." Pinder nodded reassuringly.

Shipley, however, was less sanguine. "What about the plans for expanding neurophysiology?" he asked. "How will they be affected? Are we still going to hire Evelyn Vance from Harvard?"

"Of course," Pinder answered. "Nothing's changed. As I said, Pinocchio Two will carry on in parallel. The difference now is that it can be run without the pressure to produce results to order—the way research ought to be."

Shipley detected something devious nevertheless. "So where will she fit in?" he asked. The intention had been that Evelyn would join DINS initially, with the possibility of later moving to a yet-to-be-established autonomous neurophysiology section. That was the group that Corrigan had hinted she might end up heading.

Pinder showed his hands. "Well, naturally we've had to reexamine some things to accommodate the new opportunities." So something *had* changed. "EVIE will consist of wedding VIV to

Pinocchio One, which will require Frank's people and Joe's. Pinocchio Two, which is what Evelyn Vance is being brought in for, will be an extension of it. Therefore, it seems to me, she ought to start out as part of that general group, rather than with DINS. You'll be busy enough dividing your time between both teams anyhow, Eric, without taking on more at this stage."

So there it was: Shipley would not be getting Evelyn as he had been led to believe. He didn't seem especially surprised. The rest of the meeting passed with a more detailed airing of goals, aims, and first guesses for completion dates.

When they talked it over in the lab afterward, Shipley was less stoic than he had appeared earlier. "I've felt this kind of atmosphere before," he told Corrigan. "It's the first step to politicizing the territory. This started out as a line of pure research. Now the science is going to take a back seat."

"Ah, come on, now, Eric, and admit that you're just sore about Evelyn being switched out of DINS," Corrigan said. "I think it was a bit mean too, if you want to know the truth, but I'm guessing that Jason had his orders."

"Hell, you know I'm not interested in those kinds of games," Shipley told him. "But I think you should watch out. Tyron has got 'political animal' stamped all over him. Didn't it strike you as significant that with all these changes, there still isn't a clearly defined slot heading up DNC? It's still as vague a mess as it was before."

Corrigan shook his head. "You've got it the wrong way around, Eric. Think about it. This will allow some sound consolidation on Pinocchio Two—the chance to do it right. You've got to agree that this hybrid idea is a bit of a mishmash. I mean, in the long term where can it lead? When P-Two expands to take in vision, what's left for the hybrid? Then, I'm a-thinking, it will be Frank-me-boy who'll be finding himself with nowhere to go."

Shipley remained unmoved by Corrigan's confident optimism. "We'll see," he replied neutrally.

❀ CHAPTER TWELVE ❀

Evelyn's position was confirmed, and a month later she moved from Boston to a rented apartment that Ivy Dupale helped her find in Aspinall, on the north bank of the Allegheny River. One of the better-preserved older districts of quaint streets with traditional stores and houses, it suited Evelyn's taste and was conveniently close to Blawnox.

Evelyn soon became good friends with Ivy, and she and Corrigan continued seeing each other out of working hours. They were well matched to each other's needs. He, on his way up and all set to fly, had an appreciative and willing admirer; she, the emerged fledgling, found a guide and protector. They sampled the restaurants, from the best French at Cafe Allegro on the Southside heights overlooking the Monongahela River, to the traditionally romantic, old-stone-built Hyeholde, set in a wooded estate out near the old airport. They toured the bars, took in the zoo, the theaters, and did the round of Pittsburgh's museums. Some weekends they spent at his place, some at hers.

Tyron and his group from SDC installed themselves in space provided at Blawnox, and work commenced on the initial phases of EVIE. The new, more comprehensive interface warranted going for a greater degree of realism than had been justified with MIMIC. Accordingly, Ivy Dupale's graphics group were given the go-ahead to enhance Pinocchio with an upgrade that had been in abeyance for some time: the addition of "Personal Attribute Files."

The hologram figure generated by Pinocchio was not a representation of anyone in particular, but simply a generic human form with rudimentary features and attire. The PAFs were lists of data descriptors specifying the features and physical appearance, build, and dress of an actual person: Corrigan, say, or anyone else on the research team. An individual's PAF could be superposed on the generic Pinocchio form to create a lifelike miniature of whoever was coupled into the system at a given time—or, just for the fun of it, of anyone else whose file was in the system. Having one's PAF compiled and filed for Pinocchio became something of a fad around the company, and most of the senior executives managed to find some pretext for stopping by to see their analogs cavorting in various simulated environments.

Then, one day, Therese Loel of the Engineering Systems Group, who had been one of the party that visited SDC in California, approached Pinder with a request. ESG was the "specials" part of Pinder's domain: a facility within the R & D division for designing and building customer-specified systems to order. In this it came halfway between one of CLC's regular manufacturing divisions, who made and sold standard products, and R & D proper, which was funded either internally or under specific research agreements contracted outside. Therese had talked briefly about EVIE to some of her acquaintances at Feller & Faber, a major international client of ESG's based in New York and involved in prestige marketing. CLC had supplied a package of AI-based learning software to track and predict market trends, which had proved quite successful; now, some people at Feller & Faber wanted to learn more about this new development and where it might be pointing. Could Pinder arrange for someone who knew more about the subject than she did to accompany ESG's sales personnel on a visit to the customer and give them an overview?

Pinder was keen to spread the word about the new venture, and agreed. There were really only three people who knew enough about both the Pinocchio and VIV aspects that together composed EVIE:

Corrigan, Eric Shipley, and Frank Tyron. However, Shipley's disinterest in anything connected with selling or publicity was notorious, which ruled him out. Tyron was fully committed, and in any case could hardly be used to promote CLC's private interests since he was not an employee. And that left only one. Accordingly, Pinder called Corrigan over to his office, filled him in on the situation, and told him to get in touch with the ESG sales executive assigned to the account, Henry Glinberg, who would make the arrangements.

They caught an early-morning flight up to La Guardia a week or so later. Having prepared himself for worse, Corrigan found Glinberg to be lively and alert, personable and appealing—the kind of salesman who made people feel important by listening, even when nothing they said was the slightest bit interesting. He didn't contradict, disagree, or antagonize with unasked-for opinions—preferring to win sales rather than arguments. And he dressed and groomed himself well but not flashily: enough to make a person feel respected by being worth the effort; not so much as to make them feel cheap. His company came as a stimulating change from the tech-intellectual surroundings that Corrigan had grown used to, and after an hour Corrigan could cheerfully have bought a lifetime's insurance, a new car, or anything else from him—and then done all his friends a favor by recommending their names too. It seemed to be generally considered a social virtue for somebody to be "easy to talk to"; "easy to be around"; "easy to get along with." Corrigan could recall countless occasions, from buying an airline ticket to making a hotel reservation, when he'd practically had to battle with a company's employees to be allowed to spend his money with them. Why, he wondered, was it so difficult to be "easy to buy from"?

From the airport they caught a cab to CLC's Manhattan branch office near Lincoln Center, where they met up with Mat Hamils, sales manager for the New York City area. Feller & Faber was his customer, and he would be taking them there—Glinberg was a Pittsburgh-based ESG specialist who supported customers throughout the Northeast. Before leaving to go crosstown, they reviewed the situation over coffee in a meeting room adjacent to Hamils's office.

"So in terms of spectaculars, you're saying that EVIE will bring everything together sooner—touch, vision, talk, the works," Hamils concluded. Clearly, he was thinking ahead and had customer demonstrations in mind.

"Yes," Corrigan said.

"But it's hybrid, not full direct-neural," Glinberg reminded Hamils. He looked back at Corrigan. "Pinocchio Two will be all-neural, though—right, Joe?"

"Sounds better," Hamils commented, nodding.

"But it just adds speech and hearing to the existing motor I/O," Corrigan said. "Vision won't be until later."

Glinberg frowned. "I thought you said something on the plane about a new section being organized to move the interfacing up from the medulla to the pons."

"Yes, but for vision you have to go in at the thalamus. That's another level higher yet."

"Oh." Hamils nodded that that was something they'd just have to accept. "Okay. So when will it happen?"

"It isn't scheduled at present," Corrigan replied, conscious as he said it of sounding negative. Hamils shot Glinberg a glance that said he couldn't see this as a star attraction for getting prospective customers excited.

There was a short silence. Then Glinberg clapped Corrigan lightly on the shoulder. "But doing it right takes time, eh, Joe? P-Two will be better in the end."

Corrigan acknowledged with a faint grin. "Right," he agreed.

Hamils looked at his watch. "We'd better be moving," he announced. They drank up, collected briefcases and things, and headed for the elevator.

"Do you get to see many customers, Joe?" Hamils inquired casually as they got in.

"Not really."

"The main person we're going to see today is a guy called Victor Borth. He's general manager of F and F's New York office, and a working director of the firm. A very influential person."

"I see."

"Sometimes there's politics involved in these situations," Hamils went on. "Just stick to answering questions, and keep it technical. We'll let you know when. Okay?"

"Sure," Corrigan said.

It was only when they were in the car and heading toward the East Side that it dawned on him that people who knew too much were considered a potential menace—he had been tactfully told where his place was.

The offices of Feller & Faber occupied four floors of a soaring face of copper-tinted glass in midtown. The visitors were conducted from the elevators through a reception lobby of rust-gold velour furnishings, ceramic and chrome, and art nouveau prints, into corridors flanked by designer-decor office spaces and computer displays glowing in glass-partitioned rooms.

They had arrived early to let Hamils take care of some routine matters before the main meeting, and Corrigan found himself tagging along on a quick tour. Somebody from F & F was due to attend a trade exhibition in Russia, and there was talk about a joint promotional effort involving CLC marketing people from Pittsburgh. A man called Gary had a problem with a service invoice. Pat wanted advance information from CLC engineering on a new line of image analyzers not in production yet. Could Sandra in the Manhattan office get two more sets of manuals on the stock-forecasting package? The proposal to Mercantile Bankers in London was looking good, and there should be a decision next week.

After the racks and cubicles, scratched metal desks, and tiled vinyl floors of the environment that Corrigan was used to, it all seemed very glamorous and exciting—a glimpse of the real world, where the events that shaped the news were made to happen. In comparison, the world that he was from looked woefully pedestrian and academic—a behind-the-scenes support facility to serve this, the stage.

Finally, they came to a sumptuous corner office looking out over Manhattan in two directions. It had deep russet pile, integral mahogany shelves and fittings, and framed travelogue scenes looking down over a conference area set off around a circular, glass-topped table. From the immense desks with computer side-tables and recessed consoles, the office was evidently shared by two people. One of the desks was unoccupied. From the other, a man of about Corrigan's age rose to greet them, smiling genially. He had a trim, athletic build with collar-length yellow hair, and looked aristocratically debonair in a tan jacket and maroon cord shirt worn open with a silk cravat in place of necktie.

"Nigel, how are things?" Hamils pumped his hand. "Is the world still taking good care of you?"

"Never better."

"You know Henry Glinberg, up from Pittsburgh again to see us."

"Of course. Hello again, Henry. Did you fly up this morning?"

"Hi, Nigel. Yes. Can't afford the time to stay over every time. You customers keep us too busy."

Nigel's smile broadened, easily, unrepentantly. "How would you pay the rent without us?"

Hamils indicated Corrigan. "And this is Joe Corrigan, from the DNC group at Blawnox. He's the guy that Jason sent up after Therese Loel talked to Victor."

Nigel shook hands with Corrigan, languidly yet firmly, without undue assertiveness. "Very pleased to meet you, Joe," he said. Just a simple business introduction, and yet he conveyed the impression that he really meant it. Style, Corrigan thought to himself. The art of gentility and charm. Something that didn't come very easily from talking to machines all day.

"Me too," he responded.

"Nigel Korven," Hamils supplied. "He's one of the senior consultants who take care of F and F's key clients." Corrigan took that to mean what the sufficiently sophisticated were called, in place of "salesman."

"So you're the expert from afar, who's going to tell us about Direct Neural Coupling and where it's leading," Korven said. "It sounds absolutely fascinating. Some people here are extremely eager to meet you."

"As long as they understand that it's just for information,"

Corrigan said. He was about to explain that the research was still in an early stage, but caught a faint shake of the head from Hamils.

"Do I detect an Irishman?" Korven said, changing subjects smoothly. "Over here permanently, I hope?"

"As far as I know," Corrigan said.

"Good. That's something we could use more of." Korven turned to Hamils. "Well, I think the others are just about ready for us next door. We can go straight on in." He picked up a folder from his desk and selected a few other papers. "Did you get that house in the end, Mat—the one you wanted?"

"The one up near the bridge, right. Got it for eight grand off the asking, too."

"Splendid. Your wife must be very happy about it."

"She's delighted. First thing is a warming party. You'll have to come along."

"I'd love to, Mat. I'll have to see if I can find somebody pretty to bring along."

"Somehow I can't see you without a woman around, Nigel," Glinberg said as they moved out of the room.

"Oh, but I don't keep them," Korven answered. "It's better to have new ones frequently. They're so much more pleasant to be around when they're on their best behavior and trying to make an impression." He winked reassuringly at Corrigan. "Right, Joe?"

Hamils drew Corrigan aside as they were about to follow the other two out into the corridor. "Let CLC decide what its policy is," he murmured. "We want these people to feel that we can help them solve their problems. They won't connect if you make it sound too remote."

Corrigan nodded. "I'll remember."

They went into a room a few doors away, where two more people were waiting at a large central table. Korven introduced Walter Moleno, fortyish, dark-haired and tanned, with a thin mustache: "Our man in Southeast Asia, back on one of his rare visits home."

Moleno shook his head. "It's not a place, I keep telling you, Nigel. It's a computer. They don't need VR out there. They all live in computers already. I come back for the reality experience."

"In New York? My God! A bit like going to Kansas for the views, isn't it?"

The other person was a woman called Amanda Ramussienne: probably in her mid-thirties, with high, angular features, wavy ginger hair, and alluring, green, feline eyes that caught the light in a way that made it seem to be coming from inside. Her makeup was generous but professional, and the image completed by a beige dress and gold jewelry that blended impeccably and had not come from the neighborhood mall. She spoke animatedly, with lots of expression and gestures, and in some other setting Corrigan would have guessed her background to be theatrical. Korven introduced her vaguely as an "analyst"; from the preamble after they sat down, Corrigan gathered that her work involved contact with the media.

"I had lunch with that awful creature from Time-Life again yesterday," she told Korven. He smiled a mixture of amusement at her feigned indignation and despair that she should have known better.

"You mean the fat one who smokes buffalo shit?"

"Of *course* the one who smokes buffalo shit. He definitely wants me to go to bed with him. He even had the nerve to say so. . . ." She waved imploringly at the ceiling. "What is so special about this job that I should put up with this? I mean, when is the harassment thing going to be extended to apply to customers too?"

"Why not try seeing it not as harassment but as opportunity?" Korven suggested sagely. "Most *men* would."

"If it were the sexy, good-looking ones who came on, I might," Amanda agreed with a sigh. "But why does it always have to be exactly the opposite kind?"

"Who are we waiting for?" Hamils cut in. "Victor?"

"He'll be in when he's finished a call he's on," Moleno said, nodding. "We thought half an hour here to get to know each other. Then we'll collect a couple of others and go for lunch."

"Have we picked a place?" Korven asked.

"Just downstairs." Moleno looked at the three from CLC. "It's one of those weeks, I'm afraid. Everyone's flying with both feet off the ground."

Hamils nodded. "What kind of mood is Victor in today?" he asked.

Korven turned his head toward Amanda. "Oh, I don't know. What would you say? Is the beast human today?"

She nodded. "Yes, I'd say so. He wasn't devouring anyone the last time I saw him."

"We think he's human," Korven told Hamils.

Corrigan looked at Hamils inquiringly. "Victor's okay," Hamils said. "But at times he can be a bit . . ." He looked diplomatically to the three F & F people before choosing a word. "What would you call it? Temperamental? . . ."

"Obstinate. Opinionated. Bombastic," Korven supplied, with the candid air of somebody saying what everyone else knew perfectly well anyway. "But we all love him, just the same."

"Just don't argue with him," Hamils translated. "If he gets something wrong, let it keep and tell us afterward. We'll straighten it out later."

There were a few seconds of silence, seeming to say that nothing more could make things any clearer after that. Then Amanda treated Corrigan to one of the smiles that talk-show hostesses use to get the show going again after an awkward hiatus. "How much do you know about the kind of business we do here, Joe?" she inquired.

"Not a great deal, to be honest. Something to do with marketing and forecasting, isn't it?"

"Those terms are a little obsolete now," Korven said. "You can charge more for 'econodynamic trend analysis.'"

"Ah. Yes."

At that moment the door opened as if on a spring, and a short, stockily built figure marched in and stumped to the end of the table, where he deposited some sheets of printed figures and a notepad. He had a smooth, tanned head fringed by dark locks that reflected a sheen, heavy eyebrows, and a solid, rounded face with pugnacious jaw and chin. His fingers were thick and stubby, with tufts of hair on the backs between the joints, but the nails were well manicured. He was wearing a dark three-piece with hairline stripe and—a rare sight for the day and age—a white carnation pinned in his left lapel. Mat

Hamils knew Borth, of course, but Glinberg apparently had not dealt with him directly in previous visits. Korven completed the introductions.

"So you work for Therese Loel," Borth said, taking in Glinberg with an unblinking stare that gave away nothing. His voice was blunt, direct, straight to the point.

"That's right," Glinberg confirmed.

"Harry's the ESG specialist, based out of Blawnox," Hamils filled in. "We call him in as needed."

Borth's gaze shifted to Corrigan. "But you're the guy Therese said they'd send up, who knows about the computers that let you play Ping-Pong in your head."

"Joe's from the main corporate R and D facility, also at Blawnox," Hamils supplied.

Corrigan frowned. There was some confusion already in what Borth had said. DNC coupled direct into the nervous system. The simulated Ping-Pong was something different: a demonstration that the SDC people used to show off their VIV helmet, which utilized the regular senses. But before Corrigan could frame a reply, Borth changed tack:

"Have they told you much about the kind of business we're in here?"

"We were just about to when you came in," Amanda said. Her manner had changed with Borth in the room. She was all seriousness and attention now—no longer a vivacious artiste, but suddenly the business professional.

Borth remained standing, and spoke moving back and forth at the end of the table. Presenting to a group seemed to be his natural style.

"We live in a complicated world. All the time, it gets more complicated. Everywhere you look, where people are dealing in long-term plans—in business, in industry, in technology, in politics—more money is having to be put down up-front, the lead times are stretching farther into the future, and what happens at the end of it is anybody's guess. Bigger stakes; less certain outcomes. In other words, it's all getting to be more of a gamble." He paused, looked from side to side, and showed his empty palms, as if inviting anyone who could to dispute that.

"Guess wrong, and you can be wiped out even though nothing was your fault: the bottom drops out of a market that everyone said couldn't fail; a trend turns around; the public loses interest in some fad that was going to be the rage for the rest of time . . . and nobody knows why." Borth held up a fan of stubby fingers and began ticking off examples. "How many of you remember the savings-and-loan mess years back, when they poured billions into stacking up downtowns with high-rise office space that nobody wanted? Before that there was the synthetic-fuel thing. Eight billion they blew on it—because the world was about to run out of oil. Then we're drowning in oil, and the whole thing's a fiasco. Screenpad Corporation spent eleven years making plans and tooling up, saying they were going to make paper obsolete. There's still plenty of paper around today, but they're not."

He raised an emphatic finger. "*But* . . . if you call the shots right, you can be made for life. Not that many years ago, all the pros laughed when a couple of guys in a garage said everyone could have a computer. Amspace in Texas came up with a cheap, clunky, surface-to-orbit pickup, instead of the Ferraris and mobile homes that the Air Force and NASA had been making, and they created a global space-trucking industry.

"Now look at the things that some people are telling us will be next." Borth looked around again, appealingly this time. "Nanomachines? Adaptive fiction? Bioregenerative materials? Talking houses? Where do I put my money for the big paybacks ten years down the line?" His gaze came back to rest on the three people from CLC. "You can see the problem—and believe me, it is a problem. That's where we make our business: helping people out there to make those decisions. And naturally there are other outfits who do the same thing. Sometimes we're right more often than they are. Sometimes they get the edge on us. Frankly, there isn't a lot of difference: we all hit at around the same percentage. But I can tell you this: there's *lots* of money out there, *big* money, just waiting for the first outfit that can come up with a way of doing it better. We happen to think that smarter computers is the way to go. That's why we're interested in anything new that CLC has got coming down the pike."

Borth sat down finally, indicating that he was through. He continued looking expectantly at Corrigan. Corrigan, however, having had his orders, left it to someone else to respond. Hamils launched off into a fairly standard line about Virtual Reality technologies offering new ways for users to interact with data: Through suitable presentation to the user's senses, information normally handled as abstract symbols could be transformed into the furnishings of a directly perceivable "world." Processing would then take the form of manipulating those objects via intuitively meaningful actions as used in the everyday world. Glinberg gave the commonly cited example of a bicycle. "To compute the correct angle to lean at for taking a corner at a particular speed requires solving a complicated equation of physics. But the five-year-old kid just *feels* the right thing to do, and does it. Well, the way you do forecasting at present is tackling the problem as numbers; what Joe's people are working on will give you a bike."

"So it's not one of these systems that thinks it knows my job better than I do," Borth said, assuming the position of one of his clients. "I'm still the best judge of my own business. It simply gives me a better way of seeing the angles."

"Exactly," Hamils said.

Which gave a clear and concise picture, certainly. And it was obviously the kind of thing that the customer wanted to hear. The only problem was that it bore no resemblance to what was actually envisaged at CLC. Pinocchio Two was aimed at shifting the coupling level of the existing motor interface to a higher region of the brain stem and adding speech; EVIE was a short-term kluge to gain experience with vision before the whole thing was redesigned to DNC. The kind of thing that Hamils was talking about, if it ever materialized at all, was years away in the future, at least.

Corrigan tried to inject some measure of perspective but received a firm "not now" signal from Hamils. Borth gave no indication of wanting a detailed technical explanation of either project. It made Corrigan wonder what he was doing here at all. He suspected that the reason was primarily for effect: to maintain an image of CLC's corporate responsiveness. Therese Loel knew of the huge potential market within F & F's client base, and had mentioned the DNC program simply to be sure that nothing of possible relevance was missed. Borth had asked for a specialist; the company had obliged. Now everyone was reading too much into it.

"Have you seen our research organization down at Pittsburgh?" Hamils asked Borth.

"I've been to the head office in the city a couple of times, but never out at the labs, no," Borth replied.

Hamils inclined his head for a moment. "Maybe we could offer you a trip down there to see what goes on?" he suggested. "Then Joe's people could show you the whole state of the art. What do you think?"

"Sounds good," Borth replied. "I'd like that." He glanced at his colleagues. They seemed interested. "We'll all come," he announced.

Hamils looked pleased with the morning's work. "Joe will set it up when he gets back," he said. "Okay, Joe? Can you fix that for us?"

There it was at last: a direct question. What else was Corrigan supposed to say? "Sure, I'd be happy to." He forced his expression to remain calm and composed. "That would be no problem at all. But we are in changeover mode to the new project just at this moment. . . . Could we schedule it for a little later in time?"

◉ CHAPTER THIRTEEN ◉

"You come home at some unearthly hour, and all you've done since is drink coffee. No sleep, nothing to eat. Why can't you admit that it's a textbook case of delayed shock response, following your recent emotional trauma?"

"Horace, shut up. You don't know what you're talking about. In fact, you don't know anything about what's going on at all."

"There's nothing to be ashamed of, Joe. It's perfectly normal. The symptoms were described exactly by Fenwick Zellor in—"

Corrigan flipped the manual override on the kitchen monitor panel to "off." Then he returned to his chair at the table, topped up his mug, and resumed contemplating the design of floral bunches and foliations on the wallpaper opposite.

Although he was looking away from it, he knew that above the work surface behind him was a spice rack fixed to the side of a cabinet—a flimsy, wooden affair of two shelves and supporting ends, holding an assortment of small glass jars. It was outside the range of his immediate attention—as far as could be ascertained from outward appearances, anyway—and the likelihood of anything else in the room affecting it in some way in the next few seconds was vanishingly small. That meant that it would rank low in the probability tables constantly being updated by the program that tried to guess which features of the surroundings were likely to be objects of action or change in the immediate future.

The number of discrete objects needed to make up a simulated world that aspired to be in any way authentic was stupendous. Every one of those objects had, associated with it, a list of latent attributes that might require activating at any time, according to circumstances. A book taken randomly off a shelf and thumbed, for example; a rug kicked back across the floor; a candy bar broken—all would involve the sudden revealing of new information that had previously been hidden. The number of conceivable ways in which a given situation *might* develop in the next instant was so astronomic that no method of organizing the data could make all of the possible continuations equally available for processing in the time necessary to create smooth, realistic transitions: the computers couldn't generate dirt and worms under every square foot of grass in Pennsylvania all the time, just in case somebody were to decide on a whim to pick up a shovel and dig a hole somewhere.

So what the system did was identify the most likely continuations, based on its accumulating experience of how people tended to behave, and make sure that the pertinent descriptors would always be the fastest accessible. Thus, there was a small but not insignificant possibility that the mug in Corrigan's hand might slip and shatter— and the pointers to such details as the internal structure, texture, and fracture modes of the porcelain would therefore be high in the current access tree. There was a bowl containing two oranges an arm's reach away from him on the table, and the distinct possibility presented itself that he might decide to peel one of them; subfiles defining the properties and behavior of the pulp, fruit, juice, and pips would all have been shuffled up to ready-access status when he arrived in the vicinity and sat down. Similarly for the pages of the magazine lying underneath the fruit bowl, the contents of the pockets of his jacket, slung over the back of another chair, and the details of the palm of his hand, resting on the tabletop—in case he chose to turn his hand over and look at it. But for the spice rack behind him— out of sight, and not something that a person would normally pay attention to. . . .

In a slow, natural movement, consciously suppressing muscle tension and keeping his gaze on the far wall to avoid signaling any intentions to the eye-tracking software, he set the mug down and leaned back in his chair. Then, abruptly, he leaped up and whirled around, in the same movement shooting out a hand to smash one of the spice rack's ends outward.

If his attention hadn't been totally focused, alert for every detail of what happened, he might well have missed it, even then. But for someone who knew what to look for, everything was wrong. For a brief instant—barely perceptible, but definite—there was a break in the movement of his hand just as it touched. The sting and the sound came a fraction too late. And there was a fleeting moment of blankness in the break before the detail of splintered wood and the exposed grain added itself. He stared, oblivious to the clattering of spice jars falling on the countertop and rolling off to the floor. When he pried off one of the shelves hanging by an end and snapped it experimentally, the effect was perfect. He dropped the pieces onto the counter and sat down again at the table.

So it was true.

He snorted humorlessly to himself as Lilly's words came back: "It makes too much sense . . . Way too much." Wasn't he, she had said, being just a little too insightful for someone who was supposed to be crazy?

Of course, it was too much of a coincidence that both he and she, involved in the same project twelve years ago, should have undergone similar psychologically disrupting experiences, and afterward have perceived a world severely distorted to begin with but steadily improving with time.

And that both he and she should suffer from an impaired sense of smell. The first cranial nerve, the Olfactory, serving the most primitive of the senses, is the only one to synapse in the cerebrum. They had never been able to carry the DNC interfacing level beyond the thalamus.

And that in all this time their travel options should have been limited for "medical" reasons. The preparations for Oz had included a major program of systematically recording and encoding all the architectural, geographic, and other visual details of the city—a process known as "realscaping"—in order to re-create any scene realistically in a virtual presentation. But there had to be limits. The program had covered only Pittsburgh and the surrounding area—and the effort entailed by that had been massive enough. In addition, Xylog merged its database with others compiled by cooperating organizations that had carried out similar schemes elsewhere. One of those had been Himomatsu Inc. of Tokyo, which explained how Corrigan had been able to "visit" Japan four years previously.

Why hadn't he seen it sooner? Because he had been too busy proving to himself that if he didn't fit in with the world, then he didn't need the world anyway. Because he had been trying to pretend that he could bury the resentments that came with remembering a life of success and achievement all snatched away. Because he thought he deserved better. Yet the same could be said on every count about Lilly, but she had seen it. . . . And so had he, as soon as she started questioning things. It had been staring him in the face all the time, but she'd had to spell it out. That was what had galled him.

Presumably, then, Lilly must have been right in her guess as to why they had no clear recollections of what had taken place after commencement of the preliminary tests, when the project had supposedly run into problems and been canceled. Their memories had been suppressed and a cover story manufactured to camouflage the cruder, early phases of the simulation, when the system was in its infancy of learning. The disruption had been progressively reduced as the simulation got better, and the corresponding improvement in perceptions and thought coherence offered as evidence of "recovery." The possibility of suppressing the memories of the real-world surrogates in this way was something that had been talked about often enough, but in all of Corrigan's experience the decision had been not to use it. That was why his first reaction to Lilly had been to reject the suggestion as impossible. Evidently he had been wrong.

So exactly what was going on and why? He didn't know. He would need to start practicing some real philosophy for once, and get in touch with Lilly again. But that was going to have to wait for a while, he decided. Virtual or not, there were some aspects of this reality that were simply just too "real"—and which, for the moment at least, there was nothing he could do to change. Before any more consideration of what it all meant and what he was going to do next, he would have to get some sleep. He got up, shrugged at the mess of the broken spice rack and scattered containers, and made his way blearily through to the bedroom.

❂ CHAPTER FOURTEEN ❂

Corrigan stood with Mat Hamils, the New York City-area sales manager, outside the main entrance to the Executive Building of CLC's Blawnox R & D facility. With them were Victor Borth, Nigel Korven, and Amanda Ramussienne from Feller & Faber. Five months had passed since Corrigan's visit to New York. Pinder had decided to hold things until the first implementation of EVIE was operating, and then there had been a further delay while the PAF system was expanded to handle several operators simultaneously; but finally, the long-promised F & F trip to Pittsburgh for a demonstration had been arranged.

Borth raised a hand in front of his face and wiggled his fingers. He turned his head to his two companions watching him, pursed his mouth approvingly, and nodded. He looked across the parking lot toward the main gate, and beyond at the tree-clad hills dotted with houses in the distance. The day was sunny and bright. Intermittent traffic sounds came from an unseen highway. To one side, a lawn edged by flower beds bordered the paved area where they were standing. A bee buzzed around the gladioli. Farther away, a crow landed on the lawn and cried raucously.

"I'm impressed," Borth announced.

"I certainly prefer this improvement in the weather," Korven agreed. The drive from the airport had been filthy, through heavy traffic with rain falling continually from a leaden sky. Hamils glanced at Corrigan and looked pleased.

There were still some peculiarities about the scene, however. The flowers and the grass looked normal enough close up; but with increasing distance they lost detail too quickly and became smeary, as if viewed by somebody shortsighted. The distant scenery was too flat. And although there could be no denying that the colors were an improvement over even high-resolution conventional graphics, they lacked some subtle, indefinable quality of richness and depth out in the sunshine. In some areas of sharp contrast, such as shaded spots underneath trees, or the view back inside the lobby, which was illuminated by tinted light, they were simply . . . wrong. Some correction mechanism that the brain applied to create the hues that it "knew" to be true, regardless of the raw data that the optic nerves were reporting, was not being emulated.

"Let's go for a walk," Corrigan suggested.

They stepped off the paving in front of the entrance and began following the driveway in the direction of the gate. Although their movements seemed acceptably smooth and natural, they all felt a hint of a vaguely disconnected, floating sensation that Tom Hatcher had described as "walk by wire," which resulted from motor feedback not being perfectly synchronized with vision. Borth was relieved to note that a wrinkle in his sock that had been bothering him all morning was no longer there.

A car entered the gateway and approached, slowing as it got nearer, and drew up in front of them. Driving it was Joan Sutton, one of the SDC technical people assigned to support Frank Tyron on what was now officially designated the CLC/SDC EVIE project. Tyron himself was in the passenger seat. They got out, grinning unabashedly at the amazed expressions on the faces of the three visitors.

"Fantastic! I could almost believe you're really there," Borth exclaimed.

Corrigan was especially pleased with the results of the improved Personal Attribute Files that Ivy Dupale's graphics section had been working on. Not only were individuals interacting within the simulation; they were doing it with accurate eye and facial movements superposed onto the figures being generated from the PAFs. The incorporation of regular skin-potential sensors into the VIV helmet gave face-muscle movements, and eye-tracking came as standard.

Accepting the unvoiced invitation, Borth stepped forward to examine the car, a 2007 Dodge, which was obviously the star part of the demonstration. The detail was uncanny, with paint and chrome reflecting the surroundings convincingly. When he reached out and tested, the hood was warm to the touch. There was even some realistic ticking and creaking of metalwork cooling down.

Borth grunted and moved to the driver's-side door, which Joan Sutton had left open. She moved aside. Borth peered in, then began poking around curiously. He moved the panel, column, and foot controls with a hand, feeling them resisting and responding. "This is good," he told his colleagues. Amanda came to the other door and ran a hand over the upholstery and trim.

"Better than what I can afford to drive, Victor," she declared pointedly.

Borth sniffed. Then he frowned, turned and moved his head over the back of the seat, then sniffed again. "It's got no smell," he called to those outside. "This looks like a new car. It ought to have the new-car smell that you always get. It doesn't."

"We can't give you a sense of smell," Corrigan said. "It's handled at a different level of the brain."

"Oh, is that so?"

"It was described in the information that was sent," Amanda reminded him.

"Was it? Okay."

Amanda turned on the radio, and it played a local Pittsburgh channel—injected through the VIV audio system.

"What about the parts that you don't see?" Korven queried. It was the obvious next thing. Corrigan caught Hamils's eye and winked confidently.

Borth pulled the hood release and walked around to the front. Korven raised the hood. Engine, battery, generator, hydraulics, air conditioning—everything was there, with all the hoses and accessories.

If they looked, they would find water in the radiator, fluids in the reservoirs, oil in the sump. The glove compartment had maps in it, and there was an inside to the trunk, complete with spare wheel and a jack. Within reasonable limits, the team had covered every base.

And then Joan Sutton inadvertently dropped the keys, which she had been toying with. They struck her thigh and glanced off to fall under the car, just behind the front wheel-arch.

"It's okay. I'll get 'em," Korven said, and squatted down to reach. Then he stopped, looked in farther, then pulled his head back and grinned up at Corrigan. "Gotcha!"

"What?" Borth inquired, coming around.

"This car doesn't have an underneath," Korven said, gesturing. "It's all just blank."

Corrigan sighed and showed his palms to acknowledge defeat. There was no way to anticipate everything.

To finish the demonstration they entered the Executive Building and went through the reception area, past CLC's "museum" and the visitors' dining room to a rear exit. From there they crossed a parking lot to the IE Building and went upstairs to the lab area that had been allocated to EVIE. Here they found seven chairs fitted with Pinocchio collars and VIV helmets, arranged in the same positions as the real chairs that they had sat down in at the commencement. Tyron ushered them in and invited them to take their places.

"I hope you're sure that we'll end up coming back out," Korven teased as he settled back. "I mean, I wouldn't want somebody to hit a switch the wrong way, or something, and send us into another simulation inside a simulation."

"What a fascinating thought," Amanda said. "Is it possible?"

Borth and Hamils were fiddling uncertainly with the collar attachments. There were no technicians to help this time. Since only seven working EVIE interfaces had so far been built, nobody else could be projected in from the outside.

"It's okay. You don't have to worry," Tyron said. "We cheat a little." As he spoke, the devices positioned of their own accord, and the participants found themselves in blackness, suddenly conscious once again of the helmets confining them.

Tyron's voice came again, now sounding muffled and remote from the outside. "You can take them off. That's it."

Borth and Hamils had a moment of confusion in unraveling what was real and what wasn't. One by one they all removed their headgear to find themselves in the same place, only this time there "really." The approximation had been good, but this had an entirely different feel about it. Jason Pinder was present also, along with Therese Loel from ESG, Tom Hatcher, Ivy Dupale, and a number of technicians who had been operating the equipment.

Borth was grinning like a kid stepping down from a funfair ride. A good sign. "This is it?" he quipped. "We're back now? You guys are sure?"

"You'd better be," Therese said. "It's almost time for lunch. The virtual variety isn't all that nutritious."

"Incredible!" Hamils declared. "Absolutely incredible." He directed the words at Pinder, but they were for the F & F people's benefit. "You know, you're really onto something here, Jason. There's no end to what can be done with this."

"I wonder how authentic it's possible to get?" Amanda Ramussienne said, staring thoughtfully back at the connecting gear as she stood up.

"My dear, what do you have in mind?" Korven asked her in a tone that required no answering.

The visitors were clearly impressed, and it seemed that the way was open for getting down to some solid business talk on the market area that all were agreed still held enormous potential. But things turned out to be less straightforward in the world of not-so-virtual reality. Borth put it bluntly from the end of the lunch table, back in the Executive Building a little under an hour later.

"It's nice," he told them. "And clever. Very clever. Don't get me wrong—I can see that some very smart people have put a lot of effort into this. I don't want to knock that. But when you get down to it, it's still a toy—the kind of thing that kids might get a kick out of playing more realistic games on. You guys get my meaning?" He looked around. Beside him, Pinder stared woodenly at the table. Korven continued to look smooth and imperturbable, as always. Amanda's face had taken on harder lines than her normal sultry image. Corrigan had noticed that she tended to mirror whatever mood of the moment she sensed in Borth. Conversely, she seemed the only one at F & F who could handle him. Korven and the others always went to Amanda first when there was a delicate issue to raise with him, or when he was having one of his grouchy days.

Borth went on. "What we're looking for is *real artificial intelligence.* We've explained it all before. Our clients want to predict the outcomes of complex situations. What you've shown us here is neat, but it only anticipates what the people who programmed it were able to tell it to anticipate. So it's no better than the people, and we can hire them already. See what I mean?"

It was exactly what Corrigan had tried to point out after his first meeting at F & F many months ago. But sales and management had been interested only in not cutting off options. If this was going to be a debacle, it wasn't of his making. He maintained a detached, inwardly self-vindicating silence.

Tyron shook his head. This was the first time that he had heard straight from the customer what was wanted, and it was nothing like what CLC or anyone else was in a position to supply. He was too astute a politician to get into an argument over it, but this thing had to be put to rest. "What you're asking is virtually impossible," he said, glancing from side to side for support from the CLC people. "The world of human affairs is an extreme example of complex, chaotic dynamics that are unpredictable by definition—far more so than the weather system, economy, or other things that you hear about. Even in simple models, the tiniest changes in starting conditions can produce wildly differing outcomes. Nothing known to science can make predictions about systems like that. One chance-in-a-million accident can ruin a company. A singer with a cute face can start a craze that alters the world. For most things that happen, nobody will ever know what the causes were. . . ." He looked at Pinder. Pinder nodded his endorsement. Tyron came back to Borth. "That's simply the way it is. We're up against laws of nature here. Nothing is going to change it."

Corrigan was intrigued to note that Borth didn't seem to be hearing anything especially unexpected, but doodled on a pad and nodded idly until Tyron had had his say. It was Amanda who came to the point of what this was all really about. And she did so with surprising candor.

"You're all thinking like scientists," she said, smiling in the manner of someone ending the joke they had all been playing, of pretending that they hadn't known all along. "Most of the people that we deal with are frauds, flakes, and phonies. I mean, who are we talking about? PR departments that think reality is what they say it is. Madison Avenue and political hygiene experts who make their own reality. Media crazies who never knew the difference in the first place. They all operate in worlds of manufactured images—images built on the public's credulity and wish-fulfillment fantasies, sustained by illusion and delusion. What matters is not what happens to be true, but what people *believe* is true, and what they *want* to be true."

She held up a hand to acknowledge what Tyron had just said. "Yes, sure, *we* know that most of what happens in the world happens for reasons that nobody understands. But there will always be somebody who gets the credit for having called it: the leader of whatever the current in-fad is; today's guru-of-the-moment . . . Anyone with the right *reputation*. Whether the reputation is based on fact or fantasy doesn't matter.

"Well, right now the trendy word in cocktail-party science is AI. If somebody like us can make it believable that they can bring real AI to bear on the complexity-prediction problem, it'll have the clients lining up all down the block."

"Even if it has known . . . limitations?" Therese Loel still hadn't fully gotten the message. She couldn't bring herself to say, "won't work."

"It doesn't matter," Korven interjected softly. "In this world, what you believe to be real is real. Amanda said it: *Reputation.*"

"The Rainmaker Syndrome," Amanda said. "If you dance long enough, eventually it'll rain. If lots of people make predictions, some will hit lucky, and that will be good enough for the rest. When enough people try a cure for something, some percentage of them is going to get better anyway. And there's your reputation. When it happens in the market we're talking about, somebody's going to collect a bonanza."

Borth closed his pad and looked up. "But EVIE and Pinocchio aren't it. They play at being what the world is right now. What I want to see is how the world is gonna be, say, five years from now. Show me *that*, and we can start talking deals."

◉ CHAPTER FIFTEEN ◉

In the middle of 2008, Frank Tyron left the Space Defense Command to take up a position with CLC's R & D division as "Development Manager, Simulation Graphics," reporting to Pinder. In this, he took charge of a new group that combined the people still on assignment from SDC, plus the loosely structured graphics and holo-imagery section that Ivy Dupale had been heading informally. The remaining parts of the DNC department outside Shipley's DINS lab were consolidated as EVIE and placed under Corrigan. The corporation assured all concerned that these moves represented an overdue streamlining and rationalization, needed to better serve a "fast-growing and exciting new area faced with increasingly severe competitive pressures from abroad."

There was disgruntlement within the DNC group over Ivy's being passed over in this way by an outsider. Evelyn was one of the most indignant, but being a comparative newcomer to the scene, she was hesitant about how much of a fuss it was her place to make over it. Privately, she made representations to Corrigan.

"I think it's scandalous, Joe—especially after the job she did getting the synchronization bugs out of the EVIE imaging system. Can't you talk to Pinder about it, or something?"

"My line is research," Corrigan told her. "Corporate politics isn't what I do." He also wondered if the change was entirely bad; it could represent a step toward the more cosmopolitan flavor that he felt the project could do with.

"So you won't do anything?"

"Eve, I *can't* do anything."

Corrigan was also preoccupied at this time with the problem of efficiently representing and storing the enormous amount of detail implicit in any realistic depiction of the world—which the F & F demonstration had highlighted. To represent everything absolutely faithfully was impracticable but also unnecessary, since a reality was real enough if it looked real enough. The problem, then, was to find good ways of being able to cheat and get away with it.

Fractal algorithms provided a method for generating a lot of material from minimal information—the way Nature compresses its assembly directions in DNA. The principal drawback was that to produce a convincingly realistic output, some kind of randomizing capability needed to be introduced, which meant no two results of applying the same input formula would, in general, be alike. Hence, two separate runs to generate a tree, say (or leaf, or rock, or mountain, or snowflake), from the same set of starting parameters would both look like a tree, but they wouldn't be the *same* tree. This would probably be all right for representing things like forests, skies, or general scenery where precise details didn't matter too much; but other situations demanded a different approach.

So in these latter cases there seemed to be no alternative to having to store all the detail that might be required. Even with the kinds of faster processing methods and special-purpose hardware that Barry Neinst had been exploring, this imposed severe limitations on how large a world they could hope to simulate accurately. For the world to be sufficiently varied and interesting, not all of it could be represented everywhere, all the time. Nor, of course, did it need to be. So the system was organized to concentrate on the parts making up the immediate experiences of the individuals experiencing the simulation. Thus, indeed, in these worlds the Moon was not there when nobody was looking at it; and the question of trees falling in deserted forests didn't arise, since with nobody around, forests ceased to exist.

For smoother continuity, and to reduce the occurrences of "black-hole glitches"—as when somebody opened a door to find themselves staring into a featureless void for a perplexing moment— various ways were tried for getting the system to anticipate and pre-access the branches that were most likely to be needed next. But none of them proved wholly satisfactory. Following chess-playing-machine parlance, this became known as the "look-ahead" problem. Solving it, along with "realscaping" more of the Pittsburgh area, was the main focus of the EVIE group's work through the second half of the year.

During that period, Ivy Dupale resigned from the company and got a job on the West Coast.

With Christmas approaching, Corrigan and Evelyn drove out one evening to Eric Shipley's house in Franklin, north of the city. Tom Hatcher and several others from the project were also due. It was a homey, unpretentious place, nestled in a fold of wooded hillside that provided seclusion, yet with the township center conveniently less than a mile away. It was the main house of what had once been a farm. The outbuildings were now converted or demolished, and most of the land sold off, except for a couple of acres forming a shady, somewhat overgrown garden bordered by a creek at the rear. Shipley lived there with his graying, genially disposed wife, Thelma. They had two sons and a daughter, all of them grown and gone in different directions. The children's rooms were always kept the way they had been for their frequent visits home.

Hatcher was already there when Corrigan and Evelyn arrived. With him were two of his programmers, Charlie Wade and Sue Lepez, and also Bryan Reed, one of the electronics technicians working on EVIE. There were sodas, coffee, and beer. Later on, a couple of pizzas arrived. By the middle of the evening the talk had ranged over shop topics and settled on the do's and don'ts for surviving in a popular VR game called "Sniper." Shipley drew Corrigan away to go and see an old nautical chronometer of polished teak and gleaming brass that Shipley had in his study. It was not long, however, before they were back to the subject of developments within

CLC. Corrigan sensed that this was the real reason why Shipley had taken him aside.

Most people—including Corrigan himself—had seen the consolidation of EVIE under his direction as an effective promotion, and an indicator that he was solidly on his way upward to better things. Shipley, however, wasn't so sure.

"You said yourself, once, that in the long term EVIE doesn't lead anywhere," he reminded Corrigan. "You called it a short-term stunt, a hybrid mishmash. So what does that say about anyone doing you a favor by putting you in charge of it?"

But Corrigan was still riding the wave. "Ah, come on, Eric," he said lightly. "You wouldn't want me think that you're having an attack of sour grapes, now, would you? Don't you remember, too, that EVIE was to be the main-thrust program for two years? Whoever runs it now will automatically pick up whatever comes next."

"That could be changing, Joe. There's been a lot going on involving Tyron and Pinder at the division level that we're only getting parts of. My guess is that corporate thinking has been turning away from EVIE ever since that business with Feller and Faber. In other words, they're saddling you with a lame duck."

"What else would they have in its place, then?" Corrigan challenged, his voice a touch sharper. They were still a year or more away from shifting up to the thalamus—and there was no guarantee that it would work even then.

Shipley shrugged and showed his hands. "You tell me."

"Why assume that they've got anything else at all?"

"Then look at it this way. If EVIE really is a sinking ship, whose name is being quietly dissociated from it and who'll be the skipper who goes down?" Shipley paused to let Corrigan think about that. "Then ask yourself what Tyron and his people were really brought in for. It certainly wasn't just to take over Ivy's section. That's a holding operation."

This time Corrigan said nothing but stared hard at him for several seconds. Shipley waited, holding his eye questioningly. Before they could resume, however, the long, loose-limbed figure of Tom Hatcher sauntered in from the living room, holding a can of beer in one hand and licking pizza grease off the fingers of the other. Evelyn was behind him, looking fresh and casually appealing with her long, fair hair, white top, and red, clinging slacks.

"Not interrupting anything, are we?" Hatcher drawled. " 'Cause if we are it's too bad. This is a party."

Corrigan hesitated, then grinned. "No, it's okay, Tom. Just shop as always." It was a good time to ease things up a little anyway. Evelyn squeezed past Hatcher to hand Corrigan a sausage on a cocktail stick, then snuggled close while he slipped an arm around her. Hatcher went over to look at the chronometer that Corrigan had been examining earlier.

"Say, that's some piece. They don't make 'em like that these days."

"Not a shred of plastic in it, and the knobs don't come off in your hand," Corrigan agreed.

"Can't say I'd want to carry it around on my wrist, though."

"You didn't have to. You had a ship to carry these around."

"Where do the batteries go?" Hatcher moved to admire a highly polished period revolver, mounted as a display on a board fixed to the wall nearby. "Looks like a .44 Dragoon Colt," he commented. "Probably from the Civil War."

"Right on," Shipley said, nodding.

"I didn't know you were into that kinda thing."

"I'm not. Thelma picked it up at a yard sale for five dollars."

"Does it work?"

"No—just an ornament."

"Too bad." Hatcher's interest in guns was well known.

Shipley nodded in the direction that Hatcher and Evelyn had come from. "What's going on back there?" he inquired.

"Shop," Evelyn said. "Is it ever different with this bunch?"

"Charlie's talking about his accelerator for the new look-ahead tree," Hatcher explained. "I had enough of it all day. I came here to get away."

They still hadn't found a reliable way of paralleling the human intuition for knowing what people were apt to do next. In a test the previous day, the system had properly anticipated all the things that one of the experimenters could reasonably have been expected to do with a magazine when he picked it up and rolled it—except use it to swat a simulated fly. Hence there was a hangup upon impact, in which time the velocity of the magazine fell to zero, and the fly was able to walk with impunity onto the object that was supposed to have flattened it.

Machines were good at organizing the world into neat hierarchies of computed probability. The real world, however—essentially because of the way that the people in it behaved—didn't work that way.

"Charlie's still an idealist," Hatcher said. "He just won't accept that the world isn't logical."

"Well, it doesn't work by formal, Aristotelian logic," Shipley agreed. "You see, that's purely deductive: you start with what's true, and from that the way the world has to be follows. That's what machines are good at. But in real life you start with experience of the way the world is, and then infer the reasons why and hope they come close to being true. Inductive: that's what people do—and even they aren't sure how. That's why textbook science and real science aren't the same thing."

"Is philosophy a hobby of yours, Eric?" Evelyn asked. She had been running her eyes over the shelves of books around the study.

"Oh, I dabble in a bit of everything," Shipley replied affably.

"So the universe is inductive," Corrigan concluded.

"Isn't it obvious?" Shipley said.

"I thought that philosophers have been having a problem with induction for centuries," Evelyn commented.

Shipley shrugged. "It's of their own making—as are most of humanity's problems. They started by assuming that the universe *couldn't* work inductively—because they couldn't reduce it to formal rules—when it obviously does."

"So we have to teach the simulator how to be inductive," Corrigan said. "How *does* real-world logic work, then, Eric?"

"Being ninety-percent right, ninety percent of the time," Shipley replied. "It's what science, business, war, and evolution are all about."

"What about sex?" Hatcher asked, looking away from the Colt and taking a swig from his can.

"Oh." Shipley smiled. "That's made up of all of the above."

A thoughtful expression came over Hatcher's face. "Maybe the way isn't to try and *teach* the system how to be inductive at all," he said. "I mean, if we're not really sure how we do it ourselves, we're hardly in a position to spell out the rules, are we?"

"What other way is there?" Corrigan asked.

"Maybe the thing to do is turn it the other way around."

There was silence for a couple of seconds while the others puzzled over this. "How do you mean?" Shipley asked finally.

"Let it learn in the same way as we do: by observing the behavior of real people in the environments that it creates. With EVIE, we've got all the technology you need." Hatcher paused, then went on, more excited visibly as he warmed to the idea, "Instead of the inhabitants of a world evolving in response to the environment, the environment learns to get better by watching the reactions of the inhabitants. See what I mean—it would be turning nature upside down."

"Hmm." Shipley drew back, frowning. "I'll have to give that some thought. . . . It's interesting, that, Tom. Very interesting."

Corrigan had taken down one of the books that Evelyn had noticed and was turning the pages idly. "Epictetus? I've heard of him."

"Greek slave, taken to Rome," Shipley said, moving over.

"Got freed and became a philosopher," Corrigan completed.

"He's the reason why I've never been interested in politics or prestige," Shipley told them.

"Really?" Evelyn said.

Shipley grinned. "Oh, I was kidding. But he does say some interesting things."

"Such as?" Corrigan asked curiously.

"That you shouldn't seek happiness through things that other people have control over," Shipley answered. "Otherwise you end up being enslaved to them."

That didn't seem to leave very much, as far as Corrigan could see. "What else is it that you should want, then?" he asked.

"Live for your own values and beliefs: things that nobody can take away," Shipley answered. "Then nobody can own you."

The veiled reference to their private conversation earlier would have been enough on its own to goad Corrigan into dissenting, even without his innate Irish argumentativeness. "It sounds like a pretty empty cop-out, if you ask me, Eric," he opined. "The kind of thinking of somebody who would never try going for anything for the fear of losing it. Where's the challenge and satisfaction in living a life like that?"

"It's being free, Joe. Fearing nobody. Look at the antics of some of the people we see every day and ask how many of them can say they have that."

Corrigan shook his head. "You live your way, I'll live mine. I couldn't accept a philosophy like that."

Shipley seemed unperturbed. "Maybe you should go back and get in touch with your roots again, sometime, Joe," he said. "To Ireland. There's a tradition there, too, that understands the kind of things I'm talking about."

"Oh, you don't buy that load of rot, too, do you, Eric?" Corrigan groaned. "Thieves, rogues, and scoundrels, the lot of 'em. They'd sell their grandmothers for the price of a pint—and then leave you stuck with the tab if you look the other way."

"I'd still like to go there," Evelyn said. It was something they had talked about a number of times.

Corrigan looked at her. "Well, maybe it is about time that you and I took a break somewhere." He raised his eyebrows. Her face split into a smile, and she nodded eagerly. "How about Florida, or maybe Mexico?" he suggested.

"Somewhere a bit sunnier than Pennsylvania in December, anyway," she said. "It's no better than Boston."

Corrigan thought for a few seconds longer. "Then let's make it California," he said. "There's a string of places dabbling in neural stuff on the West Coast that I've always been meaning to check out. And there's an old friend of mine from MIT called Hans Groener who's doing things at Stanford on sleep and dreams that sound interesting, but I've never had a chance to see it."

"Sure, California'll do. Why not?" Evelyn said. "I've never seen Yosemite."

"Do it," Shipley told them. "Everything's slowing down here for the holidays. And you've probably got some leave that you need to take before the year's out, Joe."

Why not? Corrigan thought. "I'll call Hans tomorrow and see what we can do," he promised.

❀ CHAPTER SIXTEEN ❀

Despite his fatigue and having been up all night, Corrigan did not sleep well. He awoke halfway through the afternoon, still feeling woolly headed and groggy. All he could remember from his disjointed recollections of the early-morning hours was that Lilly's place was north of the river, somewhere near the Allegheny Center. He cleaned up and put on some fresh clothes, then fixed himself a snack. Computer-injected hunger signals felt just the same, even if his real body was in repose, getting its nutrients from dermally transfused solutions. After that, he left without turning Horace on again, and caught a bus to the North Side.

But nothing that he saw jogged his memory as he wandered up and down the streets of the district contained in the crook of the I-279 Expressway, north of Three Rivers Stadium. Any of a score of apartment-block entrances that he passed could have been hers. Any of the streets that he walked along could have left the hazy image that was all he could piece together of unremarkable frontages glimpsed in predawn shadows.

It made sense to him now why recent years should have seen so much redevelopment around Pittsburgh. For every part of the old city that was "demolished," new, simulated scenery could be substituted that would not have to conform to anybody's real-world experiences. Nobody could walk around inside the Camelot, for example, and be puzzled by not finding things the way they used to be. The "realscaping" task was thus considerably eased.

He wanted to tell Lilly that she had been right, but everything was okay—the experiment was going as it should. Yes, their memories of the actual commencement of Oz had been suppressed, and alternative stories given to mask the transition from the real world to the illusory. But it didn't follow that something sinister was going on. Some such provision would have been necessary to ensure that the responses of the surrogates—the real-world participants coupled into the simulation—would be natural and valid.

And boy, had that part of the scheme worked as planned! Until Lilly waved the facts in front of his nose, he himself—one of the principal creators of the simulation—had failed to realize that he was inside it. She had thought to question where he had not because she had known less. He had been involved in the planning of Oz. Hence, if any deception were intended, he would have known about it. Since he didn't, there couldn't be any; and once the impossibility was established in his mind, there was no place for the possibility to coexist. The irony was that it had been able to work in his case only because of his knowledge that it *couldn't* work.

The main cause of Lilly's distress and anger was not so much the deception—she was a military volunteer, and things like that happened and could be compensated for—but the twelve years that she saw as stolen from her life. And who could blame her for that? But what he knew, and she almost certainly would not, was that those twelve years were also an illusion. The system coupled directly into post-sensory brain centers, which enabled data to be coded in a prereduced, highly compressed form that eliminated delays associated with preprocessing in the perceptual system. This meant that time inside the simulation ran about two hundred times faster than real time in the world outside. Hence, the actual time that they had spent hooked into the virtual world would be closer to three weeks than the twelve years that they remembered subjectively. Although even that was longer than the durations projected for the test runs that Corrigan had expected to be taking part in, it wasn't outrageous. They were all scientists and volunteers, after all. They would have had little problem agreeing to something like that.

He hoped that if he could find her and reassure her of at least that much, she would see things in a different light and be less likely to start doing anything rash that might disrupt the experiment. There was no reason for the test conditions to be affected by the mere fact of their knowing what they knew now, as long as they continued to act as if nothing had changed. The system could only monitor external behavior: what a surrogate did and said. Since nobody possessed the knowledge to tell it how, the system was not able to decode inner thought processes from deep inside the brain and read minds. If it could, there would have been no need for Project Oz in the first place.

The whole idea had been that the system would learn to make its animations more lifelike by imitating the behavior of real people injected as surrogate selves into the simulation. It had no way of knowing why the surrogates that it watched behaved in the ways they did—any more than they frequently did themselves. At the end of the experiment nobody would know, let alone have been able to specify beforehand, the precise structure of software structures and linkages that had self-organized to make such mimicking possible. The neural structures responsible for the complexity of human behavior in the real world had evolved by principles that were appropriate to carbon chemistry. Trying to duplicate them in code would have been as misguided as building airplanes that flapped feathers. Oz was designed to build, in ways appropriate to software, whatever structures it needed to achieve similar results. Nobody needed to know exactly what the final structures were, or how they worked. The aim was to achieve directed coevolution: the end-product, not the mechanism for attaining it, was the important thing.

That had been the theory, anyway. Whether it would work was what Oz had been set up to test. And from the bizarre goings-on going on in the world around him, Corrigan's first conclusion had to be that as far as its prime goal was concerned, the project had wandered somewhat off the rails. For, far from modeling themselves on the surrogates, the system animations seemed to be going off into self-reinforcing behavior patterns of their own, while—if his own and Lilly's cases were anything to go by—the surrogates had become misfits. That in itself didn't trouble him unduly. This was research, after all; perfection could hardly be expected from a first-time run—and especially in an undertaking as unprecedented and as ambitious as this.

Hence, it was no surprise that the animations fell short of true human emulation in some aspects. What was astounding was that they came so close. The empty stares and "flatness" were minor flaws compared to the extraordinary degree of realism—even if it did tend somewhat toward the eccentric—with which the personas that he encountered daily were able to act out their affairs and effect the continuity of leading consistent background existences offstage. So what if the system had overstepped the boundary of neurosis when it tried to make Jonathan Wilbur an embodiment of human criteria for personal success and failure; or if Maurice at the Camelot couldn't master a value system that didn't reduce to a simple profit-and-loss calculus? They had fooled Corrigan. It was sobering to realize just how effective the combined weight of suggestion and authority had been in persuading him that the defects he had perceived in the early stages were in himself and not in the world around him. Now so much seemed so obvious.

The universal ineptness at fathoming humor and metaphor that he had observed for years—processes that involved the associative genius of human intellect at its subtlest—should have given the game away. And if not that, then surely the curious and unnatural persistence of people like Sherri and Sarah Bewley when they pressed him for explanations of where they had missed the point. Of course. All the time it was the system—wanting to know how it could do better. Mind reading was not an option.

In the real world, when people acted strangely or unsociably, others tried to gain some insight to why by getting them to talk. In the same way, when the system sought deeper understandings of what motivated the surrogates, it put animations around them to ask its questions for it. And the closer the relationship, the more personal—and hence relevant to the purpose—their questions could naturally be. Maurice, his boss at work; Sarah, his rehabilitation counselor (and the earlier attempt in the form of Simon, which had failed)—both were examples of the computers trying to get close, wanting to discover what made him behave as he did. No wonder he sometimes found himself reflecting that Horace, Sarah, and Maurice sounded the same. They *were* the same. His house manager was the system in disguise, too.

And even his wife! For hadn't it been Sarah who first came up with the suggestion that marrying Muriel might be a good move—for "therapeutic" reasons? Weird but frighteningly effective, he had to concede. Acting through one manufactured personality, the system had insinuated itself into his personal world in the form of another. Corrigan could only marvel at the ingenuity of it. Already the project was surpassing anything he had imagined, even in his wildest moments of selling it to others.

And now there was the risk that just at this crucial stage when Oz was surpassing all expectations, Lilly, unless he could get to her, might jeopardize the whole thing. But he was not going to get to her this way, he admitted to himself finally. Until he figured out another way, or until she got to him again, the thing was to carry on acting normally. That meant going in to work today, just as if nothing had happened. He crossed back over the river to Downtown and decided that it wasn't worth going out to Oakland. On the other hand, it was too early to go straight to the Camelot just yet.

There was a bar not far from the Vista—the hotel where Evelyn had stayed when she came down from Boston for her job interview—that he used to frequent a lot during his time with CLC, but which he hadn't been in since his "breakdown." He knew every scratch on the countertop in that place, the prints and curios on the walls, all the scuff marks and stains in the pattern on the wallpaper. There was no way that the realscaping crews could have covered *every* place in town.

Out of curiosity, he made his way there. The street had acquired its share of changes over the years, but apart from a new door and a coat of paint, the bar still looked pretty much the same—outside. But that was the easy part. He went inside. . . .

And sure enough, it had all been remodeled. New counter, new walls, new everything. Corrigan sighed and ordered a Bushmills, straight up. It could have been his imagination, but he was sure he detected a hint of a knowing smirk on the face of the pudgy, balding bartender.

"Okay, you got me," Corrigan conceded, raising his glass.

"Ah . . . pardon, sir?"

"It doesn't matter."

There was a pay phone in an alcove by the cigarette machine. Corrigan changed a twenty into quarters and sauntered over. He set his drink on top of the phone and tapped in the number for Information International. The codes were all different from the ones used in the real world—the change had been explained as necessitated by changes in procedure by the phone companies. Corrigan couldn't remember offhand why the Oz designers had done that.

"How can I help you?" a voice inquired.

"I'd like a number in Ireland, please."

There was a confused pause. Corrigan smiled at the thought of the drastic axing and reassembly of a whole section of the system's pointer tree that those few simple words would have caused.

"Why do you want a number there?" the voice demanded, sounding belligerent. Oh, yes, Corrigan thought to himself, it all seemed so obvious now.

"What the hell does it matter why I want it?" he retorted. "Would you please just do your job."

Another pause, then a different voice, a woman's, with a believable brogue: "Directory, which town, please?"

"Dun Laoghaire."

"Yes. And who would you be wanting there?"

"There's a grocer's shop on the corner of Clarinda Park and Upper George's Street, called Ansell's, that stays open late. What's their number?" It would be approaching ten P.M. in Ireland—five hours ahead of Pittsburgh time.

A long pause. "Ah, I don't seem to have them listed anywhere. Are you sure it's still there? It might have changed."

"How about the New Delhi? It's an Indian restaurant along the street."

"No. I don't have that either."

Corrigan grinned. The system was throwing every obstacle at him that it could come up with. "Then tell me the number of the Kingston Hotel at the bottom of Adelaide Street."

"A hotel is it, you said?" The system was trapped. Corrigan could sense it, there in the voice.

"Yes, the Kingston, on Adelaide Street. If that's gone too, give me the number of the police station around the corner."

He got the number, and after parting with a fistful of coins was through. "Is this the Kingston?" he inquired.

"Yes, it is," a young woman's voice replied.

"And are you at the reception desk there?"

"I am. Who's this?"

"Just somebody who would appreciate it if you could help settle a small bet we're having here. I wonder, would you mind stepping across the hall for a moment and looking out the front door to your right, and then describe to me what you can see?"

"Oh, no, I couldn't be doing that."

"Why not?"

"It's, er . . . not company policy."

Corrigan had to stifle a laugh. His eyes were watering. "Then tell me what the large picture is above the main bar in the lounge."

"That was taken away, I'm afraid."

"I'd like to have seen them do it. It's painted on the ceiling."

A sudden shrill tone announced a disconnection. "There seems to be a technical fault," Corrigan was informed when he checked with the operator.

Still smiling, he went back to the bar with his drink. In a niche among the shelves of bottles, standing between a darts trophy and jar of ticket stubs, there was a figurine that he hadn't noticed before. It was of an Irish leprechaun, complete with hat and pipe. "So, you're still haunting me, eh, Mick?" he grunted as he sat down on the stool. It was uncannily like the one he had in his hallway at home.

❀ CHAPTER SEVENTEEN ❀

The hills behind the Bay to the east looked invitingly sunbaked after the chill and wet of winter in Pennsylvania. Below, as the plane descended on its final approach into San Francisco International Airport, fingers of houses and marinas creeping outward along the water's edge formed complex, convoluted patterns like frost on a windowpane.

Corrigan, looking casual in an open-neck shirt, light windbreaker, dove-gray jeans, and sneakers, slipped a hand over Evelyn's and leaned closer. He had been more relaxed than she had ever known him, telling stories and cracking bad jokes all through the flight. "You know, Eric was right," he said. "We've been cooped up inside CLC for too long, worrying about its politics. It's not worth it. This is the kind of thing we should be making more time for. There might be something to be said for those old books of his after all. People need to get their values straight."

She smiled and treated him to a look of mock superciliousness. "Why go back two thousand years to find that out? I've been telling you the same thing for ages."

"Have you? I never noticed."

"My point exactly."

"Then you're right too. Let the world be advised that Joseph M. Corrigan is switching to a lower-wattage lifestyle. The high-power stuff, I'll leave to the Pinders and the Tyrons. And the blood pressure that goes with it."

"Half your time would be empty," Evelyn pointed out. "No. On second thought, most of it."

"Great."

"What would you do with it?"

He kissed her on the cheek and pretended to think about it. "Oh, I'd find something."

They spent the next couple of days sight-seeing around the city. They went to the aquarium, planetarium, botanical gardens, and museums in Golden Gate Park, rode cable cars, and ate the best at Fisherman's Wharf, Japantown, and Broadway. They rented a car and drove north across the Golden Gate to the wine country, around the Bay to visit some of the researchers at Berkeley, and back across the Bay Bridge in the evening to see the SF Symphony, playing the winter season.

When they got back to the hotel, Corrigan called Hans Groener, his onetime colleague from MIT days, to confirm their visit to Stanford for the next day.

"Yes, that will be fine, Joe," Hans said over the phone. "Also, I have a surprise for you."

"Oh? What's that?"

"I talked to an old friend of yours who's out here now, and who would like to say hello again. So I invited her to join us for dinner tomorrow night and make it a foursome—Ivy Dupale."

"Hey, terrific!" Corrigan called across the room to Evelyn. "How about this. Hans knows Ivy. She's joining us for dinner tomorrow night."

"How wonderful!"

"Fine, Hans. That'll be just great."

The following morning they left San Francisco again and headed southward this time, to Stanford University. Hans was involved in sleep and dream research, which Corrigan looked on as something different and quite probably interesting, but not really relevant to his own line of work. It would be good to see Hans again anyway, even if the visit did turn out to be mainly social. But after he and Evelyn arrived at the sprawling campus with its Spanish-inspired facades of rounded arches and shady colonnades, and had talked with Hans in his laboratory for only half an hour, he realized that he had been mistaken. Hans's work could turn out to be very relevant indeed.

The DINS technology used by Pinocchio and EVIE used a configuration of electrodes inside the collar to create a dynamic pattern of ultra-high-frequency electric fields that penetrated the lower brain regions and brain stem. The fields superposed and were precisely shaped to add or cancel in different spots that could be very finely localized, which was how desired neural centers were activated selectively. However, attenuation and dispersion increased with penetration depth, reducing selectivity and hence the effectiveness of the technique. This was the main factor drat had restricted direct coupling to the medulla.

For several years, papers had been appearing in the scientific literature, reporting on an alternative approach using intersecting photon beams tuned to several narrow-frequency windows at which body tissue was found to be surprisingly transparent. It was only in talking with Hans that Corrigan first came to realize how rapidly these investigations had consolidated and were advancing. The new, emerging field was known as "Deep Selective Activation."

"The window allows photons to penetrate coherently and maintain a tight focus, below disruptive ionization energies," Hans explained. "On top of that, frequency tuning to specific neural states provides an additional dimension for fine probing. There's no need for flooding the cells with huge numbers of photons." He was lean and narrow-framed, with straight blond hair and a pale, thin-lipped countenance. The movies would have cast him as an SS officer whose sadism was a compensation for a physique that fell short of the Wagnerian Nordic ideal. In reality, Hans played American folk guitar and bred parakeets. Most of his equipment was being rebuilt currently, and his staff hidden away in offices or at computer terminals: there wasn't a lot, really, to show that day.

"I knew you were dabbling in this, but I never realized it had come so far," Corrigan confessed.

"DSA has had a boost from a lot of government work that was

declassified," Hans told him. "We've got quite a club springing up here on the West Coast. SRI are putting a team together. Todd's group up at Berkeley."

"We hoped to see him yesterday, but he's away this week."

"Hughes and Lockheed are in on it. Some department in the Air Force has been very active."

The significance of the remark didn't hit Corrigan just then. He was still telling himself inwardly that he would have to make a point of keeping more up to date with the literature in future. Get back to being a scientist again, and forget trying to turn into a corporate politician. Being back in academic surroundings was reawakening his appetite for intellectual excitement.

Evelyn was studying some charts of neural organization fixed to one of the walls. Corrigan's background was software rather than interfacing, and his personal expertise at the working level lay in the area of self-modifying associative nets. What Hans was describing came closer to the kind of work that Evelyn had had experience of at Harvard and was now doing with Shipley.

"Hans, what are these references to 'resonance modes' here?" she asked curiously. "I use this mapping system practically every day, but I've never come across those before."

Hans stepped across and looked pleased, rubbing the palms of his hands together and showing teeth with lots of metal. "Ah, yes, very good. You spotted it." He nodded approvingly at Corrigan. "You've found a smart lady here, Joe."

"And what else would you expect?"

Hans looked back and forth, taking in both of them. "This is something fairly recent that we've discovered through DSA. It's quite exciting—something that I think you will find particularly interesting, Joe. We call it associative neural resonances."

Corrigan's eyebrows rose. "Which are? . . ."

"Shortcuts to generating complex pictures inside the brain. We've found that triggering just a few, precisely selected, neuronal groups can activate entire chains of connected imagery."

"Wilder Penfield's experiments, back in the forties," Evelyn tossed in.

"Yes," Hans agreed. "Except we can do it from the outside." He glanced back at Corrigan. "You know how extraordinarily lucid dreams can be, yes? The images can be so rich in detail that it's often impossible to tell whether one is asleep or not."

"Sometimes I've been awake for five minutes before I realized I wasn't awake yet," Corrigan said.

"Exactly." Hans nodded and went on. "Obviously that information isn't coming from anywhere outside. It was already present there, in the mind. Random firings can set off whole trains of them that are linked together, which we experience as dreams—or it may be firings that are predisposed by recent repeated activity due to worry, intense emotional contexts, and that kind of thing."

"Like the way a bell rings," Evelyn said. "The complexity of the sound has nothing to do with how you hit it, or what with. It was already there implicitly, in the bell's structure."

"And with language," Hans said. "Words are just a code system to trigger associations already established in the listener's neural system from the experience of living. The information is in the listener, not the speaker. It seems to be a general characteristic of the neural system. And that is what we are learning to control. Activating just the right set of primitives can cause amazingly detail-rich images to be generated in the visual system. By 'playing' the input combinations like a keyboard, we can induce complete event-sequences to order, inside the subject's mind, without having to inject huge data streams to specify every detail. We simply reactivate what's already there. Much faster than conventional brute-force graphics. Much more efficient."

The significance was apparent immediately. Here, possibly, was a totally new way of approaching the problem that Corrigan's group had been grappling with of representing major portions of the real world. Instead of trying to supply every detail of an image, feed in just the right cues and let the subjects fill in the details themselves, from the inside.

But surely it couldn't be that simple. Hans watched the frown forming on Corrigan's face, knowing the objection that was coming.

Finally, Corrigan said, "These resonances. Are they unique—different for each individual? Or does everyone share the same ones? . . . I mean, if they're unique, they can't produce the same world for different people."

"Yes, I know what you're saying, Joe. But the fact is, there does seem to be a surprising degree of commonality. We are still very much in the fact-gathering stage, but the way it looks is that similar input code patterns do result in similar things being perceived by different people."

Corrigan was looking undisguisedly skeptical. "How could that be, now?" he demanded.

Hans refused to be put on the defensive. "How do we know that we all see the same world anyway?" he challenged. "Oh, sure, we agree on the same broad descriptions—I'm not disputing that. But how do we *know* . . ." he paused, looking first at one, then the other, to emphasize his point, "that what we're seeing is identical? We don't. You'd be surprised how much in ordinary day-to-day living, people habitually see what they expect to see, not what's there. Our tests show measures of agreement that are comparable. So the differences that we get are no worse than happen every day in the real world anyway." He shrugged and turned up his hands to make one final point. "And in any case, we all tend to dream about similar things. That says there's common circuitry at work somewhere."

"But surely the degree by which different people disagree can't be the same for all of them," Evelyn said.

"That's right—it varies as a Gaussian spectrum," Hans said. "Ninety percent more-or-less agree what it's like out there, and they define the 'norm.' But the fringe groups differ increasingly, until in the extreme cases they live in a different world entirely."

"And we call them insane," Corrigan said, getting the point.

Hans grinned at him jestingly. "Maybe you're tackling VR the wrong way, Joe. Instead of trying to shovel a whole world into people's heads, perhaps you should try inducing the right dreams, and let the machinery that's already there inside do the work. That is what it evolved for, after all. Just as the best cures use the body's own defenses."

※　※　※

Ivy arrived late in the afternoon. She was looking good, had found herself a place in San Jose, and was heading up a space-imaging program at NASA, Ames. She asked about Tom Hatcher, Eric, and the others back at CLC, but—not so surprisingly, Corrigan supposed—did not show a great deal of curiosity about the progress of the project itself. Corrigan took the hint and didn't push it on her. Evelyn got the same message.

From the university they went to eat at a place in Palo Alto that was a popular nightspot as well as a restaurant. Afterward, they stayed for a couple more drinks, and to dance. Late into the evening, while Evelyn was on the floor with Hans and the other two were taking a break, Ivy looked across at Corrigan over the rim of her glass and asked, "Are you going to marry her?"

Corrigan was used to Ivy's direct way of saying exactly what was on her mind. He had found it disconcerting at first; later it became refreshing. He grinned forbearingly. "Now, why would I want to go and be doing a thing like that?"

"You two go so well together."

"Exactly. Why go and spoil a good relationship?"

Ivy sipped her drink unblinkingly. "I think you should risk it. She wants to, you know. Women have this kind of radar. We can tell."

"There's an old Irish saying," Corrigan told her. "If you want praise, die; if you want blame, marry. People change when they feel owned. They start blaming each other for not coming up to expectations that were never realistic in the first place."

"If you're smart enough to think that, you can't be dumb enough to believe it, Joe," Ivy said.

Corrigan took a mouthful of drink, thought for a moment, and set his glass down. "Ah, enough of this heavy stuff," he said. "Have you got your breath back? This is a great one that they're starting now. Let's go back and show Hans and Evelyn a thing or two."

But Ivy's comment about he and Evelyn going so well together had struck a sympathetic chord in him somewhere. Some of the women back at CLC had said the same. For some reason, it was always the women who noticed such things—or at least, who mentioned them. And socially, it was one area where his life felt incomplete.

He was unusually quiet and thoughtful all the way through the drive back up to San Francisco.

❀ CHAPTER EIGHTEEN ❀

It was too late in the season to visit Yosemite as Evelyn had wanted—reports were that the approaches were already treacherous due to snow. So, following a suggestion of some people that they talked to at breakfast the next morning, they postponed that for another occasion, and instead drove across the San Joaquin Valley and up into the Sierra foothills to the Mother Lode country of 1849 gold-rush fame.

They toured the old mining town of Columbia, preserved as a state monument, where the buildings remained inside and out just as they had been a century and a half before, and residents wearing traditional dress still worked the old crafts. The Wells Fargo Company office was still there, whose scales had weighed over one and a half billion dollars' worth of precious metals during the gold era.

Eight miles away they found California's largest public cave, Moaning Cavern, estimated to be a million years old and large enough to hold the Statue of Liberty upright and still leave room to spare. The bones of approximately a hundred people dating back to prehistoric times had been found at the bottom, 180 feet below the surface—probably the results of unfortunates accidentally falling into the cavern, since until its opening up in recent times the entrance had been just a small, vegetation-covered hole in the surface. The guide, who was also the owner, told them that from the positions that the bones were found in, some of the victims had apparently survived the fall and tried to climb out—a tough proposition, considering the overhangs. Traces of carbonized wood suggested that perhaps others at the surface had thrown down torches in an effort to help. "Of course, it's impossible to be sure," he told them, pinching his mustache and chuckling. "But we like to think that some of 'em made it."

They drove higher into the Sierra, the wild range separating California from Nevada. In every direction they looked they saw tree-covered hills, sweeping expanses of canyon and rock, unfolding vistas of lakes and mountains. Corrigan found himself intoxicated by the feelings of freedom and openness. They gazed down at foaming creeks far below them in sheer ravines, stared up in awe at sequoias with trunks more than twenty feet in diameter. From a crag high in the Sonora pass they clung close as they stared out over the vastness, and it seemed that all of it belonged just to them.

"This time you've got to admit it, Joe," Evelyn said. "Come on. There are some things that even Ireland doesn't have."

For once, Corrigan failed to rise to the provocation. The jocular side of him that would normally have responded reflexively was suppressed by a more serious mood. "You can judge for yourself when you see it," he said.

"When," Evelyn repeated bitingly. Corrigan had been promising for the best part of a year now that they would go there one day. She didn't take it seriously anymore.

"Sure." Corrigan kept his eyes fixed on the distant ridgeline and forced his voice to remain matter-of-fact. "We can go there for our honeymoon."

She drew her head back slowly, turning to look at him. "Are you serious?"

"Oh, I know I can be an ass about most things, but do you think I'd joke over something like that?" And then he relaxed and smiled, spreading his hands to indicate that was all he had to say.

"You mean it? . . . You really, really do mean it?"

"Of course I mean it, you silly cow of an American female. So do I get an answer, or are you going to stand there looking like that all day?"

She threw her arms around his neck. He pulled her close. They kissed and hugged, rubbed and nuzzled.

"So you will, then, eh?" he murmured.

"You know I will. Didn't you? . . . Couldn't you tell?"

"I wasn't sure."

"How could you not?" She drew back, shaking her head, laughing out loud, unable to contain herself. "So when? . . . Where? How are we going to do it?"

Corrigan shrugged, able to feign nonchalance again, now that he had gotten it out. "Whatever you like. Do you want to hire a cathedral, and maybe a symphony orchestra to go with it?"

She shook her head. "Nothing like that. Something small and informal."

"Short and quick?"

"Just that. I want it just to be us. It doesn't have anything to do with anybody else."

"I was hoping you'd say that," Corrigan said. "We can go straight on into Nevada and do it while we're here. How's that?"

Evelyn gaped at him. "While we're here? You mean now?"

"Why not? If you're going to live with Irish impulsiveness, you might as well get used to it. We could make Carson City or Reno tomorrow. A couple of days there. Then a flight to San Francisco or L.A., connecting to Dublin via London. You're always saying how much you like to support wild life. Okay, then, how about Christmas and New Year's in Ireland? Your life will never be the same again."

She shook her head disbelievingly. "But . . . what about work? We're expected back there. We can't just . . ." She left it unfinished, not quite sure what she had been about to say.

Corrigan made a dismissive wave in the air. "Ah, to hell with the lot of them. They can manage on their own for a while, this once. We've both got enough leave due to us. We've been saying ever since we got on the plane: it's about time we started living a little more for ourselves for a change. Well, I'm thinking, the time to begin that is right now."

"But shouldn't we at least call them and let them know what's happening?" Evelyn asked.

"Oh, not at all. We'll make it a surprise for them when we get back," Corrigan said.

"I don't think I've ever felt so happy."

They went back to the car. As they got in, Corrigan pressed the button to disable the phone from accepting incoming calls. "There," he said. "Peace guaranteed. Come on and get in. I wouldn't want you catching a cold. You're mine now, exclusively, for the rest of this year. CLC can start taking its share again when we're into the new one."

Eric Shipley had a feeling that something unusual was in the air when Pinder appeared in the DINS laboratory, being genial and showing an uncharacteristic concern about how things in general were going. As a rule he spent most of his time holed up in the Executive Building with the others of the managerial elite who had transcended the mortal plane of solder guns, screwdrivers, and rolled-up shirtsleeves. Shipley believed that a chief's place was where the troops were—in the trenches. When managers collected together in comfortable surroundings remote from where things were happening, it usually wasn't long before they started inventing realities of their own that were far more virtual than anything going on in the labs.

"It's come a long way since the days when it was you, some programmers, and a couple of techs," Pinder said, casting his gaze around. He was referring to the group that had first experimented with adding DINS feedback to the MIMIC prototype that Carnegie Mellon and MIT had developed jointly—the combination that became Pinocchio.

"It's going to go a lot farther, too, and get a lot bigger," Shipley replied, sensing the way the conversation was headed. He might as well give Pinder his opening now, he decided, and find out what this was about.

Pinder obliged. "And the organization has to adapt to anticipate that. It was fine for handling things the way they used to be. But that has all changed. We see things going toward a more comprehensive organizational structure that will combine all the interactive environment work under one reporting function. Bring all the decision-making together, eliminate the duplications."

By "we," Shipley presumed he meant the Olympians across the parking lot. Pinder refocused away from the distance, where he stared when he was being evasive, and back on Shipley, which meant that he was getting to the point. "Don't you think that the DINS group would function more smoothly all around as part of an integrated system like that?"

In other words, apart from possible semantic jugglings with job titles, Shipley couldn't expect any promotional prospects. Pinder was sounding out his reactions to merging DINS under a larger structure that would be headed by someone else. "Integrated" was always the managerese code word for "more controllable."

Shipley thought it was plain to everyone that his interests lay in science, not in whatever satisfaction came from exercising authority over people. He was not surprised, for he had never entertained the illusion that, by the generally accepted criteria, he was particularly promotable material. Neither was he concerned. The decision was one that he had made consciously, a long time ago. He replied, "I don't think that the neural work on P-Two and EVIE would be affected much, either way. If it fits in better with other plans, then fine."

"Such an arrangement would be acceptable?"

"I'm assuming that my present group remains intact."

"Oh, no question. You and your people simply transfer under the new system as is. It's really the other sections that get reorganized more, around you. You carry on as normal."

"Okay."

"We're responding to new opportunities in a changing world," Pinder said. "Naturally, the new organization that we're talking about would benefit from the direction of somebody whose background best qualifies them to exploit those opportunities. I'm sure you see my point—the contacts and resources that Tyron's government and industrial experience give him access to are something that the corporation can't afford to ignore."

"I see," Shipley said.

What he saw was Corrigan being shoved into a subordinate position incommensurate with his ambitions, tied to a project that Shipley was becoming increasingly certain was not going to be the corporation's mainline development thrust. But he had seen that much coming for some time anyway. More disturbing now was to see these overtures being made in this fashion, while Corrigan was away. It invited suspicions of more devious motives behind them. Shipley had no idea what these might be, but his instincts detected something underhanded.

Back in his office, he brooded for a while over the situation. Then he asked his secretary, Kathy Rentz, to find out Corrigan and Evelyn's planned schedule in California, and to try to get ahold of them. Kathy checked with Judy Klein in Corrigan's office and got back to Shipley half an hour later.

"They were due back in San Francisco today, but the hotel there says they called last night and canceled the reservation. Judy hasn't heard anything."

"Dammit. . . . What about their mobile number. Did you get that from the car-hire company?"

"Yes I did. I've tried it half a dozen times at least, but it's not accepting. Sorry, Eric. That's all I can tell you."

❂ CHAPTER NINETEEN ❂

Corrigan didn't know Lilly well enough to have any real idea what she might do. She seemed sane and stable enough on the surface, but he had been confounded by human nature often enough to know not to trust first impressions. For his part, he had no difficulty accepting and adjusting to the situation—he knew the background to Oz and was committed to its success. But how might somebody else react in a world where no action could have "real" consequences, and who really believed that twelve years of a life had been stolen?

The trouble was, he still hadn't been able to trace her. He had gone to the North Side again, with no result, and got Horace to call companies listed under "Shoe Manufacture" in the city directory, to find out if any of them employed somebody called Lilly. This had produced four Lillys, none of them the right one. Either her firm was listed as something else, or she had told him a wrong story for some reason, or given him a false name for some reason, or she went by a different name at work for some reason . . . or any one of a thousand other possibilities that knowledge of human nature said happened every day. If this was the kind of thing that the machines were supposed to figure out, then good luck to them, Corrigan thought. Ten thousand years hadn't been enough for humans to even begin figuring out each other. Whether those twelve years had been real or not, he had to admit that they had certainly changed some of his attitudes.

What he needed to do, then, was talk to Dr. Zehl. It was obvious now, of course, why Zehl seemed so different from most of the people that Corrigan met: he *was* different—not an internal animation created and manipulated by the system, but, like Lilly and himself, a real-person surrogate projected in from the outside. Corrigan realized now that he had met others, too, in the course of those years. If the original plan had been adhered to, there should be fifty or so of them mixed in among the regular population.

But Zehl was not one of the ordinary surrogates. Supposedly, he was Washington based, appearing and disappearing spasmodically, and often not seen again for long stretches of time. This, along with his position as Sarah's "supervisor," told Corrigan that he was really one of the controllers, entering the simulation from time to time in an effort to keep track of how things were going. In all likelihood he was somebody that Corrigan knew, but the physical appearance of injected surrogates could be changed at will. But whoever he really was, Zehl was Corrigan's only ready channel of communication to the powers outside who had the ability to determine Lilly's whereabouts, given the nature of the situation.

Corrigan called Sarah Bewley and told her it was important that he get in touch personally with Zehl immediately. Sarah, naturally, wanted to know what he proposed telling Zehl that he didn't feel he could tell her, his counselor, and the whole thing bogged down in a mire of pique and offended feelings that got him nowhere. In any case, Zehl was out of town and not contactable right now. Corrigan called Zehl's department in Washington direct, and after some bouncing around obtained a number that had Zehl's name listed. The voice that eventually answered, however, confirmed that Zehl was currently away and couldn't be easily reached. In fact, it would be the system covering for the fact that Zehl, or whoever, was not currently coupled into the system. The number Corrigan had called was a code to activate an external flag alerting an operator, to page Zehl.

"This is the twenty-first century, isn't it?" Corrigan objected. "Are you telling me you can't get a message to him?"

"Well, maybe . . . if you leave it with me," the voice replied.

"Tell him it's from Joe Corrigan of Xylog. I want to talk

urgently about Oz. That should get him back to you minutes after he reads it."

But even a minute outside would still be something like four hours inside. The same speeding up of time that made more than a week of simulation time fly by while Zehl was absent for an hour also meant that Corrigan was going to have to wait for a response. A day for him equated to a little over seven minutes for Zehl, which meant there wasn't much time out there for anyone to hold lengthy conferences on what they were going to do. It also meant that Lilly would have free rein for a couple of days at least. But, unless he happened to run into her by chance or she decided to find him, there was nothing that Corrigan could do about that.

In the meantime, the best way to avoid having the time drag was to carry on as normal. But now that he knew the situation, he found himself in something of a quandary. Part of his nature—probably to do with his Irishness—rebelled from the prospect of obligingly continuing to act out his role as if nothing had happened, like a rat in a laboratory cage. The system had fooled him, and it couldn't be allowed to get away with it. On the other hand, he was a scientist involved with an experiment that was to a large degree of his own making, and his new awareness gave him a unique opportunity to function as a privileged observer on the inside. So he satisfied his instincts by teasing the system gently to its limits. This not only provided valuable practical data on where the limits were; but also, like playing word games with Horace and Sarah, he found it perversely and gratifyingly amusing.

"I've got a joke for you," he told Sherri. It was the middle of the afternoon, and the Galahad Lounge was quiet. "What do you call an insomniac, agnostic, dyslexic?"

"I don't know. What?"

"Somebody who lies awake all night, wondering 'Is there a dog?'"

She laughed obligingly, stared through him at the tariff list on the wall, and went away to clear some tables while she thought it over.

It was all so obvious, now that Lilly had forced him to recognize it. Strange, how the obvious was always the last thing you thought of.

Or maybe not so strange, Corrigan reflected as he replaced glasses on the shelf below the bar. When you finally see the obvious, then obviously you stop wondering. It was the same as when people were always asking why everything they lost was always in the last place they looked: who was going to carry on looking after they'd found it?

Sherri came back to the bar and looked at him curiously. "So could an anemic, myopic, skeptic be somebody with a pale face who doesn't believe he's shortsighted?" she asked.

"Could be," Corrigan agreed nonchalantly.

"So is that funny too?"

"I'm supposed to be odd," he reminded her. "Why would you care how it strikes me?"

She corrected herself. "Would they have thought it was funny back in Ireland years ago? I'm just curious."

Corrigan made a show of subjecting the proposition to profound analysis. "Ingenious, yes. Funny, not really," he told her.

"Okay," she invited. "Now tell me why not."

Normally, Corrigan would have known better than to try, and hence wouldn't have raised the subject in the first place. This time, however, he was aware that he was really talking to a trio of TMC 11s and a SuperCray in Xylog's basement. It was about time, he decided, that they began really exercising their circuits to earn their keep.

"Imagine an insomniac, and imagine an anemic," he replied. "How do you picture them?"

Sherri frowned. "I guess one of them looks whiter."

Corrigan had to make an effort not to guffaw out loud. It was pure Horace and Sarah, leaping clear over the point. "Okay, that's the anemic," he agreed. "What does the other one look like?"

"How could I possibly know?"

"All right, let's try it another way. Why can't insomniacs sleep?"

That was easy. The system almost fell over, reciting from its lookup tables. "Well, it could be from any of a number of possible causes. Metabolic malfunction, hormonal imbalance, chemical stimulation by any of . . ." Sherri broke off when she saw that Corrigan was shaking his head.

"They worry too much," he said.

"Maybe that too. But not all of them, necessarily," she answered.

"Never mind the others. The one we're talking about does."

"All right."

"Ah, now, you're accepting the fact, but you don't see the 'why.' What is it that he worries about?" Corrigan pressed. Sherri was looking bewildered. Never before had a simple question of hers led into anything like this. Corrigan made a tossing-away motion. "His boss is an arsehole, and his genius isn't being recognized at work; the car he just got fixed is making expensive noises again; his bank balance is printed in blood; and his wife, his girlfriend, and his mortgage are all a month overdue at the same time. His life is a mess. Subconsciously we feel fortunate and superior by comparison, and that makes us smile. So he's funny. The anemic isn't."

"Was I supposed to have thought all that?" Sherri asked, looking aghast.

"No. You're supposed to have *felt* it. It's the same someone-else-is-getting-it-and-I'm-not feeling that makes us laugh at banana peels and custard pies."

From the look on Sherri's face, Corrigan could have been revealing the secret of the philosopher's stone. At the same time, he might as well have been expressing it in Swahili.

"And that's it?" she said.

"Of course not. That's only the start. You want more?" Corrigan tossed out a hand. "Myopic means shortsighted, which in many contexts has connotations of stupidity and ineptness. Not funny, see? Being dyslexic might not be funny if you're dyslexic, but to the rest of us it conjures up pictures of getting everything the wrong way around: typical Irish."

"So we're superior again? Is that the idea?"

"Right. It reinforces the implication that we had before, and the way the two themes interweave is satisfying." Corrigan couldn't resist adding, "Of course, the unstated allusion to musical counterpoint is obvious, which makes the metaphor doubly satisfying."

"Yeah. . . . Right."

He went on. "Your making him a skeptic doesn't really work—skeptics are much too logical and sensible to be funny. The agnostic is funny because he doesn't know which way he thinks, which maintains the symmetry by casting him as a psychological dyslexic. And lastly, juxtaposing God with dog is delightfully irreverent, which a lot of people won't admit to being outwardly—but inside they find it hilarious. . . . So there you are. That's why it's funny. You did ask."

Sherri seemed to have so many questions jostling for attention at once that her eyes just glazed. Her eyebrows knitted, and her lips writhed. Finally she said, "I don't believe that you had to piece together all those connections. The number of permutations is too great. You'd never get through them." In its eagerness to know, the system was forgetting what was and was not an appropriate comment for a cocktail waitress.

"Not if you were a computer," Corrigan agreed. He winked. "But for people like you and me, it's easy. Right?"

"How do we know which connections to pick?"

"From the experience of life. When the person that you tell it to picks the same ones, and they don't know how either, you realize that despite your differences, there's something deep and mysterious that you both share in common."

Sherri was wearing the expression of a first-semester algebra student who had just glimpsed a textbook on tensor calculus. "You mean one joke says all that?" she managed in a strangled voice.

"Sure. In other words, you're not alone in the universe. It's a pretty good feeling to have, and you laugh. That's the other part of what makes funny things funny. Maybe it's the biggest part."

❂ CHAPTER TWENTY ❂

It was Christmas week. The jostling crowds of returning migrants making their seasonal pilgrimage home, and foreign-born kin eager to explore their cultural roots, gave Dublin Airport the appearance and feel of a refugee transit camp.

The party started as soon as Corrigan and Evelyn came through the exit from customs into the arrivals hall, where they were immediately spotted by a boisterous trio of Corrigan's former student colleagues sent to intercept them.

"There's yer man!"

"Will ye look what he's brought back with him! Are there many more like that back there, Joe?"

"You're looking just great, Joe. It's good to have you back."

They were showered with rice, which they had avoided in Reno since the ceremony had been a simple, civic one, and draped with streamers. Corrigan was treated to a swig of Bushmills from a hip flask and presented with a wrapped bottle of something. Evelyn got a bouquet and was introduced to "Mick," "Dermot," and "Kathleen."

"Ah, Mick won't be so bad, once you get used to him," Dermot assured her.

"Dermot's all right, really. He doesn't say things like that when he's sober," Mick explained.

"Evelyn, ye can expect no sense at all out of any of them, now that the three are together again," Kathleen warned.

"She's probably right," Dermot agreed.

"And it'll get worse," Mick guessed.

The laughing, taunting, and backslapping continued as they trundled the baggage cart out of the terminal building and across to the parking levels. The air was chilly after California and Nevada, but Corrigan had had the foresight to invest in some warm clothes before they left.

"And what possessed you to end up with the likes of him?" Mick asked Evelyn. He was a hefty and solid six-footer, with the complexion of a radish and prizefighter features. "America must be getting hard-up for men these days, since the last I heard of it."

"Ah, it's his blarney," Dermot told them. "You didn't swallow the line about his uncle owning Aer Lingus, did you?" he said to Evelyn. "There's a long line of sorry women who are after hearing that one."

"Wasn't that how he got chased out of Ireland in the first place?"

"I thought that was to do with the wealthy widow-woman that he was sponging off."

"The one with the mustache and the warts on the nose, was it?"

"Not her at all, at all. Another one."

"Well, shame on the man."

"It'll do you no good. Sure, he never knew the meaning of the word."

"My friends," Corrigan sighed, grinning.

"Well, shame on the two of you," Kathleen declared. She slipped an arm through Evelyn's. "You just stick close to me, and I'll show you who the decent people are. We do have a few left over here, you know."

"And what would you know about them?" Mick challenged. "She's away over the water and gets herself a Brit for a boyfriend, and then comes back to preach at us about decent people! Did you ever hear the like of it?"

"Don't listen to them," Kathleen advised.

"Joe didn't listen to us either, and look what happened to him," Dermot said. "He's come back a Yank. It's the end of him."

"America's great," Corrigan told them. "A great place if you want to make some money."

"Maybe so," Mick agreed cheerfully. "But Ireland's the place to spend it."

They piled into Mick's Toyota wagon, and after negotiating the succession of traffic "roundabouts" to exit the airport, they were soon heading south on the main road into the city, still wet from rain earlier that morning, and congested by slow-moving crawls of traffic interspersed with Atha Cliath's bright-green, double-decker buses. Despite the gray sky, the chill and the damp in the air, and the sooty countenances of the old buildings—after Boston, Pittsburgh, and the West Coast, Corrigan found it exhilarating to be back among the narrow streets with their lines of shopfronts and busy sidewalks. There were trees and Christmas lights in the windows, pubs carrying signs for Guinness stout and Harp lager, local branches of the Bank of Ireland and Allied Irish Banks, and the "To Let" signs had names of auctioneers, not realtors.

"You know, this old city might be showing its age and crumbling in parts, but it's nice to be back in a place that was built for people to live in, not automobiles to flow through," he remarked fondly as he took it all in. "It's a good thing that they never let too many planners loose to improve it."

"The only way you could improve this mess would be by bombing it," Mick growled as the lights turned back to red a second time without the line moving.

Evelyn had wanted to see Trinity College, where Corrigan had earned his degree. He had warned that the wrong end of an eastbound trans-Atlantic red-eye flight would not be the best time for satisfying that kind of curiosity, and by this time she was in full agreement. So they postponed that item, and instead crossed the Liffey via the East Link toll bridge in the heart of Dublin's dockland to follow the coast road to Corrigan's hometown of Dun Laoghaire.

Apparently, more people were gathering there to greet them.

"I didn't realize I was so popular," Corrigan said, permitting himself a small dash of self-flattery when he was told.

"And who said you were?" Mick challenged. "It's just a good excuse for a party. Sure, they don't even remember who you are."

Evelyn smiled to herself in the back with Kathleen. Evidently, immodesty did not sit well with the Irish.

Then came the cross-examination on Corrigan's work and what he had been doing—wearying after the journey, but to be expected. But behind the banter and lighthearted digs that never let up, Evelyn detected sincere curiosity and a genuine respect for his achievements overseas. Then it was Corrigan's turn to ask the questions, and the talk degenerated into a cataloging of names, and who was where and doing what these days, most of which meant nothing to her.

Mick, despite the wild-bachelor image that Evelyn had formed, was now married and working with the European Economic Community on economic modeling. Dermot said that the one thing he had in common with economists was that he didn't understand economics.

Kathleen was a systems analyst with British Aircraft Corporation, come back to Ireland for the holidays and the "*craic*." As far as Evelyn could make out, this was something of a catchall term for generally having a good time. Corrigan told her that along with reproduction and education, it made up most of the country's export industry.

Dermot seemed to have worked the most closely with Corrigan in former years. He was still with their former professor, Brendan Maguire, who had moved away from Dublin's urban environs to set up an EEC-funded research outpost of Trinity at what sounded like a remote spot, called Ballygarven, near Galway on the west coast.

"What's Brendan doing there?" Corrigan asked.

"What he's always been interested in: a bottom-up approach to AI," Dermot replied. "Your kind of thing, Joe. Now that he's got himself away from all the bureaucracy and the politics, he's able to do things his own way. Basically, he's defining clusters of agents as elementary software entities and letting them evolve. We call them his 'insects.'"

"A Minsky approach," Corrigan said.

"Exactly."

"I worked with Minsky for a bit while I was at MIT."

"I know. That's why I think you'd be interested. We'll have to try and get you over while you're here."

"I'll try and work it in," Corrigan promised.

"Brendan would never forgive you if he found out you were back and didn't go over there to say hello to him."

"How are you finding it over there yourself?" Corrigan asked.

"I like it."

"Isn't it a bit quiet after Dublin?"

"Ah, I've had me fill of this smelly city. Anyhow, there's good *craic* in Galway, which isn't too far. The scenery is grand, the women are fine . . . and the pints are as good as you'll find anywhere. That's the main thing."

"Now there speaks an Irishman," Corrigan pronounced.

"What's it like there?" Evelyn asked curiously.

"Ah, sure, there's nowhere to touch it," Dermot told her.

"Where is it?"

"Over on the west of Ireland," Corrigan said. "The Atlantic coast."

"The winds come in off the sea and over the cliffs as fresh as the day the world was created," Dermot went on, turning and extending an arm toward the window, as if it were all outside. "The mountains are wild and unspoiled, and the lakes as clear as pools of spring water."

"My God, he's getting lyrical," Kathleen muttered.

"Think of Yosemite—without California. And the people there, the friendliest you'll find anywhere in the world."

"Let's do go and see it," Evelyn said to Corrigan.

"We'll fit it in somehow," Corrigan promised Dermot.

"But it's so out-of-the-way," Mick said over his shoulder from the driver's seat. "What do you do when you want to go anywhere?"

"Why would I want to go anywhere?" Dermot asked him.

"You have to, sometimes. After all, you're here now, aren't you?"

"Well, I got here, didn't I? So it's obviously possible."

"I'll still take Dublin, meself," Mick declared. "Look at the bay out there, and Howth on the other side. You can't beat that."

"It's an open sewer," Dermot sneered. "Sure, you wouldn't have to be Jesus Christ to walk across to Howth. You couldn't sink through the pollution."

"Who has to walk, anyhow? We've got the DART."

"You need it. Walking would be quicker than this traffic."

"Do they argue all the time?" Evelyn asked Kathleen.

"Not all the time. When they do start really arguing, you'll know it."

In Dun Laoghaire, they followed the harborfront past stately Victorian terraces and arrived at the Royal Marine Hotel, where Corrigan and Evelyn would be staying. Immense in scale and magnificent in rendering, it was a fine example of the palatial resort hotels that had sprung up all over Europe around the middle of the nineteenth century—although since saddled with a modern extension in a clash of styles that reverberated all the way along the seafront.

They entered through an arched entrance lobby with marble columns and staircase, and went through to an enormous lounge, its walls adorned with huge, gilt-framed mirrors and paintings of sailing ships, and one side taken up by picture windows looking out over lawns with the harbor and its granite piers beyond. The place was packed with what looked like a dozen parties merging together and going on at once. People stood five deep around the paneled, L-shaped bar at the far end, and mixed groups, including children, filled the tables and milled about in the spaces between, while rosy-faced waitresses in maroon uniforms battled through it all carrying trays laden with bottles, glasses, and pints of black, creamy-headed stout. The hubbub of voices was overpowering. Through it the strains of a piano and accordion were coming from somewhere at the far end, and a circle off to one side were swaying and singing. Kathleen slipped an arm firmly through Evelyn's. "You'd better hang on to me in this," she said. "Ah yes, there's our crowd now, over that way. Let's see if we can fight our way through. . . . There's your ma, Joe—in the blue. Do you see her?"

"I do. She's looking well. Is Dad here too?"

"He should be around somewhere. Probably over at the bar."

And then it was all hugs, handshakes, and more backslapping. Corrigan's mother, Helen, turned out to be a fine-looking woman, with rich black hair showing a few gray wisps, and high-boned, distinctly Irish features. She was groomed and dressed meticulously in a dark-blue two-piece, and carried herself well, with elegance. Her reception of Evelyn was not unwarm—curious and expressing a natural interest with dark, alert eyes that missed nothing; but at the same time she was clearly maintaining a measured reserve until she got to know this new addition to the family better. But the news that Evelyn, like Joseph, was a Ph.D. impressed her. "Don't let him forget it," she advised Evelyn when they got a moment to talk between themselves. "He needs someone who's a match for him. These young flibbertigibbets that you see everywhere let the men turn them into replacements for their mothers, and it's the end of them."

Kevin, Corrigan's father, looked fit and hearty, with a square-jawed, pink-hued face, and wiry gray hair clipped straight and short. He was wearing a dark suit with vest, tie loosened and collar in disarray, liberally sated and jovial. "Well, he's taken his own sweet time about it, but he hasn't done badly," he pronounced, clamping an arm around Evelyn's waist. "What he did to deserve you is beyond me power to imagine, but there must be some sense left in him somewhere. Welcome to Ireland. And welcome to our house."

After that, Evelyn lost track of the introductions as they were shouted over the din or acknowledged with a wave from a table, over a frothing pint. There were Corrigan's two brothers and a sister, dozens—it seemed—of his old pals, friends of the family with names no sooner announced than forgotten, and innumerable cousins, uncles, in-laws, and aunts. And, of course, everyone was dying to meet the American wife.

"Carnegie Mellon, in Pittsburgh? Was Joe there? I didn't know that," a tall man in a tweed jacket said. "Did you know that Andrew Mellon was Irish-American?" Evelyn hadn't. "And so was William Penn, who founded Pennsylvania. In fact, he was native Irish—from Cork."

"The Irish seem very proud of their nationality," Evelyn remarked.

"Other people have nationalities," someone else chimed in. "The Irish and the Jews have a psychosis."

"The only thing you have to know about Irishmen is not to let them mix alcohol and politics," a chubby woman in a floral dress told Evelyn. "It's like driving. They can't handle both at the same time, you see."

"Where did ye say they're living now, over there? Pittsburgh, is it?"

"I thought a Pittsburgher was something you ate with chips at McDonald's."

Behind, Corrigan was unable to resist a little posturing as the worldly finder-of-fortune returned from afar. "Of course, I moved out of academics a while ago, now," he told a couple of men about his own age, both nursing pints of Guinness. "I'm managing a big AI project for one of the larger corporations—Pittsburgh based."

"That's nice," one of them said, staring woodenly.

"In fact, we're in the process of reorganizing for what everyone thinks will be a major breakthrough. Might well mean another promotion."

"That's nice."

Another woman said to Evelyn, "You should make money while you're young, and babies when you're older. People get themselves into such a mess trying to do it the other way round."

"I have relatives in Boston," her companion said. "We always try and get over there for Saint Patrick's Day. Americans do a much better job of organizing it. I think they understand it better than we do."

The drink and the talk flowed freely. As the mood grew mellower, Kevin Corrigan rose to propose the traditional Irish wedding toast: "May you have many children, and may they grow as mature in taste, and healthy in color, and as sought after . . ." he swayed unsteadily, almost spilling his drink, and Helen nudged him sternly, "as the contents of this glass."

"*Slainte!*" everyone chorused, and drank.

Then it was the turn of an uncle, also called Joe: "May the road rise to meet you, the wind be always at your back, the sun shine warm upon your face . . . Hell, there's more, but I forget what it is. Anyway, good luck to the pair of you. And let's be seeing more of you over here in future than you've managed so far. *Slainte.*"

"And may you be half an hour in heaven before the Devil knows you're dead," someone else threw in.

"*Slainte!*"

"May you live as long as you want," a woman sitting by Mrs. Corrigan followed, "and never want as long as you live."

And naturally, Mick couldn't be left out. "May you die in bed at the ripe old age of ninety-five," he said, raising his glass to Corrigan.

"Why, thank you, Mick."

". . . shot by a jealous husband."

By the middle of the afternoon, Evelyn could feel travel fatigue and jet lag catching up with her, on top of everything else. The room seemed to be rocking, and the faces and conversation were all smearing into a meaningless blur of sound and color. "I have to go up to the room and rest," she told Corrigan. "Can we make some excuse and get away?"

"Good idea," Corrigan mumbled—he wasn't looking especially bright-eyed and spiffy, just at that moment, himself. "There's going to be a party later, up at the house."

Evelyn shook her head dismally. "I'm not going to survive this."

"We're away," Corrigan announced to everyone. "Got to get a few hours' sleep. Have fun. We'll catch you later, okay?"

"Would you get that? He can't wait."

Ribald jeers and catcalls, mainly from the male company present.

"Tch, tch. What's the world coming to, at all?"

"Not an ounce of decency in the man."

"Will you give over?" Corrigan protested. "We've not even unpacked yet."

"Well, while you're at it you can unpack this as well." Jeff, one of the cousins, handed Corrigan a gift-wrapped box. Corrigan tore off the paper and added it to the pile of gifts and wrappings that had accumulated on the table, and opened the box. Inside was a figurine of a grinning Irish leprechaun, sporting a high hat and puffing a pipe. "To take back with ye's and remind you of us," the cousin said.

"It'll do that, all right, Jeff," Corrigan said. "Sure, it even looks like you."

"He needs a name," one of the women called out. "You have to give him a name, Joe."

Corrigan looked around him. "Ah, what else is he but a Mick, of course? We'll call him Mick."

Mick moved over and stared down approvingly at his namesake. "He looks happy enough to be a Mick," he agreed.

One of the men across the table started to sing, "When Irish eyes are smiling . . ." He looked at Corrigan and raised a hand invitingly for him to take it from there.

Corrigan couldn't. He was too exhausted, and the drink was hitting him the wrong way . . . and besides, he didn't remember the words. Then Marvin Minsky's line came to him, from the day when Corrigan and Evelyn had visited Boston. Grinning faces on every side waited for him to continue the song. He tossed up a hand, acknowledging defeat, and grinned.

"You've probably just been ripped off. . . ."

❁ CHAPTER TWENTY-ONE ❁

Corrigan sometimes said that Europeans had exported Puritanism and the work ethic to America in order to be rid of both, and then get back to the business of enjoying life. The Christmas week that followed became one long round of eating, drinking, dancing, and more drinking, that persisted through into the New Year. By custom, annual holidays east of the Atlantic tended to be generous, and most people saved a healthy portion of them for the year's end. It seemed that nobody was at work who didn't have to be, and Evelyn lost track of the homes that were visited, and the pubs and hotel lounges sampled in the annual tribal loyalty-reaffirmation rites. Like many visitors to Ireland, she had a feeling of rediscovering the basics of simple warmth and spontaneous familiarity that can be too easily forgotten when pursuit of wealth and what passes for success becomes obsessive. Even allowing that she was being a bit romantic and impractical for the modern world, she suspended her disbelief willingly and delighted in fond reconstructions of bygone times, doubtless illusory, sparkling with wisdom and elegance that had probably never existed; but, after all, wasn't this supposed to be the most romantic time of her life?

What marred it a little was Corrigan saying scoffingly that she sounded like a tourist. For him this was just a break. He was becoming impatient to get back to the arena. Americans, it was often said—especially those with Irish roots that were imaginary—could be more Irish than the Irish. It was sometimes true the other way around, too. Mick was not a lot of help in sustaining her romantic images of unsullied Irish charm and simplicity, either.

One evening in one of the seafront hotels, the customers sitting around the lounge began taking it in turns to sing solo. Every one of them seemed to have a party piece, which the rest would listen to appreciatively and applaud loudly—a far cry from dingy downtown bars where people went to get drunk, laid, or lost in anonymity. At one point, Evelyn felt her eyes misting as she listened to a wistful, soaring tenor voice evoking visions of homey farm cottages and green hillsides swept with rain.

"Can everyone over here sing?" she whispered, leaning across to Corrigan and Mick.

"Ah, it's the drink that does it. He'll be croaking like a rusty gate by morning," Mick told her, ruining the whole effect.

"Most of those songs were written by people who'd been away from Ireland so long that they forgot what it was like," Corrigan said.

"Or never been there, more like," Mick agreed.

"Six months over here, and you'd be writing the same about Pittsburgh," Corrigan told Evelyn.

They did visit Trinity College, finally, with its stiffly aristocratic frontages of gray, columned stone, staring down over an inner maze of interlocking lawns and cobbled courts. Evelyn was fascinated by the famous Long Room chamber of the Old Library, built in 1724, with its wood paneling, carvings, and gallery, containing hundreds of thousands of volumes going back to medieval times and before. Jonathan Swift, Oliver Goldsmith, George Berkeley, and Oscar Wilde had been students here, and again, walking among the ceiling-high shelves of cracked leather bindings and yellowing folios, Evelyn found herself reliving images of a time of tastes and sensitivities that had passed—even with the brash intrusion of a gaudily modern gift-and-souvenir shop, underneath on the ground floor.

They shopped in O'Connell Street, had lunch in the open, airy environment—with the sun actually putting in an appearance that day, reassuring the faithful of its existence—of the glass-enclosed mall by Stephen's Green. They saw Georgian squares and walked over the bridges along the Liffey, jostled through street markets, and took the tour of the Guinness brewery.

And, partly as an aid to working off the effects of a week's overindulging, they joined the crowd of afternoon strollers walking the best part of a mile out to the lighthouse at the end of Dun Laoghaire pier. The weather that day—Mick said that four seasons a day was the norm in Ireland—was fine and dry, the wind brisk, the sea air bracing.

"I think it's wonderful," Evelyn said to Corrigan and Mick. "All these people out walking just for the pleasure of it. It's more the way things should be. Back home legs are getting to be for emergencies only."

"Have you seen what the price of gas is here?" Corrigan snorted.

Back at the house, Helen Corrigan showed her the traditional way of making tea, in a pot. "I don't care what those two say," Evelyn declared as they set out cups, saucers, sugar, and milk on a tray in the kitchen. "I think they do it to twig me. It's a side of the humor that I haven't really figured out yet. But people here still have a charm that you don't find in many places around the world these days."

"Ah yes, it's the charm of them that you have to watch," Helen replied, smiling faintly as she cut slices of still-unfinished Christmas cake.

"How's that?"

"People will behave as outrageously as the world will let them. And charm is how they extend the limits. Joe can be one of the worst. But it's not a lot of good telling you that now, I suppose."

Finally, Corrigan and Evelyn said their goodbyes and au revoirs to a final gathering of relatives and friends, and loaded their bags into Dermot's eighties-vintage Rover. Then they left Dun Laoghaire to drive across to Galway on the west coast of Ireland, where, as hoped, Dermot had arranged for them to visit Corrigan's former professor, Brendan Maguire, at Ballygarven before their return to the States.

❁ CHAPTER TWENTY-TWO ❁

More rooms with fluorescent lights and pastel walls, racks of electronics, glowing computer screens. Not rooms formed of movable partition-walls and ceiling tiles, but solidly built from stone, with mullioned bay windows, modernized to a laboratory environment. Maguire had installed his research outpost of Trinity in a large old house a little above the town itself, known locally as "The Rectory."

Maguire himself was a short, rounding, Pickwickian figure with a crescent of ragged white hair fringing a balding head that had taken on the same, post-holidays, pinkish hue as his face. He had a pair of ferocious white eyebrows, and rimless spectacles that tended to sit halfway down a bulbous, purple-veined nose. He was wearing a crumpled tweed jacket of brown-and-tan check with a woven tie, plaid shirt, and baggy gray flannel trousers with turnups that hadn't been in style in fifteen years. From appearances, Evelyn would have dismissed him as a bumbling rural schoolteacher. Corrigan told her not to be deceived: it was Maguire's insistence on accurate thinking and old-fashioned rigor that Corrigan had to thank for his later successes in the States.

There was little here in the way of visually entertaining demonstrations. Maguire showed them screens of symbolic diagrams representing abstract software relationships, and charts that tracked growth and decay trends in mixed populations of numerically defined entities that he referred to as "species." The term was no misnomer. The aim of the research that Maguire and his team were engaged in was, in effect, to induce the emergence of intelligent behavior from neural-system analogs.

". . . assuming that anything that has appeared in the natural world so far can be called intelligent," Maguire said. "The notion shouldn't be so strange to you, Joe. We talked about it often enough."

"We did, that."

Dermot elaborated for Evelyn's benefit. "The idea, essentially, is to let a computer-intelligence follow the same route as we did and evolve from simple beginnings—instead of trying to reproduce in one step all the complexity that resulted from a billion years of selection and improvement."

"I've never believed that was practical, as I'm sure Joe will have told you," Maguire said to Evelyn.

She smiled. "At least a thousand times, at the last count. Top-down won't work, right?"

"That's right. We simply don't have the detailed knowledge to specify it," Maguire said. "Nobody has."

"So how far back did you go to begin?" Corrigan asked him, intrigued.

"The groupings that I showed you a few minutes ago approximate roughly to early molecular structures," Maguire replied. "We put a seed population into a simple world in large numbers and let them interact and compete. They've been running for the equivalent of several million years now, I'd say."

"And the species you have now are performing at about the level of insects?"

"Roughly, we think. The dynamics are completely different from biological competition. Making a direct comparison isn't easy."

"Pretty impressive, all the same," Corrigan commented.

"We do have the benefit of being able to guide things by conscious direction," Maguire pointed out. "We are able to introduce deliberately engineered genetic combinations when we see fit. That speeds up the process considerably. It's amazing the difference it makes when God goes into the stock-breeding business."

"It's fascinating, all right," Corrigan agreed. There was an odd light in his eyes. Listening to Maguire and Dermot had rekindled all kinds of enthusiasms from years that he had almost forgotten. He could feel the excitement of real science stirring again: knowledge pursued purely for the sake of knowledge.

"But we need a more realistic simulation of the physical environment if progress is to be sustained," Maguire went on. "One that will react back on the actions of the population more strongly and drive the selection mechanisms harder. It needs to close the overall organism-environment feedback loop more tightly."

"This is interesting. . . ." Corrigan's face took on a faraway look for a moment. "Kind of ironic."

Maguire looked at the others uncertainly. "What is he talking about?"

"The work that we're doing back at CLC right now," Evelyn answered. "On the face of it, it sounds as if it might be an answer to just the kind of problem you're talking about."

"Is that so?" Dermot said.

"In that case, you should stop messing around among those Americans, trying to act as if you were a millionaire or a celebrity or something, and get yourself back over here and help out," Maguire told Corrigan—but he wasn't being serious.

"No chance," Dermot declared. "He's been too seduced by now by thoughts of money and promotion in those big corporations over there."

Maguire snorted. "Well, don't let yourself be carried away by it all," he said to Corrigan. "Remember that the higher a monkey climbs, the more of an arse it looks."

Corrigan grinned. "Okay. But I will make sure you get all the information we can let you have that might help," he offered.

"That would be something we'd appreciate," Maguire said.

For lunch they drove down to the Cobh Hotel in the center of the town, which was where Corrigan and Evelyn were staying. Ballygarven was a small boating resort grown from a fishing village that stood at the head of an inlet where the sea twisted its way among rocky headlands and shingle beaches. Behind the town, heather-covered slopes and marshlands rose toward a ridge of granite-topped summits a mile or two away. Evelyn was doubly glad that she and Corrigan had decided to make this trip to the west of Ireland before they left. It was just as she had pictured, ever since Dermot began describing it soon after their arrival.

Food was served in the bar, which though modernized had not lost its old-world feel. Maguire steered Evelyn and Dermot to one side where there stood a table for hot food and another for salads, recommending the mussels and the lamb. Meanwhile, Corrigan went to the bar to take care of the drinks. He and Evelyn had checked in the evening before, and he already knew Rooney, the bartender. Several of the locals were in, taking a midday refreshment.

"Oh, the American's back, I see," Rooney said, taunting Corrigan good-humoredly. "Coca-Cola, is it? Or do I have to start mixin' some o' them fancy cocktails for ye?"

"Three pints, and enough of your lip, Rooney. And a glass of lager-and-lime for the lady, if you please."

"Are ye's back to see some decent scenery? Sure, don't the mountains way up above look green and fresh in the sunshine this mornin', after the rain?"

Corrigan looked pained. "What mountains are you talking about, Rooney? You don't call those humps out there mountains, do you? I'll tell you, we were in the Sierra Nevada in California just before the holidays, and there's real mountains for you. They've got one cliff called El Capitan, in the Yosemite Valley, that goes practically a mile straight up."

"Is that a fact?" Rooney said, putting a glass under one of the pumps. "And what would be the use of things as big as that to anyone at all? Our Irish mountains have got a top and a bottom to them, and that's all that matters. Why waste so much on all that useless middle? If you stand a little bit nearer they look the same anyway. But you don't have to spend half your life getting up, and then back down again." Rooney looked at the regulars in appeal. "Isn't that right, now?"

"It's fine by me," one of them agreed. "I'd never be seen dead on the top of either one of them anyway."

"You see, I was right. It's after turning into a Yank, you are. Everything has to be biggest, and that's all that matters. Never a thought for the quality of things."

"And when were you last there, Rooney?" Corrigan challenged.

"Oh, you'd be surprised if I told you, wouldn't you?"

"Go on, then. Surprise me."

Rooney set a foaming pint down on the countertop for the head to settle, and began pouring another. "Oh, I know all about the high life and such, as you might call it," he said airily. "I'm what you might call something of a self-unmade man."

"Oh? A self-unmade man, is it?" one of the locals said.

"And what might that be?" another asked.

"I started out, long ago in me dim and distant youth, as the president of a big corporation, making half a million dollars a year," Rooney said. "But would you believe, I *needed* every blessed penny of it. There was the yacht to take care of, the private jet plane, and the mortgage on the mansion. All them social clubs and country clubs and golfing clubs, with their dues. . . . And you wouldn't want to hear about the kind of wife I had to put up with, and her tastes."

"Would ye listen to the man?"

"Okay. And? . . ." Corrigan said, smiling.

Rooney went on, "But I worked hard and assiduously, and by the time I was twenty-five I'd come down to regional manager. Got rid of the house for something smaller, the car for something slower, the wife for someone saner, and I found I could manage on two hundred thousand a year. So I paid off the debts, kept at it, and I was down to a branch manager by thirty, ordinary salesman by thirty-four, and I quit the salaried professions altogether before I was forty."

"Now there's a success story for you," one of the regulars murmured approvingly.

"It's different. I'll give you that," his companion agreed.

Rooney nodded. "By then I didn't need a salary anymore. Today, I don't owe anybody anything, and this job pays me all I need. It's only four shifts a week, and I get plenty of time to read the books I always wanted to, sit in the sun when it suits me, and go fishing with the kids." He thought for a moment, then shrugged. "To tell you the truth, I probably don't need the money that much at all, for we've a small farm that could get us by. But I keep it for the people that you meet."

Evelyn and the others had come over and were listening. "Another philosopher," she said to Corrigan. "You know, Joe, this is the kind of place that Eric should be in."

"Who's Eric?" Maguire asked.

"A scientist that we know back at CLC," Corrigan said.

"He'd fit in here," Evelyn said. "You're his kind of people. You talk his values. Corporate politics isn't his scene."

Maguire nodded and pulled a face. "Well, if he ever decides he's had enough, tell him to get in touch. We'll talk to him, sure enough. We've got some good people here, including some from Europe, but we could always use more. . . . And that applies to you, too, Joe, don't forget. If you get tired of being among those neurotics over there, we'll find room for you."

Corrigan laughed and raised his pint. "I think I can handle whatever comes up, Brendan. But thanks anyway."

The next day, Dermot drove Corrigan and Evelyn south to Shannon, where they boarded an Aer Lingus jet for New York. It had been fun, and it had been interesting—the kind of break they had intended. And in another way, a lot that they had not intended. But now it was time to get back to the real world. They had a big surprise to tell everybody.

❂ CHAPTER TWENTY-THREE ❂

Jonathan Wilbur was in the Galahad Lounge again, sitting at the bar. It was early yet, with a few people at the other barstools and a group from a company marketing conference that was being held at the Camelot that week occupying some tables on the far side.

"How are things working out with Oliver?" Corrigan inquired casually.

"Oh, okay," Wilbur replied neutrally, and returned to playing with his portable electronic office. Corrigan sauntered back to the other end of the bar and checked the pressure in the dispenser. Wilbur looked up at him oddly from time to time but said nothing. Corrigan got the feeling that his behavior of late had been puzzling the system.

In the commercial showing on the TV, the couple who had arrived for dinner were healthily image-conscious, he in a satin-edged cloak and wearing a wig of constantly color-changing optical fibers, she in a *Psi-Woman* meditation jumpsuit, complete with requisite combination shoulder-purse and music/mantra player.

"Wasn't she the clairvoyant in that movie about the surgeon who put his wife's lover's brain inside the gorilla after they had the car crash?" a fat woman in a pink sombrero, sitting on another stool, asked the man with her while she stared absently at the screen and pushed pretzels into her mouth.

"Yeah. She showed the detective where the body was." The man

585

was wearing a short, embroidered cloak and matador's black hat. It was South of the Border week. Anyone in Mexican garb got a ten-percent discount in most places.

On the screen, the two guests were sipping before-dinner cocktails. Suddenly the woman nudged her husband and pointed to a faint finger-smudge on her glass. "*Body grease!*" she whispered behind her hand. The husband hurriedly put down his own glass, at the same time glancing apprehensively from side to side at the cutlery and the china. Moments later, the scene ended with a shot of the couple departing on a pretext, and then the embarrassed host consoling his distraught wife.

"She can really do it," the woman in the sombrero said.

"Huh?" her companion said.

"In real life—she's really psychic."

"Oh."

"The police use her. A documentary last week had her in it, so it must be true." The woman looked at Corrigan for support. "She can find missing stuff by looking at pictures that they take from choppers over the city."

"That's nice," Corrigan said.

While on the TV, the hostess's wise and worldly mother was educating her daughter in the use of "Bodysafe." After spraying fingertips and palms, they embarked on a tour of the house together, rapturously drenching drawer handles, doorknobs, light switches, phone buttons, toilet seats, and anything else carrying the risk of indirect contact with another human being. The ad ended with the husband and wife again, this time waving goodbye to their guests after a brilliantly successful dinner party, and then flinging their arms around each other ecstatically—presumably after taking appropriate precautions with Bodysafe.

"You know, Joe, I think you've been holding out on me," Wilbur said at last.

Corrigan ambled back to that end of the bar. "Oh? Why would that be, now?"

"I think you saw some things coming that I didn't see, and you didn't tell me."

"Is that a fact?"

"About Oliver," Wilbur said. So, apparently, things weren't going so well. "What makes people so greedy? I mean, not only in business, but all these people that we read about. How do they get like it?"

"People will continue trying to get better at whatever others continue to admire," Corrigan answered.

"Aren't there any people of principle out there anymore?" Wilbur grumbled.

"Probably. But who's interested in principles? What gets you elected is where you stand on issues. And that's a shame, because issues change but principles don't. When you know a man's character, you know where he'll stand on any issue."

Already, as a now-cognizant observer inside the experiment, Corrigan was gaining some invaluable insights on how the system was evolving. This was the way they should have done it from the beginning—with the surrogates fully aware of what was going on. It was what he himself had always advocated in the endless debates on the subject. He didn't know how the decision had come about to go ahead with it—once it was decided upon, keeping the fact secret from the surrogates would be essential. The idea of it had been to guarantee that the surrogates' behavior would be as authentic as possible. But now he was surer than ever that it had been the wrong way to go. Knowing what was going on, he could steer the system into grappling with concepts of real substance for a change, and hence into showing the beginnings of emulating real, thinking beings—which had been the whole idea. Left to freewheel in its own direction for years, it had been industriously populating its world with morons.

Wilbur propped his chin on a hand and stared across the bar exasperatedly. "Joe, why are you a bartender?"

"To get the money to pay the rent."

"No, I mean why don't *you* run for office or something?"

"I don't have the necessary lack of qualifications." Corrigan gestured to indicate the far side of the lounge. A manager from the Krunchy Kandy Corporation, which was the company staging its marketing conference at the hotel that week, was leading a mixed group of employees, all dressed similarly to himself in the pink-and-gold tunic and red frilled cap of the Krunchy Kitten, through a rendering in unison of the company's new TV jingle. "Anyway, who on earth would vote for me?"

The phone behind the bar rang. Corrigan picked it up. "Hello, Galahad Lounge. This is Joe."

"There's an outside call for you," the hotel operator's voice said.

"Thanks."

"Go ahead, caller."

"Joe Corrigan here."

"Ah, hello, Mr. Corrigan," a firm, genial voice—but at the same time, one carrying an unmistakable undertone of curiosity—replied. "This is Dr. Zehl speaking. I got a message saying that you wanted to get in touch with me."

The announcement came so unexpectedly that it took Corrigan several seconds to collect his thoughts. "Where are you calling from?" he asked.

"Does it make any difference?" Zehl—whoever he really was— had to be neurally coupled into the system again. If he were speaking via a direct channel from the outside, the mismatch in time rates would have made communication impossible.

The bar was an awkward place to have to take the call, but nobody was paying Corrigan any attention. He kept his voice low and faced away from the room, into a corner.

"Are we on monitor bypass?"

"Yes." The question would have confirmed what Zehl suspected—that Corrigan knew the situation. Zehl's reply meant that although the conversation was being handled by the system, its content was not being made available to the context analyzers. In other words, the line was not being tapped.

"So you know the score," Corrigan said. "Okay, I know what it's all about. Oz is running. We're still in it. You're one of the outside controllers."

"I see." Zehl's tone was wary, waiting to see what line Corrigan would take.

"Has anyone else in here figured it?" Corrigan asked.

"You're the first that we know of, so far."

"It's gone way past anything that was planned. I don't know how it got to be taken this far, but the results are amazing."

There was a pause, as if this was not the kind of reaction that Zehl had been expecting. "You're . . . satisfied, then?" he said finally.

"Yes, for the most part," Corrigan replied. "The memory-suppression took some figuring out at first, but I'm better off without it."

"How do you mean?"

"It works better this way. I can do a lot more on the inside, now that I know what's what. We should have set it up this way to begin with."

"Okay." There was an edge of relief in Zehl's voice. "So it seems to be working out."

"There might be a problem. One of the other surrogates has cottoned on to what's happening too. The trouble is, she doesn't know so much of the background, and she was pretty mad about the whole situation when I talked to her. I'm worried about what she might do."

"Why not talk to her? Tell her whatever she needs to know. It can't make a lot of difference now."

"That's what I want to do. The trouble is, I can't locate her. What I need you people out there to do for me is . . ." Corrigan's voice trailed off as he caught sight of the tall, dark-haired figure in a long coat, just coming into the lounge. He nodded a quick acknowledgment as he caught her eye, and turned his face back to the phone. "It's okay. You don't have to bother. I'll call you back later. Guess what. She just walked in the door."

◎ CHAPTER TWENTY-FOUR ◎

"I understand that congratulations are in order," Jason Pinder said from behind the desk in his office in the Executive Building. It was a meticulously neat office, with everything arranged logically and every need anticipated. "You never cease to surprise us, Joe. Well, give my best wishes to Ms. Vance. . . . No, that's wrong, isn't it. It's Ms. Corrigan now. Anyway, I hope you'll both have a fine future."

"Thanks," Corrigan said from the chair opposite. It was his first morning back. The summons to Pinder's office had come minutes after he appeared in the lab. Corrigan didn't believe it was just so that Pinder could be the first to offer his best wishes.

Pinder stroked his mustache with a knuckle and regarded Corrigan pensively for a moment before continuing. "I wouldn't want to spoil the romance of a time like this, but your going off without a word like that made it impossible for us to let you know what was happening. Nobody knew where you were."

Corrigan was far from sure that anyone from management had been trying to find out. Certainly, Corrigan's secretary, Judy Klein, had said nothing about being asked in the few minutes that Corrigan had had to talk with her before being called over to see Pinder. He knew that Shipley had been trying to get in touch with him before he and Evelyn left California for Ireland, but that was a different matter. Since Shipley was not expected in until the afternoon, Corrigan still didn't know what that had been about.

Pinder went on. "As you know, the whole DNC program has been the subject of top-level discussions in the company for some time now. While you were away, I was notified of certain decisions that have been made concerning revisions to our goals, and the organizational adjustments that will be needed to accomplish them."

Only then did the premonition hit Corrigan that a pie was about to hit him in the face. In the same instant, the certainty crystallized that this wasn't something that had suddenly happened in the last few weeks. He waited, saying nothing. Pinder continued:

"The change that will have the most impact as far as you're concerned, Joe, has to do with our reviews of the state of the art and the future developments that now seem likely in various fields. To put it bluntly, VIV technology is obsolete—or at least, on its way toward very soon becoming so. EVIE really can't be justified any longer as the company's main VR line. Going through the primary sensory system for vision and acoustics is a dead end. All the market indicators are for taking everything over to direct neural sooner rather than later." He showed his palms, then sat back, watching Corrigan with his marbly gray eyes to await his reaction.

It was one of the occasions when the normally smooth-working pieces of Corrigan's mind grated and jammed. First, after the success with Pinocchio One, Pinocchio Two had been enthusiastically pushed as the next logical step: extension of the existing system into the pons, in preparation for going further to the thalamus and hence being able to add DNC vision and acoustic. Then SDC had come along, offering a quicker fix through a hybrid approach using VIV technology, and that had become the mainline thrust in the form of EVIE, with P-Two relegated to longer-term, secondary status. But now, suddenly, EVIE was obsolete. What did it mean? Were the original priorities being reinstated?

"*Everything,* via direct neural?" Corrigan repeated. "That's what Evelyn's work is aimed at. So what are you saying? P-Two is on track again, after all?"

Pinder shook his head. "Fooling around at the pons—it's still years away from going to vision."

"What, then?"

"We can DNC to the thalamus right now. Scrub P-Two. Forget messing around with hybrids. Full DNC with vision in under a year."

"How?" Corrigan asked, nonplussed. This was obviously the whole point that Pinder had been leading up to.

Pinder sat forward to rest his arms on the desk, fixing Corrigan with a direct stare. He held a breath for a second or two, then exhaled heavily. "Frank Tyron has drawn our attention to some recently declassified work that has been going on in SDC for some time, which changes the picture considerably. Basically, they already have a working method that couples to synapses in the thalamus. It's called DIVAC: DIrect Vision and ACoustics. He's put a proposal to the Board for going straight to a combined Pinocchio/DIVAC system now, rather than Pinocchio combined with VIV, and shooting for a full direct-neural system in half to a quarter of the time you're talking about. The Board's reaction is extremely favorable. Ken Endelmyer's with it all the way."

Pinder sighed and made an open-handed gesture that seemed meant to indicate that it was all as much a surprise to him as to Corrigan. But Corrigan didn't believe it. This kind of thing was not hatched overnight, without the involvement of somebody in Pinder's position. Shipley, he remembered, had seen something like this coming. At his house, Shipley had voiced his suspicion that EVIE was falling into disfavor, and putting Corrigan in charge of it was not necessarily to his advantage. Meanwhile, Tyron had been talking directly to the Board. The straws that Shipley had glimpsed had been in the wind for months.

Suddenly, a lot of things came back to Corrigan that he should have seen the significance of immediately, long ago. Hans Groener, in California, had talked about thalamus-level research going on there, and had mentioned the Air Force's involvement. But Corrigan had been so immersed in his own, self-centered universe that it had barely registered.

"So . . ." Corrigan waved a hand meaninglessly while he struggled to collect his thoughts. "What about Evelyn and the pons interface that she's working on? We brought her in with the aim of eventually setting up a neurophysiology group. What happens to that?"

Pinder nodded sympathetically. "I hear what you're saying, Joe.

But the corporation has to take account of developments in other parts of the world. Not all of anyone's plans always work out as hoped. The decision is made: further major funding, either for EVIE or for further pons work, is out. But we would be prepared to keep it going in a low-key mode in case the DIVAC-based approach runs into snags—if that's something you'd be interested in doing." It didn't need Pinder's tone to convey that it equated to consignment to oblivion. Corrigan's expression said that he would not be interested. "Alternatively," Pinder said, coming to what was effectively the only option, "you could move into the mainline operation."

Just for a second, Corrigan had thought Pinder was about to offer him the job of heading it, but his use of the word "into" promptly scotched that.

"Naturally, positions will be available for you—yourself and Evelyn," Pinder said.

Corrigan swallowed dryly. His gut-feel already told him what the answer to the only outstanding question had to be, but there was no way around it.

"Who'll be running this operation?" he asked.

At least Pinder had the decency not to try to pretend that he hadn't been expecting it. It was, after all, as Corrigan could see by now, the whole point of the interview.

"Frank Tyron originated the proposal," he reminded Corrigan. "His contacts and experience are right for this kind of work. And the Board were very insistent that a program that will involve a lot of coordination outside of CLC, and especially liaison with government departments, requires someone with his kind of background. I'm sorry, Joe. I know you've done some good work, but that's the way it is." He placed his hands palms-down on the desk and concluded briskly, before Corrigan could react, "The project will be designated COmbined Sensory and MOtor Stimulation: COSMOS. We're at the beginning of a new year, and we want to get as much mileage out of that as possible. I'd like the current projects tidied up and loose ends cleared by the end of the week. There will be a meeting next Monday to brief everyone on the goals and tentative organizational structure for the new program."

Even with it spelled out like that, Corrigan couldn't bring himself to capitulating ignominiously to instant acceptance. "I'll have to think it over," he replied, too numbed for the moment to be capable of responding more effectively.

Pinder nodded. "I understand. Tomorrow morning will be fine."

Corrigan left in a daze shortly after. He didn't feel like a person at all, but more a financial statistic or a function in an organization chart, whose feelings and self-esteem faceless people in five-hundred-dollar suits and limousines could trample on at will. The indignation came later.

"Christ, Eric, they're just sweeping the two of us aside, putting us under this outsider that we don't even know." Corrigan turned and flung his hands out appealingly to Shipley, who was watching from a stool at a bench in the DINS lab. Evelyn sat listening from a paper-strewn desk to one side. "I mean, if we'd nothing of any note to show after these years, I could understand it. But there wouldn't be any plans for them to be making, without us. . . . You and I, we *made* this project. It's ours. They can't just hand it over like this."

"A lot of things have been going on that we don't know about," Shipley said. "Things that go back to before Tyron even joined the company."

"Oh? Like what?"

"I'd bet that Tyron had a lot to do with that information at SDC not being made public. He had some kind of deal worked out before he left the SDC—that he'd bring it with him into an area where it can be exploited commercially. Some people are going to make a lot of money out of this, Joe. But it won't be us."

It took a moment for Corrigan to see fully what Shipley was saying. "Surely not," he protested.

Shipley shrugged. "Why do you say that? It wouldn't exactly be the first time something like that has happened. As a matter of fact, I did some quiet checking on the side while you and Evelyn were away. There are no licenses payable for using the VIV technology that was pioneered at SDC, and I'm pretty sure the same is true for DIVAC. That means that the information can be used freely by anyone now, without restrictions. So Tyron can bring his know-how into CLC and earn himself a lot of gratitude. That's what it's all about."

Evelyn sat back in her chair. "What can you do?" she said. "I guess we're just a different kind of people. That's the way things have always been with half the world. Probably they always will."

Corrigan snorted. "Are you saying we should lie back and enjoy it? Well, you can if you want. But I'll be hanged if I will."

"What do you propose?" Shipley asked, not bothering to disguise his skepticism.

Corrigan turned away and banged the side of a steel electronics cubicle with the flat of his hand. "Right now, Eric, I don't know," he muttered. "But dammit, I'll think of something."

The den of Evelyn's apartment at Aspinall was darkened, lit only by the green-shaded lamp on the desk. Corrigan stood by the window, brooding to himself as he stared out at the lights of the city. So what, exactly, was Tyron proposing to deliver that was generating so much excitement and attention? he asked himself. Functionally it would still be EVIE. For anyone using the system, the fact that a different behind-the-scenes technology was supporting the vision and acoustics would make only a marginal difference. It was still what Victor Borth had called a "toy": something that played at imitating the world. That would be of interest to some enterprises, and no doubt Tyron and whoever he was in league with had identified some potential—possibly some quite substantial potential. But Corrigan knew that what the people with the *real* money wanted was something else. Okay, he thought to himself, so those were the rules, were they?

"Joe, are you coming to bed?" Evelyn's voice said from the doorway behind him.

"Not really sleepy."

"It wasn't really sleep that I was thinking about."

He turned and smiled tiredly in the light at the window. "I have to say my prayers first. You know how the Irish are."

She came in and moved close to him. He slipped an arm around her. "Still letting it eat away at you?" she said.

"Oh . . . just thinking."

"You can't change anything. Start thinking about moving to another job if it'll help. We'll manage."

"Just walk away? Wouldn't some people like that!"

"I know that the Irish are fighters, too. But you can't fight this."

"Well, maybe you're being just a little bit too quick on handing down that verdict."

She turned her head and looked at him uncertainly. "Why? What have you got in mind?"

He thought for a second, then said, "Let me check on a few things first, before I start going into it. Okay?"

"If you say so."

He squeezed her waist and patted her behind through her robe. "Go and get warm, then. I'll be through in a minute."

"Hurry up," she whispered, kissing him on the cheek, and left the room.

It would still be before eleven in California. Corrigan went over to sit down at the desk and called Hans Groener's personal record onto the terminal's screen. He selected the phone number and pressed a key to initiate auto-call. Moments later, Hans's features greeted him. They talked for most of the next hour about thalamus-level interfacing. The next morning, Corrigan extended his leave by a few days and caught a noon flight to San Francisco. He and Hans spent the rest of the afternoon talking in Hans's lab at Stanford, and afterward into the early hours at Hans's apartment, going through research notes and generating reams of charts and diagrams.

On returning to Pittsburgh, Corrigan went straight over to see Jason Pinder.

⊚ CHAPTER TWENTY-FIVE ⊚

Corrigan's manner had changed since his last interview with Pinder. Although it had never come close to anything that could be called servile, common sense had always caused him to hold his opinions unless they were asked for, and then to couch them with a restraint appropriate to Pinder's position. Now, however, the words poured forth as from an inspired evangelist. Pinder, aware that Corrigan was neither naive nor new to the business, listened with intrigued curiosity.

"Before the company leaps into putting up a lot of money and committing itself for years ahead, it ought to ask one last time what it stands to get in return for the investment," Corrigan said. "When you sit down and analyze it, all that COSMOS is really promising is a more sophisticated version of what we've already got in the lab down there: a full-sensory interface. The only difference is that EVIE uses VIV for its vision and voice, whereas COSMOS will shift everything to the thalamus. But essentially it's still the same thing. And that same thing is what the people from Feller and Faber told us they didn't want—what Borth described as a 'toy.' What they do want, and what there's still a huge market for out there if someone can come up with a way to achieve it, the thing that the industry has been after for decades, is *true AI*." Corrigan drew a long breath as he came to the point that he was preparing to stake his future on. "Well, I think that I can deliver it."

They both knew enough of what Corrigan was talking about to make questions unnecessary. All he needed was a cue. Pinder nodded. "Go on, Joe. How?"

Corrigan moistened his lips. "The top-down, analytical approach doesn't work. Everyone in the field agrees. The only way it's going to happen is by getting some kind of initially simple system to evolve."

"Which has been tried in enough places too," Pinder observed. "And the results have all been equally modest, to say the least."

"Agreed. But they've all been tries at equipping computers with sensory apparatuses like TV cameras, arms, legs, and wheels, and letting them loose to explore some kind of environment. But you don't realize how good biological nervous systems are until you try copying them. They were shaped by a billion years of evolution to interact with the real world. Computers weren't."

Which exhausted what everyone in the trade knew were the two acknowledged theoretical approaches. "So are you saying you know another way?" Pinder asked.

"Yes, I think so."

"What?"

"Computers do interact extremely well with their own, internal worlds. . . . So what you do is, invert the conventional approach." Corrigan spread his hands. "If training a machine intelligence in our world isn't effective, let's try doing it the other way around: by going into its world and doing it there."

Pinder frowned. "Sorry, I'm not quite with you, Joe. Doing what, exactly? Where?"

"People interfacing via EVIE interact with a machine-created version of the real world through the surrogates that they control. But the machine could also put pseudopeople of its own in there too—'animations.' You design the system to be goal-directed to make the behavior of its animations converge to that of the real-people surrogates."

Pinder sat back, seeing the implication at once and staring at Corrigan thoughtfully. "So its success would be measured through a kind of Turing test," he said.

"Yes, exactly."

"This is certainly a new one on me, Joe. I've never heard the like of it."

"What do you think?"

"It's intriguing."

Corrigan could see that he was making an impression and pursued his point further. "The system wouldn't need to know *why* the individuals that it was trying to imitate were doing whatever they did. Its brief would be simply to make its animations behave similarly, which it could accomplish from external observables. And that's what's different about this approach. In the past, we've always tried to press into service existing processing methods and associative structures—tools that were developed for other purposes. Well, very possibly they're inherently unsuitable for this kind of job and can never work. But the way I'm talking about, the system will be free to create its own organization of associations and linkages in a way that's appropriate to its goals."

"Information-processing architecture is appropriate to what information-processing systems do. Whatever it is that has evolved inside cerebral cortexes is appropriate to what cerebral cortexes do," Pinder summarized.

"That's it. And we don't need to know in advance what the final organization will be, any more than the first protoplasm needed to know the wiring for a mammalian brain. The system would learn the way children do: by trying to imitate 'adults' who already understand the way the world works, and making its own connections and associations accordingly.

"And we've got all the pieces needed to do it. Pinocchio provides the basics of a suitable vehicle for driving both the surrogates and the animations. EVIE, with the all-neural package that we're talking about for COSMOS, gives us a mechanism for coupling in the surrogates. A multitasking expansion of Jenny Leddell's Perseus system from MIT could drive the animations."

Corrigan judged this a good place to stop at for a response, and waited. Pinder stroked his chin and stared down at the desk. What Corrigan was proposing was clear enough. He was searching for the flaws. Finally he looked up.

"A world to support that kind of evolution needs to be context-rich," he said, meaning the degree of detail and its variability that the system would have to support. "The look-ahead for sudden context changes and recomputing SDVs still hasn't been solved satisfactorily. And it would get a hell of a lot worse with this."

It was an objection that Corrigan had expected. Now he could offer a radical departure from anything that had been considered so far. "COSMOS only gives us a bit sooner what EVIE would have led to anyway, eventually," he said again. "But why get involved with the primary sensory system at all? If we are set on going straight to the thalamus, we can take advantage of new effects that operate beyond that level, that will crack that whole set of problems."

Pinder looked surprised. "Effects? What effects are you talking about?" he asked.

"When I was in California last month, it wasn't just for a romantic interlude and to get married," Corrigan replied. "I also wanted to update myself on some work going on out there that I'd been following." Not quite true, but it sounded better that way. "A group at Stanford is deep-coupling to the thalamus too. One of the people involved is called Hans Groener—I worked with him at MIT. His particular angle is dream research."

"So how does it affect us?"

"Input compression. One of the things they've learned to do is to use a high-level code to activate percepts already stored in the nervous system. I think it could solve the details problem."

"Dreams?" Pinder repeated. He thought about it and frowned. "But wouldn't that make it all subjective? Everyone would experience their own world."

"To some degree, maybe. But apparently there's a commonality to the coding that has surprised everyone. So, yes, in a sense the participants would be experiencing what's partly an induced dream; but—down to any level of detail likely to matter, anyway—the same dream. So the contextual environment would be much richer than anything we've' ever contemplated before—and getting better all the time. The environment and the animations would stimulate each other into coevolving: one of the most powerful evolutionary mechanisms there is."

Pinder looked as if he wanted to believe it. But there was one more reality to be faced. "Children need years to grow up," he pointed out. "We don't have years. What prompted the decision to go for COSMOS was that it gives us something to go for now."

And that was that last thing that Corrigan had been waiting for. He nodded. "Yes, I know. And that's where the other interesting thing that Hans's people have stumbled on comes in. You know how it is when you dream—sometimes you find that what seemed to last hours all took place in a few seconds while you were waking up? Well, it seems that the effect can be achieved artificially when you go in above the primary sensory level."

"Artificially?" Pinder's eyebrows shot upward. "What are you saying? That it's possible to accelerate interaction rates?"

Corrigan nodded. "Exactly that. Time in the simulated world could run faster. So you wouldn't have to wait years for your child to grow up."

"What kind of an acceleration are we talking about?" Pinder asked, now definitely interested.

"Somewhere in the hundreds, probably. That means that the equivalent of years of growing up would take a few weeks of machine time." Corrigan sat back and extended a hand, palm upward, like someone offering the world. "There it is—all the ingredients for a true AI. And you could have it in as much time as we're talking about now for COSMOS—which the customer says is just a toy."

Pinder put the proposal to Ken Endelmyer, the CLC president, later that week, with the endorsement that in his opinion it was worth looking into seriously. Certainly, it was bold and vigorous in concept— maybe just what the whole field needed. A high risk, yes; but the potential rewards were huge, too, as they well knew. Endelmyer called in Therese Loel for an opinion. She was as intrigued as Pinder and agreed that there might be something in it. She also thought that the potential return from COSMOS was paltry compared to the market that this could open up. Endelmyer put the prospect, along with tentative estimates of what it would take to make the project fly, to the Board. Visions grew of this being pushed as the lead corporate research project, and it became a major funding issue. A month after Corrigan's talk with Pinder, orders came down from corporate headquarters to put the present plans for COSMOS on hold.

Corrigan and Evelyn had just moved to a house in Fox Chapel, a higher-income, professional residential area a few miles north of Blawnox. They threw a great housewarming party for their friends from CLC and elsewhere, and to add to the fun had one of the EVIE realscaping teams go through the house to capture the interior from all sides and angles for addition to the ever-growing database for the "simworld" of Pittsburgh and the surrounding area. So now, Corrigan explained to everybody, they would be able to relive the party all over again by coupling into EVIE when they got back to work tomorrow morning.

On the night of the announcement that COSMOS was on hold, Corrigan came home somewhat the worse after a celebratory drink or two in town. "Maybe Mister Tyron isn't so much of a big wheel after all," he said, sporting a cigar along with a satisfied smirk as he delivered the news. "It's like Vic Borth said: his field is just visual imagery. Toys. But this thing we're talking about now is going to need real know-how. It's getting out of his league."

Evelyn was less sure of that, but wrote Corrigan's brashness off to the effects of the drink and the strain that he had been under. Anyway, she didn't want to spoil the party. "Sit down and I'll get you a coffee," she said, forcing a smile. "Have you eaten yet?"

Corrigan stabbed his own chest with a thumb as he lowered himself heavily into an armchair. "If there's big money to be made out of all this, maybe I'll get to claim a share too now. Maybe we'll see who's who, eh?"

Evelyn's smile faded as she went through into the kitchen. She wasn't sure that she liked the side of Corrigan that was beginning to show itself. And she was nervous. She didn't think that somebody like Tyron would give up so easily—nor the kind of people that he had behind him.

✺ CHAPTER TWENTY-SIX ✺

Maurice came into the still room as Corrigan was changing out of his work jacket and into his street clothes. "Where are you going?" Maurice demanded. "You've got another two hours left yet."

There were times when it was fitting for Corrigan to carry on taking orders from, and working for, a computer animation, but somehow he couldn't bring himself to ask permissions or have to make excuses. "Not tonight," he said, pulling on his topcoat. "There's too much to explain, and you probably wouldn't believe it anyway. It's quiet, and Sherri can handle it. I'll talk to you tomorrow."

Far from satisfied, Maurice followed Corrigan out into the corridor. "There is such a thing as proper procedures, Joe. You might show the courtesy of clearing it with me first." Lilly was waiting by the door from the Galahad Lounge, and moved across to join Corrigan as he appeared. "Oh, so it's like that, is it?" Maurice went on behind him. "You can't just walk off the job for a date, Joe. I mean, hey, what is this? This isn't gonna go away in the morning, you know. Just who in hell do you think you *are*?"

They came out onto the street, with its usual assortment of caricatures, crazies, and zombies. "I've been looking for you all over," Corrigan muttered as soon as they were away from the doors. "You've had me worried, I can tell you."

"You know where I am. What was so difficult?" Lilly's voice was clipped and bitter. Clearly, she was not over her indignation—at the deception, and him as the only accessible target representing those responsible. The latter was compounded by his defending the situation, which she interpreted as bland acceptance. He got the feeling that she had come to him only as a last resort.

"I tried to, a few times. But I couldn't find the place again. They've changed parts of the city that weren't scaped. I tried to get you at work, but I couldn't find it listed."

"Why all the trouble? What worried you so much?"

"I didn't know what might come into your head to try next."

"Did you think I might try suicide or something as a way out?"

As a matter of fact, Corrigan had. After all, no physical harm could come to an external operator from causing an internal surrogate to permanently deactivate itself. But for all anyone knew, the knowledge and the trauma of the event might leave some adverse psychological imprint. It was something that the system designers had talked about, but in the end been forced to leave as one of the many unknowns that the experiment would entail.

"Somehow it didn't seem like you," Corrigan replied. Lilly didn't respond. He went on. "I was concerned that you might try to disrupt the experiment. Oh, I don't know how, exactly. . . . Set fire to the city, start a riot, preach revolution from street corners—mess the whole thing up somehow. And that would have been a shame, because it's all doing so incredibly well—despite the flaws."

Lilly stopped in the middle of the sidewalk and stared at him incredulously. "I can't believe I'm hearing this." She shook her head. "I've heard of loyal servants of the System, but this is unreal. I mean, they've stolen twelve years of your life, and all you can do is stand there defending them like Horatius on his bridge and say—"

Corrigan raised his hands protestingly. "No. Look, it's not the way you think. We haven't really lost twelve years."

"Not lost? What would you call it, then?"

"I didn't mean like that. It hasn't—"

"Do you call being surrounded by this lunacy every day living a life?"

"Let me finish. . . ." Corrigan looked around. There was a small coffee shop, not too crowded, a short distance from where they were standing. He took Lilly's elbow and began steering her in that direction. "We can't talk like this. Come on, let's take the weight off our feet in there. A cup of something might calm you down before you break a spring or something, too."

"... and we finally settled on a factor of 200. A day to us is only seven minutes outside. A whole week is less than an hour. So the twelve years that you're so hyped up about works out at about three weeks.... Hell, Lilly, you're a scientist. What we're going through is a unique experience. Three weeks isn't a lot to exchange for it."

Lilly, hunched over the opposite side of the small corner-table, sipped her coffee and sighed. Corrigan's words had had some effect. At least she was listening. She indicated their surroundings with a glance and a motion of her head. "So this is all an accelerated dream. We can afford to sit here and talk about it. It isn't losing us much."

"If we sat here for the next hour, it would be a whole eighteen seconds out of your life," Corrigan said.

Lilly fell quiet for a moment, reflecting on that. "You people might have told us," she said.

"Tyron didn't mention it when you were interviewed in California?"

Lilly shook her head. "They didn't tell us a great deal about it at all."

"Maybe they did tell you after you got to Pittsburgh," Corrigan said. "But then somebody sprung this memory suppression, and it got lost with the rest."

Corrigan felt more at ease for the first time in days. It seemed that he had saved the project and would have good news to report the next time Zehl contacted him. The thing now was to get Lilly back into playing her role normally. He made a conscious effort to discharge the atmosphere by being casual, resting an elbow on the edge of the table and draping his other arm along the back of an empty chair next to him.

"Out of curiosity, what gave it away?" he asked her.

"You mean how did I see through the simulation?"

"Yes."

"Oh, not because of any one thing that you could put a finger on. Lots of little things."

"But there must have been something that clinched it."

Lilly stared into the distance and tried to think back. "I think it was cracks in a sidewalk," she replied at last.

"You're joking."

"No. . . . I do remember a couple of days in Pittsburgh before it all goes blank—when the group from California that I was with first arrived. There was a briefing and some preliminary tests."

"Okay."

"Well, I spent some of my free time wandering around, taking in the sights. I like the older, East Coast cities—they're all so much alike in California. Anyway, I was standing watching something in one particular small street—it's not all that far from here—that had lots of old, cracked paving stones in the sidewalk, and I noticed that the pattern of the cracks near the base of a lamp outside an antiques store looked like the coastline of Labrador."

Corrigan shrugged. "What about it?"

Lilly drank from her mug, frowning with the effort of trying to keep clear what had happened around that time. "Soon after that it all gets lost. That was when the intensive tests began, and we were supposed to have had the breakdown and the rest of it. . . ."

"Yes. Go on."

"Much later, after all the therapy and rehabilitation, when I was out and about again, I ended up one day in that same street. The stones were still old and cracked, so they hadn't been replaced—but the pattern wasn't there." She raised her eyes and looked across at Corrigan. "And that was when a lot of other strange things that I'd been noticing started making more sense. It was a simulation. The system had the data to create realistic views of that street; it knew that the street had old paving stones, and that old paving stones would have cracks. So it put cracks in them. But it didn't put in the right cracks."

Corrigan looked at her, astonished. "And that was it?"

"That was it."

He sat back, nodding. All for the want of a nail . . . "I noticed similar things from time to time, too. I put it down to my own faulty memories." He shrugged, as if accepting the need for some kind of explanation. "That was what all the authority figures in my life had been telling me for years."

Lilly looked at him doubtfully over her mug. "You know, for someone who was involved from the start, there seems to be a hell of a lot that you don't know," she remarked.

"I'm not really in any better situation than you," Corrigan said. "We talked a lot about the pros and cons of suppressing the surrogates' memories, but as far as I was always aware, the decision was not to go with it. So what must have happened is that top management of the project set up another group to implement it secretly. . . ."

"But I thought *you* were project top management," Lilly interrupted.

Corrigan waved a hand. "Okay, maybe I should have said company top management. There were all kinds of people involved in Oz, both inside CLC and out—it was a hugely complicated undertaking. . . . Anyway, the idea was to make reactions to the simulation valid. But I always thought it was the wrong decision. Things work better if you know what's going on."

Lilly stopped him again. "Wait a minute. Are you saying that you didn't *know* about it—that there was going to be any memory suppression?"

Corrigan shook his head and showed his hands appealingly. "I couldn't be allowed to, could I? Think about it. If a surrogate knew in advance what the intention was, he'd see straight through any attempt at a cover story. If it was going to be done, that part *had* to be done by other people—without my knowing. Sneaky, yes. But what other way was there?"

Lilly tapped her spoon absently against the side of the mug, frowning to herself and watching it in a distracted kind of way. Corrigan realized that she was far from appeased. She had let herself be led into a diversion about the project's early days and cracks in paving stones to give herself time to mull over the things he had said earlier.

Finally she shook her head and said, "It still doesn't add up, Joe. You said you were one of the principal architects of this experiment, right? It practically grew from a proposal of yours in the first place."

Corrigan had a premonition then of where she was leading. Suddenly he felt less comfortable. "Right," he agreed.

"And yet, twelve years into it, you could still be taken in?" Lilly stared at him disbelievingly. "If this was anything at all like the experiment you expected, you'd *have* to have recognized it. Even if your memories of actually commencing it were suppressed, you'd know enough to figure out what all that business early on had been about. The only explanation has to be that the possibility of a simulation that would keep running for years never entered your head. Therefore, it must have gone way past anything envisaged in the plans that you knew about. Maybe the reason I saw through it first was that I didn't know what the simulation was *supposed* to be."

Corrigan had to nod—he had said as much himself when they talked before at Lilly's place. The first phase was supposed to have consisted just of progressively more elaborate tests. A comprehensive, extended simulation of the kind they were in wouldn't follow until much later. "Nothing like this was even scheduled," he admitted.

"Well, it seems *somebody* scheduled it," Lilly said pointedly.

In short, had he ever been as in control of things as he imagined? And if he had not, then who had been in control?

And still was?

✸ CHAPTER TWENTY-SEVEN ✸

The CLC Board decided to go with the proposal to attempt evolving an Artificial Intelligence by means of machine-directed animations learning to mimic human surrogates in a virtual world. The project was designated "Oz," and to begin with, half a floor was allocated to accommodate it in the IE Block at Blawnox. This did not mean abandoning COSMOS, however, since an all-neural interface as envisaged from COSMOS would be essential for coupling in the human surrogates for Oz. Hence, COSMOS was recast as a subsidiary goal in the greater plan.

The COSMOS part of the program was left under Tyron's management, as had been the original intention, and the overall direction of Oz entrusted to Pinder, with Corrigan heading up the groups responsible for developing the animation-driver software. Peter Quell, Pinder's deputy, stood in as acting head of the rest of the R & D division. The most obvious aspect of this arrangement was the temporary nature of Pinder's overseeing role in getting Oz off the ground. When he returned to his regular job as R & D chief, an opening would be left for a permanent technical director for the Oz project. And just as clearly, the only two real candidates for the position would be Corrigan and Tyron.

Corrigan remained undaunted and cockily confident. "He's just an interface man," he said to Evelyn on one of the evenings that were becoming rarer when they both got away early enough to have dinner in. "We're into big systems now. Complex, adaptive systems. And that's my territory."

Evelyn was less sanguine. "Tyron's got people behind him, here and outside CLC, who've staked a lot on seeing their man in control," she reminded him. "They're not going to go away, Joe. I mean, who are we talking about that we know? Velucci was there at the first meeting with SDC, wasn't he?—he has to be involved. Probably others from corporate, above Pinder. Maybe even Endelmyer. Certainly Harry Morgen and the others who followed Tyron. And others outside CLC, who must have had a hand in keeping the work on DIVAC in the public domain and nonlicensable. They're not just interface people. And they're not people who are going to sit back and watch while somebody throws a wrench in."

Corrigan speared a piece of steak with his fork and held it in a so-what pose. "They need what I've got," he said. "I'm the only one who can deliver Oz in the time they're committed to, and they know it. So what can they do?"

"I don't know, Joe. But be careful," Evelyn said.

The months that followed saw a lot of activity to extend the funding and support for Oz onto a wider base beyond CLC. Corrigan was too preoccupied with technical issues to pay much attention to background politics, but one day the company announced that Feller & Faber were coming in as cosponsors of Oz, which would be set up and run under a new, jointly owned corporation, "Xylog," dedicated to the project. F & F in turn were able to channel further funding from their lucrative client base, and very soon the original scheme that was to have been housed on a half-floor at the existing Blawnox facility gave way to a greatly expanded vision using more, bigger, and better machines, many more people, and occupying a site of its own elsewhere. F & F and its associates would manage the financial side of the joint venture, with somebody from CLC—yet to be designated—directing the technical operations. So in essence nothing changed as far as Corrigan and Tyron were concerned; it had all just shifted to a higher level.

All kinds of visitors began appearing at Blawnox, eager to see the work. Some of them were very strange, but all commanded influence or were in positions to direct significant flows of money. Another thing they had in common was the perception that they brought of Oz. They did not seem to have been made to understand it merely as a means to achieving AI. Rather, they took the AI for granted and saw it in turn as the engine that would power a revolutionary method for testing new design concepts, product models and styles, marketing methods, political campaign strategies—anything at all— in an artificial world running hundreds of times faster than the real thing: a Reality Simulator.

The character that Pinder and Tyron had brought over from the Executive Building was as zany as any that Corrigan had met in the last few months. His name was Roderick Esmelius, and he was from Market Resource Researches Inc., one of Feller & Faber's clients. He was tall, lean, and eccentrically theatrical, with flowing, silver hair, a suit of maroon trimmed with pink, and sporting a cane. The assistant with him, whose name was Godfrey, had dark curls, heavy, black-rimmed spectacles, and a mauve suit. He referred to the project as the "Crystal Ball," and seemed to think that it could predict election results. MRR were contemplating buying into Oz to the tune of two million dollars to try out a brainchild of Esmelius's that he was sure would revolutionize advertising. He explained to Corrigan and Shipley, punctuating his words with flourishes and pauses for effect:

"It will have the greatest impact of anything since the advent of television. The problem is getting to people, you see. There are too many distractions and alternatives to pull audiences away." In other words, the program offerings were garbage. "People are busy and more mobile these days than they used to be. They don't have enough opportunity to be near their TV." Esmelius wagged a finger and swept his gaze over the whole group as he came to the crux. "So why not let it *accompany them* permanently, everywhere? We hear about putting chips in people's heads to link them to computers. So why not a TV in the head?" He paused expectantly. Pinder nodded an amen. Tyron smirked at Corrigan. Shipley, from his chair at a terminal where he had been working, tried to catch Corrigan's eye with a look that asked if they were hearing things right; but Corrigan was too busy keeping up an appearance of relaxed, can-do suavity. He had been getting more conscious about dress lately, and was turned out in a stylish jacket of gray and black fleck, with a pink shirt and red silk tie with matching handkerchief folded in his breast pocket. Gold had appeared on his fingers, cuffs, and in his tie clip, and he had upgraded his watch.

Esmelius went on. "Just imagine, watch anything you like, any time, anywhere you like. And what a medium for advertisers: a direct line straight into everyone's head! You can't beat it."

Godfrey carried on, pitching with the same enthusiasm. "We have a number of potential investors. But public acceptance would be the key factor in a venture like this. Now, if we could show them what the public's reaction would be, *before* anyone puts up the money to actually develop the technology . . ."

"You want to know if the Oz simulation could tell you," Shipley completed. Having listened to a dozen similar lines in the last two weeks, he knew what was coming.

"Yes, precisely," Godfrey said. "Can the Crystal Ball do it? It would pay for itself ten times over, just on that."

"You'd only need to give the inhabitants the *effect* of having such technology," Pinder put in.

"Quite so," Esmelius confirmed. "All we'd want to know is their reactions."

Shipley was looking dubious and about to say something, but before he could do so, Tyron came in, looking at Pinder. "The potential for this kind of thing must be enormous. Just think of all the applications that could be emulated in advance, without the need for detailed designs or even a working prototype. All you need is the concept."

Pinder was nodding like a pigeon pecking up seed. "I agree, Frank, I agree. It could begin a whole new science for allocating development funding and priorities."

Tyron answered Esmelius, but with his eyes on Corrigan. "Oh, I'm sure that our programming specialists won't find it a problem."

"It's a natural extension to the self-adapting routines that we've been developing, based on the MIT system," Corrigan said. "The channel simply becomes an additional subgroup integrated into the perceptual data stream routed to each animation designated as implanted with a chip. The evaluation and response matrixes would be generated by the modules we've already got."

"You're saying that your people could handle it, then, eh, Joe?" Pinder interpreted, just to make sure that Esmelius understood.

"Sure, no problem," Corrigan said.

"Splendid." Esmelius beamed. Godfrey made satisfied clucking noises. Pinder could have told them as much himself without bringing them over, Corrigan knew, but it was more reassuring to hear things like this direct from the source. Also, as Tyron had made sure would not be missed but which Corrigan was not too concerned over for now, if anything went wrong, it would have been Corrigan who had said before witnesses that everything would be fine.

The two visitors stayed a short while longer to raise some further points and view what there was to see in the labs, and then left with Pinder and Tyron to meet others for lunch.

As soon as the door had closed, Shipley swung around in his chair and shook his head at Corrigan exasperatedly. "Joe, will you tell me just what in hell you're playing at? This all started out as a serious attempt to achieve AI. Now it's turning into a circus. God, even in the last two weeks we've listened to one crazy from Madison Avenue talking about turning every home into a theatrical supply company; another who wants walking advertising machines pestering people everywhere; houses full of talking appliances—and now commercial TV in people's heads. The management here ought to know better, but they've all lost their heads over the prospect of unlimited funds. This is getting crazy, Joe."

Corrigan nodded. "Yes, you don't have to tell me that, Eric. I know."

"But *you're* going along with it, for Christ's sake."

"I'm not going to be made to back down in front of F and F clients." Corrigan leaned over a table to run an eye over the printout stacked on top. "That's exactly what Tyron is trying to do: get negative reports sent back to the financial people in charge of the operation, who haven't got a clue what's feasible and what isn't."

Shipley nodded emphatically, as if that made his point. "Sure, I can see it—only too well. But what good are you doing yourself if you're not going to be able to deliver? You'll look plain dumb. And Tyron sure as hell knows that too."

Corrigan turned, looking composed and self-assured. "Relax, Eric. None of this is going to be happening anytime soon. Only the first-phase objectives have been made firm, and they're realistic. This other stuff they're talking about hasn't even been scheduled tentatively yet. It's all politics. The important thing for now is to say what the people who write the checks want to hear, and not sound obstructive. Trust me. I'm beginning to see how this game works now."

Shipley looked back at the screen that he was working on and shook his head. "Lies and deception. Promises that can't be kept," he muttered. "It's not the world we used to know."

"Well, you know what they teach in law school: If you can't lie honestly, then fake it. Got to move with the times, Eric."

"And what became of science in all this?"

"Nothing worthwhile was ever gained without some calculated risk. That's true in science too."

Corrigan opened out the sheets and stared down at them. Maybe it was all changing too fast for Shipley to keep up with. He thought about the opposition he was up against, and wondered if he could afford to keep carrying a deadweight. Nothing worthwhile was ever achieved without having to make some sacrifices at times, either.

Financial notables, brokers, celebrities from the media, even a couple of senators—all became part of the regular scene as money flowed from bottomless expense accounts. Parties and nightlife became as much a part of the routine as progress meetings and system tests during the day. From the original concept, Oz grew to a mammoth scale requiring hundreds of new specialists and thousands of square feet just for the equipment. To accommodate the project, Xylog acquired a newly completed complex centered around an eight-story main building on Southside, where some warehouses had once stood just off Carson Street. So the day came when trucks and packers arrived at Blawnox to move the labs, offices, and hardware that would be absorbed into the Xylog operation.

Corrigan was at one end of what had been the main EVIE lab, supervising the crating of the CDC mainframe that Tom Hatcher's group used for associative array development, when Pinder appeared, ostensibly to ask how things were going.

"Fine," Corrigan told him. "The installation at Carson Street is ahead of schedule. I'll be going there first thing tomorrow to start getting it all on line, and we should have the section back in business by next week."

"Excellent." Pinder clasped his hands together behind his back and gazed around. Most of the lab area was bare, apart from discarded trash and wastepaper swept into piles. Lengths of disconnected cables protruded from underfloor distribution points and hung from overhead. A work crew was maneuvering the last of the large crates onto forklift palettes. "It's like moving out of a house, isn't it," Pinder commented. "Full of ghosts and memories. Funny how places always look so much bigger with the furniture gone."

"I thought this was the ultimate in modernism when I moved in," Corrigan said. "But compared to where we're going, it all seems quaint."

"Look at the kind of money that's going into Xylog," Pinder answered.

"I guess so." Corrigan had caught the quick, sideways looks that Pinder had been giving him as they spoke, and knew there was more to this than a casual visit. Such was usually the case when Pinder came over from the Executive Building.

Pinder glanced around. There was nobody in their immediate vicinity. He motioned with a nod of his head for Corrigan to follow, and walked slowly along by the outside wall until they came to a window overlooking the rear lawns and parking lots. "I'm a bit troubled by Shipley's ultracautiousness," he said, directing his gaze straight ahead. "I know it's good science and so on, but that belongs in the labs. What worries me is the negative impact that it's likely to have on the financial backers. At a time like this we can't afford that."

It was too close to the way Corrigan's own thoughts had been running for some time for him to be capable of making much of a show of surprise. Mainly out of curiosity to see where this was leading, he replied neutrally, "Has somebody been complaining?"

Pinder made a sucking noise through his teeth. "Not in so many words. But I've seen the looks and glances. And it's something that stands to affect you personally as well, Joe. I think you owe it to yourself to give some thought to a side of things that you might not have considered very closely."

"Oh?"

"Look at it this way. Eric has done some first-rate work in the past, I know—and I wouldn't want to belittle any of that. But I have to ask, is he really suited to a senior position in the new style of organization that's taking shape? You said it yourself—it's a streamlined product of the times. And running it is going to require a management team who all share a common level of enthusiasm, personal ambition, and a conviction that the job can be done. One dissenting note could create discord throughout. Your own future hinges on the success of this in a big way, as I'm sure I don't have to spell out. . . . So give me your opinion, straight. It's not a time to let notions of personal loyalty obscure sound judgment."

Corrigan stared fixedly out at the rear facade of the Executive Building opposite. Pinder had said it—all the things that had been swirling around in Corrigan's mind, but which he hadn't been able to bring himself to admit consciously. Even so, now that the opportunity was not only there but being pressed, a deeper-rooted reluctance to wield the knife prevented him from being blunt. "I don't know," was all he could muster. "As you said, it's something that I'd probably have to think over."

Pinder waited a few seconds longer, then sighed. "All right, I'll come out with it straight. Borth has seen it too, and he isn't happy. He's told Ken Endelmyer that he doesn't want Shipley in the venture. Management's view is that his former DINS work is part of the past now, and largely irrelevant, and they have concurred."

So there never had been anything for Corrigan to give an opinion on. Pinder had simply been casting for a way to make him feel implicated. But if Corrigan had any protest to make, this was the moment to do it.

He turned and looked around the place where they had worked together, remembering feet propped on untidy desks; solder guns and birds'-nest tangles of makeshift racking; grubby diagrams tacked to pressboard; scratched keyboards and gray metal shelving. He thought of the future and Xylog: of glass-paneled corridors, deep-pile executive suites, and gleaming machine-halls. And he said nothing.

Pinder heard the silence and went on. "There is a core group from the DINS section that I'd like us to retain. Frank Tyron agrees that they're good and wants them transferred to COSMOS, but I think there's an equal case for integrating them into your side of the operation. I'm giving you first choice. What do you say?"

An offer of alliance, wrapped around the handle of the knife. He couldn't do anything to change the verdict now, Corrigan told himself. Only Tyron would benefit if he refused. It was a time for realism.

"Sure, I'll take them," he said.

❈ CHAPTER TWENTY-EIGHT ❈

The sign in gold indented lettering on a polished wood ground facing the elevators read:

Floor Six
OZ PROJECT SOFTWARE SYSTEMS DIVISION
ANIMATIONS ENGINEERING
ADAPTIVE ENVIRONMENTS GROUP
DATABASE MANAGEMENT
SUPPORT SERVICES

"Good morning, Mr. Corrigan," one of the two clerks waiting with bundles of files greeted as Corrigan emerged carrying a black Samsonite.

"Hello, girls," he returned, nodding, and headed toward the double doors leading through a glass divider to the sixth-floor reception foyer.

"Good morning, Mr. Corrigan," the receptionist said from her desk as he passed.

" 'Morning, Betty. You're looking very smart today."

"Why, thank you."

"We've got some important people coming today. Keep it up."

"Good morning, Mr. Corrigan," the young man in a charcoal suit going the other way said, halfway across the open-plan floor of work spaces and conference areas leading to Corrigan's office.

"Hello, Chris. Did we get those specs integrated for Bolger?"

"Completed yesterday. Run and checked out last night."

"Good lad."

Judy Klein was already at her desk in the partitioned outer area in front of his office. It looked like part of a set for the flight deck in a space-fiction movie, with its curvy furnishings and multiscreened computer side-table.

"Hi, Judy. 'Tis a grand day for living, to be sure, to be sure. What have we got?"

"Hello, Joe. Let's see. The arrangements for those people from Chase that Borth is bringing are confirmed. And there's a message from Amanda Ramussienne at F and F saying that she'll be coming too."

"Fine. And where have we fixed for lunch?"

"Delio's for twelve-thirty."

"That's great."

"Roger said to let you know we've signed off on the two new TMCs. There's a list of calls to be returned on your desk. And Pinder has put the meeting with Quell back to ten-thirty instead of ten. I said it would be fine. It doesn't clash with anything."

"Okay. Anything from Tom Hatcher yet on those referent transfer patches?"

"Yes. You're due to see him in half an hour with Charlie Wade and Jorrecks. He said he'll have the information then."

"Fine. I'll clear the calls first. If anything comes up while I'm down there, just put it through."

"Will do."

Corrigan went through to his own office and set the briefcase down on one corner of the broad sweep of curved, walnut-topped desk with its terminal, onyx pen-holders and neatly arranged piles of papers and reminders. The floor-to-ceiling windows formed a corner of the building, presenting fine views of the downtown Pittsburgh vista along the opposite shore on one side, and the meeting of the three rivers with the Ohio Valley beyond on the other.

The last few months had seen an intensification of the realscaping program for capturing every facet of visual imagery over the entire Pittsburgh area. Camera teams had been out every day, touring and recording all the streets, expressways, parks, and trails; from vehicles and on foot, from helicopters overflying the city, from boats out on the rivers. Back in Xylog the machines were running day and night, reducing and compiling the encoded scenes into crosslinked hierarchies of field definitions in the huge database that took up half a floor of high-density crystal-array recirculator memory cubicles. Hatcher had told Corrigan that they could reproduce any aspect of any scene out there, from any viewpoint, in any direction. Corrigan had studied the figures and experimented with some samples, and he believed it. The results of the similar but smaller-scale program that Himomatsu had carried out in Tokyo were now incorporated into the main Oz database, as was a part of the Inglewood area of California and a few other places, following experiments by SDC.

Having reviewed his priorities for the day and disposed of the calls, Corrigan went through the mail with Judy and gave her a list of follow-up actions for the morning. Then he went back out to the elevators and down past the Primary Operations Level, where the main banks of massively parallel processing lattices took up almost the entire floor, past the Interface Level with galleries of COSMOS coupling hardware for up to fifty real-world surrogates, past the Monitoring & Control Center, from where the whole operation was directed, and came out on the second floor. Finally he came to a door marked FINAL EVALUATION & TEST, which was where Tom Hatcher's group ran newly completed system modules prior to operational integration.

Hatcher's concessions to the new order of things amounted to switching to regular pants in place of jeans, acquiring a jacket, and, on special occasions, adding a necktie. But underneath, the old, easygoing casualness remained unaffected, and he was still more at home sprawled in front of a terminal with his coffee in a Styrofoam cup than listening to investment plans being expounded over pâté de foie gras. When Corrigan arrived, he was waiting with Charlie Wade, one of the old crew from Blawnox, and Des Jorrecks, the head of

Xylog's applied psychology department. There were two broad areas to discuss:

First, results of tests to evaluate different strategies for creating animations that would best emulate people. Like people, the animations would shape their lives and personalities by pursuing goals. The intention was that these goals would arise internally, according to the animations' individual natures and experiences, rather than be imposed from without. But real people rarely formed distinct goals that they pursued consciously and deliberately all the time, such as to become a doctor, lawyer, physicist, or actor, or to head a country or win an Olympic gold medal; for the most part, they simply lived their day-to-day existences following unconscious drives and desires, and the bigger things just "happened." How, then, should such a nature best be simulated? What mix of drives, fears, ambitions, aversions was needed, with what kinds of relative weightings? How should such factors be represented as a statistical distribution across a whole population? Opinions on these questions changed constantly, and the short answer was that nobody really knew. A lot would be learned when the first runs were done in full-system mode, with the animation and environmental modules finally on-line and interacting together.

The other thing on the agenda was a subject that it seemed could never be laid to rest: the question of suppressing the surrogates' memories when they began the full-system tests. Those in favor argued that it would ensure greater authenticity of behavior. Those against, who included Corrigan, maintained that they were scientists running an experiment, and scientists needed to know what was going on. "All we have to do is play role models to a bunch of dumb machines. We're not trying to impress a panel of Shakespearean critics," Corrigan said after they had been through the technical arguments yet again. "And on top of all that, it will make it a more exciting experience for everyone: the thought of launching off into the unknown—a bit like going up on a space flight to another planet, or something."

"Aw, I don't know that it would get anybody that excited when you get down to it," Hatcher said. Hatcher was for suppression but resigned to a lost cause. Corrigan had vetoed the idea, there was not enough time left now to change the decision, and that seemed to be that. "These things tend to creep up on you so gradually, day by day, that you get used to it. I asked an astronaut the same question once. He said that they trained so hard for a mission that by the time it actually happened they couldn't tell the difference anymore. But then, that was the whole idea, I guess. Pretty much the same as what we're doing."

It wasn't just a matter of authenticity. There was the question of being better able to cope in an emergency, too. "What if something did screw up in there, Tom?" Corrigan said. "We're going straight into people's heads, interacting at deep perceptual levels that wire into emotional centers. And with the speedup, if anything unexpected did start happening, it would be hours out here before anyone knew about it.

Hatcher knew all that. He thought over it briefly, failed to come up with anything that hadn't been said a hundred times already, and shrugged. "Well, that's what the surrogates are being paid all that money for. We know there's a lot we don't know, and so do the volunteers who are coming in from outside. What else can anyone say, Joe?"

"I think Joe's got a point, all the same," Jorrecks put in. "Whoever's in there needs to be able to abort the run from the inside if it really goes off the rails somehow. But how could they do that if they didn't even know they were inside a simulation? I don't think I'd want to go in there under those conditions."

"You want an ejector seat," Charlie Wade said.

Jorrecks nodded. "Yes. But of course you couldn't have one if the memory was suppressed, since there would be no knowledge of the mechanism for using it. There's no way you could get around it. Any knowledge that an escape mechanism existed would also be knowledge that there was a simulation to be escaped from, which would defeat the whole purpose." Jorrecks looked at Corrigan for support. Corrigan nodded.

Charlie Wade looked at Hatcher questioningly. "Shall we tell them?" he asked.

"Why not?" Hatcher said.

Corrigan looked from one to the other. "Tell us what?"

"As a matter of fact, we think it is possible," Hatcher said.

Corrigan looked skeptical. "How?"

"But everyone would have to do it for themselves."

"What are you getting at, Tom?"

"Well, if it was me—if I was going in as a surrogate, and let's say that shortly before the full-system phase I was suddenly told that all memories of, say, the last couple of days were going to be suppressed."

Corrigan nodded. "Okay."

"What I'd do is this. I'd plant something inside the simworld that would be significant to me in some way, something that nobody else would know about. Later, after the run was started and I was in it, I wouldn't know I'd done it, because that memory would have been killed. But I'd still know the way I think, and I'd wonder what in hell this something—this whatever—was doing there. But if some kind of crisis developed to raise the stress level to the point where I had to get out, then I'd recognize it as a signal to myself. And from there it wouldn't take much fooling around with it to figure out what I'd set it up to do."

Jorrecks looked at Corrigan inquiringly. Corrigan thought about it for a few moments, and nodded. "That's clever."

"You think it could work?" Jorrecks said.

Corrigan smiled and had to nod. "It just might, at that, Des. It just might."

Hatcher clasped his hands behind his head and stretched his length out over the chair. "Does that mean you've changed your mind, Joe? Suppression's in, after all? We can go with it?"

"Not at all," Corrigan said, waving a hand dismissively. "It's dead and buried. Forget it. We've enough else to do as things are." Hatcher knew that and hadn't really been serious anyway. Just then, the phone on Hatcher's desk rang.

"I think we're done," Jorrecks said, seizing the opportunity and rising while Hatcher picked up the receiver. "We'll leave you to it, guys." Charlie Wade got up from his chair also and collected his notes together.

"Tom here. . . . Say, hi! Yes, he sure is." He held the phone out to Corrigan. "It's Eve, for you." Jorrecks and Wade left the room with a wave and a nod each.

"Hello?" Corrigan said.

"Joe, Judy said you were probably with Tom. Just checking to see if we're still having lunch."

Corrigan frowned. Oh, yes, that was right—she had suggested it that morning. He had mumbled that it would probably be okay, and then forgotten to get back to her when Borth's visit was confirmed. "Er, look, something's come up and I'm not going to be able to make it," he replied. "I should have got Judy to call you. I'm sorry about that."

Evelyn sighed. "Oh dear. And you were so late that I never got to see you last night."

"Everything's insane. It's all hectic now we're getting close."

"I know. Maybe dinner for a change?"

"I'll try." Corrigan looked across and caught Hatcher's eye. "Tell you what, why not have lunch with Tom instead? He's up to his neck too, but I'm sure he'd like the company." He held a hand over the mouthpiece. "Like to have lunch with Eve? I was supposed to, but I'm grabbed. I know you two always find plenty to talk about." Hatcher didn't seem overly happy, but nodded. Corrigan spoke back into the phone. "He says that's fine."

"Okay. Tell him I'll stop by there at, say, twelve. Okay?"

"She says how about twelve? She'll stop by here." Another nod. "That's fine. Look, I've got a ten-thirty, so I have to go. Talk to you later, then. 'Bye now."

"Goodbye, Joe."

"Thanks. You're a pal," Corrigan said to Hatcher as he put the phone down. "Borth's coming with some people from Chase. I'm tied up to do lunch there."

Hatcher shook his head in a way that said he didn't buy that. "So? You could have taken Evelyn there too. You're a head honcho and she's staff. Hell, this outfit can afford it."

Corrigan winked. "But the delectable Amanda will be there too. There are times and places for wives."

Hatcher couldn't contain his disapproval. "I'm sorry, Joe. Maybe I'm sticking my nose in, but I just don't like to see it. Everything used to be fine with you two. You've changed a lot, you know—especially since we moved to this place."

"Hey, give me a break, Tom. What's the harm in a change of pleasant company once in a while? I do plenty of good-husbanding out of hours, when it's the time for it."

"Ain't the way I've been hearing it."

"Look, I'm not asking you to get involved or make it your business, Tom. Just a small favor to cover when I'm double committed. I happen to think that taking wives along just for the ride isn't the proper thing to do. Whether the firm can afford it or not isn't the point. I also think that honchos should set examples, don't you?"

Hatcher turned back to his terminal. "This time, Joe," he growled. "Just don't do it to me again, that's all."

❀ CHAPTER TWENTY-NINE ❀

Today was the beginning of National Color Week, and Carson Street was filled with radiantly decked people marching to express themselves through visual combinations: yellow for happy, blue for somber, red for lively, green for simple, and other mixes and hues for other natures and dispositions—real, imagined, or self-fulfilling—in between. Self-playing instruments driven by microchips were all the rage, so nobody needed to be a musician to join in the festivities with a guitar, trumpet, accordion, or trombone, and "belong." The TV shows and movie ad inserts had been plugging fiber-optic augmentations to hairstyles and clothes, and half the costumes glittered and glowed like slow-motion Christmas trees.

Corrigan stood with Lilly on a rise above the main body of the crowd, staring at the site that had once held a modern, eight-story commercial structure of shiny white tiling and green-tinted glass, with separate buildings for offices and administration. All that was left now was one of them turned into an apartment block that looked like a psychedelic gift-wrap pack, another adopted as a "temple" by a cult who believed themselves to be reincarnated aliens from Sirius, and the main building demolished to make room for a hotel that never happened, now a campground for vagrants.

Even now, Corrigan found that it needed an effort to tell himself that what he was looking at had never happened. The conditioning processes of twelve years, everything he had seen, read, and been told through all that time added up to a powerful weight of persuasion that his instincts fought against simply dismissing. This had been Xylog. He could remember how it looked in those final weeks, the hectic days and bleary-eyed, all-night sessions to complete the preparations on time and straighten out the inevitable last-minute hitches. He had made some initial sorties into the final test simulations to check details from the inside . . . And after that his recollections became confused and indistinct.

It was only long afterward, when he was well on the road to recovery, that he had learned how those final tests had damaged him, along with many others, with mental disruptions, hallucinations, breakdowns, periods of total blankness. The government intervened to halt the project. There had been hearings and investigations, and finally the project was abandoned and the site sold off. He had read the reports, watched the tapes. And here, in front of him, was what was supposed to be the incontrovertible evidence.

Except that none of that could have happened, for the simulation was still running.

"You weren't a permanent inhabitant like most of the other surrogates," Lilly said. "You were supposed to be one of the controllers—entering and leaving whenever you wanted."

"That's right." Corrigan had no explanation. He could only agree.

Lilly turned to him with an air of finality, as if that summed up everything that she had been saying since their first meeting in the Camelot. "So something that you weren't expecting must have happened during the last week or so."

"I don't know, I don't know," Corrigan groaned wearily. "It's all so confused from around that time. I can't remember."

"What happened, obviously, was that your memory was wiped too," Lilly said. "But according to you, it shouldn't have been. Which can only mean that somebody else set it up."

"You don't *know* that," Corrigan protested. "I could have agreed to something they sprung on me in the last few days. If that's the case, then of course I don't remember anything about it. That would have been the whole idea."

"You were one of the main designers," Lily pointed out. "Your place would have been supervising from the outside." She raised an arm to take in the locality of Southside around them, the river off to one side, and beyond it in the visible part of downtown Pittsburgh. "We're *twelve years* into this, and it's still running," she said. "Didn't you tell me before that this goes way past anything that had been planned? All that had been scheduled was a series of more extended testing. Nothing like this." She waited for a moment, saw that he had no immediate answer, and went on. "It's clear what must have happened. Somebody else had arranged a far more elaborate simulation than you were told about."

"That's impossible."

"Which meant that you weren't. as in control as you thought. Your position wasn't so unassailable—that's what you won't admit. Sometime during the early phases you entered the simulation on a routine visit, and while you were inside they switched over to the extended version and wiped your memory to keep you here for the duration. Meanwhile, they're running things on the outside. . . . And you're telling me not to worry, everything's going just fine? That I should trust them?"

"Oh, for God's sake, you've been watching too many movies," Corrigan retorted irritably. He had a more than gnawing suspicion that she was right, but he needed time to think. "You don't have any evidence for all this. It's pure fabrication. These weren't the sinister people that you're trying to paint—just ordinarily ambitious people in a competitive environment. You're making it sound like intrigue inside the Kremlin."

"Oh, yes? Look what they did to you. You'd already stabbed your best friend in the back. And things with Evelyn were heading for the rocks. How soon afterward did that come apart? In circumstances like that, it would have been easy for them to convince anyone who asked that you'd elected to go in as a surrogate on your own initiative—to get away from it all for a while to wouldn't it?"

"Maybe I did," Corrigan retorted. "And that would put a hole through your whole paranoia theory right there, wouldn't it?"

And he had a point. Now it was Lilly's turn to feel less sure of herself. "Why? . . . When did it finish with Evelyn?" she asked.

"Oh, it all came to a head about three weeks before Oz was due to go live. She split." Corrigan sighed. "She left me for being too pushy and ambitious. Muriel left me for being the opposite. It's true what they say about women, you know: there's no pleasing them."

"Tell me what happened," Lilly said.

◎ CHAPTER THIRTY ◎

Evelyn stared across the living room at Corrigan, shaking her head disbelievingly. Her eyes were wide, her body taut like a threatened animal, her face a mask of someone he didn't know. All of the resentment and anger that had been pent up for months was pouring out with the adrenaline flush.

"How *could* you?" she shouted. "A man that you'd worked with for years . . . after the friend he's been to both of us. How could you let them just walk all over him like that? What did you do—just stand there? Didn't you say *anything* to stand up for him?"

Tom Hatcher had told her over lunch about Corrigan's part in the Shipley affair—but in a distorted way that made it sound as if Corrigan had asked Pinder to dump him. Apparently that was the version that Tyron had been spreading around the company. But Corrigan was in no mood to quibble over details or have to justify himself.

"What did you expect me to do?" he snapped back. "Their minds were already made up. . . . And anyway, they might have had a point. Eric would never have fitted in at Xylog. If the truth were known, he wanted out of it anyway." Shipley had been offered a mundane position in the general CLC research facility, but turned it down and quit the company.

Evelyn looked at Corrigan contemptuously. "Who are you to say what Eric wanted? At least he could have been given a chance to say so himself, instead of being discarded like worn-out shoes. Don't things like people's pride and dignity mean anything to you anymore? It's a shame, because they used to."

"Yes, they do," Corrigan answered, marching in front of her. He jabbed at his chest with a thumb. "And so do my own, for that matter. All I'd have succeeded in doing would be to make a sacrificial lamb of myself. And wouldn't Tyron have just loved that! Can't you see? It's exactly what he was hoping I'd do."

Evelyn hooked a wisp of her hair with her finger and whirled away savagely. "God, if you only knew how sick I am of hearing about Tyron, Tyron, Tyron . . . the whole pack of them."

"*One* of us is going to end up as the technical head of Xylog," Corrigan said. "It's down to that: either him or me. Doesn't that mean anything to you?"

"No, it doesn't. I told you, I'm sick of all of it. Maybe Eric knew exactly what he was doing. Perhaps you should have walked out too. At least you'd have stayed the person you were."

"And what, exactly, is that supposed to mean?" Corrigan demanded darkly.

Evelyn turned back with a pained, sarcastic face. "Oh, don't start acting as if you were stupid, Joe, on top of everything else," she implored. "When I fell in love with you, it was because I admired you for what you stood for: knowledge, honesty, the worth of people as people. But that's all changed. I loved you because you were what you seemed to be. You were genuine. Now you're turning into what I never thought you'd be: a phony."

"Grow up, little girlie," Corrigan said. "It's called getting on in the world. You don't expect people to stay as techs in labs all their lives, do you? Anyone who called herself a wife would be appreciative. Will you listen to yourself and hear what I get?"

Evelyn shook her head. "Getting on in the world? Is that what you call it? Getting on would be doing better what you do. Becoming a better person. But you're trying to ape these freaks that you idolize, who have taken over the project. You're trying to be one of *them*. That's what's so sickening."

It was her last plea for him to see things from where she stood, but Corrigan threw it back at her. "Well, at least they add a bit of fun to life for a change. Is that supposed to be bad or something? It might do you a bit of good to get out of that stuffy lab and away from your notes, and find out what life is all about for once."

Evelyn rounded on him like a goaded cat. "Yes, of course, there are plenty of more *glamorous* women out there, aren't there—with more tits than IQ points," she spat. "And pricey dresses bought on someone else's expense account. Is that the attraction in all these new playpens that you've been discovering?"

"Damn right!" Corrigan yelled.

Her eyes blazed at him for several seconds, inviting him to take it back. He glowered back defiantly. The hell he would. She turned away, tight-mouthed, and went over to the phone. "Well, enjoy," she told him. "And when you come to your senses, or your 'friends' decide to ditch you the same way they did Eric, don't bother looking. Have a nice life."

"What are you doing?"

Evelyn didn't answer him. "Hello? Yes, I'd like a cab, please. It's two twenty-three Elm, Fox Chapel. . . . Right away. I'll be waiting outside."

"Where do you think you're going?" Corrigan demanded.

"It's none of your business. Probably back to Boston." She disappeared along the hall leading to the bedroom, then came back a few moments later, clutching her purse and pulling on her coat.

"What about your things?" Corrigan said. "I hope you're not expecting me to send them."

"I wouldn't want anything that reminds me of this place. I'd rather start from scratch again."

"Well, isn't that typical," Corrigan sneered. "Have you ever seen anything through in your life? The project goes live in three weeks, and you won't even stick around to see the end of what you've been working for."

"I'm not interested in the stupid project. It's changed you and it's ruined us. You stay and watch your precious project. I wouldn't want any part of a world that your kind of friends created."

Anger surged up inside him suddenly then. His pride would not permit the affront of letting her walk out first to leave him standing there with the choice of either submitting passively or climbing down. He swept his jacket up from the chair where he had draped it and opened the door before she could reach it. "Suit yourself," he threw back over his shoulder. "It won't bother me. I'm going to get very, very drunk."

"Isn't that just—"

He slammed the door before she finished, and went out the front of the house. His car screeched out of the driveway moments later.

But he did not get all that drunk. After he'd had a couple in one of the bars downtown and calmed down a little, he went to the phone and called the Vista Hotel. A minute later he was through to Amanda Ramussienne.

"Why, Joe, how nice to hear from you," she purred. "I enjoyed talking to you at lunch so much. Where are you?"

"Just a few blocks away. It occurred to me that it wouldn't be very gentlemanly to let you go back tomorrow without so much as a goodbye. Have you eaten?"

"Not yet, after this afternoon."

"I haven't yet either. I thought you might like to join me. What do you think?"

"What a nice idea."

"How are you fixed?"

"Sure, I can make it. Give me forty minutes to spruce up."

"I'll be there at eight," Corrigan said.

"I look forward to it," she murmured. There was just the right hint of a double entendre in the way she said it.

Nothing had changed when Corrigan got back to the house in the early hours. Evelyn had gone. It gave him a feeling of unencumbrance and freedom, of decks cleared for what had become the only important thing in life. Oz was *his*. He had wrested it out of what had seemed a lost cause, when every sign had pointed to Tyron taking control via COSMOS. He felt like a grimly confident general on the eve of battle. Even if his closest ally had deserted him in the final hour, nothing could take away victory now.

◎ CHAPTER THIRTY-ONE ◎

It was one of those awakenings that come suddenly, like a light being switched on, unlike other mornings when Corrigan could spend ages tugging himself free from the clutches of sleep. He felt unusually light and sprightly—more charged up than he could remember feeling in a long time. Maybe he would call Lilly and see about meeting somewhere for lunch.

After leaving the former Xylog site they had come back to Oakland, bought some wine and cooked themselves a dinner at his place, then talked on until the early hours. The suggestion of her staying over had permeated the mood of the evening unspoken. But few turnoffs could be more effective than an awareness of being in a simulation subject to monitoring and recording, and the understanding to wait for more conducive circumstances had been just as mutual, again with no need for anything to be said. The rapport they seemed to have was uncanny, he reflected as he stared up into the darkness. Or was that simply how any two real people would affect each other after twelve subjective years among animations?

Something was odd.

It could have been a difference in temperature or humidity, or perhaps a subtle change in the odor or acoustic properties. But something felt wrong about the room. And the pillow was silky. They didn't have silky pillows—Muriel thought they were too clinging.

"Lights, Horace," he called. Nothing happened.

He reached out and groped for the switch on the wall-mounted lamp above the bed. But his fingers found nothing, just a blank wall. And instead of the padded headboard below the lamp, he found what felt like a polished brass rail connected to a bedpost.

Bewildered, he pushed back the covers and sat up. The face of a clock was glowing at him from the bedside unit that the time was 6:30 A.M. There shouldn't have been a clock on the bedside unit, nor the lamp whose outline he could now make out in the light from the clock. He felt for the base of the lamp, found the switch, and turned it . . . to find that he was not in his apartment in Oakland at all.

But at the same time, the surroundings were familiar: the vanity with its mirror and lights, walk-in closet with louvered doors, satin drapes and shag carpet. . . . He was back in the house that he and Evelyn had lived in at Fox Chapel twelve years ago. The room was untidy, with the pants from one of his suits thrown over a chair along with a crumpled shirt and some socks, shoes tossed haphazardly by the closet, and clothes overflowing around the laundry basket.

He blinked, swung his legs out, and sat in confusion on the edge of the bed, trying to make sense of it. It made no sense. He got up, crossed over to the window, and peered through the drapes. The cluttered housefronts and cramped urban streets of Oakland were gone; instead, roomy, upmarket homes with wide driveways, standing comfortably secluded in wooded suburban surroundings. There was no doubt about it: this was Fox Chapel.

Numbly, he fumbled his way into a robe and went out into the hall and along to the living area. His briefcase was on the long coffee table in front of the couch, with papers and a notepad scattered in front of it, and pushed to one end were an empty coffee mug and a half-eaten sandwich on a plate. The side table with the computer monitor had been pulled forward for easy viewing from the couch, and the still-connected keyboard was resting on one of the arms. It looked as if he had been working late last night. He went over and shuffled through the papers. They were all to do with preliminary test schedules for the Oz project. He activated the terminal and checked the current date. It read Tuesday, October 12, 2010. Oz had been due to go on-line at around that time, late in 2010.

Still baffled, he went through to the kitchen. As he did so, he became aware of a different feeling in the way his body moved. He felt lighter on his feet, more lithe and supple than he was used to. The kitchen was messy, like the bedroom—dishes in the sink, more papers on the table, the things for preparing the sandwich in the other room not put away. He went over to the mirror by the shelf above the microwave and looked at himself. His jaw fell in astonishment. He was looking at himself twelve years younger and a good fifteen pounds leaner. He felt his face, ran the fingers of a hand through his hair. This was insane.

So what about the whole business of being a bartender and meeting Lilly? Had it all been a dream? No, he couldn't accept it. Dreams could be uncannily lucid, it was true, but never as real as those recollections—all the way through to seeing Lilly out to her cab and going to bed last night.

The only other explanation, then, was that he was in the middle of a lucid dream right now—dreaming that he was back in the days of the project. But surely no dream could be as real as this either. Or could it? The disconcerting realization came over him that he had no idea if he was asleep or awake, and he was far from sure how to find out.

Pain. The pain response didn't function in the dreaming state. That was why people always pinched themselves. He pinched the back of his hand. It hurt. He bit his tongue. It hurt more. He picked a pin out of an oddments bowl on a shelf by the refrigerator and jabbed his thumb with it, and it hurt like hell. Yet somehow he was still unconvinced. Perhaps it was possible to dream that you were feeling pain when you really weren't.

If he was not dreaming, and this was in fact 2010 with Oz about to go fully on-line, why was he unable to recollect anything that had happened at Xylog yesterday, or what he was supposed to be doing there today? His memories of such things were blurred and distant, as would be expected after the passage of twelve years. On the other hand, he could vividly remember going to the Southside with Lilly yesterday and seeing the site where Xylog used to be, going back to Oakland, and their cooking dinner together. If that had been a dream, why was yesterday so vague, now that he was awake again? If this was a dream, it was so real as to be scary—there didn't seem to be a way out of it.

He went into the den to check on the terminal there for any received E-mail that might give him a better perspective on what was going on. But when he activated the terminal he stopped, confused. He couldn't remember the procedure. This was silly. He stared at the screen, feeling stupid, but it was no good. He found the mnemonic for "Help," scrolled to the directions for accessing personal mail . . . and all of a sudden it came easily.

There were several items from various people, but they were too long-forgotten to mean anything. Nothing triggered any immediate associations. And then he came across a note from Judy Klein that read:

Monday, October 11, 9:35 P.M.
Joe:
Just a reminder to call Ed Meechum first thing regarding the interview scheduled for tomorrow (Tuesday). I do have the figures from F & F that Ed said he was interested in, so we should get you the slot.

Judy

He *remembered* reading that message before—years ago. It had been in the last few days before Oz went on-line, a few weeks after Evelyn walked out. That explained the state of the house. The project had been getting good media coverage, and Ed Meechum was the producer for an interview that NBC was due to shoot, describing the last-minute action. Exactly who would be interviewed had not been decided yet, and Corrigan and Tyron were both vying for the visibility. The figures mentioned in Judy's message were statistics from the tests run so far—hopelessly skewed, if the truth were known, but since when had the media worried unduly about minor things like that?—that F & F were banding around to impress their clients on the predictive power that would come out of Oz. In other words, pure hokum to reassure the investors.

But the point was, he *did* get the slot. He remembered being interviewed at Xylog late in the afternoon. It had been a circus of hyperbole and misrepresented facts, and thinking back to it now didn't make him feel especially proud of his performance at all; although F & F had been delighted. Afterward, he had gone out for dinner with Meechum and some other NBC people. Amanda Ramussienne had been there too, having come down that day from New York. They went to the Gaucho Restaurant in Station Square. Corrigan could remember it all. He stared at the words on the screen perplexedly. But how could he? How could he be remembering details—even if a bit vague—of events that weren't due to happen until later in the day? The whole situation was crazy.

He left the den in a daze and went to get a better look at himself in the bathroom mirror. Yesterday, there had been a nick on his thumb, where he had cut it cleaning up the pieces of a broken glass at the Camelot. It was quite pronounced, with a week or more of healing to go before the mark would fade. Yet today there was not a trace of it.

Something very strange had happened to him. He had definite recollections of having woken up like this, on this very day, but long ago. The recollections were indistinct and incomplete, as if being retrieved from long ago. What had happened after the dinner with the NBC people? He seemed to remember they had gone on to a club, and afterward he went back to the Vista with Amanda. And then, the next day, what? . . . He wasn't sure.

The first thing he could recall anything of after that was being in Mercy Hospital, slowly piecing himself together again. Dr. Arnold and the nurse . . . Katie, her name was; a strange Saturday-night dance, populated by caricatures representing the system's early attempts at constructing people; Simon, the counselor, and the time when Corrigan had dug a hole in the hospital lawn. . . . And after that a succession of memories over the years, becoming progressively clearer until the last few days, when he was forty-four, working as a bartender in the Camelot, and met Lilly.

But the person looking back at him out of the mirror was a young man of thirty-two. The computer said the date was Tuesday, October

12, 2010. There was a message in the system from Judy, put there last night, that corroborated it. Had that whole sequence of the last twelve years that he thought he remembered been nothing more than a creation of his mind? Was it possible for a mere dream to be so compelling?

He went back to the den and used the phone to call Lilly's number. The call failed to connect, and he got a message asking if he needed information. That was right—the codes used in 2022 had embodied a new system of multifunction options that confused everybody. He was unable to recall any of the numbers that he had used in 2010, not even his own or Xylog's. Neither could he remember how to get a directory on the phone's miniscreen, so he had to go through the Operator.

"Information. What city, please?"

"Pittsburgh. Do you have a listing for Essell, please? Lillian Essell. The address is 7H Beech Ridge, on Boer Way."

"One moment. . . . I'm sorry sir, I don't have that name listed."

"It's on the North Side. I've been there."

"Well, it's not here. That's all I can tell you."

"How about the Camelot Hotel? Downtown on Fourth Avenue."

"Camelot, with a C, as in King Arthur?"

"That's it."

"No, I don't have that either. Downtown, you say? I've never heard of it."

"One more, then. Do you have the Xylog Corporation?"

"Xylog? You mean the place with the big computer project that's been in the news? I'm sure I have. Do you want the number?"

"Not right now. It's okay. I was just checking something. Thanks for you help."

"Thank you."

Corrigan hung up and stared at the phone. So nothing of the world that he remembered as of yesterday existed out there. Lilly, the Camelot, everything else . . . it had all been a fabrication? He walked slowly back to the kitchen and put on some coffee, forcing himself to try to think.

A dream so vivid that even now it eclipsed his recollections of the world that he found himself back in? The only explanation he could conceive was that in his sleeping fantasies, he had acted out how, unconsciously, he would have wished the project to evolve over years; and—as happens with dreams—his mind had created some bizarre images and interpretations.

Had the project become such an obsession with him as that? If so, then perhaps this was a warning sign, and this time he should take heed. Maybe what some people had been telling him was true, and he was letting himself get unhinged over the business with Tyron. Evelyn might have had a point, he reflected uncomfortably.

But if the whole business of being in the simulation had been a dream, how could it have included a distant memory of reading a message from Judy Klein that he had seen for the first time only a few minutes ago, after he got up? Obviously, the only answer could be that it hadn't been the first time. He must have got up sometime in the middle of the night, checked the mail at that time for whatever reason—and then gone back to bed and forgotten about it. Except that he hadn't quite forgotten it, and his mind had woven it into the dream. That was it. That was how it must have happened. He nodded to himself as he took his first swig of coffee, feeling relieved and unburdened inside now that he had straightened it out.

He washed, shaved, and dressed, and in the process decided that he would eat breakfast out, on the way to Xylog somewhere. It was a pity about Lilly, though. He could have gotten along well with Lilly, he told himself. It seemed that in the process of creating her, his subconscious had fashioned an ideal woman. He was going to miss having her around, even if they did argue a lot. It was funny how somebody could feel that way about a creation in a dream.

And then, as he fastened his tie and put on his jacket, he thought about Evelyn. Again, as if he were really reaching back over years, he remembered distantly how he had acted, and all of a sudden it made him feel shabby. He no longer felt any of the anger or resentment that had raged so violently in him only a week or two before. He could understand how she felt, see the bitterness he had caused, feel her hurt. And God, she had tried. . . . Why had he been so incapable of seeing all this before? Could a dream bring about such changes?

Before leaving, he went back to the den and retrieved Judy's message again in order to call Ed Meechum. But then he realized that he had no idea what the figures from F & F were all about. He would have to wait until he got to the office and reminded himself, he decided.

❀ CHAPTER THIRTY-TWO ❀

For a dream, it was having the strangest effects. In it, he had not driven a car at all during his recovery and rehabilitation process, and later his therapists had discouraged him from acquiring one. By that time he had become used to not owning a vehicle, and living close to the city in Oakland had given no cause for change. But now, on the way in from Fox Chapel in his Mercedes, he felt as if he really hadn't driven for years. He was clumsy on lane changes, getting blared at a couple of times, and found himself uncertain about what should have been a familiar route that he had been taking every day since the move from Blawnox to Southside. Coming in on Route 28, he forgot that he had to exit onto East Ohio Street to get to 279 South, and instead carried on over the Veterans Bridge into the crosstown tangle, where he took a wrong ramp again and ended up in the early-morning downtown pileup, from which it took him fifteen minutes to extricate himself. The main problem was that the city he still remembered himself as living in for the past twelve years had changed more than he'd realized, and he had difficulty recalling the real one. However, he did remember his reserved parking slot at Xylog, found it, and after leaving his car, went up to the sixth floor.

"Good morning, Mr. Corrigan," the receptionist greeted, smiling, as he came through the glass divider from the elevator hall on the sixth floor.

"Good morning . . ." He couldn't remember her name. Nodding an awkward smile, he went on toward his office. Judy was at her post outside, looking relaxed but professional as usual.

"Good morning, Joe. I thought you said you'd be in first thing today. I was here extra early."

"Oh, yes. . . . Sorry about that. I got stuck in traffic."

"Did you get my message about the figures for Meechum?"

"Yes, thanks."

"Called him yet?"

"Not yet. I just wanted to check through them with you first. Remind me what they were about, would you?"

Judy looked at him strangely for an instant, but turned to her keyboard, tapped in a code, and brought a file up onto one of her screens. "It's the statistical correlations that Borth had done for the tests that we ran last week," she said.

Ah, yes, it came back to him now. To impress one of Feller & Faber's moneyed clients, Borth had commissioned a marketing analyst to massage the data from some test runs of "proto-animations" (i.e., primitive creations that had not evolved inside a full simulation yet) in such a way as to suggest that the buying patterns of real supermarket customers were already discernible. It was mainly fiction and wishful thinking, but the client was happy. Also, it would be good publicity material to slip into the interview with Meechum.

His memory refreshed, Corrigan asked Judy to get ahold of Meechum and went into his office. Inside, he stopped and looked around at the walnut-topped desk with its onyx penholders, shelves of reference books and reports that he liked to keep handy, diplomas and pictures framed on the wall. . . . Already, the sights of familiar things were triggering more memories and associations. The dream was beginning to fade at last; he could get back to being himself, and on with the important business at hand. There was a memo board with some cartoons and other clippings that, on the whole as he looked at them, struck him as somewhat immature and slightly silly for the office of a prospective technical director in this kind of operation. He made a mental note to get rid of them that morning. Also, on a shelf of a wall unit close by, was the figurine of an Irish leprechaun that cousin Jeff had given to Corrigan and Evelyn as a wedding gift during their honeymoon visit to Ireland. He frowned at it, puzzled. He was certain that Evelyn had put it on the window ledge in the den back at the house. What was it doing here?

Then the call tone sounded from the comm unit on one side of the desk. "I've got Ed Meechum," Judy's voice called through the open doorway.

"Okay." Corrigan activated the screen, then hesitated, confused by the display of icons and options that it presented. After a few seconds Judy turned and leaned across to peer in at him.

"Aren't you going to take it?"

"Er . . . I'm having a block today. What do I do?"

"Just hit Enter. It's on Auto Accept." She said it in the same tone that she might have used to tell him that turning the wheel steered the car.

"Oh, right. . . . Ed, hi."

Meechum's features appeared on the screen: lean, toothy, and with thinning hair, but at the same time healthy and vigorous, with a pink-skinned, open-air complexion. "How's it going, Joe? Got some news for me?"

"Yes. We've got the figures. Want me to copy them through?" The eerie thing was that he remembered saying something like this before. How could the "dream" explain that? . . . Unless he had somehow projected it into the dream in anticipation, because he knew he was due to call Meechum. How could one stupid dream have gotten him feeling as rattled and confused as this?

"Great," Meechum said. "How do they look?"

"Oh . . . I haven't really had a chance to go through them closely, Ed. But from what Borth says, they look like what you wanted."

"Me? Hell, it's you who's been pushing them on me, Joe."

"Oh, yes. Right."

"I've had Frank Tyron on me as well this morning, wanting to get a plug in about the new version of the interface hardware," Meechum went on. He winked conspiratorially. "But I remembered what we agreed yesterday." Corrigan had no idea who agreed what yesterday. "You're all set for filming at four o'clock. Is that okay?"

"How long are we talking about?" Corrigan asked.

"For the interview?"

"Yes."

"What I already told you: forty-five minutes, probably cut to around ten minutes' air time." Meechum looked pleased with himself, as if he were waiting for congratulations. He was saying that he was on Corrigan's side, and they both understood how everything stacked up.

Corrigan sighed inwardly. There was serious work to do and a major project with all kinds of unknowns confronting them. Getting the job done was going to need all the talent they could muster. Suddenly, the whole business with Tyron that had been dragging on and interfering with everything forever seemed so unimportant and idiotic. Why exacerbate it any further?

"Hell, there's time enough in that for both of us. Why don't we simply get Frank in on it too?" Corrigan said.

Meechum stared out of the screen incredulously. "Tyron? You mean you want to let him on the show? You don't mind? You're saying you'll hand him half the action?"

"Why not? He's done a good job on the COSMOS interface. It'll give you some good stuff."

"Well, sure . . . if you say so." Meechum shook his head as if this was all too much for him. "You want me to just go ahead and fix it with him, then?"

"Yes, do that."

Meechum nodded, shook his head again, then decided to drop it. "I was thinking, Joe, afterward, we could get a cocktail someplace and have dinner. Maybe that place in the mall along by the river, the Gaucho, was it?"

That was where they had gone in the dream, Corrigan remembered. Had it been somehow prophetic, in the paranormal kind of way that he'd heard tell about but never had any time for? Could there be something to it after all? He wondered if he was tied in some inexplicable way to acting out those things that he remembered, or was he free to alter them if he chose? Try it, he told himself.

"I've had enough of the Gaucho, Ed," he replied. "Let's make it somewhere different this time. How about the Sheraton? It's practically next door."

"Suits me."

Which seemed to answer that question.

"I'll get Judy to fix it," Corrigan said. "So we'll see you here later."

"Four o'clock."

The screen cleared, and Corrigan looked up to see that Judy was waiting just inside the doorway, holding a folder and some papers. He motioned her in. She approached and placed the wad on the desk. "Gary called through while you were on the line. He's on his way."

"Gary?"

"Gary Quinn."

Oh, yes. He had been one of Tom Hatcher's software engineers, Corrigan recalled. "What for?" he asked.

"What for? To talk about the spec you wanted to change. There's the file, with a fax that came through from Cindi in Blawnox." Judy watched uneasily as Corrigan sat down and turned the sheets. From his actions it was clear that he wasn't sure what he was supposed to be looking for. "Joe, you'd been here talking about it for an hour when I left last night. It's the spec for the second-level attribute cross-linkages. It has to be approved and sent through to Keith before lunch today."

"Oh, yes. . . . Right. I just need a minute to recap. It's okay, Judy. You can carry on."

But Judy stayed where she was, looking worried. "I have to ask, are you feeling all right today, Joe? You've been burning it at both ends for months. . . . And now this thing with Evelyn on top of it all. Let me slot you in sometime today for a check."

"No, it's all right. I guess I hit the bars a bit last night. Probably a reaction, eh? Everything's still hazy."

Judy shook her head. "What's happening to everybody this morning? Tom Hatcher was supposed to be here too, but his secretary says he hasn't showed up—not even a word. And the full simulation is scheduled to go live in three days' time. It's crazy."

"Maybe Tom's been feeling the strain and doing some unwinding too," Corrigan said, forcing a grin. "Be an angel for me, would you? Fetch me a strong, hot coffee, black with nothing, and I'll be fine."

☸ CHAPTER THIRTY-THREE ☸

Somehow he muddled his way through until the late morning, when Amanda Ramussienne called. She was still in New York.

"Joe, hi darling," she crooned. "Look, I hate to do this, but I'm gonna have to break your heart. Something's come up that I can't do anything about, which means I'm stuck in town and can't make it down there today. Promise you won't hold it against me for the rest of time."

So it appeared that lots of things were free to change: Here was one less complication to deal with. Corrigan decided he could live with that. He forced a resigned grin. "Well, too bad. Life happens, I guess."

"And I was *so* looking forward to it! You still have that promise to keep."

"We'll get by." Corrigan had no idea what she meant. "I appreciate your letting me know."

"You're so understanding. I'll make it up with interest."

"I'll be here."

"Well, it's all a panic here. Have to go. You'll do great on the interview with Ed. I wanted to be there. So sorry again, Joe." She winked a promise; blew him a kiss, and vanished.

Corrigan sat, staring at the blank screen, wondering what had possessed him. Looking back from where he saw things now, the whole business with Amanda felt grubby and sordid. Had the phoniness and gaudiness always been that transparent? And then the full realization dawned on him that it hadn't all happened *then*; it was *now*. It was possible that he could straighten things out with Evelyn.

Then Judy came through to remind him that he was due to have lunch with somebody from another F & F client. The name meant nothing. "What's it about?" Corrigan asked.

"He's the one who thinks Oz could be used to try out an idea he's had for using media superheroes to promote products to adults the way they do already with juveniles," Judy said.

Corrigan remembered him. A complete flake. He had talked without stopping all through lunch, without telling Corrigan anything he didn't already know. Corrigan couldn't face the prospect of repeating it. "You know, maybe you're right," he told Judy. "Maybe I'm not feeling myself today. Can you fob him off for me? Tell him something vital has come up on the project—anything."

"Leave it to me," Judy said.

Corrigan went off to a coffee shop in Station Square to think and be alone.

For he was unable to avoid a conviction that had been steadily growing inside him all morning that the impressions that he had woken up with that morning of having lived years past today were not the result of some extraordinarily vivid dream or fabrication, but that it *had* happened, somehow, and now he was back at the age of thirty-two again and had lived this day before. But how could that be? Things like that simply didn't happen.

All he could think of was that the life he remembered living after having the breakdown and Oz being canceled had, in fact, been real, but distorted in the process of his gradual recovery—in other words, exactly what he had been told it was. In that case, everything he was experiencing now was an illusion, perhaps taking place in the course of some kind of catastrophic relapse manufactured out of his stored experiences from long ago. So was he really back in Mercy Hospital or somewhere in 2022, thinking that he was back in 2010, before he had the breakdown? But if everything he was experiencing was the product of a deranged mind, then anything was possible and his situation was a total solipsism, with no possibility of his being able to prove or disprove anything by any form of investigation or experiment, one way or the other.

But then, on the other hand, would a deranged mind be capable of thinking it through this logically? In which case it was real. But since time travel didn't happen, if it was true, it followed logically that it had to be a delusion. Unless, of course, he was only *thinking* that he was being logical. . . .

At that point he gave it up as hopeless and went back to the office.

One corner of the main reception lobby had been turned into a mini TV studio. Meechum was on a couch in the center behind a low, glass-topped table, with Corrigan sitting in an armchair on one side and Tyron on the other. The crew had set up lights and improvised a background from drapes, potted plants, and a sign bearing Xylog's corporate logo.

After a short introduction, Meechum turned to Corrigan and picked up his main theme. "Tell us, Joe, isn't it like being God, in a way? I'm told that Oz will be a world in itself, inhabited by computer creations that behave exactly as real people do. As the manager of Xylog's software division, you're the person largely responsible for those creations. How does it feel?"

Corrigan stared down at his hands for a moment, reflecting on all the hype and exaggeration and wishful thinking masquerading as fact that had been dispensed on the subject. A public circus was not the place where science should be conducted. It was time to make a start on setting the record straight right now.

He looked up. "Let's clear up a lot of wrong information that has been put out about this, that shouldn't have been," he said. "We are not about to create an artificial world that's going to model how people in the real world think and behave—the products they'd buy, how they'd vote on this issue or that issue, what they like, what they don't like, or anything else like that. Human behavior is one of the most complex phenomena ever studied. For forty years now, some of the most intensive research going on in the world has been aimed at trying to emulate the full versatility of what we call 'intelligence,' and for the most part it's got nowhere. All we're doing at Oz is exploring an alternative approach to achieving that: an Artificial Intelligence— a process that functions something like the way we do. That's all. Whether such an AI—assuming that we're successful—could form the basis of a lifelike simulation of the real world is a question that lies way in the future and is one that we're not even considering yet."

Meechum was looking a bit taken aback. He accepted as a matter of course that part of his job was to be a paid hack, and he had been ready to help plug the product in whatever direction his guests chose to steer things. But this sudden shrinking of a current sensation down to lifelike proportions was something that he had not been prepared for. "That's, er, something of a more cautious assessment than a lot of the things we've been hearing," he commented.

"My first role is as a scientist," Corrigan said. "I'm simply reporting the facts as to what the goals of the Oz project are, as currently formulated. I can also speculate on what it might lead to in times to come, if you like. But that wasn't your question."

On Meechum's other side, Tyron was following with a mixture four parts bewilderment to one of confusion. His first reaction on hearing of Corrigan's offer to share the show had been one of suspicion, and he had arrived ready to outdo anything Corrigan might try adding to what had already been said to please the ears of the project's financial backers. It did cross his mind as he heard this that Corrigan's intention might be to throw him off stride and steal all the thunder, but the fact remained that in the meantime, right off the top of his head, he didn't have a lot to say that was wildly inspirational to counter it. So when his turn came, he took up the theme that Corrigan had set and concentrated on the new interfaces and associated hardware that formed his main contribution to the project, the principles underlying its operation—which were fascinating—and what it could reasonably be expected to accomplish.

Meechum grew more relaxed as it became evident that the animosity that he had been waiting to see surfacing between them was not going to happen, and the rest of the interview went well. But it was Corrigan who set the tone, while the other two responded. Although he was physically the youngest, his unswerving dedication to principle and insistence on frankness inspired everyone watching. When they were getting up after the cameras stopped rolling, Meechum said, "Joe, that makes more sense than anything I've heard in ages. You carry a wise head on young shoulders."

Pinder, who had come down from the top floor to watch, walked over to Corrigan while the NBC people were packing away their equipment. He seemed intrigued in a guarded kind of way.

"You handled that . . . interestingly, Joe," he said. "Interestingly, but well. Very commanding and positive."

"Thanks."

"It was more down to earth than I expected. You, ah, seem to be taking a more sober view of things all of a sudden."

"I try to be realistic," Corrigan said. "Fooling yourself isn't going to help anyone in the long run."

"There could be some flak from Borth's people. It wasn't the crystal ball that they've been painting to their clients. This could burst a few balloons."

"Probably better now than later, then," Corrigan said. "Investors are the worst ones to fool."

Pinder looked at him curiously for a second. "Ed tells me that it was your suggestion to put Frank on the show as well."

"Sure, why not? Frank and his people have done some neat things. The idea was to make the show interesting, right?"

Pinder cast an eye around and lowered his voice reflexively. "What I'm saying is, it isn't exactly the best strategy for the longer term from your point of view—with things being the way they are." In other words, as they both knew, Pinder's term as acting technical chief of Xylog would end soon. Corrigan was not optimizing his chances of stepping into the slot by sharing the limelight.

"Let's get the ship launched first," Corrigan replied. "When we know it floats, then we can worry about who'll play captain." Which was what Pinder thought he had been hearing, but he had wanted to be sure.

"You've changed in a big way, Joe," Pinder told him.

Something about Pinder had changed too. He was too wary, feeling his way with probing questions that seemed somehow out of character. The assertiveness that Corrigan remembered was missing. It was almost as if Pinder hadn't known Corrigan as long as Corrigan had known him, and was unsure what kind of reactions to expect. But then, from Corrigan's distorted perspective of things, it had been a long time for *him*. Maybe he didn't remember Pinder as well as he thought.

And, indeed, Corrigan did seem to have undergone a change in his personality that appeared permanent. For by the time the party sat down to dinner in the Sheraton, the twelve years of pseudolife that he remembered himself as having lived were just as clear in his mind as when he had woken up that morning, while his recollections from yesterday and the days before, although jogged and reawakened to some degree by the events of the day, were for the most part just as remote.

However, as if to compensate for the loss of detail from his immediate past, he seemed to have retained the maturity that had developed in the course of living through years that were still ahead of him. This expressed itself as a charisma that affected everyone present at the table in the same way that it had enabled him to dominate—without domineering—the TV interview earlier.

Among those present was a Graham Sylvine, from a department in Washington that prepared appraisals for scientific-policy reviews. He had been following the Oz project for some time, and appeared in Pittsburgh without warning late that afternoon. He reminded Corrigan of somebody, but Corrigan was unable for the moment to put his finger on just who. "The next phase will be the first full-system run, is that correct?" he asked Corrigan.

"That's right," Corrigan confirmed.

"What does that imply, exactly?"

"So far we've only been testing parts of the simulation as separate pieces. Next we bring them all together as a full system. Also, we'll be introducing the first real-world surrogates: operators coupled into the simulation to act as models for the animations to learn to emulate."

"Did you hire actors?" a woman across the table asked.

Corrigan smiled. There had in fact been some talk about doing just that. "We wondered about it," he replied. "The problem was that it might all work too well and we'd end up with a world full of actors. So we decided to stick with ordinary people just being themselves."

"I take it that you won't be one of these surrogates," Sylvine said.

Corrigan shook his head. "They're on a full-time commitment. I'll be going in and out of the simulation to keep an eye on how it's going, sure—but my place is really on the outside, watching the whole thing."

"What kind of risk is there in all this connecting into people's heads?" another woman asked. "It sounds horribly spooky to me."

"Naturally we wouldn't be proceeding without testing as thorough as it's possible to make it," Corrigan replied. "But I'd be less than frank if I told you that we know everything. Of course there are uncertainties. That's how you learn. Life and progress toward better things couldn't exist otherwise."

"Well, what we've been hearing today sure makes a change from all the PR bull," Meechum said. "Now I'll be frank with you, Joe. Listening to you talking today has been the first stuff about this whole project that I've really believed for months."

"It's about time, then," Corrigan said.

Sylvine was vague about when he would be returning to Washington. He asked Corrigan a series of technical questions about the basis of Oz and what it might lead to. The surrogates seemed of particular interest to him. He wanted to know what kind of world they would perceive from the inside. Also, he raised the possibility of memory suppression and was intrigued by Corrigan's account of how the possibility had been considered and rejected by the Oz designers. It occurred to Corrigan that perhaps this constantly recurring issue was of more concern to him unconsciously than he realized, and maybe that was what had caused him to cast himself as a subject of it in the dream.

The person that Sylvine reminded him of, Corrigan realized as he watched him, was Dr. Zehl—Sarah Bewley's supervisor in the dreamed simworld. He wasn't quite sure why, although it certainly had nothing to do with physical similarity. Perhaps it was that Zehl, too, had been from Washington; or maybe his tendency to appear suddenly, without warning.

The woman who had inquired about risk was still watching Corrigan and thinking to herself. When a lull presented itself, she asked him, "Do you really think that we do progress toward better things, Mr. Corrigan?"

Corrigan wiped his mouth with a napkin. "Certainly we do," he answered. "Evolution is a self-improving process. Hence change is for the better, by definition."

"I'd have to think about that," the woman said dubiously.

"I never realized before that you were so much of a philosopher," Pinder said to Corrigan. He had been watching Corrigan and saying little throughout, still showing much of the interest and curiosity that had been evident earlier.

"That was one of the things I learned as a bartender," Corrigan replied unthinkingly.

Pinder looked surprised. "Really? I never knew you had been a bartender. When was that?"

For a second or two Corrigan was flummoxed. "Oh . . . that was way back, when I was earning my way as a student in Ireland," he said finally.

He looked around, grinning. Everyone smiled back. He could become anything he wanted, he realized. He was a young man again, free to relive a crucial part of his life—and as far as he could see, with the benefit of all the accumulated experience of having lived the next twelve years before.

Maybe this was a dream, and maybe it wasn't; he had all but given up trying to tell. But either way, it seemed he had no way of breaking out of it if it was, or of changing the situation if it wasn't. So he might as well make the best of it. This time around, then, he decided, it would be a great ride.

He tried calling around to locate Evelyn when he got back later that night, but nobody he talked to could give him a lead. It seemed that everybody he'd known in Boston had either moved or was out of town. None of the few that he did manage to get through to had heard from her.

❂ CHAPTER THIRTY-FOUR ❂

"I just thought you'd like to know, Borth called Ken Endelmyer at home last night," Pinder said from the screen of the comm unit on Corrigan's desk. The NBC interview had been aired as part of a current-affairs documentary following the six-o'clock news the previous evening. "I'm assuming that he wasn't very happy."

"Which was pretty much to be expected," Corrigan answered. His tone was matter-of-fact, with no second thoughts or regrets. "I still think it will do more good this way in the long run, after the dust settles."

Pinder rubbed his chin as if still pondering something that he had spent a lot of time on, and nodded. "I've been thinking about it since yesterday, and I have to agree. The air needed clearing. Things have been getting out of control for a long time. So the other thing I wanted you to know is that if things do get rough, you can count on my support. As you say, it will do everyone more good in the long run."

"Well, thanks: I appreciate it." Corrigan said.

"I'll keep you posted if I hear anything more," Pinder promised, and hung up.

Like the others at the TV interview the day before, and at dinner in the evening, Pinder too had succumbed to following Corrigan's lead, almost as if their roles of senior and junior in the line of command had been reversed. And it had happened so naturally and easily, Corrigan realized, that he didn't even think about it.

There had still been no sign or word of Tom Hatcher since yesterday, which was odd, considering that they were in the last days of preparation before Oz. Already some critical decisions had had to be delayed, and the software section-heads were getting anxious. Corrigan was wondering whether he ought to have somebody check with the police, when his desk unit buzzed again and Judy came through on voice.

"Ken Endelmyer's secretary at Head Office is holding. Also, I've got another reporter on the line, wanting to talk to you: a Lola Ellis from *Futures* magazine in L.A., but she's here in Pittsburgh right now."

Corrigan sighed. "Let's see what himself wants and get it over with. Slot the reporter in when you can for later." The Meechum interview had apparently made an impression—this was the third journalist this morning asking for more information.

"She's being very insistent," Judy said. "She seemed to think you'd recognize the name."

Corrigan grinned as he signed some letters that he had been checking when Pinder called. "A good try, but I've never heard of her. Fix an appointment, will you, and put Celia through. Oh, and could you try calling Tom's place one more time, Judy?"

"Will do. You're through," Judy's voice said. At the same time Corrigan's schedule for the day appeared on the screen, with Celia's face framed in a window in one corner.

"Top o' the mornin'," Corrigan said, accentuating his brogue.

"Hello, Mr. Corrigan. I'm sorry to drop this on you at such short notice, but Mr. Endelmyer would like to meet with you rather urgently. Could you get over here for, say, eleven o'clock this morning?" Coming from such heights, it was an order couched as a request merely for form. God, Corrigan thought to himself, he must really have stirred things up. He saw on his schedule that he had a couple of things fixed for around then, but they would just have to be shifted.

"Yes, that will be fine," he replied.

"We'll see you at eleven, then."

The window with the face vanished, and Corrigan called up a color bar to indicate to Judy the appointments that would have to be changed. Her voice came through again a moment later.

"Still nothing from Tom. I've put Lola Ellis in to see you here at four-thirty this afternoon. Uh-oh . . ." Judy had just seen Corrigan's changes flagged on her monitor outside. "What's this? Has something come up for this morning?"

"I have to report to the general," Corrigan said.

"What's up?"

"Celia didn't say. Firing squad, probably."

Judy paused just long enough to be discreet. "I thought you were very good. But you did rock the party boat a bit."

Corrigan snorted. "Well, maybe this is where I get told that I'm not going to get my captain's hat."

"That would be a shame," Judy said.

"Ah, not a bit of it," Corrigan told her. "We can always go and work in a bar."

But to Corrigan's surprise, the summons was not for him to be shot. He arrived to find that Victor Borth had come down unexpectedly that morning from New York. Pinder was there also, along with a couple of the other CLC vice presidents. It turned out that Borth had not contacted Endelmyer the night before to vent fury about Corrigan's performance, but to commend it.

"I was gonna get him fired," Borth admitted candidly. "I was as mad as hell." He made a short, stabbing gesture toward where Corrigan was sitting. "This turkey had loused everything up. It was going to be panic out there—backers running in a stampede to get out after some of the things he said." Corrigan caught Pinder's eye across the table. They shrugged at each other, both equally at a loss as to guess what might have changed things. Borth went on. "Then I get a call from Milton Perl." Perl was Chief Executive Officer of Berrenhauser Trusts, one of the major backers, who had marshaled a consortium of commercial banks and investment houses behind the project. "And what do you know—Milt loved it! You see, they *had* been getting bad vibes for some time over the whole project, and they *were* talking about pulling out—the whole shooting match, the consortium, the works. Those guys aren't so stupid. . . . I mean, you don't get to be worth that much if you don't know your head from your ass, right? They knew it wasn't going to happen the way they'd been hearing it. 'Vic,' Milt says to me, 'I've been worried.' See, his people *knew* that nothing even close to this has ever been tried before in history, and that there are all kinds of questions nobody has answers to. But they also know that you never get anywhere if you won't take risks. 'We were willing to take a risk, Vic,' he says to me. 'But in return we expected honesty. All we wanted to hear was somebody tell us to our faces that there could be no guarantees. Then we'd know we were all on the same side and working to solve the same problem, right? But that wasn't what we got. Instead, all we got was bullshit.'"

Borth pointed at Corrigan again. "Until *he* said it! And now Milt and his friends are happy people." Borth spread his hands and treated everyone to an uncharacteristically appeasing smile. "Okay, I admit that I laid it on a bit, too, at times. But I'm not one of these tech-whiz geniuses. I guess a lot of people got carried away in the excitement, eh? But now everybody's feet are on the ground again, and this is a good time to reappraise things."

Endelmyer looked startled. "Reappraise things? What are you saying, exactly?"

Borth raised a restraining hand. "Oh, it's okay, Ken. Don't get me wrong. I used the wrong word. 'Consolidate' might be better. The project stays, no question. But Milt does want to go over the goals and purpose again, now that people are making sense, so we're probably talking about putting back the start date."

"I hope he's not asking for a redesign," Pinder said apprehensively.

"Nothing like that," Borth assured everyone. "Like I said, Milt is a happy man today. But he does want to be clear on what the limits are and what can realistically be expected. As far as Oz goes, the technical design, organization, and operations stays with CLC, the way we've always agreed. The only thing that Milt *did* insist on in that area . . ." Borth leveled a finger at Corrigan again, "is that he wants *him* in charge of it."

They stayed for the remainder of the morning discussing details, and then went to lunch, which Borth insisted on standing. And so there it was. After months of rivalry, backbiting, and infighting that had produced nothing but tension and bad feelings all around, Corrigan accepted, as the talk flowed around him, that in under a day he had attained everything he'd wanted. And it had not had to be fought for or conceded grudgingly, at that, but was being thrust upon him eagerly. Just a little integrity had worked wonders when the compounded results of suspicion and fear of failure had been about to bring disaster.

And it was all due to this extraordinary situation that he found himself in, whereby he was able to apply an older man's experience to a young man's circumstances. If it had proved this effective in the course of one day, he wondered if there was any end to where it might lead in the years still ahead of him.

Back in his own office that afternoon, he found himself wondering if this might explain the phenomenon of genius, that the world had been baffled by for as long as people had been around to think about it. He had convinced himself by this time that his experiences of the day before had been nothing more than a peculiar form of déjà vu, brought on by the sudden activation of a heightened level of consciousness at which he was now functioning. Events since yesterday were diverging so rapidly from anything in the "dream" that any feeling of having lived this time before had for the most part already left him.

But the altered perspective and perspicacity of vision that had accompanied that strange sensation of regression—the calm, inner confidence that he knew where he wanted to go and why, knew how to get there, and that it would not be the end of everything if he messed it up anyway—remained. He felt like a mouse that had been raised to some privileged vantage point from where he could watch the others still scurrying about in the maze. He could see where all the courses led, what lay at the end of every decision path, and in which direction changes would alter them.

Perhaps, far from being unique, this altered state of perception that seemed, as yet, beyond the ability of physics and psychology to explain, was something that had happened to many individuals of exceptional achievement and ability throughout the past. If so, it was little wonder why so few of those affected had cared to speak out. Far better to be an Einstein or a Da Vinci without the complications of trying to explain what would probably never be believed anyway, than risk being locked up as insane. And then again, maybe many of those who did try to convey their experiences had been put away, excommunicated, burned, banished, or whatever for just that. It was often said that the borderline between genius and madness was very thin. And as he got to thinking more, it struck him as significant how much of the world's religious teachings could be interpreted as coded references to undergoing a mystical rebeginning of life: "born again;" "life after life;" "inner enlightenments" that can only be experienced, not described. Suddenly, it all took on a new meaning.

Through the afternoon, he went mechanically through the routine of taking calls, seeing visitors, checking on the project, and dealing with queries from Judy. There was still no word from Hatcher, and he told Judy to check with the police to see if there was any record of an accident. Pinder called to let him know that the rumor was already going around the top floor of Corporate HQ that Corrigan was tipped to be the technical director of Xylog. The news must have got back to New York ahead of Borth, too, for Amanda Ramussienne was on the line a half hour later.

"I see Pittsburgh is in the news," she crooned from the screen, giving him one of her special sultry looks through half-closed lids.

"Why? What's happened?" Corrigan asked.

"You don't watch it?"

"No time for trivia. Anyhow, I only believe the advertising. What's happened?"

"Oh, I assumed you'd know about it. There was a shootout at the airport there—less than an hour ago. A maniac went wild and shot some police officers. Anyhow . . ." She smiled a seduction. "But, as a matter of fact, if the rumors I hear are anything to go by, you are getting famous down there too. There's a whisper that you're going to get the tech-chief slot at Xylog."

"Who whispered that, now?"

"Oh, a little bird."

Corrigan shook his head despairingly. "Nothing's confirmed. We'll see how it goes."

Amanda became more serious. "So there is something to it, then?"

"It's looking promising," was all Corrigan would say.

She brightened up. "So when are you coming up to New York again? We need to celebrate."

"I told you, nothing's definite."

She pouted. "Well, what's wrong with *practicing* celebrating? I need your kind of company."

An icon indicated another call waiting, with a message caption superposed from Judy that read: MILTON PERL, BERRENHAUSER. "Amanda, sorry, but I have to go," Corrigan said. "Something's waiting."

"Let me know soon, then?"

"Sure. 'Bye."

Perl was calling to suggest that he and Corrigan ought to meet sometime and get to know each other better. Corrigan agreed, and they fixed a dinner spot for the end of the week. Then Endelmyer's secretary came through again to advise that a meeting was being scheduled for the following week to reappraise Oz, and the Board would like Corrigan to present his assessment and proposals.

But commercial and material success were by now beginning to look mundane to Corrigan. Carried away in his inner speculations, he found himself wondering about the possibility of devoting himself to more profound callings. He experienced a conviction of being destined for greater things: things that would shake the world, rewrite a chapter of science, shape history. . . . And then Judy buzzed through to say that Lola Ellis from California had arrived and was waiting outside.

As soon as Judy showed her in, Lola wearing a blue coat and carrying a white purse, Corrigan knew that they had met before, but something looked wrong. And she obviously knew him, for instead of acting like somebody being shown into the office of a stranger, she stood waiting expectantly . . . yet at the same time showing apprehensiveness, as if unsure whether he would know her.

Ellis, Essell. Lola. . . . Of course! He should have gotten it from the name alone. She was twelve years younger too, of course, but he should have known the features well enough.

It was Lilly, from his dream life. A twelve-year-younger version of Lilly.

But that made nonsense out of everything that he'd come to terms with over the last two days. For she didn't belong here. How could somebody from a dream fabrication suddenly walk into this life?

He nodded to Judy, and she left, closing the door. Corrigan and Lilly stood, staring at each other.

He shook his head, nonplussed. Lilly watched his face, giving him that same uncanny feelings that she had always been able to that she was reading the thoughts going on behind. Then she nodded, and he realized in the same moment what she had been looking for and had seen there.

"It's happened to you too, hasn't it?" Lilly said.

❀ CHAPTER THIRTY-FIVE ❀

Idiotic fantasies! Megalomaniac delusions!

Corrigan asked himself yet again how he could have allowed himself to be so carried away by it all. All he had needed to do was check the list of Air Force volunteers who were coming to Pittsburgh to see if it included a Lillian Essell from California. If it did, then she had not been a fabrication concocted in his head. Neither, then, had the rest of the simworld existence that he remembered.

They walked slowly along the embankment by the river between the Gateway Clipper Landing, where the tourist riverboats berthed, and the Smithfield Street Bridge. The day was dull and overcast with a hint of rain on the way, the river gray and sluggish. On the far side, the evening traffic was building up on the Penn Lincoln Parkway at the foot of the vertical, rectangular foothills of downtown Pittsburgh. They had got out of Xylog to be on their own and try to think through what it meant. Corrigan had been silent for a long time. Lilly stared ahead, her hands thrust deep in her coat pockets, leaving him all the time he needed.

Yesterday she had woken up to find herself twelve years younger, back in the hotel where the Air Force volunteers for Oz had been lodged that long ago, the day after her arrival from California. She remembered going to Xylog with the others, but her recollections of exactly what took place were vague, since, like Corrigan, she was recalling them from a perspective of many years later; soon after that they ceased completely, and the next thing she knew was being confused and slowly coming together again in the same kind of way as he had experienced.

And then she found herself suddenly about to relive that day again. As before, she had come to Xylog yesterday—and might even have bumped into him if he had happened to go across to the DNC Training Lab in one of the other buildings, where the new arrivals were being briefed and introduced to Oz. Like him, as she grappled with the weirdness of the situation and began experimenting, she discovered that she was not bound to relive what she remembered but could change things. Unlike him, she had thought to seek him out as part of what she, too, had been tempted to rationalize as a "dreamworld," and find out if he existed in this one. In a group from outside the company confined to a different building, she hadn't been able to get near him in the day yesterday, and he disappeared for the evening after the TV interview. So this morning she invented Lola Ellis.

There was no question that they had met in the simworld. When they compared experiences, they found that they remembered the same places, the same people, the same events, the same conversations together. The simulation had happened. There could be no doubt about that. But if that was the case, how could the simulation have not yet started?

One explanation, of course, was that the whole thing *had* been an internal creation in Corrigan's mind, and still was: that what he thought he was hearing and thinking now was just as much a part of it as everything else. In that case he was totally insane, there didn't seem to be much he could do about it, and the only choice open was to go with the ride and wait to see where it took him. But he had been around that same weary, frustrating loop enough times, and since no logical process could help if he accepted that as the answer, he rejected it through pure Irish obstinacy if nothing else. In any case, he told himself, if he were going to go to the trouble of going insane to invent an alternate reality to escape into, surely he would have made it a more entertaining and hedonistic affair than this.

A chill breeze was starting to lift off the water, the kind that nipped the ears and found chinks in clothes. Corrigan directed their steps across the court by the riverside parking lot, toward the Freight House—a onetime railroad terminal building, now converted into a complex of shops and restaurants. "Let's head inside and get a coffee or something," he muttered. "Maybe a bite to eat."

"Did you have lunch?" Lilly asked.

"No chance of missing it in this job."

He went over the facts in his head one more time. The simulation had been real—the way they both remembered. It had been taken to a degree of realism that went beyond anything he had known was planned. Their memories of going into it had been suppressed and a cover story manufactured to disguise the cruder early phases, which again, as far as he had ever been aware, had not been the intention. He was supposed to have been one of the controllers, able to enter and leave intermittently at will, fully aware of what was going on. The only explanation there could be to that much was that another design group that he didn't know about had been organized somewhere, who had vastly extended the scale and concept of the operation, added the memory-suppression option that he had declined, and then sprung it on the surrogates unannounced—as they would have to if the memory suppression was going to serve any purpose.

Fine, so far. That much was what Lilly had already tried to tell him. But it still failed to explain how he and Lilly could be carrying recollections of their experiences inside a simulation that had not yet begun. The only answer to that was, they could not.

They came to the entrance into the mall. Corrigan stopped to gaze at the gaily stocked shops and booths, the decorations and colored lights, the crowds of evening shoppers; he went back in his mind over the events of the last two days. It was uncanny, but there was only one explanation left.

"When you woke up yesterday, you were back in a hotel, right?" he said.

"Yes."

"Not at Xylog. But if we were back in 2010 after coming out of the simulation, why didn't you find yourself in a lab somewhere, where you must have been to take part in Oz in the first place? And how was it that I found myself back at home in Fox Chapel?"

Lilly shook her head. She had been going through the same convolutions as he in her own head, and had tied herself in similar knots. "Everything was so confused from around this time. I've just about given up trying to make sense of it," she replied.

Corrigan began moving again, leading them over to an open-fronted store with counters displaying ladies' jewelry, perfumes, and cosmetics. "It needed to be confusing," he said, not looking at her but studying the items arrayed on the shelves. "To disguise the crossover while the system was still learning. We thought we were recovering from perceptual dislocations. But all the time it was the world that was getting better, not us." He smiled in a peculiar, crooked kind of way. "It's got a lot better since then, hasn't it, don't you think?"

"What are you talking about?"

"It needed those cover stories so that the surrogates wouldn't cotton on—the *first* time around."

Lilly caught the emphasis. "I'm not sure I follow. . . ." But her voice was little more than a whisper, her eyes suddenly fearful. A part of her, at least, followed him, all right.

Corrigan picked up one of the sample bottles of perfume from the counter and dabbed it on the back of his hand. He sniffed, then extended his arm toward Lilly. "Like it?" he asked her.

She started to shake her head and say something, then checked herself and lowered her face. There was no smell at all. Nothing. She straightened up slowly, shaking her head, refusing for a moment longer to face what it meant.

Corrigan nodded. "I can't smell it either. The first cranial nerve, the olfactory, synapses directly in the cerebrum. We never could get the sense of smell right, could we?"

For what it meant was, they had never come out of the simulation at all. It was still running.

And not only that. Somebody on the outside was *rerunning* it from the beginning.

In a small room off the Monitor & Control Center on the third floor of the main Xylog building, a small group of people listened tensely to Tyron's aide, Harry Morgen, just up from the gallery of interface cubicles on the level below. Tyron was there, so was Borth, John Velucci from CLC Legal, and also Joan Sutton, the other technical specialist who had first followed Tyron from SDC. A technician standing beside Morgen had brought a hardcopy of the trace report that he had asked for on returning from the simulation. Things were not going according to plan.

"She tried to contact him in Xylog," Morgen informed the others. "Now she's due to see him, posing as a journalist."

Tyron was peering at a screen showing a status update on Corrigan, revised in the last few seconds. "His behavior is way outside his computed assigned norms. The system can't make sense out of it. His SDV index is down to fifteen percent."

"What does all that mean?" Borth asked.

"That something unexpected is motivating them," Tyron said.

Joan Sutton was shaking her head in a way that said this confirmed all she had been fearing. She was the one who had urged more caution all along, and opposed the latest extension of the original plan, which had thrown everything into a new dimension of risk and uncertainty.

"The forced reset was too soon," she told the others. "It should never have been attempted at this stage. The erasure function was too much of an improvisation, to say the least. With the time-rate differential there was no chance for a rational evaluation."

"The opportunity was too much to let slip by," Tyron insisted, defending the decision that had been at his urging, and also for Borth's benefit. "We had to go with it."

As the representative from the top floor of Corporate HQ, Velucci was the de facto chairman of the proceedings. "That's all history now. Time's running. What's the recommendation?" he asked them. This kind of briskness had become routine. In the five minutes that they had been debating, the simulation had already moved into a new day.

"Too many uncertainties. Shut it down now," Joan Sutton said without hesitation.

"I disagree," Tyron said. "I say, send Harry back inside, maybe with you, Joan, to give a second opinion. We can still get a lot of mileage out of this."

Morgen nodded. "I support Frank."

"We can't quit now," Borth pleaded. "This is where all the backers get their payoff. It's worth hundreds of millions."

"What about the people in there who are being rerun?" Sutton demanded. "They'll sue for every cent in the company."

"We've got enough money to keep them sweet. We've got lawyers. We can handle that when the time comes," Borth said.

Impasse. Everyone looked toward Velucci. He got a connection to Endelmyer at CLC's Head Office on one of the conference screens, summarized the situation, and requested a ruling.

"Are they in any immediate risk?" Endelmyer queried.

"No," Tyron answered firmly.

"We don't know," Sutton said.

"That's pure speculation," Morgen said.

"Any risk that we can positively identify," Endelmyer corrected.

"No," Tyron said again. This time Sutton remained silent.

"Is there evidence that they suspect?" Endelmyer asked.

"Nothing that Harry actually saw—only the SDV index," Tyron replied. "But that was yesterday their time. That's why I want to send him back in. Joan can go with him."

"As ourselves," Morgen interjected. "There isn't time for messing around through personas." Tyron nodded that he agreed. All heads turned back toward the screen.

"They knew what they were getting into. As Victor says, any objections can be straightened out afterward," was Endelmyer's decision. "Send Morgen and Sutton in. We keep it going."

Corrigan and Lilly came out of the west end of the commercial court on Station Square and began walking quickly back along Carson Street toward Xylog. All thoughts of coffee and sandwiches were forgotten. Of course Sylvine reminded him of Zehl, Corrigan told himself. It was more than simply that they were both from Washington, appeared at short notice, and asked lots of questions.

Corrigan had already tagged Zehl as an external controller coming into the simulation, and something in Corrigan's subconscious had identified the same habits of speech, posture, and mannerisms in Sylvine. Sylvine was Zehl! It was the same person from outside, cloaked in two different identities. The difference was that this time, Sylvine hadn't instantly come across as being somehow more "real" than the others around him. The animations were getting good. Stunningly good!

There was an anger in the forced pace of Corrigan's tread on the sidewalk stones and the taut set of his face that Lilly had not seen before. It was an anger of the worst kind—the kind directed at one's own foolishness. While he had been fondly living fantasies of glory and success, believing himself to be in control of his imaginary project in its imaginary world, somebody else, outside, was very much in control of the real one.

"They must have been setting it up since before Xylog was formed," Corrigan muttered darkly. "Nothing like the scale of this was expected until way in the future. That was why I had such a hard time accepting it. Now I can see what's been going on."

"What? Tell me how you read it," Lilly said.

"This is what Borth's clients wanted all along—a simulated world that they could test marketing ideas in. And somebody told them they could have it. That was why the backers poured all that money in."

"You mean Tyron and company?"

"It has to be. Borth's no doubt in on it, Velucci certainly, maybe Endelmyer himself. I don't know. . . . But they've got friends in SDC. There could have been a whole department working on this behind a security screen. They must have done it the way you said once: waited until I went into the simulation on a routine inspection, then invoked the memory suppression to make it permanent and concocted some story to say it was my own decision. That gave them total control. And they've been in control of everything out there for the last three weeks."

They crossed the exit from a parking lot without slowing down, forcing a car that had just begun moving out to stop abruptly with a squeal of tires.

"*Hey, asshole! You try'na get yusself killed or sump'n?*" Nothing abstract or unreal about this world. It was eerie.

"That much I follow," Lilly said. "But how do we suddenly find ourselves back here again—before the project has even started?"

"The backers didn't get what they had been expecting," Corrigan replied. "They got the crazy place that you and I remember." He tossed a hand up as they walked. "No good for their purpose at all, not even close—*to begin with.*"

Lilly walked a couple more paces, then came to a dead halt when what he was saying finally hit her.

"Ohmygod!" she gasped. Corrigan stopped and looked back. "But it was getting better, wasn't it," she said.

He nodded. "Faster than anybody ever dreamed it could—certainly much faster than anything I'd ever have dared bet was possible. We did a better job than we realized. Finally, after about three weeks of run time—twelve years in the simulation—it had got itself almost right. Not completely. There were still some flaws. In particular, the animations weren't copying the surrogates but had gone off on a zany tangent of their own instead; but for the most part, the realism that it achieved was incredible. And then somebody out there said, if it can get this close in three weeks, starting from scratch . . ."

Corrigan saw from the look on Lilly's face that she had already completed the rest for herself. What somebody had said was that they could do so much better still if they could start all over again, only this time with the benefit of everything that the system had learned the first time.

"They've reset everything back to the beginning," Lilly said. Corrigan nodded. But it still didn't add up. Lilly's face creased in puzzlement. "But how could they hope to run it again with us knowing what we know now?" she said.

Corrigan shook his head. "We weren't supposed to. They've got memory suppression. All that was supposed to have been erased, so that we'd start out again yesterday with clean slates, really believing that it was the real world, just before Oz was due to start. But they screwed up somewhere. That suppression didn't work. And now they're all set to run the whole thing through again—only this time from more realistic beginnings."

Lilly stared at him aghast. "The whole thing? You mean . . ."

"Sure. Why not? It's only a few more weeks. But the returns they stand to collect are enormous."

"That's out there!" Lilly choked. "It might only be a few weeks to them. But in here . . ."

Corrigan nodded curtly and took her arm to resume walking. "Exactly. If we don't find a way out of this, it's going to be another twelve years!"

◈ CHAPTER THIRTY-SIX ◈

Lilly was still struggling to come to grips with it when they arrived back at the main entrance to Xylog. "They can't," she protested as they ascended tie front steps. "No way. Not another twelve years. There's got to be some way of telling the outside that they've screwed up."

Corrigan nodded curtly. "Graham Sylvine."

"Who's he?"

They went through the glass double doors into Reception.

"One of the people that I had dinner with last night—supposedly an observer from Washington. But he's really that Dr. Zehl from before that I told you about—the same person. One of the outside controllers."

The receptionist at the desk smiled inquiringly. "Mr. Corrigan, right?"

For the first time in two days, Corrigan registered that her face was new. The plaque on her desk gave her name as Chris Iyles. "No Nancy?" Corrigan said.

"She left, I guess. I'm her new replacement."

"Hi." Newer than you know; Corrigan thought to himself. Every synthetic personality was one less real one to get right. The system didn't have attribute files on everyone. He gestured at the screen to one side. "A Graham Sylvine from Washington was here yesterday. Can you find out if he's still around?"

"Do you know who he's with, Mr. Corrigan?" the receptionist asked, turning to call up a schedule of visitors.

"He's been all over—here and at Head Office. That's all I can tell you."

"One moment."

Lilly flashed Corrigan a questioning look. He explained, murmuring, "Twenty-four hours to us is only seven minutes out there. It's not practicable to give advance notice when you're coming in, which is why they're always showing up unexpectedly. But once you are in, there isn't any great haste about having to get out. So he could still be around somewhere."

But no. "I'm sorry, Mr. Corrigan, but it looks as if Mr. Sylvine left yesterday," the receptionist announced.

"Damn! . . ." Corrigan drummed his fingertips on the desktop. "Is Jason Pinder's secretary still here? She should have his Washington number." With the imminence of the project, practically everyone was working late.

"I don't understand," Lilly murmured. "He's not going to be there, is he? . . . Is there even a Washington here?"

"It'll activate a code to have him called on the outside," Corrigan said. "I used it with Zehl."

"She's not at her desk right now, Mr. Corrigan."

"Here, let me." Corrigan swiveled the unit and entered his own ID, which gave him access to Pinder's files up to "Restricted" level. He keyed through several layers of indexes, found the database for personal contacts, and located the record for Graham Sylvine. It gave a Washington number. Corrigan selected it and initiated the call.

Lilly looked away and watched the receptionist with a fascination that she tried not to show. Even now she was unable to detect any hint that it was an animation. Surely this wasn't possible.

A legend appeared on the screen to say that all personnel had left for the day, which was confirmed by a voice-over. Callers were invited to leave a message. Corrigan snorted softly, but he had expected something like this. "Joe Corrigan from Xylog, Pittsburgh, for Graham Sylvine," he said. "Tell him . . ." He paused. "Tell him that it won't wash this time either. He'll understand. The memories from last time have not been erased. Repeat: have not been erased. We need to talk. Get in touch ASAP." Corrigan hung up and stood staring at the screen. He was clearly dissatisfied, but just for the moment no immediate continuation suggested itself.

"That's it?" Lilly said, echoing what he felt. "That's all we can do?"

"The time differential," Corrigan muttered. "If it takes him five minutes to respond and connect back in, that'll still be tomorrow morning for us."

"There aren't any others?" Lilly said.

"Maybe Pinder," Corrigan said, half to himself. He found it difficult to believe that somebody of Pinder's seniority would have been misled into becoming a memory-suppressed surrogate. Therefore, Pinder would be participating in a fully aware state, probably having decided out of sheer curiosity as much as anything to see the launching of the rerun for himself, from the inside.

Corrigan's eyes, shifting around restlessly, came back to the terminal. He reached toward the keypad, then hesitated and shook his head. "No, let's do it from my office upstairs." He glanced at the receptionist. "Thanks, Chris."

"You're welcome." Lilly still had her visitor's badge from earlier. The animation nodded a smile as they went on through toward the elevators.

Upstairs, Judy was still at her desk and had a sheaf of messages. "Joe, where on earth did you go? The whole world's been calling. There are a couple of urgent—"

"Later. Can you get Jason for me right away? Whatever he's doing, it's more urgent."

"Tom called in at last, but he wouldn't leave a number. He said he'd call back."

Corrigan stopped. It was the first time he'd thought about Hatcher since he and Lilly figured out the situation. And suddenly he knew why Hatcher hadn't shown up for two days. Hatcher had been scheduled to enter the simulation as an observer periodically, just as Corrigan had. And the same thing had happened to him. Tom had been there, somewhere in the simworld, all those "years." And yesterday he had found himself back at the start of it, just like Corrigan and Lilly.

"How is he?" Corrigan asked.

"Acting weird. He didn't say why."

"If he calls, put him straight through."

Corrigan went through into his office with Lilly and closed the door. "Let's assume I'm right and we weren't supposed to remember anything about having gone through this once before, but something's gone wrong. Pinder will be able to decouple straight away and let them know. That way we don't have to wait for Sylvine to get back to us."

Lilly sank down into a visitor's chair, but Corrigan carried on prowling about the room. "No, that isn't it," she said, watching him. "You're just mad as hell at what's been going on. You can't wait to get at them."

Corrigan stopped pacing and looked at her, then emitted a loud sigh. "Hell, what else do you expect?" He folded his arms and propped himself back against the desk. "They've been working some secret deal with Borth and his backers all along, and taken control when they got me inside the simulation. They've stolen the damn project. My project! . . ."

The call tone sounded from the desk unit. He straightened up and turned to accept. Judy's voice came through. "Jason for you. He's across the river at Head Office."

"Thanks. . . ." Pinder's face materialized. "Hello, Jason."

"Yes, Joe? I've ducked out of a meeting, so this had better be good."

Corrigan was still in two minds as to whether Pinder had been a party to the conspiracy. If he had, then much of what Corrigan thought he remembered didn't add up. But those memories were from what had been twelve years ago to Corrigan, and it was impossible to be sure. Giving the benefit of the doubt where due, he decided to play things low-key.

"It's no good, Jason," he said, shaking his head. "We know. You'd better tell the others. There isn't anything wrong with the set, as you've seen for yourself. In fact, it's way ahead of anything that I'd have bet on. But we know it's being rerun. The memory tape from last time didn't get wiped. It's still there."

"Joe, what are you talking about?"

Now Corrigan was irritated. He'd played it straight with Pinder, and he would have expected at least the same in reciprocation. "Look," he said tiredly, "acting dumb is unbecoming, as well as being insulting to the intelligence. We know what's going on, and we want out. I'm not saying you were involved personally, Jason, but some people out there are going to have to do a lot of explaining. I've had twelve years of this shit, and I'm not in a very patient mood for talking. So get yourself out of that cubicle and go and tell whoever's running things to shut it down—*now!*"

But Pinder, far from conceding anything, glared back with a look of outrage. His jaw clamped tight, his mustache quivered, and even on the screen his face turned visibly a shade redder. "Who in God's name do you think you are, and who do you think you're talking to like that?" he spluttered. "Allow me to remind you that you are not a director *yet*. And if this is a foretaste of how it's likely to go to your head, I have a strong mind to recommend to the Board that they reconsider."

For a terrible moment, Corrigan did wonder if he had made one almighty, god-awful mistake. But no, there could be no doubt. The memories of the simulation were clear in his head. Lilly was there, right behind him. There was no flaw in the argument. They had to be in a rerun, for all the reasons they had figured.

Conscious of Lilly watching him, Corrigan's mind wallowed as if in a gel. This sudden change in demeanor of Pinder's had thrown him completely. Earlier today and the day before, Pinder's disposition had been almost deferential, acquiescing to Corrigan on just about every point that had been raised. Corrigan remembered thinking to himself how their roles seemed almost to have reversed themselves, and in his headiness he had attributed it to the transformation that he then believed himself to have undergone. But now . . .

Then Corrigan realized what was happening. He swallowed hard and blinked. Pinder was being belligerent, yes; but at a deeper level nothing had changed. Corrigan had come on the line spoiling for a fight, and Pinder was simply responding in kind. He was still taking his lead from Corrigan. Corrigan stared disbelievingly. No wonder there had been something naggingly but undefinably different about Pinder, which he hadn't been able to put his finger on in two days. Pinder wasn't going to be of any help. Pinder really didn't have any idea what he was talking about. Not *this* Pinder.

"I'm . . . I'm sorry," Corrigan mumbled. "It's a misunderstanding on my part. I guess all this last-minute stress has been getting to me. I'll explain tomorrow."

Pinder's face relaxed immediately. Unnaturally so. Real feelings didn't just evaporate that quickly. Here was further proof if Corrigan needed any. He wondered how many other clues he'd been surrounded by for two days without noticing. "Very well, Joe," Pinder said. "I'll get back to my meeting. I hope you feel better tomorrow." The screen blanked out.

Corrigan sat down shakily on one of the other chairs. "*Jesus!*" he breathed, shaking his head.

"What is it?" Lilly asked.

He waved vaguely at the screen. "That wasn't Pinder. He isn't coupled in as a surrogate at all. That was a system animation."

"Never!"

Corrigan nodded. "He's been acting out of character since yesterday—only marginally, but it's there. You'd have to have worked with him to spot it. It even took me until just now."

"But how? . . ." This time Lilly was incredulous. "How could the system possibly learn to mimic somebody that accurately who wasn't in the first run? He wasn't there. He was never a surrogate."

"The system had a Personal Attribute File on him that it had been building up before then—from early experiments and calibration runs that he took part in. Practically everyone in the company tried it. It got to be a fad." He shook his head again, still having trouble accepting it himself. "God, they're getting close! . . . The whole idea of Oz was that the animations would improve by modeling their behavior on that of the surrogates. Something wasn't right the first time around, and they went off in their own direction instead. But near the end, some of them were getting amazingly good—remember Sherri at the Camelot?" Corrigan stared at Lilly wonderingly.

"People like Zehl were reporting back, and it amazed everyone else too. Then somebody got the idea of rerunning the whole thing—going back and *starting out* with everything that the system had learned. Think what *that* could produce. They'd stand a strong chance of actually being able to deliver what the backers had been expecting—but which nobody who understood the technicalities had taken seriously. So they gain control and collect all the accolades from the people with the money, while I'm stuck here on the inside. Neat."

"But you have to come out sometime," Lilly pointed out.

Corrigan shrugged. "Then what? What do I do, cry foul? File a lawsuit? With the money they've got behind them now, they can ride all of it. . . . At least, that's the way they'd figure it."

Lilly looked at him for a few moments longer, as if waiting for something. "Well?" she said finally.

"Well what?"

Suddenly, everything that she had been fighting to control since waking up the previous morning came boiling out. She had sought out the one person she knew who offered a hope of making sense of anything, and he was acting as if the situation were no more serious than missing their stop on the subway and having to ride it out to the next. In reality, the sheer enormity of it had numbed him past the point of being able to react.

"*For Christ's sake, Joe!*" she exploded, rising up from the chair and coming nearer. "These people have as good as abducted you and taken control of the project. We're just about to start all over again from the beginning. And you're just sitting there like . . ." She turned away to get a grip on herself. Corrigan heard her draw in a long breath. She turned back again, her hands turned upward and extended. "Surely you're not saying that all we can do is wait like a pair of dummies until someone outside decides it's gone far enough? There must be some way of getting out of here. There has to be a way we can do *something*!"

"Pinder can't help us. All we can do is wait for Sylvine to get the message," Corrigan said.

"Sylvine won't do any good either," Lilly answered.

"Oh? And what makes you say that?"

Lilly looked at the desk, then at the wall. Finally she brought her gaze back to meet Corrigan's and shook her head as if it should have been obvious. "There isn't any reason for them to be in a hurry, is there, Joe?" she said. "As far as they're concerned, the longer we're in here, the better. So why should they rush to shut everything down when the results are way past all expectations? Just because Sylvine comes out and tells them we've sussed it? Come on."

Corrigan looked back at her long and hard. It was obvious. "No reason at all," was all he could say.

He slumped back in his chair and spread his hands, indicating that he had nothing more to say. Then the desk unit buzzed. Corrigan accepted, and Judy's voice came through. "It's Tom." At once, Hatcher's face appeared on the screen. He was unshaven and looked haggard.

"Tom! Where are you?" Corrigan exclaimed.

"It doesn't matter. Look, I'm gonna have to make this quick, Joe, but it's important, so listen. First, let me see if I'm right about something. Did a very peculiar thing happen to you yesterday— yesterday in the morning? Like, I've seen all this before?"

Corrigan nodded curtly. "Yes. . . . Yes, it did."

"Okay. We're talking the same language." Hatcher saw Corrigan's mouth starting to open and cut him off with a wave of his hand. "Not now. I need to get together with you. I'll see you at your house—say, half an hour from now. You know and I know that nothing else in this place we're in matters, right? So is that okay?"

Corrigan nodded. "Half an hour."

"I just want to tell you one more thing in case I don't make it. Do you remember that talk we had, way back, with Charlie Wade and Des Jorrecks about ejector seats? Well, you went into the sim a day before I did, so you won't remember. But I do. You and I talked about it again after the phase-two tests were started. There were some funny things going on then that you'll have forgotten about, that we didn't like. We agreed that some insurance would be good to have. Do you hear what I'm saying, Joe? *The ejector buttons exist.* We planted one each, the way we'd talked about before."

Corrigan stared incredulously. "You mean—"

Hatcher looked around warily, as if worried about being watched. "Gotta go, Joe. Your place, half an hour. See ya." The screen blanked.

Lilly looked at him, not bothering to ask the obvious. He rose and ushered her to the door. "I'll tell you on the way," he said.

Judy swiveled in her chair as they came out. "Do you want to see any of—" But Corrigan declined with a wave.

"Sorry, Judy. We have to leave right away. Thanks for holding the fort. Talk to you tomorrow."

Judy eyed Lilly suspiciously. Corrigan paused, staring at her. Her eyes shifted from Lilly to him, her brows rising inquiringly. He peered, trying to pierce the veils to penetrate to the person inside. Was she? Wasn't she? . . . But it was no good. For the life of him, he couldn't tell.

❄ CHAPTER THIRTY-SEVEN ❄

They drove northward in Corrigan's simulated Mercedes, along simulated Route 28 by the simulated Allegheny River toward the simulation of Fox Chapel. Had the sign indicating the Blue Belt exit at Millvale really leaned over to one side as he was seeing it? Were the cracks and faces of the rock outcrop to their left exactly like that, or was the computer adding in its own details? Because his subjective recollections stretched back over twelve years, he couldn't know from memory how much of what he was seeing was authentic. Lilly was evidently pondering the same issues.

"This is your car," she said after a period of silence that had lasted since the Fort Duquesne Bridge. "I mean, not just the same model and color and everything that you drove now"—she was still seeing events from a viewpoint projected twelve years forward—"but *your* car, the one that you'd owned and gotten to know."

"Yes," Corrigan said. He could see where her thinking was heading, but it was easiest to just let her follow it through.

She motioned with a hand. "So what should there be inside that glove compartment in front of me?"

"I honestly can't remember. Have a look and see."

Lilly reached out and opened the compartment door. "Map of the city, another of Pennsylvania, black flashlight, insurance certificate, pen, wiping cloth . . . another pen, empty envelope, and an owner's manual," she recited, taking out the items and showing them briefly.

"Sounds about right," Corrigan said, glancing at her and nodding.

Lilly shook her head. "But this is what I don't get. How does the machine that's managing this simulation *know* what was in *your* car? When we were at my place, you talked about how a lot of detail can get filled in by a person's subconscious—like in a dream. But that isn't happening here. I'm seeing the same things as you, but the information can't be coming from my subconscious, can it? I never knew what was in your glove compartment."

Corrigan shrugged. "No big deal, really. Think about it. I'm comatose inside a COSMOS cubicle at Xylog, and my car is right outside in the parking lot. It wouldn't take somebody very long to inventory everything with a camera and input the images to the system." He paused to let her take that in, then added casually, "When you woke up this morning, where was it, exactly? Tell me again."

"A hotel that the Air Force put us in."

"After you arrived from California to take part in the project."

"Yes."

"And I assume that you put on some regular clothes out of your wardrobe, and picked up the purse and that blue coat when you were leaving. Right?"

Lilly glanced down at herself. "Well, sure. Of course I did. What else?"

Corrigan gave her a sideways grin. "Then how come I see a blue coat and all the right things? *I* don't know what was in your closet, do I?"

It took Lilly a few seconds to see what he was driving at. "The bags, all my things? . . . You're kidding!" she said disbelievingly.

Corrigan nodded. "Same thing. A crew goes out to the hotel, scans the rooms and itemizes the contents. Do the lot in under an hour. If the truth were known, that's probably why they put you in a hotel in the first place. Don't make any mistake, Lilly. There's heaps of money riding on this. These people are doing it right."

Lilly still couldn't buy it completely. "But you didn't wake up in a hotel room with just a few things," she said. "You were at home. There's no way they could have captured the whole of something like that. Every piece of junk in a desk drawer? The contents of a file cabinet? It's simply not feasible."

"It wouldn't be as hard as you think. Practically all of us who were on the project got our homes realscaped just for the hell of it, to make realistic test environments. So a lot of what would be needed is in the databank already. But you're right—it couldn't be perfect. I want to find out what differences you and I see when we get there. There could be something in that house that can get us out of this, regardless of what anyone outside decides. That's what Tom Hatcher was telling me back at the office."

"Okay. Then now suppose you tell me what that was all about," Lilly suggested. "Hatcher was the one who ran a lot of the software development at Xylog, right?"

"That's him. Well, there was something that he and me and a couple of others talked about once when we were arguing about memory suppression." Corrigan grunted as he braked to avoid a Buick making a sudden lane-switch without signaling—probably under the influence of a random number.

"Okay. And? . . ."

"One of the things that came up was how to get yourself out of the simulation—say, in some kind of emergency—if we had gone with suppression; in other words, if you didn't even know you were in a simulation. We called it the ejector seat. But can you see the problem? If your knowledge that it exists gets erased as part of the suppression, it's no use to you. But if you know about it from before the period that was suppressed, then you must know also that you're in a simulation, which defeats the whole object of having any suppression in the first place."

"How do you use a button that you know you're going to forget about?" Lilly summarized.

"Exactly."

She sat back in her seat, thought about it, and then looked across at him. "There's no way you can do it."

"Tom came up with a way whereby maybe you can. His idea was

to plant something of personal significance in the simworld environment that would take on a new meaning when you know that you're looking for it. In other words *you* know the way you think, and when the need became strong enough, you'd realize that you would have put something close by somewhere—something that you'd recognize when the time came. So for as long as the simulation was running normally, it would effectively be invisible. Get the idea?"

Lilly did, but its relevance was less clear. From what Corrigan had just said, the notion had been purely hypothetical—something to think about if the decision had been to use suppression in the project. But—as far as Corrigan had been aware, anyway—the decision had been not to use suppression. So why would he have implemented an ejection button? She tried to think back to what she had overheard Hatcher say from the screen.

"Back in your office just now, he said something about you and he talking late into the project. You went into the simulation a day before he did."

Corrigan nodded that she had got it. "So my memory erasure went back a day earlier than his did. Something was going on that aroused our suspicions enough for us to decide that maybe an 'out' button would be a good insurance. And what he's telling me is that we went ahead and put them in somewhere. It means that there is a way out, Lilly, whether Sylvine and the rest of them out there feel like cooperating or not. All we have to do is find it."

They drove along a road of comfortably aloof homes lying in upper-middle-class seclusion among shrubbery and pines, and turned off into the driveway of a low-set, contemporary composition of lacquered timbers and stone chimney breasts, with brown shingles, a screened porch, and large expanses of glass.

Corrigan parked without saying anything, got out, and walked around to open the passenger door. Outside a house a short distance farther along, a man who looked like the occupant was standing with a woman by the mailbox at the end of a driveway. They looked across while pretending not to as Lilly climbed out of the car—unwilling to permit anything approaching eye contact, even at that distance, but too intrigued to miss anything. Then the gazes averted, and the chins began to wag.

"I think I'm the sensation of the street already," Lilly said as they began walking up toward the house. "How long is it since Evelyn left?"

Corrigan snorted. "Three weeks. You know, it's funny. I can remember how smug and self-satisfied I felt when we picked this place. Now I think I'd prefer that flat in Oakland. Better neighborhood. Less insufferable people."

"Drunks, deadbeats, students, dancers? Even bartenders."

"Exactly."

The dog from next door was out front, secured by a sliding chain to a line that gave it the run of the lawn on the far side of the scattering bay laurel and flowering dogwoods separating the two properties. It was a shaggy gray mass of indeterminate origins, and had paused to watch them hesitantly, as if unsure what it was supposed to do. Corrigan stopped and looked at it strangely for a couple of seconds. Then he held out a hand and called jovially, "Hey, Bruce, old fella. How's it going today, eh?" The dog scampered as close as its chain would permit, tongue lolling from jaws panting wide in delight and tail wagging. Corrigan grunted to himself, followed Lilly up to the door, and let them in.

"I never knew you were a dog person," she said as he closed the door.

"I'm not. That was an experiment. Checking out the system."

"What do you mean?"

Corrigan cocked his head and pointed back over his shoulder with a thumb. "Its name isn't Bruce—I don't know what its name is. And it never acts like that. It hates me." Lilly frowned uncomprehendingly. Corrigan moved to the hallway window beside the door and looked out. The dog had gone back to investigate something under a shrub by the lawns; the two people across the street were still talking.

"The system is operating right on its edge," Corrigan murmured. "You see, it *didn't know* what to make the dog do. Somebody must have got a shot of the next-door dog when they were here realscaping the house, but they didn't know what name it answered to, or how it behaves. So the system took its cue from me. That's what it was designed to do." He inclined his head, still gazing out across the road. "Are those animations of real neighbors that somebody got views of, or are they characters that the system invented? I don't know, because I've never talked to anyone around here. But the system couldn't be aware of that. If I did know what the guy who lives there looks like, I'd be in a position to catch it out. If I walked across and went into his house, do I know what I ought to find there, or could the system get away with making up an interior of its own? It can't tell. You see, again, we've got it right on the edge."

Lilly looked out of the window, and then uncomfortably back at Corrigan. "This is getting weird."

"Hell, it's been weird for a long time, Lilly."

He helped Lilly out of her coat and hung it, along with his own, on the rack by the door. "That's interesting, Joe," she agreed after she had absorbed what he was getting at. "But how is it supposed to help?"

"I'm not exactly sure yet. But when something's stretched to its limits, that's when you find where its weaknesses are." He led the way into the kitchen and tipped the old filter and grounds from the coffeemaker into the trash bin. "Anyhow, simulation or not, it activates the same taste centers. Let's get the pot on."

"I could use one." Lilly looked around at the mess he had left that morning—the sinkful of dishes; papers from work spread over the table; bread, cheese, pickles, and mayonnaise for his sandwich still not put away. "Boy, you sure have been on your own for three weeks," she commented.

"Ah, don't start giving me any of that old bilge," he warned. "It's been hectic at Xylog. And since I woke up yesterday I've had other things on my mind than housekeeping."

Lilly opened the dishwasher and shook her head despairingly at the pile of crockery and kitchenware inside. "Where's the detergent?" she sighed.

"I can't remember. It's been twelve years since I saw it. Try the cupboard under the sink."

Lilly opened the door and squatted down to look. "The stupid thing is that there's really no need for any of this. Why go to the trouble of creating a simulated world and build in all the limitations of the real one? You could just have a code word or something that gets this done in an instant." She found the detergent, stood up, and poured detergent into the dishwasher while Corrigan loaded items from the sink. "You could make life really comfortable, when you think about it."

"Magic words, eh? You're right. That's exactly the kind of world we could create. We haven't scratched the surface of this business yet, Lilly."

She switched on the machine and began collecting assorted jars and dishes together to either throw out or put in the refrigerator. "You see what I mean," she said. "Look at all this. Why is it necessary to have stuff dry up and go bad? Couldn't we have a simulation without mimicking the effects of microbes?"

"Why stop at that?" he asked her. "Maybe you'd never get too hot or too cold, cut your finger, get a bruise, or catch flu, either. Talk to anyone anytime, and be anywhere in an instant."

"Well, why not?"

"People might never want to come out of it." Corrigan shook his head and set down two mugs that he had found for the coffees. "There's all kinds of things to find out. The whole thing's being rushed too fast, and for all the wrong reasons. That's how we come to be stuck in here." Which brought them back to the immediate issue at hand.

"You said we were here to look for the clue to a way out that Tom says you planted somewhere," she said.

"Mmm."

"What kind of thing are we looking for?"

"I don't know."

"That helps."

"The clue to the magic word." Corrigan poured the coffees and handed her one. "It was twelve years ago, Lilly. I hadn't planned on it happening this way. It was supposed to have been just a few days."

"What did you mean in the car when you talked about us seeing different things when we got here?" Lilly swept her free hand in a circle. "I see a sink, refrigerator, table with things on, a window over there, and the door we came in there. Isn't that what you see?"

"Oh, sure. But you'd expect that. Everything superficial would have been captured when the guys were here realscaping the house. Possibly Tyron's people came to get additional detail, too, at the same time that they did the car—after I was inside the simulation. So for stuff like that, the system has objective data that it can feed in the data streams to both of us. But at a more subtle level there are things that exist in my memories that it doesn't know about. Will my mind fill in the details subconsciously so that I see them and you don't? Or will I not see them, although I know I ought to? How will the system handle it when it's driven to the limit?" He sipped from his mug and looked around the kitchen casually.

"For instance . . ." Corrigan moved over to the microwave and took down one of the recipe books from the shelf just above. It was called *Cooking the Good Old American Way*, and showed big, elegant houses and a riverboat scene. "They did a thorough job," he commented. "This book of Evelyn's did have that picture on the front. But they had to stop somewhere. He opened the cover and showed Lilly the endpaper and flyleaf inside. "What do you see there?" he asked her curiously.

She looked, then raised her eyes to meet his uncertainly as if suspecting a trick and shrugged. "Nothing. It's blank."

He nodded. "That's what I see too. But what I know, and what you and the system don't, is that it was a gift from an aunt of Evelyn's, and it had an inscription inside. . . . You see—we've carried out one experiment already."

Lilly gaped. In two days, nothing had brought home to her the reality of the situation that they were in more effectively than that one, simple demonstration. Corrigan was straining the system's rules, watching for where the cracks would appear. Lilly realized then that he had a twofold strategy: either he would find the "magic word" and get them out; or failing that, he would find a way to crash everything from the inside.

She watched, still struggling to overcome the eerie feeling of it all as Corrigan replaced the cookbook. He opened one of the kitchen drawers and rummaged idly among the contents, but nothing caught his eye as the kind of thing that he had vaguely in mind. It was the usual assortment of utensils and implements that could have been imaged and recorded straightforwardly. He needed something that would let his mind work spontaneously, without prior expectations. He wandered around, taking pictures off the walls, lifting ornaments from their niches, trying to create opportunities for stumbling on details that a realscaping crew with finite time to contend with would have missed. The watercolor of a schooner that he took down from above the breakfast bar was just blank pasteboard on the reverse side. Was anything supposed to be written there—a date, a caption, an inscription? He couldn't remember. Was the maker's mark that he found on the underside of the vase from the ledge by the pantry the authentic one that had always been there, or had the system improvised it? He had no idea. He lifted a wooden-handled carving knife from its fixture on the wall—a relic from his student days that had followed him over the years through all his digs and apartments from Dublin to Pittsburgh. The handle had a deep, L-shaped gouge in it, dating from a time long forgotten, which had been hidden facing the wall. He held it out to let Lilly look at it.

"Tell me what you see," he said.

"An old knife. It's got a worn blade, a polished wooden handle held by brass rivets."

Corrigan turned the knife over in his hands. "Anything different this way?" He turned it again, showing her the first side once more, then the other.

"No. Should there be?"

"To me, there's a deep gouge in the handle. You don't see one at all?" He had found something.

"No. Nothing." Lilly looked up at him disbelievingly. "My God!" she whispered.

Corrigan had forgotten that gouge. But his subconscious hadn't, and it was filling the detail in, inside his head. The system had known nothing about the gouge, since it had faced the wall and not been captured in the imaging; therefore, the data to define it were absent from the optical input being generated for Lilly.

"Now it's caught in a direct conflict," Corrigan said. "It knows that you and I are seeing different things, violating its primary reality criterion. It can't resolve the issue by deleting what I see, and it can't correct what you see because it doesn't have the information to draw it. And either way, even if it could, that would violate its consistency rules."

Lilly shook her head helplessly, as if it were her problem. "So how will it handle it?" she asked.

Corrigan shrugged. "I have no idea. The system has been evolving its own associative structures. That's what it was designed to do. Its internal complexity will be so great by now that neither I nor anyone else could tell you what it'll do. It's going to be interesting finding out." Lilly looked around uneasily, as if half expecting the house to cave in. Corrigan grinned cheerfully and took her arm. "Come on," he said. "Let's take a stroll around the house and see what else we can find."

They went out through the living room and into the den. It was getting dark. Corrigan switched on the light and gazed around at the desk, the terminal, shelves of books, ornaments, pictures and other hangings on the walls. Finally he went over to the bookshelves and began peering more closely at the titles. "Now, I can't remember exactly everything that was here," he said. "But it seems the kind of place that I might have stuck a reminder to myself. . . . Ah! Now, see this one, for example." He took down a thin, green-covered volume with the title *The Stories Behind the Flags*. "You see, I can't remember where this book came from at all. It could be something that Evelyn put there and didn't tell me about, or I forgot." He glanced at Lilly pointedly. "Or maybe I put it there for a reason, just before Oz went live, and the memory got suppressed along with everything else from those last few days. See my point?" He rippled through the pages idly with a thumb.

Lilly caught glimpses of the pages, replete with text and illustrations. "The pages are all there," she said, indicating with a hand. "Surely the people who scanned the house couldn't have gone through every one."

"No need," Corrigan said. "You just get the titles from a high-resolution scan of the room, and the system obtains the contents electronically from a library." He nodded toward the file cabinet in a corner. "I bet you'd find a lot wrong in there, though. Nobody's going to wade through that lot."

"Are you going to look?"

"Oh, we'll get to it. Meanwhile, what about this book? Is it the clue to the magic word?"

Lilly turned up her hands. "I don't know. How do we find out?"

"We experiment. . . . Maybe all you have to do is say the right words in the right place, like in a D and D game. Maybe it's the title." He raised his voice and recited, "'The Stories Behind the Flags.'" He waited a moment, then shrugged. "Maybe the name of a flag. How about, The Stars and Stripes? . . . Old Glory? . . . Irish Tricolor? Union Jack?" He looked back at Lilly. "You see. Nothing happens."

"Just like D and D games," she remarked.

"Maybe we have to type it into the system." He went over to the terminal, sat down and switched it on, and began entering any phrases and references to flags that came to mind.

"This could take until the next ice age," Lilly said bleakly as she began to get the idea.

"I told you, having to try and hit on the right thing from twelve years back doesn't help. If it was a connection that meant something a couple of days ago, the way it was supposed to, it would probably be obvious already."

He carried on resolutely. Lilly looked around the room, searching for anything that might suggest itself. She was about to say something when the headlights from a car turning into the driveway outside came in through the window.

Corrigan stopped what he was doing and got up to cross the room and peer out. A familiar tall, loose-limbed figure, yellow-haired in the glow from a nearby streetlamp, straightened up from behind a Ford parked next to Corrigan's Mercedes and headed with tense, agitated footsteps toward the front door of the house.

"Well, there's one lot of questions we won't have to worry about for very much longer," Corrigan said, letting the drape fall back. "Tom's here."

✸ CHAPTER THIRTY-EIGHT ✸

The bell started ringing when Corrigan was halfway to the door and carried on ringing until he opened it. Hatcher looked as if he had been in a private war. His hair was tousled, his face showing two days of yellow stubble, and his eyes, which in all the years they had worked together Corrigan had never seen other than mild and mockingly easy-lazy, mirroring the way Tom ambled through life, were red-rimmed and glazed. He was wearing a gray, hooded zipper jacket, torn on one side, over a stained khaki shirt and blue jeans.

He gestured back toward the driveway and said without preamble, "Can I move the car into the garage? I need to get it out of sight, off the street."

"Well . . . sure, Tom." Corrigan went past him to open the garage door, while Lilly watched from the doorway. Corrigan heard the door of Hatcher's car slam behind him, and the engine start. He fumbled with the keys and had to try several before he found the right one to open the door. Hatcher drove in past him and got out; Corrigan closed the garage door from the inside and led the way through a side door into the kitchen. Lilly joined them from the hallway a few seconds later.

"I was right, wasn't I? It happened to you too," Hatcher said, again wasting no words on preliminaries. "You couldn't remember which key opened the garage. It's been twelve years since you did it last, right?"

Corrigan waved a hand to indicate one of the chairs by the kitchen table. "Why don't you take a load off your feet before we get into this, Tom? You look beat. We've just made some fresh coffee."

"What does it matter—any of it? We're not really here. None of it's really here. Coffee? You act like . . ." Hatcher checked himself, then indicated the surroundings with a wave of his arm. "Just to be sure that we're talking the same language—we *do* both know what all this is, right?"

Corrigan nodded. "It's the simulation. We know that. And to save any more comparing of notes, yes, we both went through twelve years of it. And yesterday we woke up back at the beginning, all set to start over."

"Her too? You mean she's not a . . ." Hatcher threw up a hand in a way that said call them anything you want.

"This is Lilly Essell," Corrigan said, his tone making the point that bizarre circumstances didn't excuse bad manners. "Space Defense Command, Inglewood. Lilly's a scientist with OTSC—one of the surrogates recruited from outside. She was involved with DIVAC development. We met in the simworld the first time around."

Hatcher sighed, sank down onto the chair, and nodded wearily. "Excuse me, Lilly. . . . Yeah, man, could I use some coffee."

Lilly had already taken down an extra mug and was filling the three of them from the pot. "Thanks," Hatcher acknowledged as she set one of them down in front of him. Some of the fury that Corrigan had sensed when Tom came into the house was abating, but his movements were still tense. He picked up his mug and sipped from it, clasping it in both hands. "Having those freaks around for too long," he said by way of explanation. "That's what it does to you."

"It's been tough all around," Lilly said.

"This is the Tom Hatcher that we talked about," Corrigan told her. "Worked with me on software for years. Now he runs a big slice of the development work at Xylog."

"I've heard a few things about you, Tom," Lilly said.

"Well, wait until you hear my version before you make your mind up. You know how it is with these Irish guys." Hatcher's voice had dropped. The forced humor was an offering to placate.

"Hi," Lilly conceded with a nod.

Hatcher turned his head back to look up at Corrigan. "I figured out how it must have happened. You remember how it was between you and Frank Tyron back then? There was a group who had him all set up as their man to run COSMOS as a way of cashing in on the work done at SDC. But you screwed that up by selling the company on Oz, and the war changed to which one of you would move into Jason's slot when he went back to Blawnox. You remember all that?"

"How was I supposed to forget?" Corrigan said.

Hatcher went on. "They had another group somewhere that we didn't know about—probably back in SDC—that they kept updated with all the research work that we did. These other guys worked it up to a full-world sim and added in a memory suppressor. You, me, and the others who were part of the regular schedule got wiped as soon as we were inside, and the Tyron campaign committee has been running a gimmick-tester for Madison Avenue ever since. That's how come all that money kept pouring in. And now somebody has decided to restart the whole thing. But this time there isn't going be a discontinuity at the changeover that needs to be camouflaged. The simulation has gotten good enough to merge in smoothly with reality. We weren't supposed to know anything about that, but this time the suppression screwed up."

Corrigan made a sign that there was no need for Hatcher to go on. "Okay, we pretty much figured it out the same way, Tom," he said. "I found myself coming together again after supposedly being messed up in the head by a project that was canceled years ago. After years of being a convalescent, I ended up working as a bartender." He looked across at Lilly. "Lilly was on the right track before I even suspected."

The news seemed to deflate Hatcher, as if something that he had been pinning a hope on had collapsed. "So you're not . . . you're not just in here as an observer right now?" he said. "You can't decouple and go stop this from the outside?"

Corrigan looked surprised. "How could I? We're both in the same situation. You just spelled it all out. . . ." His voice trailed away as he realized that Hatcher had been asking him again to double-check:

Was Corrigan *really* a memory-suppressed surrogate? Or did he know more than he had let on? In short, had Corrigan been a party to the group that had sprung this?

Hatcher's manner became more subdued. "I had to ask," he said. Clearly this had been one of the reasons why he had contacted Corrigan.

"I understand," Corrigan said.

Lilly caught Corrigan's eye in a way that asked if any of this mattered. Weren't they missing the whole point that this was supposed to be all about? Corrigan got them back to it.

"On the phone earlier, you said we put in ejector buttons. What was that all about?" he said.

Hatcher took a long drink from his mug. "By the time we got into the serious tests, some funny things were going on. More strangers being brought in from outside that we hadn't expected. Installations and integrations that weren't scheduled. We couldn't get a straight answer out of anybody. . . ."

Corrigan could only shake his head. "I don't really remember." It was all mixed up in the confusion of half-memories from immediately after that time, twelve years ago.

"We didn't like it, Joe. And the more we talked it over, the more we agreed there was no way we were gonna go into the sim with all these guys we didn't know pressing buttons on the outside, without taking out the kind of insurance that we'd figured out for memsupped surrogates. You went into the simworld that night—the day we talked about it. Your memory must have been wiped back to take out that day, which is why you don't know anything about it. But I wasn't due to go in until a day later. So I remember us talking about it."

Lilly, who had been looking from one to the other as she tried to follow, raised a hand to hold everything there. "Wait a minute, let's see if I've got this straight. You're saying that sometime between the time that you two talked and the time Joe went into the simworld, he placed some kind of escape device in here that only he would recognize when the right time came. But he's not only forgotten what it was; he's even forgotten that he ever had the intention."

Hatcher made a face. "Well, I can't *know* for sure that he did. But from the way we talked about it, yep . . . I'd be pretty sure that he did."

Lilly still wasn't clear as to the problem. She shook her head. "But I thought you said that you *both* set up one. Your memory wasn't wiped that day. So why do you need Joe, anyway? Don't you know what *your* escape button was?"

To her surprise, Hatcher set down the mug, showed both his empty hands, and shook his head helplessly. "There's nothing there that I can recall. Maybe I didn't get around to implementing it until the next day—because I knew I wouldn't be going inside until then. Then that day got wiped, just like the day before it did with Joe, so I ended up remembering saying that I was going to do something, but not what I actually did."

Lilly looked at him dubiously for a moment or two. "Then it doesn't sound as if it was very effective, does it?" she commented. "I thought that was the whole idea."

"We were thinking in terms of something that would only need to have some kind of significance after a matter of days," Corrigan said. "We never dreamed it would have to mean the same years later. Things get fuzzy over time. Who can remember what was and wasn't important twelve years ago?"

Hatcher shook his head, and all the pent-up feelings that had been simmering boiled up again. "You take it all so cool, Joe. They're in charge right now, goddammit! Doesn't it *mean* anything, what these people are doing out there?" His voice rose. "It might be only a few more days to them—that they think they'll be able to buy their way out of when it's over. But it'll be more *years* for us!"

"Tom, I do know that," Corrigan said, trying to calm him.

Hatcher didn't seem to hear. "Do you know what it means to me?" he asked, pointing at his own chest. "What those twelve years were for me in there? I didn't end up convalescing and meeting lots of people as a bartender. I figured out early on what was going on. Only, those . . . 'people' I was dealing with didn't know any better. They thought I really was crazy, and they weren't about to let me out."

"*What!*" Lilly gasped. "You mean, all that time? . . . You were shut up in an institution or something?"

"They called it a 'remedial care center.'"

Corrigan stared, horrified. Whatever the reasons in the cases of the other surrogates, it explained why he had never bumped into Tom during those years in the simulated city. Surely, though, he thought to himself, a case like Hatcher's would have been monitored by a contact from outside, as had his own by Dr. Zehl.

"But aside from animations, there must have been outside controllers showing up too," he said. "You could tell them apart. You'd have been looking for it."

Hatcher nodded cynically. "Oh, sure, there were several of those—usually passing themselves off as 'supervisors' to the regular animations, or some such. But they could only ever see it from the angle that it was just a few days. They're probably the ones who told the animations to keep me off the streets—they didn't want to risk me meeting other surrogates and blowing the whole thing."

"One of them showed up at Xylog yesterday," Corrigan said. "I called his number and left a message saying we know the score and want out. But it'll be tomorrow before we hear anything back."

Hatcher sighed, closing his eyes for a moment. "You think they're really going to take any notice?" he said. "Come on, Joe, let's get real. They've got high stakes riding on this. You and I don't even come into it anymore. You're wasting your time."

Maybe. But at least Corrigan had been looking around constructively for the hope of a way out, Lilly thought. Perhaps if Hatcher had kept a cooler head in the previous run, he might not have ended up as an interesting test case for animation counselors to sharpen their notions of human psychology on.

"We're not *just* waiting for the guy from Washington to call back," she said. "Even since we got back here, we've been looking for the whatever-it-is that you say Joe set up somewhere. Did you? I mean, have you even *tried,* instead of saying it was all too long ago and you can't remember?"

Hatcher made a tired throwing-away motion in the air. "Ah, there's no way you'd even know where to start. The possibilities are endless. What am I supposed to do—go running all over the place like some kid chasing clues in a treasure hunt, because people like them won't talk to me? The hell I will." He waited for Corrigan or Lilly to disagree, and when they said nothing, waved a hand to indicate the house. "Show me I'm wrong. How did you two make out? Find anything?"

Lilly shook her head and drew back with a sigh. "No. We didn't."

Corrigan reversed one of the other chairs and sat down on it straddle-legged. "Okay, then suppose you tell us what else you've been doing since yesterday that didn't work either," he suggested. "At least we're not driving around looking like a survivor from the Burma Railway. What happened to get you into that mess?"

Although the question had to come sooner or later, Hatcher sat with his shoulders hunched, contemplating the mug between his hands for some time before replying. At last, instead of answering directly, he went back to the morning of yesterday.

"Suddenly, the whole crazy nightmare was over. I woke up at the start of a day I'd lived twelve years ago when the project was about to go live. It took me half a day in a daze to be sure that it hadn't all been some kind of way-out, unheard-of lucid dream."

"I had the same problem," Corrigan said. "In fact, it had me fooled until Lilly walked into my office a few hours ago—even after the last experience. Would you have believed it could get as real as this?"

Hatcher shook his head. "No way. This is scary."

"What put you onto it?"

Hatcher looked at Corrigan curiously for a second. "Did you talk to Barry at all since this flip-back thing happened—since yesterday?"

"Barry Neinst? No, I've had all kinds of things going on. What about him?"

"It isn't him. Not the real Barry that you and I knew. The one who's been walking around Xylog since yesterday is an animation."

Hatcher waited for Corrigan's reaction. It was not as strong as it might have been had it not been for Corrigan's own experiences with Pinder and Judy Klein. He just nodded and said, "I've seen it too."

Hatcher went on. "There were some things that Barry and I talked about twelve years ago that the Barry yesterday didn't know anything about. And in any case, after twelve years of dealing with animations, you can tell."

Corrigan nodded to say that Hatcher didn't have to go into that. They had been there too—they knew what he meant. "So what did you do?" he asked.

"The first thing? I just walked out. Screw it. I wasn't gonna be part of the game anymore. . . . Then I got in a car and went driving—out, away from the city. I wanted to see just how far they'd extended the realscape. And do you know something—you can't tell. It just goes on and on. Somewhere there's a join where it stops being a replication from the image banks and turns into a synthesis that the system will keep spinning for you for as far as you wanna go, but you can't tell where it is. It'll just keep painting highway. Stop at a Waffle House and go inside for a coffee, and it'll create an inside of a Waffle House—it knows how. And it'll put people in there who'll talk to you all day. Kind of strange—like some of those games you can play that keep generating landscapes that go on forever."

"Not forever, surely," Lilly objected. "What happens when you come to somewhere you know? I mean, suppose I decided to drive back to L.A.? I might get taken in by a lot of invention along the way, but not when I got there. Even if they mapped in a few blocks around Inglewood, there couldn't have been anything as comprehensive as what was done for Pittsburgh."

Hatcher was nodding in the slightly impatient way that said yes, anyone with a brain functioning on the positive side of imbecile level knew all that. It wasn't intentional, Corrigan told himself. Tom had spent too long surrounded by animations that he knew were animations, and by the sound of it, hating them. Tact was not a habit that could be regained instantly after years of dealing with elaborate mimes that had no feelings.

"Last night I had a ball just being out around the city again, even if it was all a fake," Hatcher told them. There was a strangely satisfied, yet at the same time malicious look in his eye as he spoke. Corrigan had never seen Tom quite like this. Here was something that they had never really stopped to consider in all their debating about the project and its possible consequences: a personality being radically altered in a space of what, in the outside world, had amounted to only a few days. He wondered what alterations had taken place in himself—perhaps irreversibly—that he was even now unaware of.

"Where did you go last night?" Corrigan asked uneasily.

Hatcher's expression broadened into a smile that Corrigan wasn't sure he liked—the smile of a chain-saw murderer bragging about his exploits. "Here, there—what does it matter?"

"What did you do?"

"I was getting even, man!" Hatcher's voice began rising again, with an edge to it that said his patience was being stretched. Maybe he'd had enough of interrogations in the last few years. "I had a lot in my system that I needed to get rid of. Smashing bottles can be very satisfying, even if it wasn't them that got you mad, and they don't know they're being smashed."

"Okay, okay." Corrigan put a hand up to his brow and nodded, not really wanting to hear all the lurid details spelled out. So what had Tom done? Started a fight? Broken up a bar? Heaved bricks through a jeweler's window? A lifetime's instincts tried to feel shocked, but they were overridden by the intellectual awareness that in a simulation such acts carried no more moral significance than shooting monsters on the screen of a video game. In fact, now that the worst was out, Corrigan found himself tempted to smile.

Hatcher looked across at Lilly. "Then, today, I asked myself what you just asked—only, I wasn't about to go driving for days to get to L.A. or anywhere else to find out. So I went out to the airport, walked up to the ticket desk, and said I wanted to go to Vancouver."

Lilly was catching the changing mood on Corrigan's face and did smile. "That's one way to give them a hard time," she said. "How did they handle it?" But Corrigan had stiffened at Hatcher's mention of the airport.

Hatcher snorted. He seemed to be enjoying reliving the experience. "By getting flustered and irrational and stupid," he replied. "First they tried to say the flight was canceled. Then, when I said okay, I'd take the next, they said the airport there was closed—there had been a freak blizzard, and the area was a national emergency." Corrigan recalled the antics that he himself had forced the system into when he put the call through to Ireland. Hatcher showed an upturned palm. "Would you believe, the turkey of a supervisor there tried to talk me into making it Japan instead? Who ever heard of a passenger showing up at an airport, who wants to go to Vancouver, being told maybe they ought to try Japan instead?"

"That was because it's in the bank," Corrigan said needlessly. The parts of Tokyo realscaped by Himomatsu had been merged into Oz as part of the project.

"So, since you're still here, what happened?" Lilly asked.

Hatcher sighed heavily and pushed himself back from the table. "Well, it got kinda noisy. First, airport security showed up, then the cops came muscling in . . . and I guess after all the crap I went through last time, the freaks just pushed me too far. But I'd probably gone there with trouble in mind anyhow." He reached inside his coat and drew out a handgun—a large one, .44 or .45.

"Oh, my God," Lilly breathed. It was what Corrigan had feared.

Hatcher held the weapon between his hands above the tabletop, staring at it for a few seconds as if savoring the memories that it evoked. Then he looked up at Corrigan with a challenging expression and shrugged nonchalantly. "I started blowing 'em away. There's probably something about it on the news if you turn it on."

Corrigan groaned—not at the news so much as from the realization that his letting-up of fears had been a delusion. Tom was still very much borderline—right on the edge.

Hatcher interpreted his frozen expression as censure and rose up from the chair. "What's the matter, Joe? Don't you understand?—*I've had it* with animation freaks! There was *no way,* they were gonna shut me up inside anywhere again. . . . But it doesn't matter a shit anyway. They're just walking bundles of code. It doesn't mean a goddamn thing—any of it." He stood, waiting for a sign that they understood. But despite himself, just for that instant Corrigan was unable to return anything but a blank stare while his mind fumbled for the right thing to say. Lilly seemed to be affected the same way.

Hatcher looked at them and colored, angry now. He pointed back toward the front door, indicating the direction to the outside of the house but meaning the outside of the whole simulation. "Do you expect me to just walk around and carry on being a good guinea pig for those guys out there? I'm telling you, I'm getting out, and it won't be with any of their permission." He grinned crookedly as a new thought struck him, and turned the gun toward Corrigan. "I could get you outta here too, if you want, Joe—real quick."

Corrigan's reaction was reflexive. "Don't point that bloody thing at me. Look—"

"What's up, Joe? You're getting this confused with reality. All that happens is the impact function of the bullet transforms as a superposition into the physical subfile of your physical matrix and makes it nonviable, and you'll wake up in a cubicle. Why put up with any more of this shit?"

"Tom, you just let me handle it in my own way, okay?" Corrigan said tightly.

"We know how you feel, but why don't we just relax and—" Lilly began, but Hatcher thrust the gun back inside his coat and was already moving toward the door. There was a look in his eyes that hadn't showed earlier—final surrender when a last hope had failed to materialize.

"I came here because I thought you might be on an open wire out, Joe," he said. "But it seems you're just as trapped in here, and I sure as hell am not gonna sit around waiting for them to call me. Okay, you solve it your way, and I'll solve it mine. This isn't gonna get us anywhere. Sorry I messed up your evening. So could you just let me have my car?"

"Now don't do anything—" Corrigan began, but Hatcher cut him off with a laugh.

"I don't believe it. Joe. You still haven't gotten it into your head. . . . There isn't anything stupid that I can do. All those years must have got you really conditioned. Maybe I had it better after all." He crossed the kitchen and opened the door leading to the garage. "Now the car, Joe—please?"

They watched the Ford drive off with a squeal of tires, and only then did Corrigan notice for the first time that one side of its front fender and the wing were mangled. He went back inside with Lilly, and they ate an uninspired meal of bachelor-fare oddments from the refrigerator.

Afterward, they resumed poking around the house for possible clues to an escape switch, but the enthusiasm went out of it as they soon found that Hatcher had been right about one thing: with no idea what they were looking for, the possibilities were virtually unlimited, and so was the amount of time that finding it was likely to take. Finally they agreed that it would probably be smarter to await a response from Sylvine as a first option. They retired early, Lilly taking the guest room, and drove back to Xylog first thing the next morning.

That was when they learned that Hatcher had hit a truck head-on at what witnesses said must have been eighty miles per hour, shortly after leaving them the previous night. According to the accounts, his car had been accelerating as it crossed the central dividing line, and had made no attempt at evasion. One driver, still in a state of bewilderment, who had been following a short distance behind told the police, "It was like nothing you ever saw—like it was deliberate. There wasn't a piece left big enough that you could have made a planter out of. Nuthin'."

Shortly afterward, the police released a statement that the driver of the Ford had been tentatively identified as the "Greater Pitt Gunman," who had left a security guard and two city policemen dead, along with four others wounded, in the airport shooting earlier the previous day. Since then, there had been twenty-three further incidents of multiple shootings in public places, and reports were coming of other, similar happenings around the country.

◈ CHAPTER THIRTY-NINE ◈

Corrigan watched across his desk while detective Yeen from city police headquarters checked over the notes that he had made. "And you didn't talk to him at all yesterday? The last time that you did see him, did he seemed to be acting normally?" Yeen's tone sounded dubious, as if he were giving Corrigan a chance for second thoughts.

"We had a meeting scheduled for yesterday morning, but Hatcher didn't show up," Corrigan said. "I got a message late in the day that he'd called, but I was in a hurry and didn't return it. That really is all I can tell you." And neither was he really interested, nor especially inclined to make any effort at pretending that he was. None of this was going to make any difference. Besides which, some of Hatcher's cynicism seemed to have rubbed off on him. There was something mildly degrading about the thought of acting out a charade to placate an internal construct of a computer. After seeing what this whole creation had driven Tom to, he was as ready as Tom had been to blow the whole thing sky-high from within. The problem was figuring out how, and that would take just a little more patience yet.

"The car was heading north on eight, which passes close to Fox Chapel," Yeen commented. "At least one person remembers seeing a brown Ford with a damaged front wing just a few streets from where, you live."

Corrigan shrugged and held up his hands. "He might have stopped by the house before we got back. All I can say is that I didn't see him."

"We?"

"Lilly—Ms. Essell, who's sitting outside. She's a journalist from California, writing an article about the Oz project. We went back to talk about it in the evening. Yesterday was too hectic earlier."

"And she's still here this morning. Did she stay at the house?"

Corrigan sighed, wishing for an instant that he, too, could simply pull out a gun and dispatch the whole irritation. Already, he was understanding a lot better how Tom had felt. If he made up some other story and it didn't fit with Lilly's, there would be no end to this. He had other things to do.

"Yes," he replied testily. "In the guest room. She also happens to be an old friend."

The detective's eyebrows rose, but he didn't pursue the point. "So you can't really be of any more help?" he said.

Corrigan spread his hands in a suggestion of being tactful. "That is what I've been trying to say."

"I see." Yeen got up and put the notebook back inside his zippered document holder. "I appreciate the time, Mr. Corrigan. You will be available here if there are further questions?"

"Of course."

Corrigan walked around the desk and opened the door. Lilly was sitting outside in one of the visitor chairs opposite Judy's desk, where she had waited the previous evening. "Is there anywhere that I could have a few words with Ms. Essell?" Yeen asked Corrigan as they came out.

"There's a room just along the corridor that you could use if it's free," Corrigan said. "My secretary can show you the way. Judy, could you check the small conference room and take Mr. Yeen and Lilly there if it's free?"

Judy rose from her seat. "You've got some urgent messages," she said, handing Corrigan a couple of slips. "One from Endelmyer, one from Pinder. They both want you to call back straightaway." Corrigan nodded and took them.

"Would you mind answering a few questions, Ms. Essell?" Yeen asked Lilly, his tone not really leaving a lot in the way of options.

"Well . . . I guess not." Lilly met Corrigan's gaze as she got up, but Yeen had left them no opportunity for agreeing on details.

"I'll see you later," was all that Corrigan could say. Just like in the books. Somebody must have fed the system detective stories, he reflected as he watched the two of them follow Judy away around a corner.

A sandy-haired, wide-browed, bearded figure in a black, V-neck sweater with a white-stripe diagonal design approached from the other direction and caused him to turn. It was Barry Neinst. He looked solemn, but although it was he who had come to see Corrigan, he hesitated longer than would have been natural, letting Corrigan set the tone of what was appropriate by speaking or acting first. As had been the case with Judy, Corrigan could detect nothing from outward appearances that told him if he was talking to an animation or a surrogate. It was only their subtle differences in manner that set them apart. Corrigan waited curiously, deliberately refraining from offering any cue. Finally, the system capitulated, and Barry said:

"I don't know what to make of it—about Tom. It's just . . . too terrible. I mean, what do you say? . . ."

"What can you say?" Corrigan answered. "It's been a lousy morning. Life goes on. Tomorrow might be better." Barry's eyes widened into circles of confused surprise behind his spectacles. In some half-amused, cynical way, Corrigan enjoyed being no help at all, watching the system dither and flounder.

"I guess you're right," Barry said. In a matter of seconds the about-face was complete. Yet such shallowness had been there all the time in the animations that had been all around him since yesterday, Corrigan reminded himself. So adept was the human mind at the art of seeing what it expected to see. "There's nothing we can say that'll change anything, eh?" Barry went on. Already the system was trying out the new line, fishing for confirmation that it had got it right.

Corrigan obliged. "Not a thing." His eyes strayed down to the two slips of paper in his hand. The project—this unreal version of it, anyway—was no longer of any interest, and neither, therefore, were the concerns of unreal Pinders and unreal Endelmyers. He wondered what way of dealing with them would entail the least distraction from the things that did matter. Perhaps simply to ignore them.

"Let's just hope he hasn't started too much of a craze," Barry said.

Corrigan looked up, only half hearing. "Who?"

"Tom."

"What about him?"

"All the others."

"Other what?"

"Haven't you seen the news this morning?"

Corrigan's brow creased. "No, I haven't. What's happened?"

"Oh. Then you don't *know*!" Barry moistened his lips and moved a step closer. "Since it was on the news last night, more people have been driving their cars into oncoming traffic. It's as if a lot of people out there suddenly discovered a new way of solving their problems that they hadn't thought of before. When I was driving in, the count was up to fifteen. The whole city's going crazy. People are afraid to go out."

Corrigan stared at him in astonishment. First the shootings that had been breaking out since the incident at the airport. Now this. He thought back to the way Pinder and the others had behaved yesterday and the day before, the plasticity of Meechum, Borth, the CLC Board. . . . An instinct told Corrigan that there was some kind of pattern behind it, connecting them all. But before he could give the matter any further thought, the phone on Judy's desk rang to announce a voice call.

"Excuse me." Corrigan picked up the handset. "Yes?"

A man's voice said, "Is there a Ms. Klein there, please?"

"She's away from her desk at the moment, I'm afraid."

"Is there a Mr. Corrigan?"

"This is Joe Corrigan speaking."

"Good morning. My name is Ulsen. I work with Mr. Sylvine, at the Advisory Office of Advanced Technology in Washington. . . ."

"Yes! Good morning. Could you hold for a moment?" Corrigan covered the mouthpiece and made waving motions. "Sorry, Barry, but I have to take this inside right now. Can I catch you later?"

"Sure. But we need to go over the initialization checklist for tomorrow."

"It may have to be postponed with this other business. I'll let you know later this morning."

"Okay." Barry shrugged and turned to leave, just as Judy reappeared from the direction of the conference room.

"Judy, can you switch this through? I need to take it inside," Corrigan said as she came back to her desk. She nodded as she sat down, and tapped a couple of keys. Corrigan went into his office and picked up. "Hello? Mr. Ulsen?"

"Yes. You left a message yesterday for Mr. Sylvine to call you?"

"That's right."

"Well, he's out of town right now and not due back for some days. Can you tell me what it's about? Maybe I can help."

Corrigan thought quickly. Seventeen or eighteen hours had gone by since he had made the call from Main Reception, when he and Lilly returned to Xylog the evening before. In the world outside, that would be a little over five minutes. Sylvine had no doubt decoupled after the dinner the evening before that (an additional seven minutes earlier) to make his report, which was why he wasn't replying. Although "Ulsen" might not necessarily be playing an active role in the simulation, he was coupled into the system, since he was able to synchronize with Corrigan. But he would be a temporary liaison, there to provide a contact of sorts; he would be able to disconnect and talk to the outside.

Corrigan said curtly, "Look, whoever-you-really-are. No bullshit, okay? I know the score. The memory erasure of the first run didn't work. Get this whole thing terminated immediately. Do you understand?"

There was a long, creaking pause. "I'll have to consult—"

"Consult, nothing. There isn't anything to consult about. In case you aren't aware of it yet, one of the surrogates just checked himself out. The rest can follow. Whoever's behind this are facing enough lawsuits to paper CLC's Head Office with already. You tell them that it stops *now*! Out." Corrigan slammed down the phone and stood looking at it. He was conscious of a feeling of anticlimax. So that was it? After all the talk, all that he had been able to do amounted to no more than issue a demand into a phone and hang up. And now, back to the interminable waiting. All of a sudden, Hatcher's uncompromising solution was beginning to look clean and decisive by comparison. Not prepared even to consider the demeaning passivity of waiting, he had gone straight over to the offensive. Probably he was causing consternation outside, right at this moment. Anything that Corrigan might do now would be merely a supporting action.

Then the sound of new voices came from outside the office door, which Corrigan had left open. He looked away from the desk and saw that Harry Morgen and Joan Sutton had arrived. Morgen was talking to Judy and pointing at a configuration on her screen that looked from a distance like Corrigan's call-log format. Sutton was standing behind him, gazing about at the surroundings as if she had never seen them before. Then Morgen, in the process of uttering something, brought his right hand up to touch his temple with a finger in an odd, flicking motion, vaguely suggestive of a lazy salute. Corrigan had seen that mannerism before somewhere.

Corrigan walked slowly across the office and stopped in the doorway, studying them. Neither they nor Judy had noticed him yet.

Then he remembered where he had seen that temple-touching mannerism before: Zehl! Dr. Zehl had had the same unconscious habit. And, therefore, Graham Sylvine—since Corrigan had already concluded that they were the same person. So Morgen had been the outside controller who had masqueraded as Zehl and Sylvine. That much made sense—Morgen was a firm Tyron follower. The only thing that didn't answer was if *this* Morgen was another animation re-created from system profiles, like Pinder and Barry Neinst, or a projection of the real person, coupled in. If he was real, then maybe Corrigan had his channel to the outside standing here, right in front of him.

◎ CHAPTER FORTY ◎

Judy stopped what she had been saying as she saw Corrigan moving out from the doorway of his office. "Oh, here he is now." Morgen and Sutton turned toward him and exchanged perfunctory greetings. Corrigan watched their faces as they spoke. As with Barry Neinst, there was no way of telling from outward appearances.

"People over at Head Office are trying to get hold of you, Joe, but you haven't been getting back to them," Morgen said. "With the project about to go live, that seems strange. Is everything okay over here?"

Corrigan was conscious of their eyes searching his face like mapping radars, almost as if they were trying to divine the true person behind the surface imagery as much as he was of them. Considering the events since the previous evening, Morgen's remark seemed curiously insensitive. And Corrigan thought he knew why. Here was his opportunity.

"He was one of our key people," Corrigan said. "And now the city's making a fad out of it. It *does* alter the perspective of things a bit."

His vagueness was deliberate. Involuntarily, Joan Sutton glanced at Morgen with a bemused look, and he returned one that was just as mystified. *They didn't know!* And in that instant Corrigan knew that they were real-person surrogates. The way that Sutton had seemed awed by the surroundings should have told him sooner.

For had they been Morgen and Sutton animations—permanent

denizens of the simulated world—they would have been present since yesterday, and hence aware of what had been dominating the news. But Morgen, as Sylvine, had left only twelve minutes ago, outside-time, which would have given him barely enough time to report from his last visit, agree on the next objectives, and reenter. The fact that he had reappeared so soon, as himself, and bringing Joan Sutton with him, suggested that something irregular had been detected by the controllers on the outside. That would fit with why they were checking on Corrigan's behavior.

He looked at them coldly, making no attempt to hide the rancor that he felt. "You don't know what's been going on, do you?"

Morgen tried to feign a puzzled look. "How—"

Corrigan cut him off with a disdainful wave. "Don't try any acting, Harry—it'll save us all a lot of breath." He nodded back toward the doorway of his office. "Let's go inside." He extended an arm. Morgen's face was apprehensive. Sutton shot him what looked to Corrigan like an accusing look, and he sensed that all was not smooth between them. They went through. "Hold all calls, Judy," Corrigan said, and followed.

Inside, he closed the door behind him and turned on them. "Now let me guess what's been happening outside. The trait-assimilation parameter settings in the first run were wrong—yes?—which caused the animations to go off on self-reinforcing patterns and create a screwed-up world in which the surrogates—" Corrigan indicated himself with a finger and interjected in a scathing voice, "such as *me*! . . . instead of providing the models, became misfits. Yes, *Doctor Zehl*?" He glared at them and found that his breathing was heavy. Morgen had paled. His skin looked clammy in the pale light of the office. The system was picking up his physiological responses and projecting them perfectly. Even Corrigan marveled.

He went on. "But even so, the results were so far beyond anything we'd ever imagined that somebody out there decided to run the whole thing again from the beginning with the parameters reset. But that's where you messed up. You see, the erasure of the first run didn't work the way it was supposed to. We still remember it—all twelve years of it."

They stared at him numbly. He continued. "But yesterday, Tom Hatcher decided he'd had enough and wasn't about to go around again. And do you know what he did? He got a gun and blew away a heap of computer-code cops and security guards out at the airport. By nighttime, it had become the rage all over the city. Later, Tom ran his car up to eighty and pointed it head-on into a truck, so he's out of it already, and probably giving everyone out there hell." Corrigan's face creased into a mocking smile. "And guess what—this morning there's screwballs doing the same thing all over Pittsburgh."

The expressions on the two faces in front of him were completely stunned, causing Corrigan's smile to widen derisively. "You see what it means?" he said to them. "Now the parameters are *over*compensated. The animations are slavishly copying whatever the surrogates do—if you'd looked hard enough around the dinner table, you might have seen it yourself when you were here a little while ago as Graham Sylvine. With surrogates acting rationally in the way everyone assumed they would, that might have been okay. Oz could have worked. But what the experiment never bargained for was any of them going off the rails the way Tom did. Now you're about to create another world full of lunatics, only this time psychopaths and suicides." Corrigan tossed out a hand in a dismissive gesture, and the smile vanished from his face. "So it's over, and lot of heads are going to roll out there. Get it terminated."

"I did try and tell you," Sutton began, looking at Morgen. "I said that the—"

Morgen waved her aside in a way that said all that could wait until later. "It was the pressure from the F and F consortium," he told Corrigan. "They insisted on going straight to a full-world implementation, and they funded additional outside programming to do it. That was what they'd always wanted—a virtual world. They weren't interested in developing AI. We had to go along to get the backing."

Corrigan looked at him disdainfully. "What do you take me for? I've grown twelve years in the last three weeks. Come on—I want *out!*"

But Morgen persisted in the line that had been agreed upon in his excursion outside. "Look, Joe . . . I know that the way it's been done has been a bit underhanded. . . ."

"*Underhanded!* By Christ, I—"

"Hear me out, please. Look, I know you've had a raw deal. But that can all be straightened out. As you just said, this whole project, this process of yours, has worked out way, way better than anything anyone ever dreamed of. If—"

"Right! *You* just said it: this process of *mine*!"

"I understand what you're saying, Joe. But let's not allow the project to suffer just because you're feeling sore in the short term, right now." Morgen showed both palms hastily. "Don't get me wrong—I'm not saying you don't have good reason. Rerunning and knowing what we know now, it might actually get so close to reality that you can't tell the difference. That was the original success criterion, remember? And we're almost there already. After this we can do more realscaping and expand the territory. Maybe tie in a whole list of remote places." Morgen forced a jocular tone. "Hey, remember that time you wanted to visit Ireland, and Zehl had to pull rank?"

"Somebody seems to have it all figured out," Corrigan remarked sarcastically.

"See it through," Morgen urged. "You'll be more than compensated. It's already been agreed. We're only talking about another few days."

That was too much. "*For you!*" Corrigan exploded. "A few days for you! Don't you understand what I said a minute ago? Suppression of the first-run memories *didn't work*. For us, you're talking about years. I want this thing stopped now, and I want out. So get on with it."

Morgen shook his head, still unwilling to give up but at a loss for a continuation. "Is there a choice?" Sutton asked him. "From the sound of it, it's all about to go off into a different brand of craziness in the other direction anyway. It's time to hold, analyze the data we've got, and reevaluate."

Still, Morgen wavered. After a few seconds of waiting, unyielding, Corrigan pointed out, "You might as well. It can't work now, whatever you do. I'll just start tossing people out of the windows, and by lunchtime everyone'll be doing it. What use is that going to be to your precious backers? It's over. Accept it. Get us out."

Finally Morgen capitulated. "I can't make the decision. It has to go back to the people outside."

"Okay, but you don't have to decouple. Use one of the direct gate codes," Corrigan said. As a transient observer, Morgen would be able to signal the outside via a special calling number like the one that Corrigan had used to leave messages for "Sylvine." Probably he had recourse to other means, too.

"Better do it, Harry," Sutton murmured in a tone that said he might as well get it over with. Morgen hesitated, then drew a pocket communicator from his jacket and tapped in a numeric sequence to flag a precoded message that would be transmitted practically instantaneously. Hence he was able to get information out straightaway, which was the option that Corrigan had not had access to.

"You might as well tell them to reduce the time-acceleration down to unity, too, while you're at it," Corrigan suggested. "Communication would be a lot simpler. It won't make any difference now. This run isn't going anywhere."

While the time-rate differential existed, however, and allowing for even a couple of minutes' deliberation on the outside, there would be a considerable delay before any response became known. Joan Sutton was at boiling point, tight-mouthed and sending Morgen daggers looks. Corrigan guessed that she had opposed the decision to reset the simulation and been overruled. Corrigan decided it would be easiest to leave them to it. He had said all he had to say for the time being.

He moved back to the door and opened it to look out. Lilly was back sitting on her chair opposite Judy's desk. Yeen was standing nearby. He came across when Corrigan appeared.

"Er, Mr. Corrigan," he said. "There are one or two inconsistencies between your account and Ms. Essell's—that we'll need to go over." Corrigan did his best to look surprised. "I must ask you to be available again later today."

"Very well," Corrigan said.

"If you do have reason to go elsewhere, you will leave details of how you can be reached?"

"Of course."

"Then that will be all for now. Thanks for your cooperation. I can find my own way out, if that's okay."

Corrigan smiled apologetically. "Sorry—company rules. Judy, would you take Mr. Yeen back down to Reception, please?" Judy got up and walked away with Yeen in the direction of the elevators. Corrigan shrugged at Lilly in a way that said none of it mattered. The sound of Joan Sutton's voice rising came through the doorway behind him. Corrigan half closed the door behind him and went over to Lilly.

"I think we might have cracked it," he said in reply to her inquiring look. His voice lowered. "Two of the outside crew showed up as observers while you were gone. I've told them the game's up. They're on the line back to base right now."

She gaped at him. "Cracked it—already? You mean we're getting out?"

"Right. There'll probably be a bit of a wait before anything happens, but they know it's blown. And thanks to Tom, we know how to wreck everything from the inside now, if they try to be obstinate. They don't have any choices."

Lilly was about to reply, but then she looked away toward his office door with a puzzled expression. Corrigan realized that it had suddenly gone curiously quiet inside. He went back, pushed the door open, and looked in. Morgen and Sutton had vanished.

❀ CHAPTER FORTY-ONE ❀

Harry Morgen stood facing Frank Tyron in the Monitor & Control Center on the third floor of the Xylog Building. Sutton was with him. They had just come up from the gallery of interface couplers on the level below after breaking one of the cardinal rules for transient observers visiting the simulation: effecting entry and exit in such a way as to risk confronting the inhabitants with abnormal phenomena. Endelmyer had heard the news about Hatcher and was on his way over from CLC headquarters across the river with John Velucci from Corporate Legal. Rumors were flying around the building that the whole Oz simulation was about to self-destruct.

"It doesn't matter anymore," Morgen insisted. "Time is more important now. The longer Corrigan has to wait in there, the more likely it's going to get that he'll start doing something to sabotage the whole works. You have to believe me, Frank—he's mad as hell and he'll do it." Morgen pointed to the lanky, yellow-haired figure with a pallid, tired-looking face covered in unshaved growth, who was sitting by one of the consoles along the wall, a blanket drawn around his shoulders and clutching a mug of hot, black coffee. "He showed them how to do it. We overcompensated on the TAPS. Now half the animations are shooting each other and crossing over highways. It's an asylum in there."

Hatcher's chest heaved with laughter that was stifled by the thermometer in his mouth. The medic standing by him took it out and nodded that it was okay for him to drink the coffee now. He had flatly refused to be taken to the medical department for a rest and checkup as stipulated in the exiting procedure, and come straight up to the M & C floor instead. Nothing would make him miss what happened now, and that was final. Jason Pinder was hovering nearby, watching him anxiously, genuinely concerned.

"We're initializing real-time resynch now," a supervisor called from where he was standing behind two of the console operators. "T-by-tau is dropping at one per second. Should have reintegration in about three minutes." It meant that the simulation's accelerated time was being slowed to bring it back into synchronization with the real world.

Despite all these signs that it was over, Victor Borth was not ready to concede final defeat just yet. He turned from where he had been listening with his back toward Tyron and the others, and spread his hands appealingly. "This is crazy," he told them. "Somebody tell me I'm not hearing this. Are you people saying that two guys can screw up a whole project of this magnitude? I mean, what does it take to keep two guys sweet? All they've got to do is name it." He turned and walked toward the side of the room where Hatcher was sitting. "Hey, you. Tom, is it? What's the biggest thing you've ever dreamed of getting out of life? Cars? Boats? Broads? You could be a millionaire, know that? Everybody's got something. You could have some of the most powerful people anywhere on your side for the rest of your life—anything you wanna do. There has to be room for us to talk, right?" Hatcher shook his head, sighed, smiled wearily to himself, and looked away.

Of more concern to Tyron than Hatcher's future right now was the matter of his own. He was the one who had convinced the consortium of F & F's client-backers that a functioning pseudoworld was feasible; he had coordinated outside development of the advanced system that went past the original specification drawn up inside CLC; and at his instigation, Borth had organized the flow of funds to support it. If he delivered as promised, the wherewithal to smooth over all these embarrassments would be forthcoming. He'd have the leverage; he'd have the friends. If he failed to . . . No, they were all in it too far. There could be no backing down now.

He had authorized temporary resynchronization to permit direct communication with Corrigan from the outside. Now he decided that a more direct form of intervention was needed. He turned to the operators at the section monitoring operation of the COSMOS neural-coupling interfaces on the floor below. "Initialize another two units." Then, curtly, to Morgen, Sutton, and Borth, "We're going back in."

Borth looked taken aback. "All of us? You mean . . ."

Tyron smiled thinly at him. "Why not? You've been saying for a long time that you'll have to try this thing yourself someday. Well, now's your chance. Use your arguments on the guy who matters."

"T-tau one seventy-five and falling," the supervisor reported.

"Come on," Tyron said, striding across the floor in the direction of the way out to the main corridor. Borth followed, and after a moment of faltering Morgen and Sutton fell in behind. "And anyhow, we still have the final argument," Tyron tossed back at them over his shoulder as he reached the doors. "We've got the switch out here, and he doesn't."

They disappeared, and the doors closed behind them. Some of the operators exchanged curious looks. Others shrugged. Pinder leaned closer to Hatcher with a worried expression. "How do you feel?" he asked.

Hatcher stared dully across the room and considered the question. "I'm not sure," he said finally, looking up. "How is the victim of a successful suicide supposed to feel? . . . Not bad, considering, I guess."

❀ CHAPTER FORTY-TWO ❀

For Corrigan this was the most unreal part since the beginning of the entire experience. The full-scale Oz project, culmination of everything he had been working toward for the past several years, was about to go live in the next couple of days. Technicians and managers assailed him constantly for decisions about last-minute details; Endelmyer, the president of the corporation, was demanding that his calls be returned. And none of it mattered. There was going to be some delay no matter how quickly events moved in the world outside. His only choice was to either make a dramatic exit as Hatcher had done, or wait it out.

Judy had been away from her desk seeing Yeen from the building, so Corrigan was spared having to improvise some other pretext for getting her away from her desk to cover for Morgen and Sutton's abrupt disappearance. One other detail that he did need to justify to keep things from getting difficult, however, was the continuing presence of Lilly. It seemed odd, at a time like this, to have to give consideration to satisfying the pseudocuriosity of a computer animation, but it was the easiest way of keeping things simple in the meantime for himself.

When Judy returned, Corrigan informed her that Lilly wanted to spend the rest of the morning going through her notes and listing any final questions before going back to California, and would be using the small conference room that Yeen had questioned her in. Lilly disappeared accordingly, and the routine calls and queries continued unabated until late morning. Then Judy announced that Mr. Ulsen was on the line from the Advisory Office of Advanced Technology, Washington. Corrigan told her to put the call through.

"Mr. Corrigan?"

"Yes."

"Ulsen again. How are things in there?" At least there were no attempts at pretense this time.

"Never mind the niceties," Corrigan growled. "Morgen and Sutton are back out, so you know the score. What's the situation?"

"Your request is understood and appreciated, Mr. Corrigan. A delegation is on its way back into the simulation to talk to you."

"That wasn't a request, dammit. And there isn't anything to talk about. Do you intend doing as I said, or do we start unhinging the whole works from the inside here?"

"Please understand that I am merely an intermediary. I have no personal authority in this. It's all gone way over my head."

"Then just get back out there and tell whoever is in charge to shut down the whole operation—now. That's all there is to it. End. Period. Do you get the message, Mr. Ulsen?"

"Yes, I understand perfectly. But I have been asked to remind you of the reality of the time-rate differential. Some finite time will be required however urgently matters are expedited out here, and that will translate into a delay that may seem unduly protracted."

"All you have to do is restore tee-tau to unity. Then we'd be able to talk direct and wouldn't need an intermediary. It's perfectly simple."

"That is already being done. But as I'm sure you appreciate, it will still necessitate a considerable delay at your end. All we're asking is for you to bear with us."

Only if the intention was to talk. But Corrigan had already said that there was nothing to talk about. He was just about to launch into another outburst of invective when he saw Pinder hovering in the doorway of the office. Pulled in two directions, he wavered suddenly. "Be quick about it, then," he muttered to Ulsen.

"Thank you for your understanding."

Corrigan put the phone down and looked up. Pinder came in, closing the door. His expression was accusatory, yet at the same time questioning—unable to condone but reluctant to prejudge. Corrigan had been expecting it. Pinder had been involved when the police appeared with the news about Hatcher, and gone over the river to convey the tidings to Head Office. The calls from on high had begun soon afterward, and now he was back as an emissary to find out what in hell was going on.

Pinder opened. "I was prepared to overlook your indiscretion of yesterday, Joe, but this is going too far. Don't you realize, *the president of the company* has been *personally* trying to contact you since first thing this morning. And you don't seem to give a damn. What on earth's gotten into you? I told you the last time that you are not the technical director yet. Now I think I'm beginning to realize just how unsuited you'd be to that task. Now, are you going to at least cover while we get the project up and running, or do I put in Frank Tyron as acting coordinator, effective immediately?"

Corrigan stared at him indifferently, feeling like Archimedes having to put up with the babbling soldier from Rome while trying to ponder things that mattered. On the other hand, Archimedes had gotten himself killed. There could be no letup yet; the game had to continue. But he had learned how to deal with animations.

He forced an expression of shocked surprise. "Surely you're not referring to the project . . . not at a time like this, after the news about Tom?" He shook his head to say he knew that Pinder hadn't meant it—giving him the opportunity that any decent person would have to put it another way. "We're not imagining that tomorrow's schedule still stands?"

Pinder faltered while unseen circuits hastily recomputed weighting evaluation matrixes. His change of stance was as abrupt as yesterday's, or as Barry Neinst's a few hours earlier.

"Well, of course, I didn't exactly mean to imply that. Naturally we must observe a proper sense of priorities. . . . But there are certain interests with a considerable stake in the outcome, who don't share our dimension of, shall we say, 'personal involvement'—as I'm sure you appreciate. If the schedule is affected—as it has to be, of course—we still owe it to them to be kept informed."

"I'm working on it now," Corrigan lied. "But I don't have a full picture yet. Yeen should be getting in touch again at any time."

"Very well. But in that case please call Endelmyer back and inform him of that much."

Corrigan sighed beneath his breath, nodded, and entered the code into his desk unit. Anyway, it would be as easy to turn Endelmyer's animation around too, he reasoned. The features of Endelmyer's secretary appeared on the screen. "Hi, Celia. Joe Corrigan for himself," he said.

"Oh, at last. I'll put you straight through."

Then Judy's voice came from outside on another line. "Sorry to interrupt, but Harry Morgen and Joan Sutton are back with Frank Tyron, wanting to see you. Victor Borth is with them. They say it's urgent, and you know what it's about."

"All right!" Corrigan exclaimed with relish, and forgetting all else, sprung up from the desk and headed for the door.

"Joe? . . . Joe Corrigan, where are you?" Endelmyer's puzzled voice said from the screen.

"Hello? No, it's me," Corrigan heard Pinder splutter behind him as he went out. "Well, he is, but he's just gone. I don't know what's happened to him. . . ."

Whereas Morgen's approach had been conciliatory and placating, Tyron immediately launched into the offensive—possibly because Morgen had got nowhere; more likely to maintain a firm image of the heavyweight in front of Borth.

"What do you people think you're playing at?" he demanded. "Don't you realize that the information that's coming out of this is already priceless? You're sabotaging what could be the biggest breakthrough in the whole field in the last fifty years."

"Everything's on this now," Borth pitched in, pushing his way forward beside Tyron. "If it blows, Xylog folds—the whole works. If it flies, we've got the oyster. You have to see this one through now."

Corrigan, furious, pointed an arm in the general upward

direction to indicate "out there." "That's all you can think about, even after what you forced Tom Hatcher into?"

"Unavoidable collateral," Tyron said. "It's a shame it has to happen, but there's some in every operation."

"*Unavoidable collateral!*" Corrigan exploded. "Is that what you call it? It's still all just—"

Tyron brushed it aside with a tired wave. "Look, he's okay. I just talked to him. If you want to be part of the Big League, you've gotta start thinking in big terms, Joey boy."

Judy, who had been listening bemusedly from her desk, gasped. "Tom, okay? But how could he be? I don't understand. . . ."

Tyron ignored her. Corrigan, however, was a person whose habits died hard. "Let's do this somewhere less public," he said. He looked back at the open door of his office, but Pinder was still talking at the screen in there. There was still the room where Lilly was ensconced. "Come on. This way." And before anyone could object, he began herding them away. "Don't worry about it, Judy," he threw back as they disappeared around the corner. "I'll explain it all later."

Lilly was sitting in a chair to one side of the room, apparently thinking to herself, when Corrigan came in followed by the others. Tyron halted when he saw her, a frown of puzzled recognition on his face. She seemed unsure of whether she had met him before or not.

"Yes, you know her, Frank," Corrigan said, reading the situation as Morgen came in last of all, closing the door. "This is Lillian Essell, one of the Air Force volunteers that you interviewed in California a month ago. Except for her it's been twelve years. I'm not sure if they've made that clear to you yet, out there—the memory suppression of the first run didn't work. It was a neat idea, but you messed up. We still remember everything."

But Tyron was already waving a hand impatiently and grimacing. "You don't understand. The rerun is showing some amazing things already. Just stay with it for a few more days. There's—"

Corrigan slammed a hand down on the table in the center of the room. "*Days for you!*" he stormed. "That's the whole point I'm trying to tell you, but you don't seem able to space for get it into your head. It's going to be years all over again for us!"

"Not years," Tyron argued. "The contradictions are beginning to show now. It can't go much farther. You've got to push it to its limits. That's the only way we'll learn what we need to know to make it better."

"So that *you* can deliver what they want, while I'm the schmuck locked up inside it? What do you take me for? I might be Irish, but I'm not all Kerry green. The answer's no—no way. Forget it. It's over. We're getting out."

Tyron's expression changed to something approaching a leer. "Well, it's a pity you feel that way, Joey boy, because when the chips are down you don't really have that much of a choice. We can exit at any time. . . ." To prove it, Tyron vanished before their eyes and reappeared a moment later ten feet away, on the opposite side of the table. He pointed a finger at Corrigan. "But you depend on an external disconnect." He shrugged with a grin of emphasized unapology. "And we've got the switch out there. You don't."

Lilly stood up and broke in, "That's not true. What about Tom Hatcher? We can get out anytime."

Tyron shrugged again, evidently having already considered the point. "So go ahead and opt out," he told them. "That won't score very high with the people who own the show, will it? So the simulation loses a couple of surrogates. So what? There are still four dozen others. The show goes on, with you or without you."

"You talk as if you think it's yours," Corrigan said.

Tyron leered again, more broadly this time. "You quit now, and it will be," he answered.

Corrigan shook his head, bunching his mouth grimly, and threw out an arm. "Oh no, it isn't as simple as that; at all. Haven't you heard? You've created another crazy world out there. Ever since Hatcher showed them how, they've been wiping each other and themselves out all over Pittsburgh. What use do you think a simulation like that is going to be to anyone?"

Tyron made a show of being unperturbed. "We overcompensated on the assimilation parameters. So we set them back a little. It's no problem."

Corrigan's neck reddened. He was about to reply, when the door opened again and Pinder appeared. Pinder moved a pace into the room and stood, looking around at the company perplexedly. "Will somebody tell me what the hell's going on around here?" he demanded. His eyes singled out Corrigan, and he was about to say something further, when he noticed Lilly beside him, and her visitor's badge. "Who are you?" he asked her.

Pinder was an animation. He would know nothing of what was being discussed in the room. Corrigan knew more about what Lilly was doing there than any of the others. He gave the only answer that he could: "Her name's Lillian Essell. She's a journalist from California, doing a piece on the project. I told her she could use this room for the morning."

Pinder waited a couple of seconds to see how that explained anything, and when nothing more was forthcoming, shook his head, refusing to add another layer of complication to what there already was. "I'm sorry, Ms. Essell, but this is strictly an internal company matter. I must ask you to leave us, please."

Lilly looked questioningly at Corrigan. "My office is empty," he said. "Use that for now. You know where it is." He moved with her to see her to the door. She nodded, happy to let them get on with it. Pinder stood aside and held the door for her to leave. But just as he was about to close it behind her, he saw Ken Endelmyer and John Velucci approaching along the corridor. They halted just outside the room. Endelmyer looked at Pinder strangely. Pinder looked strangely at him.

"What are you doing here?" Endelmyer asked, looking puzzled. "I thought we left you outside. How did you get inside?"

"Inside what?" Pinder replied, just as puzzled. "I've just come across."

"Across what?"

"Across from HQ. You asked me to."

"I did? When?"

Pinder tried desperately not to look like a subordinate suddenly confronted by a superior who has taken leave of his senses. "Ten minutes ago. You wanted me to get over here and see what the problem was with Joe."

"No, you were already here," Endelmyer said, looking equally suspicious. "*We've* just come over from HQ—to join Frank and the others here. But we left you outside in the Monitoring Center."

"Outside?" Pinder queried.

"Outside Oz—outside the simulation," Endelmyer replied.

Pinder looked uneasily around the room in a silent plea for somebody to tell him that he wasn't the only one for whom this was getting insane. The others returned looks as devoid of expression as a fog bank.

Then Corrigan realized what had happened. Pinder, the animation, had just left an Endelmyer animation in HQ, across the river, and now had run into the real Endelmyer, who had entered the simulation as a surrogate; and since Pinder knew only the animation Endelmyer, he was presuming this one to be he. The real Endelmyer, on the other hand, had come over from HQ in the real world, and by the sound of things had talked to the real Pinder before being coupled in. Corrigan groaned inwardly. It could only get worse. Nothing was going to sort this out now.

Pinder looked back at Endelmyer. "Outside the simulation," he repeated. "That's very interesting. I'm not quite sure I follow, though, since the simulation isn't due to begin until tomorrow." His voice was polite and inoffensive, like a student not wanting to say that the professor was wrong when it was obvious. "Perhaps you could explain?"

"Tomorrow?" Endelmyer blinked, nonplussed. "It's been running for three weeks, Jason. What in God's name are you talking about?" He sent an uncertain look around the room in his turn, then moved in through the doorway to appeal to them all directly. "Is Jason not making sense, or is it me?"

Tyron hadn't quite seen it yet either. "I understand you, but not him," he said, but sounding distant as if fearing that he might be missing something. "Of course, it's been running for three weeks. We just came into it."

"You're all mad," Pinder declared flatly.

"What kind of talk is this?" Endelmyer demanded. "First Hatcher flips. Then Corrigan won't talk to anybody. Is there something we don't know about this process that affects . . ." His voice trailed away when he saw that Corrigan was staring past him, out into the corridor, with a look of open disbelief. Endelmyer turned to follow his gaze, and his jaw fell. Another Endelmyer and another Velucci were coming along the corridor from the elevators.

"Ah, there you are, Joe," Endelmyer called ahead, seeing him. "I figured that maybe you were having bigger problems over this Hatcher business than I realized, so John and I decided to follow Jas—" He stopped in midword and came to a dead halt as he saw who was with Corrigan, just inside the doorway of the conference room. The Endelmyer and the Velucci inside stared at the Endelmyer and the Velucci outside. The ones outside stared back. All of them seized up.

Joan Sutton came out of her stupor first. "Frank, freeze the animations," she said sharply.

At the far end of the room, Tyron fished out a communicator and hammered in an emergency code. "Control? Do we have synchronization yet? Hello? Does anyone out there read? This is critical. . . ." All attention in the room focused upon him. Perspiration showed on his forehead. His eyes were wide with alarm behind his spectacles.

"Will somebody tell me what in Christ is going on here?" Borth demanded darkly.

"Oh shit," Harry Morgen groaned as the truth slowly dawned.

"Who are you talking to?" the animation Endelmyer asked, moving in through the door and pointing at Tyron. "I *demand* an explanation!"

That was enough to shock the other Endelmyer into life. "*You* don't demand anything around here. *I* run this company."

"Come in, control. Does anyone read? . . ."

In the middle of it all, Corrigan slipped out into the corridor. He walked quickly back to his own office, past Judy, who was talking with Betty, the sixth-floor receptionist, and straight in through his own door. Lilly was sitting in a chair to one side of the desk, contemplating a figurine of an Irish leprechaun that she had taken from the shelf above. She looked up before Corrigan could say anything and asked him, "Didn't you tell me that somebody gave this to you and Evelyn as a wedding gift? But I saw it at the house, too, last night. How do you come to have two of them?"

"Jesus, can you believe women? We've no time for things like that right now. The whole . . ." Corrigan stopped speaking abruptly and jerked his head around to look at her as he realized what she was saying. "Are you sure?"

"Yes. It was on a ledge in the den." That was right. On the morning of his mysterious awakening, when he came into work and looked around his office, Corrigan himself had thought that it ought to be at the house. But he hadn't been sure because it had been twelve years ago. Then, with everything else going on, it had completely gone from his mind to check in the evening. He took the figurine from her and turned it over in his hands, staring at it.

"You said, something that would be meaningful when you looked for it—something that would become significant when the time came," Lilly said unnecessarily. "And it was there the last time, too. We saw it in the shop window. You told me you had one just like it at home. You said that it haunted you." Yes. And he had seen one when he was out by himself, in the bar, Corrigan remembered. The system had been prodding him, reminding him all the time that the leprechaun was there. Because that was what, sometime in that lost day that he had forgotten, Corrigan had told it to do.

"By God, Lilly, I think you might be a genius," Corrigan whispered. He walked quickly around the desk and sat down, still holding the figurine. From outside, the sounds came of voices rising in an angry clamor. What would he have expected himself to do with it? he asked himself frantically. What associations did he have with leprechauns? A word? A phrase? A code that would have a special meaning only to him?

And suddenly he smiled as he remembered his cousin Jeff giving it to him in the lounge of the Royal Marine Hotel in Dun Laoghaire, and himself and Evelyn talking to a somewhat cynical Marvin Minsky years ago. . . .

"I wonder," he muttered aloud. Working quickly, he activated his desk unit and keyed it into "System" mode. A command prompt appeared on the screen. Lilly came around to stand behind him and watch. He entered the word IRELAND.

Nothing happened.

He tried LEPRECHAUN.

A cry of alarm came from Judy outside.

"What are you doing?" Lilly murmured tensely by his ear.

"Shhh." He entered MICK.

The system responded with: "WHEN IRISH EYES ARE SMILING . . ."

Corrigan's face broke into a wide, triumphant grin. He completed: YOU'VE PROBABLY JUST BEEN RIPPED OFF.

There was an instant's delay that seemed eternal. Corrigan stared at the screen, vaguely aware of Judy coming in through the doorway, waving her arms wildly at something behind her.

And then the screen changed to:

CONGRATULATIONS!!!
YOU ARE NOW IN CONTROL OF THE
SYSTEM PRIMARY COMMAND EXECUTIVE. ENTER:
"OUT/OUT" FOR IMMEDIATE DECOUPLING (EJECT)
"AB" FOR GENERAL SYSTEM ABORT
"OV" OVERRIDES ALL EXTERNAL COMMAND
FUNCTIONS UNTIL UNLOCKED
"DF" LISTS OTHER DIRECTIVE FUNCTIONS
"VM" SWITCHES TO VOICE MODE
(COMMAND EXEC ANSWERS TO "ROGER")

Lilly gasped, awed. "Joe, is this what I think it is?"

"Joe," Judy's voice came, strangled, fearful. "Out there—Betty. Something's happened to her." Corrigan looked past the doorway and saw that Betty was standing by Judy's desk, inanimate like a mannequin, her mouth open and arm raised in the middle of a gesture. Tyron had gotten through: the controllers outside had deactivated the animations. From outside the building there came the distant, muted sounds of multiple vehicles crashing. Corrigan looked back at Judy suddenly as the further implication registered.

"You're real!" he said in astonishment.

"What are you talking about? Of course I am," Judy said. "Do something about Betty." She must have volunteered for the rerun and had her memory suppressed, just like the others the first time. She didn't know anything about the first run.

Farther back, Tyron, Endelmyer, Velucci, and Borth were coming across the area of open floor beyond Judy's desk, looking grim and purposeful, with Morgen and Sutton following. Behind them, just before the corner to the corridor, another Endelmyer, another Velucci, and Pinder were standing immobilized.

Corrigan hurriedly tapped OV into the pad, followed by VM, and then said aloud, experimentally, "Roger, do you read?"

"Loud and clear," a voice answered. It was in his head, but he heard it in his ear.

"I'm in full exec access now?"

"You've got it."

Oh, boy. He was going to enjoy this. "Define operand class: all current surrogates," he instructed. "Exceptions by name: Corrigan, Essell, Tyron, Morgen, Sutton, Endelmyer, Velucci, Borth."

"Specify operation?"

"There's nothing to worry about, Judy," Corrigan muttered. "I'll explain later." Then, louder; "Disconnect them, Roger."

And Judy vanished—as, in that same instant, did all the other bewildered surrogates all over Pittsburgh who had just seen the world around them turn into statues.

Tyron strode into the room ahead of the others. "What do you think you're doing?" he barked at Corrigan.

Corrigan ignored him. "Roger, put SPD generic on my screen." A format appeared specifying the set of Surrogate Physical Descriptors that the system used to manage the interactions of each projected persona with its environment. Speaking quickly, Corrigan directed, "Operand class by name: Corrigan, Essell. Zero reaction coefficients of M-sub-M, M-sub-P, and delete spatial conflict restrictions."

"Get away from that. . . . *What the?* . . ." Tyron came around the desk and grabbed at Corrigan's shoulder to pull him away from the screen, but his hand met no resistance and went straight through. Corrigan had in effect turned himself and Lilly into ghosts.

Tyron brought the communicator up to his mouth and snapped, "Control, do you read?"

A harassed voice answered, "We seem to have problems. Nothing's responding out here. I don't know what to tell you."

"You don't have control anymore," Corrigan said. "I do."

"That's impossible," Tyron declared. He stepped forward, moving through Corrigan's body, but struck his knee on the edge of the chair, causing him to curse. Corrigan smirked and waved a hand invitingly toward the touchpad. Tyron stabbed savagely at several keys and saw that it was ineffective. The others closed around the desk, all seemingly talking at once so that Corrigan was unable to understand what they were saying—not that he cared a great deal anyway.

"Roger, display Global Dynamics. Reset k-sub-g to twenty percent."

"Done."

The plant out on Judy's desk straightened itself up visibly. Papers that had been lying on the desk and in other places around the office and outside suddenly lifted and began blowing about in currents from the air-conditioner vents. Velucci, who had been walking around the edge of the room behind the others, seemed to unglue from the floor in midstep, went into a strange, floating leap that carried him toward the wall.

"*Jesus Christ!*" he yelled, losing his balance and falling in slow motion over a chair. The others felt giddy and strangely light on their feet. Sutton tried to sit down on the nearest chair, but everything about the movement felt wrong; she misjudged the distance, succeeding only in tipping the chair over, and she and it went down together. Corrigan had reduced the gravitational constant to a fifth of normal.

"What do you think you'll achieve by this?" Tyron snarled. "You'll pay—you realize that, don't you?"

"Just having a little fun, Frankie boy. What *you* don't realize yet is that it doesn't matter anymore—any of it," Corrigan said. He looked back at the screen. "Let's see, now . . . Roger, reset all mu-f to zero."

"Done." Which reduced to nothing all the coefficients of mechanical friction.

Velucci, who had been hauling himself back up with the help of a bookcase, went down again as his feet shot from under him, tilting the bookcase and burying himself under a torrent of volumes coming off the shelves. Sutton sprawled flat on her back as the floor she had been pushing herself up from turned into ice. Morgen felt the treacherousness beneath his feet and reached out instinctively to steady himself against the wall, but his hand skidded away and he fell over into Endelmyer, taking them both down in a heap on top of Sutton. Tyron managed to stay upright, but his spectacles slid off. Pictures fell from the walls as their fastenings came out. The drawers of a file cabinet standing in the corner slid slowly out and tipped the whole unit over on its front with a crash. More crashings and breaking sounds poured in through the doorway from all over the building. In her chair across the room, Lilly had started to laugh uncontrollably.

Tyron, unable to contain himself, his face contorted with rage, swung a fist at Corrigan's head. Corrigan laughed derisively as it passed harmlessly through; at the same time, the opposite reaction sent Tyron's legs off in the other direction, and he fell through Corrigan, over the chair, and became entangled with Velucci, who was floundering like a beached whale.

"Roger, rotate k-sub-g vector field ten degrees northward."

"Done."

So now gravity was no longer vertical, and all the surfaces that had been horizontal were, in effect, sloping. Everything on the desk slid to the edge and then over in a slow cataract to join the collection of anything loose—books, pens, folders, furnishings, wildly flailing and protesting CLC executives—accumulating against the far wall. The desk slid across behind them, followed by the chairs that Corrigan and Lilly had been sitting in. They could stand and watch from where they were, their bodies had no effective mass for gravity to operate on—vertical or otherwise.

"Continue rotating at ten degrees per minute, Roger," Corrigan said.

Tyron tried pulling himself up the tilted floor, but his hands slid futilely. "You'll regret it, Corrigan," he screeched as a tide of oddments from the room swept him back down again.

Corrigan shook his head. At last he grasped the meaning of the words that he had borrowed from Eric Shipley long ago but never really understood. "No," he said. "None of you control anything that's important to me anymore. I'm free. You'll get out of this, Frank, but you'll be trapped in your own slow-motion tumble dryer all your life. Have fun." Corrigan looked away. The desk unit and screen had gone with the desk, but it didn't matter. "Roger, operand class by name: surrogates Corrigan, Essell," he directed.

"Specify operation?"

"Out-out. It's time to go home."

And Corrigan was instantly in a reclining position, feeling stiff and cold, his head and neck restrained. He opened his eyes sluggishly and saw cables and pickup assemblies connected to banks of apparatus indistinct in the reduced lighting. Already his senses were overwhelmed by a level of clarity and detail that he had long forgotten was normal.

"Done," a synthetic voice from a speaker somewhere announced matter-of-factly.

❂ EPILOGUE ❂

The irony of it all was that in those first two days, it was the *animations* that had behaved rationally and commendably. In his TV interview, Corrigan had set the precedent that personal integrity was more important than dishonest gain, and in succession the system-generated analogs of Pinder, the CLC Board, then F & F and its clients, had followed him. It was only when the real people got involved that the old, familiar human formula had reasserted itself of rivalry, hostility, aggression, and mistrust. That was when Corrigan knew he could no longer be a part of it, and whatever happened from there on didn't matter.

He still had his wife, of course—their supposed splitting up as told to him in the simworld had been contrived simply to account for Evelyn's absence, since after her return to Boston nothing could have induced her to have anything further to do with the Oz project. But Corrigan could only think of her as a stranger from long ago.

He did go up to Boston to see her. And she found great changes in the person who, just a matter of a few weeks before, she had come to despise. The self-assuredness that had turned into arrogance, and the pride that had soured into conceit were no more; but neither were the blithe youth and roguishness that had captured her, with which they might have grown together. At the same time, she, to him, had become childlike. For with Corrigan, it had not been a matter of space for a few weeks. A chasm existed that no amount of sacrificial forbearance could hope to bridge. They mended the space for wounded feelings, confessed to some regrets, and promised that they would remain friends. Three days later, Evelyn filed the papers finalizing the arrangement.

By that time, the notices of impending lawsuits, corporate and private, were already flying between CLC, F & F, F & F's clients, various members of the funding consortium, and dozens of involved individuals from all of them. Corrigan was advised that he had a solid case for millions. There was deceit with malicious intent, conspiracy to defraud, violation of patent rights, criminal abuse and neglect, willful and malicious misinformation and withholding of information, violation of just about every employment act, violation of contract, breach of rights, technical assault and abduction; in addition, a case charging the entirety of his collateral domestic and marital problems would be indefensible. Corrigan listened as the words echoed around him: force and counterforce; strengths and weaknesses; attack and defense; strategy and counterstrategy . . . And somehow, in spite of all his earlier passions, none of it seemed worth the real cost anymore. In the end, he just walked away.

The green slopes rising up to the mountains behind Ballygarven were splashed with purple patches of heather. On the neck of water beyond the town, a fishing boat trailing a cloud of screeching gulls chugged its way out past the headland toward the open sea.

Wearing jeans, sturdy boots, and an Aran sweater, Corrigan arrived on foot at the Cobh Hotel at a little after noon, having spent the morning on his own, walking on the cliffs, looking at the ocean, feeling the wind, and thinking. Brendan Maguire was already there at the bar with a pint of stout, talking to Rooney and a couple of the locals. Dermot Leavey was with him.

"Ah, here's the American himself now," Rooney said as Corrigan joined them. "A pint, Joe, is it?"

"A well-earned one, I'll have you know. And enough of this 'American,' if you please. Can't a man take a break to see somewhere else for a while without it following him around for the rest of his life?"

"Here, this one's mine," Maguire said, producing a five-pound note as Corrigan reached toward his pocket.

"So did you have a good wander around this morning?" Dermot asked.

"I saw a lot, anyway."

"You'll be joining Brendan and his crowd up at the Rectory, I'm told," Rooney observed, holding a foaming glass under the tap.

"That's the way it looks," Corrigan said.

"Aren't we after telling you the last time you were here that you'd get tired of all that paranoia and dashing around soon enough?" Rooney said.

Corrigan held up a hand in a what-can-I-say? gesture. "Well, here I am. I guess I'm learning how to be a self-unmade man."

Rooney grinned as he set down the glass. "Oh, you remembered that, did you? Ah well, working up there with them professors and all only gets you halfway there, you understand. Next you have to go all the way and try your hand at tending a bar. You'd be astounded at some of the people you meet. It's the only form of true philosophy left."

"Is that a fact, now?" Corrigan smiled distantly to himself and left it at that.

"Ah, yes, talking about philosophers . . ." Maguire felt in the inside pocket of his jacket and pulled out several folded sheets of paper. "This came through over the fax from your friend Shipley in Pittsburgh. It looks good. He's interested, and his approach is just the kind of thing we could use. I've already got approval for another senior slot, so I can't see there'll be a problem."

"That's great. Let's hope it works out." Corrigan picked up his beer and closed his eyes while he treated himself to a long, steady swig. It was cool and refreshingly tart after his exertions. Working with Eric again would be good. He was glad that he had been able to do something to make amends for the way things had ended last time. In a strange kind of way, he really was getting a chance to live a part of his life over again.

"Oh yes, Joe, and there was an American in here asking for you while you were out," Rooney said.

"Oh, really?"

"A woman—quite a nice-looking one, too, if you want a professional's opinion."

Corrigan was suddenly all attention. "When?" he asked, putting down his glass with a thump. "Where'd she go?"

"About ten, ten-thirty, I'd say. I've no idea where she went. Paddy might know something."

"He's got a different one after him every time," Dermot muttered, but Corrigan was already halfway out and didn't hear.

He found Paddy, the owner of the hotel, checking an order list at the front desk. "Rooney says you had somebody in looking for me this morning," Corrigan said.

Paddy looked up. "Joe. . . . Ah, yes. An American woman, it was. Didn't give a name." He turned to the pigeonholes on the wall behind. "She did leave something for you, though. . . . Here we are. I told her we expected you back for lunch, and she went off to look around the town." Paddy handed Corrigan a slip of paper. "Said she'd be back about now."

Corrigan unfolded it. Written neatly with an ink pen were the words:

> *I'm assuming this is real, but have gone to buy a leprechaun just in case. Back later.*
>
> L.

Corrigan smiled, and at that moment Paddy's voice said, "In fact, if I'm not mistaken, here she is now."

Corrigan looked up, and through the double, paned-glass doors saw a figure in a white raincoat and tan skirt approaching the bottom of the steps. She was tall, with dark wavy hair, and walked elegantly. He went out through the doors as she approached, and waited for her at the top, smiling.

"I wondered when you'd show up," Corrigan said.

Lilly didn't ask what had made him so sure that she would. There was no need. In the way that it had always been between them, most of their conversation remained unvoiced.

That was why they had made no elaborate agreements and plans when she left Pittsburgh to return to California. He'd had a no-longer-viable marriage to disentangle himself from; she'd had the Air Force. Neither needed to ask or be told that they would pick up again where they had begun, when the time was right. It had been too obvious to need saying that the place would be here.

"How did things go with Evelyn?" Lilly asked him.

"She's fine. Do you remember I told you there was always that attraction there between her and Tom? Well, they got together, and it's working out okay. In fact, I talked on the phone to Tom yesterday."

"I'm glad," Lilly said.

"How about you?"

"No real problems. What happened at Xylog?"

Corrigan shrugged. "Everyone's fighting like mad dogs there. I just left them to it. They're welcome. Some things aren't worth making lawyers millionaires over."

Lilly nodded. "Somehow I can't see Tom feeling that way," she said.

"Oh, he's going for the throat—every ounce of blood he can squeeze. Then he says he and Evelyn are going off to see all of the real world and enjoy it. After that, who knows? I shouldn't think we'll lose touch."

Lilly turned and took in the scene of the town with the sea and the mountains. "It's pretty," she agreed. "So did you get fixed up with the project that the professor of yours from Trinity is running here?"

"It looks like it. And he got a fax this morning from Eric Shipley. They're both interested, so it looks as if Eric might be moving over with Thelma too."

Lilly turned back, they looked at each other for a moment, and she moved a step nearer. Corrigan slipped an arm around her shoulders and drew her close for just a second. Then he reached out with his other hand and pulled open one of the doors. "In fact, Brendan's inside now," he said. "Come on and start meeting some new friends. They're all real this time, I promise."

"You're sure?" Lilly checked dubiously.

"Oh, definitely. No computer on earth could simulate these people."

They went through into the hotel. With their unique experience of sharing a world that most people would never know had even existed, they were natural companions for life. That much didn't need saying. And there was no particular rush to figure out exactly what they intended doing with it. Here, time ran to suit itself.

❋ ABOUT THE AUTHOR ❋

James P. Hogan (1941-2010) was a science fiction writer in the grand tradition, combining informed and accurate speculation from the cutting edge of science and technology with suspenseful story-telling and living, breathing characters.

Born in London, he worked as a digital system engineer and sales executive for several major computer firms before turning to writing full-time. His first novel, *Inherit the Stars,* beginning his celebrated "Giants" series, was greeted by Isaac Asimov with the rave, "Pure science fiction . . . Arthur Clarke, move over!" and his subsequent work quickly consolidated his reputation as a major SF author.

He wrote over thirty novels, nonfiction works and mixed collections, including Echoes of an *Alien Sky* and *Moon Flower* (both Baen). His earlier works include the Giants series (Baen) the New York Times best sellers *The Proteus Operation* and *Endgame Enigma,* and the *Prometheus* Award winners *Voyage from Yesteryear* and T*he Multiplex Man.*